Other books by Fred Patten

Best in Show: Fifteen Years of Outstanding Furry Fiction (2003)
Reprinted as:
Furry! The World's Best Anthropomorphic Fiction! (2006)

Watching Anime, Reading Manga:
25 Years of Essays and Reviews (2004)

Already Among Us; An Anthropomorphic Anthology (2012)

The Ursa Major Awards Anthology:
A Tenth Anniversary Celebration (2012)

What Happens Next: An Anthology of Sequels (2013)

Five Fortunes (2014)

Funny Animals and More: From Anime to Zoomorphics (2014)

Anthropomorphic Aliens: An Interstellar Anthology (2014)

The Furry Future : 19 Possible Prognostications (2015)

An Anthropomorphic Century: Stories from 1909 to 2008 (2015)

Cats and More Cats: Feline Fantasy Fiction (2016)

Gods With Fur

And Feathers, Scales,...

Edited by Fred Patten

Gods With Fur
And Feathers, Scales, …

Production copyright FurPlanet Productions © 2016
Cover artwork copyright © 2016 by Teagan Gavet

Published by FurPlanet Productions
Dallas, Texas
www.FurPlanet.com

Print ISBN 978-1-61450-324-8
Electronic ISBN 978-1-61450-333-0

Second Edition Trade Paperback September 2018

This book is dedicated to the

Furry Writers' Guild

Founded in April 2010 by Sean Silva, to support, inform, elevate and promote quality writing in anthropomorphic literature.

Creator in 2012 of the annual Cóyotl Awards, voted on by its members for excellence in anthropomorphic literature.

Editor since 2014 of the anthology *Tales from the Guild,* a collaboration of the FWG to showcase the writing of its members.

And a great place for all authors of furry fiction to hang out online together.

http://furrywritersguild.com/

Table of Contents

Introduction

by Fred Patten

What is a god?

A god. Not necessarily an all-powerful, monotheistic god. Some peoples have had other gods; a divine father of the gods, with several children. Think of Zeus, king and father of the (Greek) gods, and his children; Aphrodite, Apollo, Ares, Artemis, Athena, Dionysus, Hermes, Perseus… (Zeus was lusty.) Zeus himself had a father, Cronus, and a grandfather, mad Uranus; his brothers were Poseidon, god of the seas, and Hades, god of the underworld. The Germanic and Nordic peoples had similar gods: Odin or Wotan, the king-father, and his sons and daughters; Baldur, Freya, Heimdall, Loki, Thor… Loki's daughter Hel, goddess of the dead, should not be ignored.

Some people have too many gods to count. In Japan's Shinto faith, everything has its own god. This is often used for fantasy-drama or comedy in modern anime. The Japanese *shinigami*, death god, is usually depicted as a demon (see *Death Note*), but it is more closely analogous to Egyptian mythology's jackal-headed Anubis, who leads the souls of the virtuous dead to the afterlife. (The souls of the unworthy dead are eaten by Ammut, the goddess Ma'at's pet demon, depicted as having the head of a crocodile, the shoulders of a lioness or leopardess, and the hindquarters of a hippopotamus.) In the shinigami's case, it leads the soul of a newly dead up or down, depending. There are gods for everything in Shinto. In the Shinto anime TV series *Kamichu*, junior-high-school girl Yurie, who has recently become a goddess (but she doesn't know of what yet), is introduced to a gathering of some other gods and goddesses. She learns that there is not only a new god of video-tape recorders, but that the VHS and Betamax formats each have their own gods. Today there must be gods of DVDs and Blu-Ray as well.

What does this mean for furry-dom? An all-powerful god or goddess can take on an animal form at will, or transform a man into an animal. Witness Zeus' becoming a bull and a swan to seduce Europa and Leda; or Artemis' turning the hunter Actaeon into a deer to be torn apart by his own hounds. Many small-g gods have been divine animals, such as the famous trickster-gods; the African Anansi, the spider, and the North American Coyote and Raven. Odin had the two all-seeing ravens Huginn and Muninn (Thought and Memory) on his shoulders. To the North American Ojibwe, the trickster Nanabozho was a human who usually appeared as a giant rabbit, although he often impersonated other animal-gods such as Great Porcupine or Big Skunk (who in the legends did not appreciate Nanabozho's impersonations) in his scams. The traditional Oriental Zodiac features twelve animals—rat, ox, tiger, etc.—but are they only animals, or have they become something more, akin to the Platonic ideals of those animals—or those animals in divine form?

Here are 23 new stories of these Gods With Fur. Some are of gods who have taken on animal form, while others are of gods who are animals. There are stories featuring traditional gods, and stories featuring the gods of an author's fictional world, such as M. R. Anglin's *Silver Foxes* books or Kyell Gold's *Forester University* books. Some of the stories are set in original worlds with original anthropomorphic gods. We hope that you will enjoy this divine diversity.

The Mesoamericans—the Mayas, Aztecs, Toltecs, Zapotecs, Tlaxcalteca, and other pre-Columbian North and Central American peoples—had many gods. The important ones were mostly human, but many of their minor gods were animals. The nineteen months of the Mayan calendar included several named after animal gods such as K'ayab the turtle, Muwan' the owl, Xul the dog, and Zotz the bat.

According to Wikipedia, "In Aztec mythology, the Centzon Totochtin are a group of divine rabbits who meet for frequent drunken parties." They are the children of Patecatl the fertility god and Mayahuel, the goddess in charge of the maguey plant, a principal ingredient of tequila. So non-stop drunken parties with booze and sex comes naturally to them. But what happens when one of the Centzon Totochtin—the four hundred rabbits—decides that there should be more to life than drunken revelry?

400 Rabbits

by Alice "Huskyteer" Dryden

Eighty-Six-Rabbit woke up with a hangover. As far as he could remember, he had woken up with a hangover every morning since he and his three hundred and ninety-nine siblings, the Centzon Totochtin, were born of the union between Patecatl, god of fermentation, and Mayahuel, goddess of alcohol. It didn't seem to be getting any more enjoyable.

He wobbled his nose, sending ripples of pain across his skull like wind through a field of maize, and lolloped unsteadily over to the big obsidian mirror. His eyes might have been two beads of dried blood, the skin inside his ears was pale, and when he poked out his tongue it was frosted with white.

"This has got to stop," he said to himself.

"Hey! Keep the noise down!" Three-Twenty-Three-Rabbit staggered into the burrow, still clutching an empty bottle which had, at some stage, contained pulque. "What a night, huh? That was one amazing party. Wasn't it?"

"Was it?" Eighty-Six-Rabbit eyeballed his brother. Late-born and late-numbered, Three-Twenty-Three was ranked among the lowest in seniority of the four hundred sibling gods. The real big quesos, Twelve-Rabbit and upwards, wouldn't even have given him the time of day. He had a nerve, telling Eighty-Six to keep it down.

"What was so great about it?" Eighty-Six asked. "Tell me one thing."

One of Three-Twenty-Three's ears drooped. He pushed it upright with a paw, only for the other to flop down over his eye.

"Well…there was…how about…" He scratched his whiskers. "Actually, Eightsy, I can't remember the first thing about it. And that's what made it so amazing!" he finished triumphantly.

"Don't you ever want to do something different with your evenings? And don't call me Eightsy."

"Different?" Three-Twenty-Three's eyes bugged out as he thought. "Like… drinking mezcal instead of pulque?"

"No, I mean, like dancing. Playing rubberball. Going to watch a human sacrifice. We could even just stay in and talk. When was the last time two of us had a conversation that wasn't about who took the last aspirin?"

"But what about our duties?"

Each of the rabbit siblings was in charge of a particular aspect of drunkenness. Eighty-Six was the god of attempting to chat up your best friend's betrothed. His favorite sister Fifty-Five was the goddess of attempting to chat up your best friend. Three-Twenty-Three, being a more junior rabbit, was responsible for the inability to tie your shoelaces. Since shoelaces would not come to Mesoamerica for another three hundred years, he was frequently at a loose end.

"We don't all need to be at every single party, all the time. I'm pretty sure a few of us could take the night off every now and then."

Eighty-Six became uncomfortably aware that Three-Twenty-Three was wearing the expression of someone who has opened a bottle of pulque, only for the god Quetzalcoatl to fly out of it in the form of a winged serpent.

"I just think there might be more to life than getting drunk," he concluded.

"More to life than...!" Three-Twenty-Three's eyes bulged, and he clapped a paw over his mouth. Eighty-Six thought he was probably going to be sick, but instead he went haring out of the burrow and down the warren, tripping over his paws and crashing into walls as he tried to hop and thump his hind foot for danger at the same time.

"Two-Rabbit, Two-Rabbit!" he yelled. "Come quick! Eighty-Six-Rabbit has lost his mind!"

Two-Rabbit was the leader of the siblings, and, on the frequent occasions when their parents were busy with other affairs of fermentation and alcohol, represented their ultimate authority. None of the three hundred and ninety-nine had ever seen One-Rabbit; legend had it that the moment he was birthed he had embarked upon a binge of such divine proportions that his corporeal elements had fractured across space and time, allowing him simultaneously to attend every party since the age of the Jaguar Sun, as well as those yet to come. This bending of the laws of the universe was thought to be the origin of the term 'bender'.

"This had better be good," Two-Rabbit pronounced, glaring at Eighty-Six, Three-Twenty-Three, and sundry brothers and sisters who had popped out of their burrows to see what was going on. "I'm trying to draw up the duty roster for the party Tlazolteotl, Goddess of Sexual Misdeeds And Their Forgiveness, is holding tonight."

That was a top gig. The rabbits drew themselves up, trying to look alert, bright-eyed, and ready to party; not easy when the effects of the last party are still draining from your system.

"I'm just saying." Eighty-Six swallowed. "I know we do important work, helping people relax, enjoy themselves and make stupid, regretful decisions, but we've been doing it since we were born and, frankly, it's getting a bit dull. Tiring, too. I'm sure we'd all be better for a night off every once in a while. Maybe stay in and read a good codex. The humans have invented this stuff called cocoa, it's quite nice apparently…"

Two-Rabbit's bloodshot eyes looked him disapprovingly up and down, and Eighty-Six trembled.

"Eighty-Six-Rabbit, you are a deity. An anthropomorphic personification of drunkenness, no less. Anthropomorphic personifications of drunkenness don't get bored. We don't get tired. And we don't put our feet up with a mug of hot mashed beans when we could be out partying!" Her glare swept the assembled rabbits, daring them to disagree. "Am I right?"

There were hasty cheers. Paws punched the air.

"Party! Party! Party!"

With a twitch of her ears, Two-Rabbit silenced the chant.

"Eighty-Six-Rabbit, I am disappointed in you," she said. "This is not the behavior I expect from a rabbit of double figures."

Eighty-Six waited to see what punishment would be meted out. He had heard that Two-Rabbit could demote her siblings to more menial jobs, though it hadn't happened for centuries. He didn't fancy being the divine personification of slamming your finger in the taxi door, or of why not make it a vindaloo instead of a madras.

"Since you think so little of our sacred customs," Two-Rabbit continued, "you are welcome to try this crazy notion of 'sobriety'. But you will try it away from here, so none of your brothers and sisters are tempted to follow your example. Depart, now, and return when you have learned some sense."

Eighty-Six hopped slowly up the warren and into the world above, his white tail bouncing as he went. His sibling gods watched him go with twitching noses and quivering whiskers, but nobody said a word. Only Three-Twenty-Three mouthed something that might have been 'sorry'.

* * *

"Sobriety," Eighty-Six-Rabbit said out loud. Until Two-Rabbit used the word, he had not even known how to describe the opposite of drunkenness. Now, for only the fourth time in his life, he was sober to watch the sun go down.

That first drink-less night had been hard. It wasn't just the longing for pulque, a hunger and thirst rolled into one that no amount of cocoa, maize or beans could sate. Only his fierce determination had kept Eighty-Six dry. In the end, he had broken leaves off a maguey plant and drunk the honey-water, the base from which pulque was made, just to get the faintest shadow of the taste which had been mother's milk to him.

What was a divine sober rabbit supposed to do in the evenings? It was all very well to talk about rubberball and priestly ceremonies, and on the second evening, when he felt a little less like a dried-up husk of last year's corn than he had on the first, Eighty-Six tried both these entertainments. But they were no fun without his brothers and sisters there to talk to. Besides, whenever someone in the audience opened a bottle of pulque, he felt the pull of his divine duty to keep them company, and he had to move away before one of his siblings showed up.

The next night he tried going to a dance, but it seemed nobody could do anything fun without involving alcohol, and he crept away early. He made himself a nest in the grass and tried to sleep through the partying hours, but he was too used to keeping nocturnal time to get much rest. As soon as the sun rose he started walking, in the hope of tiring himself out before the next empty night.

Foregoing pulque was still hard, but he had become used to his body's grumbles about it. Worse than the pain of sobering up, right now, was the pain of homesickness. He missed his brothers and sisters powerfully. Of course they had argued; how could they not, with three hundred and ninety-nine of them, plus the mysterious One-Rabbit who may or may not have been present, all crammed into a burrow, and all in a permanent state of either inebriation or its aftermath? But Eighty-Six, like all rabbits, was a sociable creature. The world felt very cold and silent without the warmth and noise of his family. He wanted to sing off-key with Two-Hundred-Four while Thirty-Three played the log drum. He wanted to be grabbed round the middle by One-Hundred-Fifty-Three, who got all huggy after the first few bottles. He wanted to discuss the question of life, the universe and everything with Forty-Two. He wanted to form a line with his paws on the hips of the rabbit in front and conga until his feet left the earth and they were dancing across the sky, the way they did at particularly good parties when the entire tribe was gathered together. That always really annoyed the Four Hundred Gods of the Southern Stars, snooty, fun-hating bunch that they were.

He missed his job, too. He hadn't asked to quit, just to take a little time off every now and then. Sure, it had been hard, but at least he went to bed feeling as if he'd achieved something. On the occasions when he could remember going to bed, that is. He had been good at his job; everyone had said so, even Two-Rabbit, before she cast him out. Who was encouraging partygoers to chat up their best friends' betrotheds now? Three-Twenty-Three, probably. He was bound to be making a mess of it.

Weary of his wandering and his thoughts, Eighty-Six lay down on the side of a hill and stared at the sky. He had never before noticed the colors, how the daytime blue faded through yellows and pinks to the deep red of blood, then a rich indigo across which trod the moon and the stars. The breeze brought him scents of flowers and the nighttime noises of scurrying animals.

With a bottle in his paw and few dozen of his favorite siblings around him, it would have been just perfect.

Maybe if he went back and told Two-Rabbit he was really, really sorry...

"No," Eighty-Six said to the moon and stars. He'd only been trying for four nights; he wasn't about to admit defeat. He just needed to stop hanging around the places that reminded him of home—and anywhere alcohol might be found. Let Two-Rabbit wonder and worry about what had happened to him, if she cared. He had already discovered sunsets. Now Eighty-Six was going to find out what else there was in the world.

After that night, he avoided human and divine company alike. He wandered the arid regions and the lush, tropical forests, climbed cloud-capped mountains, and swam in the turquoise sea. Lonely though he was, he could not help noticing the new clearness in his mind, and his sharpened senses. The foods he ate tasted better than they had done when his tongue was dulled with pulque. He was awake for sunrise and sunset, and he could enjoy both without screwing his eyes up in agony. When he hopped and skipped in the sand, he neither lost his balance and fell over nor felt as if his head might be going to come off.

Above all, he could think properly. His brain was like a cocoa bean freshly popped from the woolly enclosure of its pod, all glossy and gleaming. He could remember things he had long forgotten, like obscure minor deities with seven-syllable names. He composed little songs and poems in his head as he travelled. To pass the time, he listed his siblings in numerical order, analyzed their characters, and remembered a nice thing about each of them. The sights he had seen and the thoughts he had had during the course of one day, he actually remembered when the sun came up again. What's more, they were worth remembering.

It was in this state that he happened upon Tlacuache, the opossum, whose place in the world was to create rivers. No one was entirely sure how this task had fallen to him, but he was pretty good at it, for an opossum. One moment Eighty-Six saw something gleaming in the distance, the next he heard a rumble, and before he knew it a river was flowing past him, with Tlacuache panting after it.

"Oh, no, you don't, friend Rabbit," said Tlacuache when he saw him. He held up a pink paw. "I know who you are—you're one of the Centzon Totochtin. Well, I can't get drunk today. I have to finish this river. Isn't she a beauty?"

They admired it together as it coursed across the plain, straight and wide, and glittering like a lost temple full of treasure.

"Don't worry, Tlacuache. I'm not here in an official capacity. I'm...taking a break."

The opossum's beady little eyes grew beadier and littler, but he didn't press Eighty-Six for the details.

"Want to help me for a while?" he offered.

"Sure."

So they drove the water across the plain, herding it along the correct path as it carved a channel and flowed into it. Sometimes Tlacuache grabbed himself a fish, while Eighty-Six-Rabbit nibbled the plants that sprang up along the banks. When evening came they rested and watched the sunset together. Eighty-Six, exhausted from his hard work, fell asleep at Tlacuache's side. In the morning, when Tlacuache asked if he would help him again, he readily agreed.

Together, they brought water down from the mountains and across the deserts. Plants sprang up in their wake, and little fish jumped for joy in the currents. Eighty-Six and Tlacuache caught the fattest and least cautious of them for dinner. With each river, Eighty-Six had lasting, physical proof that he had helped to do something good. His old job never delivered that, although he supposed there were a few happily married couples out there who, without realizing it, had Eighty-Six to thank for their union.

The opossum was peaceful company, and he called Eighty-Six-Rabbit simply Rabbit, as there was no need to distinguish him from his brothers and sisters. He taught his new friend to make cocoa, and they drank it while they watched the sun sink into their river, turning it blood-red, and the moon rise to coat the ripples in silver. Life was…cozy.

One evening, as they dangled their feet in the day's newborn river, Eighty-Six-Rabbit told Tlacuache all that had happened. The opossum listened quietly, with the occasional nod or hiss.

"I'm sorry for your troubles, Rabbit. I really am," he said at last.

"It's not your fault."

"Well, it kind of is. You see, I invented pulque. Didn't you know?"

Eighty-Six-Rabbit supposed that he had known, once, before the fog of alcohol took the knowledge from him.

"I gave it to the humans and they really ran with it. Hit it right out of the rubberball park." Tlacuache whiffled his nose. "I sometimes wonder if I did the right thing."

"Keeps them busy, I suppose."

Tlacuache nodded. "Beats all that war stuff. They haven't got the recipe quite right yet, though. Mine's still better."

"Yeah?"

The opossum produced a bottle. "Try for yourself…oh. I suppose not."

He sighed deeply, pulled off the bamboo stopper with his teeth, and upended the bottle. Eighty-Six watched his white throat bob as he swallowed. It had been a long day of river creation; he was hot, tired, and most of all thirsty.

"I suppose one can't hurt," he said. "Just…open it quietly. I don't want any of my siblings showing up."

When he woke, the sunlight stabbed at his eyes, and he slammed them shut again. Why was his burrow so bright? Then he remembered, and cautiously raised his eyelids to see Tlacuache peering anxiously down at him.

"I guess your tolerance isn't what it was," said the opossum, helping Eighty-Six to sit up. "Are you all right, Rabbit?"

"What did we do last night?"

Tlacuache didn't answer. Eighty-Six stared out across the landscape. It was moving and shimmering, and it continued to move and shimmer even after he blinked hard and rubbed his eyes. He held a paw in front of his face. It was in perfect focus.

He looked again. From horizon to horizon, a wide band of shining water ran. It looped. It meandered. It went back on itself. It even flowed briefly uphill, though as Eighty-Six watched it ran out of energy and fell back, leaving a lake behind.

"Yeah." Tlacuache scratched the back of his head and yawned. "We made a river."

* * *

Eighty-Six-Rabbit said goodbye to Tlacuache, and apologized for the river.

"Don't worry about it! Happens to me all the time!" Tlacuache said. "Are you sure you want to go? You've been a big help."

Eighty-Six took a last, wistful look at the bright morning and its brand-new river, then shook his head.

"No—I need to go back and do my duty. Two-Rabbit was right; you can take the drunken rabbit god out of the party, but you can't take the party out of the drunken rabbit god."

And he hopped away, while Tlacuache watched him go from the river bank.

It was a long journey back to the warren, and all Eighty-Six wanted when he arrived was a nice eight-hour nap in his burrow, but when he arrived he found that Ninety-Two had promoted herself into it. By the time he had kicked her out, with a great deal of noise and foot-thumping, it was evening, and the rabbits' duties were beginning. Eighty-Six checked the roster and found he had been already been assigned to a party in the Underworld, which suited him fine; he was feeling pretty low anyway.

The Lord and Lady of the Underworld welcomed them with open arm bones. As the pulque began to flow, Eighty-Six felt himself growing loud and brash and happy, just like he used to be. Warmth spread through his body. Why had he cut himself off from who he was? This worked. This was right. He couldn't escape his destiny? Well, then, he would embrace it. He would be the loudest, brashest, happiest drunk of the family. He would drink more and party harder than any other rabbit.

He shook himself from ears to tail, and resumed his role as if he had never left it. Now he had tasted Tlacuache's original recipe, the regular mortal pulque was as water to him, and he downed it at a rate that astonished his siblings and had the Lady of the Underworld checking the cellar anxiously in case her supplies ran out.

As he urged a recently deceased spirit to try it on with the long-dead fiancé of her best friend, on the grounds that the best friend was scheduled for several decades more of a long and happy life, he felt the thrill that comes with doing your job, and doing it well.

It was a long, loud and successful party, which broke up only when the God of the Morning Star had to leave in order to create the new dawn. Then Tonatiuh, Lord of the Sun, said he'd better be going too, and the rabbits went home. Except for Twenty-Rabbit, the deity of Risky Showing Off, who accompanied Tonatiuh for a while in the hope of persuading him to bounce the sun along the sky instead of carrying it as usual.

The resulting hangover wasn't easy to shake. It took several bottles of pulque, so that when Eighty-Six arrived at the next night's party he was already feeling lively. It was only a mortal wedding, but it ended up lasting nine days, during which time no fewer than fifty of the guests made advances on their best friends' betrothed. Of these, thirty-two were coldly rebuffed, six were slapped, eight were removed from the happy couple's Atemoztli card list, and four discovered that they and their best friend's betrothed had, in fact, been made for each other all along.

From then on, Eighty-Six's status as the guarantor of a great evening was legendary. Gods and goddesses booked his presence at their parties months in advance. He did feast days, wakes, birthdays and religious ceremonies, although for some reason he was never in great demand at engagement parties. He drank and danced with his brothers and sisters, and carried on long after they had collapsed. He slept through sunset and partied until the morning star had faded into the day. He had no time to sober up between parties, so he suffered no aches, pains or troubling thoughts, and he forgot that he had ever wandered the world as a solitary rabbit. Once or twice, when the room was whirling hard around him, he even thought that he glimpsed the shadowy form of One-Rabbit, always dancing a few steps ahead and out of reach.

He might have gone on this way for all of eternity, if one evening he hadn't staggered, pleasantly buzzed, into the wrong burrow, and found Three-Twenty-Three frantically splashing water over his ears.

"What's wrong, bro?"

Three-Twenty-Three turned his bedraggled head.

"Oh, hey, it's the poster boy for alcohol poisoning. Don't worry. You wouldn't understand."

Eighty-Six took a seat with the exaggerated care of the drunk pretending to be sober. "Try me."

"I'm tired, Eightsy. My throat's like sandpaper and if you picked me up by my tail, my eyeballs would fall out. I don't think I can get through another night of this."

Eighty-Six crinkled his forehead. A memory from the dim and sober past was thundering towards him, flooding his mind with the force and brightness of a river flowing true.

"Have you ever seen a sunset?" he asked his brother. "Really seen it?" He reached out a paw to smooth Three-Twenty-Three's rumpled fur.

"Hey, knock it off. I'm not your best friend's betrothed, you know."

"Oh, please. I mean: let's take the night off."

Three-Twenty-Three stared at him with bulging eyes, just as he had so long ago, but this time the eyes were filled with hope.

Eighty-Six made cocoa, and the two rabbits sat cozily together as their siblings set off for their assigned parties. They enjoyed a pleasant conversation, went to bed early, and awoke to watch the sun come up. Nobody appeared to have noticed their absence, since three hundred and ninety-nine rabbits are hard to keep track of, although Eighty-Six's favorite sister Fifty-Five did tell him that if he didn't wipe that self-satisfied smirk from his muzzle and stop looking so indecently cheerful, she would clock him one.

That night he threw himself back into the proper lifestyle as if the break had only sharpened his thirst, and the next night, and the next. The night after that, he noticed that One-Four-Four was looking a little ragged around the edges, and he took her dancing. When he woke refreshed, Two-Hundred-Eighteen, who had feasted on flatbread and milk before going out and thus remained more sober than his siblings, asked him if he fancied playing a board game.

Word spread, and soon more of his brothers and sisters came in secret to question him about the mysteries of time off. Eighty-Six found himself writing down cocoa recipes, and then organizing a rubberball league. In order to fit all this into his daylight hours, he drank less at night, so he spent less of his free time feeling like a hollowed-out gourd. He even began, when he found one of his siblings drinking hard on the eve of an important match, to tap them on the shoulder and suggest they call it a night.

It wasn't long before he extended his services to the human and divine partygoers, whispering a hint into receptive ears that stopping now would result in an evening of slurred speech and pleasantly lowered inhibitions, rather than an embarrassing scene, apologies, cleaning bills, and nicknames like Mixcoatl Who Should Not Mix Pulque And Mezcal.

Curiously, he was more in demand than ever before.

As he hopped down the warren on the eve of the rubberball finals, feeling better than he had for centuries, he caught sight of a paw sticking out from one of the burrows. It clasped a bottle of pulque, and it trembled. Automatically, Eighty-Six reached for the bottle.

"You!" The head and shoulders of Two-Rabbit emerged from the burrow, followed by the rest of her. Her eyes glowed dull and red, and her upper lip was pulled back to show her buck teeth. Eighty-Six noticed for the first time how sharp her claws were—for drawing up the rotas, he supposed.

Eighty-Six had known he was living on borrowed time. His actions could not forever escape the notice of Two-Rabbit, who made it her business to know the departures, arrivals and blood alcohol levels of all her siblings, and now he had delivered himself to her on a golden platter. If he apologized right now, and downed a few pulques for good measure, he might escape demotion to God of Projectile Vomiting, which was the nastiest thing he could dream up at the moment.

Instead, he tightened his grip on Two-Rabbit's bottle, and drew it from her grasp with a firm, practiced motion.

"How dare you, Eighty-Six-Rabbit? I'm going to make you the God of Being Projectile Vomited Upon! What have you got to say for yourself?"

Two-Rabbit was larger than the other siblings, so that Eighty-Six had to stand on his hind legs to look her in the eye, and speak the six words that would undoubtedly seal his doom.

"When did it stop being fun?"

Two-Rabbit's top and bottom teeth clicked together. Eighty-Six covered his eyes with his paws and braced for the attack. When it didn't come, he peeped cautiously through his claws at Two-Rabbit. She was shaking.

"When...when One-Rabbit left," she whispered. "When he left me in charge of you all. I draw up the rotas and then I have a drink to forget what a dull job it is, and to wash away all the complaints I get from rabbits who think they deserve to go to different, better parties, and then I have to get up and do it all over again, day after day until Huitzilopochtli is born of Coatlicue to destroy us all."

Eighty-Six blinked. He hadn't known about Huitzilopochtli, and he didn't much care for the knowledge.

"I've worked so hard," Two-Rabbit continued, staring glassily at a point above Eighty-Six's head, "and I still can't keep up with One-Rabbit. I can't even keep up with you!" She swung her gaze back to her brother. It was filled with loathing, but also, Eighty-Six thought, with fear.

"Me? I haven't had a drink for..." Eighty-Six tried to work it out. He hadn't deliberately stopped drinking; it had just happened, as he found other things to do. "It doesn't matter!" he burst out, as it dawned on him that it really didn't. "We don't need to be drunk all the time. What's fun and free about that?"

"I think you'll find," Two-Rabbit said, shuffling her paws, "that 'drunken rabbit god' is both your classification and your job description."

"We're the gods of partying! You said so yourself! Shouldn't things be a little more relaxed? Why can't we party because we want to, not because we have to?"

"This is anarchy, little brother. We were put into this world to preside over social situations where alcohol is present." Two-Rabbit was sounding dangerously like her usual self again.

"And we're doing it. Have you heard anyone, god or mortal, complain that their parties didn't have enough drunken rabbits? Someone's always in the mood, even if they're not on the rota. It just works. This is what you were afraid of, isn't it? This is why you sent me away when I suggested we might all drink a bit less. You didn't want anyone to sober up and discover the secret—that we don't need the rotas, and we don't need you."

It was a long time since Eighty-Six had made such a long speech. With three hundred and ninety-eight siblings, he hadn't had much opportunity. That was probably why his mouth was so dry.

Two-Rabbit lay on the floor of the warren, deflated. Her ears lay flat and limp along her back, and her eyes were like obsidian mirrors.

"Then what am I supposed to do?" she asked.

"There's a whole world out there, Two-Rabbit. Take a break. Wander. Learn to play the turtle drum. You can even make rivers!"

"That's disgusting, Eighty-Six."

"Not like that!" He cocked an ear. Somewhere in the distance, above his head, he heard the sound of rushing water. If Two-Rabbit hurried, she would catch up with Tlacuache before night fell. "Go on! Quick, before anyone sees you!"

Two-Rabbit hesitated. "You'll be all right without me?"

"Of course. We're drunken rabbit gods! We're always all right!"

He touched noses with his sister, then Two-Rabbit hopped away to where the golden late-afternoon light was spilling into the warren. She didn't look back.

Eighty-Six was still holding the bottle of pulque he had confiscated from Two-Rabbit. He inspected it. Talking Two-Rabbit around had been hard, thirsty work. If ever a rabbit deserved a drink, he deserved one now.

"Come on, Eightsy!" Three-Twenty-Three scampered past him. "The first match is about to start!"

He put the bottle down, and lolloped after his brother. Maybe he'd feel like a drink tomorrow, and maybe he wouldn't. Maybe he'd party all night and maybe he'd stay in. There was room in his life for both. And for sunsets. Always for sunsets.

In Norse mythology, an unnamed eagle lives atop Yggdrasil, the gigantic world-connecting ash tree. Its roots are the home of Níðhöggr the dragon. There are other semi-divine animals living in Yggdrasil, including Dáinn, Dvalinn, Duneyrr, and Duraþrór, four stags, and the goat Heiðrún, who eat Yggdrasil's branches.

As Poul Anderson and Ron Ellik put it in their chorus of "The Childish Edda":

> Yggdrasil, where nine worlds flash, is a noble piece of ash
> That shelters Norns and Gods and all that crew;
> There's a dragon gnaws the base of an eagle's resting place
> And four harts, a goat and squirrel complete the zoo.

Composed, according to Anderson in his 1999 Operation Luna, by them "on an overnight drive long ago", to the tune of the folk song "The Ballad of Jesse James". The whole song is often sung at s-f conventions.

One of the most insignificant animals in Yggdrasil is Ratatoskr, Drill-Tooth, the squirrel who runs up and down the giant tree to carry news and messages between the eagle and the dragon. Ratatoskr has a reputation as a gossip and a liar, deliberately stirring up trouble between the eagle and the dragon for unknown reasons—out of boredom or maliciousness, perhaps out of frustration at being dismissed as insignificant by all the others, or more ominously to hasten Ragnarok, the Final Battle.

In "Contract Negotiations", Ratatoskr doesn't intend to cause trouble as much as to get the eagle and dragon to take him more seriously, and to support his growing family. Matters start to escalate out of control.

(One of the most popular fanzines in s-f fandom from November 1964 to May 1967 was the bi-weekly Ratatosk, published by Bruce Pelz, to spread the news and gossip of s-f fandom.)

Contract Negotiations

by Field T. Mouse

"You awake?"

Ratatoskr chittered, rolling onto his bare, furry back and hiding his whiskered face with russet paws. It was October, the heart of autumn, and Sol's light was bold and rich. The ethereal rays came from sharp angles, knifing through the open bedroom window and splashing inky shadows to the sides. Eventually, the red squirrel let his arms fall aside, sensitive blue eyes squinting heavily as he slowly blinked the fog from his mind. He'd dreamt about something last night but couldn't remember it. Reality was too clear and present.

The anticipation of another long day in Yggdrasil, the World Tree, was preemptively draining. *I'm a glorified message boy. Up and down, back and forth, expected to deliver anything I'm given. No questions asked, rain or shine. I don't think the other gods appreciate just how much I do for them.*

"Rata?" pressed the feminine voice beside him, more firmly than before. "You really need to-"

"Are any of us truly awake?" he opined, pulling himself together. "Perhaps life is but an elaborate dream, and we are both the dreamers *and* the dream? It must be so. For how else would I find myself in bed with such a fine squirrel as yourself?" He wriggled onto his side and flashed his mate a charming, bucktoothed smile, the same one that had first caught her attention many moons ago. "No, I wish to never wake up."

She gave him a harmless punch.

"Ow," he squeaked. "And here I was expecting a kiss!"

"You're going to be late, 'honey-tongue.'"

"I'm never late, acorn," he cooed back, wrapping an arm around her. He pulled her close, flush to his body. The female squirrel squeaked but didn't resist. She, too, was adorned in nothing but her pelt. "You, on the other paw…" She was supposed to come into heat last week. She hadn't.

"I have an appointment with Freyja today," she said quietly, burying her nose in his neck-fur. "Then I'll…we'll," she corrected, "know for sure." She pulled her head back, locking eyes from mere inches away. Hers were a shimmering emerald green. "She has a knack with these things."

"I would hope so." Freyja was the goddess of fertility, after all. "I really wish I could go with you, but-" He stopped, breathing of his mate's scent and trying to control his thoughts. *It's too early for daydreams.* "I suppose this is my fault, Brigida."

The other squirrel touched her nose to his. "Are you apologizing?" She seemed amused. Ratatoskr was rarely sheepish.

"Should I?"

"It takes two to tango, dear."

"True," he mumbled, their whiskers tangling.

"We both wanted to start a family eventually," she reassured. "Right?"

"Also true."

"So, the timeline's been sped up by a few years. No big deal."

"Except it changes everything," he insisted seriously. "We're lower gods. We have our place, just as the higher gods have theirs. They float. We orbit." He took a deep breath. "To create new life and have it orbit us? How might that change the balance of our universe?"

"Don't be so dramatic." She rolled her eyes. "We're not the first gods to have offspring."

"I know, but-"

"You'll make a good father," she assured.

He skipped a beat. "You think so?"

"I know so."

Ratatoskr closed his eyes for a moment. *We've barely known each other two whole years. Only been mated for one. Less than one, actually. We haven't had enough time together! Now, more stress, more responsibilities. Are the rewards really worth it? Are we ready for this? Am I mature enough?* He blinked as he realized, "If you are with child, I suppose we'll need a bigger place?"

"Definitely." She sighed and withdrew from him. Her paws bunched up the bed-sheets. "We're in a small, one-bedroom abode."

"It's not small. It's cozy," he defended.

"I know you've lived here a long time, but-"

"Yeah. It's not enough." He'd always resided on the east face of Yggdrasil, always waking up to the sun. He sat up, the sheets and covers slipping away from his rich, earthy pelt. He swung his legs out of bed and bounced upright, padding directly to the room's sole window.

The first thing he did was shut it. It was a bit *too* cool in here. Afterwards, he gazed out upon the glory that was Yggdrasil. It was hard not to be impressed. The ancient ash tree was a hundred times bigger than any living thing in the sprawling, mountainous forest it towered over, with as many branches as there were planets in the sky. Branches wide and sturdy enough to support dwellings like the one he was in. They pierced the heavens, creating paths to other worlds and dimensions. The base of the behemoth was stabilized by three incredibly strong roots that tapped into the underbelly of existence. *Such wonders above and below. And me stuck in the middle.*

"Are you alright, Rata?" Brigida asked worriedly, remaining in bed. She saw the pensive look on the male squirrel's face. "It's not-"

"It's not you," he reassured immediately, giving her a lingering glance. "It could never be you, love. Perish the thought. If your condition is what we suspect, my pride will be so great that I will surely fall from it."

The words caused her to blush, though her reddish brown fur prevented it from being obvious. He could tell, though. He saw the way her ears self-consciously flattened, the way her eyes moved downward.

"It just puts things into perspective, is all. I need a moment to think," Ratatoskr breathed. Life had always been somewhat of a lark to him, light and breezy. What was the point of being alive if you weren't having fun? *Parenthood is serious, though. It's going to change you.* There was that word again. His whiskers twitched. *Change. Growth. Evolution. Gods are supposed to be solid, not malleable! What if I don't want to be changed? I like who I am, who I've been.* His bushy tail fluttered. *Don't consider it change, then. Consider it progress.*

Outside, the tapered, oval leaves of Yggdrasil made for a fiery kaleidoscope of reds, browns, and yellows. Stirred by a faint breeze, they rustled musically and refracted the light a million times over. It was like being surrounded by living, breathing fields of stained glass. The ash's helicopter seeds were preparing to release, too, promising to litter the eternal forest, ensuring it would be forever choked with trees. "We'll need to relocate to another branch. You're right about that," he told his mate. "But I'll need a 'raise' to manage it."

"Is that going to be a problem?" The gods living in and about the World Tree didn't use traditional currency. Rather, they were gifted or allocated resources and powers based on their current standing in the hierarchy. The more esteemed your position, the more power you were bestowed. And the more power you had, the more privileges. Like having a bigger home, for instance.

Brigida had her own job, working for the four buck brothers, Dainn, Dvalinn, Duneyrr, and Durapror, but Rata's influence as 'personal messenger' to the Tree's two most-powerful gods would be easier to parlay into favors.

"I mean, if it's-"

"My bosses are impossible," he stressed, combing a paw through his ungroomed head-fur. They were also mate-less and childless, so he wasn't sure how sympathetic they'd be to his and Brigida's situation.

"As impossible as you? Surely not." Ratatoskr had a reputation for being a bringer of gossip and stirrer of silly trouble. There wasn't a shred of juicy information he overheard that he didn't share with her. There were things

Brigida knew, through him, that could cause scandals across the heavens. She liked that.

"I'm a god, Brigida. Comes with the territory." He stood up straighter, chest puffing out slightly.

"I would ask you to prove it, but then you'd *really* be late," she teased.

"That I'm a god?" He chuckled, giving her a look born of prolonged intimacy. "As if I haven't proven it already. And I thought we established my punctuality."

"Did we?"

He just looked out the window, again.

"I met them at the Midsummer celebration a few months ago," Brigida said, staying on topic.

"Eagle and Nidhogg?"

"Mm-hmm." She finally got out of bed herself and shuffled over to him. Her fur was a more fiery hue than his earthy one, her tail impossibly fluffy. "They seemed alright."

Rata turned and put his paws on her hips. Together, they stood silhouetted in the light pouring through the window. "They put on airs in public, just as anyone does. But behind closed doors, they're rather demanding. Petulant." He searched for other adjectives. "One of them is oblivious. The other one's snooty. He won't even tell me his name!" *Predators are so full of it.*

"You're good with words, Rata. You're a messenger. A communicator." She blew at his whiskers. "A manipulator."

"Am not!" he said half-heartedly.

"I couldn't stand you when we first met."

"I remember."

"But you didn't give up. Look at us now."

"Believe me, I've been looking since I woke," he breathed, eyes drifting over her figure again. "And not everyone is as forgiving as you are."

"See? You know how to flatter a soul."

"Must be unintentional," he assured.

"You're not that innocent."

He smiled and added, in regards to his bosses, "Getting them to agree with me? That's easy. But I need them to agree with each other." The smile faded. Any status or power increase for an Yggdrasil resident had to be ratified by both 'chief' gods. And Unnamed Eagle and Nidhogg were rarely on the same book, let alone the same page.

"What happened to the 'dreamer and the dream'? The power of positive thinking?"

"The dreamer requires tea." His stomach growled. "The dream is breakfast."

"Well, you know where the kettle is," she said simply. "And the cupboards."

"You're not joining me?" he asked, unable to hide his disappointment.

"I'm going to lay back down for a while." She was anxious about her appointment with Freyja, and her appetite was subsequently nowhere to be found. "The buck brothers gave me the day off."

"Very nice of them."

"They're pretty reasonable. And they actually get along," she jabbed.

"Well, unlike my superiors, yours *are* related by blood. So, they have an excuse," Rata pointed out.

Brigida giggled. "Didn't know one needed a reason to be civil."

"We're all animals at heart," he told her.

"That we are," she breathed. "I guess I'll see you this evening, then?"

"Are you shoving me out the door?"

"You're going to be late," she repeated.

"Am not." He went to her, kissing her forehead and adding, "I love you, Brigida."

"I love you, too, Drill-Tooth."

"I hate that nickname."

"Do you?" she said with a knowing smile.

"Makes me sound old."

She put a paw over his chest and added, "Just remember: the mediator between head and hands is the heart. It'll be alright as long as you can bridge that gap."

"I'm the heart?" He gave a bucktoothed grin. "The rest of Yggdrasil would laugh if they heard you say that."

"I guess they don't know you're a closet romantic."

"Don't you go telling them," he pleaded as he gathered his clothes and padded for the kitchen. "You'll ruin my reputation!"

* * *

"Messages, today?" Ratatoskr asked, crossing his arms impatiently. He stood contrapposto in front of the fearsome reptile. The massive cave beneath the World Tree was deathly dark, save for candles and torches that were clustered about, illuminating the three main super-roots that dug into the soil of the multi-verse. There were gaps that led to the surface, but being under the shade of the tree's mighty branches, not much natural light made it through except in winter when there were no leaves to block it.

"Hmm? What? Who's there?" Nidhogg spun about, his thick, spaded tail stirring the musty air.

"Rata," the squirrel replied, angular ears cocking. It was never totally quiet down here. Everything echoed. The squirrel swore he could hear intermixing plainchants, but he was never sure where they were coming from. Maybe it was his imagination. *Or maybe they're dirges. If I weren't so accustomed to it, this place would be creepy.*

"Ah, yes. Messenger." It wasn't that the dragon's hearing was bad. It was that he was always distracted. He was a textbook scatterbrain. A hungry one, at that. His sharp teeth glistened in the glow of golden firelight as he finished a particularly tasty morsel. "Mm-f! Mm-h." Nidhogg was fond of devouring sinful souls, which existed as balls of red, pulsating light. When he bit into them, ruby juice flowed out. It looked suspiciously like blood.

Rata wondered if the 'souls' felt pain. *I suppose it wouldn't be a punishment if they didn't.* He tried not to dwell on such things. It wasn't his problem, after all. *Besides, there's nothing I can do about it.*

The dragon picked his sharp teeth with an overlarge splinter. He enjoyed gnawing on the roots of the World Tree itself, much to Unnamed Eagle's dismay. He was always scolding Nidhogg for it in his messages, and Nidhogg would respond how the tree was too big and magical for him to actually kill and, really, weren't the roots a delicacy he'd earned the right to enjoy? Wasn't he a god? Didn't that entail special privileges? And why did the roots taste so good if they weren't meant to be eaten? Nidhogg loved rhetorical questions. Asking them meant no one could tell him he was unequivocally wrong.

"I'm glad you're here," Nidhogg said, wiping at his snout.

"Are you?" Rata deadpanned, finding that hard to believe.

"Yes." The hulking reptile, being more beastly than not, waddled over to the squirrel. He didn't bother with clothes. Or modesty. Thankfully, he wore his genitals on the inside. Rata wasn't a prude, but he didn't find the god very attractive. "I've got several important messages today."

"Oh?" He read all of Nidhogg and Eagle's correspondences. They sealed their scrolls with ribbon instead of wax, making them much easier to break into. *It's almost like they want me to read them.* It would be a stretch to classify most of them as 'important.' They usually consisted of boasts and bickering and a whole bunch of godly minutiae, which Rata would use to needle them with. It was fun, no mistake! But, sometimes, he wished they'd put a bit more wit and spice into their messages. *Give me a few more ingredients to work with!*

"They're around here somewhere." The dragon huffed and puffed. "Here you go." Nidhogg shoved a collection of crinkled scrolls at the squirrel. Three or four of them. His letters tended to be sloppier than Eagle's perfectly composed ones. This, too, had been brought up in the correspondence, to which the dragon would insist 'the gift is more important than the wrapping.' Which had led to a weeks-long argument with Eagle about whether the dragon's words were gifts or not.

"You got soul-juice on this one," the squirrel complained, turning one of the scrolls end over end before tucking it in his satchel. "Ick!"

"Eagle won't notice."

"He has *eagle* eyes, Nid," Rata reminded.

Nidhogg snorted indignantly, nostrils flaring. "If he has a problem with the neatness of my messages, he can put that in a message to me!"

"I'm sure he will," the squirrel muttered, double-checking the rest of the scrolls before stowing them away. One of them caught his eye. It looked too crisp and clean, almost like it hadn't been written on yet. He peeked inside and, sure enough, it was blank. *Strange. Must've been an accident. Nidhogg is always in a rush.* He was the exact opposite of Unnamed Eagle, who was overly-ponderous.

The squirrel raised a paw to tell the dragon he'd given him an unwritten message, but the subterranean god had already resumed his meal. He never seemed to get full. As prey, Rata knew never to interrupt a predator when they were eating. *Not unless you want to get eaten yourself. Which I don't.* So, he shrugged and tucked the empty scroll away. "Later, Nid."

"Mm-f, mm!"

Clambering up one of the thick roots with his bushy tail flittering as a counterbalance, Rata left the underworld and began the long journey to the top of Yggdrasil. As a squirrel, he wasn't afraid of heights. He was instinctually attuned to them. But, still, it was a haul.

The ascent consisted of varied spiral walk-ramps built into the outer layer of the trunk. They had guardrails on them for safety. Eventually, they segued into proper stair-steps before finally giving way, when the trunk tapered too thinly to support them, to nothing but bark and branches itself. That final stint was always hardest. Climbing with claws and paws and hoping you didn't miss your foot-hold? It was especially perilous in inclement weather, like thunderstorms and blizzards. Eventually, a ladder would lead up to Eagle's courtyard.

It was almost an hour's travel, one-way. Luckily, the squirrel kept in good shape. He rarely got winded and would nibble on nuts and treats to keep his energy up as needed. He found the journey downward to be quicker and easier than the journey up. It figured that Unnamed Eagle would be harder to reach. His whole persona was built on being enigmatic. He was distant in every form and fashion, right down to concealing his name from everyone for some paranoid reason.

Rata had plenty of time to think during his commutes. As he scaled the grand, spiritual tree this particular morning, he thought about his mate and the child they were almost certainly going to have. *And the 'raise' I need to afford it.* It was clear that his bosses weren't going to listen to him. He knew that based on experience and observation. They were lost in their own private kingdoms. And even if they weren't, why should they care? *Aside from being tone-deaf, they have all the power. They're predators. I'm prey. Nature's never been fair. They aren't about to allocate me more jurisdiction without a good reason.*

He stopped and leaned against the ramp's guardrail, gazing out at the colorful, temperate scenery, trying to draw inspiration from the majesty of it. It only partially worked. After a moment, he pulled Nidhogg's mistakenly empty scroll out of his satchel. The breeze stirred through his fur, mimicking the schemes that were beginning to swirl about his mind. *They won't listen to me. And they won't listen to each other.* He pulled out a canteen of water and downed a good quarter of it. He wiped at his lips. "Hmm…"

What if one of them wanted my services exclusively? The other would throw a fit and try to prevent it. They would fight over me. After all, they think they own me, right? A smile crept onto his muzzle. *It'd become an escalating tug-of-war, and then I'd step in with a compromise that seems to favor each of them but actually favors me more.*

If I did get caught trying to trick them, which I won't, they'd have to admit they'd been duped by a lesser god. I mean, what's my power? Communication? Gossiping? Hardly cause for worship. They wouldn't want anyone to find out about that. Besides, I've served them loyally for years. They owe me some degree of leeway. I just need to get them to see that.

He strained his fuzzy ears to make sure no one was coming up or down the ramp. He knew both Nidhogg and Unnamed Eagle's cursive by heart. He'd been reading their messages long enough to easily forge their handwriting. Not that he'd ever attempted such a thing! But, well, as luck would have it, he had a blank piece of godly stationary with Nidhogg's official stamp on it.

He'd felt that his bosses had taken him for granted for some time now. It would be nice to see how much they 'cared.' He'd always felt he was the brightest member of their little triad, anyhow. *Is it even a contest?* Those two, in their isolated chambers, were slightly out of touch. *They've lost a step or two compared to me. I'm in a relationship. I'm about to have a child. I know the gossip of the entire Tree. I'm the one in touch with reality, not them. That means I'm the smartest. Now, I can finally prove it.*

He fished in his satchel for something to write with.

After I find some ink…

* * *

The very top of the tree was perfectly manicured. The elevated wooden courtyard was framed by stylishly scraggly branches and colorful leaves. Three-quarters of the space was open-aired, but there was a segment with a roof for inclement weather. Occasionally, a breeze blew and stirred the leaves loose, and they skittered in circles from one side of the space to the other. Eagle's avian servants would quickly flap out, sweep them up, and duck back into the shadows.

"What is this?" Eagle asked imperiously, staring down from his slightly-elevated perch. It kept him a few feet above the floor. Where Nidhogg's voice was gruff and growly, Eagle's was high-pitched and squawky. Rather than machismo, he projected an erudite over-education, as if he had knowledge of many things. He certainly claimed to. But Rata suspected much of it was bluff and bluster.

Above them, the sky was a cloudless, brilliant blue. To the sides were endless horizons, worlds upon worlds. Nine of them, in fact. Rata often wondered what was going on in all those places. Things beyond imagination? Things to sate appetites both beautiful and gross? It wasn't his position to find out. Those realms were forbidden to him. He could only survive here. His soul was tethered to Yggdrasil. He'd strongly resent that if he weren't so resigned to it. *At least I have Brigida. I don't recall how I muddled through all those years without her.*

"Messenger!" the chief bird scolded, flapping his wing-arms impatiently. His feathers were a mixture of celestial gold and white, and he wore a simple, loose tunic made of comfortable off-white fabric.

"What is what, master?" Rata asked, jarred from his thoughts. Unnamed Eagle preferred to be addressed as 'master' by those subservient to him. Which, apparently, was everyone on the tree. He was an ego with wings.

"Nidhogg writes..." The eagle's keen eyes quickly scanned the scroll, as did the eyes of the feral hawk that inexplicably perched on his shoulder. He scoffed. "I suppose 'writes' should be used loosely. Barely legible. Have you seen this?"

Rata nodded. "Same as always."

"I've been telling him to take lessons."

"He gets defensive when he's told what to do. Also, he does have feral paws," the squirrel defended. "Makes it a little hard to-"

"That's no excuse!"

Eagle's hawk shrieked in agreement. The little, jet-black bird always seemed to be grumpy.

Eagle nodded, affirming the affirmation. "Quite right, pet." Then, to Rata, "So, why, all of a sudden, would he want your services to himself? He wants you as his...personal secretary?"

"Really?" the squirrel went, feigning surprise.

"Does he even know what a secretary is?" Eagle continued. He hated having his authority challenged in any way.

"You'd have to ask him." Rata's tail gave some over-exaggerated flutters. He tried to play up his cuteness as much as possible. *Even Eagle has to recognize cute, right?*

"Maybe I will. Maybe," the Eagle emphasized, "I will put that in my next message."

"You should!"

Eagle tilted his head. "He hasn't mentioned any of this to you, has he?"

"No, master, I swear it," the squirrel replied truthfully, putting a reddish paw over his heart.

"Mm." The eagle's honeyed brows furrowed. "You've been my primary messenger for several years, now. I rely on you." He cleared his throat before he became too complimentary. "I have too many important thoughts to convey to the Tree."

"Right." The red squirrel tried to keep the sarcasm out of his voice.

"Obviously, I can't deliver them all myself. There aren't enough hours in the day." It wasn't just Nidhogg he communicated with. There were other gods, as well. But he and the dragon were tethered together in an odd way. They were like the sun and moon of the World Tree. "He's always looking for ways to inconvenience me." He clacked his beak together. "Scaly bastard."

The feral hawk churred.

Eagle's eyes widened. "I know! He doesn't have an original thought in his pea-sized brain." Turning his attention back to Ratatoskr, Eagle said, "I can't have him stealing you from me. It would set a bad precedent in the Tree."

"Well, if he's that intent on it," the squirrel started.

"Perhaps you should be *my* secretary," Eagle interrupted.

"Yours?"

"Of course, that would be somewhat of a promotion. I'd have to create a new position for you. And then hire a new messenger to replace the spot left open by your move. And for the love of the gods…" He trailed off, shaking his head. "So much paperwork! That's probably why Nidhogg is doing this. Either he robs me of a valued servant, or he forces me to deal with the red tape. Either way, I'm inconvenienced." The avian reached for a scroll and some ink. "He's about to get an earful."

"Don't you mean eyeful?"

"Mm?" Eagle went, already writing.

"Also, to be clear, he can't steal me from you," the squirrel asked, "but you can steal me from him?"

"We both know who's *really* in charge here, don't we?" Eagle spread his wings as if the answer were obvious. "If he and I switched positions, I could do his job in a heartbeat. There's no way he could do mine."

"Have you seen the amount of souls he eats? It gets pretty messy."

Eagle ignored that, continuing, "This is a shot across my beak. It demands a response."

"If you insist, master." Ratatoskr tried to suppress a smile. He was both relieved and surprised. The forged message had aced the test! Eagle had more than taken the bait. *I so do love stirring the pot!*

* * *

"Eagle wants you to be what?" The dragon squinted and read the message again. He often had trouble with the bigger words. "His secrecy?"

"Secretary," Rata corrected.

"Oh." It was an hour later, and Nidhogg seemed blindsided. He swung his long-necked head about with consternation. "What brought this on?"

"I don't know, Nid." Rata shrugged and made a dismissive sound, straddling a tendril of one of Yggdrasil's roots. "You know Eagle."

"Hah. Do I?" The dragon scoffed and paced back and forth on all fours. His blood pressure began to rise. "He's jealous of our bond. Always has been." He stopped. "We have a bond, correct?"

"Oh, of course!" the squirrel squeaked. "We're best, uh...buds?"

"He doesn't have a bond with anyone!" Nidhogg taunted. "Cause he's... he's-"

"Anti-social?" Rata supplied.

"That! Yes. And he's-"

"Introverted?"

"You are a mind-reader, messenger." He lifted a front paw and gestured between himself and the rodent. "We are scarily alike."

Ratatoskr snickered. "That is scary, yes."

Nidhogg settled back on his haunches and scratched at his scales. Dry bits floated off and fell to the cave floor. "He sits up there alone all day, seeing all, knowing all. Or claiming to," the dragon added bitterly. "He thinks he's better than me. Just because he reads books in his luxurious home. My life could be a book. I've done more than he ever has. My days are just packed!"

Rata quirked a brow and looked around at the dark, deadened underrealm. A single cricket chimed.

"Shut up, you!" Nidhogg bellowed at the hidden insect.

Rata raised his paws and tried to calm the reptile down. "You're letting Eagle get under your scales. Just calm down."

"How can I? He shows me no respect! You've been mine for as long as you've been his, and he asks no permission before claiming sole rights to your services? He's always been jealous that someone as 'lowly' as me would be on his level. How petty! There are secrets about the World Tree that I deserve to know." The dragon began to pant so hard that smoke threatened to billow out of him. He violently clawed at the root Rata was reclining on.

The startled squirrel yelped and scrabbled to safety. Nidhogg often got worked into a tizzy over Eagle's correspondences, but he rarely took it this personally.

"I won't let him strong-arm me this time!"

"He has wings."

"I won't let him strong-wing me, either!" Nidhogg corrected, eyes glowing red. "Where's my quill and paper?"

* * *

"He says he needs you more than I do?" Eagle asked incredulously, golden eyes scanning the unrolled scroll. "Unbelievable."

Eagle's pet hawk whistled sarcastically.

"That's it exactly, pet. Listen to this, messenger," Eagle said, waving the piece of paper at the squirrel.

Ratatoskr cocked his ears, pretending he hadn't already read the entire scroll on the journey upward from Yggdrasil's base.

"He says I have more servants than him to begin with, so I can spare you. Hah! Doesn't he realize there's much more to do up here than down there? Nothing goes on in those caves."

"Not really, no," Rata agreed. *Nothing that should see the light of day, anyway.*

"All the activity happens here! I spend my days peering into the Nine Realms," he emphasized dramatically, "making sure they're stable. If they're not, I have to document it and alert the proper gods to enact a remedy. Even if things are okay, I *still* have to log what I observe. It's a lot of responsibility, keeping records and making sure the multi-verse doesn't fall apart." His feathers ruffled. "Keeps me up at night."

"I wouldn't want to do it."

"No, it takes a special individual," Eagle confirmed, sitting taller on his perch. He gazed into the distance heroically. "I'm the lighthouse in the storm. I'm the watchtower before the battle." He flapped his wing-arms, his tunic stirring. "Nine worlds vs. three roots?" The eagle made a face. "I require a much larger staff than Nidhogg."

Rata rubbed at his whiskery cheeks, trying to seem subservient. He curled his tail downward. "If he spent a day in your feathers, master, he'd change his tune."

"No doubt, messenger. No doubt. I am glad you are on my side. Nidhogg and I are only partners on paper. In practical terms, I run this Tree." He tossed the dragon's unrolled, messily-written scroll. The breeze caused it to skitter aside. Eagle trilled with annoyance. Air rushed in and out of his nares. "Hmm. Wait a minute..."

"What?" Rata's tilted his head.

"The scroll. I need it back."

One of Eagle's avian servants, a chickadee, quickly retrieved and returned it before flapping back into the shadows.

Ratatoskr blinked. Just how many servants *did* Eagle have?

"How did I miss it before?" The eagle sniffed at the letter. His eyes lit up. "It's faint. I thought it must be flowers in the breeze, but no, there's perfume on this."

"There is?" The squirrel leaned forward, nose twitching. "Are you sure?"

"Positive."

"Huh." *I should've noticed that. Why didn't I notice that? Was it making me think of Brigida? Was I too busy reveling in my scheme? The only way you can outsmart higher gods is by having a better attention to detail. Don't get cocky, Rata!*

"He doesn't wear perfume." Eagle raised a brow. "Does he?"

"Not normally, no," Rata joked.

"Then there's only one explanation. He's fooling around on the job, isn't he?"

"Well..." Ratatoskr hesitated. As a purveyor of juicy gossip, he was bursting to spill the beans. It was expected of him. *But do I have any beans to spill? Telling fibs is one thing when I know they're false, but what if there's a kernel of truth to them?* "When you live in the realm of the dead, you sorta need a little jolt of life to keep you going."

"I hope that is not a justification."

"Look, I've never walked in on anything. I can't give you any proof," the squirrel said honestly.

"But you have suspicions?"

"I guess?"

"Tell me. I want all the details." The eagle adjusted himself while his hawk pretended to look away.

"I don't have any," Rata insisted.

"You always have details, messenger. It is your job."

"Speaking of jobs, I thought we were concerned about securing my professional services?" Ratatoskr insisted, trying to keep his 'plan' on track.

"That can wait. I want to know who Nidhogg is consorting with."

"I honestly don't know."

"I don't believe you."

"Well, I don't!"

"You do."

"Don't!"

"Do!"

Rata frowned. "You ever been down there?"

"Of course I have." Eagle folded his wing-arms across his chest. "Just not recently."

"Sure, it's big, dark, and spooky, but it's lit solely by firelight. And there's all this hypnotic, ethereal moaning going on." He cleared his throat. "It's actually kind of romantic." *Aside from the smell.*

The eagle chuffed. "Nidhogg? Romantic?"

Rata twitched with agitation. *This isn't supposed to be about Nidhogg! This is supposed to be about me!* "I never see any ladybirds up here," he baited, trying to turn the tables. "Why is that?"

Eagle stuttered. "I'm...I'm the most visible figure on Yggdrasil. I will not debase myself by frolicking," he said, choosing his words carefully, "in broad daylight."

"I suppose you wait for night for that." The squirrel gave Eagle a slow look-over. He didn't look like someone who'd enjoyed intimacy recently. All that tension! *I almost feel sorry for him. Almost.*

"I'm still waiting for those details, messenger," he said, not letting the rodent off the hook. "I know you know what Nidhogg knows."

"Even if I did know what he knows, if he knew that I knew and you-"

"Stop, stop!" Eagle demanded, waving a wing-arm. "You're not going to fool me with wordplay."

The squirrel sighed. *No, but I'd like to.* "Perhaps you'd like the 'details' in writing?" the squirrel offered with a cheeky glance. "Then you can look at it after dark, when you're alone."

"Yes. Then I can-" Eagle stopped short and squinted. "Just what are you implying?"

"Nothing!" The rodent held up his paws, eyes widening innocently.

"That because I don't consort with every goddess in the Tree, I'm not as popular as that infernal wyrm?"

"I don't know why you wouldn't be."

"And that because of his reputation as being 'one of the guys,' he feels he can have what and who he wants? Including your professional messaging services?"

There we go! Back on track!

"Being popular with minions is one thing. I'm popular with the upper echelon. They all respect me!"

"As do I, master," Rata said with a bow. "It would be an honor to work more closely with you."

"Obviously."

"But Nidhogg can be quite persistent..."

"Has the beast threatened to devour you if you don't agree to work solely for him? He's always using violence as a negotiating tool. Sex and violence." He clucked his tongue. "That's all reptiles are good for."

"Well, he was speaking with a mouthful of tortured souls. So, he *may* have, yes."

"Figures." Eagle sighed, shaking his head. "Threatening other gods? Even if they are extremely *minor* ones," Eagle added. "There's no excuse for it.

Rata scrunched his face. "Mm. Thanks for sugarcoating that."

"I shall have to ask Thor to smite him."

"I wouldn't go that far." As much as he liked taking shots at his bosses, Rata didn't want them replaced. Better the devils you knew. *In a perverse way, I need them as much as they need me. I can game them. There's no guarantee I'd be able to do the same to their replacements.* "Besides, what does Thor have on you? You overlook nine worlds, remember? He just parties and smashes things with that hammer." *Or something.* Rata had never actually met the guy.

"This is true." Eagle settled on his perch and gazed beyond the courtyard and into the vast branches that led to the other realms. "I have much more finesse."

Rata followed his eyes. There was a moment of silence before he asked, "Do you ever wonder what's going on over there? In the other worlds?"

"Which one?"

"I don't know. Any of them. All of them."

"I know enough. My eyes are very powerful. I can see into them, see things most would only dream of."

"But you can't experience them. Not really. None of us can." The squirrel allowed himself a moment of sincerity, confiding, "It's not fair we're stuck in this tree all our lives, performing the same tasks over and over."

"That is our lot," Eagle said stoically. "We are gifted long life and mythical status. In exchange, we have our roles to play, and we must play them no matter what. Civilization relies on it. They draw comfort from it. Without us, they would crumble. Make no mistake, many would kill to be in our positions."

"I was born a god. I didn't aspire to be one," the squirrel whispered, his tail fluttering in the light breeze.

"Sometimes, greatness is not sought. It is thrust upon us." Eagle exchanged a glance with his hawk and cleared his throat, feeling naked in the presence of so much sentiment. He returned his attention to Ratatoskr. "Anyway, you're right. I don't need to go to Thor. He'll only think less of me for not being able to handle all this myself." He raised his voice, trying to get back into the spirit of the argument they'd been having. But the moment of shared existentialism had derailed his furor. "I shall write Nidhogg a *most* stern letter."

"Sterner than the last one?"

"I imagine so."

The feral hawk let loose a piercing cry, trying to inspire his owner.

"What'd he say?" Rata wondered.

"The pen is mightier than the sword," Eagle replied.

* * *

"How did Eagle find out about my companions?" Nidhogg demanded angrily, scales burning with embarrassment. He tore up Eagle's note and then stuffed it into his maw and ate it. He didn't care if it tasted dry. "Did you tell him, messenger? How could you?" he mumbled with his mouth full. He sounded wounded. And hungry.

"I didn't!" Rata held up his paws, feeling bad. He stood on the cave floor this time, gazing upward at the burly beast. This whole scheme was supposed to be fun! Now, suddenly, he was having heart-to-hearts with Eagle and hurting Nidhogg's feelings? "I swear, I know nothing about it. I mean, I had suspicions, but-" He blinked. *Wait.* "Companions? Plural?"

"How did he know?" Nidhogg roared.

"It was just a lucky guess." Ratatoskr closed his eyes as the dragon's hot breath ruffled his head-fur. "One of your scrolls had perfume on it." He paused, trying to tread carefully. "You weren't doing anything kinky with ink and paper, were you?"

"Of course not!" The dragon slunk back, eyes darting. "I was-"

"What?"

"I was writing a love letter, okay!" the dragon insisted.

The squirrel blinked. "Really? I didn't know you were that serious about anyone."

"Well, I am." The dragon scuffed the ground with a paw.

The squirrel scuffed his foot-paws on the cave floor, curiosity piqued. "So, more than one, or-"

"I have a life, too, you know. I keep telling everyone that."

"I never said you didn't."

"He'll make fun of me, now."

"Eagle?"

"Yes."

"Why should he care?" Rata continued, trying to comfort the reptile. "I mean, I have a mate. You have your-" He gestured with his paw, awkwardly. "Whatevers. It's perfectly normal, perfectly natural! He's just jealous. He's probably lonely, too."

"I don't know why. He's got a fancier home and more prestige."

"But you're more relatable," Rata told Nidhogg. "Your heart's always in the right place."

"Thank you, messenger. That means a lot."

"No problem."

"Mm." The dragon rumbled. "See, we work well together. It should be permanent. He would steal you from me? Deny me a friend? I should dispense with messages entirely. I should go up there myself and knock his feathery ass off that ridiculous perch!"

"Nid, if I may?" Rata raised a paw. He'd worked his bosses into enough of a flurry. After all, Nidhogg had just expressed his gratitude! *That's what you wanted, wasn't it? Respect? Well, that and more power.* It was time to initiate the compromise.

"What?" the dragon asked.

"He's probably expecting that."

"So?"

"Eagle's a serious type. He hates surprises. You could knock him off-guard much more easily by doing that."

"Doing, uh…what, again?"

"Surprising him."

"Right! Yes!" The dragon nodded and then asked, "How?"

"I'm not going to lie," Rata said before outright lying. *Or is it closer to the truth than you care to admit?* "I have the best job in the multi-verse. I'm flattered you both want my services. But instead of trying to keep me for yourselves, why can't you share me? Isn't that what we've been doing all these years?" *Besides, who else is insane enough to take this job and put up with you two?*

"Go back to normal, then?" The dragon squinted. "After all he's said? Where is the victory in that?"

"Peace is its own victory. Besides, you can claim to be the bigger beast. The wise, reasonable one. Tell him you'll share me, but *only* if he gives me a raise in powers to mirror your appreciation."

"A raise?" Nidhogg squinted.

"Yeah, like...you know."

The dragon blinked. "I don't."

"A promotion."

"Why?"

"Don't you appreciate me? Haven't I worked hard for you?" Ratatoskr argued seriously. "Don't I deserve it?" The squirrel faltered. If he told the dragon the truth, the scheme would unravel. *A day's worth of mischief gone to waste.* He'd be relying, instead, on the higher god's graciousness. *Do dragons even have grace? And if they do, would I trust it more than my own wiles?*

Nidhogg tilted his head, waiting.

"Brigida's pregnant," Ratatoskr sighed. "I'm, uh, going to have a family, now." The squirrel avoided eye contact. "I can't handle it unless I have more resources. A bigger place to live, more food, more..." He trailed off, gesturing with his paws. "Things that us lower-tier gods don't have access to. I'm not asking to be as high as you! I know that's not possible, and I wouldn't want the responsibility. But maybe I can be...mid-tier? Or something? What's it gonna hurt?"

Nidhogg settled on his haunches and stroked his chin.

Ratatoskr's tail twitched.

"Upon reflection, I no longer require the services of a messenger," the dragon stated.

The squirrel's heart froze. *Did I misplay my paw? Did I push him too far?* "What?"

"My correspondences have grown to require the handling of an *express*," he emphasized, "messenger." Nidhogg gave a toothy grin. "The position is open for applicants."

⚹ ⚹ ⚹

Distant stars began to wink into sight as the sun set on Yggdrasil, the panoramic sky a swirl of vivid oranges and pinks. A bit of purple snuck in, too, tempering the visual warmth and better reflecting the feeling of the air, which held an undeniable chill. Winter was on its way. There was no denying that.

Eagle, keen eyes dilating in the changing light, exchanged a dubious look with his pet hawk before the two birds glanced at the rodent. "Express messenger?"

"I'm willing to take on the title, master," Ratatoskr said, bowing eagerly. In the shroud of heavy shadow, his reddish fur looked a deep shade of brown. "And, as I must, all the privileges that come with it."

"I'm sure you are." Eagle leaned back on his perch. "So, does this mean you'd be delivering our messages more quickly?"

Rata straightened. "Well, no, but-"

"Does it mean you will be on call twenty-four hours a day?"

"I, uh, hadn't planned on-"

"Is that because you already deliver your messages as quickly as possible or because the promotion isn't needed?"

"It *is* needed," he stressed.

"Why?"

"Nid's agreed to it, master," the squirrel insisted lamely.

"But I haven't. And you're skirting my question. You may play me for a fool, messenger, but I assure you I am not. I want the truth."

The squirrel twitched at the rebuke. "Sorry." He sighed and trailed off. When it came down to it, here and now, he found Eagle was more intimidating than Nidhogg. He wasn't as strong or violent, no. *There's a genuine distance between me and Eagle that makes his authority more official. I respect his opinion more.* "It's just that-"

"If you wanted a promotion, why didn't you ask for one?"

"I wasn't sure you'd give it," the squirrel replied quietly.

"Why not?"

The squirrel shrugged. "I wasn't convinced of my value to you. You have more important things to worry about."

"I assure you that the well-being of all the gods in Yggdrasil is something I 'worry' about," Eagle said with clear compassion. He skipped a beat before confessing, "I talked with Freyja today. She stopped by during your last trip to the roots."

"Oh."

"Seems your reputation for getting up to mischief is truly warranted!"

"The motivation was love, not mischief," the squirrel said sheepishly. He tried not to smile. He failed. "Though it was as enjoyable as the latter."

"Congratulations." Eagle nodded. "To you and your mate."

"Thank you…"

"You seem surprised?"

"Not surprised. Caught off-guard. I'm just not used to being thanked." It was more humbling than he'd expected. Now, he'd been thanked by both Nidhogg *and* Eagle. Everyone's cards were on the table. "And, to be honest, I thought I was-"

"Tricking me?"

The squirrel nodded.

"You were, at first. I was confused by Nidhogg's strange 'request' for a personal secretary. And even more confused by your passivity about the whole thing. I had a hard time believing you'd want to spend every single day beneath the ground."

"Wouldn't exactly be ideal, no," Ratatoskr echoed.

"So, I figured you were letting us fight over you. I didn't suspect you'd actually started the whole thing until I heard of your growing family, which would be a strong motivation to seek a more prestigious title." Eagle preened at his feathers. "I'm not as aloof as I look."

"Then why do you act it?"

"As I intimated earlier: we have roles we must play. Mine is that of the leader, the straight man. The rock."

"And Nidhogg's, what, chaos?" Ratatoskr paused. "So, what does that make me?"

"Though you're striving for a higher position amongst the gods of Yggdrasil, you've always have more freedom than the rest of us. Your role is more fluid. You get to move about the entirety of the tree, get to have a personal life. The fate of universes does not rest on your shoulders. You're a wild card. You don't have it that bad."

"No, I don't," the squirrel confessed.

They both went silent, listening to the breeze filter through the Tree, as well as the vocal night-bugs that accompanied it.

"Well," Eagle eventually said, taking a deep breath, "I believe your shift is over for today, *express* messenger. The sun is nearly set."

"That it is." Rata craned his neck and glanced at the Nine Worlds. At night, they glowed with enough dreams to rival the crescent moon. Biting back a warm, heartfelt smile, he adjusted his satchel. Before he left, he asked, "Surely, you've time for a little fun?" There was no ribbing in his voice. Just genuine concern.

The Eagle's beak betrayed nothing. But his eyes glinted with playfulness. "Go home."

"Of course." *Home, to Brigida. We have much good news to celebrate! My promotion. Her pregnancy. Our future.* "Thank you, Eagle." He paused and realized that for all the complaining he'd done about his superiors never thanking him, he rarely thanked them in return. "Really."

"Now!" Eagle said, shooing the rodent with his wing-arms. He wasn't comfortable with so much overt emotion. "I will have many more messages to be delivered tomorrow."

"And I will be here to deliver them," Ratatoskr promised smartly. It's not like he had anywhere else to go. And with a family in the making and a new branch to move into and a better understanding of his bosses, why would he want to be anywhere but Yggdrasil? It was the World Tree! His whole universe was here. For the first time he could remember, the squirrel god was fully at peace with that.

M. R. Anglin began writing her Silver Foxes *series, set in the anthropomorphic world of Clorth, almost ten years ago. There are four novels now:* Silver Foxes, Winds of Change, Prelude to War, *and* Into Expermia; *all available from CreateSpace and Kindle.*

A rough summary is that Clorth is inhabited by anthropomorphic animals of all species, but the nation of Expermia is extremely racist (or, in this case, speciesist). Expermia was ruled by a silver fox aristocracy for over two thousand years, and after several centuries of isolation, it is still dominated by foxes who have expelled all other species. Now Expermia is emerging from its isolation; but, based on past events, the rest of Clorth fears its militaristic government is about to start a war of conquest. The series focuses upon the tensions between the multispecies Kingdom of Drymairad and its neighbor, Expermia, which has just begun to let outsiders visit under carefully controlled conditions but is paranoid about non-foxes.

Up to now, the Silver Foxes *series has been about Clorth's society and politics. "On the Run from Isofell", Anglin's first* Silver Foxes *short story, introduces Clorth's gods and Skitter, a flying squirrel with a mission.*

On the Run from Isofell

by M. R. Anglin

The jostling of the pick-up bumping over dirt and rocks was so relaxing that Skitter almost didn't hear the whisper telling him it was time to disembark the truck bed he had been hitching a ride on. He rubbed his eyes and yawned. The sun beat down on his round, fur covered ears and made the skin under his brown fur itch. An endless sand sea stretched out across the landscape until it met the sky at the horizon—a sky so blue it dazzled Skitter's eyes. Wind blew through his fur and clothes and whistled through the sand. Ash gray trees and cacti poked up through the barren landscape.

It was so mind-blowingly beautiful that Skitter nearly fell into a trance watching it. He shook his head and stretched, his arm flaps almost catching the wind and launching him into the air. As a flying squirrel, one wrong gesture on a windy day—or on a fast moving truck—could mean take off, so he kept his arms close to his body as he knocked on the window to the cab.

"Excuse me." Skitter shouted at the driver, an otter named Darren who had agreed to give him a ride. "I have to get off here."

"Here?" The otter's voice was muffled. He opened the window and blinked in the wind. "But there's nothing around." He tried to glance at Skitter while keeping his eye on the road. "We'll be in town soon so hang tight."

Skitter sat back on his tail . . . then shifted position so he could move it out of the way. Darren was right; there was nothing out here. But he was sure that he heard Kadaiel tell him it was time to get off. And he knew better than to second-guess Kadaiel. If Kadaiel wanted Skitter to get off here, here was where Skitter was getting off.

He got to his feet. The special toga he wore fluttered in the wind. It had openings on the sides to allow his arm flaps to catch the air currents. He stepped onto the edge of the bed, stretched his arms to the sides, and jumped.

"Hey!" Darren slammed on his brakes. The truck squealed to a halt. Skitter had heard that some of the people on the mainland drove hover cars, but Darren's car had wheels. He said it made it easier to traverse the desert.

Skitter's flaps caught the air and lifted him up. But the wind he had felt earlier had died down, so Skitter parachuted to the ground and landed on packed dirt.

"Are you crazy?" Darren slammed his door before marching over to Skitter. "You could have gotten yourself killed."

"It's okay, Darren-lo." Back on the island of Kasate, where Skitter was from, the suffix "lo"—"li" for females—was a term of respect. "You didn't have to stop for me. I—oh!" Skitter stiffened. "Wait! I'm sorry. I didn't even realize . . ." He pulled money out of his pocket. "Here's some gas money. Thank you for the ride."

Darren stared at the money. "I don't want that."

"But you brought me all this way . . ."

"Forget it." Darren beckoned to Skitter. "Back on the truck. We've got a few more miles to go until town."

"But this is where I'm going." Skitter pointed down the dirt packed road he had landed on. It snaked its way through the desert. "I'm supposed to follow this road all the way down."

"This one?" Darren pointed at the road. "But there's nothing down there. It's just desert."

"Sure looks like it, doesn't it?" Skitter put his hand on his hips as he studied the path. "Guess I'd better get moving."

"Stop!" Darren jerked Skitter to a halt. "Don't you know what's down there?"

Skitter paused a moment, his eyebrows arching up. Maybe Darren was a little slow. "You told me it was desert."

"That's the road to Expermia . . . you know, the land foreigners never return from . . . at least not alive." Darren waved his fingers in a spooky kind of way.

Skitter stifled a sigh. It was official. Darren *was* a bit slow. "I'm sure that's not the case." He brushed Darren's hands off of his shoulders.

"You don't scare easy, do you?" Darren rubbed his hands over his head. "Okay, okay. I was exaggerating. But Expermians are not friendly to foreigners—what they call 'Outsiders.' And that's only if you even make it there. That desert walk is a killer, and I'm not joking about that. You could die out there."

"Really?" Skitter's eyes grew wide as he looked down the road. Imagine a path so treacherous it could kill someone by walking it. It must be the heat and the sun . . . it was pretty hot out here. A smile came to Skitter's lips. Maybe . . . just maybe, this was his time to take the final journey to Kadaiel's side and . . .

"No, no, Skitter. Not yet," came the whisper, and Skitter was certain it was chuckling.

Skitter sighed. Too bad. "It's okay, Darren-lo." He turned to Darren. "I won't die here. Kadaiel says it's not my time yet. But there's something he wants me to do down there."

"And why do you look so disappointed about not dying?" Darren gave a grunt. "I should have known this was going to be a strange day when Dabae asked me to give you a ride. Leave it to his student to be as weird as he is. Wait there a moment." He made his way back to his truck. "I can't believe this kid is only thirteen. He's causing me so much trouble . . ."

Skitter glanced down the dirt path as Darren's muttering fell away. He wanted to get going, but Kadaiel didn't seem to mind the delay. He took a deep breath and waited.

"Here we go." Darren returned holding a container with a strap on it. "Dabae told me you might pull something like this. He said if you were insistent, I'm supposed to let you go. He also said you don't think these things through."

Skitter cocked his head, his ear twitching a bit. "What do you mean?"

"Water." Darren handed him the container.

"Oh, thank you." Skitter slung it over his shoulder.

"Now listen." Darren knelt so that his face was level with Skitter's. His eyes were hard and serious, commanding Skitter's attention. "Like I said before, this road leads to Expermia, but it doesn't lead to a formal border. A border's not necessary. Most folks die of heat and thirst before they get anywhere significant. But there's a little shop on the side of the road that marks the edge of Expermia. If you can get supplies there, you might make it to where you're going. If not, your best plan is to turn your tail around and head southeast toward the town I was telling you about. It's small, but the area around it is flat so you should see it if you're within a few miles of it."

"Thank you, Darren-lo." Skitter turned to face the road. It was nice that Darren worried about him so, but there was nothing to worry about. If Kadaiel called him to do something, how bad could it be?

Skitter's fur prickled with excitement as he started down the road. This was it. He was on his first mission from Kadaiel without Dabae to guide him.

"Be careful out there, Skitter," Darren called as Skitter walked. "I don't want Dabae to have to bury one of his acolytes."

"I'll be okay." Skitter waved at him over his shoulder. "I told you; Kadaiel said it's not my time yet."

Darren shook his head. He returned to his truck and took off.

Skitter turned his attention back to the road. "You know something, Kadaiel? Some people say I'm flighty, but a lot of times they don't listen. I'm sure I told him what you said about it not being my time once before."

And though Skitter didn't see anybody, he was sure he heard Kadaiel laugh.

* * *

Skitter had never been afraid of dying—rather in a way, he was looking forward to it. Dying meant he was on his way to see Kadaiel and live with him forever. But just because he wasn't afraid of dying, that didn't mean he wanted to die. For all his life, he had thought that if he were given the option to choose his death, drowning would be on the bottom of his list. But now another option was added to his list of undesirable deaths: dehydration. But worse than dying of dehydration was living through it.

He smacked his lips as his tongue stuck to the roof of his mouth. His tongue felt like the sand on the ground, and his saliva was thick and sticky. It had only been a few hours since he left Darren, but the sun beat relentlessly on his fur. Heat from the surrounding air smothered him and drifted up from the sand, burning his sandaled feet. His toga would have been soaked with sweat if the dry air hadn't sucked it up as soon as it came out of his pores. There was no escape from the desert's torment.

Skitter plodded down the road, longing for the water he had long since finished. It was only through Kadaiel's whispered directions that he hadn't lost the road. The heat was making him drowsy and loopy all at once. And he was hallucinating. Often he'd see images of water shimmering in the distance. But every time he rushed toward it, there would be nothing but sand. Even knowing, he saw a shimmer with what looked like mountains in the distance.

Skitter was beginning to hate those water-illusions.

A dark mass appeared on the edge of the road. As Skitter plodded closer, it took on the form of a small, wooden building that was bleached gray from the sun. The wood siding was cracked and split, but it held up a tin roof that sparkled in the sun.

"Probably another fake vision." Skitter glared at it as it approached. "It will disappear soon."

But it didn't go anywhere. Skitter came to a halt next to it. Outside was a cart full of a peach colored fruit with red splotches on it. Inside was packed with groceries, food, and drinks.

"I made it!" Skitter tore toward it. "This is the place Darren-lo was talking about!"

He burst in, darted straight for the refrigerators, and grabbed an ice-cold bottle of water. Condensation dripped from it as soon as he took it out of the case. He downed the whole thing so fast, he got an ice-cream headache.

"It's totally worth it." Skitter clenched his teeth as the headache faded. Then he flung open the door to the refrigerator and allowed the cold air to waft over his hot fur.

"Hey! You! Outsider!"

"Now let's see." Skitter heard someone calling, but he didn't know anyone out here that would call out to him. "I'm going to need much more water to keep going." He scooped up as many bottles as he could carry.

"Yo, Outsider!"

Skitter's stomach rumbled. "I'm going to need food, too." He surveyed the shelves of food and caught sight of a selection of nuts on display. "Oooo! Hazelnuts! And almonds. My favorite!" He glanced at his full hands and then the nut display. "I gotta put this down." He ambled to the check-out counter.

The fox behind the counter stiffened his whiskers as Skitter unloaded his hands.

Now Skitter knew better than to stare at someone different from him, but this brown fox had ears so enormous, Skitter couldn't help it. They must have been the size of Skitter's head. Plus his brown hair had turned a shade of red at the end—as red as autumn leaves. His nametag read, "Phain."

"Listen, you Outsider!" Phain's angry tone snapped Skitter out of it.

"Sorry. I didn't mean to stare. Is it alright if I leave these here a second? I'm going to get more stuff and come back to pay for it all." Skitter swung around to the nut display.

"Wait a second!" Phain caught Skitter by the shoulder. "You can't do that!"

"Oh!" Skitter paused a moment. "Is there a basket I can use, then?"

"I mean that." Phain shook the empty water bottle Skitter had drunk. "This is unacceptable."

Skitter scratched the back of his head. "I was so thirsty, but I'll pay for it with the rest of my stuff."

"We don't serve Outsiders here."

"But I have money." Skitter reached into his pockets. "What currency do you use?"

Phain thrust his chin in the air. "We don't sell things to Outsiders, and we don't take their money!"

Skitter raised an eyebrow. "So you're mad that I drank the water, but you won't let me pay for it? That doesn't make any sense."

"It's my establishment, so it's my rules." Phain bared his teeth. "Now, you stole from me. What are we going to do about that?"

"I'm trying to—" Skitter's ear twitched. A shadow fell over him. He turned to see that two foxes with large ears and bi-colored hair had approached him from behind. They cracked their knuckles.

Skitter blinked at them. They towered over him, their ears pinned back. They wore tunics with two splits up both sides and baggy pants underneath. Long pieces of cloth held in place by silver pins dangled from around their shoulders and waists.

Skitter gazed at them and their clenching fists. "A . . . are you going to beat me up?"

"We don't take kindly to Outsider thieves around here." Phain grinned.

Skitter's ears fell. His tail flopped on the ground. He had never been in a situation like this before. What was one to do at this point?

A bright light dazzled his eyes. He tilted his head to see behind the two thugs and spied a creature, the species of which he couldn't determine, standing behind them. It had a fiery sword in its folded hands, and its gold eyes were narrowed.

Skitter hissed in a breath through his teeth. "Beating me up is not a good idea. I don't think Kadaiel wants you to do that."

"We don't care what Kadaiel thinks," said one of the thugs.

"Yeah." The other snickered. "Bring your Kadaiel around here. We'll beat him up too."

Skitter stiffened. Could it be that these people had no idea who Kadaiel was and how dangerous it was to badmouth him? Sure enough, the creature behind them—some sort of cat . . . a white leopard, maybe?—growled. He raised his sword to strike.

"Wait, wait, wait!" Skitter raised his hands. "Don't! Please. I'll leave! You don't have to hurt anybody!"

"It's too late for that!" the first thug said, and the other laughed in agreement.

Skitter turned his eyes to them. "I wasn't talking to you."

The two thugs furrowed their brows.

"That's it!" Phain rumbled deep in this throat. "I don't know what game are you playing, Outsider, but it's over now. Get rid of him, boys!"

"Excuse me!" Another fox, this one Skitter's age, shoved his way between the two big foxes. He was brown and had the largest ears Skitter had ever seen—even larger than Phain's. Seriously, they must have been twice as big as Skitter's head. And his glasses were two large round circles set on his snout. His two front teeth peeked out of his closed mouth. He wore the same type of clothes as Phain and his companions, but unlike Phain, his hair wasn't two colors. He had a bag full of food and drinks in his hand. He shot a glare at each of the foxes and slammed down a bill. "I'll take three waters." He slid Skitter's empty bottle and two unopened ones in front of Phain.

Phain snorted. "That one's opened."

"I can see that." The fox adjusted his glasses. "These make sure of it. And you can take my money. I *am* an Expermian citizen."

"You're a feisty one, aren't you?" Phain jerked his head. The two brutes moved aside.

Once they did, Skitter glanced behind them. The creature snorted through his nose and disappeared.

Skitter sighed from relief. Everyone was safe.

"Here." The big-eared fox tossed Skitter one of the unopened bottles. "Use that to get out of Expermia. Outsiders don't belong here." He turned on his heel and walked to the door.

"Wait!" Skitter scrambled after him. As he darted out of the door, he nearly crashed into a vixen his age. She had brown hair and fur, freckles on her snout, and olive green eyes. Her tan dress reached down to her shins and had a slit on either side that went up to her waist. Underneath the dress she wore a pair of brown pants. Like the other Expermians Skitter had seen thus far, she also had the same cloths hanging around her waist. They were held in place by silver pins with an engraved design on it. She gazed at Skitter with large eyes.

"Let's go, Cherraine." The fox handed her the extra bottle of water before marching toward a sand bike. It was a typical bike, but like Darren's truck it, too, used wheels instead of hover-jets.

The vixen took one last look at Skitter before she trotted after the fox.

"Wait a second." Skitter followed them.

"What do you want now, Outsider?" The fox unloaded his supplies into the sidecar.

"You saved those two big guys when you intervened." Skitter took his hands. "Thank you so much." He pumped them up and down.

"Saved them?" The fox pulled his hands out of Skitter's grasp. "I think I saved you."

The vixen, whose name seemed to be Cherraine, grabbed the fox's hands. She shook her head, pointed at Skitter, and then at her eyes. She gestured and her mouth worked, but no sounds came out.

"What?" The fox exhaled through his nose. "Cherraine, I don't understand you."

"Doesn't she talk?" Skitter studied her.

Cherraine stiffened. She released the fox's hands, dropped her eyes, and shook her head.

"I'm sorry." Skitter lowered his head.

"We have to go." The fox stuffed the rest of his things in the sidecar. "Cherraine."

Cherraine glanced at Skitter then tapped the fox on the shoulder. She pointed to Skitter then the sidecar.

"No, no, no!" The fox stomped his foot. "We are not taking him with us!"

Cherraine made a gesture as if to ask why.

"Because he's an Outsider! I've already stuck my neck out for him once because you insisted. Why are you so keen on him anyway?"

Cherraine clasped her hands and pleaded with her eyes.

"It's okay, Cherraine." Skitter smiled at her. "I don't think I could come with you anyway. I have a job to do."

"Oh, yeah?" The fox leaned on his bike. "What job?"

Skitter shrugged. "I don't know yet."

The fox clicked his tongue. "Outsiders." He sat on his bike. "Let's go, Cherraine."

"Hey, what's your name?" Skitter said as the fox put his bike in gear.

"Why do you need to know?"

Skitter shrugged.

Cherraine elbowed the fox before climbing up on the bike behind him.

"Name's Touval," said the fox.

"Touval!" Skitter smiled at him, revealing his own large, front teeth. "I'm Skitter. I'm sure we'll see each other again."

"Skitter?" Touval stifled a snicker. "Really?"

Skitter nodded.

It took a moment for Touval to wipe the smile off his face. "Well, Skitter, I doubt we'll ever see each other again." He sped off.

"I like him." Skitter watched him go. "So, Kadaiel. What do I do now?"

A faint whisper came to him, "Start walking."

Skitter groaned. "I don't want to be thirsty again."

Kadaiel said nothing.

"Okay." Skitter took a deep breath. He got back onto the road and headed down it. It might be difficult and even painful, but there was nowhere in the world Skitter would rather be than where Kadaiel wanted him to be . . . even if it was panting with thirst in the middle of a desert.

* * *

Skitter shot up to a sitting position. The moon and stars shone down on him. He had collapsed on the sand somewhere around sunset and had fallen fast asleep, but a noise had woken him in the middle of the night.

A howl tore through the still night. It was the same noise that had woken him up, but this one was much closer. A snarl rolled through the air.

Skitter swung around. A brown animal that went on all fours crept closer to him. Its teeth were bared and glistened with saliva. Its fur was on edge.

"Wow!" Skitter got to his feet. "I have never seen anything like you before. You are a beautiful creature!"

It snarled and leapt.

"Back! Back!" A figure jumped in between Skitter and the animal. He had a lit torch in one of his hands.

"Touval?" Skitter blinked at him.

"Get out of here! Nantük always travel in packs." Touval waved the torch at the creature. "Go to my bike. Now!"

Skitter glanced over his shoulder. Cherraine sat on the sand bike a short distance away. She beckoned to him furiously. Skitter darted to it. Cherraine motioned to the sidecar, so Skitter jumped in, squashing some of their supplies in the process. Touval threw the torch at the creature, darted to the bike, hopped on in front of Cherraine, and took off. The creature galloped after them but soon fell behind.

"What did I tell you?" Touval shouted at Cherraine as he drove. "I told you he'd be nothing but trouble. Why did you insist on following him? We've lost half a day of traveling because he walks so slow."

Cherraine ducked her head but held on tight to Touval.

"Cherraine . . ." Touval sighed. "And you!" He shot a glare at Skitter. "You are so danger-prone, Outsider."

"I would have been fine." Skitter tapped his knees. "Kadaiel said this wasn't my time to go yet . . . though, being attacked by that thing would have hurt a lot. So thanks."

Touval took a moment to stare at Skitter. "Whatever." He shook his head. "Weirdo."

Skitter let a snicker escape him. That wasn't the worst thing he had been called in his life, and Touval probably wouldn't be the last to say that about him.

* * *

It was surprisingly cold in the desert at night. Goosebumps rose in waves on Skitter's skin as the wind from the bike's motion washed over him. He had bundled himself in his tail and had started to feel cozy when Touval pulled the sand bike to a stop.

"We'll camp around here tonight." Touval surveyed the area. "But we need a place far enough from the road that we don't get seen."

"Why don't you want anyone to find you?" Skitter buried his nose in his tail.

"I . . . uh . . . it's . . ." Touval turned away, scratching his cheek. "It's none of your business, that's what."

Skitter cocked his head. This whole situation was getting more interesting as time went on.

Cherraine gasped. She tugged at Touval's clothes and pointed into the distance. When Skitter looked, he saw an orange, flickering glow on the sand. A whisper beckoned him to the light.

"Firelight." Touval tapped the seat of his bike. "We should head off and travel a bit more. We don't want to—hey! Cherraine!"

Cherraine had hopped off of the bike and darted toward the fire.

"She's got the right idea." Skitter jumped out of the sidecar and trotted after her.

"I am surrounded by crazies! Get back here, you two." Touval darted after them.

When Skitter caught up to Cherraine, she was standing before the fire staring at a figure sitting next to it. It was a white Alsatian—what some people call a German Shepherd. He wore the same type of clothes as both Touval and Cherraine . . . actually, the same kind of clothes as all the Expermians Skitter had met thus far had worn.

"Hello." The Alsatian smiled at them. "Come by the fire and get warm."

There was something about that voice that made Skitter's heart jump. He dashed to the Alsatian's side before he realized that he was snuggling next to a stranger. But the Alsatian didn't mind.

"My name is Josaif," he said. "Touval, Cherraine, thank you for defending Skitter those two times. It allowed me to set all this up for you before you got here."

"You know this kid?" Touval pointed at Skitter.

"I've been traveling with him for a while now," Josaif said. "Isn't that right, Skitter?"

"That's right." It wasn't until the words left Skitter's mouth that he realized that he had been traveling alone all this time—well, alone except for Kadaiel. But somehow he didn't feel as if he had told a lie, either. He turned to the stranger. Josaif looked at him with laughing eyes. It made Skitter want to jump and shout for joy. Who was this guy?

"If you had waited a few moments once you had chased the nantük away from Skitter, you would have seen me." Josaif stoked the fire. "I was shooing off the rest of its pack."

"You were?" Skitter's eyes widened.

"I was." Josaif nodded.

"Then you must be a fast traveler," Touval said.

"I am," Josaif said and offered no more word of explanation.

Skitter studied this stranger. If he concentrated, he could almost recognize him, but the truth seemed to be hidden.

Josaif chuckled to himself. "Skitter, are you thirsty? If you are, you should drink."

"All I have is the rest of my water bottle." Skitter pulled out his bottle. There was only a fourth left.

"Drink," Josaif said.

Skitter shrugged. He was thirsty and looking at his water was making his tongue stick to the top of his mouth. He downed the contents . . . at least he would have. But the little bit of water he had didn't seem to end. There must have been more water in there than he thought. He drank until his thirst had disappeared. When he looked at his water bottle again, the water level had not dropped.

Skitter's eyes bugged out of his head. "What th—!" He turned to Josaif. "You . . . you . . . Kadaiel?"

"Shhh." Josaif put a finger on smiling lips and winked at him. "Now, please sit. I give my word that you are safe." He looked into Cherraine's eyes. "And I'm sure you'll find the solution to your particular problem soon."

Cherraine's eyes widened. She plopped down on the ground.

"We don't need your help, thanks." Touval caught Cherraine's hand. "Let's go."

"Sit down, Touval." Josaif motioned to the ground. "If you go farther, you'll find yourself in trouble."

Touval crossed his arms. "Why should I believe you?"

"You don't have to." Josaif smirked at him . . . but in a good-natured way. "But you should."

Touval snorted. He sank to the ground. "All these stupid Outsiders . . ." he muttered. "I'm only staying because it's too dark and dangerous to go any further."

"You are wiser than you think you are." Josaif leaned forward to look him in the eye. "Both you and Cherraine are welcome to me."

Touval's fur stood straight on end. His face flushed, and he looked away.

Josaif leaned back on his hands. "Why don't you go to sleep? Skitter and I will keep watch."

"Yeah, right." Touval crossed his arms. "As if I would sleep with Outsiders watching over me." He glared at Josaif through narrowed eyes.

* * *

"It didn't take him long to fall asleep." Skitter let his eyes wander over Touval's still form.

"He's been awake longer than he should have been." Josaif laid his hands on his knees. "The poor thing has taken on too much for one his age."

"Is it my business?" Skitter looked up at Josaif. "Can I ask what he's been through?"

"You'll find out soon enough."

Skitter drew up his knees to his chest. "So how come you came . . . I mean, how come you're visible to me? You're not usually. And how come you didn't let me know who you were at the beginning?"

"Because sometimes I like to surprise you. You make the most delightful face when you're surprised."

Skitter couldn't help but smile.

"So, Cherraine, my dear." Josaif's voice rose. "Would you like to tell me why you've been calling out to me all this time?"

Skitter turned to the place where she had been sleeping. Cherraine pulled herself onto her hands. And by the way she blushed, it was obvious that she had been eavesdropping. She looked Josaif straight in the eye, shrugged, and shook her head.

"Of course you have been calling to me. You've been calling to me ever since this terrible plight has befallen you." Josaif gave a grin. "You just didn't realize that it was me you were calling."

Cherraine's eyes widened.

"Now come, Cherraine." Josaif patted the ground in front of him. "Won't you sit and tell us what has happened?"

Cherraine got up from her place and sat where Josaif had indicated. She glanced at Touval and bit her lips together. Her eyes darted around the camp for a moment before she nodded to herself. Then she looked into Josaif's face and gestured with her hands.

"No, no, dear." Josaif held up his hands. "Use your words."

Cherraine blinked at him.

"Um, sir . . ." Skitter played with his tail. "She can't talk."

"Of course she can talk." Josaif's ears turned forward. "She is just unable to at the moment. Her voice was stolen from her."

Cherraine's mouth dropped open.

Skitter let his whiskers twitch. "I don't understand . . ."

"Cherraine, would you be so kind as to allow me to look inside of your mouth?" Josaif said.

Cherraine started, her ears shooting straight up.

"I'm sure he'll be able to help you, Cherraine." Skitter held the tips of his toes.

Cherraine clamped her mouth shut. She shook her head so hard, her hair slapped her cheeks.

"But why not, Cherraine?" Skitter got to his knees.

Cherraine shook her head even harder. She scrambled to her feet and darted to her sleeping bag. She climbed in and pulled it over her head.

"Cherraine!" Skitter got to his feet to chase after her.

"Let it go, Skitter." Josaif put his hand on Skitter's shoulder. "I knew she wouldn't trust me all at once. She feels that there's more to me than she can see, and it scares her."

"But why?"

"You'll find that out soon enough." Josaif leaned back. "Go to sleep. I'll watch over you tonight. You won't see me in the morning, so don't be alarmed. Continue on with your journey."

"Okay, but . . ."

"But?"

"Is there something you can do to help Cherraine and Touval?" Skitter tapped his fingers together. "I know I only met them today, but . . ."

"Skitter!" Josaif said with a laugh. "Why else do you think I called you into this desert?"

Skitter's face beamed.

"I have given you the authority to help them, Skitter." Josaif put his hand on Skitter's head. "Whatever you need, you'll be able to do it."

"Thank you, sir." Skitter curled up at Josaif's side.

Josaif stroked Skitter's hair. "Skitter, you are a joy to me."

Skitter curled his tail around his body and smiled.

* * *

"Finally awake, are you?" Touval stood over Skitter with his hand on his hips.

Skitter stretched and ran his hands over his fur. The sky was a soft purple but turning a shade of rose and mandarin at the horizon. Josaif was nowhere to be seen.

"When traveling in the desert you need to leave before it gets too hot." Touval said, raising a finger in the air. "It was nice of your friend to leave us breakfast. We've already eaten, so you can eat on the way."

"Thanks." Skitter rubbed his eyes.

"We can't wait for your friend, though." Touval scratched his hair. "And I'm not sure how we're going to find him . . ."

"He said we wouldn't see him this morning." Skitter got to his feet. "We can go on without him."

Touval studied him for a moment. "If you say so." He picked up his sleeping bag. "I can't believe I slept in the presence of Outsiders." He headed to the sand bike.

"Where's Cherraine?" Skitter glanced around the expired campfire.

"On the bike." Touval jerked his head toward it. "She must have had a bad dream or something. She's acting weird this morning. Not very sociable at all."

Skitter's ears went back a bit. He knew what had upset her. He found her sitting on the bike, clutching her sleeping bag like a stuffed animal.

"I wish she could tell me what's wrong." Touval strapped his sleeping bag on the bike.

"There is a type of language that uses hands to speak." Skitter raised his hands. "I know a little bit. I can teach you if you want, Cherraine."

"You see!" Touval thrust his face into Cherraine's. "I told you. You can learn sign language. It's a perfectly acceptable way of communicating!"

Cherraine shook her head hard. She turned away from them.

"She's been like this ever since she lost her voice." Touval kicked a tire. "She's so stubborn!"

"She wasn't born without a voice?" Skitter's ears pricked.

Touval nodded. "She probably doesn't want to learn sign language because it's an Outsider invention."

Skitter let his ears flatten. "Why do you two hate Outsiders so much?"

"Because we're Expermian."

Skitter stared at him.

"It's silly, isn't it?" Touval shrugged with a smile. "I don't see the logic in it myself. There's so much we can learn from Outsiders. But the higher-ups decided that a proper Expermian must hate all Outsiders, and so we do."

"That's stupid." Skitter climbed into the sidecar.

"It is, isn't it?" Touval's smile faded. "But I suppose Cherraine and I are not proper Expermians anymore." He fell silent for a moment before forcing a smile. "And I guess that's fine by me. You're the first Outsider I've ever met, but for the life of me I can't seem to hate you."

"I don't mind not being hated." Skitter chuckled. "But, why do you say you're not proper Expermians?"

Touval and Cherraine glanced at each other. Both their ears fell.

"Because we're running away." Touval ducked his head. "We're running from Isofell."

"Who's that?"

"I suppose an Outsider wouldn't know about him." Touval bit his bottom lip. "He's the Expermian god of Trainers, knowledge, and wisdom. I've served him all my life . . . until now."

Cherraine clutched her sleeping bag.

Skitter crinkled his nose. He had a good idea of where this was going. "What changed?"

"I . . . I didn't want to lose Cherraine." Touval ran his hands along the bike. "She is more important to me than following Isofell."

Cherraine put a hand on Touval's shoulder. He held on to it.

Skitter raised an eyebrow. He wasn't following this at all.

"Cherraine was chosen by Isofell a little while ago." Touval placed a hand on her cheek. "When a fox or vixen is chosen, Isofell takes his or her voice. I tried so hard to find a way to get her voice back before the priests found out, but . . ." He cleared his throat. "We had to run before they took her away."

Skitter turned to Cherraine. Tears brimmed in her eyes. Just looking at her made a lump grow in Skitter's throat. He knew he wouldn't like the answer to his next question. "What happens after a person is chosen?"

"She has to go to his temple to be dedicated to him." Touval moved his glasses to his forehead. "They have to do whatever he says. The Chosen stay in the temple forever. They're not allowed to get married or have children. Their lives belong to Isofell, and their families never see them again." He wiped his eyes. "But . . . Cherraine and I have been promised to each other since we were kids. She's always been there, and . . . and . . . I don't want her to go away."

Cherraine threw her arms around Touval and clutched him close to her. She buried her face in his clothes.

"She doesn't want to go either." Touval held on to her.

"That's awful." Skitter bowed his head. "So what are you planning on doing?"

Touval wiped his nose with the back of his hand. "My parents live in a town near the mountains. They're planning an expedition to the Cursed Mountain soon. See, there's this city hidden in amongst the mountain's heights that scholars have been trying to find for ages. In fact, Cherraine was visiting me at the university archives and helping me with my research when this happened."

"You're in university already? At your age?" Skitter appraised Touval. "You must be smart."

Touval stifled a smile as he adjusted his glasses. "That's what people say about me, anyway. I'm there to learn the basics of document restoration and preservation. Once I learn that, my parents will take over. They can teach me much better than the university can, and—" He halted when Cherraine tugged at his tunic. She gave a little pout and motioned to him to continue.

"Right . . ." Touval cleared his throat. "Anyway, *Mamai* sent me a message saying *Papai* might have found a clue to the Hidden City's location. That's where we're going."

Skitter raised an eyebrow. "To a Cursed Mountain?"

"It's not really cursed . . . at least my research doesn't lead me to think so." Touval gazed off down the road. "But something did happen there in ancient times that made people say it is. Whatever it was chased all Expermians off the mountaintops. That's why we live in the desert to this day. And there's a power that remains on the mountain heights . . . some say it's Rophim, our chief god, while others say it's something or someone else. Either way, it's such a place that not even the gods will tread there. I'm thinking that we might can appeal to that power to save Cherraine . . . or at the very least we can go to a place where Isofell can't get her."

Skitter studied the two foxes from ears to tail. "So you're willing to go to a place your people think is cursed—where your gods won't even go—so you can be together?"

Touval shrugged. "Yeah."

And Cherraine nodded.

"That's . . . that's terribly romantic." Skitter clasped his hands together. "Completely unnecessary, but terribly romantic."

"Unnecessary?" Touval's ears pinned back, and Cherraine growled. "Didn't you hear what I've been saying? What do you even know about it, anyway?"

Cherraine glared at Skitter, crossed her arms, and snorted through her nose.

"Touval, Cherraine, I haven't known you long, but I can see you're both smart." Skitter shook his tail. "So how can you be afraid of a god who's nothing but stone?"

Both Touval and Cherraine stared at him in disbelief.

"Think about it . . ." Skitter glanced around until he found a rock. He held it in his hands. "If some craftsman carves the image of one of your gods out of this, would you seriously bow down to it? It's a rock."

"*Something* happened to Cherraine!" Touval motioned to her. "Isofell took her voice. She's not making that up."

"I know something has her voice, but it's not Isofell." Skitter clicked his tongue a few times. "It's likely that some evil spirit is pretending to be Isofell so that you will do what it wants. Question is, what *does* it want?"

Cherraine slapped her hand over her mouth. She gaped at Skitter.

"Wait." Skitter scanned her face. "You know, don't you? You know what it wants."

Cherraine nodded.

"What is it?" Skitter said.

Cherraine shook her head.

"Come on, Cherraine. You can tell me." Skitter leaned in closer to her.

Cherraine shook her head. Tears started to pool in her eyes.

"That's enough!" Touval stood in between them.

"But . . ."

"Leave her alone!" Touval's tail bristled. "What do you know about any of this? We've done nothing but help you, and you respond by insulting our gods and talking as if you know it all. What makes you an expert on all this? You don't know us!"

Skitter started. Had he offended them? He hadn't meant to. He picked up his tail and began to play with it. "I'm not an expert, but Kadaiel is," he said in a softer voice.

Touval furrowed his brows. "Who's Kadaiel?"

"He's the god I serve. He's the one who sent me here to meet you . . ." Just the mention of Kadaiel's name made all Skitter's reservations vanish. "Only I didn't know that at the time."

Touval put his hands on his hips. "And what makes you so sure *he's* real when you think our gods aren't?"

"You met him last night . . . Josaif? That was him."

Touval's ears fell back. "What?"

"That's the reason Cherraine was acting so strange this morning." Skitter scratched his ear. "Last night, Kadaiel wanted to release her voice, but she got scared."

"Is that true?" Touval swung around to Cherraine.

Cherraine stiffened. She lowered her eyes and then nodded.

"Kadaiel is . . ." Skitter paused to look at the sky. "Oh, I hope it's not bad to say this about him . . . but he's a jealous god. He doesn't want his servants to worship anyone but him." He grinned at Touval. "And I think he likes you."

"But he's an Outsider's god, right?" Touval pushed his glasses up. "What would he want with Expermians?"

"But he said that you're welcome to him last night, remember?"

Touval's ears fell. "That's right. He did." He started playing with the piece of cloth hanging at his shoulder.

Cherraine grabbed Touval's arm. She shook her head at him and clutched his arm so hard that her nails started to sink into his skin.

"Ow! Cherraine! What's the matter with you?" Touval pried her hands off.

Cherraine held herself. Her skin underneath her fur paled. Her hands trembled.

Touval studied her a moment. His face softened. "Cherraine . . ." He took her hands. "Your hands are clammy. What's wrong? Why are you so scared?"

Cherraine only shook her head.

Skitter's ears pricked. There was a whisper on the wind that he could only just catch. "Cherraine, are you afraid that Isofell will come after you if you try to appeal to Kadaiel?"

A squeak escaped her. She clutched at Touval.

"You don't have to worry about that." Skitter patted her arm. "Kadaiel is stronger than anything in the world. You'll see that before this is all over." He narrowed his eyes. "Or maybe you already have."

Cherraine gazed at him and then dropped her eyes.

"Enough of this. None of this talk is getting us anywhere. Let's go." Touval mounted the bike. "The sun is already up."

Skitter nodded. He hopped into the sidecar and settled in as Touval took off.

* * *

A fox clad in Expermian garb knelt beside the extinguished remains of a campfire. His name was Temaine. He wore an orange tunic over his clothes and held a spear with a laser head. His tunic distinguished him as a priest, and the ornament on his spear specified he worked in Isofell's temple. Only a select few had the skills to be one of Isofell's guard-priests—strong, brave, chosen by the Head Priest, and blessed by Isofell with intelligence. But that didn't stop those two brats from escaping his clutches last night.

"They were here." Temaine glanced around at the landscape.

"How did we miss them?" Another guard-priest snorted. "We must have been all over these dunes during the night."

"No clue." Temaine examined the camp. There was evidence of four people here. "They had help."

"They'll need help when Isofell runs out of patience," said the second. "I'll call this in."

"Tell them we'll keep on tracking them." Temaine surveyed the road. "It seems they're headed to the mountains."

"Toward our main temple?" The second snickered. "I thought this Touval kid was supposed to be smart." He went to his sand bike to call in his information.

Temaine narrowed his eyes as he watched the road. There was something strange about this. A power he had never felt before lingered around the camp. It set his teeth on edge. Something was coming down the pipeline . . . something was about to happen. And he surely wasn't looking forward to meeting it.

* * *

The further Skitter and his new friends traveled, the more the landscape changed. Mountains appeared in the distance and loomed larger as they went. It took some days before a town emerged on the horizon—a dark, cardboard like cutout against a skyline that had become laced with towering mountains. But it wasn't until the next morning that they drove into the town nestled in the foothills of the Expimer Mountains.

"Here we are," Touval shouted over the roar of the bike. "This is Parainmont, the premier location for all researchers and seekers of knowledge. It's my hometown."

Skitter gazed around as they went. The buildings and the roads were covered in dust and sand—all except one: a white and brown edifice that gleamed in the sun. It had spires that towered above the rest of the buildings and was decorated with murals of a red fox holding a book as well as foxes with silver fur surrounding him.

Foxes and vixens in white with yellow and brown tunics over their Expermian clothes milled to and fro in front of it. Many of them had books in their hands. A work crew standing on scaffolding busied themselves cleaning the dust and grime off of the building's murals.

"What's that?" Skitter pointed to the building.

"It's Isofell's main temple." Touval rushed past it. "All true seekers of knowledge come here at least once in their lives to seek Isofell's guidance and to be blessed with wisdom. I practically grew up there."

Skitter looked over his shoulder at the temple. "If you're running from Isofell, why did you come to the location of his main temple?"

"It's the only place we can go." Touval sped down the road. "We can't get the proper supplies for going into the mountains to find the Hidden City anywhere else. Plus, this is where my parents live. It's a calculated risk. If we keep a low profile, we'll be out of here before anyone notices."

Skitter took one last look at the temple before it disappeared among the buildings. A fox dressed in fancier clothes than the others emerged from the temple as Touval turned a corner. He wore a red tunic and had a squarish biretta that looked curiously like a book on his head. As soon as he emerged he looked in Skitter's direction. Even from a distance—even though he had only glimpsed him for a moment—Skitter knew that priest had spotted them. The sight of him made Skitter's tail twitch. It was as if an unspoken war had been declared between the two of them.

He turned in the sidecar and snorted through his nose as if getting rid of an unpleasant smell. Cherraine caught his attention out of the corner of his eyes. She was watching him. But when he turned to her, she averted her eyes and clutched onto Touval.

Skitter smiled. He could see the wheels in her mind turning—considering whether or not to risk it all in an appeal to Kadaiel. He leaned back in his chair. Between Cherraine's indecision and the priest's appearance, Skitter was certain that something was going to happen soon. They wouldn't make it long without being discovered. Skitter crossed his arms. Whatever was going to happen was coming soon, and he had to be ready for it.

* * *

The sand bike disappeared around a corner, its passengers obscured by the buildings surrounding the temple. They weren't in view for very long—merely a few seconds—but it was long enough. Hairan narrowed his eyes.

"That's him," came a voice in Hairan's ear. "That's the enemy."

Hairan adjusted his biretta. As the Head Priest of Isofell, he had heard Isofell's voice in the past. But that didn't mean it didn't unnerve him every time he did hear it. Particularly lately. Isofell's voice was harsher than usual—angry. It made Hairan's insides tremble.

"Lord Isofell." Hairan focused to keep his voice from cracking when he spoke. "That's a child. How could he be an enemy of yours?"

"He's an Outsider!" Isofell snarled, nearly making Hairan scream. "He has defied me, and he has kept a Chosen from me . . . all in the name of a foreign god." He paused a moment. "You're lucky I don't destroy all of you for failing to capture them before now."

Hairan turned to his left. The guard-priests he had dispatched from the capital at Isofell's behest approached him.

"Lord Hairan, sir." Temaine dropped to his knee.

"You've failed me, Temaine." Hairan clutched his staff. Because of this guard-priest's failure, Isofell's wrath hovered over all their heads.

"Forgive me, my lord." Temaine bowed with his forehead to Hairan's toes. "I don't understand it. Although we had them in sight, we could not catch up to them during the day . . . and at night they disappeared. We could find no trace of them until the morning."

"Is that so . . ." Hairan furrowed his brows. That was odd. The guard-priests were masters of the desert—Temaine especially. He could track a flea in a sand pile. Unless . . . unless there was another power at work.

"It's the Outsider!" Isofell's voice hissed in Hairan's ear.

Hairan slammed the butt of his staff to the ground. "Let us depart. We shall descend on them now, take the Chosen, and eliminate the threat. Isofell has spoken."

"Sir!" Temaine bowed his head to the ground. He got to his feet and took off to prepare his men.

Hairan faced the direction in which Touval had ridden off. There was something about that Outsider that didn't sit right with him. He clenched his teeth together. There was more to this whole thing that he could see, and what he did see was unnerving . . .

* * *

Touval pulled up to a small storefront, though Skitter couldn't tell what the proprietors were selling. Piles of books, papers, pictures, and statues were bundled in the windows, not leaving any space for curious patrons to look inside. The sign overhead read, "Restorations."

"Messier than I remember it." Touval dismounted his bike.

"Where are we?" Skitter hopped out of the sidecar.

"This is my parents' place." Touval helped Cherraine off of the bike. "We have to stay for about a week. If we keep out of sight, we'll make it . . . that is, if my parents actually leave when they said they will." He opened the door and walked in.

A bell rang as they entered. Skitter gazed around. It used to be a store, but now it was a place that housed books and parchments, pictures and ancient carvings. Everything looked old and full of history, so Skitter couldn't understand why it was all tossed about all willy-nilly. Didn't these people care about all these old, delicate items?

But all Skitter could see of anyone were the tips of two large ears dancing above the counter.

"What on Clorth?" Touval took his glasses off to clean them. "*Mamai?*"

"Hm?" A vixen popped her head from behind the counter. She had brick colored fur, black ears not quite so large as Touval's, and brown hair that faded to a shade of yellow-green at the ends. She wore a yellow dress similar to Cherraine's. "I thought I heard the bell, but . . . Touval, what are you doing here?"

"The expedition? You told me to come." Touval rolled his eyes. "This is my mother, Tillin. Don't mind her. She's a little scatterbrained at times . . . actually, both my parents are."

"I am not scatterbrained." Tillin tapped her forehead. "But I know I had it here. I'm usually so organized when it comes to my restorations." She ducked back behind the counter. After a moment she popped her head back up. "Wait a minute! Who's that?" She pointed at Skitter.

"His name is Skitter." Touval motioned to him. "I met him on the way over here, and we've been traveling together."

"Pleased to meet you, Tillin-li." Skitter gave a little bow.

"You picked up an Outsider?" Tillin crossed her arms as she watched Skitter.

"Do you mind?" Touval said.

Tillin studied Skitter for a moment before shrugging. "I'm supposed to, but . . . meh! My mind's too full with other things." She went back to searching behind the counter. "By the way, Touval, I know I asked you to come on the expedition, but I wasn't expecting you until the weekend. Don't you have exams?" She peeked up from behind a counter for a moment before ducking back down. "Although, this does explain why we haven't been able to reach you."

"You tried to reach me?" Touval leaned over the counter.

"We've had to cancel the expedition, Touval." Tillin stood up, scratching her hair. "We've had a break-in. The scroll I was restoring and the ones your father was translating have gone missing. He's off searching the bazaar hoping that someone sold it for quick cash."

"But we have to go on that expedition, *Mamai!*" Touval slammed his hands on the counter. "We have to! Cherraine—"

"Cherraine? Cherraine . . ." Tillin tapped her chin. "There was something about her that I had to tell you . . ." She suddenly gasped. "That's right! That's the other reason we tried to contact you . . ." Her ears fell. "Sweetheart, something terrible has happened to Cherraine."

"I know." Touval lowered his ears.

"You do?" Tillin said.

"Of course." Touval motioned to Cherraine.

"Cherraine?" Tillin placed her hands on her cheeks. "You're here!" She darted around the counter and threw her arms around Cherraine. "I'm so glad you're alright! Your parents are so worried about you!"

Cherraine squeezed her.

"What's the matter, dear?" Tillin searched her face. "Why won't you speak?"

Cherraine raised her eyebrows. Touval exchanged a glance with Skitter.

"Don't you know, *Mamai?*" Touval cleared his throat. "Isofell took her voice."

"She's a Chosen?" Tillin's ears shot up. She gazed at Cherraine. "Her parents didn't tell me that."

Touval furrowed his brow. "But didn't you say that something terrible had happened to her?"

"I was referring to the fact that she had disappeared." Tillin put her hand on her hips. "Becoming a Chosen is not a terrible thing, Touval."

Touval fell quiet. He crossed his arms before saying, "It is if I'm losing her."

"Oh!" Tillin's ears fell back. "Oh, you're right. I didn't even think about that." She caressed Cherraine's ears. "You poor thing."

"That's why we have to go on this expedition, *Mamai*." Touval clenched his fists. "We have to."

Tillin studied her son for a few moments. She looked at Cherraine and then at the mountains in the distance. "Oh, I see. That's why you ran. You want to get to the Hidden City, and appeal to . . . hm . . . but Touval, my love, that's dangerous. Even if the stories are true and there is another power up there, if Isofell caught you before you made it—"

"I don't care!" Touval slammed his fists on the counter. "I don't care."

Cherraine slipped her arms around him. Silence flooded the room.

It was Skitter that broke it. "May I ask a question?"

Tillin swung around. "Who . . . oh, you . . . you. I'd forgotten you were there. Go ahead."

Skitter peeked behind the counter where Tillin had been searching. "What were you looking for when we came in?"

"A parchment that I was restoring." Tillin ran her eyes over the place. "I was sure I had it in here. My husband believes that parchment holds a clue to the location of the Hidden City."

"But you said there was a break-in." Skitter cocked his head. "Wasn't it stolen?"

"Here's the thing about that . . . I'm not sure you can call it a break-in. It was more of a . . ." Tillin paused. "Hm . . . well, actually, I'm not sure what you would call it."

Skitter waited for her to continue. But when she fell silent, staring at the floor in thought, he said, "What happened?"

"Hm?" Tillin picked her head up. "Oh, yes, of course. Well . . . I was in the basement where I do all my restorations. Everything down there is kept at the perfect conditions to ensure the most minimal impact to ancient documents, so I know I wouldn't have had that parchment out unless I was down there. My husband was upstairs attempting to translate some other pieces of related parchments that I had restored. All of a sudden the ground shook. I heard my husband scream so I rushed upstairs to see what was the matter. Before I made it to the stairs a wind blew through the basement, crashing everything to the ground and throwing me into the wall. I think I blacked out. When I came to myself, the parchment was missing, and both the basement and the storefront was a terrible mess."

"Was and still is," Touval muttered.

Skitter stifled a chuckle and let Tillin continue.

"My husband told me that after the shaking, the lights went out and he felt someone snatch the parchments right out of his hands." Tillin tapped her hands together. "The whole thing is baffling. No one who respects knowledge would dare steal such valuable scrolls. I can't fathom it."

Cherraine gasped. She slapped Touval's arms. She pointed at Tillin and then at herself.

"What?" Touval watched her a moment.

"What is she doing?" Tillin ears angled to the side. "She looks upset about something."

Cherraine kept gesturing. Her movements became bigger and more exaggerated.

"I think she's trying to say something to us." Skitter studied her. "But I can't tell what she wants to say."

"Stop, Cherraine. Calm down." Touval caught her shoulders. "We don't understand."

Cherraine took a deep breath. She took a step back and then pointed at herself.

"You?" Touval motioned to her. "Are you trying to tell us something about you?"

Cherraine nodded. She paced around the room, looking at the different scrolls and books.

"You were looking for something," Tillin said.

Cherraine pointed at her nose and nodded. Then she picked up a book and pointed at it.

"And you found it," Touval said.

Cherraine pointed at her nose. Then she waved her hands around furiously.

"And . . . now you've lost me." Touval ran his hand through his hair.

Cherraine snorted through her nose. She pointed at Tillin and then at herself.

"Hm." Skitter studied Cherraine and Tillin. "Are you saying that what happened to Tillin-li happened to you?"

Cherraine beamed. She pointed at her nose and nodded.

"You found a document, and then the lights went out, the wind blew, and when you woke up the document was gone!" Skitter said.

Cherraine pointed at her nose.

"So that's what this is about!" Skitter slammed a fist in his palm. "There's something in that document that Isofell—or whoever—doesn't want anyone to know about! So he took your voice so you couldn't tell!"

Cherraine clapped and nodded.

"And that's why you don't want to learn sign language because if you found another way to communicate, he'd take that too!" Skitter said.

Cherraine took his hands and jumped up and down with him.

Touval raised an eyebrow at Skitter. "How did you get all that?"

"That is ridiculous!" Tillin crossed her arms. "To stop the spread of knowledge goes against every tenant that Isofell teaches us."

"Technically, I don't think it's Isofell at all, but . . ." Skitter shrugged.

"There's an easy way to figure this out." Touval faced his mother. "*Mamai,* what did the parchment say?"

"I don't know. I just started restoring it. There wasn't even enough for your father to start translating. The only thing I could understand was a certain drawing. It was . . . odd."

"What was it?" Touval said.

"I think it may have been a reference to what caused the Great Migration." Tillin knit her brows. "As far as I could tell, there was a figure in the picture that all the ancient Expermians were running away from. But the figure wasn't any of the Expermian gods."

Skitter's tail twitched. He didn't know why, but he felt that figure was the key to everything. "What did it look like?"

"It was . . . male . . . and fuzzy . . . and . . . white, maybe?" Tillin tapped the counter with a finger. "It was definitely an Outsider."

"What species?" Touval said.

"I'm not so familiar with Outsider species so I'm not quite sure." Tillin closed her eyes for a moment. "Maybe a wolf . . . or a dog . . . or jackal . . . definitely a canine of some sort."

Cherraine clutched Touval's hand. She pointed to Skitter and then motioned to the air around him.

"You know what it is, don't you?" Touval grunted. "If only you had your voice."

"Your voice!" Skitter faced Cherraine. "You see it now, don't you?"

Cherraine averted her eyes from Skitter.

"There's no more running, Cherraine." Skitter took her hands. "You have to let Kadaiel help you because none of this will get resolved unless you let him restore your voice."

Cherraine ducked her head. She squeezed her eyes shut and took a trembling breath. When she opened her eyes, she looked at Skitter and nodded.

"Are . . . are you sure, Cherraine?" Touval searched her face.

Cherraine smiled and nodded.

"Wait!" Tillin cocked her head. "Who's Kadaiel?"

Touval waved her off. "I'll explain it later, *Mamai.*"

"Ready?" Skitter said. Cherraine opened her mouth as wide as she could.

Skitter peered in. At first he didn't see anything of alarm, but then as if someone had snapped his eyes into focus, he saw it: a black, slimy mass spider-webbed across her tongue. Skitter pinched the stuff between two fingers. He pulled. It stretched but stuck on Cherraine's tongue. He got a better grip and yanked. The stuff stretched longer and longer until it snapped off. Skitter fell back on his tail. The black stuff dissipated into smoke and disappeared.

"Ow!" Cherraine fell back onto the floor. "That hurt!" She rubbed the base of her tail.

"Cherraine!" Touval's ears stood straight up. "You're talking! It worked."

Cherraine gasped. "I am!" She jumped to her feet. "I'm talking! Skitter!" She took his hands. "I know what it's all about. You won't believe it! Or maybe you will."

"Stop rambling and tell us!" Touval said.

"Okay, okay, okay . . ." Cherraine took a deep breath. "It was—"

The door burst open. A group of foxes barged in, filling the entrance and blocking off the exit.

Skitter's fur stood on end. It was the priests of Isofell. They'd been found.

* * *

Cherraine yelped and ducked behind Touval as ten priests barreled in. One of them, the one wearing a red tunic over his clothes, stood before the others. Skitter recognized him as the Head Priest . . . the same one he had seen before. He had red fur, eyes as blue as midnight, and his red hair peeking out from under his hat faded to a shade of yellow-orange at the ends.

"It has come to my attention that a Chosen of Isofell has taken refuge here." The Head Priest scanned the store. His eyes fell on Cherraine. "There you are! Honestly, you didn't have to come this way to Isofell's main temple to dedicate yourself. The one in Silver Sait would have done nicely."

"Don't touch her!" Touval backed away with Cherraine behind him.

"Touval." The Head Priest turned his eyes toward him. "I cannot tell you how disappointed I am to see you here. From the moment of your birth I knew you were special. I watched you grow with pride as if you were my own son. Isofell has lavished you with a double portion of his blessings. How could you betray him in this manner?" He locked eyes with Touval.

Touval's eyes opened wide. They glazed over. "I . . . I . . . don't know . . ." He hung his head. He shook all over. "I . . . I'm sorry." He fell to his knees. "Forgive me, lord Hairan."

"There now, child. It's alright." Hairan held out his hand to Touval. "Submit yourself to Isofell. He will restore you."

Touval remained still a moment. Then he reached out a trembling hand to the Head Priest.

"Touval?" Cherraine snatched Touval's hands. "Touval, what's wrong with you?" She tried to pull his hand down.

"I've never seen him like this," Tillin said under her breath. But she didn't move from where she stood.

Skitter felt his fur prickle. Something wasn't right here. Just two seconds with this fox had drained all the fight out of Touval.

"And as for you." Hairan turned his eyes to Cherraine. She stiffened. "You can speak, but I know you are a Chosen. Come with me. You will have a good life in the temple."

Cherraine stood stiff. Her entire body trembled. "N . . . no. I . . . I don't want to."

"You will come now." Hairan narrowed his eyes at Cherraine. She trembled all over, her voice cracking.

Skitter shivered from head to tail. A power had trickled into this room. It wound itself all around Touval and Cherraine, and set Skitter's teeth on edge. It permeated the room, making it feel like Skitter was choking on something.

"That's enough!" Skitter stomped his foot on the ground. Immediately, the oppressive atmosphere vanished. Cherraine fell to her knees.

"No! I don't want to go!" Touval lurched away from the priest. He collapsed on the floor, panting and trembling. "He made me say things. I couldn't say what I wanted to."

Hairan swung around to face Skitter. His teeth were bared to the gums. "You!"

Skitter regarded the fox without a word.

"I know about you." Hairan bared his teeth at Skitter. "Isofell also warned me about an Outsider who seeks to turn his followers away. He will not stand for that! You are marked now. You will learn the true power of our gods."

The other priests shook their spears and shouted.

"I already know the true power of your gods." Skitter approached the Head Priest. He had to look up to see his face. "So for your own sakes, I'm going to ask you this nicely: please leave Cherraine and Touval alone."

"Begging will avail you nothing!" The Head Priest raised his hands and chanted. The other priests joined in. The sun seemed to darken. Over the priests' heads came a dark mass that converged into a figure of a fox. It rose over their heads until it touched the ceiling.

"Isofell!" Tillin dropped to her knees with her face to the ground.

"Oh, no!" Touval trembled where he had fallen on the ground. "The gods have come down on me."

Cherraine whimpered behind Touval. She buried her face in his fur and started to mutter something.

"Wow." Skitter gazed up at the dark mass towering above him. "That is kind of impressive. I can see why Expermians are so afraid of you."

"Silence, Outsider!" Isofell's voice grated against Skitter's ears. Even the priests cowered in front of him. "You will wish you never defied me!" He rose his fist and brought it down on Skitter's head. Skitter watched him but didn't move. The fist slammed onto . . . something . . . Skitter felt the shockwave from the strike, but his fist didn't touch him. Isofell pounded and pounded, but to no avail.

Isofell snarled at Skitter. He thrust his face into Skitter's and roared. It was all Skitter could do to keep from backing up or flinching—not because he was scared, but because the wind that came from Isofell reeked of all sorts of rotten things.

But the fact that Skitter remained motionless infuriated Isofell. "Get him! Kill him. Now!"

The priests brandished their spears. Skitter heard a high pitched whine as they charged.

"Lord Isofell." Tillin raised her head from where she lay.

"Who dares intrude on my judgment?" Isofell growled.

"Please hear me!" Tillin pulled herself to her knees. "I and my family have been ever faithful to you. We've followed your words to the letter. Please. This sort of violence is not like you. In the ancient texts you've always pursued knowledge, spurning the battle and war the other gods—"

"Enough!" Isofell swept his arm toward her. A searing wind blasted over Skitter's head. It slammed Tillin into a shelf of books. She collapsed on the floor. The books cascaded over her, and the bookshelf teetered and toppled.

"Tillin-li!" Skitter caught the bookshelf before it slammed into her.

"*Mamai!*" Touval darted to her, but Isofell held out his hand. Touval slammed into an invisible wall. "No!" Touval slammed his fists against the barrier.

"Where do you think you're going, Touval?" Isofell sneered, showing a row of sharpened teeth. "Did you think you could escape after betraying me?"

"I . . . I don't care!" Touval backed away, holding out his hands to protect Cherraine. "I won't let you take her."

"And how will you stop me?" Isofell smirked.

Skitter glanced over at Touval. He wanted to help, but he had to get to Tillin—make sure she was unhurt. He shoved the bookshelf away from her and dove under the books to see if she was alright.

Touval clenched his teeth together. "I . . . I'll appeal to another power." He trembled all over. "I'll appeal to Kada—"

"Silence!" Isofell curled his fingers as if grasping something. "Don't you dare say a foreign god's name in my presence!"

Touval clutched at his throat. He made a choking sound as he rose into the air.

"No! Touval!" Cherraine clutched at him. "Oh, please. Oh, please, come save us. Come now!" She clasped her hands together.

"There is none to save you!" Isofell tightened his grip. Touval squirmed into the air.

Skitter threw a book off of Tillin's face. She was breathing, but her eyes were closed and there was blood on her forehead. She groaned. "Touval . . . please . . . my son . . ."

Skitter tapped his teeth together. Fur rose all over his body. His tail shivered and bristled, and he trembled all over. He faced the thing hovering above him.

"I've had enough out of you!" Skitter looked Isofell square in the eyes. "Release Touval now!"

Isofell laughed at him. "And why would I do that?"

Skitter stood to his full height. "Because I am a servant of Kadaiel!" He narrowed his eyes. "And I command it!" He stomped his foot.

The earth trembled beneath his feet. Isofell lurched back as if struck, and all the priests fell backwards onto their tails. Touval dropped to the ground.

Isofell righted himself. He snarled at Skitter. "Why you little—" He reached his hand toward Skitter . . . and then froze. His eyes widened then darkened. His teeth bared to the gums. The room dimmed in response. Skitter shivered as a cold tendril ran over his body. He had never seen or felt such unadulterated hatred in his entire life.

The priests too halted where they lay after being thrown back. Their ears fell backward. All of them watched something behind Skitter's back. Cherraine let out a cry of delight.

A breeze—cool, refreshing, and smelling like rain—wafted past Skitter. Light—soft and fresh—shone on his shoulders. His trembling calmed, his fur settled, and his teeth stopped tapping.

Skitter turned. Josaif stood there, staring at the spirit with a steely gaze. He approached, patting Skitter's shoulder as he passed.

"Spirit styling yourself as Isofell." Josaif held out his hand. "Return what you have stolen."

Isofell grunted. He clenched his teeth and tensed his arm, trying to hold it back. But slowly, his hand extended toward Josaif. In it was a leather packet. He held his fist over Josaif's outstretched hand, and one by one his fingers opened. The packet fell into Josaif's hands.

Josaif lowered his hand then narrowed his eyes at the spirit. He snorted through his nose and turned his back on it.

"Continue, Skitter." Josaif put a hand on Skitter's shoulder.

"Yes, sir." Skitter faced the spirit. "In the name of Kadaiel, whom I serve, vacate this premises immediately!"

A blast of cool air slammed into the spirit. A sharp, piercing cry shattered the air. The spirit flew out of the building and disappeared.

"As for you . . ." Josaif turned to the priests. "You have raised your hands against *my* two servants whom *I* have chosen." His voice lowered almost to a growl. "Leave now, or your lives are forfeit."

The priests gaped at Josaif for a moment before scrambling out of the store.

Josaif watched them leave. He took a deep breath and released in in a sigh. "Soon . . . very soon . . . I will make things right in Expermia again." He smiled at Skitter before turning. "Well done, Cherraine!" He grinned at her. "It's lovely to hear your voice again."

"Thank you." Cherraine giggled as if someone was tickling her.

Josaif stood in front of Touval. "Come, Touval. Stand to your feet. You are exceedingly brave for one so young."

Touval stood before Josaif and adjusted his glasses.

"So many questions in your eyes." Josaif put his hand on Touval's shoulders. "Continue to seek the truth, and I will answer them all. But in the meantime, I have a question for you: will you leave behind your fears and follow me?"

Touval gulped. Josaif patted his shoulders before turning to Tillin still lying amongst the books.

He bent over and held out his hand to her. Tillin groaned. Her eyes opened, but once they fell on Josaif her groaning stopped. She watched him for a moment before taking his hand. He hoisted her to her feet.

"How do you feel, my dear?" Josaif patted her hand.

"I . . . I feel good." Tillin touched her forehead. "I . . . I'm not sure what . . . I . . . I'm a bit confused . . . I . . ."

"I believe this belongs to you." Josaif handed her the packet he had taken from Isofell.

Tillin took it from his hands.

"Both you and your husband are welcome to me." Josaif pressed her hands between his. "Will you tell him that?"

Tillin nodded.

Josaif smiled.

The sky cleared. The sun blazed forth, but the soft, cool light was gone. Josaif was no longer there. But judging by everyone's wide eyes and opened mouths, nothing was the same.

* * *

Hairan ran all the way back to the temple, burst into his chambers, and slammed the door behind him. He slid to the ground and cowered behind the door. He had never seen anything like that—the power, the glory. It set every strand of fur on his body on edge.

"What was that?"

Hairan swung around with a curse. He hadn't realized Temaine had come in with him.

"Lord Hairan, what was that?" Temaine looked at him through wide eyes. "That . . . that Outsider god. He was more powerful than Iso—"

"Shh!" Hairan slapped his hand over Temaine's mouth. "Don't say it. Do you want to be marked by the gods?"

"But what *was* that?" Temaine shook from head to toe.

"Be quiet!" Hairan looked around. "Go tell the rest of the guard-priests to keep their mouths shut. We will not breathe a word of what happened to anyone. And we'll have to make sure Touval doesn't talk either."

"But that god was defending them. He . . ." Temaine dropped his voice. "He defeated Isofell. How can we fight against that?"

"It's an Outsider god. What does he have to do with Expermians?" Hairan adjusted his biretta. "I suspect that once the Outsider leaves, his god will leave as well. And besides, it was one Outsider god against Isofell, the . . ." He lowered his voice. ". . . the weakest of our gods. I doubt this new god could stand against Rophim and the rest. I will speak to the High Priest in charge of Rophim's temple and have him inquire of Rophim. I'm sure together we can handle the threat."

"Somehow I doubt that," Temaine muttered.

Hairan swung around. "What was that?"

"Nothing!" Temaine stood up straight. "I'll talk to the men now before this story gets out."

Hairan watched him stride out the door, but inside his stomach dropped. Temaine had voiced the doubt he had no courage to say aloud. But doubt or not, there was nothing he could do about this situation. His only options were to fight alongside the gods he had grown up with or align himself with an Outsider's god. And there was no way he was about to submit himself to the same god an Outsider would worship. He'd rather die than do that.

* * *

"He came!" Cherraine clapped her hands together. "Josaif really came. I called to him, and he came!"

Skitter turned to Cherraine. "So he was talking about you when he said 'my *two* servants.'"

"I decided I would trust him when we got into town. I saw the priest watching us, and I realized we couldn't run anymore. I had seen Josaif when he sent his servants to defend you at the shop where we first met. I tried to tell Touval, but I guess he didn't understand. He thought I wanted him to help you." Cherraine clasped her hands. "From that moment, I decided that I wanted to follow Josaif, but I was afraid of what Isofell would do . . . and I didn't think Josaif would accept me."

"Wait . . . I . . . what just happened?" Tillin dropped to her knees. The packet she had been given fell from her hands. "Isofell . . . he tried to kill Touval . . . and . . . . and . . . that . . . that Outsider. He . . . he . . ."

"*Mamai!*" Touval rushed to her. "*Mamai*, I thought I lost you."

Tillin blinked. She stared at the top of Touval's ears a moment before throwing her arms around him. "Touval! I've never been so scared in my entire life! I've never seen anything like that before, and I . . . I don't know what going on anymore!"

"I do!" Cherraine bounced on her toes. "It was Josaif. That's what Isofell didn't want me to tell anybody. I was helping Touval in the archives when I found a journal of a scholar who had seen a mural when he was searching for the Hidden City—I'm sure it's the same one depicted in the parchment. Josaif was the figure the ancient Expermians were running from."

"Josaif?" Touval cocked his head. "But how could these ancient documents talk about him when he was right here?"

"You can see for yourselves." Cherraine pointed to the packet Tillin had dropped. "Isn't that what Josaif returned? I think those are the parchments that Isofell stole."

Tillin turned her eyes to the packet on the ground. She and Touval exchanged a glance. He nodded at her. She picked up the packet and undid the string. "Oh!" She cried out. "Cherraine's right! These are the missing parchments. And here's the one I was working on." She spread it on the floor.

"*Mamai*, what are you doing?" Touval hissed a breath in through his teeth. "Those are delicate. You can't have them on the floor."

But Tillin wasn't listening. "Touval, look!"

Touval leaned over the parchment. Skitter peered over Touval's shoulder. The parchment was yellowed and had holes in it and the text was illegible. But Tillin had started to restore the drawing at the top of it. It was faded, but Skitter could make out a white figure standing with his arms stretched out. Lightning erupted from its hands, striking the area surrounding him. Masses of Expermians—though not all of them foxes—fled before him.

Touval slowly sat up straight. "So . . . Josaif was the reason ancient Expermians fled the mountains?"

"I . . . I don't know." Skitter peered at the parchment. "This is the first time I've seen or heard anything like this."

Tillin ran her hands across the image of Josaif. "According to your father's and my research, Touval, the ancient Expermians staged a great rebellion against . . . someone . . . we've never had a concise answer as to who they rebelled from before. But if our interpretation of this parchment is correct, it may well have been Josaif. This mural depicts what happened in response to that rebellion."

"Does that mean that Josaif was there before the Expermian gods were?" Touval said. "That the ancient Expermians used to worship him first?"

"If that's the case, these parchments could rock all of Expermia to its foundations." Tillin fell silent for a moment. "No wonder they tried to suppress this information."

Cherraine studied the floor for a moment. "Do you know what question has been bothering me since my voice was stolen? Why did Isofell change so suddenly?"

"What do you mean, dear?" Tillin kept her eyes on what she was doing.

"You said it yourself when Skitter was facing Isofell." Cherraine played with her hair. "He's changed. He used to be gentle and a pursuer of knowledge, but now he tried to kill Touval and stole your parchments. Why?"

"That wasn't Isofell." Skitter turned to Cherraine.

Touval turned to him, mouth agape. "How can you say that? You saw it, Skitter."

"Didn't I tell you before?" Skitter gazed at the ceiling a moment. "I think an evil spirit is pretending to be Isofell to get you to do what it wants. Even Josaif said so."

"Then what happened to the real Isofell?" Cherraine said.

"I don't think there ever was a *real* Isofell." Skitter crossed his arms. "I think that spirit . . . or maybe different ones . . . made up those stories and images of your gods and convinced your people they were true. That way, they could get your people to do what they wanted—including rebelling against Kadaiel."

"Either way, it's a moot point, don't you think?" Tillin gazed at the packet in her hands. "Whether it's Isofell or not, we've had an encounter with someone today . . . someone powerful."

"You're right, *Mamai*." Touval fell silent a moment before his ears shot into the air. "We have to find *Papai* and leave . . . immediately." He hopped to his feet.

"Leave? Why?" Tillin started to carefully return the parchment back to the packet.

"Are you kidding me?" Touval clutched his hair. "Didn't you see what they did to try and stop Cherraine from talking? Did you not witness what I did? This isn't the end! They're going to come back, and who knows what they'll do now that we've defied them!"

"Oh! Oh, you're right." Tillin gathered the packet. "But if we're leaving, I can't leave my tools behind. And your father . . . he'll need his books and notes too . . ." He scrambled to her feet.

"*Mamai!*" Touval watched as she started scrambling around the room, gathering this and that. "What are you doing?"

"I have to pack. We need to prepare." Tillin scrambled down the stairs. "I can't leave my documents . . ."

Touval pulled on his hair. "*Mamai*, we have to go now—" He started after her.

"Touval, relax." Skitter pulled him to a halt. "You don't have to be so afraid."

"Yeah." Cherraine took his hand. "Josaif will be with us. And Skitter!"

"That's right, and—" Skitter's ears pricked. He caught a whisper in the air. "Oh . . . actually, I won't be."

"What?" Cherraine swung around to face him. "Why?"

"I've done the job Kadaiel wanted me to do, apparently." Skitter turned to the east. "He wants me to go that way until I hit the ocean."

"But . . . but . . ." Touval's ears fell.

"Oh, Skitter." Cherraine lowered her head.

"I'm sorry." Skitter's tail flopped. "I'd like to stay with you, but I have to go where Kadaiel tells me."

"Well." Touval lifted his ears. "At least let us pack you up with supplies before you go. We'll have to get some too, if we're going to be on the run."

Skitter cocked his ear. Kadaiel gave his approval. "Thank you. I'd like that."

"We have to leave now." Touval headed to the door. "*Mamai*, come on!"

"I'm ready." Tillin appeared with a pack on her shoulders and another in her hands. "Everything we need to restore and translate on the road is in here. Here, Touval." She handed him the pack in her hands. "That's all your most precious possessions . . . your microscope, your favorite books . . . your maps . . ."

"*Mamai!*" Touval took the backpack. "That . . . that's thoughtful of you."

"Of course." Tillin shouldered her pack. "I know you'd be devastated if you left behind things you needed . . . or wanted. We won't be coming back for a while at least. We have to be ready for everything."

"I'm . . . impressed." Touval smiled at her. "I didn't know you thought that way."

Tillin raised her chin. "I told you I wasn't scatterbrained."

Skitter snickered. Touval exchanged a glance with him and smiled.

* * *

"Are you sure you can't come with us, Skitter?" Cherraine held her hands in front of her.

They were at the bazaar, a place where Expermian merchants sat under covered tarps to sell things to other Expermians. Skitter saw everything for sale from pots, to vases, to fruit, to guns and mountain climbing gear. Tillin had gone to find her husband while Touval, Skitter, and Cherraine stocked up with supplies. Touval had even gotten Skitter a hat with a cloth hanging on the back to keep the sun off his neck.

"I wish I could stay, Cherraine, but Kadaiel told me I have somewhere to be." Skitter stretched. "I have to glide across the ocean to get there."

"Glide across the ocean? Will you be okay?" Touval studied Skitter's frame. "You don't look too sturdy."

"I've trained my whole life for far-flight." Skitter shook his arm flaps. "I can't wait to get to land, though. Gliding over the ocean is tough."

"I hope we'll meet again, Skitter." Cherraine took his hands.

"Me too." Skitter looked at Cherraine and then Touval. His stomach sank at the thought of leaving them. "Where are you going to go?"

"There's a ruin in the foothills that researchers use as a basecamp when they set out on an expedition to the mountains." Touval turned to the mountain range in the distance. "No one ever stays there long because it's so close to the Cursed Mountain. I doubt Isofell or the priests will come after us. We'll stay for a while until we figure out what to do. My guess is that we'll keep searching for the Hidden City . . . nothing else for us to do."

"I hope you find it." Skitter gazed at the mountains. "I'd like to see this Cursed Mountain and Hidden City you've been talking about."

"Maybe you'll be able to join the expedition once we figure out where it is." Touval put his hands on his hips. "Now that we have the parchment back, we can start looking."

"I hope I can," Skitter said.

"Thank you so much for all you did, Skitter." Cherraine threw her arms around him. "Stay safe."

"I will." Skitter patted her back before pulling away. "Say goodbye to Tillin-li for me, Touval." He extended his hand.

"I will." Touval shook it. "If you ever come back to Expermia, try and find us."

Skitter nodded. He shouldered the pack they had bought for him and set out down the road.

He sighed as he went. He was going to miss them.

"Well done, Skitter." Josaif appeared beside him.

"Thank you, sir," Skitter said. "Where are we going next?"

"You have quite a trek ahead, but your next assignment will be in a nice, tropical place." Josaif smiled at him. "You'll like it there. Just make sure you don't rush your trip across the ocean."

"Yes, sir! I won't," Skitter said.

If the gods know all, as they must, then they must be aware of this anthology. Here is a welcome from one of them to you.

To the Reader…

by *Alan Loewen*

And so you have found me.

What? After all this searching, you hesitate? You draw back? You searched for a god and now you have found one, and yet you clutch your electric torch in fear.

Is it that I wear the mundane form of a fox? Or maybe you searched for a god of greater power, one who does more than sit in some great underground labyrinth surrounded by books and scrolls and clay tablets?

Well, there are gods and there are gods: angels and demiurges, powers and principalities, outer gods and primal gods, and then the Logos from which all comes forth.

Me? I am the Librarian, though some would call me a kitsune or Oinari or the Cadmean vixen or the Teumessian fox. So many delightful names and so many that even I have forgotten them just as those races of humanity who named me have faded from memory.

But their tales are all here, all around us.

And you have come searching for gods and your quest has been answered.

I have a book for you.

Look down. You hold it in your hands now.

You say they are only stories written by your own kind? Of course, you foolish mortal. How can beings that transcend time and space communicate with you except through a human amanuensis? How can that which transcends the senses be described, except that a human mind filters it down to what you can grasp and smell and see and hear? Do you not know the meaning behind your word, inspiration?

You look at me and see a fox, but the old gods have always looked this way. Cernunnos, the horned hunter of the dead, Ra, the eagle-headed Sun god, Pan with his goatish features, Ganesha, the elephant god of fortune; and so many,

many more, all wearing the guise of animals. And yet how little you know. If you were to see me as I really am, I would blast your mind into oblivion.

And so here I sit, a lowly fox surrounded by her books and her tea set.

But back to the book you hold.

Let me tell you a secret. There are worlds within worlds. Your scientists are just beginning to understand that universes nest within universes and touch each other through countless dimensions. Worlds without end.

Amen.

And so you and others who read this book will think they are creative tales engendered within the mind of the author, but here is the reality. Yes, yes, here is the truth as hard as it may be to grasp.

In other worlds uncountable, the tales that you will read?

Come closer. Let me whisper this in your ear.

They are all true.

"First Chosen" plunges the reader deeply into Egyptian mythology. What—or who—is important here is Wepwawet, Anubis' father. Anubis has the head of a jackal; Wepwawet has the head of a wolf. Wepwawet faded into obscurity as wolves were hunted into extinction in Egypt by 3000 B.C.

The protagonist of *"First Chosen"* is Onuris (formerly Pinhasy), a meek acolyte of the deities of grain and corn around 2000 B.C. Pinhasy/Onuris is chosen by Wepwawet and Anubis to be Wepwawet's first High Priest in a thousand years.

It isn't easy re-starting a religion that's been dead for a thousand years. Wepwawet and Anubis help him. So does lioness-headed Sekhmet.

First Chosen

by BanWynn Oakshadow

Acolyte

"Grant thou that I may be like unto those favoured ones who are in thy following..."

(The Egyptian Book of the Dead)

Setting sun, blazing shield of fire crowning a single hill of stone lost among endless dunes. A fiery crown shimmering... inexorable. An aura of gold in the gathering night. Two shadows step out into the fading light. The Heads turn. The First a jackal, with long, pointed muzzle and tall ears. The other is not a jackal, the canine silhouette's blunter muzzle and lower, broad ears are of the wolf. He cannot look away, cannot close his eyes. The silhouettes lock gazes with him. Though he suspects the identity of one shade, does not know the other; only that they know him. They have touched his ka, that which is bound to the body, and which the body shall not survive without. His akh is not destroyed, and he is relieved, for the akh is the shadow form that shall walk the paths of the Dead until reaching the Land of the Dead, until the physical body decays to the point that the akh fades away. He feels his ba, the spirit which infuses the physical form so that it lives, flutter around him, pulling...a tearing sensation...

* * *

Deep in the temple of Neper and Nepit, god and goddess of grain and corn, a young acolyte lifts his head with a gasp and stares about him in panic until the familiar confines of the room come back to him. Shaking his head, he fights to clear the fear brought on by his dream, even as he tries to remember each aspect of it to relate to the priests later. Six dreams now of the setting sun, the hill of stone, and the unidentified dog-like creatures. Each different, yet linked one to another.

Reed torches, producing more smoke than light, reveal the clay tablet before him, half covered in the hieroglyphs of his dedication. He checks it to make sure that the surface has not dried while he dreamt, and satisfied returns to his duties. Fingers calloused by years of repetitive work still cramp as he uses his stylus to press the forms of each word into the yielding surface until the horns summon him to evening rituals.

With solemn reverence, he sprinkles the linen cloth with sacred water and places the almost finished tablet upon it. Muttering the prayers of Reverent Dedication to the Preservation of Learning, he folds the damp linen about the tablet which he then places in the sandalwood box along with forty-seven others, all baked hard as stone. A moment to contemplate the culmination of eight years of study, and he closes the box, and begins the journey to the outer temple of acolytes.

He is late for the evening Obeisance of those he serves. Onuris's voice joins those of his brother acolytes in reciting the Hymns to Nepet and Nepit, but his mind wanders, returning yet again to his dream. The single hill, the sun setting, the wolf and jackal. Unbidden, years of study sift through possible interpretations for each element of the dream and, in spite of himself, he cannot help shivering.

"… Homage to thee, Nepet, Lord of Corn and of Grain. He who tends to that without which no man can live. Praise to He whose hoe plows the furrow and makes it fertile. Praise be unto Nepit, goddess of Corn and of Grain. Praise thee who scatters the seeds that they may take root and grow. She who causes the soil to bring forth that without which no man can live. Praise be Nepet and Nepit who, together, cause the stalks of Corn and of Grain to become laden and ready for harvest, and make possible that man and beast shall not starve and die."

* * *

Dreamer

"Prepare thou for me all the ways which are good…"

(The Egyptian Book of the Dead)

He heads towards the middle region set aside for the dwellings of the priests and for training rooms and libraries. Places for learning the spells and medicines granted by the gods to aid the lives of men. The middle rings of the temple are forbidden to acolytes, and few venture even this deep into the temple but rarely. Onuris's feet know the way well. He has been there many times.

Many acolytes are jealous that a mere commoner such as Onuris has a privilege denied them.

Unlike the others he studies with, Onuris's family did not purchase his place in the priesthood. The priests had chosen him. His father supervised the cutting and moving of great blocks of stone. When he was a child, Pinhasy was playing in the quarry. He had fallen and struck his head. His father paid for priests to come and either heal him or prepare his akh to journey into the next world. Though he has no memory of it, he has been told many times how he opened his eyes and muttered to the priest, "Jackals walk the streets of Bubastis. The Crook does not stroke the earth."

He regained consciousness several days later and Pinhasy was well and whole again within a few months.

The following year in Bubastis, a persistent mould afflicted the barley seeds held back from the harvest for replanting. The wheat harvest was not affected but almost no barley grew that year and famine took many inhabitants of that city. The priests of Nepit and Nepet, god and goddess of grain and corn, came to his father's house and took Pinhasy away with them. When they returned to the temple, he was renamed Onuris, that he begin his new life by cutting loose his past.

His feet know the way to Inyotefoker, a priest skilled in divination and in walking the dreaming world. That his last five dreams, and now this sixth one, were different, occurring during the day and disturbing him with their vividness, is seen by his fellows as a deception.

It is not with a sense of privilege that he arrives at the priest's door and requests permission to enter. Inyotefoker looks up from the papyrus scroll he is reading and narrows his eyes when he sees who knocks at his door.

"What? Again? After only three days?"

"Yes, holy one. Like the others, today while I worked upon my tablets."

"Again I ask. Are you sure that you wish to report yet another dream of this nature to me?"

"Yes, holy one. I have taken an oath to report to you all my dreams that seem in any way unusual. I cannot betray that oath even to save myself scorn and ridicule."

After Onuris describes all that he can remember of his seeking, Inyotefoker closes his eyes and is silent for a long while. He opens his eyes and looks at the young man with a bit more warmth.

"Again the symbols are blatant. But, I suggest that, if you are making them up, you should create something a little less dire for yourself. Have you ever experienced and known your ka or ba outside of a dream?"

"No, holy one."

"Then how did you recognize them in the dream?"

"I do not know, holy one. I experienced the dream just as I told it to you and in the dream knew them as ka and ba."

The diviner shakes his head and sighs, "Very well, you may return to your duties."

"Yes, holy one. Thank you."

"And Onuris?"

"Yes, holy one?"

"Try not to dream so much."

"I will try, holy one."

* * *

When he wakes, a low ranking initiate priest follows him, unspeaking and deaf to any attempts at communication with him. Perhaps on Inyotefoker's advice, or it might be others wishing to humiliate Onuris and show him as a liar before the priests. The priests are following him in shifts, but there is always one watching him with grim intensity, even when he is moving his bowels. He accustoms himself to their presence and ignores them.

He has just finished the 48th tablet and is admiring…*he is among the dunes of the desert. Atop the greatest of the dunes, Onuris can see the disc of gold and the black profile of a Wolf Warrior of the Necropolis, Guardian of the path of the dead, lunges and bites him. His ba and ka are torn from him, scattered across the sand. His akh begins to fade.*

Inside the temple the priest calls for others to aid him as he tries in vain to save the tablet. Onuris's cheek falls upon its surface, but next he takes it in his hands and rips and pounds it beyond usefulness.

When he is able to move again without shaking, the priests guide him back to his mat while the High Priests considered the 'occurrence'.

* * *

Onuris lays the stylus down and stares in reverence at the clay tablet just finished. Critical eyes scan the surface seeking imperfections. Each hieroglyph is crisp and perfect. Each word as it should be. Still he holds his breath and seeks errors in the work. It is difficult to believe that it is finished. That eight years of dedication, study and labour as an acolyte have come to an end.

Fifty clay tablets: Hymns to Nepet and Nepit. Rites and spells for the dead, Rights and Responsibilities of the Priesthood. Treatises regarding the deification of the Pharaoh. Spells of protection, fertility and death… So much knowledge studied under the holy teachers and then recounted by his own hand in wet clay. The Word was the Thing. They were One.

It is only when it rests, safe and perfect, in the chest with its forty-nine brothers, that he realizes his exhaustion and pain, he stumbles to the temple to recite the Hymns to Nepet and Nepit before he is allowed to collapse on his mat.

* * *

Outcast

"I have come and I have done away the offensive thing which was upon Nepet and Nepit."

(The Egyptian Book of the Dead)

This time his mind does not wander. This time each word seems rimmed in silver and flares in his mind.

This time his voice is full and steady as he completes the Rite.

*"His sister hath protected him, and hath repulsed the fiends, and turned aside calamities. She uttered the spell with the magical power of her mouth. Her tongue was perfect, and it never halted at a word…*This is not a rite he knows! This is no reverent prayer to his god and goddess! *Beneficent in command and word was Isis, the woman of magical spells, the advocate of her brother. She sought him without pause, she wandered round and round about this earth in sorrow, and she alighted…*

He struggles to turn the prayer back to its proper form to no avail and is forced to hear himself blaspheming the very deities that he is to rise in service to…

in strength and stature, and his hand was mighty in the House of Keb. The Company of the Gods rejoiced, rejoiced, at the coming of Horus, the son of Osiris, whose heart was firm, the triumphant, the son of Isis, the heir of Nepet and Nepit."

This time the words hammer into him and he is filled with a feeling that he is too exhausted to recognize as anger. Why was he reciting hymns to Osiris that make Nepit and Nepet low and near meaningless among the gods?

The last stanza rings over and over in his head as he shuffles to the dormitory and curls up on his mat. Asleep before even closing his eyes.

Behind closed eyes he sees the linen shrouded corpse of a god. At his head he sees the sister, Isis. But at the feet of the corpse is a dark one, the head of a jackal. The dark one speaks Words and seven spirits come at his Words and array themselves around the divine bier.

Beside Anubis is a god of canine aspect, but of grey and white. He is powerful, heavily muscled, he wields a mace. At his will are summoned his seven servants armed and armoured. Armed and fierce they are and they repel all shadows that attempt to reach the incumbent form of the god.

His screams do not wake him though they reach the far halls of the outer temple. He does not feel the frightened eyes of those who peer into the room but fear to come closer to the thrashing form growling and frothing on the floor.

He does not feel the priests who hold him down or the wooden trowel forced between his teeth. He does not feel the cool glass beads laid upon him or taste the liquids dripped past his lips, or smell the incense burned over his heart.

As he struggles, all he sees becomes yellow and bright until it sears to his core. A disc of gold and in that disc a shadow. A shape he knows. In his dream the Wolf turns to him and opens its mouth as if to speak.

He wakes with one last scream and even as the priests ask him what he has seen he cannot remember. Only a disc of fire, the jackal and the wolf.

* * *

He walks step by dignified step. This is the first of fifty trips he will make today between the room of studies and the temple of the acolytes. One trip for each tablet. Each tablet carried in solemn reverence to the temple and placed as an offering before Nepet and Nepit. Each trip finishing with another Rite of Purification before beginning the next. After fifty trips, Nepet and Nepit will have sanctified his work as an acolyte and the tablets will be incorporated into the walls of the temple as it expands, that the walls themselves will be the Words of the gods for the Word is the Thing.

He is bedecked by jewellery, cosmetics. Scents rare and sacred enhance the oils rubbed into his skin. Beeswax melts in his hair and makes it shine. His kilt is of fine white linen.

Before him, a priest walks with measured step and the smoke of incense trails him as he chants the sacred prayers. Behind him, another priest marks each step with a silver gong and also chants the sacred words. He himself is silent. The words of a mere acolyte are unfit for the ears of a god. Not yet is he a holy servant of Nepet and Nepit. But soon.

They reach the chest of sandalwood. The Rites of Opening are performed and he lifts the lid so that he may bring forth his first offering to his god.

His cry of despair is drowned in the clang of the fallen gong and the exclamations of the priests.

There is no need to pull back the linens to see that the chest does not contain fifty perfect offerings of knowledge inscribed over eight years.

Each of the tablets has been broken into pieces. The chest contains only rubble.

* * *

Onuris kneels before the statues of Nepet and Nepit in the outer temple. He waits.

There has been an investigation. The priests seek to learn who has committed sacrilege by desecrating holy offerings. All know that Onuris is not well liked, and even despised by many of his fellow brothers, but none believes that one of the other acolytes hates so much as to be driven to commit such an atrocity.

Each is questioned. All claim ignorance and the Order of Diviners has been called to discover who has done such a thing. There are whispers that Onuris has done it himself. Has he not been claiming prophetic dreams? Has he not had a fit but days before? Was not his deception about to be revealed by Nepet and Nepit Themselves?

It is Inyotefoker himself who casts spells over the chest that he might see in the heart's eye what had transpired there.

Come what may, Onuris will never again walk to Inyotefoker's room to relate another dream.

Inyotefoker the blind. Inyotefoker the mad.

No sooner does he cast his spells than he screams in a voice that makes water flow down the legs of many in that room. Though he claws his own eyes from his head, it is not before others see that those orbs have become white as alabaster and as blind as stone.

No human voice rips his throat to decry, "*Mere mortals do not look uninvited upon the face of a god.*"

* * *

Kneeling before the gilded statue of Nepet and Nepit, Onuris waits for a decision. The Order of Judges retires to decide the fate of the acolyte Onuris. The Order of Diviners shall offer interpretations of events and cast many spells and auguries.

No longer does the unfamiliar weight of gold pull on his ears. No longer does silver glint around his eyes, nor does beeswax gleam in his hair. His loins remain ungirded, bare even of the rough linen of an acolyte.

Until a decision is reached, he is neither acolyte nor chosen of Nepet and Nepit. Until a decision is reached, it is if he does not exist.

He hears footsteps approaching behind him. There is no voice to tell him of his fate. He waits. A touch on his shoulder, not a hand but the tap of a reed.

He stands and turns.

Three priests stand before him. They do not speak. He cannot see their faces for each has covered his head with linen. They do not speak to him. If he speaks, he knows that they will not hear him. He cannot see them and knows that they do not see him. The reed shows that they will not touch him. If he touches one of them he will die for the transgression. One moves to stand between him and the statues of Nepet and Nepit, blocking the god and goddess from him with his body. The other two step aside, opening a way for him to the exit.

A decision has been made. Nepet and Nepit have rejected him. Onuris the acolyte is no more.

Jackal

"May he grant that I see the sun-disc and behold the moon unceasingly every day; may my soul go forth to travel to every place which it desires…"

(The Egyptian Book of the Dead)

He who has been Pinhasy, renamed Onuris and returned to being 'Pinhasy the beggar' puts aside the hard crust of bread and crumbles of cheese that are his meal. Moments later a jackal runs over his feet and steals his cheese. He rises to give chase and is knocked over by a wolf who takes his meager hunk of bread. He rushes after them, watching as they slow down and Pinhasy runs faster. Then they sprint again and he watches as his meal is carried away. Bread is food for the body. Life itself. What need for the body when it is an empty husk devoid of the eternal?

Cast out from the temple. Sent forth naked as a slave and the way behind him barred forever. Months of wandering, seeking a way, a light. Seeking a reason to live in a world where he can find no answers. Earning a coin here or a meal there through the medicines he learned in the study of the deities who have rejected him. Who have measured him, and found him wanting.

A flawed cup tossed aside by his master's hand.

Days and nights of emptiness and longing.

Months of walking with no destination.

The sounds of the city, the people, smells of cooking, the temples, most of all of the temples. They feel distant and muffled. Cut off from him by a veil of despair.

The setting sun washes the stone buildings in hues of orange and red. The lush valley of the Nile slowing its pace in preparation for the coming night. Beyond it, to the west, the edge of the desert glows gold.

Thoughts of food forgotten, he rises to his feet and begins walking once again. At last, he knows where he needs to go.

He steals a small, thin reed boat with covered goods in front and back. There is a wedge of cheese and a loaf of still warm bread atop one covered load of goods. He thanks the gods for their providence and has eaten all by the time before he is half the way to the other shore. After having starved for so long he should have known better than to eat so much so fast. He bends over the side of the boat, and his stomach empties itself, giving his meal to the fishes. He takes no notice of the protective canvases, until the jackal and the wolf step out from under them. They take a very long time to eat his food, waiting until he is looking at them before they take the smallest nibble.

No moon lights his way as the city falls behind. Her face will not rise until much later. Through the night farms and the smell of dark moist soil, giving way to scrub and cracked earth. The morning sun at his back lights the first dunes in lavenders and lapis lazuli. His footsteps hiss as they meet the first questing tendrils of the relentless desert sands.

The sand creeps between bluffs of tawny, sun baked clay and stone, in relentless hunger to engulf all in its path. Relentless, insatiable. Pinhasy knows that this is his destiny. Westward, ever westward. Though the sun rises at his back, the setting sun is his goal. Westward, towards the Necropolis. To the city of the dead.

He sleeps through the hottest part of the day but does not eat or drink. Food and drink are for the living and for the ahks, the transfigured spirits of the dead. They are of no use to the dying or to spirits bound for the Eater of Souls.

Evening comes and he is no longer alone. Beneath the sands are the still forms of the poorest dead. Around him, the furtive shadows of the jackals prowling the necropolis, lurking among the departed. Windblown drifts reveal leathery, skeletal limbs curled as an infant in the womb with eyeless, grimacing faces. Poor in life, no tomb but the eternal sands for these. Doomed to poverty in the life beyond as well. Yet even these have an afterlife beyond the reach of a failed acolyte denied by his god.

One whose akh was fit only to be devoured, and soon.

This is not the place of his dreams. No hill of stone. No blazing crown of the sun. But he has not come seeking dreams. Only death. It is not the place of his dreams, but it is enough.

Among the dead, the acrid scent of urine where jackals have marked the stones burns his nose. He continues to a place less astringent. Jackal paws whisper in the sand. He ends his journey, lays himself down, and waits for the dogs of the dead. The sun completes its journey across the sky, bringing the shadows of that time between day and night. His lips crack and his tongue swells in his mouth until it feels like leather and dead already. In the darkness, shadows whisper, paws skitter in the sand, yips and pants and the occasional growl as they circle, moving closer.

He watches as the Moon rises, a mere crescent of silver in the indigo sky. He watches as the shadows in the night circle about him, closer. Circle until he hears their panting breath and smells them in the night. Wolves, golden in the night's light. He watches them, seven in all, as they sit about him in a circle. Watching. Waiting.

He waits for the first of them to take him. He hopes the ending will be quick. If he dared, he would pray that they go for the throat rather than rending him to pieces in agony. If he dared. But he dares not pray. He is rejected. The unfit vessel.

Watching. Waiting. One, with silver in his eyes reflecting the sliver of the moon, seems to laugh at him. Its mouth open in a mockery of a grin.

Still they sit. Still they laugh.

Despair makes way for another feeling. Anger brings tears to his eyes. Tears that slip down his cheeks to fall and be swallowed by the ever thirsty desert. Even in this is he to be denied? Even in this will the gods deny him?

Seven shadows, lined with silver. Seven shadows laughing with the moon in their eyes. Seven figures sitting among the tombs of the dead. Seven wolves; blunt-muzzled heads, shorter ears, fur the lightest gold on their chest, the gold growing deeper as it rises up their sides until it is brown atop their heads, down the center of their backs and tails. Seven jackals; long muzzles, tall thin ears, blacker than the night. They shift. Shadows of one lay over another. It is impossible to know which vision is true, and which is illusion.

The moon rises high in the night as he waits. Waits to be taken and devoured. Waits for an ending, and still they sit. Still they laugh. He watches the moon appear and disappear among the tombs of stone, their shadows shortening and lengthening again as they mark her path.

The mockery becomes too much. Lurching to his feet, he faces the foremost among the dogs of the dead and raises his fists to the night, "Take me! I beg you! Take me and make an ending of me!"

* * *

Before him a single wolf sits, no sign of the other six or of the tombs that blocked the moon.

He stands alone, facing a single wolf who does not flee his apparent madness, but pants and seems to laugh at him still. He shakes his head and stumbles as dizziness threatens to overcome him. He puts a hand out to steady himself against the side of a crypt made of only shadows.

* * *

Slave
"I am helpless in the regions of those who plunder... "
(The Egyptian Book of the Dead)

He does not have the strength to flee or threaten when the wolf rises to its feet and approaches him, panting, gliding like a shadow, eyes never leaving his.

He does not flail or yell or threaten as it draws close and circles him so close that he feels the brush of fur against his calf. He had given himself. His offer, made in a dream, had been repeated while awake. Trembling, he waits for the feel of teeth, the rending of flesh and the flow of blood.

He does not feel the bite. There is no pain at all, but he can feel the flow of warm blood running down his leg to feed the sand. At least this gift has been given him; to be too mad at the time of his death to feel the pain of it other than in his soul.

He smells an astringent odour, at once strange and familiar. The smell, he realizes is all about this place. Not the coppery scent of blood, but something else. He looks down and locks eyes once again with the wolf. The wolf with his lifted leg and stream of warm urine splashing against his leg. Not blood at all. Piss. The piss of the dog. The animal is in his shadow and the moon should not be reflected there, yet it sits in those copper eyes and laughs at him.

"Take me!" he begs. He meant to die. Now, even the honour of his death had been taken from him by the gods. The wolf and the jackal have marked him and even this foul eater of the dead laughs. Showing him that even this creature looks down on him and laughs at his prayers.

He starts to shuffle forward. Heading deeper into the desert. Away from the City of the Dead. He will not dishonour their remains with his own.

The teeth he expected before close upon his leg now. Not rending and tearing. Not even biting, but holding. Halting his escape. There is no laughter in the eyes of the beast now. Something much colder, ancient and unknowable, resides there now.

The teeth release his leg. The wolf steps back from him and sits, its tongue lolling from its mouth. Mocking him. Daring him. He turns to face it and takes a step back. Before his foot even touches the sand, the animal is there, jaws clamped on his ankle, this time piercing the skin. Holding him.

He does not fight and, when his foot is released, places it back where it was before. The wolf resumes its seat, watching him and laughing at him with its eyes. He does not move again but watches the grey and white-furred wolf. When he can no longer face the mockery in its eyes, he drops his own. Humbled even by a beast. He does not realize that he has been carrying even a small sense of self, a tiny crumb of pride until that too is taken from him.

He falls to his knees, a cast off vessel, and an empty one as well. His body jerks but he does not struggle as canine jaws rip the kilt from his waist. Slaves do not wear clothes. And with it, his name.

* * *

He sits and watches the sun sink behind the dunes. The shadows begin as muted hues washes color from the crests of sand. Mauves and oranges soon to be mirrored in the sky. This has become his favourite time of day. The quiet period between waking from dreams he cannot remember and the arrival of his master. This period of rest belonging neither to the furtive hunters of the burning day nor to the furtive stalkers of the silent night.

He is attuned to the rhythms of the desert, to the ebb and flow of life in the ocean of sand. No longer is it a foe to be fought or a killer to be feared. He does not feel the heat or dryness trying to draw the life from his body. He has become of the desert. His skin is dry and leathery. Dark as oiled wood and pulled tight across his skeletal frame. Muscle has leached away leaving sinew and tendon, long bones and rounded joints. His skull gleams, reflecting the sun. His hair is gone, seared away in a time he cannot remember. If he had a mirror to look into, he would see something more akin to one of the dried corpses he had once lain among than to a living man.

Yet he did live. Each night his master comes to him and leads him to his next service. Each night he cries or screams as he struggles to understand why he is being tortured so. Each morning his master leads him to food and water. Enough to keep him in his body and no more, and then leaves him to sleep upon the sands until the following night begins.

* * *

That first day he tried to leave. When the wolf left, he fled. Fleeing the desert he turned back to the city, to the world of men. This slavery to a beast… this humiliation and denial of even his least prayers…this was unbearable.

The wolf had found him so fast that he was sure that it had known that he was going to flee and waited for him. Sharp teeth closed upon his calf sending him sprawling face down in the hot sand. He had struggled to stand but the animal was everywhere, biting and snarling. Teeth piercing his flesh and pulling at his limbs until he surrendered and quit trying to rise.

Grey-furred legs before him, casting him in the shadow of the beast, he looked up at it. Standing there, still as stone, watching him…a low growl still echoing in its chest.

He made it to his knees and started to stand when the animal had snarled at him. He remembers being frozen like that. Kneeling in the sand while the desert dog had paced around him, sniffing at him, even in his most private places. When he had tried to protect his manhood from the inquisitive nose, he had received painful bites and low growls.

When he had finished examining his slave, the wolf had nosed and pawed at him until he rose up. His torturer led him to the peak of a high dune. From that peak he was in full view from all directions. He went up the dune a man.

He came back down no more than an object, it; lower than priest, man, animal, snake…anything that moved, bred, ate, or shat was above him. All had been taken from him; his priesthood; poor but free man; and now, his identity as a man. At the peak of the rise, the wolf had ripped from him the last two, leaving an 'it' rather than a 'who'.

With bowed head, he followed the master whose violation of him had denied him even the least place in the city.

He has never tried to escape again. Instead, he has learned to shut off his mind. He locks himself away deep within dark recesses and hiding places he had not known were in his skull. Though his body shuffles after his canine captor, he is far away.

Empty

"To speak the name of the dead is to make him live again. To speak the name of the dead restores the breath of life to him who has vanished."

(The Egyptian Book of the Dead)

He learns not to feel the hunger, the pain, the terror...for a while. All these things come back to him in the light of day. In the light, when he is alone. Waiting for his master. He learns that the wolf was to bring him low and then lower before releasing him to his jackal master.

He remembers the first day of his learning. Along with his bread, his jackal master had brought a scroll. He had torn it to shreds unread and given those pieces to the wind.

His master did not return for seven days, nor did food.

The day following that, a book was resting beside his bread. He spent that day tearing the pages out of the book one by one, tearing them apart and casting those away. He had tossed the cover away without bothering to see where it landed.

He did not see his master, or food, for two weeks.

The morning after that, there was a scroll next to his bit of bread.

He had unrolled it and read some bit of the path of the dead to where Osiris held reign. The scroll described the eleven gates blocking the path by a goddess. All who sought to reach the land of the dead must know the name of all eleven goddesses in order to proceed.

* * *

—The Twelfth Hour—
The Book of Gates:

The Alabaster Sarcophagus of Seti.
The Ante-Chamber of the Tuat
The Gate Of Saa-Set: The Second Division of the Tuat.
The Gate Of Aqebi: The Third Division of the Tuat.
The Gate Of Tchetbi: The Fourth Division of the Tuat
The Gate Of Teka-Hra: The Fifth Division of the Tuat
The Judgment Hall of Osiris: The Sixth Division of the Tuat.
The Gate Of Set-em-maat-f: The Sixth Division Of The Tuat—continued.
The Gate Of Akha-En-Maat: The Seventh Division of the Tuat.
The Gate of Set-hra: The Eighth Division of the Tuat.
The Gate Of Ab-ta: The Ninth Division of the Tuat.
The Gate Of Sethu: The Tenth Division of the Tuat.
The Gate Of Am-netu-f: The Eleventh Division of the Tuat.
The Gate Of Sebi and Reri: The Twelfth Division of the Tuat

* * *

He rolled up the scroll and slept. The following morning, the scroll was gone, replaced by another, and his hunk of bread was half again larger than he had been receiving.

The sun is almost gone, he has been busy while waiting for his Master. A dagger had been dropped instead of a scroll, with no purpose he could perceive. Three who loot the dead he had found and killed with the blade. The next scroll explained the proper steps in using the sacred dagger. He hunted again with new purpose. Defilers were easy to find.

He separated first the male member and pouch of his seed, then both arms, both legs, finally the head which he quickly held to face the dismembered corpse for those few seconds that ka and ba may see the utter end of himself as his akh is destroyed.

In those times between night and day that he cannot rest, he goes out and hunts the desecrators. Other four-legged warders move like shadows, unseen and unheard. Nameless, he becomes as them, and takes up their duties to be his own as well.

His Master takes notice, and the jackal now brings a piece of cheese to drop with the bread beside the fountain, along with something new to study. Evening is still shimmering strands of its glory lancing out across the sky. He begins to slow himself, preparing to again slip away within, prepares to again die the small and temporary death left to him.

He is tired, too tired. He has endured this half-life as long as he can and ceases to hide himself away in the deepest shadows in his mind. He no longer has the strength to run away, not even in his mind.

When his master arrives to lead him away, he has surrendered. There is no will left in him that is his own.

Even until now he has seen himself as a vessel. Flawed, cast off, empty. He was still something. Now that is gone as well. He is nothing.

The jackal watches him for a long time before guiding him into the night. He has no way of knowing that only now is he truly an empty vessel. Now the vessel is ready to be filled.

He notes without wondering that they are among the stone crypts of the wealthy tonight. They have been here many times before. He follows where he is led and arrives before a low mound in the sand. At one end of the mound, paws have been busy. A ramp has been dug down into the sand, revealing the stone door of the crypt, ringed round with its spells of protection and warnings. The warning on this one is not uncommon, *"May any who seek to enter or defile this sacred place be covered by a donkey and its seed spilled within them!"*

Upon reading those words he shudders and whimpers, he is carried back to the day, long ago, when he had tried to run and the wolf had taken him, making him too low to have anyplace to run to.

Unlike all of the other times, his master nudges and nips, forcing him to hands and knees. For a moment, he thinks that his unmanning would be performed upon him again, but the jackal keep pushing until he is prostrate, face almost buried in the sand.

The sound of Her voice comes very near to ripping asunder his sanity. It is everywhere and nowhere.

"*Know thee that any mortal whose slightest gaze upon me pollutes and they shall be cursed to die the Death of a Thousand Stings!*"

Sekmet! She must be Sekmet rather than a shadow of Her. He closes his eyes and buries face further into the sand, but too late. For the briefest of seconds, from the very corner of one eye, he sees merest thread of Her skirt…

He is in a long tunnel with many side passages. Left with only the smallest memories of being other and 'it', he knows that he is on the path of the dead and he is unworthy to be there. For one-thousand days, he wanders without direction. In one tunnel he finds a mace too heavy to wield, in another, a bow and full quiver of arrows which he carries away with him. Not knowing how to count days in this place, he only knows that later, he hears the call of frightened souls, and sees ahead of him the god Ba-Pef trying to reach many akhs on the Path to the Underworld, that he may terrify and bring anguish upon them to such a degree that he will be able to devour them.

Putting arrow to bow, he shoots at and hits the god, and he is wounded. He runs a short way and ducks in a small side tunnel, and shoots him again, giving him yet another wound. He follows from a distance, and every time Ba-Pef assaults travellers of the Path, he shoots him and leads him away. He remembers the first scroll and uses the eleven names to hunt him along the whole path.

When the last arrow is spent, he is still on his knees, face in the sand.

Again her voice filled everything and his sanity was getting torn away from him. Whether through observation or some intervention of his master, Her voice lowered to no louder than any man, yet more beautiful than all the desert sunsets of a hundred years drawn together.

"*Child, does it not have a favourable vision of My voice? This one is different. I had to see for myself before I gift it with such as this. I will give it my blessing for my having tricked it into seeing the smallest of glimpses my dressage. When you begin to be remade in truth, I grant you one use of my symbol to heal any sting of scorpion or bite of asp. One time only, and it shall be gone.*"

"*Your master informs me that he cannot speak by voice to you and wishes you to know that while you were seven days here kept alive by him, you were in truth, one-thousand days in the Path of the Dead and defended over five-thousand akh that were then able to pass to the next step of their journeys. The bow and quiver shall be returned to you with my Blessing."*

He examines the symbol around his neck for five days, stopping to sleep, eat, or to void his bowel and bladder, and then resumes his study. When his teacher arrives, he shakes his head, the jackal drops a new scroll and pads away.

A gold scorpion on a gold rod hanging from a simple gold chain. He knows what it is, what will happen when he uses it. He is searching what he was, lost all of that to become 'it'. But, even as an 'it', he still has a sense of self. Is he ready to kill the last of Onuris in exchange for the unknown?

The third scroll contains the knowledge he seeks.

On the fifth day, he rises as he sees his master coming to get him and falls in to walk beside him. He has come to a decision.

The work of many paws has dug a ramp down to the doors of a sand buried tomb. There is but a small crack at the base of the doors. He sees no way in.

He kneels and then prostrates himself. The jackal sits and he falls to his knees before it. He knows what is coming. He does not need to look at his hands and arms and feet to see the stings of numberless scorpions; large, black wounds with a single puncture in the center of each. Punctures turned to silver scars, or crusted with blood and pus, or still seeping their poisons onto his skin. Every night a new wound as his Master calls up another scorpion to sting him.

He ensures that the amulet is still around his neck, holds his hand palm to the sand, and prays. *"Blessed Hedete that this one so low dares to speak thy name is desecration for you whose carapace is of the purest gold, glowing with full light of the sun, I plead that you may send one of your children to me that my master be able to show me that it is learning, and not torture, that he has offered day after day for years whose number I do not know. Thy Mother, Sekmet the divine and sacred, has given unto me her symbol that shall cure me of even the most powerful of scorpion stings. It seems that she hints of a great poisoning will come to be on me. I grovel in the sand and beg of you that you shall allow one of thy sacred children fill my veins with venom, for that they are your children, their venom is far mightier than any other. Strike me blind that I may learn to see.*

He leaves his palm flat and still as sand begins to move in tiny trickles that grow as they get closer. From the sands emerges a large golden scorpion. It takes its place in the centre of his hand, and strikes.

He screams.

Fire. Burning, consuming his flesh. His blood boils as the poison courses through his veins, filling him with agony. Almost he flees before it, to the refuge he has built in his skull, but he does not have the strength. Helpless, he is overtaken by it and carried away. The world swirls into shapes and colours that he cannot bend his senses around. A shining gold mountain looms before his blind eyes. A mountain of legs and claws and a poisoned whip of death. Claws that could crush the largest ox close on him and tear him away.

As he is carried down the ramp to the crypt he sees himself thrashing and flailing on the sand, bloody foam frothed around his mouth.

The scorpion scuttles through a crack in the wall of the crypt and he is surrounded by darkness and death. The claws release him and he is alone.

At first there is surcease from pain. Solitude, darkness, coolness, comfort. Now comes reason and some small measure of awareness.

This time he does not flee. This time is different. Always before there has been pain, torture until dawn. This time he does not flee.

He remembers seeing himself on the sand and knows that out there the pain still exists. It dawns on him that he is both here and there and so what lays on the sand must be his body with his ka keeping it alive. He reasons that since the body yet lives, that he cannot be akh, the transfigured spirit, and so must be ba, the soul that resides in the body until death transforms it.

He is afraid. Ba, ka and body should not be apart like this. If the body should die, how will it be transfigured? How will his akh travel to the Devourer of Souls and be destroyed? Even worse, that he would exist in eternity with no afterlife and no ending.

He must get back to the body. He must be re-joined by dawn, while not having any means to tell how far away dawn might be.

Panic looms in the darkness of the tomb as he scrabbles on hands and knees, feeling for the door, seeking the crack in the stone that granted entry to the scorpion.

Knees feel hard stone and a dusting of the ever-present sand beneath them. Fingers brush stone wall. He stands and follows the wall. Two paces, three. The door must be near. Four paces. Maybe back the other way. Two paces and fingers find empty space. He gropes in the darkness and discovers that a corridor turns from the wall he has been exploring. A corridor that he has somehow missed.

He is afraid to cross the empty space of the chamber. Afraid of losing even the meagre comfort of a wall against his hand. With the fingers of his right hand caressing cool stone he turns into the first corridor on his right. The mound did not appear to be large enough to contain many chambers.

Miles he has walked and many chambers have been explored. Each of them empty.

Another takes him to where it began even though it has been straight and true only moments before.

He falls to his knees, wishing that he dared pray. There is no one to pray to. He is alone.

Huddled on the floor, eyes closed to the darkness, he cries out to the one who may listen.

"Master! I am lost! I cannot find my way. Come to me, master. Lead me from this darkness."

* * *

Scholar

"Beam of light, sun and moon. Shining beast, man and woman. I am passing through."

(Egyptian Book of the Dead)

An orange glow pierces the veil of his closed lids. Opening them he finds himself on the floor of a small stone crypt. Reed torches burn in their scones on the walls. Four fat pillars support the roof, each carved and painted with messages he knows, but is too tired to read. Rotted reed baskets and clay urns hold the remains of grain and wine and bread. Food for the dead. Tools and jewellery surround the wood sarcophagus. The empty, dried husks of slaves huddled in the corners. The walls and ceiling are painted with the spells of the Book of the Sun and the Book of the Moon and of the Book of the Dead. One large door stands at each end of the chamber, which must truly be the one under the mound of sand. One door is carved of stone and has a small crack at the bottom. A crack just large enough to pass a scorpion. The other door is a magnificent work of gold. Shining like day in the meagre light of torches it calls to him. It draws him, urges him to open it and pass through, with a need so strong that tears wash down his cheeks.

At the foot of the sarcophagus sits his master, jaws agape, tongue lolling, silver eyes twinkling not with laughter, but with victory.

He rises to his feet and tries to reach the golden portal but his master blocks the way. The jackal does not growl or bite. It moves to place itself between his own and his goal. He does not fight, though the need to pass the door does not diminish. Past them waits the Devourer of Souls and beyond that is Osiris.

When it is sure that he will remain in place, the jackal sits and stares at the space between the sarcophagus and the golden doors. He looks where the jackal stares but sees nothing. Nothing but the dancing of shadows as torches flicker.

He starts to turn back to his master but a low growl warns him and he turns his gaze back to the shadows. At first indistinct, he sees that one shadow does not move with the light of the torches, but seemingly of its own will. Not daring to blink he watches as it takes shape before him.

A man...or a pale shadow of one. So translucent as to almost not exist at all, he sees a man in rich garb pacing the walls, beating them with his fists, clawing at them with torn nails. His mouth is stretched in a long wail of despair.

Again and again the figure approaches the golden doors. Time and again, his feet turn him away from the gateway and to another section of stone wall.

He who learns watches the shade and knows that he too searches for a door.

That somehow he does not see the shining portal. He searches just as the jackal's slave has this very night.

One night that defeated him. Broke him.

How long has this shade been searching?

With a warning growl that he should not move, the jackal rises and approaches the lost soul. There it becomes as easy to see the shroud of the wolf surrounding the jackal. The jackal is not his master, but is his teacher. The Wolf is his master and the jackal the instrument of his will.

It takes a ghostly hand in its jaws and gently guides it to the portal of gold. As soon as fingers brush the surface, the doors open. He who is now but a slave cannot watch as the figure passes through. The light from beyond shatters his mind and he knows no more.

* * *

When he remembers his body, he uses the last of his ability to think, and takes the symbol from around his neck, laying that gold scorpion over the still bubbling and oozing wound left by the other gold scorpion. Instantly both sting and symbol are gone. So is the memory of the wolf.

At first there was bread beside the small spring where he rested. When he used the scrolls and books, there was more bread. When he began using the dagger to kill defilers, there was water, bread, and cheese. After proving himself on the Path of the dead a dried strip of meat was added to that. Beside them now is a bow with a quiver full of arrows. Drawing an arrow, he sees that the tips are gold in colour and inscribed with a scorpion.

A gift from Sekmet...from a goddess.

His master brings a book and waits until his slave takes it and begins his studies. He reads, eats, and drinks, then continues reading before he curls up to sleep as dawn begins to spread across the sky.

It has been many nights since he watched his master in his role as guide. He does not know how many. Counting would be fruitless because time itself no longer matters to him. There is no past...the past belongs to one who was Pinhasy. There is no future...for he has not even a name to hang one on.

In the new book, *The Book of the Day*, he learns about death, the gods, his master and himself. He has seen his master guide the akh of the lost to the land of the dead. The jackals do not prowl among the dead to devour them. Guardians of the tombs, their breath smells of rot not because they fed upon the dead, but because they fought decay, snapping and tearing at it to keep it from those they protected.

He sees ones whose akhs are so pale that not even his master can reach them. Souls lost and doomed never to reach their destination. These are the ones found in crypts defiled by robbers. The places where the desiccated corpses have been broken apart for the jewellery they wore. He learns that though ka and ba are transfigured at death to the akh of the afterlife, they are still bound to the body just as in life. If a body rots away, is destroyed or comes to harm, the eternal akh will be eternal no more and would fade away.

He passes beyond the golden doors with his master, and the soul he guides. He watches a jackal and a baboon take the heart from the chest of the akh and place it upon a golden scale with a feather on one plate. Only when the scales balance perfectly does the jackal permit the soul to move on. He knows that Ammut; She who is lion, hippopotamus and crocodile, the Devourer of Souls waits below for any hearts that do not balance.

He does not want to pass back through the doors to the world of the living. His master is forced to bite and snarl and pull on him until his flesh rips before he allows himself to be taken back.

* * *

While looking for defilers of the dead with his bow, he notices that the mummified corpses in the sand, are beginning to smell of rot. He looks around and sees a shadow that is not aligned properly with the tomb it is using as camoflague. He shoots one of his arrows into the shadow. There is just enough time to know that his hit scored before he begins to rot, though he yet lives.

He watches helpless as his flesh falls from the bones of his arms and a skeletal hand grips his bow, even as the shadow becomes the giant serpent, Apep.

The decay stops and he sees himself heal in a few heartbeats. A shadowy outline of a Wolf swinging a mace, a whisp in the shape of a Jackal with a crux, and he between them with another arrow knocked. He watches the serpent until it becomes visible by its movement. He looses another arrow, aiming at where he thinks the back of its head should be. Vile rage and hate in the scream tell him that the arrow flew true. He can not be sure, but he believes he sees the hint of a smile on two muzzles as they drift into nothing.

He spends half of his sleeping period locating the remains of those struck with the rot and moves them to where they will become as leather again. He believes that even these with no ba deserve respect.

Sometimes he does not travel but dreams. Dreams of what was. Often, he is back in his cell at the temple. Always before him is the Book of the Dead. As he reads it, the jackal is there. Pointing, guiding, showing. Turning pages that cannot be read because they are blank. Large sections of the Book of the Dead that are missing. Empty, because they have not yet been written.

In dreams he has watched as the jackal-headed god treated the dismembered body of mighty Osiris that it might be whole again and saw how this should be done for the dead that their akhs might be eternal.

He learns much at the side of his master.

* * *

Supplicant
"I have come to you, my lord that you may take me so that I may see your beauty, for I know you and I know your name... "
(The Egyptian Book of the Dead)

He kneels by the spring. No longer smelling the water. Far past being maddened by the sound of its trickling even as his lips shrink and crack for want of it. No longer does his belly cramp with hunger. No more do his eyes grow blurry with lack of sleep.

Three days and three nights he has knelt here. Unsleeping, unmoving. Without food though it sits at his side. No water though it gurgles at his back. No shelter from the sun overhead. Three days since he has sent away the one that was his master.

From student to outcast. From outcast to slave. From slave to student. And now time to become slave once again. No shame is in him. If the Master accepts him as the lowliest of His slaves, he knows that it will be a greater gift than any he ever dreamed.

Three nights of deprivation. Of offering to the Master.

Three days of endurance. Apology to the Master. Begging forgiveness for his pride.

How foolish the student Pinhasy had been. Seeking to ask a place at the feet of one god while blinding his eyes and heart to the Call of another. He does not ask, even of himself, why Wepwawet has called to him. He knows only that now he hears.

* * *

111

Night falls. The moon is full, rising like a silver mirror to turn the desert into a sea of mercury. Though he has not moved for three days, he rises to his feet. Though he has not slept or drunk or eaten, his mind is clear and fever bright. Naked, he walks the sands. Climbing the hill until the lights of the city of Cynopolis shine below him, the City of the Dead at his back. He turns his back on the welcoming light of the city and faces west towards the land of the dead and kneels.

Into the night he calls:

"*Anubis, Protector of Tombs, I am here. I would be thy servant. I am yours.*"

The jackal that was once his master pads up the hill and sits behind him. He does not pause, but calls again to Him whom he would serve.

"*Anubis, Opener of the Ways, I am here. I would be thy servant. I am yours.*"

A second jackal glides out of the darkness to sit beside the first and again he sends forth his voice.

"*Anubis, Weigher of Souls, I am here. I would be thy servant. I am yours.*"

"*Anubis, Steersman of the Boat of a Million Years, I am here. I would be thy servant. I am yours.*"

"*Anubis, Embalmer of Osiris and of the Dead, I am here. I would be thy servant. I am yours.*"

"*Anubis, Who Commands the Seven Guardian Spirits, I am here. I would be thy servant. I am yours.*"

"*Anubis, Guide of the Dead, I am here. I would be thy servant. I am yours.*"

With each call another dog of the desert joins its brethren until seven in all sit behind and around him in an arc of shadows. Seven jackals circling him, just as on that night so long ago when he sought to die at their jaws. Prostrating himself in the sand, he cries again.

"*Anubis, Jackal Ruler of the Nine Bows, I am here. I would be thy servant. I am yours.*"

A Voice, thunderous and fearsome, calls from the sands, "*Why do you to call unto me and not your master? Who are you to speak my names and not those of thy master?*"

The Voice is all around, battering his ears.

"*Show that you are worthy to serve. How relentless was your search for knowledge of the books and scrolls loaned to you. If you can identify your master and call unto him as is proper, then you shall be worthy to speak. Go to the spring now and spend the full day in awareness of your hunger, your thirst, the heat of the sun, the empty loneliness of the night.*"

He waits for all the shadows to fade before lifting his head, then standing to trudge back to his place.

The following day was longer than the thousand he spent on the Path of the Dead. He went through all he had learned until he believes that the knowing is his.

With confidence, he calls into the night:

"Upuaut, who Opens the Way to the enemy in War. I would be thy servant. I am yours."

A golden wolf and a sable jackal pad up the hill and sit behind him. He notes that the jackal is his teacher.

"Upuaut, whose sharp arrow is more powerful than any other god's alone. I would be thy servant. I am yours."

A second wolf and jackal glide out of the darkness to sit beside the first, and again he sends forth his voice.

"Wepwawet, Lord of the Necropolis, protector of the dead. I would be thy servant. I am yours."

"Ophoisancient, Opener of the Ways to the sky, of the dead, of the paths of choice and actions. I would be thy servant. I am yours."

"Wepwawet, whose standard precedes that of kings, and whose staff leads beside, and with, the Apis Bull. I would be thy servant, I am yours."

"Wepwawet, who is known to lead the deceased through the underworld and to guard over them on their perilous journey. I would be thy servant. I am yours."

"Upuaut, whose head is that of a wolf of grey and of white, and for whom was named Lycopolis, City of the Wolf, in his honour. I would be thy servant. I am yours."

With each call another wolf and a jackal of the desert joins its brethren until seven of each in all sit behind him. They rise and begin to circle, seven wolves circling him, seven suns. Seven jackals circling him in the opposite direction, seven moonless nights. Prostrating himself in the sand he cries again.

"His name opens the ways, all paths through the underworld."

"Who guides the choices and paths taken in life that the Living Pharaoh be divine in his Power."

"Who in the "Book of the Dead" and the book of "That Which Is in the Underworld" is a mighty warrior and blesses the armies of Pharaoh, and is also as a scout who brings into being an "opening a path" to the enemy and allows Pharaoh's armies to proceed without distance or time between."

"I would be thy servant. I am yours."

A voice, thunderous and fearsome, calls from the sands, *"What are you to call unto me? Who are you to speak my names?"*

The voice is all around, battering his ears. Inside his head driving everything before it. There is only the Voice demanding. Shaking on the sand, he lifts his face far enough to speak in a shattered voice. Before he can speak, his face is driven back into the sand by the power of the voice.

"Tell me who you are. Tell me why four gods and goddesses have claimed you for their own."

"Tell me who you are that you use your bow to wound two gods."

"You whose names are many and are holy. I repent of my pride. I repent of my greed in not releasing all that was me that you could sculpt me as you

113

wished. I am too low to know the ways of gods. To try, hubris. I would be thy servant. I am yours. I am only what you would make of me. I have no name but that which you would give me."

Seven wolves and seven jackals, poised to rend him to pieces should his answer displease the Master, howl their approval.

"You who were born Pinhasy, becoming Onuris the Acolyte, who was thrown down and low, Nameless; who was a man; who was nothing, the lowest; who became the student of one of My Father's sons."

"That man long dead, learning from the dead, and protecting them, who has learned the Rite of the Opening of the Way."

"Then rise, you who would be first priest of Wepwawet. Rise and face your god."

Terrified to look upon the face of a god but too obedient to hesitate he rises to his knees and lifts his head to look upon his Master.

Seven feet tall, covered in short, sleek fur, growing thicker and longer from pectoral upwards. Dark storm-grey on back, lightening around sides to silver down his abdomen. Silver of the moon causing grey fur to roil like storm clouds. Eight feet of divine magnificence…each muscle supple, defined, strong and perfect. Sandals of silver upon his feet, cords of silver snaking up his calves. Legs, long and lithe and broad of thigh. Each a perfect column to support the heavens. Waist girded in white linen kilt and silver girdle. A tail, slender and waving, a dark serpent tufted at the tip like a lion's. Abdomen flat and rippled with plates of muscle, navel a perfect well of mystery. Shoulders draped in a pectoral collar of gold and lapis and carnelian. Bands of silver with glass beads and precious gems encircle biceps and wrists. Strong hands end in long, dark-nailed fingers bearing rings of glass and gold. One hand holds his mace and the other his bow.

He almost finds it impossible to lift his gaze any higher. Overcome by the magnificence before him, he is sure that he will die should he dare to see the face of a god. A god! Standing before him. Physical and manifest. The male smell of him, musky and spicy is filling him until he cannot breathe. The perfect form and symmetry of what he has seen burned into his vision forever. The thunder of that voice like the roar of the flooding Nile in his head. He does not want to look but his god has commanded him and he cannot disobey. He lifts his eyes and knows that he is less than the worms that corrupt flesh. Less than the dung of the least creature that crawls on the earth.

Somewhere beneath the pectoral, short grey and silver fur gives way to rich, thick, flowing mane, silver fur ascending to cover the fur of his throat and chin. Above… he cannot look… he must… he watches the pulsing of the great veins in the neck of the god, stealing himself to look into his face.

Wolf. Not desert dog. Not beast. Not the delicate grace of the jackal. Stolid, feral anger storming in his eyes. Wolf, god of War, defender of the Dead. His gaze stabbing into him, seeing his fear, acknowledging it as unimportant. Gaze commanding obedience. The sharp extended muzzle ending in the squared nose of the wolf, nostrils flared wide. The tips of white teeth poking just past black, shining lips. Broad, blade-shaped ears rising over the head and even over the quicksilver and blue striped Nemes headdress adorning it.

What he sees is not a merging of man and animal but something different. Something whole and perfect in its own right. Not man and animal but Wepwawet…his Master.

"I am without name, my Master. I am your slave. I am your servant. I am your priest."

"No! Not yet are you priest, servant or even slave."

The hand of his god clenches on the shaft of his mace, the muscles of his arm flexing.

The terror of rejection is overwhelming and he struggles to understand as his Master speaks.

"I called unto you long ago, but you could not hear. You were not ready to hear, and were unfit to serve me. Even then, on your day of ascension, your thoughts and soul were about you and not the Ones you proclaimed to serve!"

"A gift I gave that you that you might earn the knowledge of how I set your feet upon my path. But you remained blind as you cowered and sought to drive away my gifts."

"I called again, but still you were unfit to hear my words. My Child made you low that you might learn the humility that would guide your feet upon my path."

"I heard your call among the dead, but your cry was for yourself and not me. I sent My Father's children that you might grow the strength required to walk upon my path."

"You refused to see, and so I sent the scorpion to teach you, and you learned how to see my path."

"Finally, you call to me. Finally, your cries are mine and not your own. A vessel made by me to use as I see fit."

Wepwawet stares at him, flecks of gold and silver moving in them hold his gaze.

"From this point and for all of time, you are mine. As My Child marked and made you his slave, so do I make you mine Eturum."

* * *

Builder
"O grant ye that his father, the Lord of his god-like companions may bear witness on his behalf."

(The Egyptian Book of the Moon)

Anubis studied the new priest, "As you are but the lowest slave, so shall you do the work of a slave, asking no questions, immediate obedience, excepting that my son bid you otherwise."

"This night you shall build an aisle for me, reaching from a dock that you shall build. Thus shall you honour and celebrate the dead that are brought unto me, and the care of those who follow me. You will make floors of quartz-veined black marble polished mirror smooth. The ceiling you will plaster and tile that each of the gods is represented with due honour as the cherished dead are brought from pier to temple, and unto me with all care and honour. The walls you shall leave empty, but for the stout pillars to hold up the heavens. I will pass my hand over them, and they shall thereafter be gold and written so that each pillar shall teach in steps, what must be relearned. They shall reteach the honoured dead as they progress the way along the course. Who have forgotten who I am, and turned away from eternity. At the end furthest from the Nile, you shall stop and rest for the day."

"For this task, you shall begin your work of cutting stones and hauling them one hour after dusk. Construction shall begin as soon as the first stones arrive. You shall have one night minus the last hour before dawn to complete the procession."

"For this task, you shall have the assistance of four of my children."

At that, four of the seven jackals, stretch, grow and took on the mien of their Master. They are smaller and do not radiate the divinity that surrounds him, but are formidable.

Anubis appears to be finished with the one who has faint memories of being called…something…a name…Onuris. That bit of knowledge helps him not at all to complete The Master's will. He turns away walking into the dunes, discarding that useless information. Not understanding how such a thing was possible did not daunt him. He was no one. He was nothing. He was a tool, used by his master to his master's own ends.

He kneels motionless, the four Children standing behind him. At last the thinnest sliver of the sun had fallen and he begins counting.

With a nod, he heads down to the Nile. The Four Children fall in behind him. They will go where he directs them to go, will do what he directs them to do, but they will not act on their own. It is not only the construction that is being evaluated. The Slave knows this, but cannot allow such thoughts to slow him down.

A large ship with a flat coursed deck, and painted all in black with gold and blue, waits for him, and he knows that it is his to order. First he directs that enough large stone blocks be brought to create a proper pier where the water-logged, sagging excuse for one is collapsing under the strain. Three Children he sends on that task. The fourth stays with him as they walk to choose the best site for construction.

When he returns to the beginning, a proper stone pier has taken the place of the rotting flotilla of rotting reeds. There is also a stack of the same stone to the quantity of twenty-three blocks.

Taking one from cutting and hauling and putting both of the remaining Children to the task of constructing, he measures lines and angles and how the terrain will affect them. One smallish dune would cause the aisle to deviate by less than one knot of a hundred knot line. He orders the dune dispersed, and the construction continues in a straight line.

That what they are doing is impossible does not deter him from his assigned task. Boatload after boatload come at such a rapid pace that it seems that the boat had only disappeared around a bend when it appears loaded and heading back to him. No sooner is the last available stone set when a new load arrives. It is in this manner that they work through an endless night.

The faint hint of rose warns of imminent dawn. In near panic, he searches around him for the next stone, but none waits for him. Thinking only on his failure does he turn around and see the completed aisle. He smiles…and collapses.

* * *

When he comes back to himself there is no sign of the Children, but a luxurious, rich meal waits for him. He eats dried fish, fresh fruit, dark bread and a crumbly but delicious bit of cheese…while he reads from The Book of the Sun.

He reads until dusk and his Master comes. He trembles at the feet of Wepwawet, arms outstretched and face in the sand.

"You have not slept excepting when your mortal shell could take no more and tumbled you into the dark. Even then, you picked up that which I would have you learn rather than taking any sleep by choice. I am pleased, Eturum. You may yet be the one I have been searching thirty-seven of your generations to find."

He watches as Wepwawet walks away, but he has not been summoned and so does not move.

The footsteps have been another test. *"Eturum, the aisle is truly what I wished for, and thought was beyond human skill to build."*

Risking rage and punishment for forgetting his place, Eturum mumbles something into the sand.

"Filth! Do you think me so low as to bend down that your words may not grace my ears? If you would say something you believe important enough to say, say it! If not, do not speak! Am I understood, he who is on the razor's edge of no longer remaining Eturum?"

"I understand you, my Master. I was saying that I do not know if I am human. I am not who I was. Do not remember what I might have been. I don't know what I am other than your slave, and so do not know what I can and cannot be capable of in your service."

"Well thought out and well spoken, Eturum. Take these memories. When I return you can tell me who you were and are."

In a handful of seconds, Eturum relived every second of being Onuris.

When his Master returned, he motioned for Eturum to look him in the eyes. *"Who were you?"*

"I do not know, my Master"

"I gave you the memories."

"They were not important to keep, and so I shredded them and let them flutter away."

"What were you?"

"I do not know, my Master. How could I have been a person or thing before being yours? I looked at each moment and found it flawed and so I destroyed it and scattered it to the winds. I do not know what that says about who or what, but the words 'prideful' and 'ignorant' whirl about each other, and now being spoken, they tear and fly from even that memory."

"Eturum, you are no longer my slave. In serving me well you have served yourself. Take this box and bejewel yourself with what is inside, including the gold hemmed wrap of senior servant and no longer that of a slave."

"Are you he…my broken and empty cup? We will wait and see."

* * *

Jackal

"I have balanced the place whereon he standeth, and I have made a path for him, and it eternally shapes filth to purpose."

(The Egyptian Book of the Moon)

Anubis commands, "This night, you will go again among the tombs and find defilers of the dead. Offer fit reward to those of false tongue stealing eternity for coin. You will take none of my children, but instead bring with you he who shall help you to build back what was mine. Though he is your Master, tonight you work as a team, each learning from the other. Isis, steered by the venom whispers of Set, is set to take this side of the Path of the Dead. Set plots to make impossible for akh to reach Osiris and the Afterlife. Conflict brews and now is the time for Wepwawet to return and take up his arms. He who was my father is Wepwawet, who then dwelt within me, and is now Wepwawet, my son.

"There among the tombs, you shall find seven defilers and bring them to me, one at a time and alive, that they may be of use in the defence of the very dead that they have been enemy to. All seven must be delivered to me no later than two hours before dawn."

"Know that Sekhmet, goddess of warfare, pestilence, and the desert, is influenced by Isis and is no longer your friend."

"Wepwawet, like myself, is an Opener of the Ways from this world into the next."

Seven golden wolves in Children form step from the shadow arrayed as a spear point, and Wepwawet at its core. They are built similar to Him, but less feral, sleeker and faster than a viper's kiss. Gold rather than grey; cream on belly and chest turning gold as it goes back to finally become a brown stripe running from the top of their muzzles down their backs to the tips of their tails. Wepwawet does not pause at Anubis, but approaches Eturum and circles him several times. Sniffing disdainfully, he looks at his father, *"Are you sure that this is the one? It seems too…base and formless. It performed well with the assistance of our Power, but what use is it without them?"*

"To determine that is one of the goals of this night's labours, my son. Learn quickly how to bring two into one that the pair of you work together with such symmetry that, together, you become one instrument."

Anubis then turns his attention back to his children and begins to direct them in the building of some extension at the end of the procession.

As he turns back to his strange, divine Master it is to see the grey back of Wepwawet racing across the sands and disappearing over the crest of the nearest dune. Eturum races to catch up. The wolf stays ahead of him, and he continues running as fast as possible, long after his lungs burn, his legs quiver and he grows dizzy.

The specks of light dancing before him slow down and, after several deep breaths, took up their normal pace as stars in the night sky. A shadow moved to block the stars.

"You appear ill or injured, but I smell neither on you."

"I am not ill," Eturum pants, "nor injured. I have crossed the limit of what my body is capable of, and so it has taken away my consciousness before permanent damages was done."

"You have limits of speed and distance? Physical limits?"

Eturum nods.

"From here on, you shall teach me about your body by apprising me of changes, limits, and anything else that may help me to learn all that there is that I must know, if you are to work at my side!"

"How fast can you run?"

"I ca…"

"Show, do not tell."

Eturum settles himself, digs in his feet and sprints as fast as he is able to in shifting, dry sand. He is forced to stop, bent over and panting.

The Wolf god pads up, *"Why have you stopped in apparent distress?"*

After several deep breaths, Eturum is able to answer, "That is the fastest that I can run in this sand. I cannot maintain that speed over long distances or for a long time without resting. I will show you the fastest pace that I am capable of over long distances."

He sets off at a steady lope that he can maintain for over an hour without resting.

In that manner they approach the City of the Dead and slow to a silent step by measured step into their hunting ground.

The first capture is disappointing. The thief was around the corner of the first building they reached and his back was to the pair. The wolf whispered a phrase and the thief, who had been working blocks loose from the back of the crypt, fell into a senseless sprawl.

Directed to by Wepwawet, Eturum lifts the man high enough to drape over the deity's shoulder. Remembering the Wolf's command, he explains how easy it is to lift their prey from the sand, but becomes more and more difficult, the higher he has to lift the limp load.

"*Then you could not carry him yourself?*"

"I could but it would be a matter of many hours, possibly a day or more."

Eturum no longer wonders that his life has moved him to a point where working side by side with deities no longer seems insane.

They reach what was now a partially constructed temple. Seven fat pillars circle a large, round indentation in the floor. Before they return to their hunting, Anubis bids them wait, and has Eturum watch as he lifts the reaver and causes him to come awake.

The man begins begging, pleading, struggling, but as Wepwawet begins invoking the First Arit and pushes such that the tomb robber's back comes into contact with the pillar and begins to sink into it that the man begins screaming in truth.

"*The name of the Doorkeeper is Sekhet-her-asht-aru. The name of the Watcher is Smetti. The name of the Herald is Hakheru. The Osiris Ani, whose word is truth, shall say when he cometh unto the First Arit: "I am the mighty one who createth his own light. I have come unto thee, O Osiris, and, purified from that which defileth thee, I adore thee. Lead on...*"

It takes a long time for him to sink fully into the pillar. Only then does the screaming cease.

The hunters turn and began their second trip to the tombs that night, when Wepwawet stops, listens to something Eturum cannot hear.

"*We are under attack! Return to the temple where one of my Father's Children shall armour you appropriately. Your dagger and bow shall serve you well.*"

He moves to the horizon before Eturum could count to five. He also sees seven packs of wolves, each pack made of seven wolves.

Eturum sprints to the temple where one of Anubis's Children stands ready with a silver suit of armour. In a very short time he rushes down the aisle to the pier. He does not know why, but does not turn from what he feels is the will of his Master or Master's Father.

He arrives to see the boat at the pier shake and one side to start to split. He rushes to the damaged side of the boat with drawn bow. There is nothing that he can see. Keeping watch, a hippo comes near the surface, showing the head of a wasp. Without pause he fires, sinking a blessed arrow in one eye of the goddess Ahti. Pain and rage cause her to writhe and flail, causing more damage than her intended attacks. He takes one more shot and leaps back to the new pier of stone blocks.

The deity makes many attacks, almost always collecting an arrow for her efforts. When she dives for the foundation, his bow sends the arrows into the depths.

He kneels and sets the bow aside, waiting with his dagger in hand for Ahti to make another attempt to kill him. She is so fast that she almost reaches him. When his dagger slices through the entire width of one of her many faceted eyes Ahti screams, almost deafening him. As he watches, she flees upriver.

The feeling of malevolence he had not been aware of dissipates.

Returning to the temple, he feel no impulse to hunt elsewhere. Without questioning, he sees Anubis and his Children battle on the Paths of the Dead. Wepwawet's wolf packs are doing battle alongside Osiris against an army far too large to defeat, yet even as he watches he sees that the army grows smaller from moment to moment.

His Master's doings are no business of his. With all Children gone as well, the temple is vulnerable. He takes it upon himself to run circuits around the temple while watching for new shadows between sand and sky.

Drawing an arrow and knocking it he calls, "Be warned that I am a servant of my Masters, and if you be no friend of theirs, turn back or be struck down!"

The shadow moves closer. He looses an arrow. When it does not stop the shadowy figure still advancing toward the temple, he fires more.

As fast as he can draw, knock and loose, he brings a storm of arrows until the shadow steps into the light of the temple, revealing Wepwawet, his master with more than twenty arrows piercing his flesh and gaps in his armor.

Devastated with shame, he casts the bow away and falls to the floor spread-eagle silently weeping that he has dishonoured himself so. Failed to the detriment of He whose service is the only center of his life. He does not beg or plead. His words are unfit for a god's ears to endure.

"*What should be done to you?*"

The servant waits for permission.

"*You may answer.*"

"Your father should take me up and sink me into one of the pillars as is done with other filth."

"*That is among the most horrible of fates. Are you sure? Tell me all that you have done since you were left alone.*"

"Somehow, I thought to defend the pier. As soon as I was armoured as you commanded, I ran to that place and saw that the boat for carrying stone blocks appeared to be under attack. I boarded the vessel and saw a hippo with the head of a wasp and knew her to be Ahti trying to sink the boat. I wounded her several times, but had to jump back to the pier. I failed you the first time by allowing your boat to be destroyed. The arrows appeared to harm her, but not severely, but for the first of my shots, which struck her eye. I lay down my bow and drew my dagger, kneeling low so as to remain unseen until she came in deliberate search for me. I cut her eye clean across its width. For the second time I failed you, for I was unable to keep her from escaping.

I took my bow back up and ran to the temple. It was undefended with all Children gone. I failed you the third time in thinking that I was, in the least measure, able to act in a Child's place. My vision is poorer at night, so I watched the crest of sand against the sky, looking for unusual or moving shadows. I gave warning, and failed in the most grievous of ways, fired my bow at a moving shadow. I shot with the intent to kill whatever cast it before it could reach the temple. In so doing, I struck my Master in many places until you stepped into the light. My greatest failure, an unforgivable one."

"Then shall I list your failures that I can better decide. In the first, I deliberately gave you no target and over five days of mortal travel away cast my will to you, and you answer without hesitation or doubt."

"In the second failure you did battle with a goddess, a minor one, but goddess all the same. Your loss was of a reed boat already stove in. With bow you wage battle against the goddess and, with your dagger, injured so mightily that she is forced to flee and the Air of Doom dissipated."

"Without being told to do so, you took it upon your mortal self to guard this temple. When a possible threat appeared, you warned and then sent forth arrows with such skill that a squad of mortal soldiers would be decimated by the count of fifteen men."

"We have known that these conflicts were coming long ago. We used them to see if you truly were my instrument. You proved that you were by defending the pier. Did you have the courage needed to be in my service? Did you have the mind and skill to plot and execute strategy? A near blind goddess is the answer to those two. Did you have the courage and sense to take matters into your own hand, doing service that you believe necessary without command? Every arrow that has pierced me as well as those in the sand are badges of honour.

My decision about your punishment is this. You are to keep the armor and wear it with pride in the knowledge that those who see it shall know that you are in my service and I am pleased with you."

"Come, we have more sacrifices to gather." Wepwawet's armour disappears, and he shakes himself in the manner of a wet dog, sending arrows in all directions.

"I know your thoughts, my servant. If it were not as apt as you picture it, I might strike you. But it was of good humour and I shall let it pass…until the next time."

It seems to Eturum that his master has some sense of humour. Then he hears a chuckling in the back of his skull.

They head back to the Necropolis and make three more trips before dawn, with Wepwawet carrying two each trip. Each is tied in such a way as to see the fate of the one preceding him.

The second prey is treated as the first, this one to the speaking of the Second Arit.

"*The name of the Doorkeeper is Unhat. The name of the Watcher is Seqt-her. The name of the Herald is Ust. The Osiris Ani, whose word is truth, shall say [when he cometh to this Arit]: "He sitteth to carry out his heart's desire, and he weigheth words as the Second of Thoth. The strength which protecteth Thoth humbleth the hidden…"*

One after another are all seven defilers brought to Wepwawet that he might call from the Seven Sacred Arits and empowers all seven pillars.

And he speaks the sixth of the Arits.

They bring the last of the prey to the almost finished temple well before the limit set by Anubis.

Eturum is not exhausted, as he expects he should be. His limbs are light, he is not panting or sweating. The latter had disturbed Wepwawet who was alarmed that the human's body was wasting vital water in such a way. It took much reassurances that the process was natural and would not end in death as long as he could replace the fluids when he was able.

* * *

Harvester

"*O grant thou that I may continue to advance, and that I may attain to the sight of Ra…*"

(Egyptian Book of the Dead)

The Guardian of the Dead is joined by the second Opener of the Ways. Eturum is instructed to touch a certain pillar and joins the two gods in reciting the Seventh and final of the Arits. The proper words appear, written in fire across his mind as the seventh thief is pressed into stone, making of him one of the Seven Sacred Guardians of the Moon's Eye.

"*The name of the Doorkeeper is Sekhmet-em-tsu-sen. The name of the Watcher is Aa-maa-kheru. The name of the Herald is Khesef-khemi. The Osiris scribe Ani, whose word is truth, shall say [when he cometh to this Arit]: "I have come unto thee, Osiris, being purified from foul emissions. Thou goest round about heaven, thou seest Ra, thou seest the beings who have knowledge. Thou Holy ONE! Behold…*"

With the speaking of the final word, the circle in the ceiling positioned over the round indentation in the floor began to shimmer metallic silver all around its rim and also the rim of the depression.

"*Wepwawet, your servant returns changed in body. I would know the thoughts that caused you to do this thing.*"

"*When you speak a task for me, you pass it to Eturum also. At that point, he ceases to exist as an identity. His only thoughts are how he may best assist me in the task you have given. When there is no task or other requirement, he reads volume after volume of lore. His mind picks up what he does not understand and stores it until he is ready to understand. He sees no "me" in himself. He is our tool in all ways. Making him physically more capable does nothing to him as self, but improves the tool we have made of him.*"

"*If the mortals are as he is, should we not take and train others as well?*"

"*Remember, you, that we searched over a thousand years to find one who had the potential to become what he is so close to being.*"

* * *

"*On this night, my son shall carry for your use one hundred vessels of perfectly blown glass. You have no need to return to me with each reaper's capture. Instead you shall use the gift I have bestowed upon you to treat thieves and charlatans. With the assistance of Wepwawet, this gift will draw forth the spirit of those who are abominations unto me. The spirit than shall pass without resistance into one of these one hundred flawless globes of perfectly blown glass, there to bide until such a time as I or my Brother wish that they shall be released.*"

"*You shall not return to me until all of one hundred contains a soul. You must return before dawn.*"

"*If you follow the instructions that I have given unto you, a full day and night of rest, water and food as well as my approval shall reward you.*"

At that, Eturum's stomach clenched, his vision became blurry and knees weak and unsteady.

"*Thus do I release you of the illusion that you are well and that your needs are met. Now know you that if you fail me, you will die before the fall of another night, and the Opening of the Door shall not be given you.*"

"*Succeed and you will begin walking the steps which last one full day and one full night that shall raise you above Wepwawet's servant, and become the first and always highest of my son's priests.*"

As soon as he is dismissed, Eturum begins the run to the tombs in the same easy lope that served him so well the night before. He has run thus for less than an hour before falling between one stride and the next.

From outside his body he sees Wepwawet turn him over and urge him back to his feet, but sees him as ba, ready to join ka to become akh. By the power of his divine will did he restrain the three essences that were Eturum and force them back into flesh, while silently calling out to Anubis.

* * *

Eturum wakes to the room swirling overhead slowing until he was able to identify it as the eye in the ceiling of the temple. Three of the Children come to him with a ewer of honeyed milk, fruits, roasted goat, cheeses and bread, placing the woven grass trays where he can reach them. He touches nothing, not having his Master's permission. Instead, his eyes followed the Children and wonder where the other four were. Mere moments later he sees one running along the crest of a dune. Less than a minute later, another runs in the opposite direction along a different dune.

"Eat, drink and refresh yourself, Eturum. I am not cross nor disappointed in you. It is you who has surprised us. You have performed each of your tasks, no matter that each called upon you to exceed in different ways so well, that I overestimated what the vessel of flesh that you walk in was capable of. I cannot punish you for striving so hard to please me that you would push yourself to the precipice of death and over. If not for Anubis, you would be lost to us."

At these words he tries to rise to his knees so that he can prostrate himself before Wepwawet, but the world spins away into darkness.

* * *

Reborn

"I am light. Gaze on me. Moon in darkness, sun in morning. Light is what I will on earth, along the Nile, among the people."

(The Egyptian Book of Days)

The depression beneath the circular opening with silver rim in the ceiling is filled to near its limits with quicksilver. Obeying what he feels to be true as he had at the pier, he moves to stand in the very center of it.

As one Wepwawet and Anubis enter the pool at opposite ends.

Anubis stands at his feet, his Master at his head.

"My Servant, I would have you lean back against my hand which shall support your head and you keep your body still and in line with itself. I shall lower you to beneath the surface of the quicksilver of the Moon, that all imperfections and impurities be cleansed from your body."

"I will then tap you on the forehead and you shall then open your mouth and breathe in that which shall cause your death. Struggle not nor resist the command to inhale, else you shall die beyond death, gone forever and never having existed."

"Have you anything to say before we begin this point of no return?"

"Only that I shall do all in my power to obey you to such a degree that I do not cause you to regret your choice."

"Well said." That from Anubis.

The first part is easy and he tries not to think beyond. He feels the outer layers of skin sloughing off. If his hair had not already been cleansed away, it

125

would remove itself here. Every pore in his skin is explored and cleansed. Time seems to stop as the cleansing goes on and on.

When the tap on his forehead comes, it is so unexpected, that he inhales automatically. The effort is to not struggle as the sacred fluid does to the inside of his body what it has done to the outside. His body no longer holds him and he rises into the stars to look down where two blazing lights minister to the tiniest, most insignificant spark. Allowing himself to drown was the easy part. The difficulty is to leave the stars and once again be trapped in the insignificant cage of flesh and bone.

When he is lifted to stand again, the mercury spills from every orifice: mouth, eyes, nose, anus, penis, ears…

Wepwawet strikes him on the back and he inhales…and screams.

He is mortal flesh holding immortal amounts of power.

The two gods hold him as the power blazes through him bringing scream after scream, until the power has been bled off to where the remaining amount can be contained in mortal flesh.

Released, he leaves the pool. He walks around the circumference, both gods watching. Between one step and the next, he who is now a golden wolf pads on his four paws. Changing back from wolf to man, he signals the Children to dress him. Two of the Children clothe him and another applies his jewellery and cosmetics. He does not call for weapons or armour, and reaches out, without looking, and his staff of office is placed in his hand.

Calling for a pedestal, ink and quill, and the Book of the Dead, he begins to write and does not cease until every blank area shown to him in his dreams is filled.

He turns and prostrates himself before Wepwawet, holding the staff over his head. "My Master, I am yours to command. Any that I command shall be those commanded by you through me. Any that I bring harm or healing to, it shall be your will guiding me. I am but a vessel that is filled at your will."

Wepwawet smiles, *"My cracked and empty cup has been remade."*

* * *

Pharaoh

"And so shall travel Pharaoh through the netherworld on a boat of the sun god Ra, and rise and have his victory over the dangers of the Underworld and of all those who rise against him."

Amduat (The Book of the Netherworld)

As Eturum prepares to begin the trek to Pharaoh, his Master bids him wait. *"After the battle was won with the aid of my wolves, Osiris could not thank me directly. Instead he granted to those wolves who fought and survived the ability to take the form of a mortal man at will. Seven of these I place at your command. Hide their secret from all who have no need to know."*

"Know you that your ascension was only the beginning. My cup is whole but nearly empty. Next shall my priest become my warrior as well."

Across the valley of the Nile cries of dismay echo from every temple. Every temple but one. As priests in all temples up and down the Nile began to read of the Book of the Dead found unfamiliar texts as well as expected to ones. Rites unchangeable are altered. Entire passages are changed and huge amounts of new writings have appeared. Runners are sent between the temples and acolytes hide themselves as holy ones representing the entire pantheon of the gods gather in panicked meetings that only increase the confusion. The panic grows as dawn approaches and priests try to decide whether to perform their rites as they have always been done, or to include the new texts as well.

Morning rituals begin across the land. Rites that seem to stumble rather than to flow. Rites in which the tongues of priests fumble through chants that they have performed flawlessly each dawn leading up to this day. At first, the noise from outside the temples is too weak to breach the temple walls, but that noise grows as voice after voice raises confusion, awe, dismay and fear over what the morning sun reveals.

Across the Nile, past the city, high on a stony hill in the City of the Dead stands a vast and elegant structure that had not been there the day before. Across the expanse of the open desert wafts chanted rites from the buildings that had never been heard before. The people gather outside those temples they had always counted on for direction and answers. Rumours spread like oil on water that the priests are as surprised and as lost as those seeking explanations. Panic mounts.

Those priests not conducting or participating in the sacraments send runners anew and prepare themselves to call on Pharaoh, for it is impossible that his own people have not already seen what must surely be the temple to the dog god, Anubis.

Eturum laughs to himself at all the panic over some words in flawed books. Chickens in the yard chasing worms while the barn burns. A war has begun, no mortal clash, but a fight between gods and goddesses, with the afterlife of every man in the balance. These priests are blind. He pictures a fat doughy priest covered with gold jewellery and bright jewels. He can see the expression on the priest's face when the wall falls in, crushing him and adding him to the foul compost already below. The Children chuckle. Seven special Children are his to command and to lead the pack as wolf. Of the seven, three travel with him.

* * *

Holy guards surrounded Pharaoh, forcing a space between him and his priests and followers. Order grows harder to maintain and had almost reached the point of crisis when officials called from the doors of that great chamber asking instruction on how to deal with a priest and his strange guards requesting entrance. Horns are sounded and the voices of holy eunuchs sing the entry of the high priest of Wepwawet.

The audience hall of great Pharaoh is packed. Representatives from every temple attend their divine leader. Each tries to hide the fact that they know little more of the strange events than the lowliest worker, and are as confused as those outside gaping open-mouthed at the impossible temple on the hill. Those who are of high enough office to warrant their presence press the priests for answers that they do not have to give. Slaves pause in their serving and have to be beaten back to work as they overhear theories expounded by one priest only to be vehemently denied by another. Foremen from many of the greatest Pharaoh's projects wait pensively for instruction on whether or not to continue their labours that day.

Reavers of the dead have been captured and are brought before Pharaoh. They are being questioned about what they had seen and heard in the night as they went about robbing the corpses in the desert. None admit to seeing or hearing anything. Each speaks of their innocence and ignorance.

Pharaoh orders each to be tortured, then and there. Even as they are brought to the brink of death and beyond each maintains their ignorance if not their innocence. Pharaoh's rage grows as it seems his entire empire conspires to deny him the answers to the questions he places before the priests, several of whom grow increasingly nervous as Pharaoh's gaze begins to travel between priests and torturers with growing intent.

Once the defilers of the dead has received just payment for their deeds, does Eturum step forward.

The strange priest with gold-hued skin is virtually ignored as everyone tries to push back and away from the three wolf-headed beings that move with the priest. One on each side with mace and bow, in violation of the Law prohibiting weapons being brought into the presence of Pharaoh. The third, striding behind the priest, holding a large, silver tome.

Upon reaching Pharaoh, the two Children guards drop to one knee, one fist on floor and looking down at the stones. The third child kneels and holds up the tome. The priest bows deeply, but did not prostrate himself as he should. But all is chaos and even if improper, their calm is an island in the chaos, and Pharaoh reaches out to cling to it.

He signalled that they may rise. Rather than order the Children to abandon their weapons and risk being ignored, he turned them to his advantage.

"Priest, I thank you for bringing the Guardians into my presence and believe you would not have done so, unless you saw the necessity. I hope that they can help to create order where there is none."

The Children turn away from the priest and to the crowd instead. Silence moves like the rings on water when a pebble is thrown.

"Who are you, Priest? Why are you unknown to us? What is your relationship to the strange temple that grew in the space of a single night? I would have answers!"

"It is my humble privilege to answer Pharaoh's questions that they may shine more glory upon him. We are not here to trouble Pharaoh, but to bring him answers, gifts, and knowledge."

"I am Eturum, first High Priest of Wepwawet in a thousand years. My responsibility is to assist he who is the true son of Anubis, Lord of the Necropolis, who was before that Wepwawet's true son. He who made Osiris complete when his body was sundered, Guardian of the dead, Warrior of Pharaoh... they who shall teach that Pharaoh's mortal body shall become eternal that his akh may be in the presence of Osiris for all time."

"You asked that we bring order to chaos. I show my humble will to obey Pharaoh in all things, except that they conflict with the will and words of my Master. There are among these priests charlatans who follow none but themselves, lies and greed. Would Pharaoh have that I bring them to his attention?"

Pharaoh is unsure exactly what was happening, but however strange, this bizarre group seems to be the least insane thing that has happened all day. He waves his hand that this priest proceed.

Eturum turns and approaches a priest that looks no different than the others. He reaches out and touches the forehead of the priest, who bursts into flame and begins to scream.

Everyone begins moving in panic when Pharaoh orders silence...except the torch who had been a man still screaming.

Eturum grabs the wrist of a priest who does no more than pull away while wailing. The Priest of Wepwawet forces the man's hand into the flames of the other priest. He too screams for a moment and then his face relaxes in amazement.

"Great and Holy Pharaoh, there is no heat. I am unharmed."

Eturum turns to a Child to carry the flaming and screaming priest outside. Even then, he can be heard inside. Care is taken to place him where Pharaoh can see him.

Eturum looks at another priest. "This man is a true and loyal servant of his god and shall lay down his own life to save yours in two years and three months' time. Anubis has suggested that I inform you of this that you may ponder the wisdom of elevating him to your inner circle. His mind is sharp, his dedication is total."

He touches the priest's forehead. The man's flinch is infinitesimal. He is unharmed.

"I apologize for doing that to you, honoured one, but it was necessary to show that those who burn are truly guilty and that the innocent cannot be harmed." He bows to the priest, "Can you find it in yourself and the will of your god to forgive me for using you in this way?"

"It was well thought and well done, my brother in service to the gods. Before all else, must come the safety of Holy Pharaoh. Your demonstration has reduced the panic."

Without turning, Eturum reaches back behind him and touches another forehead; more flames and screams. The panic reduces.

Moving through the crowd, he touches those who were the most devout of servants both to their gods and of Pharaoh.

No fool, Pharaoh begins ordering these men to form an arc between him and the crowd, with the third Child at the center.

Guilty 'priests' begin to back up and the Pharaoh's guards are called to hold them while Eturum touches them and turn them into living torches. After the first, guards struggle to be the one who grabs a man and carry them outside to a garden of seventeen living torches.

* * *

Chosen

"I have come daily, I have come daily. I have made myself a way. I have seen that which has been created by Wepwawet."

(The Egyptian Book of the Day)

"Glorious Pharaoh, there is worse in your court. Do I have your permission to bring them to your attention?"

In the distraction one of the Children runs to the side, drawing attention while another dove onto the raised dais forbidden to all. He grabs one of the two who are Pharaoh's most trusted guards and wraps arms around him.

Pharaoh startles and begins to stand when Eturum assures him that he is not under attack or in danger. To the contrary, his life is being saved.

"This guard that you see beside you was killed this morning and the body hidden in a grain basket." He reaches out and touches the man, whose visage changes.

Pharaoh has him dragged away and orders that he shall not die for three days of constant torture.

Eturum and the Child stepped down.

"I most humbly regre…"

"Enough! You are like no other Priest. How is this so?"

"It is because I am a First Priest, taught by Wepwawet and Anubis in flesh as well as in spirit. The learning has not been dissolved by age after age of teaching, with bits being lost along the way."

"I come to tell you that we have built for you and those Holy Pharaohs that come after, a temple where your body shall be made eternal upon your passing."

"Amduat ("The Book of the Netherworld") is given unto you that you be strong and victorious in your travels through the underworld and the enemies there that you shall face before your passing. Along with the tome, do I give unto you one of the Children of the gods as a Guardian to you and only you."

"How effective a guard is this...Guardian?"

"If you will call up twenty prisoners sentenced to torture and death, yet still undamaged, and arm them, I would demonstrate."

The twenty are brought forth and taken to the center of the aisle leading to Pharaoh's dais. All others back to the walls not only to give Pharaoh an unimpeded view, but also to get clear of impending combat.

"I do, now show me the worthiness of this Guardian."

The Child handed his weapons to the human guard and strode forth.

Without looking back, Eturum speaks three words, "Kill them all."

It takes less than one minute before the Child reclaims his place on the dais and his weapons from the other guard.

"This Guardian will serve as Pharaoh bids him in all ways possible. He does not sleep and will guard you even then. His nose is near perfect and will detect almost all poisons. He has other qualities that should be shared only with Blessed Pharoah."

"May I have a table placed before your dais and have permission to use it?"

"The final gift we bring, to show our duty, honour and dedication to Pharaoh is this, the tomb which shall be built for you." He unrolls the scroll, to show the tip of a spearhead of four equal triangles. The head of the spear grows out of the sands, its white peak pierces the sky.

Stories set in an anthropomorphic mixed-species world usually have a completely original religion, when they have a religion at all. Kyell Gold asks how a major religion of our world might be modified for an anthro world.

Gold also presents an anthro therianthrope: a wolf who is sure that he's really a stag and tries to become one.

"All Of You Are In Me" is set in Gold's Forester University universe, the setting of many of his award-winning novels.

All Of You Are In Me

by Kyell Gold

Hi. Thanks for checking out my video. I'd be a good parent for an at-risk kid because I already have a grown daughter, so I've been through that, but more important is what I've been through myself.

I'll go back to the beginning for this, and the guys at New Families say that it's important for you to hear my whole story. There's some stuff that's… well, I'll just tell it.

I was eight, I guess, because I was holding that little plastic deer in my paw as we knelt in the pews, and I remember my ninth birthday was when Mom told me that I was too big a wolf to take toys to church. The sermon that day was one of those bits from Luke where Jesus talks to his disciples, and a lot of it was about giving up material possessions, and then he goes on to talk about how He will come back when we least expect Him and how we have to keep the house in order. And Peter asks, "Lord, is this just for us or for everyone?"

And Jesus says that the disciples are like his managers that he puts in charge of the workers at the house, or something, and then he goes on to say, "You number twelve and all the peoples of the world are manifest in you as they are in Me, that you may go forth and spread My word."

Eight-year-old me looked down at the deer (it was a G.I. Joe, I think) in my paw and then up at the front of the church. If you've never been in a Catholic church, the altar's surrounded by the twelve Aspects of Christ. I had always looked at Jesus Dog when praying (the portrait was almost always as a wolf; Dad said that in the original texts, that aspect was Wolf, but when the churches changed from Latin they made it Dog so the coyotes would feel included), but when I heard that line that day, I looked up at the Jesus Stag and I really understood how all the twelve species could be part of the same person. I felt the thrill when I looked at the Stag that I never had looking at the Dog.

It was easy to pray to Him all through the rest of my childhood. I mean, my parents couldn't see who I was looking at when I knelt in church, or who I was envisioning when I said my prayers at night. Our Bible was inclusive, so it had pictures of all Twelve, and I would sit and look at the Stag for a long time. Mom and Dad were happy with how much time I spent with the Bible, which made me feel a little guilty. Not enough to stop, though.

When I was ten, I found a couple branches in the forest that looked just right and brought them back to my room. I put them on top of my head between my ears and stared at myself in the mirror.

I'd always thought there was something different about me, but until eight-year-old me prayed to Stag Jesus, I didn't suspect what it could be. When I put those branch-antlers on my head, they looked right, and I got that same feeling of warmth and…and rightness that I got from Stag Jesus.

That was the first time I thought that I might actually *be* different inside. There wasn't a lot of recognition of trans-species folk in those days. It was the mid-eighties and I was still two years away from understanding that "gay" was more than just a schoolyard insult.

But I could stand in my room with those branches held to my head and feel like they were part of me, and if I lay my ears back and squinted, I could almost see what deer-Isaac would look like. The way I thought of it then was that I had the soul of a deer.

Mom threw the branches out a few months after that and I pitched a fit. But I didn't dare mention the branches so I yelled about her cleaning my room without my permission. She thought I was crazy, but I couldn't—I didn't have any way to talk to her about what I was really mad about. I found a couple more branches that summer but they never looked right to me.

My first high school girlfriend was a doe. I liked to pretend I was a stag while we were making out. But she eventually dumped me for a real stag, and that was, um, that was really tough. I was thinking…

This was teenage me, okay? And they were just thoughts.

I was thinking about killing myself, because I thought I'd never be able to be a stag on the outside like I was on the inside. And I had the Bible there, you know, the big one with all the pictures, and I was crying on the Stag Jesus and saying, "Why did You make me like this if I can't ever be happy?"

I was frustrated and mad and hopeless. But I never acted on any of those thoughts. I got through that time with the help of Stag Jesus. His calm smile and the antlers reminded me of what He said to the disciples, about "all of you are manifest in me," and I thought that that meant there was at least a bit of Him in me as well, in my soul. And that gave me some comfort. Enough to get me through that time. I knew—I knew He still loved me even if Andrea didn't.

Yeah, I still remember her name.

Anyway, I threw out the branches in my closet after that, and I stopped pretending I could be a deer. On the outside, anyway.

But I still dated does. I met an elk a couple years out of college. We really hit it off, got married, and I thought that might do it for me. You know, lots of mixed-species couples adopt one kid of each species and I was really looking forward to having a deer—an elk, I mean—as a son or daughter. In retrospect, yeah, it was because I wanted to feel like a deer. But that doesn't mean I'd love them any less.

But Vi had three sisters and a brother who all had children, and she didn't want two children. She grew up sharing everything and she wanted our son or daughter to have their own space. I'm an only cub, and my parents really wanted a grandchild. So it made sense to have a wolf, and we went through a surrogate so Stacey is really my daughter.

She's great, by the way. I came out to her when she was home from college the other day. It's her sophomore year and she's doing great, really smart. She doesn't quite understand, but she did better than Dad did, and she doesn't blame the divorce on me.

Oh yeah. Vi and I aren't together anymore. She decided she wanted to have another kid when Stacey was getting rebellious. Vi went through this whole thing about not understanding wolves, and I tried to get our priest to talk to her about all the species being one and so on. I told her I would love to have a son or daughter elk, but… the fact is we hadn't really been connecting for a while, and it wasn't really either of our fault. She married an elk and they've got a kid now, so she got what she wanted.

I never told her about how I feel. I didn't tell anyone until I turned forty a couple years ago and realized I didn't have any reason to hide it anymore. I didn't have a wife, I worked from home, and I lived in Crystal City, where it's more acceptable. Transitioning, I mean. And everyone asks if Shada Jamison influenced me. Well, yeah. I mean, she was all over the media, and she was not only going from mouse to tiger but also male to female in the bargain, and I'm not transsexual, just transspecies. But yeah, Shada and all the acceptance around her really made me believe it was possible.

But it was more than that, too. Even though I put away those childish branches, I never gave up thinking about being a deer. I still prayed to Stag Jesus every Sunday and I read up on some of the teachings of the Church about different souls. Believe it or not, the Church is actually really forgiving about that. They believe that your soul can belong to one Aspect of Jesus while your body reflects another, and that's meant to be a test to teach you how to appreciate and relate to others.

There was a computer program online like ten years ago that would show you what your children would look like if your species could interbreed. I put in Vi's picture with a picture of Ray Brighton, this elk who plays football for the Sabertooths, and pretended that the result was my son. Yeah, there's also a photomorph of what you would look like as another species and I made myself a white-tailed deer, but that was back in my mid-twenties and it wasn't as good. I never liked that picture as much. But the one from ten years ago, that one I kept.

So on my fortieth birthday, I realized I was happiest when I was praying to Stag Jesus, imagining myself as a stag. And there was something our priest said, about how people should not pray for God to do things for them, but for the strength to make changes in their own lives. I realized that if I wanted to make this change in my life, I was going to have to do it. I found a therapist and spent a year preparing for my transition, and that was good because there were a lot of things I hadn't thought about, but my therapist was great about walking me through it.

She recommended a place where I could get prosthetic antlers, and there's a fake nose they make that is pretty comfortable. That's what you're seeing here. With fur styling I can pass for a deer at a distance, and even close up with people who rely on scent more than sight.

More importantly, I'm identifying as a deer. That's who I am. I'm the same Isaac I always was, but now my outside matches my inside. And more than anything I'd love to have a deer or elk child to love and call my own. I'm still a churchgoer and I have a community, so I'd be a great single parent. As you can see, I've been through a lot and come through it stronger, with my faith and my confidence in life. I pray that you'll see fit to entrust me with your child.

* * *

The slender fennec fox, looking as fashionable as any runway model in a slinky royal blue dress with a creamy white ribbon slung over one hip, dropped three boards at their table, a single sheet of paper clipped to each. "Three veg menus," she said. "Can I get your drinks started?"

"We were looking at the menus outside," Isaac said. "I think we're ready."

When she'd taken their order and left with a swish of her fluffy tail, Isaac turned to Brady and smiled. "See, that right there. She didn't even look twice at me. That's awesome."

The big white-tailed deer in the open peach-pink collared shirt smiled back. Across from them, a rabbit in a light jacket with the logo of a movie studio wore a more tentative smile, the smile of the new guy at the party trying to fit in. "Not a lot of people expect a guy who looks like a deer to not be a deer."

Isaac's ears, pinched in to narrow them, still flicked back when he was uncertain. "But if I was just a wolf wearing antlers, she'd have maybe stopped to ask. People used to tell me I was wearing a 'great costume.'" He grimaced.

"So," Brady said, a little louder than necessary, "you got your adoption video in?"

"Yeah." Isaac exhaled. "They said to speak honestly and from the heart. So I told my story. About how I transitioned, how it's been part of my life since I was eight, how I've always wanted a kid, how important church is." He paused. "I didn't want to tell them about being depressed when I was a teenager, when I thought about killing myself, but the fox there said that a story like that would let them know that I understand depression. A lot of the at-risk kids struggle with that."

"Whew." Alfie shook his head.

Brady elbowed Isaac. "Did you tell them about your experimental phase in college?"

"No." The stag laughed and nodded toward the rabbit. "Do you have to tell everyone about that? Did you tell him about the month I was into Hinduism, too?"

"Alfie was asking why I hung out with such a straight guy, so I had to tell him you weren't always that straight."

"For like six months." Isaac held up a finger to the rabbit, who wore a smile.

"Until my antlers dropped." Brady reached up to rub the base of his current set. "Then you magically rediscovered does."

"Did he give you his antlers?" the rabbit asked. "He just throws them out now."

Isaac looked down at the table as Brady roared with big, booming laughter. "He actually took them without asking me. I didn't care, but it was weird."

"So you knew?" Alfie looked between them. "You guys have been friends, what, twenty years?"

"Twenty-three, on and off." Isaac fiddled with his fork. "There were a few years when Stacey came along…"

"His wife didn't like me a whole lot," Brady filled in. "To be fair, that was when I was in my 'out and proud' phase. I wore fishnet halter tops a lot."

The rabbit's eyebrows rose. "Still have any of them?"

"Probably in a box from the last move. We can dig one up."

And then the waitress came back with their food and the conversation shifted to whether the small café was going to survive, other places like it, Brady's spring pea casserole and Isaac's potato hash, and the movie Alfie was working on now.

"Do you miss meat?" Alfie asked Isaac as they were settling the check.

"I've been vegetarian for years," Isaac said. "Made things easier with my wife to start out. I've had meat a few times with Stacey—my daughter—but no, I don't really miss it."

"Huh." The rabbit shook his head. "If I had to give up a whole section of my diet, I don't know if I could. Like bread or something."

"I didn't have to," Isaac said. "It felt right to. It's not like I'm sacrificing something."

"Yeah, okay." Alfie smiled at Brady and tossed three twenties down. "I'll get ours. You ready?"

"Sure." The stag reached over to hug Isaac. "Friday night *Daredevil?*"

"I'll get more beer." Isaac hugged back, then extended a paw to Alfie. "Nice to meet you," he said.

"Same here." The rabbit shook. "Take care, and good luck with the whole…deer thing."

Isaac tilted his head very slightly, adjusting for the weight of his antlers. "The adoption?"

"Uh. Yeah, that. And—"

"All right." Brady grabbed his boyfriend's arm. "Let's go before you say something even more stupid."

Isaac watched the stag and rabbit leave the café, and when the waitress came back he gave her the cash and his credit card. "The balance on the card, please."

She ran it in less than a minute; he scrawled his name on the pad and sauntered out into the warm Crystal City afternoon. Crowds swirled around him, and instinctively he scanned eyes to see who might be looking askance at him, listened for conversations to see if anyone was talking about "that dressed-up wolf" or "that antler freak" (both things he'd heard often in the first six months of presenting as a stag). In this crowd, in upscale Crystal Lake, most people were focused on themselves, or their phones, and if any glanced his way, they glanced away again without registering surprise or disgust.

Waiting at the corner, he saw an impressive rack of antlers a bit ahead of him. He perked up and then recognized Brady. As he tried to push through the crowd, Brady half-turned to listen to Alfie, and the rabbit's words came to Isaac's ears. "Look, he's a nice guy. I feel for him, you know? But you can't just slap on antlers and pray to a different Jesus and bang, you're a deer. Biology doesn't work that way."

"It's more complicated than that," Brady said.

"I mean, if he was going for the surgeries, you know? But he opens his mouth and he's still got those big fangs, and his eyes don't look quite right either."

"It's not about—"

And then Brady turned just a little more and his eyes caught Isaac's. Alfie, oblivious, went on. "Special effects are all about detail. When you can see through the costume, it's not—what?"

Brady had elbowed him, and as the light changed and people streamed past them, both of them turned to look at Isaac. For a moment, he was back in those early days before he'd pinned his ears, when the weight of the antlers still caught him by surprise. Then Alfie muttered, "Aw, shit," and looked away, and the pity in Brady's eyes was too much.

Isaac turned and pushed against the tide of people, not even scanning them now to see who was looking. He got to a clear space next to the patio of the café and stood there with his eyes closed. Behind his closed eyes, Jesus

Stag smiled with hands outstretched toward him. *Let go of your anger. Feel the weight of your antlers. All of you are in me.*

He'd relaxed by the time the large hand fell on his shoulder. "Hey," Brady's voice said. "Look, Alfie's an idiot. Sorry about that."

Isaac turned, not squirming out of the embrace but not returning it. "No," he said. "He has legit questions. It's not something everyone understands."

"But he should try harder." Brady exhaled. "Anyway, I'm only sleeping with him because he promised me a job in the studio, and he's only sleeping with me because I give him free training at the gym. You won't have to see him all that often. You don't have to see him again if you don't want to."

"No, it's fine." Isaac thought again about the Stag's warmth and let it shape his lips into a smile. "I'd like the chance to explain to him, if he's interested in listening."

"Okay, well." Brady squeezed Isaac's shoulder. "We cool?"

"Of course." Now Isaac did reach out to hug his friend back. "*Daredevil* Friday. You can bring Alfie if you want."

"He'd have to binge the first five. But maybe." Brady looked back and rubbed his chin. "Maybe if I guilt him about how bad you felt."

"Don't do that." Isaac patted the stag's arm. "I don't want pity. I just want to be a normal guy."

"Ugh. You and your high road." But Brady said the words with a smile, and waved as he headed back along the sidewalk, the crowds parting for his stately physique.

* * *

Isaac had never found the Catholic Church on Guildstern Avenue completely empty. Even on days like this Thursday night, when he went in needing to pray for reassurance, there were always at least a half-dozen others in similar supplication.

He took a place in the third pew back, farther forward than where he and Brady customarily knelt, but in the same direct line to the Stag Jesus portrait at the front of the church. After crossing himself, he bowed his head, his antlers a comforting weight pulling his head forward.

Lord, he said, *it's been two weeks and I haven't heard a whisper from the adoption agency. Give me the strength to hold off the doubt that they're going to reject me. Give me the courage to be a father again. Give me the confidence to be the deer that I am. And,* he added, remembering Alfie and the two conversations they'd had since that brunch, *give me the patience to continue to help others understand me and Your plan for me.*

As always, the Stag filled him with warmth and certainty. He stayed for a good half hour, trying to keep the feeling so that it would carry over into the rest of his life, reciting things he was thankful for and burdens he needed help with.

I am in You, he concluded with, and as he always did, he imagined the Stag's answer: *I am also in you.*

Outside the church, Isaac pulled out his phone to check his mail. Still nothing. All he wanted was an acknowledgment that he was an approved adoptive parent.

But, he reminded himself as he slid the phone back into his pocket, there were a number of other reasons they might be weighing his application. Single parents were approved less often than families. He didn't have a pile of money, like a lot of single Crystal City parents. He was in his forties, which was on the old end of the age distribution. And his transition, of course, was unusual.

To balance that out, he had recommendations from Stacey and Vi, a nanny lined up, a job that was steady, and a background that would let him relate to at-risk children.

The stag walked past a young couple, lions, male and female. They met his eyes, smiled in the way you do when you pass someone on the street, and resumed their conversation.

Another little victory, he thought. Like the rabbits in his office including him when discussing vegetarian snacks, like being shown the extra headroom cars rather than being told "you'll have to take those off when you drive," like Stacey calling him with a new fur coloring treatment she was excited about and thought he'd like. The little victories were all in him, little bursts of rightness that bolstered his soul as if each one was the Stag reaching out through the world to tell him I made you this way and I bless you.

If this adoption agency didn't work out, there would be others. The stag lifted his head, balanced the weight of his antlers, and walked proudly on.

One of the most popular gods of the Native North Americans is Coyote the Trickster. Every tribe has its own humorous legends of Coyote, sometimes a man but usually a wild canid trying to get laid. He brought fire to humans, but that was more by accident than design. Usually he is tricking his fellow animals and man, or trying to—when his pranks don't backfire on him. His name is from the Nahuatl word cóyotl, meaning "barking dog".

Many Native American legends are being forgotten today, but Coyote's are still fresh, lively, and often risqué; probably due to the spread of the wily wild dog into urban areas in recent decades. (During a 2007 heat wave in Chicago, a coyote entered an open Quiznos sandwich shop, jumped into the shop's cooler, and wouldn't come out. TV news crews recorded Animal Control removing him.)

"Yesterday's Trickster" tells about how Coyote sets out to remind a modern woman of just who he is—and learns something about himself, as well.

Yesterday's Trickster

by NightEyes DaySpring

The modern world wasn't something that agreed with Old Man Coyote. He had helped humanity build it by giving the humans fire, but that had been long ago. Things were good for a long time after that, but the arrival of the Europeans had changed everything. He had done what he could for the people who originally called this land home, but his efforts hadn't paid off. At least his children were doing well for themselves in this new world, living in the shadows of the cities.

It wasn't the arrival of the Europeans that he hated the most about how the world changed, either. It was the arrival of automobiles. The woman that just ran him over with her SUV while he checked out a particularly juicy bit of roadkill was the most recent reminder of why he hated cars. She hadn't even bothered to stop; not that it would have helped, but didn't she at least want to make sure she had gotten a clean kill? He hoped that she had spilled whatever she was drinking at the time of impact into her lap. She looked shocked to see him when he glanced up at the sound of squealing breaks as her SUV barreled into him.

Lying dead on the side of the road also didn't suit Coyote. He'd been dead before. The last time, when he'd been caught in a steel trap after eating poisoned food, an old Navajo man took his lifeless carcass home and skinned him for his fur. The man had used the pelt to keep his bed warm, but sensing there was power he couldn't possess, the Navajo man buried Coyote's bones a distance from his home. A few months later, Coyote had resurrected himself from the desert dust.

Being dead didn't bother Coyote, just the pointlessness of his misfortune this time. He'd done it so many times that he just considered it an extended nap. It gave him time to recharge his magic. Now lying bleeding in the blazing sun, barely able to breathe, that did bother him. He would have to wait for something to come and finish him off, and that he was not doing, at least not today.

He pushed himself forward with just one working leg, inch by inch, his broken body aching in protest. He managed to drag his wounded form off the road into the dust and gravel at the side. Afterward Coyote panted in the shade of a scrub bush, exhausted. He could feel his physical form slipping away.

"No," wheezed the canine. The word came out as a bark. "Not today."

He propped himself up with his unbroken leg, and threw back his head into a yipping howl, calling down primordial magic. The sound was weak and faint. When he was young, before the Europeans had come, this had been easy. He could will himself to shift forms and heal. Now it was much harder; but as he kept up the howl, it became easier, his voice stronger.

When he finished, he let himself flop to the ground where he panted for a minute, momentarily tired. Finally he got up, shaking out his dusty coat.

A trail of blood and guts led from the road to where he stood, but turning to look back at his tail, he seemed to be in good shape. All four of his paws were whole again. Coyote was back in action.

Unfortunately the roadkill he'd been investigating also was struck by the SUV, and it disintegrated. It was inedible and a waste of good jackrabbit. Now what was he to do for his lunch?

Coyote shook himself again and looked around. The two lane road was deserted. The SUV, having faded into the horizon, left nothing else behind to mark its journey. Scrubby vegetation stretched on for miles, and mountains stood in the distance on two sides. The sun hung heavy and hot in the sky with few clouds for shade. Coyote was alone. If he wanted to eat, he would have to hunt for his meal.

He considered. Did he still know how to hunt? Once he'd been a great hunter. He taught his children and the Native Americans who revered him all he knew. That had been long ago. Now no one revered him. Even the few Native Americans remaining, clinging to the land the Europeans hadn't taken from them, didn't hunt much anymore. Coyote had gone on so long tricking people out of food, when he couldn't scrounge up a good meal, that his skills had grown rusty. Once he walked the land like a ghost, silent and deadly; now his paws crunched in the desert sand.

He started off in a trot, following the road, listening and sniffing for signs of life. He stayed off the hot pavement and stuck to the embankment. Nothing moved, and no cars came. For over an hour, Coyote trotted down the side of the road, searching, but only insects buzzed by. There were no interesting scents for him to follow. Thirst began to pull at him. His healing magic was powerful, but it had taken a lot out of him. He needed to find water soon.

Eventually he came to a small town. A gas station and some houses clustered around the road. Outside of a small bodega sat a familiar looking SUV. Coyote stopped and considered, listening to the growling in his stomach.

The sun was high in the sky, so no people were out right now. Glancing around, he walked over to the SUV to sniff around. The vehicle smelled like a typical truck, but in the front, there was the distinct scent of blood, and he could see a dent in the fender.

"Ha!" he barked. He could get revenge against... a woman who didn't carefully watch for wildlife while driving down a deserted, desert highway? Hadn't he been trying to take advantage of someone else's lack of attention and fallen for the same trap?

The sound of bells jingled as the front door of the bodega opened. Coyote startled and ran for the side of the building. Two women emerged talking.

"Sorry I couldn't get here yesterday," the woman who drove the SUV was saying. "I hurried over as fast as I could. I even hit something on the way here and cracked the front fender. Poor thing didn't make it." From the shadows, Coyote watched the two converse. The SUV driver was short with dark features and a naturally tanned complexion. She might have some blood of the native people in her, but the other woman was fully Native American and older. She had tanned skin from years of being in the desert, although she still possessed in her aged frame a youthful vitality. Her long, graying hair was tied back into a braid.

The Native American woman shrugged. "I appreciate your making the journey, Sophia. You sure you want to head back to Phoenix tonight?"

Sophia nodded. "I'll be fine, Emmy. It's only four hours. Good luck with your beading. I appreciate the necklace."

"I'm still trying to figure out those blasted computers. Anyone willing to come all the way out here to fix mine deserves something a little extra for their trouble. Now, you said you cracked the front fender?"

Emmy walked over to the SUV and pointed to the dent that Coyote's skull had made. "I'll call my insurance when I get home."

"What did you hit?" asked the older woman.

"I think it was a coyote."

The native woman frowned. "That's bad luck. Coyotes are bad news, and not just for ranchers. Many of the old stories talk about the trouble Old Man Coyote can bring."

Coyote perked his ears and wagged his tail from where he watched the two. Someone still taught the old myths! He felt his heart leap. His assailant had led him to some place special. What was the name of this town? It might be worth him returning in his human form.

"I'm sure things will be fine. That old dog must not be doing well, if he's getting hit by cars."

Coyote growled mentally. His power had waned so much since the Europeans had come; he couldn't show his abilities like he used to. It wasn't his fault people had stopped believing in him!

"I guess so," said the older woman. The sound of the phone ringing inside caught her attention. "I need to get that. Good luck with the truck."

They hugged each other goodbye, and he watched the older woman walk back inside, while the younger woman pulled her keys out of her purse. Nobody believed in him anymore, huh? Perhaps it was time to change that. He darted out from his hiding place, a low growl in his voice. Sophia turned as he rushed forward. At first she registered surprise, and then fear. With careful skill he leapt up and felt his jaws close around the woman's keys. There was a tug from her, but his momentum carried them down and she released her keys before he even landed, hitting the dirt and scrambling away with them.

"Hey!" yelled the woman. "What the hell!"

Coyote ran toward the brush that surrounded the town, pursed by the woman. With a trickster's skill, he weaved through the bushes, leaving her behind. He slowed then and circled back to see what she would do now. The woman was visibly shaking.

"Emmy!" stuttered the woman.

The native woman came outside carrying a cordless phone. She took one look at her shaking friend, and spoke quickly into her phone. "Samuel, let me call you back."

Coyote's keen ears picked up a surprised "What!" from the receiver before Emmy disconnected the phone. She glanced around and walked quickly up to Sophia. "Are you okay?"

"A coyote, a coyote," mumbled the distraught woman.

Emmy glanced around. "A coyote?" she said with caution.

"A coyote just stole my keys! It ran up to me and ripped them out of my hands."

The older woman was quiet for a minute. "You better stay with me tonight. Let me get you something to calm your nerves."

"Was that thing rabid?"

The woman shook her head. "I don't think so. I think we have a spiritual problem on our hands."

Sophia blinked. "Pardon me, but a what?"

Emmy didn't elaborate. Instead she walked back to the bodega and locked it up, before leading the woman away.

Coyote's blood was pumping loudly in his ears. He tracked the two as they walked away from the store, the keys dangling from his mouth. Oh, this was going to be good. He was finally going to get some respect. He wanted to go up the mesa and sing, but if he did that, he wouldn't be able to track his latest victims.

He stomach growled, reminding him he had physical needs to attend to; otherwise he was going to need to use more of his dwindling magic reserves.

* * *

The older woman lived in a simple cinderblock house on the edge of the town. It was surrounded by a carefully maintained and fenced yard. After determining the two weren't going anywhere right away, Coyote buried the keys near the house. Then he back-tracked to the bodega. He was disappointed to find the dumpster outside locked against animals. Sniffing around, he encountered one of the local cats. It would have made a decent meal, except it took off at high speed after sighting him. He'd chased it past a few houses, but it escaped to safety through a cat door.

He did find some runoff from the town that had a horribly dusty and soapy taste to it. He didn't know who out here bothered to waste precious water and wash their car, but he was thankful someone had. With nothing better to do, he hunted for rodents taking advantage of the waste humans often left behind. After three tries, he was able to catch a small mouse that he gulped down hungrily. It didn't cure his hunger, but it gave his stomach something to work on.

Wandering the perimeter of the settlement, he found a sign with the town's name on it: Rock Mesa Springs. It looked like many other small desert towns, but it had a certain charm to it. It clung to existence off a small highway. Coyote hadn't bothered to learn how the new people built their homes, but he knew they loved to be near highways. This one wasn't like the larger roads he'd seen that people called interstates. From the few cars that passed through the town, it wasn't an important route either.

Returning to the house, he wandered around the chain-link fence until he found a part of it loose enough to let him through. The dirt yard it protected smelled vaguely of the woman and something canine, probably dog. Creeping up to the side of the house, he listened carefully, hoping the walls weren't too thick to block out the sound.

Thankfully a window had been left open, and he could listen in. The two were talking about silver and beaded necklaces. The scent of dog was strong near the house, so he kept quiet. Even if he changed into his human form to approach the women, the animal would smell who he was. He needed to think of what the next step of his plan would be.

After a few minutes the conversation faltered, and Sophia changed the topic. "What do you think I should do about my keys? Do you think the coyote dropped them somewhere near the store?"

"I doubt it. This is not wild coyote behavior," said Emmy. "This is spirit behavior."

"I guess," Emmy responded, the doubt obvious in her voice.

Coyote considered his options. This woman had wronged him, but it wasn't an intentional evil. Europeans were always so careless about the natural world today. They didn't understand the ways of the past. They didn't care to, either.

"Perhaps we might do an offering to appease the trickster god. I'm sure he'll appreciate it."

His ears shot up. An offering? This Native American woman really knew the old ways. He had to stop his tail from wagging and thumping against something to give away where he was. He didn't want to disturb her dog.

"An offering isn't going to fix this. I'm still going to need to call a locksmith," Sophia said.

"Not necessarily. If you let me take care of the spiritual side, this might work out."

Sophia made an annoyed sound. "If you don't mind, I'm going to go see if he dropped the keys somewhere near the store. I appreciate you trying to calm me down, but I can't sit and wait here. It was just a wild animal."

"If that will make you feel better, go ahead," suggested Emmy.

There was the sound of movement in the house, and Coyote ducked behind the structure. From around the corner, he watched Sophia walk out of the front door and down the street. He considered following her, but her search would be fruitless. He was more curious about the old woman and her offering, but he knew her dog would eventually pick up his scent. It surprised him that the animal hadn't noticed him yet.

What type of dog was it, he wondered? He sniffed around the yard. It had a strong scent, possibly suggesting a big dog. He inhaled deeper. No, it wasn't a dog at all. It was a wolf.

He let that register. A full blooded wolf wouldn't take kindly to him hanging around this house. This was definitely the type of animal that didn't like him, and if the woman had trained it right, it would defend its pack from him.

The sound of the front screen of the house being pushed open caught his attention. The door closed automatically, and there was no other sound. Coyote felt the fur on the back of his neck stand up in apprehension. Had the woman let the wolf out? Carefully he looked around the corner of the house toward the front, but there was nothing there.

The sensation of hot breath on his tail told him exactly where the wolf was. He spun to confront the animal. He wasn't afraid of Wolf's children, but they were never kind to his own children. Teaching one some respect would be a pleasure, but the animal before him had not assumed a threatening position. Instead it sat, tongue rolling in the heat, looking amused. It had gray and tan fur on its face that spilled into white on its belly, and dark gray on its ears and back.

Coyote also could easily read the magic behind it now that he saw the animal. It was not a wolf's intelligence that drove this creature.

"I'm honored by your presence, old one," barked the wolf.

"You're a skinwalker," Coyote said surprised.

The wolf wagged her tail. "I did not think my form would fool you."

It was all in her scent, if he paid careful attention to sort out the smells. The pelt that granted her the ability to transform, the work she did with silver, glass, and stone. Her magic was just a tiny fraction of his, but she had to have sensed and possibly scented him when he approached the house. She let the younger woman leave so she could confront Coyote in her canine form.

She was pretty, for a wolf. She was larger than him, her muzzle broader, her ears rounder. The gray on the very tips of her ears came from age, but she was still a formidable hunter. Coyote had always dreamed of a mate like this, but he never could settle with one woman. He'd tried before, but always the feeling of new land under his paws called to him.

"It has been many years since I've encountered a human blessed by Wolf's protection."

"The women in my family have always honored the great, gray hunter. Many years ago, he chose to honor my great, great grandmother with this gift."

Carefully he circled her, but she turned, not letting him get behind her. He laughed, and let his form slip. His tail grew shorter, his fur longer, and his ears more rounded. With a broader muzzle he barked at her. "So why did you choose to face me like this?" he asked.

Her courage faltered slightly at seeing him change into the form of a wolf, but she stepped forward bravely. "Stories of your deeds have colored my people's history. I know Sophia doesn't believe, so it's logical for me to meet you in her stead."

"If your friend doesn't believe in me, can you really make right for her?" asked Coyote, stepping closer to the wolf.

She growled to force him to keep his distance. "What is it that you want from her, anyway?"

Coyote didn't have something in mind, but he knew of something that the native woman had that he could ask for. "From her, nothing. From you, though, I will take your lovely pelt. My magic is not what it used to be, and your pelt will help me out immensely."

The wolf's ears fell back. "For a set of keys, you want my pelt?"

"Yes," woofed Coyote, with a grin on his now broad muzzle.

The wolf turned away from him to trot toward the door. "I will hire her a locksmith, if that is your price."

She was not to be fooled apparently. "Wait!" he called out to her. "I would be happy to trade the keys for something else. Something you can willingly give me."

She stopped, and looked over her back. "What do you want, old one?"

Coyote let his form slip back to its natural state. His tongue rolled from his muzzle. "I want you to tell Sophia the truth. My power fades, and without new people learning about me and the other spirits, someday we'll fade back to the heavens. I'm not afraid of leaving, but what the world will be like without us worries me. The new people must learn of the old ways."

"I'm not sure how much you listened to our conversation, but I already said a spirit was about."

The old trickster let himself wag his tail. "She doesn't believe like you do. I need her to believe. If I ever hope to restore balance to this land, people must know how important the land is."

The wolf gave him a skeptical look, but he stood proud. For so long, he'd let people forget about him and his deeds. Wolf, Eagle, Raven and the others hadn't been better, but if the guardians of the land wanted people to treat the land right, they needed to revere it like the spirits who protected it. Coyote knew this, but he had never tried to teach the new people this lesson.

"And what will I do?" she asked him.

"You know the old stories, don't you?"

She bobbed her head, the closest a wolf could come to nodding.

"Good. You'll follow my lead."

* * *

The coyote on the doorstep did not sit well with Sophia. She froze at the gate and sucked in her breath, her hand tightly gripping the fence.

"You," she whispered. "Why are you here?"

Coyote let his muzzle hang open, grinning. That was an obvious question.

"Go away," she said flailing her arms around.

Coyote got up and reached down to pick up her keys.

"Wait, I need those!"

He glanced up at her, with her keys in his muzzle. He titled his head at the woman.

She twisted her hands. "Why me?" she asked.

He dropped her keys. "You hit me with your SUV," he barked out. The sound carried. The woman at the gate's eyes went wide. "It hurt... a lot!"

The woman opened her mouth to say something, but nothing came out. She took a step toward Coyote, and her legs buckled out from under her. After she hit the dirt, she didn't move.

* * *

"Will she be okay?" he asked Emmy. The older woman was hovering over Sophia, where she fell in the yard.

"I think so," she said. "Was your plan to just scare her to death?"

"No!" he yipped. "I didn't think she'd do that."

"You can't just go revealing yourself like that to people. The world doesn't believe in you or me anymore."

Coyote huffed. "Obviously. If it did, my powers wouldn't be so depleted. People would treat the land better."

Emmy got up and walked back into the house. A minute later, she returned with a glass of water. She knelt down next to Sophia and cradled her head. "Sophia, Sophia." She shook her gently. "Sophia, are you okay?"

The woman groaned, and Emmy held out the glass and she took a sip. She sputtered. "I think the heat got to me," she whispered.

Coyote inched closer to look at her, and she jerked when she noticed him. "Oh god!" she shrieked.

Emmy grumbled and reached out and pushed Coyote away. "You've done enough damage to her in one day. Give her keys back, and let her go home."

He yelped surprised. "Me? She ran me over!"

"It was an accident," Emmy said. She looked down at Sophia. "It was an accident, right?"

Sophia blinked a few time, trying to process this. "Yes," she finally got out.

"There. Are you happy, Coyote?" asked Emmy. She was glaring at him.

Happy was not the word to describe how Coyote felt. Perhaps he should have done something more exciting, like stealing the woman's car. He could take the form of a man. How hard could driving a vehicle be? People did it all the time, so why couldn't he?

Disappointed, he walked over to pick up the keys. He then carried them and dropped them into Sophia's lap.

"There," he said, sitting down near the woman. "You can return home."

She picked them up. "Uh, thank you?" The expression on her face was a mixture of awe, fright, and confusion.

He huffed and got up.

"He doesn't expect me to pet him, does he?" Sophia whispered to Emmy.

"I think that would be unwise, unless you want to lose some fingers." Emmy cleared her throat. "Before you go, Coyote, I left you an offering at the back door of the house."

His ears perked, and with a bob of his head, he turned to trot around the house, leaving the women to themselves. Had Emmy actually given him her pelt? No, he knew she wouldn't part with that. Wolf would be angry at him if he tricked her out of it. He much preferred his sleeker canine form anyway.

The smell of meat caught up to him even before he rounded the corner. There on a plate sat a sizeable piece of beef. He stopped, surprised. It took him a minute before he walked up and sniffed at the food.

It smelled good and fresh. She'd even given it to him on a plate! Someone had given him a meal on a plate, and he hadn't had to turn into a human? This was certainly a new one. With reverence, he gingerly picked it up and moved it before he dropped it in the dirt to start tearing off chunks. The meat was cool and tasty, although the fact he had to rip it up himself gave it a sandy after-taste. Still, he felt happy and relaxed when he was finished.

Sated, he crept under the open window. The two were talking inside the house. He knew Emmy would know he was listening.

"Is Coyote always so temperamental?" Sophia was asking

The old Native American woman laughed. "He can be. He makes a lot of mistakes on his own. If you've got a few minutes, let me tell you about how he and Eagle stole the sun."

Coyote groaned inwardly and trotted off. He knew how that one went since he'd been there. Things had worked out in the end, hadn't they? He would come back later to talk to the skinwalker. If he wanted to spread news of the spirits and respect for the land, he needed someone to help him. Maybe he could get Wolf to assist. This could be something he and his brother could do together.

He had started the day trying to eat roadkill, and ended it by eating steak! Maybe the modern world wasn't so bad. Speaking of that, he glanced toward a nearby house where a beat-up pickup truck sat with the windows down. It was time to upgrade his skills. Hopefully the owner wouldn't mind if he borrowed the truck to take it for a spin. He was on a roll today. What could possibly go wrong?

Are there Gods above Gods?

Don't be distracted by wondering who Celea and Ajax are, or why they are fighting the Great Druid. Don't even wonder about the world inside the ruined temple, or about Stheneleos Magus CCLXII and The Toucan God who dwell there.

Wonder instead about when magic becomes divine power. Wonder about the rules that bind Gods.

Wonder about the Gods of Necessity.

The Gods of Necessity

by Jefferson Swycaffer

Celea and Ajax sprang up, their camp-site forgotten, and took to their heels, running for their very lives.

It was, all taken with all, a situation they were more than familiar with. Perhaps they'd been foolish for lighting even the smallest of fires. Or, like as not, their enemies would have come upon them anyway, for the scouts of the Great Druid liked to comb through the forests, peering and studying, collecting samples, and always, always on the alert for enemies of their highly singular creed.

Celea had only a moment's warning, the faintest sniff of druid-scent. Fortunately, she and Ajax were long accustomed to keeping a raw-nerved watch. Only Druids could have come so near before detection; only Celea and Ajax could have a hope in the world of escaping.

The chase was conducted in something very near to silence. Cold, still air might have magnified any little sound, and small crusts of snow clung to the ground, ready to reveal by crunching noise or by outline and imprint, the foot that trod upon it. The forest was of pines and firs, with the usual clutter of deadwood, always a risk of cracking noisily under a careless step.

The two adventurers—who, if asked, would have preferred to have been called freedom fighters—tore away from their primitive camp at top speed, and in different directions. That was established practice. One might be captured, but, with average luck, not both. Their footfalls were speedy, yet subtle. A deer might have grazed nigh, and heard nothing.

Nor did the Druids call out, or signal to one another by audible means. They had their own arcanum, and means by which knowledge came and went. Celea had reasoned upon it being a form of mental telepathy. Ajax thought it might be communication via the issuance and detection of smells, sly chemical wafts of odors from secret scent-glands.

Celea, being of the skunk-kind, knew better, but never seemed able to convince Ajax. Ajax, of leonine form, possessed a keen nose, although not as discerning as Celea's. He kept his stubborn doubts.

She, black with white, had certain advantages in a forest flight: her skills were of the stealthy kind. She knew when to sprint at the top of her speed, and when to sink to earth, to bury herself in loam and mould, to draw into herself her bodily and spiritual presence and to *not be*.

Ajax was fonder of a more sanguine approach. Tall and broad and ferocious, and as white, pelt and mane, as the drifts of snow, he was less adept at stealth. He had his bow strung by the third great bound through the tree-boles. He chose his moment skillfully, and sent two arrows back the way he'd come, with cunning accuracy and deadly effect.

Two Druids fell. They did not cry out.

Even the little forest birds seemed to take no notice of the chase, but continued fluttering and singing, their high, peeping calls untroubled by the wars below.

A lady skunk and a he-lion, running on two legs, not four, with a great deal of skill and cunning in just these sorts of unpleasant complications. They'd left their packs behind, which mandated a long, slow circle, or pair of countering circles, for Celea had run to the left and Ajax to the right.

The Druids were all of a species, and it was a new one on the land: they were a kind of sleek weasel, flex-spined, with short legs but long, agile arms and dexterous, creeping fingers. Their eyes were cold and slitted, not as acute by daylight as by night. The Great Druid had formed them, and made them his slaves, so fully dependent upon his will that they believed in his every word and obeyed out of joy, not coercion.

Not so the villages that fell under their dominion, for there, dread magical work began, and the slow conversion of years. The lands under the Druids grew men and women whose children were more like the Druids than like themselves, and their plantings were directed with unquestioned exactitude.

There was no deadwood fallen beneath the trees tended by the Druids, and nor did birds sing in the boughs of those trees.

Celea, for her part, made the most of her stealth, but also knew when it was the right time to bound upward and fire off the casting of a magical attack. The problem was that magic takes time, and a brisk chase through the forest affords little luxury for concentration and preparation. She was restricted to those effects she had stored up ahead of time, and these were never many.

She brought herself to a harsh halt against the rough bark of a tree—automatically, she categorized the species of Fir, for the Druids were not the only respecters of nature in the world. One, two, three…six Druids came tumbling after, breaking from behind the trees, revealing themselves to her aim.

She held a flake of fired clay in her fingers, a little chip of decorative ceramic-work, which she had worked and baked in a kiln, in a distant land and a happier time. She wished for a thousand of these, but was down to her last five. They would not soon be replaced.

The Druids neared. She broke the little paten with a deft snap of her fingers.

Magic *happened*. There was a leaping, surging effect, difficult to make out with the worldly senses but unmistakable and highly emphatic as sensed by the soul. Dire, sullen, blistering forces, something like heat, yet wholly distinct, flooded out and engulfed the six in pursuit. Four died, and two were left curled and sobbing, like caterpillars splashed with vinegar.

It was not very different from what the Druids would have done with her. They were fond of planting trees in people, bringing about a long, lingering, and grievously painful death.

This was the kind of war that had few truces or parleys, and many an ambush and snare. Peace was not likely. Victory, for Celea, would be seen in the diversion or delay of the Druids' advance over the land. If they could be pushed away to the south, then perhaps some of the remaining free people could be brought to safety in the east.

Until the Druids took up their march again.

Now Celea ran, and now she hid herself again, pushing herself down in the dirt and ferns beneath a fallen pine. She left her scant collection of magics in her belt-pouch, and fingered a short, sharp, silver-hilted knife.

* * *

Ajax, in his quarter of the woods, also had work to do with the blade, but his weapon was an arm-and-a-half long greatsword, with which he was accustomed to doing devastating work in close quarters.

A pack of Druids came upon him, and he, grinning, let them think this was a good idea. Seven mighty swings of his sword changed their minds, save that there were no minds left when he had finished.

Then, pragmatic as ever, he ran. He wanted to roar, a huge exultation of triumph and joy, but, on consideration, felt it was unwise to broadcast his location so exactly. He roared inwardly, in his spirit, and felt much better for it.

Bounding over a fallen tree, he found himself in the midst of a fresh party of Druids, too many for him to count in a hurry.

(Too many, Celea might have teased him, for him to count at all. She was the educated one of the pair.)

Surprise worked both ways: four Druids were fallen before they had even had time to comprehend the presence of the warrior who had sprung so suddenly into their midst. There were nine remaining. Ajax was almost certain it was nine. It might have been ten. He made a face.

Dead Druids were easier to count than living ones.

The blade-work began in earnest. The wretched beggars were lithe, Ajax had to give them that. When they couldn't parry, they dodged, all too often seeming able to bend around the long, deadly arcs of his sword-sweeps.

Often, but not always. He cut them down, one by one, and paid for it with his own blood, for his own skills at dodging, while accomplished, were only mortal. His luxuriant white pelt and mane were soon splashed, striped in glorious red, the gore as often his own as the Druids'. Certain of his injuries were telling, so that, before the end, he was wielding the two-handed sword in only one fist. He was as a hound among rats, or a bear among hounds, or even a dragon among bears.

He won.

He won, but he paid for it.

The count was fifteen, or so he would claim later. For now, he was much impaired as a warrior, and so it best behooved him to scout and slink and creep over the forest floor. He'd gone a fair distance along before it occurred to his weary brain to bandage himself up, stanching the bleeding, not only to spare himself the loss he could not afford, but also to prevent himself from leaving a carmine trail through the pines, a trail it took no Druid's skill to follow. He threw dignity to the wind, and tore his loin-cloth—his only garment—into strips to bind up his wounds.

Celea had seen him naked before, and for the opinion of the Druids he cared very, very little.

When he got back to the camp, whence he and Celea had fled, no Druids were in evidence. He circled the clearing slowly and at a distance, keeping to the shelter of the woods. Before too long, he was certain: he was alone.

He trod heavily out of the circle of the trees, and examined what the Druids had left of the camp. They'd done some despoiling, and most of the supplies had been looted. Still, some of the necessities of the trail had been left, either untouched, or merely fingered and forgotten. There was a small medical pouch, from which he renewed his bandaging. A scrap of canvas, a corner of their tiny lean-to tent, could be sacrificed to fashion a new loin-cloth.

Then he lay himself down, just for a bit of a rest, and straightaway fell into a deep, unrouseable slumber. That was how Celea found him when she, too, completed her wide circle through the forest.

There were no Druids remaining...of this scouting party. But the next party would be less than five leagues distant, and would know, as they always knew, just what had happened.

Telepathically projected thoughts, she was certain. Cues of scent couldn't explain their transferred knowledge, especially at such distances, and nigh-instantly. But Ajax clung to his notions...

* * *

"Where am I?" Ajax asked, rousing in the dead of the night.

"The forest," Celea said.

Ajax pondered that. "Good forest, or bad forest?"

"As yet, still good. The Druids haven't started planting."

Ajax shivered. The plantings of the Druids were not pleasant to look upon.

"You hurt?"

"No."

"I think I might be, a little."

Celea didn't know whether to laugh or to sob. He was, and not a little. "I've changed your bandages, and put what magic I could over your cuts. Is it good tactics, I ask, to use your left hand as a shield?"

"Better than my right."

"You're going to lose that arm…some day. But not today. I've done what's needful."

"Magic?"

"Yes."

"Good." He went back to sleep.

Celea did laugh, then. The gigantic lummox had a child's faith in her magic, thinking it to be a cure for all sores and sorrows. He didn't comprehend the limitations, the rules of necessity, the costs and the compromises.

If he were to lose his arm, she might even craft a magical replacement for it. But he would not like living with the result.

In the morning, they were still alive, and that was as much as they could have hoped to ask. They packed themselves up, binding most of their kit on Ajax's broad back, although Celea insisted on taking more than her usual share of the load. That Ajax did not contest her in this indicated, more clearly than anything else, how deep were his hurts.

They plodded onward, making their own trail, with such skill that even the Druids would not easily follow them.

"I forget," Ajax said, his voice dimmed and his words slurred. "What are we looking for here?"

"An old temple."

"Right." A long silence followed. Then, "Why?"

"Might be something useful inside."

"Right."

"Magic, or weapons, or just money. Maybe an Oracle. It'd be nice to have the Gods on our side."

Ajax straightened, just a little, and his words took on slightly more force. "The Gods *are* on our side." Then he slumped, and continued putting one foot before the other. Celea was forced to lead the way, as Ajax was beyond caring. On his own, he would begin to lose his way, moving about in circles.

But she had to smile. Circles might be better than straight paths. She didn't know where the fabled temple was, only that it was said, by repute, to be somewhere in these hills.

At one point, as afternoon drew toward evening, she paused, imagining the sound of words. They were strange words, and she took great care to memorize them. Where they came from, she did not know, and what they might have meant, she had no idea.

She was a magician, but of the practical order of the craft, not a theoretician, and sorely lacking in the deepest secrets. Effects were what she wanted, and of several strong and subtle results, she was mistress. The causes were almost as mysterious to her as they were to Ajax.

He was done. His bandages were crusted with old blood, and wet with new. There was nothing to do but make themselves a camp.

If the Druids came upon them, they would die. Celea didn't need an Oracle to tell her how likely that was.

* * *

By a peculiarity, they were left alone. The Druids may have prowled, but some fate protected the little camp where Celea tended Ajax's hurts. Snow fell lightly over the forest, which was good, as it hid away tell-tale tracks, but it was also bad, for, in the cold, Ajax took on a burning fever of the flesh. Celea was obliged to keep a small fire burning, for warmth and to melt snow into water. Ajax was gripped by a powerful thirst, and a series of delirium-dreams, during which he didn't know where he was. He didn't even know who Celea was, and, betimes, mistook her for a foe. He was weak, now, and that spared Celea from some hurt, for Ajax batted and snapped at her. In the fullness of his strength, he could have harmed her severely. Now, he could scarcely swing his fists.

Food was scarce, and Celea, among her other duties tending Ajax's illness, had to go out gathering. Some days, she brought back a little handful of reeds or seeds, pine-nuts or roots. Her magic turned the vegetable matter into meat, which she shared, favoring Ajax with most of what there was. On other days, she brought in nothing at all. She scouted a wide circle around the little camp, always coming and going by a different way, so as not to beat down a trail.

One day, some distance from the camp, she found a circle of stones, and, nearby, the ruins of the ancient temple or oracle which she had sought. She spent some time exploring it, in time finding a doorway within. The opening was blocked by a drift of forest litter: fallen branches and high piles of pine-needles. She might have cleaned it away and gone farther within, but the hour was late, and she worried for Ajax.

Over the next three days, she moved the camp, only a little distance at a time, until she had carried him into the shelter of the temple buildings.

There wasn't much left: a low edifice, of cold, bare stones laid in even courses, with a lonesome, empty doorway, blocked by a mound of debris. The circle of standing stones was to one side, and, through the forest, there was the barest trace of an ancient roadway, laid of the same smooth grey stones.

Celea took some time cleaning away the opening to the door, so that she might peer within. There was only a small, square chamber, floored with the same detritus that had closed the doorway.

Within the little room, perhaps once a guardroom, she labored to build up a larger fire, and to lay down a mattress of branches and pine-boughs for Ajax's sick-bed. He was as ill as she'd ever known him, but his inner strength was still immense. He did not want for vigor, nor for a will to live. Even so, he suffered, and was often far-gone into the realms of fever and madness.

On the next day, as sunlight sifted into the little room for perhaps the first time in an aeon, Celea was able to see a tiny, shadowed altar in the back corner.

With proper reverence, she made an obeisance to the spirit of the temple, and went so far as to place a small offering on the altar. She knew that the ghosts of such places oft were restless. It seemed the proper duty of a guest to make a gesture of propitiation.

She had no expectation of the grand revelation that followed.

The entire rear wall of the entry chamber folded itself away, the massive stones swiveling about, each pivoting above the next, so that the whole of the wall parted, not unlike a stage-curtain being drawn to left and right.

Beyond was…

A world.

Broad stairs descended, and tall columns speared upward. A vast space was revealed, a grand hall, with stairways and balconies, and innumerable passages receding to unguessable depths. All was clean, with the look of polished marble, and light, soft and golden, gleamed from candle-sconces high on every wall and pillar. What might, from the outside, have seemed only a sketchy ruin under a hillside was, instead, a palace within the land.

Celea all but held her breath. Magic was all about her, a pure and elegant form of arcane power, morally neutral in its tone and mode: it was neither the healing magic she preferred to wield, nor the deadlier and darker kind of necromancy and destruction she was sometimes required to employ.

It was as clean and innocent as light itself.

After a time, two little spots of motion introduced themselves into the architectural marvel, moving from out of a distant recess, entering into the light and the magic.

They crossed the vast floor, a tall figure and a small one. Slowly, solemnly, they drew near.

The tall one was a black-furred creature, much like Celea in appearance, even to such details as the white counter-colored breast and stomach. He was masculine in appearance, and neither of Celea's skunk-form nor Ajax's lion-form, but something vaguely in between. He wore leather-armor pauldrons over his shoulders, and a belt and breechcloth. His eyes were great and wide and knowing.

The smaller one was only a bird—but what a bird! Green-feathered, with a bright yellow beak as long as a warrior's knife.

Coming to a halt, they looked up the stairway, regarding Celea with an immortal calmness.

"I am Stheneleos Magus CCLXII," the tall, dark entity said, in a high-pitched, echoing voice. "Beside me is The Toucan God. We find ourselves the tenants of this buried land. Be welcome."

"Yeah, yeah, c'mon in," The Toucan God squawked, his voice raucous and harsh. "Bring your boyfriend. It's okay. Haul him right down the stairs. It's warm here. Maybe he'll get well. It could happen. Or maybe we'll wrench the souls out of your bodies and sacrifice them to the nether powers of the night of the spirits." He emitted a raspy noise, lifting his head and opening his beak in something like a smile. "It's all the same to us, innit?"

Celea's first instinct was to run. She overrode this with an effort of self-control.

She'd come in search of an oracle. It seemed to be that she had found one. "Are you Gods?"

Stheneleos Magus CCLXII tilted his head a bit, in a gesture Celea was unable to interpret. "He is," he said, indicating The Toucan God, "but I am not."

"Oh, yes, he is," The Toucan God shot right back. "He's got too much tied up in the humility and penitence racket to admit it outright, but he's a God, all righty. Now go. Go! Hustle. Bring your sweetie in. Don't let his head go bump, bump, bump on the stairs."

Panic still fluttering in Celea's heart, she turned and did as she was bidden. She was no mighty warrior, but at need, she was able to heft Ajax in her arms. There seemed so little left of him, he was almost as light as a child. She carried him, most carefully, one step at a time, until she came to the polished ballroom floor, beneath the light of a cluster of candles and little fairy-lanterns. A second trip sufficed to bring in their meager packs and supplies. Before long, Ajax was snuggled up in tenting and blankets, the empty leather packs folded under his head for a pillow.

"Thank you for your hospitality," Celea formally intoned.

"Do not thank us yet," Stheneleos Magus CCLXII said.

"That's right. We ain't your hosts yet. At this point, you're just an intruder. You're kinda welcome, and we're right glad to see you, but we can still throw you out again, or just kill you. Still all legal."

"You invited me to enter."

Stheneleos' gaze was level. He said nothing. The Toucan God flapped his short wings and capered about on the floor. Celea looked at him and wondered if there was enough meat on his bones to make a meal for Ajax. If there had to be killing done, perhaps… She didn't actually put her fingers on her magical weapons, but she knew exactly where they were.

"If you are to have the right to stay, you must answer a riddle," Stheneleos explained.

"It's a hard one, too!" The Toucan God shrilled, a noise that may have been meant as laughter.

Celea was no stranger to riddle games. She nodded, once, most solemnly. Stheneleos nodded in return. Celea, watching him, found her opinion changing. These two *were* Gods. The power of magic was great in them, but there was more beyond: the sheer numinous gleam of sacredness, of miracle, of the mastery of time and space, of creating and of ending, flooded out from the two as light from a flame. If Celea, in her power, represented a candle, these two were immense bonfires of might, all but rivalling the brilliance of the sun.

Stheneleos began to intone: "A light unseen, a sight unweaned, a field ungleaned—"

But The Toucan God was having none of that. "No! Hold it right there, pokey! Not that old chestnut! Nossir! The *hard* one. I don't like the look of this here stinker-belle. How do we know she's even housebroken."

That was so preposterous, Celea couldn't even take offense. "I do have some mastery of the social graces, my Lord."

Stheneleos's mouth twitched in a small, private smile. The Toucan God jumped about, from one leg to another, an odd hopping little tarantella. Celea wondered how many years had passed since the last time anyone had danced upon this dance-floor.

Stheneleos took a breath, and began again.

"An Italian is in England, speaking to a Belgian who is in Guyana. It falls to a Scotsman to explain how."

The Toucan God tittered. He bent and tapped the end of his beak on the mirror-smooth marble floor. He looked at Celea from one eye, then from the other. Just as she had wondered how much meat he had on his bones, now he seemed to be weighing her up for the slaughtering, dressing, and carving.

But she shrugged, and gave the best answer she could.

"Guglielmo Marconi created the radio that broadcast a message to Honore Lesseps, across the Atlantic Ocean. James Clerk Maxwell derived the mathematical equations governing electro… Electro…" Celea drew a breath, and concentrated. "Electro-magnetism, which explain the phenomenon of radio transmission."

It was a pretty little speech, given that she did not understand so much as a single word of it. Where were "England" and "Guyana?" Who were all of these people? What in the world was an "equation," and what possible nonsense was meant by "electro-magnetism?" This all reeked of a kind of magic she had never studied, nor even been introduced to.

The Toucan God, if he had seemed animated earlier, now went into paroxysms of outrage. He flew about in short leaps, fluttering his wings more in agitation than for ascent. He cursed, and his language was nothing good to behold. Before long he was delivering himself of blasphemies that led Celea to clasp her hands over her ears, while thankful that Ajax was in no position to hear. He had a goodly enough stock of swearing words already, the rogue of a soldier that he was.

Stheneleos made a small, polite bow. "You are welcome to this hall, and the environs of this palace. You are also entitled to our granting of three wishes."

"Three…?"

"Three wishes."

"Wish for more wishes!" The Toucan God snapped, and followed it with a whistle.

Celea wasn't so foolish as to fall for that. That story was as old as magic itself, and Celea knew the moral lesson. Wasn't there, somewhere, a man, trapped forever in a short loop of time, wishing for more wishes, over and over, gathering them up, but never free to exercise them?

She also knew better than to wish for something vast and dramatic, such as the defeat of the Great Druid and the expulsion of the Druid-kind from all the forests of the world. To be sure, it *was* what she wished, more than anything else. But a canny instinct told her that it would not do to challenge these two with so extensive a request.

Her magical training informed her that one of the wishes was already spoken for, and must not be wasted. She looked at Ajax, his fur matted, his breath coming in short, shallow gasps. Should she expend one of the wishes for his recovery and health?

No. That was a decision that was easy to make, but hard to live with. His life was already forfeit, dedicated to the cause she and he had undertaken together. He'd sword-slaughtered a bevy of Druids, at entire risk to his own life, and he'd do it again. His life was never more than a short knife-stroke from its end, and nor was hers.

He'd get well on his own, or else he wouldn't. Wishing for his life was as foolish as wishing for rain.

"I need time to think," she said. "May I come and go? I would go out gathering."

Stheneleos shook his head. "You have no need to search for food. We will provide your ordinary needs. That is the rule of conventional hospitality, by which we are bound."

Celea, smiling to take away any possible sting, asked an obvious question. "You are Gods. How are you to be bound?"

The Toucan God, in disgust, waddled away, leaving the room. His little talons rattled on the marble floor. Before long, Celea and Stheneleos were alone, with the sleeping Ajax in his blanket-nest an unhearing, unknowing presence.

"What do you know of 'Free Will?'" Stheneleos said. For Celea, it was like being back in school again, when her old tutors delighted in answering questions with more questions.

"Free Will is the joy and limitation of mortal souls, deriving from the *moral sense*, whence arises the conflict between desire and The Good. Animals are not said to have it, but the knowing races do. I know right from wrong, but am still able to choose my actions. Sometimes, when it seems fitting, I may choose to do wrong, even if I determine, in my thoughts, that it is for the higher good. The headsman who strikes at the neck of a condemned murderer is not doing murder, nor is the soldier who puts an arrow through his foe-man. But such striking and slaying is not, in itself, a good thing. Free Will is the calculating of the proper act, in a maze of possibilities, and in the blindness of the ultimate outcome."

"You have Free Will?"

"Yes...or so I believe."

"The one by your side? Your partner, Ajax?"

"Well... No. No, but, you see, that's really complicated. He doesn't, but..." She drew a deep breath. It was a mystery that took a fair amount of explaining. "And...ah..." If it were possible for a furry face to blush, Celea would have. "He isn't my lover. We just fight Druids together."

"Tell me this secret."

How could she cling to Ajax's privacy at the same time she hoped to ask these two Gods, these Oracles, for information? They had promised her the granting of wishes: how dared she withhold the answers they sought?

"Ajax was born without Free Will. Without volition. He's a slave. That's his nature. Anyone can say to him, 'Follow me,' and he must follow. 'Lift that weight and bear it for me.' He lifts and bears. 'Tell me all you know.' He tells. 'Take up a sword and slay my enemies.' He slays. That was how he was when I first met him..." She shrugged. "He tried to slay me. He was under someone else's orders and commands. He was born without volition, just as some are born without an arm or without a leg. Now, some cunning artificers are able to craft a synthetic arm or leg, nothing very sophisticated, but enough to grab the end of a rope, or stump about on. I know the magic that provides a semblance of volition. I cast that spell over him, mornings, and he is free, for the length of the day."

Stheneleos Magus CCLXII heard that, his face blank, betraying no emotion. When Celea had finished, he asked, "Does The Toucan God have Free Will?"

Celea actually laughed. "There can be no doubt of that!"

"Do I?"

Now Celea was serious again, and she bowed her head in respect. "You are a God. Of course you do."

His voice sank low, and he, in return, bowed before Celea.

"Perhaps I know the same spell."

Celea's eyes went very, very wide. She might have said something, although what would have been fitting, she couldn't have guessed. About that time Ajax shifted about in his blankets, and, breath rasping, started to awaken.

* * *

The two Gods of the Oracle were as good as their word: food was provided, and water, and other comforts and amenities. There was a place, a room in the immense palace, where water fell endlessly from high overhead. It was a good place for washing, even if the water was snow-melt. Nor was the indoors waterfall something that seemed intentionally contrived. Instead, it seemed—and Celea confirmed this, later, by climbing—that a wall had cracked in some high place, letting in the stream from outdoors.

She also traced the stream as it seeped away from that room, as it drained out into the depths of the palace. That was her first indication of how vast it all was.

Food was the first thing; without that providence, she would have had to go out into the forest to hunt. But between Stheneleos and The Toucan God, a pleasant variety of fruits and grains, melons and gourds, grains and seeds was carried to the two guests. Stheneleos bore baskets and bowls in his muscular arms; The Toucan God relied upon a kind of levitation, moving things about by the power of his magic, an expression of his divine will. It was left to Celea to cast the food-magic over the offerings, so that the vegetable fare took on the characteristics of flesh, raw and dripping and bloody. Ajax couldn't have survived a day on a vegetarian diet, and Celea preferred a mixture of fruit and meat.

In all the land, whether ruled by the Druids or in the Free Lands ruled by none, no magical spell was more important. It meant that predation was not absolutely necessary for the survival of the carnivores.

It was not unheard of…but it was no longer needful.

Day by day, Ajax recovered his strength. Soon, he was able to get up from his bed, first tottering like a little child, then striding about, finally stamping and swinging his arms.

Celea introduced him to the two Gods. Ajax, wide-eyed in superstitious awe, stammered out the appropriate reverences.

There was always a strange mirror-image affair when he stood before Stheneleos Magus CCLXII. The two had much in common. Stheneleos was black and white, and Ajax white throughout. But they were of a height, and had the build and brawn of warriors.

Ajax was bereft of Free Will, but had a counterfeit of it graced upon him each morning. Stheneleos was a mystery, but, little by little, Celea came to the conclusion that he, too, exercised freedom of volition solely by dint of a magical artifice.

"When are you going to make your damn wishes?" The Toucan God shrieked. His address went from loud to louder, and his outrage was perpetual. Since no form of apology or propitiation would calm him, Celea and Ajax, perforce, ignored his cries, and continued to adhere to the proprieties that guests owe their hosts.

"We've got wishes?" Ajax asked.

"Yes. Three. Kind of traditional."

Ajax rubbed his jaw with his hand. "Well, I wish..."

"Ajax!" Celea's shout was accompanied by a particularly pungent emission of scent, something akin to burning hair and cat spray. But it was too late... and, a moment later, it was too late *twice*.

"Oh, poop," Ajax said, his voice very small and filled with contrition. That didn't make things any better.

Where it came from, didn't matter. It was an indoors avalanche of dung. Manure, fewmets, ordure, scat. Horse apples and cow pies and rabbit pellets. Some was dry and crumbly; some was fresh and syrupy. It lasted for a good two minutes, sinking deeply into their fur and skin. It worked its way into their eyes, and, inescapably, their mouths. Celea gagged, and was roundly sick. Ajax spat and spat again, but somehow kept his stomach from turning. Before long, it was impossible to tell that Celea had been black and white, or Ajax white all over: both were stained a ghastly melange of browns, brindles, and tans.

Almost...almost...Celea blundered by crying aloud, "I wish you hadn't said that." It was close.

The Toucan God laughed immoderately the whole time, his raucous cries of villainous joy high and rasping, a cacophony of wicked delight that bordered upon insanity.

Stheneleos Magus CCLXII stood fastidiously aside, and waited out the storm. When it was done, he politely ushered the weary pair to the indoors shower, where they rinsed themselves thoroughly clean. They lingered in the water for a good long while, no matter how cold it was.

Ajax scrubbed Celea's back. In time, Celea was able to put her fury behind her, and return the favor. Ajax was who he was, and it was as pointless to expect wisdom of him as cowardice: he was made absolutely without either.

When they stood away from the ice-water shower, they found that Stheneleos had made up, slightly, and in his gentle way, for The Toucan God's rowdiness: their clothing was cleansed and refreshed. Back on the ballroom floor, their little camp had been swept up also, and there was no trace remaining of the flood of muck.

167

"You know," Ajax said lightly, "one of these days my mouth is going to get us in trouble." It was as close to an apology as he knew how to make.

* * *

"That Toucan God... Loud son of a bird, isn't he?" Ajax muttered. Days had passed, and his injuries seemed healed. He and Celea were exploring the depths of the palace, walking to re-build Ajax's strength.

"I can't tell... He's a God... But I think he may be putting on an act."

"Only pretending to be furious all the time?"

"Yes. He certainly hasn't acted upon it. He hasn't changed us into beetles, or even shut us out into the forest."

"He could, any time he wants."

"Yes... He and Stheneleos both claim to be bound by the rules of hospitality, but what can bind a God? At any time they want, they could change the rules around, making us appear to be in violation. You know, 'Oh, how improper of you not to bow three times to the east before going to bed at night. You have offended and must pay.'"

Ajax wasn't so certain. "Are Gods allowed to be that capricious?"

"The same question pertains: who forbids them?"

Ajax frowned, trying to work through thoughts that were too deep for him. He was a better swordsman than philosopher. "Are the Gods just like people, then? Fickle and selfish and hypocritical? I thought there was a kind of, I don't know, nobility to them. When they make promises, they have to keep them. If Gods are just the same as we are, they ought to be running the place. We should be their slaves."

"Some have said there are Gods above the Gods, higher powers that rule them, higher entities that enforce their vows."

"And there might be another, higher echelon yet," Ajax said, although his voice was suddenly light and mirthful, "until you rise to the top-most level of all, and the one God superior to all others."

"A mightiest of Gods?"

"Yes," Ajax nodded. "Necessity."

Celea had to give that a great deal of thought.

About them, the palace seemed to have no end. The architecture was largely of a given style. Another world might have called it Georgian, or perhaps Palladian. Lines were largely parallel, although there was a flair for arches and domes. A subtle flavor of asymmetry pervaded, such as arcades with doorways on the right, going into chambers of various sizes, and arches on the left, opening down to lower levels. Stairways were grand, by and large, although some regions were meaner, and the steps were narrower and steeper.

Certain features were asymptotic to infinity: there was one stairway where the risers were higher and higher, until the way was too steep for exploration to proceed. Another place, its counterpart, had steps that fell away into unguessed depths, and where Celea and Ajax dared not risk descending.

Most of the palace was well-lit and clean...but not everywhere. One region seemed to have been shattered, perhaps by an earthquake: the floor came to an abrupt end, and dropped down into a darkened chasm. Ajax, being the impetuous soul he was, found something to drop, to listen for a clash or clang or perhaps a splash. There was only silence.

Once, on one of their forays, they felt the pressure of an unseen gaze, that eerie sensation of being watched. For Ajax, it was no more than the subtle trigger of a warrior's sense of danger, but for Celea, it was the tripping of a magical spell of detection, one of the many subtle protections she kept around herself.

They were deep within the vaults of the palace, some dozens of levels downward and past a mile—Ajax counted his paces—from the ballroom where they camped. Around them were the same familiar arches, domes, corridors, and branching staircases. The place could have housed an army... or a nation.

Ajax made a little motion with his fingers.

Celea emitted a tiny whiff of scent. She was of skunk-kind, but her glands were tremendously sophisticated. This waft was quick and faint, of black sage mixed with whortleberry, and Ajax knew what it meant, just as Celea knew what his hand-sign meant.

Someone was about, and had taken an interest in their presence.

Without making it obvious, they diverted their steps, circling broadly back toward the environs they thought of as safe. But something alien and eldritch was behind them, and, as they walked, not seeming to hurry, it drew nearer.

They heard its sounds first: fluttering and flapping. At first they thought it might be wings. The Toucan God? But the sound was heavier and faster-paced. Then there were sighings of wind, hot little breaths of air. Finally, wet flopping noises, as of something immense hunching its legless way over the marble floors.

Celea and Ajax gave up their pretense: they ran. Instead of separating, as they had in the forest, they clung together, side by side and matching strides in their flight.

Whatever it was that pursued them hastened itself also, and a harsh, hot, wet wind blew from behind. In a race down one long, bare corridor, the pair dared to glance, just once, back behind them to see what it was.

They rather wished they hadn't.

They were pursued by something unworldly, a shape without shapes, something that unfolded and boiled, neither liquid nor solid. Something like a vast set of bellows expanded and squeezed; an apparatus akin to a deck of playing cards in mid-shuffle scraped over the floor; little strings of bright color, like beads on a wire, might have been eyes.

The mental emanations, which had been subtle, now erupted, overt and hostile. The thing radiated hatred the way a forge emits heat. It was as deadly a threat to the mind—and to the soul—as it could ever have been to the body. Celea would rather have been cut apart by the swords of a dozen Druids than allow herself to fall into the grasp of this thing.

Ajax pulled ahead, a bit, in their headlong flight. Celea was, quite ridiculously, reminded of the old joke. "I don't have to be faster than the bear; I just have to be faster than *you*." But her blessings upon him were uncountable as he slowed again, very slightly, so as not to outpace her. In fact, she could tell that he was giving thought to a stand, which would have been more than a little ridiculous, given that he'd left his sword back at their camp in the ballroom. Not even Ajax would contemplate turning and making a fight against such a monstrosity using his claws and his teeth only.

Could he?

Celea knew him too well. In a dim, determined, business-first part of her mind, she began to assemble the elements of a magical spell, one she might cast quickly and in the throes of desperation.

Hadn't Ajax said it? The highest of Gods was *necessity*.

Then, ahead of them, they saw something worth running for. Stheneleos Magus CCLXII and The Toucan God stood, side by side, in the middle of the long, straight corridor. It looked like a rescue, or at least the hope of one. Celea wondered if they would demand one of the remaining two wishes in return for protection.

She sped by on one side of Stheneleos, at the same time Ajax streaked past The Toucan God. Then they began, little by little, to slow their pounding steps.

They halted, and turned about.

They were in time to witness the power of the Gods.

The Toucan God favored a flashy, splashy, colorful kind of effect, as many-colored as his plumage and his bill. Flames coruscated, blitzing out in whorls and whirlwinds, accompanied by a rainbow of mists and smokes. Brilliant lights lanced and danced, piercing in hue and deadly in effect. A low thunder rolled, shaking the floor and walls of the corridor, echoing throughout this region, at least, of the palace. There might have been other corridors and chambers so far removed that no sound reached to them, but here, at least, the kettledrum-hammerbeat was overpowering. Outdoors, even in a forest, it would have been heard for five good miles, up hills and down valleys.

He jumped and danced and sang and squawked, his wings flapping, his little talons clicking like castanets. He turned his head backwards and forwards, sometimes almost all the way around. He gave voice to oaths of the mightiest potency, rare slogans and daunting invocations, until the words themselves took on a mighty force of their own.

Where his pyrotechnics struck, the walls and floors themselves were torn up. Gashes opened, and knife-slices gaped. But the true object of The Toucan God's wrath was the immense and fluid entity that still rushed onward. The colored blasts ripped into it, shearing parts away from the whole, blasting holes through the center, and causing entire structures—organs or organelles or merely working parts—to flash into flame and wither into ash.

Stheneleos Magus CCLXII, his expression as dour as ever, seemed less interested in the appearance of lordly might, and more devoted to its exercise. He stood stock still, with one hand raised, his heavy, blunt fingers—each hand had only four, Celea noted then, for the first time—gripping only empty air.

Yet about him was a power of the spirit, a vast, calm declaration of pure will. The monster raved with hatred; Stheneleos rebutted, in a wordless denial, reaching out with a manipulating grip of pure personal mastery.

A lesser deity might have spoken, and the lower his prominence on the scale, the louder his shout. "No!" But Stheneleos made his rejection an element of the world's nature. He did not cry "No!" but, rather, the very earthly definition of the situation—entity, corridor, Stheneleos—was a negation.

The entity could no more advance against him than ice could be hot, fire cold, clouds solid, or the mountains infirm.

His hand closed, slowly, the fingers squeezing together.

The monstrosity fell apart under The Toucan God's assault, and vanished away to Stheneleos Magus CCLXII's grip.

Stheneleos was still and silent. The Toucan God danced around a little more, cackling and whistling and clapping his beak open and closed.

* * *

The four were back in the ballroom. Food had been given to the two guests. The two Gods showed no indication of any need or desire to eat. There was warmth and comfort.

"What was that thing?" Ajax wanted to know. He was *very* careful not to express it in the form of a wish.

The Toucan God sneered. "We call 'em 'Dimension Weasels.' Nasty bastards. It'd have turned you inside-out, quick as winking. Imagine that, why don't you? Your guts sliding over the floor, your face mashed all up against itself, your hands trapped in a pocket of skin, while your lungs puff and blow somewhere outside of your rib-cage."

Celea and Ajax each pulled a frowning face of revulsion. The Toucan God laughed immoderately.

"It is time, I think," Stheneleos advanced, "for you to decide what your remaining two wishes shall be. Then we will allow you to depart the palace."

171

"Not that we won't miss you or anything," yipped The Toucan God, "but you can't stay, unless you stay forever. And you don't have the power that would take. If you manage to skill yourselves up—you know, learn the eight forbidden words, read the four lost books, eat of the Fruit of the Tree of the Knowledge of Truth—then come back, and we'll let you be one of us. We'd make a fair little pantheon, don't you think?"

Stheneleos spoke, then, very solemnly. "I do not think that will be your fate."

The Toucan God laughed, then, oddly, lowered his head and turned his head aside. "No, that ain't how it's prob'ly gonna happen. Million to one odds. Not impossible, but, hey, never draw to an inside straight."

Celea and Ajax had no idea what that meant. It was one more mystery from a world that was not their own.

"Only eleven point seven five to one," Stheneleos murmured. The two adventurers didn't understand that, either.

The Toucan God seemed a bit nettled, but didn't deign to address that point, and so the pair of guests remained ignorant.

"I wish," Celea said, as formally as she might, "for any information you are willing to give me that will be helpful to us in our struggle against the predations of The Great Druid."

Stheneleos and The Toucan God looked at one another as if in silent mutual consideration of the merits of the wish. The Toucan God, eventually, made a short, quick nod. Stheneleos held out a hand, which, somehow—it was a miracle and Celea knew enough not to question it—held a heavy, black, leather-bound book.

"Here is wisdom."

Celea received it from him.

"Thank you," she said, and meant it. She had no way to know what it contained. It might have been full of platitudes—"Strike where the enemy is weak, and withdraw where he is strong"—but it would, in fact, contain wisdom.

"Yeah, yeah, yammer yammer, yada, yada." The Toucan god made a noise very much like a man spitting. "Whatever. You could have asked for your soul's peace, or for a diamond worthy of a king's treasury, or four extra arms—mighty useful, I can tell you—but, no, you hadda go the 'wisdom' route. I tell ya, it's saps like you that make the God Biz a bummer."

Even Stheneleos looked a bit scandalized at that.

"Your third wish?"

Now Celea laughed. "It was determined already, made obligatory by the iron laws of necessity. I wish for you to give to me the answer to the riddle you asked me when we first met—and to give it to me..." She paused, and counted on her fingers. "...*Eight days before we met.* Only that way can I have had it to give to you. I still have no idea who the Italian was in England, or what in the world Electro… Electro…" She laughed again. "What it was that the Scotsman figured out."

Stheneleos Magus CCLXII nodded, and said, very softly, "That wish, of course, had already been granted." He smiled. "It was granted eight days before we met."

"Hmph. Hadda be." The Toucan God snorted. "Cheating, I call it, but how ya gonna argue with magic? You guys got at least one thing right: the supremacy of *necessity*. When you gotta, you gotta."

"Why did it take you so long to make up your mind?" Stheneleos wondered. "You've been here with us, in the palace, for nearly a fortnight."

"Well, we needed the time for Ajax to get better. If I'd just made my wishes, one, two, and three—with no dung involved, thank you *very much*—we'd have had to leave again, out into the cold forest, with Ajax still cut-up and fevered. Staying a while was also, for us, a necessity."

"And so the Gods learn wisdom from the mortals," Stheneleos Magus CCLXII said softly, although there was a twinkle in his eye that hinted he'd known it all, all along.

Slowly, from the far side of the ballroom, the lights began to go out, and a cold wind slithered in from the open doorway in the vestibule behind. Celea and Ajax hurriedly gathered up their supplies and equipment, and scurried away, dignity forgotten.

For dignity, there was no necessity.

What if there weren't any gods? But there was an Employee's Handbook that told each animal, each bird, each reptile, each insect, each fish, and so on, exactly how it was supposed to act? Who is responsible for supervising those actions?

Mauli is a Supervisor in charge of making sure that the butterflies in her area perform according to the handbook. She is not above engaging in some not-so-friendly rivalry with the Supervisors of other species in her area. Is there an overall Corporation in charge of everything? Who is its CEO? Mauli is a butterfly atheist, so why does she care about making sure that the handbook is adhered to? And where do the humans fit into all this?

The Precession of the Equinoxes

by Michael H. Payne

"Let's go, Bix!" Perched on the branch of the river birch, Mauli smacked a foreleg and a midleg against the cocoon hanging beside the shredded remains of her own. "Time and tide don't wait, so we're on the Goddamn clock here!"

"Yeah, yeah," came a yawning voice from below the layers of silk. "Gimme another five minutes, will you?"

Mauli pointed several of her eyes at the sun drifting slowly up from the one-third position in the crystal blue eastern sky and smacked the cocoon again. "Spring began at exactly 10:06 AM local time, Bix, and if there aren't butterflies swirling in Goddamn prismatic splendor over every meadow in this forest before we hit noon, Corporate's gonna be all over my cloaca! So get it together!" She spread her orange striped wings and leaped into the air, just exactly the right amount of a breeze blowing to rustle the leaves around her.

Which meant the wind sprites were on the job, and Mauli checked that item off her mental list with more than a little relief. It was enough of a nightmare dealing with the *actual* plants and animals in the world without having to cross over into the metaphysical, too.

Just another perk of being a Goddamn supervisor...

At least she was catching colors moving now among the river birch's spiky branches. Moths and butterflies less goldbricking than Bix crawled from their assorted pupae and waved their wings to dry them. She focused the majority of her eyes on the grass at the base of the tree, but no cottontails were hopping around down there. Just as well: in her sixty-three reincarnations working the spring shift, Mauli had seen small mammal supervisors come and go, but the current guy—

"Supervisor Mauli! Supervisor Mauli!" The voice made Mauli wince, but before she could duck in among the peeling birch bark, Teb was swooping up, his wings yellow with a light iridescent green around the edges. "This is so wonderful! Just like you said it would be!"

With an effort, Mauli kept herself from sighing. She didn't mind the way Teb had attached himself to her right after she'd given the first-time hatchlings their orientation—where to crawl, where not to crawl, what to eat, what not to eat—but she could've done without his obvious brown-nosing. "Keep your proboscis coiled, kid," she said. "It's just another job."

"What?" Teb's wings froze, dropping him a whole bodylength before he caught himself and rose back into place, his antennae spread wide in shock. "But Supervisor Mauli!" He extended one foreleg, touched the other to his chest, pressed his middle pair together in front of his thorax, and swiveled his head to face the sun. "As woodland creatures, we have the duty and the privilege of manifesting the divine in the everyday world! We further have the duty and the privilege of spreading beauty, edification, and amusement to all who would gaze upon—"

He went on quoting the employee handbook, but Mauli arched her wings and let the breeze carry her silently away. She had *way* too much to do right now without getting caught up in all that newbie crap... especially when she glanced at the branch where she'd just done her own annual chrysalis slip.

"Damn it, Bix!" She swooped down and kicked his cocoon, still hanging there as solid and undisturbed as the day she'd watched him spin it. "Don't make me come in there!"

"All right, all right!" The cocoon wobbled a little. "See? I'm starting to get, y'know, my enzymes secreting and everything!"

Wishing she had the vocal apparatus to growl, Mauli flapped away, but not before Teb had caught up with her. His mouthparts unfurled to start vibrating—no doubt ready to begin chapter two of the handbook—but Mauli whirled on him and planted a foot in the middle of his chest. "I have time for exactly two things right now, Teb: getting this meadow up and running, and nothing else." She dove for the lower branches. "And you have two choices, too, see? You can help me, or better yet, you can leave me the Hell alone!"

"I'll help, of course!" he chirped, and Mauli rolled a few dozen of her eyes. After all, a self-appointed intern was just exactly what she needed, wasn't it?

Flitting from tree to tree, she checked in with the heads of the other insectoid groups attached to her sector. She was glad to see that the rates of web spinning, bark gnawing, and swarm forming were all within the norms for the first couple hours post-equinox.

Within *her* norms, at least. "Forgive me, Supervisor Mauli," Teb said when Mauli had given Chettik six tarsal segments up in return for the arachnid's eight, "but with this many spiders, shouldn't the webs be more evenly distributed here?" He gestured to the thickest stand of trees she had jurisdiction over. "That would allow—"

"It's the first day of spring, Teb, not Halloween."

"But the employee handbook says—"

"It does, yeah." Mauli held up a foreleg the way he had earlier. "Right on the front page, and I quote, 'The proper running of the world is above all else an intensely local phenomenon.'" She used that foreleg to poke him in the chest again. "Which means it's the supervisor's call, kid. I decide how much spider web we use, where we put it, and how sticky it is. Y'understand?"

Teb's antennae went wide and flat, and a way too familiar snooty voice spoke from below: "Might I suggest, Supervisor Mauli, that you adopt a less confrontational tone when instructing your interns?"

Mauli almost let her own antennae droop, but no. She wouldn't give that Goddamn rabbit the satisfaction of seeing it. "Supervisor Kiloa!" Forcing her mouthparts, she gave a big, insectoid smile and looked down at the chubby gray cottontail looking up at her, his nose flicking like he smelled something sour. "All's well among the small mammals, I take it?"

"As frolicsome as always, Supervisor Mauli." His whiskers flicked. "I assume you have the various semi-random phyla under your jurisdiction corralled? Or at least pointed in something resembling the correct direction?"

"Well, of course!" Mauli let her grin move closer to the sort of expression she'd seen wasps give their prey. "After all, us insectoids aren't anything like you mammals, are we? We're hardly worth even thinking about in the grand scheme of things, right?" She started counting off on her tarsal segments. "Except for, y'know, taking care of plant pollination and garbage removal and being the Goddamn basis of the carnivorous food chain and everything!"

Kiloa just sniffed. "I see no need for either your self-righteous tone or for your casual blasphemy."

"Blasphemy?" It took Mauli a few sputtering wingbeats before she could go on. "You telling me you believe there's a Big Boss, Kiloa? 'Cause I've been doing this job longer'n you've been alive, and I'm telling you right now: if there *was* a Goddamn God, I'd know about it!"

"Of course." Every part of Kiloa seemed to frown. "Because the CEO of all creation would want nothing more than to poke around in the mud and the slime with the likes of you."

"You supercilious, fur-bearing bastard!" She zoomed down to flap herself furiously in Kiloa's face. "Without me and my team, there'd *be* no spring, you got that? And while I know it's too much to expect blood bags like you to be grateful, maybe you personally could manage to act like a professional for once and think of us as full partners in this whole Goddamn enterprise?"

His eyes narrowing, Kiloa gave a puff, tumbling Mauli abdomen over antennae.

"Supervisor!" Kiloa heard Teb shout from somewhere. "Have a care, sir!"

"I always do," Kiloa said. Mauli focused on his voice as she got her wings going the right way and her balance back. Looping around, she glared down at him, but the rabbit was turning and hopping away. "Because unlike *some*," he continued, "I know my place in the cosmic order, and I put my utmost exertion into maintaining that place."

Mauli flexed her proboscis to start letting him know exactly what she thought about *that*, but Kiloa was going on in a loud but bored-sounding voice: "All else aside, however, I came to inform you that a small party of humans appears to be settling into our meadow for something of a picnic." He looked over his shoulder, his expression pinched like he'd bitten into a lemon. "And while I have my finest troop of cute and fuzzy bunnies standing by to gambol about for their edification and amusement, I couldn't help but notice that *your* river birch still has at least one lumpy, large, and unopened chrysalis hanging from it." Facing forward again, he shook his head. "Very sloppy, Mauli. Not at all what the protocol requires."

Teb gasped behind her, but Mauli kept her full attention on Kiloa. "Here's a thought, Bucktooth: how 'bout you keep your Goddamn whiskers on your own snout, huh?"

With another sniff, Kiloa loped back into the tree shadows, and Mauli took off flapping for the river birch.

"All right," Teb was babbling beside her. "We can still pull this out. We'll get a group together to lead the humans away from the tree. Then we'll—"

"No." Mauli could see the humans now through the trunks and branches: two parents and a girl child, she thought from the different layers of clothing they were all wearing, striding across the grass from one of their automobiles, pulled off at the side of the dirt track that passed for a road in this part of the woods. "It's you and me, kid, and we're drawing the little one straight to Bix's cocoon. Got it?"

"Supervisor?" Fortunately, Teb didn't whisk himself in front of her, or she would've smacked him all the way down to the ground. "But we're not ready!" Several of Mauli's eyes caught the way he clutched his forelegs to his chest. "We're supposed to be filling the air with color and radiance! We'll be the laughingstocks of the entire organization if we—!"

"Damn it, Teb!" Mauli brushed her antennae against his, shocking his head around to stare at her. "We haven't got time for this! So you're either following my lead, or you're hanging back and letting me do my Goddamn job!" Snapping her wings, she vaulted over a sapling and dropped toward the humans, where the male was spreading a red and white checkered cloth over the grass.

A flutter at the edge of her vision: she glanced over to see Teb still with her, his face set with a grim sort of determination she hadn't imagined he was even capable of.

She couldn't keep from grinning, but then they were coming into range of the humans voices. "Careful, Alice!" the adult female was calling, setting down a large wicker hamper on the blanket.

"Yes, Mummy!" the girl called back, but she was staring at the forest. Mauli was sure she could smell the excitement flooding from the child. And with good reason, too, the way the trees and wildflowers were so absolutely Goddamn dew-bedecked all around them.

Hitching her wings, Mauli drifted in front of the girl and angled herself so the morning light would reflect off her stripes. The girl caught her breath, and when Teb's green and yellow flashes washed over her as well, the girl spun toward her parents. "Mummy! Daddy! There's butterflies! May I please go in a little ways and look for more?"

"All right, Alice," the male answered, grinning from where he and his mate were unpacking the hamper. "But stay close. We'll be ready to eat in a few moments."

"Yes, Daddy!" She whirled back, but Mauli hadn't waited; she was already under the tree canopy and heading inward.

The girl gasped and began lumbering along behind, Teb doing a more than credible job of herding her. Besides, Mauli was sure the sparkle of his green wingtips would hold the girl's attention better than her own dusty orange.

At least the river birch wasn't far from the tree line: flying in that scattershot way human children loved to follow always made Mauli a little dizzy. Bix's cocoon hung about halfway up the tree—after this many reincarnations, Mauli had finally found the best place to position her chrysalis, and she always made sure to settle in with Bix right there where she could keep watch over him. She skimmed past, gave the cocoon the slightest tap, and pulled herself out of the way into the thick leaves higher up, the human's thudding footfalls coming to a stop.

A rustling told her that Teb had followed her in, but she raised a foreleg to stop him from speaking, all her eyes focused on the scene below. The girl took another step closer to Bix's cocoon, now vibrating quite distinctly; then the silk split down the middle and Bix crawled out, the girl's mouth tightening into a tiny 'o'.

"Reach up," Mauli muttered. "Come on, girl; you know you want to."

Almost as if she were in a trance, the girl lifted her arm, fingers shaking as they extended toward Bix. And Bix—because, yes, he was a lazy idiot, but when the spotlight turned his way, he was every inch the Goddamn professional—Bix crept right out onto her index finger before unfurling his wings.

Teb gasped, and Mauli couldn't keep from grinning again. Huge and glinting with metallic blue and vermilion, his wings seemed to blossom from his back, with the girl staring and more firmly rooted to the spot than the tree. Bix flexed his wings up and down, up and down—just hard enough, Mauli knew, for the girl to feel the breeze of them wafting across her face—

then he arched away lightly, delicately, spiraling into the air like the perfect combination of every graceful thing the whole Goddamn world had to offer.

Casting her glance around, Mauli found Kiloa and his bunnies standing up in a patch of wildflowers two trees over, their jaws hanging open as wide as the girl's. Mauli sent Bix a quick directional pulse from her antennae, and he shifted his flight; taking the girl's attention with him, he drifted over the rabbits, and she gave about the most delight-filled squeal Mauli had ever heard.

Fortunately, Kiloa wasn't quite as stupid as he sometimes acted: by the time the girl was looking, his whole group was gamboling away like nobody's business. The girl took a step toward them, and they scattered, the human male calling, "Alice! Time for sandwiches!"

And just like the handbook said, when the girl looked around, she was alone with the trees and the grass and the flowers, the sun shimmering through the leaves to cast shadows just exactly as warm and deep and mysterious as they were supposed to be. A single bird warbled somewhere up in the canopy, and Mauli made a mental note to send Tingford a bouquet of molted beetle casings for being right where he needed to be right when he needed to be there.

The girl stayed still, her mouth open like she was trying to inhale the whole place, then she turned and ran stumbling toward her parents. "Mummy! Daddy! There was butterflies! And bunnies! And… and *everything!*"

Silence drifted down over the meadow, and Mauli relaxed her grip on the branch she was clinging to. "And *that,*" she told Teb, her new intern still staring at the empty glade, "is how you Goddamn do the pathetic fallacy."

"Well, technically, that wasn't the pathetic fallacy since it involved more than inanimate—" Teb's voice crumbled; he shook his head and waved a foreleg. "But how?" he finally got out. "How did you know that would work?"

"Wrong question, kid." Mauli stretched. "But you flew with me into all that without a clue what was gonna happen, so you get an answer. Besides, it's simple: when you got the best in the business working for you, you set things up, and you let them do their jobs." She nodded toward the path the girl had taken. "She's never gonna forget what she saw today, and whether she becomes a biologist or a painter or an auto mechanic or a magician's assistant getting sawed in half eight times a Goddamn week, she's gonna carry this moment in her heart forever like an ember or a seed. Just like the handbook says."

Teb was staring at her like she'd grown an extra set of antennae. "You? Quoting the handbook? Correctly, I mean?"

His obvious distress started a little tickle way down in Mauli's thorax, and slumping back, she let herself laugh till her spiracles ached. "Damn, Teb!" she finally wheezed. "The look on your face!"

"Well?" Waving his upper arms, he set his middle pair akimbo, his tarsal segments balled against his abdomen. "Ever since I hatched, you've done nothing but disparage the handbook! I'd begun to think you had no use for the protocols whatsoever!"

Mauli straightened up. "Remember a little earlier when you asked me, 'How?'"

A spiky wariness still shimmered around his antennae. "You said it was the wrong question." His proboscis relaxed. "Very well, then, Supervisor. What's the *right* question?"

"'Why?'" She spread all her arms. "Why do we go through all this Goddamn rigmarole, anyway?"

"Why?" Confusion replaced everything else in his expression. "It... I mean, you might as well ask why the sun rises and sets! We spread beauty, edification, and amusement by manifesting the divine! It... it's what we *do!*"

"The divine." Flicking her mouthparts, Mauli made as rude a noise as she was able. "Next you'll be telling me about the CEO of all creation."

"Well?" he said again. "*Someone* has to be in charge of the Corporation, and that someone's probably human-shaped! Why else would humans get special treatment? Or are you saying the protocols wrote themselves?"

Wondering how long had it been since she'd had someone in her sector willing to argue with her, Mauli grinned and let the scent of the pines deeper in the forest wash over her. "*We* wrote the protocols, Teb. The animals and the plants and the rocks and the wind: we are the Corporation, and we are the divine. Humanity used to be a part of it, but they decided one day that they'd outgrown nature, that they didn't need it anymore. And that's when things started going wrong."

If bugs could blink, Mauli knew Teb would be doing that. "I don't understand," he said.

"That's 'cause it makes no sense." Mauli looked through the waving branches to where the girl and her family were sitting on their blanket and eating their sandwiches. "Humans separated themselves from the rest of the world and turned into something so wild and different, they could destroy the Goddamn planet if they wanted to and barely even notice." She couldn't stop a shudder. "The protocols exist to remind humans where they come from, to make 'em look around every once in a while and think about what they *really* are instead of what they think they are." Turning, she gave Teb a shrug. "'Cause we miss 'em, see? We want 'em to come back, and we know it's not gonna be any good till they do."

Teb had frozen in place, but Mauli could almost smell the thoughts spinning furiously through his head. "I... I never imagined—I mean, the handbook doesn't mention *anything* like that."

"Yeah, well..." She jerked her head toward the rest of the meadow below them. "I'd be surprised if half the supervisors out here know the real reason we do this stuff." Flexing her wings, she leaped into a hover. "But c'mon! We've gotta grab Bix before he crashes into a high-tension line! There's three more Goddamn months of spring to get through, y'know!"

Primitive man attributed everything to the gods. The gods created the world, the oceans, fire, disease, the harvest, and everything else. The ancient Greeks attributed the winds to Anemoi, the wind gods. Aeolus, the storm god, was the king of the Anemoi. There were four Anemoi for the four compass directions: Boreas, the cold North Wind, bringer of winter; Zephyrus, the mild West Wind, bringer of spring; Notos, the warm South Wind, bringer of summer and autumn (the ancient Greeks recognized only three seasons); and Eurus, the East Wind, to complete the directions. They were sometimes depicted as winged men and sometimes as horses; the Spartans sacrificed horses to the Anemoi. When the Persian Empire under Xerxes tried to conquer Athens in 480 B.C, the Athenians prayed to Boreas to sink their ships. The ancient Assyrians and Babylonians of Mesopotamia believed that disease was brought by the demon-god Pazuzu, who had the body of a man, the head of a lion (usually snarling ferociously), the talons of an eagle, the tail of a scorpion, prominent wings, and an erect penis with a poisonous snake's head. It was probably not a coincidence that disease-carrying prominent-winged mosquitos come from the swamps of Mesopotamia, in modern Iraq.

"Deity Theory" is set in a parallel universe where the deities are all anthropomorphic animals. They and the humans have their own dimensions. As human civilization evolves, belief in the gods is replaced by science. But science arguably doesn't explain everything. "We can cure disease, but where did it come from in the first place? We can predict the weather, but never control it. We know what chemical reactions are, but not why they react that way." When a plague strikes the human dimension that science has answers for but can't cure, one person travels to the Great Animals' dimension to find the causes of everything.

Deity Theory

by James L. Steele

Abby twisted the cork from the glass bottle, shook a capsule into her hand and stared at her palm. She had taken one of these pills almost every night for the last fourteen years. Tonight she thought of all those people in the school, coughing and moaning and screaming at things that were not there. Nobody had died yet, but she had heard on the radio this morning that thousands had already perished in the plague sweeping the globe.

The scientists were at a loss to explain it. The population density was intentionally kept low to prevent the spread of disease, so by all logic and reason this plague should not exist.

Over the last few weeks Abby thought of the jackal while she listened to the news broadcasts. She remembered him prancing about Canvas, bragging about what he just made to the tiger and the cheetah and even the lion, arguing with them over how many of their plants and animals were dying, how it wasn't right to make something that affected what someone else created. None of it made sense then, but now it added up.

In her hand Abby held a choice: to sleep peacefully and wake up to a nightmare, or to visit Canvas again and find out if her intuition was right. She had not been to Canvas in eight years. This was the first time she wanted to go back.

She tipped the pill back into the bottle, corked it and set it next to the radio on the shelf. She removed her clothes. When she was a little girl, she often broke into hot sweats whenever she went there. The village only had electricity for six hours a day, and she didn't want to waste it laundering a few pieces of clothing. She could wash them in the river, but the scientists advised everyone not to risk it, as the plague might be waterborne. She thought she knew better, and now was the time to prove it.

She slipped under the thin blanket and lay her head on the pile of clean clothes. She used to have a pillow, but two weeks ago a stray dog had wandered in and chewed it up, along with several books and her winter blanket, and there would not be a supply train from the city for another month.

The sun was setting. The warm wind blew the curtain inward and waved it around. Her brother's mat was on the other side of the narrow room, empty. The farmhands were living in the makeshift village far away and dared not come back until the scientists could figure out a way to treat the plague.

The village scientists had been pleading with the city for extra electricity for days to expand their research, but their village was only three-hundred residents. Their labs were not expected to make any kind of breakthrough, which was ridiculous because it was Abby's village that had first isolated the proton more than a decade ago.

She was thrilled not to have to take night shift, but she shivered in the summer heat thinking about the sick she needed to tend in the morning. The spasms, the bleeding, the hallucinations, the mucus everywhere... The scientists insisted the plague was not airborne, but they also did not know how it was transmitted.

Abby knew. Her nerves calmed, and she began to slip across. The heat of summertime faded, and a new, more intense heat replaced it. The sleeping mat and the pile of clothes under her head now felt like sand. Canvas felt just as real as the world she left.

She opened her eyes. She was lying down in the desert this time. She rose to her feet, conjured loose clothing for herself, and took in her surroundings. There was nothing but majestic sand dunes as far as she could see in all directions. She was hoping to appear in the forest, but it seemed her childhood ability to be anywhere she wanted at will was weaker now.

Returning here after so many years was a strange sensation. As a child, this was her private playground. Now she felt like a stranger in an unfamiliar country. Canvas felt dangerous, and she disliked the change. She couldn't see them from here, but she remembered where the forest would be and ran in the direction of the trees. She glanced back and was relieved to see her bare feet still left no footprints in the sand.

When she was four years old, she had described the sensation to many doctors and scientists, but none could come up with an answer for why she was always so sleepy during the day. It wasn't until a few years ago she concluded that she never really went to sleep when she came here. She wasn't dreaming, but going to a real place where she was awake and alive, and yet Canvas also had dreamlike qualities. She could will things to appear, become invisible, fly—all the expected elements of a lucid dream.

The doctors had diagnosed Abby with "chronic dreams," her being the very first to have the condition. The pills they prescribed inhibited them. Without the pills the doctors designed for her, she would never have been able to concentrate on her schooling. From her pre-school years all the way into her late teens she cheered every time the train arrived, bringing the raw herbs and chemicals the apothecary refined, distilled and combined to make the medicine that allowed her to sleep peacefully.

Now she was back. This had been her second home, and she had wandered these deserts and forests and mountains and oceans and observed everything that went on. She explored every corner of the place, completely invisible to all the inhabitants. When she knew the pills worked, she occasionally skipped her medicine just to come back. Now that she wasn't prisoner to Canvas every night and was free to come and go as she pleased, it was a playground as large as the imagination, all for her to enjoy in any way she wanted.

When she graduated primary school and had to help with the housework and the harvest, Canvas seemed like something she needed to leave in her childhood. She had taken her medication every night all through secondary school and grew up into a happy, normal young lady.

She heard voices over the next dune and crouched low as she climbed it. She peeked over the crest. The valley between the next two sand dunes was wet, and there was a giant snake with purple and green scales down there. He was coiled up and screaming at the heron flapping just above his reach.

"I told you to stop bringing rain here!" The snake's fangs were as tall as Abby. "This is the only place I can sculpt the sand the way I like it!"

As he shouted, the heron's wings created wind and blew the dry sand in Abby's face. The dunes on either side of them were visibly wearing away.

"And stop that! I wanted no wind here! It destroys my work! It took me years to mold the sand to look like this!"

"Your desert needs rain just as much as the tiger's forest. More so now that you have plants and animals to care for."

"Well, move the shark faster! Maybe it will only take me a few weeks to fix it all!"

Abby ventured to look to her left, the direction the heron's wings were blowing the wind, and sure enough it was raining on that side of the desert. She remembered the myth: the shark had a massive stomach and used it to swallow vast quantities of the ocean. She was unable to deliver it anywhere, but her lover, the heron, drew up the wind and cast her aloft, carrying her around the world so she could spread the rain.

"I don't know how you tolerate this place," shouted the heron. "Why do you surround yourself with emptiness? Don't you want things to grow here? If not for me bringing a few showers here, nothing would."

The snake coiled up, stretched into the air and snapped his jaws at the bird. The heron was about the same size as the snake, though it was difficult to appreciate the size of these Animals because her sense of scale was so distorted here. The heron easily flew out of reach and flapped harder, creating more wind that blew the sand around.

"You let the tiger in and he created those things," shouted the snake. "It's because of you there are sharp plants here I can't touch!"

"Serves you right for encroaching on his forest. How many trees were swallowed by your sand?"

"It was an accident! I apologized!"

"And then you made creatures that lived in those plants. Admit it. They gave you something new to do. Now they need water, so live with it."

Abby realized she was afraid of them. Afraid of being seen. She never felt like this when she was a child. This place felt different now. She was vulnerable, exposed, and helpless. She had never really been aware of the myths she had read. She only knew that the tiger was responsible for the forest, the snake created the desert, and so forth. She paid no mind to the enormous power these Animals had over Canvas, how their whims meant life or death in her world, and to even look at them in the wrong way risked displeasing them.

Now she was aware of exactly who the Great Animals were. Her adult mind knew what they represented, and what they could do to her if they saw her. Disturbing their activities could bring famine, drought, quakes, or worse. It made more sense now than when she was young. This wasn't a playground; she could have done great harm to her world.

She couldn't stay here, and she didn't want to risk walking around them. She didn't feel hidden anymore, and if she were seen, her presence might displease one of these Animals, and who knew what the consequences would be. She closed her eyes and willed herself to appear in the forest. It wasn't as easy as it had been years ago. It took special concentration and patience now, whereas before it had happened as instantly as a whim. The snake and the bird were still arguing and sparring, and after a few minutes of concentration she was under a canopy of trees.

The trees were beautiful. Perfect. Branches were straight and upright, nothing was broken, and the trees seemed to give off a light of their own. She heard two more voices and crept through the trees carefully. The underbrush was orderly and straight, and her feet made no sound when they stepped on a plant. When she raised her foot, the plant she stepped on came back upright exactly as it had been. Nothing broke or wilted here unless the Great Animals themselves broke it.

As she approached, the voices became clearer. She knew them. She'd spent hours watching and listening to these animals, and she could pick out any of them. She passed through a curtain of rain, and now it was raining through the trees. The rain was coming from a large shark suspended in the air between two trees by a violent uplift coming from the desert. A tiger thrice as tall as Abby was sitting on the clean forest floor, shouting up to it.

"Why not?" said the tiger.

"I can't give you any more rain. There are other places that need it as much as you do. The cheetah needs it for the plains. She wants more game to hunt. The bear needs it for the mountains. Hunting is better when there's snow."

"I can make the trees bigger! And I have a new idea for creatures that thrive on the excess water!"

"If I do that, the trees will drown. You have plenty of water. Make do with what you have, tiger."

The updraft suddenly shifted, and the shark was propelled above the canopy. Abby heard the heron's distinct flapping overhead, pushing the shark along, taking the rain with her.

"Wait, don't go! I want to show you what I have in mind!"

"Save it for next time, tiger," said the heron from far overhead. "We have other places to be."

The tiger growled, leaped to his feet and dashed deeper into the forest. "Wait! Wait!"

Abby watched him disappear through the trees, chasing the curtain of rain the shark took with her. Abby willed her clothes to dry, then she ran in the opposite direction. She was sure the lake was around here, but it had been so long since she'd been there she didn't remember the way.

She passed a pack of wolves laughing and playing and hopping around between the trees. The wolves were as tall at the shoulder as she was. They seemed friendly now, but when they were hunting one of the small animals they created in the tiger's forest, they were scary. When she was a little girl, she always avoided them unless they were between hunts, when they were laughing and rolling about like this.

She ran through still more trees. She never became tired in Canvas, but she was frustrated. She leaned against a trunk, looking at her feet, which in this distorted, dreamlike realm appeared far away.

This wasn't working. She couldn't remember how to get to the lake. She was sure it was in the forest, and she had found it many times, but that was years ago. Now she wished she hadn't abandoned this place as a childhood plaything that needed to be discarded because she felt she needed to be an adult.

Wandering wouldn't help her find who she was looking for. She thought about the other large animals here. The smaller ones were minor, a product of these large Animals' whims. When she was a little girl she had watched the cheetah create a colony of prairie dogs. When she woke up, the things were everywhere, as if they had always been there. Indeed, scientists and researchers had produced records going back generations that stated they had always existed, but Abby remembered the animals and those records did not exist until the cheetah created them the day before.

She thought about where the jackal would be. Like the tiger, she only recognized the animal from books. They did not live in her village, or even her country. The jackal was one of the Great Animals that did not seem to have a home range. The snake had the desert, the cheetah had the plains, the tiger had the forest, the crocodile had the water, but the jackal wandered, just like the pack of wolves and the heron.

She remembered the mantis. The mantis had created the lake as part of the forest, but also separate from it. The mantis was tired of his creations falling prey to whatever forest creatures the tiger created, so he made his own refuge. Now she remembered the only way to find it was to will herself to be there.

Abby thought about the lake and willed herself to appear. It had been so easy years ago. Now it was an intense effort that required concentration and physical willpower. It was working, but it took more thought than she remembered. When she opened her eyes, she was behind a small cluster of trees surrounding an isolated body of fresh water.

Sure enough, there was the jackal. Somehow he had found the lake, and he was rolling on the ground laughing at the mantis. The jackal was as tall at the shoulders as she was.

"This isn't funny!" shouted the mantis. She was three times taller than Abby, and her mouth never seemed to match her words. "Make it stop!"

"Don't you like it?" said the jackal, lolling his tongue on the ground as he lay belly up. "It's my newest creation! Look how fast they spread!"

"Jackal, you're free to create as many of these things as you want, but I never gave you permission to use my insects!"

"Oh, cheetah will love them! He's been making too many things for himself to hunt. The plains are crowded. I'm just trying to help keep things under control. Can't reason with you people any other way. Even you've been a bit too productive lately. Can you imagine what would happen without me? This place would be overrun with creatures!"

The mantis lunged. The large dog rolled away and shouted from a distance. Abby's consciousness extended to the lesser insects around her, the ones the mantis had created both in her image and variations thereof. They were full of something else. Something bad.

The mantis chased the dog around the lake, him laughing at her the whole while. Abby closed her eyes and conjured a weapon. Something that would work here. In her hands she felt a bow and arrow. It was perfect, as it would let her affect the outcome of this quarrel without drawing attention to herself.

She crouched between the trees, set the arrow and drew back. She waited for them to separate long enough to get a shot in. Their scuffle came close to her, the jackal scampered away, still laughing, and she let the arrow loose. It struck the jackal on the side. No blood came out, but the canine was clearly startled. He fell, unable to move. The mantis rushed in, snatched the jackal up and screamed at him.

"Release my insects!"

The jackal hung from her scissor-like grip, kicking the empty air.

"Now!"

Abby was still low, watching through the underbrush. The bow and arrow had disappeared, and she remembered from her childhood that these animals may not bleed or sleep, but they do feel pain. It was probably the only thing keeping one of them from overrunning everyone else.

The other insects started behaving differently. Abby became aware that they had been freed of whatever the jackal had placed in them. The mantis sensed it, too, for she let him drop to the ground.

"Leave! If I find you here again, I will make you suffer!"

"Please... Please... There's something..." He screamed and writhed in wordless agony.

The mantis just now noticed the arrow sticking out from his side. She leaned over it, grabbed it in her mandibles and pulled it out. The jackal was visibly relieved.

"What is this?" said the mantis, turning the arrow over in her forelimbs.

Abby closed her eyes and willed herself to wake up. She felt her clothes fading away, the air around the lake yielding to the smell of wheat and corn drifting in through the window.

She opened her eyes and raised her head. It was still dark outside, and she was covered in sweat. She threw off the cover, stood up and groped around the shelf for the switch on the radio. She flicked it, but there was no electricity. Gasping for breath and desperate for a drink of water, she threw on some dirty clothes and dashed out of the house.

The village streets were deserted. Most everyone who wasn't already sick was indoors, hoping to avoid the plague. The houses were old, most of them were crooked, and the windows were shuttered. Nothing was over two stories high here, though she'd heard the buildings in the city could be as tall as five.

She turned a corner, skidding in the dirt and dashed down the next road. The horses in nearby stables grumbled at her passing. She hopped over a sleeping dog in the middle of the street. The airyard was just on the other side of the buildings here. Normally there would be balloons and zeppelins lined up in the field, ready for takeoff, but none dared land here now.

A little further up the street was her usual work. The town's master seamstress was a prickly old woman named Mrs. Zin, but she had been alive for a long time, she knew everything, and Abby enjoyed being around her. She always learned something every time Mrs. Zin opened her mouth. For weeks the boiler in the back had been shut off, the steam valves empty, and the flywheels that ran the sewing machines idle. Life in the village had stopped to care for the sick.

Abby turned another corner and opened the gate to the school. She slowed to a fast walk, tried to compose herself, and walked through the main door.

The hospital had been overwhelmed last week, and all victims of the plague were treated in the school. There was little anyone could do but try to alleviate the symptoms and hope the patient recovered while the scientists a few buildings down worked on what this disease was and how to cure it.

Oil lamps and pillar candles lined the tables down the hallway. It was just enough light to see her way down the hall and into the lunchroom. A hundred people lay in sleeping mats on the floor. Several nurses were walking from patient to patient. At first Abby didn't know what she was hoping to find here, but something was different. There were no sounds of moaning, no coughing, no choking, no rambling as the patient suffered hallucinations. A few of the patients were sitting up now. Abby walked to the closest one, a farmhand who had fallen ill three days ago.

"Are you all right?" Abby said.

He took a breath. It was clear, clean. "Yes… I think I am."

Moments later, several nurses followed by three doctors and every scientist in the village ran inside the lunchroom and walked from patient to patient. Some of the ill were standing up, marveling at how easy it was now. The lead scientist ran from the lunchroom and down the hall. Abby knew exactly where he was going and ran after him. She turned a corner into the schoolmaster's office, where the scientist was winding up a telephone on the wall.

"I need to reach the office of the power plant, please. Emergency." A few seconds of silence. "Hello, this is Doctor Hagim from the village of Nariss. We need electricity, now!" He was silent for a moment longer. "Our village was struck by the plague, and now the patients have recovered! I examined them myself just a few hours ago, and they were bleeding and coughing! Now it's like they were never sick! I need electricity so I can run the x-ray machine and MRI!"

Abby leaned on the doorframe while he waited for an answer.

"What?!" said Doctor Hagim, leaning closer to the mouthpiece. "Please, can you give us anything?… Fine, fine, shut us off an hour early tomorrow. Thanks!"

He hung up the earpiece on the hook and faced Abby. "What are you doing here?"

"What's happening?"

"Patients all over the country are cured. The power plant is overwhelmed with requests. Nobody's sure what's happening. We might have an hour to take whatever readings we can."

"That's wonderful."

Doctor Hagim nudged past her and speed-walked down the hall. Abby stared into space for a few minutes. It worked. What she thought she learned as a kid… it was all true. She came back to herself, turned around and ran back down the hall. As she did, the electric lights turned on, and she shielded her eyes from the sudden glare but did not stop running. Squinting, she turned the corner. The doctors and scientists had pulled a few volunteers from the group and were leading them out the front door now. The patients were walking upright, in full command of their body. Abby caught up to Doctor Hagim.

"Doctor, can I ask you something?"

"What is it, Abby? Make it fast."

"What if I told you I tried something a few hours ago. Something drastic."

Doctor Hagim met her eyes. Abby lost her nerve and turned her face down to her bare feet.

"Uh… have you ever given thought that maybe disease isn't caused by microscopic animals? Maybe some of the new theories could be true? That the forces of nature are not controlled by anything in this universe, but happen somewhere else? That they're controlled by people… somewhere else?"

"Deity Theory," he said.

"Yes. Disease, the wind, the rains, that they're all—"

"Deity Theory was created to describe the way a few isolated tribes survived without science centuries ago, not a current school of thought that needs to be tested. Did you try praying? Is that what you're trying to tell me?"

Abby lifted her head and met his eyes. "I did."

"To whom?"

"Anyone I thought might help. And now…"

"Science cured your sleep disorder, Abby. Centuries of research went into that medicine."

"Then what happened to the plague?"

"We're going to find out. We'll find the answer. We always do. If you want to help, come to the hospital, otherwise you may return to bed."

"Thank you, doctor. I think I'll go back to sleep. Doesn't look like anyone needs me here now."

"I hope not. I'll sleep a lot better when we figure out what happened. Goodnight."

Abby watched everyone leave the school and migrate to the hospital. The recovered patients were marveling at their newfound strength. Many were walking to the well to draw water from it. She was now alone in the schoolhouse. She listened to the sound of her breathing for a minute, then turned around and wandered down the hall. She absently extinguished the lamps and candles as she passed them. At the end of the hall she stopped at a door. The schoolhouse had five classrooms, more than enough for their village, and Abby was in front of her old grade school room now.

She turned the knob and walked inside, shutting the door behind her. The single electric light in the ceiling cast a gloomy, yellow haze over the desks and chairs. A few open books were still on the desks, school having been cancelled in a hurry as the plague worsened. Class hadn't been in session in weeks, and the air in here already smelled old and dusty.

Miss Weiss. Abby remembered her talking for hours at a time about prehistory, how people long ago discovered the telescope and then the microscope, the first scientific instruments. It was said they were invented before the wheel. People in that primitive society looked at various things, and one of the first discoveries was the cause of disease. Microscopic animals were everywhere, and civilizations all over began to devote their societies to escaping them.

The telescope led to other instruments that measured the weather patterns, and people began to time their crops to the cyclic seasons. Other people invented filters and studied the sun. Parallel experiments in chemistry revealed the inner workings of the world around them. The electron was harnessed centuries ago and had been used to further the advances of science ever since, though it was not as reliable as the steam engine.

But, Abby learned, there were a few civilizations in isolated places of the world that did not begin with science. They began with superstition, fear, and storytelling to explain disease, rain, and the changing seasons. Their creation myths and tales of Great Animals had been published as curious glimpses of the direction civilization could have gone, and Miss Weiss had gladly let Abby borrow that book. She devoured it as a child, practically memorizing it. She had seen the characters in person, and knowing nobody else had made Canvas feel that much more special.

She turned around in the room, meeting the eyes of every portrait on the wall. Great scientists throughout history; men and women who contributed something to the whole of civilization. They were hung chronologically around the room: the man who invented the telescope and microscope. The woman who identified the first disease. The man who recorded the first correct anatomy of a human being.

It had taken just thirteen-hundred years to go from simple hunter-gatherers living in tribes to the modern steam-age, and another fifty years to tame the electron. The societies who began with Deity Theory were still in the hunter-gatherer phase when modern society found them.

Abby recited the first passage from the book of myths as she met the eyes of the woman who invented the first practical steam engine. "In the beginning, the Great Animals created a Canvas. Then they set to work filling it with whatever they desired. If we displease them, they will fill their Canvas with pain and misery. But if we honor them, they will fill it with joy and wonder."

* * *

Abby awoke in the mountains, and the disorientation made her dizzy. She hadn't dared to come back in months, but the winter had been extremely mild, and spring had brought no rain. The meteorologists all across the country had stated all their calculations predicted the rain should be coming north, but it had stayed to the south. People in the southern regions were suffering from floods while those in the north faced famine from their lost crops. Scientists all across the country were releasing balloons with radio transmitters into the atmosphere to try to figure out what was happening, but all readings were coming back confirming the previous findings. According to them, there was no reason the rain should be south.

She conjured some warm clothes for herself and stood up. The last time she was here, during the plague, she didn't like the way this place made her feel. She felt exposed, in danger, and just one glance away from being discovered. She remembered playing with the lesser animals that roamed the land and living under the water for hours at a time, observing how this place worked and what wonders the Great Animals could do. Now she was an adult, and that somehow changed everything.

She had appeared exactly where she wanted to be. From here, she could see everything, and she looked over the land and found where the rain was. She concentrated, lifted off the ground and flew down towards it. There was no breeze hitting her in the face, and her clothes did not flap against her body. When she young, this feeling was exotic and exhilarating. Now she feared it.

She dared not fly very far, so she settled down on the forest for cover and ran the rest of the way. She passed the pack of wolves again. They were rolling on the ground, laughing and howling as they chased one another and stepped on each other's tail.

She passed a red fox that was half her size. The book of myths mentioned this creature, but it had been so long since Abby had thought about Canvas and the book of myths she did not remember what his domain was.

She left the forest and ran for the curtain of rain that was hovering over the southern region of the plains. She willed herself to remain hidden, but she still felt exposed and vulnerable. All around here were the mindless beasts of the plains, created by the cheetah to hunt. She only knew what a cheetah was from depictions in books, and he did not seem to be around.

As she neared the curtain of rain, the ground became saturated and spongy. The swamp turned into an ocean, and Abby concentrated hard to keep her feet above the water as she ran.

She entered the curtain. The water was deeper here, and she was having a difficult time not falling in. Without realizing it, she was standing on an open ocean in the middle of the plains.

A few treetops poked up from the water on the horizon. She saw animals there. One of them looked like the cheetah in a tree. As she neared, she saw the heron in the same tree, a few branches across from the cheetah. The shark wasn't in sight, but there was a tiny vortex of air a few paces from the tree, and the rain seemed to be radiating from the top of the vortex.

The cheetah clung desperately to the branch. He was larger than any one of the giant wolves Abby passed, and yet the tree branch did not bow under his weight. "You couldn't have had this fight over the snake's desert, could you?"

"Then I would have both the snake and the tiger yelling at me," said the heron. "The snake would whine about his precious sand dunes, and the tiger would yell at me for drowning the cacti and scrub he created in the snake's domain. At least this place you made entirely yourself."

"Just apologize to her!"

"I won't apologize. If she thinks the wind isn't as important as the rain, we're through."

"Really, who else would you want to be with? You two are perfect for one another."

"The fox has been making partnership offers since we came here. Maybe I'll go down and see him."

The cheetah laughed. "The fox? What would you two possibly do together? He spends all his time in a burrow. You're in the air!"

Abby had let herself sink below the water just enough for her eyes and ears to be above it. By now she had ventured a bowshot from the tree branch.

"Might be a good change," said the heron. "Sometimes I am weary of carrying her around. Why couldn't I have been like the bear and claimed my own domain?"

"We need her rain. Without the two of you, none of this would exist."

"That's the problem. Everyone needs us, but what about us? I love her, I really do, but what if I want my own domain? What if I want to create something?"

"You already do. You make storms out of her rain."

"I still need her rain. I'm talking about a place of my own."

Abby looked upwards. Rain did not fall from clouds here, but from the shark. She couldn't see the shark through the thick rain far overhead, but she could discern where the center of the downpour was. If this was a lover's quarrel, and if these two were anything like her parents, then all they should need was a push for them to make peace.

She conjured up another bow and arrow and rose partway out of the water. She set the arrow, aimed at the center of the rainfall high above, and let it fly. It whistled into the rain, struck something with a thunk. The rain faltered, and a shark fell from the sky. She careened down and splashed into the ocean a few dozen paces from the tree. As soon as the shark touched the water, the rain ceased.

The heron gasped, took to the air, kicking up an enormous gust of wind that made whitecaps in the floodwater, and soared down from the branch to where the shark had fallen. She flapped harder, blowing the water away from the fallen bird, making waves that washed over Abby. She sank below the waves and tried to hold herself still.

The heron's beak was moving, but she couldn't hear what she was saying. The shark's mouth was moving as well, and the heron was now holding the shark in her wings. The shark returned the embrace. The cheetah was still in the tree, looking on, tail twitching. Abby let go of her breath, closed her eyes and willed herself to wake up.

She heard a grumble behind her, opened her eyes and spun around. She was face to face with a crocodile three times her size. Abby thrashed, swam backwards, forgetting she didn't need to swim here. The crocodile wiggled her tail and pursued her, opening her mouth. Abby closed her eyes and willed herself to wake up—wake up—wake up now!

"What... who are y..." The Animal's growling words faded, and the gentle breeze through the window replaced it. Moments later, she heard raindrops.

She bolted awake and ran to the window, forgetting to cover herself. Rain was coming from the south. She smiled. She pounded the windowsill and laughed as more drops pelted her face.

"Abby?" said her brother from his sleeping mat. "Abby, what's...?"

Abby couldn't stop smacking the frame and laughing. Her brother rose from the floor and joined her at the window. She grabbed him and jumped up and down. Her laugh was infectious, and he started jumping and laughing as well. They hugged as the rain came down harder. When it became too hard, she pulled the shutters, turned her back to the wall and slid down to the floor, laughing. The rain still pelted the metal roof, and it sounded like life itself had returned.

A shirt hit her in the face. She pulled it off and watched her brother. "It's dark, and the lights are out, Omar. Nobody will see me." A dress hit her, and she just held it in her lap. Omar was putting on his slacks. "Where are you going?"

"To get the equipment ready. We have boilers to clean, rainwater to distill, valves to test. Months of dry weather, anything can go wrong."

"In a downpour?"

"Have to start now. You should prepare some things, too. Can't celebrate until the harvest is over."

"I know."

He was putting on his shoes. Abby leaned against the wall, enjoying the sound of the rain hitting the shutters and the roof. She watched her brother and smiled.

"How do you think they'll explain this?"

"What do you mean, Abby?"

"They never figured out what happened to the plague. Now this... The rain came back. They still don't know why it didn't come north."

"They'll figure out someday."

"That's it. That's all they ever say. Science explains everything that happens in the world. But don't you ever wonder? We can cure disease, but where did it come from in the first place? We can predict the weather, but never control it. We know what chemical reactions are, but not why they react that way."

"They don't have all the answers. But we're always learning them."

"Do you ever wonder what science is? Who created these rules in the first place? What if they're not predictable laws, but someone's whims? Maybe we've been going about it wrong all these years."

"We must be doing something right," he said as he stood and walked to the door. "I'm waking father. You should wake mother, tell her what's happening and to prepare."

"I will. Have fun out there."

The rain was still coming down in sheets. Omar walked out and into their parents' bedroom. Abby leaned her head against the wall and smiled. She then promised to take her medicine and never venture into Canvas again.

* * *

Abby awoke beneath a tree in the plains. She rose to her feet and immediately started running, looking in all directions. The feeling was stronger this time—that she was an intruder, vulnerable, helpless, and one wrong step away from angering someone. She was hoping it wouldn't be as bad as last time, but it was worse every time she returned. Nothing would have made her come back except a problem big enough to tear the town apart, and just a few weeks after the rains returned, it happened.

Neighbor was turning against neighbor. Her own mother and father were arguing from the minute they woke up to the moment they went to sleep. Abby even argued with Omar a few times, and it wasn't like them not to get along. He was sleeping in the farmhands' houses now, far away from her. She didn't like the strife that had appeared between them, but they were not the only ones.

The radio had been buzzing with reports of the same kinds of things happening all over the world. Strife, bickering and hatred. Psychologists were at a loss to explain it, but the last time it had been recorded, over a century ago, towns had turned against one another, the sixteen nations had started to ignore old treaties and fight over resources again, industry turned to making weapons of war.

Abby had a theory. She had resisted the prickle of curiosity until it had grown into a dire need to know for sure. Now she was back in Canvas, and she would not leave until she found the wolf pack.

The book did not say what the wolves did, and Abby had never been sure what their role was, but if she was right, the source of the world's problem was within her power to fix. She created loose clothing for herself as she ran along the windless grassland. She passed by trees, looking everywhere, hoping to find them quickly so she could leave before the feeling of danger consumed her. The wolves could be anywhere, but they were most often in the forest, and she was headed in that direction.

She stepped out of the grassland and entered the tiger's domain. Here she slowed down and tried to look between the trees as she ducked through them. It was always so clean here. She wondered if real forests looked like this, as she had only ever seen drawings of them in books and periodicals.

It seemed quieter here than usual. She didn't remember this place being so quiet before. There should be animals running about, but so far she hadn't seen a single one. In all her previous visits, she could barely walk fifty paces before coming across some Great Animal. It only added to her feeling of dread.

Finally a sound came through the branches, and she veered towards it. Snarling, yelping, howling, and snapping teeth. She had never heard these things in Canvas before, and a chill ran up her neck. A few dozen more strides between the trees, and she saw the wolves.

Two of them were at one another's throat. Three more were circling each other, snarling. Two more were gnawing on another's legs. There was no blood, but there was pain. The forest was full of it—all of Canvas was full of it. The feeling billowed over Abby like steam from a train.

Abby hid behind a trunk and watched the pack turn on one another. Opponents changed every few seconds—the attacked became the attackers, landed one bite or kick or swipe on another wolf, then that wolf would turn around and strike back.

Abby crouched low, still holding the trunk. The bow and arrow wouldn't work this time; she needed something to quell a fight, but she didn't know what they were fighting over.

She closed her eyes and concentrated. Sometimes in dream worlds, knowledge came to her because she willed it to come, and she hoped to do the same thing again. Through the growls and snarling, she began to hear purpose.

… there had been disagreement over who should tend to the newly created animals they made for the forest…

… one of the wolves claimed ownership of them…

… but they had always treated their creations as joint ownership before…

… it caused a schism in the pack. Everyone now claimed ownership of the various things they created, and now they were fighting over ownership.

Abby opened her eyes. The pack was fighting harder than ever. Now she realized the two closest to her had both claimed the coyote as their own. Three more claimed each had created the maned wolf, and Abby sensed they had created it together many years ago—no one wolf had created anything, and that was the point: they couldn't create anything on their own, but together they made wonderful things.

She wasn't sure how to solve this. She panted harder, watching the wolves fight, sensing the repercussions of their strife seeping into her world every second. She was wasting time, but nothing was coming to her this time.

"Don't be afraid."

Abby spun around and was face deep in a chest of white fur. The tiger! Abby stumbled backwards around the tree and towards the pack of fighting wolves. She heard wings flapping behind her. She didn't have to turn around to see the heron had landed on the ground behind her. Her eyes darted to the side. The crocodile was on dry land, crawling into the space she had just backed away from. She passed a couple of fighting wolves, and they forgot their dispute at the sight of her. The tiger was walking in her footsteps, haunches raised, stalking her. Everyone towered over her.

The cheetah was somewhere, watching her. The fox was also here. The snake was behind her, coiled around a few tree trunks. Other Animals were here. Dozens more—most she had only fleeting memories of. Everyone had been watching the pack of wolves fight, just as helpless and bewildered as she was.

Abby couldn't breathe. She closed her eyes and willed herself to wake up.

"Who are you?" said the tiger.

"Nobody created her," said one of the wolves.

"You don't belong here," the heron said.

She felt a few paws touching her, some furred, some scaly, some feathery. She pushed them away and willed herself harder and harder. Feathers were touching her cheek as her clothes began to fade and the voices became the cold night. She opened her eyes. She was on her sleeping mat, under the blankets, wrapped up tight to escape the strife that had consumed the world. She was sweating and panting.

A shadow moved in front of her. Abby gasped and pulled the blanket up over her nose. Feathers were backlight by moonlight, and a long beak turned into view as well. The heron was here, the giant bird took up all of Omar's side of the room. She spread her wings and looked about. Abby shivered as sweat dripped from her eyebrows. The heron turned from the window and aimed her body at Abby.

"What happened?" said the bird. "Where am I?"

Abby shivered harder and covered her face.

"Where have you brought me?! I have never seen you before! What do you create?! What is your domain?!"

Abby tried not to shiver, but she realized hiding under a blanket was childish, and she had to reply or she risked displeasing this creature and dooming all of mankind to windless skies, or never-ending tornados and hurricanes.

"I'm sorry."

Everything was still for a few beats.

"Sorry for what?" said the heron.

"My name is Abigail Hibi. I've been coming to Canvas for a while. I was the one who shot the jackal. I shot the shark from the sky. I had to. I'm sorry!"

"Shot? That was you?"

"I'm sorry! I'm so sorry, please, I had to stop the plague and make the rains move again! People were dying! I didn't know what else to do!"

"The rains? You mean when the shark and I were fighting?"

The heron was listening to her, and Abby felt a little better now. She pulled the covers from her head and faced the silhouette of the heron from her pile of clothes.

"Yes. The rain was stalled over the plains. None of it was reaching us, and it was drowning the people in the south. I had to help."

"What are you talking about? Nobody was harmed by that. All the animals left the flooded areas. Those in the dry regions moved south to find the water."

Abby stopped shivering. She pulled the blankets down the rest of the way and sat up against the wall. The heron was huge in this tiny room. Her eyes were used to the glow of moonlight, and now she could make out the Animal's face.

"I don't understand it myself," Abby said, "but now I know it's true. You control the wind. The shark makes it rain, and you're the reason it goes anywhere. Everything you do there affects us here. You, the Great Animals, are the reason we have physical laws here."

"Where is here? And what do you mean physical laws?"

Abby was at a loss to explain this, and stammered for a moment before speaking again. "The world you created... I called it Canvas when I was a child. I used to go there every night in my dreams. They put me on medicine so I could sleep and I didn't go back until there was an emergency."

The heron did not reply, and her face was impassive. Abby hoped it meant she was at a loss for words and not weary of this conversation.

"The world you created," Abby said. "Canvas. Why did you make it? Where did all of you come from?"

"We came—"

Abby's door slammed open and her mother stood in the frame. "Abby, what is the meaning of this noise?!"

Abby froze. She waited for her mother to look at Omar's side of the room. Instead, her mother stared deeper into her.

"Who are you talking to this early!?"

Abby looked at the heron. The bird was facing Abby's mother. "Who is this? Who created her?"

The woman in the doorframe did not take her eyes off Abby. "Abby, I'm not kidding! What is the matter?!"

"I'm sorry, mum. I forgot my pill. I must have been talking in my dream."

Her mother's stare became harder. "Take your pill, go to sleep, and if you wake me again I will shove the whole damn bottle down your throat so you'll never wake up again!"

She turned, slammed the door and stomped back to her room. Abby could hear the faint sound of her weeping through the wall.

The heron rose, stepped closer to Abby and wrapped a wing around her. "She can't hear us now."

"How?"

"I think I understand a little better now."

The heron's body shrank, drew inward, softened into that of a woman instead of the imposing figure of a giant animal. Now instead of a large heron standing in the bedroom, she resembled a compromise between a bird and a woman. Her face was still birdlike, but her stature was very human. Her body was still covered in feathers, but her wings now resembled arms, with wingtips that functioned like fingers.

"You visited my world in dreams. Your world is also like a dream to me. Everything you've told me matches what the other Animals have said when they saw you. Tell me everything."

* * *

Scientists have been struggling to understand why their instruments have picked up no wind readings since the wee hours of the morning. One need not consult mechanical devices. One only needs to step outside and feel that there is no breeze. None at all. My friends, I assure you that this is not local to our broadcast area. All across the globe, there is no wind. Furthermore, airplanes do not rise, even when traveling fast enough. Balloons do not rise. Various other devices that rely on the wind in any way simply do not work. It is as if the laws of physics on which air travel depend no longer hold true.

Various houses had the radio tuned to the same frequency, but most were not listening to it. As Abby walked with the heron, who had taken on a humanlike body of similar proportions to her own, people were out on the streets.

Two men burst from the door to the apothecary's shop. The first man, Magreer, was shouting to the whole town that Patel was a cheating thief for charging twice for a medicine what the apothecary the next town over was charging. Patel followed him out to the street and pulled Magreer around and argued the price in his face.

The price was the same it had always been, he was saying.

Magreer was shouting back that it was always robbery.

They went back and forth like this for a while. The heron was watching, listening, head tilting and staring in a very birdlike way. Nobody could see the heron-woman but Abby. The heron had hidden them both from view, and being able to view what people were like when they thought nobody was watching was a perspective she would not wish on anyone. Patel threw a punch at Magreer. The two men went down to the dirt in a brawl.

"My apothecary," said Abby. "Patel. He makes my medicine. Never heard him raise his voice to even his own son. Look at him now."

The heron hurried them along. Another radio came into hearing range as they moved down the street.

… have established the rains have stopped as well. No rain has fallen anywhere on the globe in the last twelve hours, which baffles scientists.

Further up the road, a man was struggling to keep his horse from kicking him. He was rearing up, resisting every effort.

"That's Mister Kjold. A farmhand. His horse has been agreeable for years, and now all of a sudden…"

The heron was taking in the sight as they walked by.

… just received word that the solar time does not equal the measured time in any part of the world. My friends, it's as if the rotation of the Earth has stopped. Those of you with pocket watches, check them now, and compare that time to your local sundial. You will confirm they do not match. For example, it is currently nine-thirty-six in the morning in the city of Eastlake, but the sundial reads eight-forty-one, and the sun is still not moving in the sky.

Even further up the road were young girls throwing rocks into the school building. Then two women were arguing about how one looked at the other this morning. They began pulling hair and swinging kitchen equipment at one another.

… power plant is running at maximum capacity, but output is less than half what it should be. Those of you able to hear this broadcast, consider yourselves lucky. It is as if the electron has decided not to do what it always has done since the beginning of time.

Women were beating dogs that had wandered into their line of sight. Children were kicking neighbors, and pets were turning on their owners. The heron watched each incident with an impassive expression.

… on a similar note, it also appears as though combustion is not predicable either. Foundries and factories the world over are reporting an inability to maintain a fire, or set anything alight. Trains all over the world are halted due to the inability to light a fire in the boiler. Some boilers are lit, but at greatly reduced flames relative to what they should be. It is a baffling mystery that authorities are still working on. This on top of the strife that seems to have engulfed…

The broadcast became static, and then the power went out.

They were walking by the town hall now, and Abby stopped at the sundial. The clock tower read nine-fifty-six, but the shadow on the sundial read eight-forty-one. The heron stepped up to it, standing opposite Abby, and compared the two.

"This lack of harmony," Abby said. "It's the wolves, isn't it?"

"Yes." She was staring at the sundial. "We all recognized everything we were doing needed to work together. The wolves took charge of making sure of that. When they fight, everything stops. This is exactly what we see in my world when it happens."

"What about the electricity? What's happening?"

"It's the fox," she said. "He wanted to create lights in the sky to impress me. He's been trying to convince me to be his mate since he arrived. Now that I'm gone... he has no reason to do so anymore."

"That one act of trying to win you over created the laws of electromagnetism that we use to make radios work. Notice the wind. There is no wind."

"I can't make the wind blow here. I can change myself, but I can't change this world."

She looked up at the clock tower, then turned to the sun. Abby let her take in the sight for a moment with nothing but the background noise of violence to fill the gap. Finally, Abby spoke up.

"I don't know how, but it's because of you we have physical laws. Until right now, they have been predictable and constant. If those laws change, we die."

"This is unbelievable," said the heron.

People were running around them, threating each other with weapons, cursing, destroying houses and businesses. It was like watching a radio drama happen before her eyes. She was a narrator. She was an observer. None of it touched her.

"Nobody created you," the heron continued. "Nobody created this world. The fox's electricity, the horse's fire, my wind, my lover's rain... All of it added up to create something bigger. We never thought..."

She lowered her eyes to the sundial. The shadow hadn't moved the entire time. The sun was still as high in the sky as it had been hours ago. She turned to the sun now.

"And the lion. The lion! He isn't running across the dome of our world to bring light to everything! They've all stopped! The other Animals are panicking! They don't know what happened to me, so they've stopped everything!"

"The jackal creates disease," Abby said. "Why?"

The heron met Abby's eyes. They were still birdlike and expressionless, but far less intimidating now that she was Abby's height.

"The jackal came to... to Canvas late. We were already making creatures in our image by then. He didn't want to do what everyone else was doing, so he started creating animals too small to see."

"What is Canvas?"

"It was a place we created to do as we pleased."

"Where did you come from?"

"Another world already created by other Animals. We wanted to make things of our own, in our image. This must be the reason leaving that world was forbidden. They didn't tell us it would affect events somewhere else, or creatures would emerge from it we did not intend."

She followed a man running from one building to another, carrying a torch, screaming. He was trying to light things on fire, but the fire was not spreading. Nothing was lighting up. This angered the man even more, and he used the torch to club the nearest person he could find.

"We have to go back," said the heron. "You must take me back, please!"

Please? Abby thought. She was silent for a moment, staring into the bird-woman's unreadable expression. "I can only visit Canvas in dream. If I take medicine to fall asleep, I won't dream."

"Then show me more. Let us walk until you can sleep."

"I would show you the city, but the trains aren't running, and it's many days walking."

"I will take us there," said the heron-woman, walking around the sundial to Abby's side. "As you could will yourself to appear anywhere in my world, so I can in yours."

She took Abby's hand in her wing and closed her eyes. Moments later, the village of Nariss faded away, and the city of Eastlake came into view.

Everything that was happening in Nariss was also here, but magnified. People were running about, demolishing windows, buildings, electrical poles, animals, and each other. Horses had broken away from carriages and were running in circles, kicking anyone that came near.

There was no fire anywhere. Water was not flowing from any of the open hydrants. Abby noticed some beverage mugs in a corner tavern overturned, but the liquid was still inside as if the glass were upright.

"The crocodile," said the heron, noticing where Abby's attention was. "She isn't making the water flow now. They're all upset, and they have no idea what's happening here..."

As they wandered the streets and observed the chaos and looting and violence, Abby did not feel like she was in the presence of a vengeful deity who demanded respect. The heron had been surprised at every turn, and had even been polite to Abby.

Abby thought less of the rioting and more about the idea that the Animals were ignorant of their power over this world. Everything they had done was an accident. The book of myths was wrong. Now that she thought of it, something had been explicitly omitted from the book: who was making these observations about the Great Animals? Who wrote the myths?

There had to have been people like Abby in the past. People who went to Canvas in their dreams and told stories about what they were seeing. They assumed the deities were vengeful and knew about what they had created, but the Animals had no such knowledge. The sacrifices, the pleas, the prayers; all were for nothing.

She had once felt in awe learning about the men and women who figured out the laws of aerodynamics, electromagnetism, and thermodynamics. Abby's vision glazed over as she realized she was walking with a creature who created those laws, and this bird didn't even know she had done it. All the heron wanted to do was help her lover spread the rain across the land. From that simple act of compassion had arisen a whole system of mathematics describing lift, pressure, turbulence, and drag.

The myths always portrayed the people sacrificing and pleading to these Animals to keep things as they were and to fill their Canvas with joy. A person in Abby's position coming from a primitive culture would do the same out of fear, but Abby had an idea.

"We need to bring them all here."

The heron turned, met Abby's eyes. Abby held her gaze, then took her feathered hand as they watched chaos engulf the city.

* * *

Abby awoke on the roof of one of the farmhand's houses. The harvest was over, the fields bare, so there was no one here now. The sun was high in the sky, and the light was overwhelming.

She felt the heron's wing around her, gently raising her up to a sitting position. On the roof, and on the ground below, were the Great Animals. There were over a hundred of them, all assuming a form that was between human and animal to make themselves appear less intimidating. All the wolves, the tiger, the lion, the fox, the jackal, and many others. Even the desert snake was here, somehow finding a way to assume a disarming human form and still appear snakelike.

The wind was not blowing. The sun would stop in the sky for as long as the lion was here. The strife that had engulfed the world had long ago eased, and so long as the wolves were in harmony when they left Canvas, this world would still be in harmony.

Abby had a tremendous headache from traveling to Canvas and back so many times over the last few weeks. Though she had slept every night, she never rested, and now had a difficult time remaining on her feet. The deity of the wind helped her to her feet and held her upright. Abby spoke to all the Animals.

"By now all of you have seen what happens when you change something in Canvas. Anything you do can lead to thousands of deaths here. You saw what happened to the people when the wolves began fighting! Imagine what would happen to them if the horse made fire impossible, or if the heron and the shark started fighting again!"

She had their complete attention. Over these last few weeks Abby and the heron had brought the others here to see the results of their whims. They had seen for themselves what happened when they no longer performed their habits, and what the result was when they resumed. The wolves were the first to try it. When they realized their fighting caused Abby's world to be in disharmony, they made up and were harmonious again. They then returned to Abby's world and saw the change.

Animal after Animal saw what their role was, and how it affected the people inhabiting it. Everyone understood what it meant for Abby's people. She made sure to show them. She guided them to the most relevant sights, most of which she had only read about in books. The Animals made it possible for her to travel there and show them.

Abby realized on the day she stood at the sundial with the heron that Doctor Hagim was wrong. The book of myths wasn't a chronicle of dead possibility; it was a glimpse into a potential future. The relationship was just starting, and Abby decided she did not like the future the myths represented— one full of fear and sacrifice and subservience to omnipotent beings who cared nothing for how their actions affected anyone. She had the power to build this relationship on understanding and compassion, and she did not waste the opportunity.

Now they stood outside the village of Nariss, on and around the farmhand's house, waiting to meet the people whose lives they affected. They had followed her lead this whole time. They recognized the people were fragile, and if any of them made the slightest change, people would die. Their first reaction was not to swell up with power and demand respect, but to be careful where they stepped. Abby cultivated this reaction in her every word and deed.

"No one person created us," Abby resumed. "The sum of your individual creations made us, so we are all your children. The world you created is my world. It's yours to take care of and protect, and so are all the people in it. It's time everyone knew who created the laws that make my world. It's time they met you and understood you, even thanked you. They will be eager to know who you are, just as you are eager to know who they are."

Knowledge came to Abby. The Animals had made themselves visible to all now. The sun was stuck in the sky. Within hours, reports would be going out that electricity, fire, the progression of the day, wind, and everything else they took for granted had ceased.

The Great Animals were silent, waiting for Abby to lead the way, eager to meet everybody who relied on the laws their whims had created. Abby was certain the people were ready to understand who created those laws. Science had done an excellent job preparing them for this moment, and Abby hoped she had done a good enough job preparing the deities as well.

What is the difference between a Trickster and a God? If the Trickster is all-powerful enough, does it matter?

Read "Questor's Gambit" and decide for yourself whether Questor is a God or a Trickster? Then decide whether this story is funny-animal fantasy or uplifted-animal s-f? Is Questor a being in the unimaginably far future who has evolved into godlike power? Or does he only appear as one to make Commander Wilker happy?

And does it matter?

Questor's Gambit

by Mary E. Lowd

Commander Bill Wilker's angular muzzle split into a wide collie grin, and he smoothed down his ruff of fur that spilled regally out of the collar of his Tri-Galactic Navy uniform. "That's a goddamned beautiful lookin' planet," he said.

And it was a goddamned beautiful planet on the viewscreen. It was green and round and blue—everything that a planet should be, not like the desolate lava balls and crater-faced lumps in the last several star-systems. This planet practically screamed, "Shore leave!" and Bill Wilker was ready to take up that cry.

"I should lead a reconnaissance team down to the surface," Cmdr. Wilker barked to the Captain. "Check it out. Take some readings. Scan it." He wondered if those blue oceans looked as enticing up close as they looked on the viewscreen. He wouldn't mind a swim.

"Easy, Commander," the captain meowed. He was a Sphinx cat, and his naked pink ears twisted about, as if he could pick up clues about the planet by listening closely to every sound happening on the bridge of the starship *T.G.N. Initiative*. Though, clearly, the only way to really get a handle on a beautiful planet like that was to set paw to ground.

Still, Cmdr. Wilker respected his captain for being cautious. He was a smart cat. That's why he was the captain.

Captain Pierre Jacques made the rounds on the bridge, leaning over each junior officer's shoulder in turn to see the readings at their stations.

"Come on," Cmdr. Wilker said. "They've all reported. It's safe. We should send a team down."

Captain Jacques' pink and gray skinned tail lashed. He leaned closer into the station manned by a black cat and pointed at her commscreen with a claw. "There," he meowed. "What's that? It looks like life signs."

The black cat confirmed, "Yes, those are probably some sort of tree or other vegetation—unusually complex for plant-life, but clearly chlorophyll-based—."

The captain paced the bridge, and a rumble rose in his throat, not clearly a purr or a growl. That meant he was about to authorize the reconnaissance team. Cmdr. Wilker knew it. He knew his captain better than anyone.

Cmdr. Wilker looked again at the beautiful sphere on the bridge's main viewscreen, readying himself for the captain's order. Then the screen fell dark.

All the lights went out.

The bridge of the *T.G.N. Initiative* had gone as dark as the space surrounding it.

Junior officers meowed and barked, filling the darkness with a cacophony of interrogative uncertainty, but Cmdr. Wilker's strong, calm bark rose above it, silencing the rest: "Captain, what do we do?"

The air on the bridge chuckled, a deep, resonant sound that Cmdr. Wilker could feel vibrating the very deck under his paws. Then a shining crescent appeared in the darkness on the viewscreen, split down the middle, showing itself to be an eerie, disembodied cat's grin, and said, "Don't ask *him*. He's a trivial, unimportant feline. Ask *me*." The glowing form of a feline body—pink, purple, and swirly, dressed in a shimmering toga—took shape around the crescent grin. "I'm Questor; bow to me, mortals."

"I bow to no cat!" Cmdr. Wilker barked, but when he saw Captain Jacques' reflective eyes glaring at him in the dull pink glow from the viewscreen, he ducked his head and apologized, "I'm sorry; I should let you handle this, Captain."

In the midst of chaos, Captain Jacques remained one cool cat: "Greetings, Questor. I'm Captain Pierre Jacques of the Tri-Galactic Navy Ship *Initiative*. We're on a voyage of peaceful discovery. Your transmission seems to have coincided with a loss of control on my bridge. If your transmission is the cause of my ship's system failures, please rescind any effect you may be having on my ship so that we may converse *peaceably*."

Cmdr. Wilker wished he could keep his cool like that. *One. Cool. Cat.*

But Questor wasn't having any of it. He rolled his eyes dramatically, sighed, and then the image of his body on the viewscreen stepped surreally down onto the bridge, taking physical form. He was followed by dancing lights that flitted about, throwing colorful shadows in every which direction.

"Of *course*, I'm the cause," Questor intoned. "I am the day. I am the night. I am the stars. I am your god." He circled around the captain, finally stopping in front of him, nose to nose; captain to strange visitation; cat to cat. "Bow to me."

A lesser cat's ears would have flattened in irritation, but the captain was not a lesser cat. Apparently, neither was Questor. He clicked his claws, and his shimmering toga was instantly replaced by a Tri-Galactic Navy admiral's uniform. "I order you to bow to me."

"You are no admiral," the captain returned, and the two cats descended into rapid-fire verbal sparring. Cmdr. Wilker was fascinated by their stand-off, but he recognized Capt. Jacques' strategy—this was intentional distraction. While the cats argued, Cmdr. Wilker edged his way to the back of the bridge and conferred in whispers with several junior officers in sequence: the black cat confirmed that while her bridge console wasn't working, Questor showed no life-signs on her handheld unimeter—more like a rip or twist in space; Lieutenant Natalie Vonn, the yellow lab security officer, offered to attack Questor, with her blazor or bare-pawed, since the black cat thought shooting energy at an energy life form might be a bad idea.

"You know what?" Cmdr. Wilker said. "Let's risk it. You've got your blazor; use it."

The black cat rolled her eyes, but Lt. Vonn said, "Yes sir!" and pulled out her blazor.

Before she'd even pointed the weapon at Questor, the mauve-furred cat raised his voice and said, "Not so fast." Questor's slitted eyes flashed like twin pulsars, and Lt. Vonn disappeared. One moment there was a yellow lab holding a blazor; the next, she was simply gone.

"What the hell have you done with my officer!" Captain Jacques yowled, finally losing his cool.

Questor gestured carelessly to the ship's viewscreen behind him, and an image appeared of a naked feral dog, cowering and whimpering behind bars. The poor creature looked like Lt. Vonn would have if dogs and cats had never been uplifted—four-legged, wild, able only to bark and howl without meaning. "I sent her to another universe… one more appropriate to her level of *civilization*."

The image disappeared, and Cmdr. Wilker felt a horrible sense of relief. He knew she was still suffering, but he couldn't help his sense of relief at not having to see it. *So awful.* "Bring her back!" Cmdr. Wilker barked. "You can send me instead!"

Captain Jacques held out his paws as if trying to hold down and steady the situation. "Clearly, you are powerful," he said to Questor. "Bring back my officer; restore power to my ship; and let us start again. My crew is on a mission to discover new life forms, and you are possibly the most fascinating one we've ever seen—"

"I'm not a life form. I'm a god. Bow to me. *Pray to me.*" Questor's Cheshire grin shone like a newly discovered crescent moon—it was filled with danger and unknown risks.

"We are an enlightened people," the captain said reasonably. "We've evolved past the need for superstitions like gods and prayer."

Questor seemed amused. "Evolved? Enlightened?" he asked. "You think you don't… *need* me."

"Of course, we don't need you," the captain agreed. "But we'd be very interested in getting to know you. Learning about each other. *Once you return my officer.*"

Questor rolled his eyes dramatically and waved a paw. Lt. Vonn reappeared suddenly, still in the act of aiming her blazor. She fired at Questor, but the energy bolt passed harmlessly through him and scorched the deck behind him.

"See?" Questor intoned. "*Uncivilized.*" He glared at the yellow lab with her blazor, and she whimpered like a puppy rather than a Tri-Galactic Navy security officer. Cmdr. Wilker wondered how much she remembered of what Questor had done to her, sending her to that horrible alternate universe.

"Now that you have your *precious* officer back," Questor said as his body faded eerily away, leaving only his grinning teeth. "Let's see how much you *don't need* me." The teeth winked out like stars dying, and the actual stars returned to the viewscreen, studding the velvet black sky around that goddamned beautiful blue-green planet. All of the bridge's stations came back online with blinking lights and reassuring beeps.

But then the stars on the viewscreen swirled, and the blue-green world spun away like a ball flying far, far out of reach. Cmdr. Wilker's heart raced at the sight; every fiber of his being shouted that he had to help his captain get their ship back to that planet.

The terrier at the pilot's station barked, "Captain, we're spinning out of control, and we're gaining speed!"

"That's obvious," Captain Jacques grumbled. "Can you at least keep track of where we're going"?

"The computer will store the data necessary to calculate our location…" As the pilot terrier spoke, the swirling stars slowed, and a golden-orange nebula grew on the viewscreen until it engulfed them. The ship came to rest with the crenulated dust of the nebula glittering dully all around. The terrier's triangular ears drooped, and he shook his bearded face. "…but without a fix on the stars, it could take days to process the data."

There were no stars visible. Only nebula.

"Set a course out of the nebula," Cmdr. Wilker barked, shooting his captain a quick look to make sure that he approved. It was the obvious move. He might as well take care of it, giving his captain extra time to think.

Unfortunately, an hour later, the nebula dust was just as thick, and the captain was deep in thought, sitting in his captain's chair. His eyes were closed so he could focus. Cmdr. Wilker was sure the little cat would have a brilliant plan when he woke up.

Two hours later, the terrier pilot barked, "There's a ship—or space station—ahead of us. It's large and mechanical. The size of a small moon. Should I give it a wide berth or approach it?"

While the captain roused himself from his deep thoughts—or possibly his shallow catnap—Cmdr. Wilker paced the deck. The foreign ship could be dangerous, but it might have important information. "Are there life signs on the ship?" Cmdr. Wilker asked.

The black cat—Lt. Libby Unari—answered in the affirmative.

"Good," the captain meowed, now fully awake. "Approach the vessel and open a communications channel." As they approached, the alien vessel grew on the viewscreen—its surfaces were triangular, giving it the overall shape of an icosahedron, but each face was riddled with bars and latticework, complex patterns of wiring, rather than a smooth hull.

Looking suddenly cheerful with his pink ears standing tall, the captain added, "Fascinating! That meddlesome Questor may have inadvertently aided us in our mission of exploration!"

Rich chuckling filled the bridge, and Questor's eerie Cheshire smile appeared on the viewscreen beside the alien vessel just long enough to say, "Don't be so sure, my dear little captain."

The terrier at the helm barked, "Sir, I'm picking up transmissions from the vessel, but they're aimed away from us—they're not answering our radio signals."

"Can we get any information from those transmissions?" the captain asked.

"They're not in a language the computer recognizes." The terrier looked really gloomy as he added, "And it probably means this ship has allies nearby."

Cmdr. Wilker looked around the bridge and saw that all the junior officers—Lt. Unari the black cat, Lt. Vonn the yellow lab, the gray tabby at the tactical station, and the shaggy poodle running scans of the nebula—looked similarly gloomy. "Hey now," he barked, his muzzle splitting into an infectious collie grin. "You say 'allies' like they're our enemies. We don't know that—they might just be calling all their buddies in to come check out the cool new ship they've met! This could be the start of an entire new alliance between the Tri-Galactic Navy and these... triangular-ball-ships."

There. That pep-talk ought to lighten everyone's spirits, Cmdr. Wilker thought, swishing his tail. And everyone *did* look a little more hopeful.

Then Lt. Unari's panel lit up and chimed with alarms. "I'm picking up an unauthorized teleportation beam..." Her black paws worked the panel, tracing the source of the beam. "And now there's an extra set of life signs... in..."

The comm-channel from engineering opened up, and they all heard the voice of chief engineer Jordan LeGuin meow, "Captain, we have an intruder down here." He sounded very stressed.

Lt. Unari looked up from her control panel, her green cat eyes troubled. "That's where the extra life signs are—engineering."

Captain Jacques gestured to Cmdr. Wilker and Lt. Vonn—"Get down there, on the double!"

The two dogs wasted no time; the collie and yellow lab jogged through the corridors of the *Initiative*, drawing their blazors as they moved. "Lowest energy setting," Cmdr. Wilker woofed as they approached the doors to engineering. "We want to try to keep this peaceful. If we can."

Lt. Vonn led the way with her blonde head low and her blazor held high. Her brush of a tail kept eerily still. She was a consummate professional, trained in three different forms of martial arts. Cmdr. Wilker would have trusted her with his life, but he hoped he wouldn't have to.

Inside engineering, the various canine and feline junior officers had backed around the edges of the room, many ducked behind the zephyr drive coils that pulsed with soft blue light. In the middle of the room, Lt. Jordan LeGuin—an orange tabby wearing techno-focal goggles and with fur fluffed out so far his tail looked like a bottle brush—was hissing and spitting at a segmented figure twice his size that was messing with the central control pylon that reached from the floor to the high ceiling of engineering.

At first, Cmdr. Wilker thought the intruder was wearing body armor, but as he stared at the smooth, gun-metal gray plating of the segmented body, he realized that he was looking at a creature that was truly alien: exoskeleton, at least six limbs, a mandibled face with hundreds of wriggling mouth parts, and glittering domes of compound eyes—this was an arthropoidal alien.

No one would have uplifted a hideous creature like that. Would they? No—this species had to have evolved to sentience by itself. But the Tri-Galactic Navy was out here to contact alien life, and this intruder certainly counted.

Cmdr. Wilker held out one paw and lowered the blazor in his other, knowing that Lt. Vonn still had him covered. "We're on a mission of peace," he barked. "Please, you've taken us by surprise. Come with me, and speak to our captain. Our people could learn so much from each other."

The alien emitted a sound like fireworks, whistling and crackling bursts that the ship's computer was apparently unable to translate. Then another pair of limbs unfolded from the alien's body, bringing the total count up to at least eight. These arms hinged like a praying mantis's, but they spewed shiny sticky silk like a spider's spinnerets. The stream of gooey material knocked Lt. LeGuin to the deck, glommed onto his orange fur, dripped over his uniform, and stuck him firmly to the floor.

"Fire!" Cmdr. Wilker barked, and Lt. Vonn's blazor blared. The energy beam bounced off of the alien's metallic carapace and hit one of the zephyr drive coils, breaking it. The yellow lab launched herself bodily towards the insectoid intruder, but before she could lay paws on it, a stream of sticky silk hit her hind paws, and she found herself glued in place.

This fight was not going well. As Cmdr. Wilker knelt down to check on Lt. LeGuin, the alien returned to messing with the central control pylon. Lt. LeGuin was clearly shaken and might need his fur shaved to unstick him from the floor, but he seemed otherwise unharmed. Cmdr. Wilker needed a new strategy for dealing with this alien.

Lt. LeGuin whispered to Cmdr. Wilker, "You need to get the alien away from that pylon. It could damage the hyper crystal that powers the zephyr drive."

Cmdr. Wilker looked up at the arthropoid and considered his options. Lt. Vonn had ruled out blazor attacks and paw-to-paw combat for him. It wouldn't do any good to draw the alien's ire and get himself stuck to the deck like his security officer and chief engineer.

Unless... If he turned off the artificial gravity, then spewing silk would jet the alien backwards, away from the central control pylon.

Unfortunately, before Cmdr. Wilker could open his muzzle to tell the computer to shut off the gravity in engineering, the arthropoidal alien succeeded in jimmying open the panel on the front of the towering pylon. It reached into the opening with fearsome claws and grabbed the glowing yellow crystal from its chamber. Then the arthropoid and the hyper crystal disappeared in a shimmering field of quantum energy.

"Doggarnit!" Cmdr. Wilker barked. He tapped the comm-pin on his uniform, opening a communication channel to the bridge: "Captain, the alien has teleported away, taking our hyper crystal with it."

The captain's voice answered through the comm-pin, "It's worse than that, Commander. I've been receiving reports of intruders all over the ship—our security teams can't keep up."

"We should get out of here," Cmdr. Wilker said. He looked down at the tabby engineer stuck to the deck and asked, "Do we have any back-up crystals?"

"Two," he meowed. "In storage bays three and twelve."

"Not any more," the captain's voice responded. "They've stripped us clean of anything valuable and portable. We're dead in the water. But the good news is that they're leaving us otherwise alone."

Cmdr. Wilker didn't think that sounded like very good news. "So far," he said. "What if they come back?"

Across the room, Lt. Vonn was struggling against the gooey silk holding her in place. With a sickening sound, she pulled herself free, leaving behind most of the blonde fur from her hind paws. It looked painful, but she didn't even limp.

"Let's not give them the chance," Lt. Vonn barked. "We should launch a full scale attack—"

The captain's voice cut her off: "That's not a good idea. An entire fleet of similar vessels is on their way, and they've already stolen our entire stock of electron torpedoes."

Lt. Vonn's muzzle drew into a tight grimace, her blonde ears far back on her head. Cmdr. Wilker understood how she felt. He wanted to attack these arthropoids with all he was worth too. But he had to be smart.

"Captain, I'd like to lead a stealth mission onto the alien vessel," Cmdr. Wilker barked. "If we can steal back one of our hyper crystals, we can hot-paw our way out of here. We'll have sustained heavy losses in terms of machinery, but right now, I think we'll be lucky if we can just get out of here without any loss of life."

"I agree," the captain meowed. "Make it happen!" The communications channel to the bridge chimed off.

With the help of a junior engineer and a vibro-scalpel, Cmdr. Wilker got Lt. LeGuin unstuck from the floor. His arms sported a few bald patches, and his uniform had a few holes in it. But he could function, and Cmdr. Wilker would need the orange tabby's expertise for navigating a foreign vessel. No one knew ships like Lt. LeGuin.

Meanwhile, Lt. Vonn assembled an arsenal—she holstered a blazor rifle on one leg and an electron pulse cannon on the other. On her back, she strapped a curved, two-handed vibro-sword. She did not look like a yellow lab that you wanted to cross.

The three of them—orange tabby in techno-focal goggles, yellow lab armed to the teeth, and collie in charge—headed to the tele-bay and teleported over to the alien vessel in their own shimmering field of quantum energy. Based on their scans of the icosahedral vessel, Lt. LeGuin had picked a location for them to teleport to that he believed to be an empty maintenance bay.

There had been no life signs in the chamber, so Cmdr. Wilker's heart nearly stopped when the shimmering quantum energy cleared from his vision to show an arthropoidal alien with mouth parts squirming, staring right at him with those mounds of glittering eyes. It raised one of its spinneret arms, and Cmdr. Wilker threw himself in front of his two subordinate officers to protect them.

But instead of gooey silk, the air exploded in pink and purple confetti. When the confetti cleared, the arthropoid was gone, replaced by a pink-and-purple striped Cheshire cat, laughing hysterically on the floor.

"Oh my," Quester purred. "You should have seen your face! That loooong muzzle of yours, hanging open!" He rolled about the floor in laughter, hugging his fluffy tail to himself.

"That was not funny," Cmdr. Wilker barked. Then he remembered they were on a stealth mission and lowered his voice to say, "I thought you claimed to be a *god*. It seems to me that you're no better than a cosmic trickster, playing stupid pranks on us."

Questor's wide Cheshire grin grew suddenly serious. He picked himself up off the floor, dusted off his faux Tri-Galactic Navy uniform, and squared off against the mortal collie *questioning* him. "I am a god, and this is no prank. This is a warning. A dire warning. You think you're playing games here? These Arhcidopterans do not take kindly to intruders in their home nebula."

Cmdr. Wilker stood nearly twice Questor's height, but he suddenly felt small staring into the pink-and-purple cat's eyes. Those eyes had sparkled when he laughed, like stars dancing now they were as hard and dark as twin singularities. The anger in those eyes could suck him in and destroy them all.

Cmdr. Wilker cleared his throat and said quietly, "We didn't intrude. You sent us here."

"You think they'll care?"

An inarticulate growl of rage broke out behind the commander, and he turned to see Lt. Vonn with her hackles raised. Her paws hovered over the butts of the holstered weapons on each of her legs, but the memory of what Questor had done to her before stayed her.

Questor laughed again; the sound rolled through the air, rich and velvety. "Your guard dog has learned some manners. Let's see if you can learn something too."

Confetti filled the air again. When it cleared, vanishing as if it had never existed at all, Questor was gone too.

Cmdr. Wilker wished *Questor* had never existed at all. Then they'd all be back where they'd started—about to explore a goddamned beautiful blue-and-green world. Maybe discover some new flowers that no one had ever seen before. Maybe go for a swim and discover a brand new form of sea life.

Instead, Cmdr. Wilker led his stealth team through the winding corridors of this mechanical insect hive, ducking behind sticky cocoon-like structures whenever one of the arthropoids passed by. The walls sloped inward, meeting at a point for the ceiling. Apparently, the arthropoids really liked triangular structures.

At every junction between corridors, Cmdr. Wilker looked back at Lt. LeGuin for directions. The little orange cat scanned with his uni-meter and silently gestured which way to go.

Cmdr. Wilker's herd-dog instincts told him that he should be behind his crew, watching their backs and protecting them, but he had to trust Lt. Vonn with that role. He knew the yellow lab had them covered from the rear. Her blazor may have proved useless in the *Initiative's* engineering bay, but a blazor rifle was ten times more powerful. If that wasn't enough to protect them, the electron pulse cannon strapped to her other leg worked on an entirely different principle. A pulse from it ought to leave one of these giant insects curled on the floor, contorted by spasms of pain. If all else failed, Cmdr. Wilker knew the yellow lab was not above paw-to-claw combat, and the vibro-sword strapped to her back would be able cut them all free from sticky silk if need be.

Cmdr. Wilker knew he was leading a tight team, and they were prepared for dangerous missions. Nonetheless, he was infinitely relieved when the little orange tabby looked up from his uni-meter and said, "There's a hyper crystal in the chamber at the end of this corridor, and I'm not picking up any life signs."

Excellent, all they had to do was nab the crystal, call back to the Initiative, and teleport the hell out of here. At least, that's what Cmdr. Wilker thought until he'd poked his long collie nose through the chamber door. Except, it wasn't a small chamber on the other side; the space opened out above and around him. There were no arthropoids nearby, but he could see them flying through the open space in the distance. He hadn't realized they had wings.

Lt. LeGuin stepped up beside Cmdr. Wilker, and the wide open space in front of them reflected eerily in the lenses of his techno-focal goggles. The vessel was a hollow icosahedron—small chambers and corridors lined the outer shell of the vessel, but the heart was nearly empty. Spires rose from the walls, pointing towards the center, and a few latticed bridge-ways crisscrossed the space. Far above their heads, where the bridge-ways met in the very center of the yawning open space, a massive knot of silk like a giant cocoon pulsed, beating like a heart.

Cmdr. Wilker wondered what was inside it—a queen? a nursery? He hoped he would never find out. "You didn't detect any life signs nearby," Cmdr. Wilker woofed quietly, "but I guess you didn't detect any *walls* either."

"Woah…" Lt. LeGuin's soft voice was almost a purr. "I thought the uni-meter was malfunctioning, but it wasn't… This vessel is *amazing*."

Lt. Vonn shouldered the small cat aside and pointed her blazor rifle out at the empty space as if she could fend off an entire ship with it. "We don't have time for marveling at feats of engineering," she said. "No matter how amazing. Now where's the crystal?"

Lt. LeGuin lifted his uni-meter to scan again; the device's screen flickered with yellow and green lights. Then the orange tabby pointed at a bulkhead to their left built like a metallic honeycomb. "It's over there."

Cmdr. Wilker put his paws to the metal surface, expecting it to be cold, but it was warm against his paw pads. He felt around the edges until one paw slipped into a groove. He pressed in, then pulled outward. The honeycomb panel came off in his paws. Underneath, the hyper crystal glowed, bathing the alien landscape in soft comforting light—the light of the crystal that would take them home.

"Careful," Lt. LeGuin meowed. "They've already wired it into their own machinery."

"Is that a problem?" Lt. Vonn asked.

Cmdr. Wilker eyed the crystal warily. It didn't *look* like it would be hard to remove.

"It means that when we take it out, whatever it's powering will shut down." The little cat's words were matter-of-fact, but they carried a heavy weight.

"Right," Cmdr. Wilker said. "So we need to be ready to teleport out of here on the double." He put a paw to the comm-pin on his navy uniform to call back to the *Initiative* and let them know to be ready. The comm-pin clicked, but the *Initiative* didn't respond. "Is something blocking the signal?" Cmdr. Wilker asked.

Lt. LeGuin checked his uni-meter; red and yellow lights chased each other over its screen. "Maybe. There is a strong electro-magnetic field here."

"Can you counteract it?"

The lights on the uni-meter screen reflected off Lt. LeGuin's techno-focal goggles, and tiny lines of blue text streamed across the goggles' lenses, combining with the reflections in a dance of colors. After a minute or two, Lt. LeGuin said, "It's not working, but I've located the quantum energy trace of a tele-bay on this vessel. If we can't tell the *Initiative* to teleport us home, we may be able to teleport ourselves from there."

Lt. Vonn grumbled. Her blonde ears were far back on her head, and the black skin of her mouth was set in a tight grimace. The fur around her collar was standing up, all prickly.

"How far is the tele-bay?" Cmdr. Wilker asked. He could tell that Lt. Vonn was picturing how dangerous it would be for them to fight their way out of here; he didn't like the idea of fighting their way through an army of arthropoids on their own turf any better than she did. But if they could just get back to the *Initiative*, it would all be okay.

Then a purring voice whispered in Cmdr. Wilker's ear, warm breath stirring the long fur of his ruff, "Or will it?" It was Questor's voice, and the eerie shape of that crescent moon grin followed it. Those shining teeth hovered by Cmdr. Wilker's ear, far too close for comfort, and whispered again, "Are you sure that your communications are malfunctioning? Or is it possible that something has... *happened*... to the rest of your crew?"

Irritated, Cmdr. Wilker snapped, "Is this how gods behave? They torment and taunt?" The collie was trapped on an alien vessel with a critical mission to accomplish. He did not have time for this cat's games.

Pink and purple tabby swirls materialized around Questor's grin, looking as much out of place in this giant honeycombed chamber as they had on the *Initiative*'s bridge. The odd cat had disposed of his faux admiral's uniform, returning to the shimmering toga he'd first appeared in. He was also lying across the air, hovering several feet about the ground. He stretched and rolled in the air, as if he were nothing more than a cat sun-bathing on the beach. Perfectly normal. Perfectly bizarre.

Questor stepped down from his invisible couch and stood on the ground, looking up at the much taller collie. "You hurt me, dear mortal. I'm not *taunting* you. I'm *warning* you."

"You use that word a lot," Cmdr. Wilker said. "Yet, I don't see how that was a warning."

The Cheshire cat sniffed and took several steps away. When he looked back, already fading into transparency, he said, "If you'd rather return to a ship full of cocoons with no plan for how to handle the situation, *be my guest*." His voice was hard and cruel by the final words, and their sound echoed after the sight of his shining teeth had entirely disappeared.

"I wonder what that meant," Lt. Vonn woofed, but before Cmdr. Wilker could say anything in response, the yellow lab disappeared in a shimmer of quantum energy. Lt. LeGuin followed a moment later, and then Cmdr. Wilker felt the warm numbness of quantum teleportation begin to tingle in his own chest. He flung himself at the honeycomb panel and ripped the hyper crystal free of its wiring, consequences be damned.

To his own eyes, it looked like the alien vessel around him blew apart in a million tiny shards, though it was really his own atoms and particles that tunneled through space to where the *Initiative's* tele-bay, in all its comforting familiarity, reformed around him. The solid weight of the hyper crystal, still grasped in his paws, made Cmdr. Wilker feel profoundly grateful.

To who? he wondered. This was the kind of moment when one might thank the gods for letting him return home, mission successful. Yet it was a god—ostensibly—who had put him and the *Initiative's* crew in danger in the first place.

No, Questor was not a god.

Or was he?

Thoughts for another time, Cmdr. Wilker told himself firmly. He held the glowing crystal out to Lt. LeGuin and said, "Get this crystal back to engineering." He turned to Lt. Vonn and said, "Escort him there. I'm heading to the bridge."

"Here, take this." Lt. Vonn pulled a hidden vibro-dagger from her boot and held it out to the collie.

"Thanks," Cmdr. Wilker said, hoping he wouldn't need it. He watched the yellow lab, with her blazor rifle held ready, follow the little orange tabby out of the tele-bay and into the corridor. That Lt. Vonn sure as hell was one prepared dog. Cmdr. Wilker admired that.

On his way to the bridge, Cmdr. Wilker tried several times to contact the captain—or any bridge crew—with his comm-pin. No answer. But he pushed his worry aside and kept hurrying through the halls.

He saw a cocoon—just like Questor had warned—stuck to one of the corridor walls. Then two more. It was only a few of them, but they were the right size to hold a dog or cat. It took every bit of Cmdr. Wilker's willpower to pass those cocoons by, hurrying on to the bridge instead of stopping to tear the hideous silk away with his vibro-dagger and release whatever—*whoever*—might be trapped inside.

He could do more good on the bridge, Cmdr. Wilker told himself. Once Lt. LeGuin got that hyper crystal hooked up, someone had to pilot the *Initiative* out of here. When the ship was safe, then Cmdr. Wilker could worry about the crew.

No matter what Questor had said, no matter what Cmdr. Wilker had seen in the halls, he still wasn't prepared for what he found on the bridge. The corridors had been almost eerily quiet—without the ship's alarms blaring, Cmdr. Wilker had dared hope that all would be well on the bridge. It was not.

The door to the bridge slid open, and a squealing screech like a chainsaw cutting through metal filled the air. Two of the arthropoid aliens skittered and zipped through the room, occasionally opening their wings to fly short hops. The bridge felt very small with two large insects buzzing around it, nearly bouncing off the ceiling and walls.

A third arthropoid near the back of the bridge was carefully, patiently wrapping a struggling black cat—Lt. Unari—inside a cocoon, stretching the shimmery strands of silk around her using four different angular limbs. The terrier at the pilot's station had already been replaced by a squirming silk cocoon, and the remaining science officers on the bridge—a spaniel and two more cats—were stuck to the wall behind their stations like flies in a web. *But where was the captain?*

A red bolt of blazor fire streaked across the bridge. The energy bolt hit one of the arthropoids in its wing, and the alien shrieked in pain. Another bolt of energy struck the arthropoid in its antenna, breaking the appendage and leaving it dangling.

Based on where the blazor fire was coming from, the captain had to be hiding behind one of the consoles. As Cmdr. Wilker watched, the small Sphynx cat jumped from behind the console, tucked into a roll, and then ducked behind the cocoon at the pilot's station. He started firing again immediately, but he only aimed at the aliens' peripheral appendages—antennae, wings, the claws at the end of their limbs—anything but the smooth metallic carapace that had simply reflected Lt. Vonn's blazor fire earlier.

This explained why two of the aliens were buzzing around the bridge like crazed hornets. They were trying to capture the captain. From where he stood, Cmdr. Wilker couldn't tell who was winning. He raised his own blazor, ready to assist the captain, but before he could fire, the two bugs fell onto the captain in a way that made the score much more clear. In a flurry of strangely-jointed legs, the arthropoids wrapped the captain in silk. Within moments, the fight was over.

A burning rage inside Cmdr. Wilker told him to bark and howl and gun these insects down, but that wouldn't help the captain. One more cocoon on the bridge wouldn't get the Initiative out of here.

The arthropoids hadn't seen Cmdr. Wilker, so the collie stepped slowly away. As he left the bridge, his gaze fell on the viewscreen: the *Initiative* was surrounded by icosahedral ships. Even if he had control of his own vessel, it would mean a space battle to get out of here.

Cmdr. Wilker didn't have a plan yet, but he kept moving, heading instinctively toward engineering. That was the heart of the vessel. With the bridge lost, he should be down there. Maybe, he thought, Lt. LeGuin could find a way to reroute the ship's controls and pilot it from engineering.

It would probably help to have a few more paws on their side, so Cmdr. Wilker stopped at the next cocoon he saw and hacked into the sticky shell of silk with his vibro-dagger. What he found underneath dropped him to his knees, and the vibro-dagger fell out of his paw, clattering to the floor. He had imagined the cocoons to be some sort of stasis—a way to neutralize enemies. Nothing more. He had been so wrong.

The officer inside the gashed open cocoon had been a calico cat, but she wasn't any more. Her furry ears with their orange-and-black splotches were unchanged, as was the splish of white fur that ran down to her pink feline nose. Her eyes though… her golden cat's eyes had split and multiplied into unholy domes of facets. A pair of many-jointed antennae rose between her ears, and wriggling nubs and feelers had grown around the edges of her mouth. She was no longer a cat. She wasn't quite yet an arthropoid. Is that what she would become if Cmdr. Wilker left her here? How far gone was the rest of the crew? If he got them home, could the Tri-Galactic Navy doctors reverse this horrific process?

Was there anything left on the *Initiative* worth saving?

All was lost.

Cmdr. Wilker threw his head back and howled. Eventually, the howl took the form of a name, and Cmdr. Wilker cried all his anguish into the one word, "QUESTOR!!!" The meddling feline might not be a god, but Cmdr. Wilker could curse him like one.

As the collie's howl died away into a heartbroken whimper, the air around him tinkled and chimed like it was filled with invisible bells. "You *called?*" The Cheshire cat's voice sounded like a smile, even when that eerie crescent of teeth was nowhere in sight.

Cmdr. Wilker's vibro-dagger rose from the floor as if lifted by an invisible paw. It floated up to the gashed cocoon and begin skillfully cutting the silk away, dancing merrily through the air, seemingly of its own accord.

The disturbing hybrid creature beneath the silk still wore her Tri-Galactic Navy uniform, but it had been torn where two extra pairs of angular limbs had burst through the fabric. The limbs were shaped like an arthropoid's many-jointed arms, but they were covered with orange-and-white splotched fur. When the last of the cocoon's silk fell away from the hybrid creature, Cmdr. Wilker was horrified to watch the calico-that-was step away from the cocoon and begin twirling through the corridor, moving as if she were jerked about by marionette strings.

Questor's disembodied voice purred, "The Archidopterans do lovely work, don't they?"

A strangled sound escaped from Cmdr. Wilker's throat. It was the only sound he could muster as a reply.

"Cat got your tongue?" Questor asked, his crescent grin finally glinting into view. "Of course, you won't have a tongue much longer—once you're an Archidopteran, you'll probably have a proboscis or some such. Delightful, isn't it?"

Questor's pink-and-purple feline body, still dressed in a shimmery toga, took form around his grin. When he was fully opaque and solid, Questor stepped up to the calico-that-was, grasped one of her bizarre insect claws in his own paw, placed another paw between her various limbs, approximately at her waist, and they began to waltz.

It was hideous. But also upsettingly graceful.

"Help us," Cmdr. Wilker woofed, so quietly he didn't expect his tormentor to hear.

"What's that?" Questor meowed, still dancing. "Do what?"

"Help us," Cmdr. Wilker repeated, woofing louder. "You sent us here; you can send us home."

"My dear puppy-dog," Questor meowed, finally stopping his waltz. "I can do so much more." He clapped his paws, and in a flash of light, the hybrid creature beside him returned to her original form—a calico cat in a pristine Tri-Galactic Navy uniform. "All you have to do is accept me as your god and pray to me."

"*Please*," Cmdr. Wilker barked, beseeching Questor with all his heart. "*Help us.*"

Questor's ears flattened, and his eyes flashed. He clapped his paws again, and the calico cat returned to her hybrid form. "That's not what I want, and you know it!" he meowed, sounding more like a petulant kitten than a supreme being. "Don't plead. *Pray.*"

In exasperation, the collie cried, "What's the difference?" The fate of his fellow officers—every dog and cat on the *Initiative*—depended on this whimsical feline, and Cmdr. Wilker didn't understand what he wanted. Was it a question of semantics? If he spoke eloquently enough, could he persuade Questor to save them? The captain was so much more eloquent in his speech… Why couldn't it be the captain here, instead of him?

Or could Questor see into his heart and tell that Cmdr. Wilker still doubted that the Cheshire cat was anything more than a troublesome, powerful, space anomaly?

Cmdr. Wilker wasn't a religious dog, but he believed in forces greater than himself. He knew who had uplifted his people, raising them from mere feral animals and guiding them into sentience, giving them the gift of a civilization among the stars. And it wasn't this Cheshire cat.

"Would it help you to believe in me," Questor asked, "if I looked like this?"

Cmdr. Wilker didn't know if Questor could see into his heart, but it seemed as though he had read the collie's thoughts. The swirly stripes of pink-and-purple fur, the wide Cheshire grin, the triangular ears—all gone. Questor stood before Cmdr. Wilker in a new form—an ancient form actually. Brown hair topped his head, but his face was naked skin, like the captain's. Instead of a muzzle, his flat face sported a nub of a nose and thin, smiling lips over flat teeth.

Cmdr. Wilker had seen paintings, statues, holograms—but he had never seen a real human in the flesh. His heart opened in a way he'd never felt before, a way that felt completely natural and right. This was who he owed his love and loyalty to; this was who had designed him. He bowed his head before the human Questor and said in the simplest, sincerest woof: "Please, my god, help me."

Questor laid his human hand on the crown of Cmdr. Wilker's head and patted it twice. His long fingers scratched behind Cmdr. Wilker's ear, tangling in the thick fur of his mane, and the collie's tail began to wag, an instinctive response to his master's love and praise.

"That's a good dog," Questor said in a fluting voice, much smoother than his previous feline meow. Then light flashed all around, and suddenly Questor was gone. Only his voice remained, a lingering whisper in Cmdr. Wilker's ear: "*Don't forget me.*"

Cmdr. Wilker rose to his feet, feeling disoriented. He was on the bridge. The cobwebs of silk were gone. So were the cocoons. All of the bridge officers stood at their stations, perfectly normal cats and dogs with their ears flattened or twisting about in confusion.

When Cmdr. Wilker looked at the viewscreen, the icosahedral ships and the thick nebula dust were gone. They were back in clear, empty space, and the goddamned beautiful blue-green world hung in front of them like a gift—a ball his master had fetched. It looked even more goddamned beautiful than before.

"What the hell happened?" Captain Jacques meowed. "Where'd the big bugs go? And where's that damnable purple cat?"

Cmdr. Wilker wanted to pretend nothing had happened. Now that Questor was gone, he felt a strange shame over his feelings and actions. Even if he had saved the ship by praying to Questor, he was a Tri-Galactic Navy officer and should be above *begging*. Still, the captain deserved an answer.

"Questor sent us home," Cmdr. Wilker woofed.

The captain's naked ears stood tall and straight with surprise. "Really? Why?"

Cmdr. Wilker's tail tucked between his legs as he said, "I told him he was a god and prayed to him."

The captain must not have noticed his first officer's shame, for he exclaimed, "How clever! You must have done a masterful job of convincing him. Well done, Bill."

For the first time, the captain's praise felt thin and hollow to Cmdr. Wilker. It was probably just how shaken he felt—the last few hours had been very upsetting. He would feel better soon.

"Do you think he'll come back?" the terrier pilot asked.

The captain turned to the row of science officers and said, "Let's put together a science team to analyze the ship's data from our encounter with him. Perhaps we can come up with counter measures to contain and control him if he does."

Cmdr. Wilker hoped that would work, but in case it didn't, he added a silent prayer to Questor: "*We're okay now. Please, leave us alone.*" He didn't know if that would work either.

"You look exhausted," the captain said to Cmdr. Wilker, placing a furless paw on the collie's shoulder. "Would you like a break? Go to your quarters and get some rest?"

Cmdr. Wilker considered the offer carefully, but before he could respond, Lt. Unari said, "Captain, we're receiving a video-communication from the planet."

"Can you put it on the main viewscreen?" Captain Jacques asked.

Moments later, the image of the blue-green world was replaced by the image of a grinning, green-furred, otteroid.

"I thought you said there was only plant-life on this world?" Captain Jacques asked Lt. Unari.

The black cat looked at her computer scans, back up at the viewscreen, and then back at the computer scans. "I think that creature *is* plant life— sentient photosynthetics."

Looking more closely, Cmdr. Wilker realized that the otteroid's spiky green fur looked very grass-like.

"Welcome to our world," the otteroid said, and everyone on the bridge drew a sigh of relief that the computer was able to automatically translate her language. *So much better than insects that screamed like inarticulate chainsaws.* "We have a wide range of recreational opportunities available—especially if you enjoy water sports." She gestured behind herself and Cmdr. Wilker realized the green otter was standing in front of a waterfall, cascading water into an intricately-winding complex of live trees that had been grown into the shape of water slides. *It was the most fun-looking thing he'd ever seen.* "And we welcome visitors."

This was how a mission was supposed to go. No gods, just happy aliens and fun times. "We should send a team down," Cmdr. Wilker woofed to his captain, tail swishing eagerly. "I'd be *happy* to lead it."

Do you know Norse mythology? Do you really know Norse mythology?

Fenrir the giant wolf, the Father of Wolves, Odin's Bane, is a favorite villain of Norse mythology. Here is his story, from his point of view.

Fenrir's Saga

by Televassi

Yes, skald, you speak of me, but you never get my story right. The tales of Fenrir stink as soon as you give them a sniff. Why would the gods keep a ferocious wolf in their home; one that was predicted to kill Odin? No one is that stupid. How was Fenrir tricked into allowing himself to be shackled not once, but *three* times? I'm not enough of a beast to fall into a trap; I never needed to break some chains just to prove to them my strength.

I can smell your questions, story-teller: 'why didn't the gods just kill me?' Do you really believe that the gods didn't want to defile their holy places by spilling blood? I know the answer - it's an in-joke between them all. Asgard's foundations are soaked with the stuff. As for my bound state now? I don't believe that Gleipnir is so strong because it was forged from the sound of a cat's footfall.

Let me tell you three things. I know I didn't take Tyr's hand; he was my friend. I know my vengeance will be the end of Odin's world. 'Ragnarok' is what he calls it, but he has such an ego to think that his death will be the end of everything. Finally, if Vithar—that pathetic *runt*—tries to stop me? I'll have crunched his skull into powder by the time I'm done with him.

But to the telling! You may not have the wolf's nose to sniff out lies, but I promise to speak the truth. The problem with prophecies is that those who see them believe them to be true. This is why I am called the Father of Wolves, and how I came into conflict with the All Father, Odin. It's time everyone knew the secrets of the gods.

* * *

Fate rarely gives what you want; I've always wanted children. There are two ways to do that. The first is like mortals, but with magical beings it has unpredictable results. Loki, my deadbeat father, is a great example. He sired

225

me from a bout of sex whilst trying on his wolf shape with some Vanir witch who was into that. When I was born—a fully formed wolf, complete with fangs and fur - she abandoned me.

Like all misbegotten things I found my way to the Ironwood, a wild edge of creation that made a fine hunting ground, but it was not a place that promised a desirable mate. It was a realm that harbored wild and fierce things under its twisted branches and decaying trees. I loved how the icy wind swept through my fur, and hearing the wordless silence of the creaking boughs, and above all, hunting, chasing, killing any trespasser.

I was always aware that the forest would not satisfy my wants. A wolf has to range far if he wishes to find a mate, so when I was suddenly pulled, kicking and screaming through the void, to Asgard, home of the gods, I could smell the second option.

Now I haven't forgotten myself; the second way to make children is by runes, words of raw power that can do extraordinary things. Using them would be less unpredictable, and most importantly would let me shape my children to my will. I'll tell you a secret. Despite my wolfishness, I've always envied men—how you stand tall, how you have hands that can make wonderful things. I wanted my children to be like you; wolves but human—all the best bits. I needed runes for that, and Asgard held them. That is where my tale begins in earnest.

I lay on the stone floor and wrinkled my nose, folding my tongue up over my snout. Ugh! It stank here! Of sweat, of stale ale, rot, mold… but underneath them there was something, like the power in the air after a thunderbolt, or the energy in a howling wind.

Before I had time to investigate that smell, two figures advanced upon me. They were formless to my sight, nothing but shadows, moving like men but with the manner of beasts. One seemed to have something equine to its gait, the other one strode like a deer. They smelled like something impossible, like the thunder of a waterfall. I slunk back against the wall, snarling and baring my fangs, but they didn't flinch. They lunged for me and I tried to bolt between them, but their hands closed around me, crushing me. Their strength was something else—I couldn't even wriggle in their grip.

They pulled me into a golden hall that gleamed like the sun. I stared at the vaulted ceiling and sharp gables, too used to seeing the boughs of trees sprawling out in chaotic directions. This was something entirely else to me. Everything here was controlled, everything had a strict place, and it smelled of that strange power too.

I first saw him on a golden throne - a wolf, but bigger, more muscular, and with sharper fangs. He wasn't like me. He had the shape of a man, but perfected with a wolf's frame. I burnt with jealousy; he had hands instead of paws, a slender muzzle suited for speech, a broad chest—even his hind legs were lengthened so he would never skulk about the earth on all fours. He was a noble creature. I was nothing, a common animal, but an animal who knew my nature well. He wore his wolfishness like an ill-fitting cloak; his ears were lifeless stubs of flesh that stood motionless atop his head, his snout never twitched at tell-tale scents that were floating about the hall, his tail was limp, and his hackles…I could go on.

"Behold Asgard, centre of the nine realms, and the golden hearth of the Aesir. You stand before Odin, the All-Father, Delight of Frigg, Eagle-Head, Mighty God, Lord of the Earth, Battle Wolf, and Lord of the Aesir." He paused to take a breath. "For this time alone, I will forgive you for not kneeling." He bowed his head—faintly.

From the way he kept stealing a glance at me from the corner of his eyes, I knew he tracked me like prey. I think he expected me to be overawed by the surroundings, but I had no care for such gaudy things; I wished only to crunch them up with my teeth, knowing they were his.

"I offer an apology for the manner of your arrival. Thor has never recognised his own strength," he chuckled, his lips pulling back to reveal the tips of his fangs. I looked behind me, but there was no one there.

"I have heard tales of you; my ravens have flown all across the realms. I've heard mortals who whisper, calling you the 'Father of Wolves.'" He bowed his head as if to honor the title. I would have laughed if I had not suspected that the invisible brute 'Thor' lurked behind me. His breath stank of carrion. "Quite the splendid title, I must say." It was poor flattery—the way his hackles began to bristle betrayed him. Oh, he *hated* a rival.

"It seems a shame for such a wolf-god to have no hall of his own." Behind his black lips, his fangs were yellow and crooked—used too much for speaking, not enough biting. I decided it was best to put my tongue to speech, resistance no longer lay best in silence.

"A wolf cares nothing for the nine realms. I am of the Ironwood; you would call that a home. The forest is my hall, and it's where I only care to be." I let the words fall from my tongue like leaves shed in autumn; no matter what mortals wish, the truth they heralded was that winter was coming. "Your words are sweet-smelling, yet they are but vapors to me—they are no meat when I try to bite them." I think Odin realised I was sharp then, at least in the way a predatory beast is. My words cut both ways—in showing my disdain for titles I'd given him a veiled insult. He seemed to like that.

"You cannot reject what you don't know. Do you wonder what power keeps the winds and snows at bay here, what fuels the hall's hearth-fires, or what power pulled you here?"

He'd clearly not spent long as a wolf—the wind and whirl-rain are nothing when clothed in a thick pelt, but I sensed that a point lay at the end of his speech so I held my tongue.

"All through beloved Ironwood you have run, but you never found a she-wolf to lie with. The thought of feral children displeases you, does it not?

Dumb, brutish beasts, shadows of yourself." He laughed softly. "You seek something like me, don't you? Something tall-backed and towering?" He stood up, grasping his spear beside him, and on two legs slowly stepped down towards me. His claws made no sound. "I will give you what you crave—a suitable means to sire your children. In return, I ask for your word, so I know you bear no ill-will." With a claw, he pulled away at a tangled knot of fur underneath his muzzle. "It is only an oath; an honorable promise," he explained.

"Do you think I'm a liar?" I snapped, crunching my teeth together. The sound echoed through the hall. "If you want a demonstration of loyalty, I'd happily prove myself against your enemies," I growled, licking my fangs. I always enjoyed the prospect of blood; all battles were really a chase in the end.

"We are not at war," Odin snorted, shaking his head. "I would not have a new conflict bubble up on a beast's whim. A simple oath, one sworn in the runic tongue, will do."

Hearing that, I felt cold. I was so blind. With every word Odin had set a snare; now he clasped it around my throat and he dared me to seal it shut, else he'd just kill me.

"I'll swear it," I said, feigning a smile. My compliance meant nothing—I was young, I was too much the hunter, never the prey. It is not a wolf's nature to know how to evade a snare, and I couldn't see a way out from this one.

"I see no reason to delay," Odin stated, marching forward. There was a malevolent glint to his yellow eyes, and he swung his tail slowly back and forth behind him with all the arrogance of someone who had gotten their way. I hated the way he looked down at me; a triumphant sneer pulling at the corners of his muzzle.

"Shall we begin?" he asked, rubbing his victory in. Despite my anger, some part of me was eager to see how runes were cast. Though I smelled their power here, it was like a drop of ink washed down a stream, so diluted you cannot see the colour.

With a different voice, one that spoke inside every corner of my body, I heard it.

"Ehwaz!"

Instantly, Odin's breath smelled like the thunder of a waterfall. Somehow I felt the word pull on my soul. My eyes became entranced by Odin's as he stood there, the locks of his grey mane billowing about him. I felt sick, I felt lightheaded, and no matter how much I willed it, my body would do nothing.

Growing numb, I dimly felt Odin's hand, his touch filling the air with the scent of singed hair, even though there were no flames. Lightning sparked from between the tips of his claws, writhing between the hairs of my pelt like serpents. They burrowed like worms into my flesh. I howled as he pierced me, arcing towards my soul, searing everything he touched, rewriting my nerves. I cried. I curled my tail. I whined. I was a fool to think I'd only speak some words! I understood what *Ehwaz* was. It was a rune, with the power to force me into slavery.

I remember Odin's sneer as he left his mark. I was his—no longer a wolf, but his pet, his dog. When he released me, I collapsed on the floor. The great hall didn't seem so golden then. My claws skittered across the stone as I writhed haplessly, instinct firing my nerves, trying to outrun the pain.

I shut my eyes when I felt tears come. I had been robbed. My freedom was gone. I was no longer Fenrir of the Ironwood.

Somewhere, I smelled Loki's amusement.

* * *

When the tears ceased welling I opened my eyes. The golden hall was deserted. Its bronze hearth-fires had burnt low, allowing darkness to skulk about the building's corners like a scavenging beast. Despite the light, Odin's throne glittered before me. A soft whine escaped my muzzle as I remembered how I had been sullied. I smelled my shame all about me; something of the All-Father's scent lingered upon me. I growled at the foot of the throne, disgusted at how empty my defiance felt.

I didn't know what to do. I followed my instinct to cast about for a scent. I smelled something fresh—a scent I had hitherto not known. Like deer, but stronger, less flighty.

On the steps to some antechamber at the back of the hall, a great black horse sat. He seemed a noble breed, with high aquiline features and a luxurious mop of braided hair that fell down his back. It was a mane that would be the envy of any proud beast, studded as it was with silver bands woven into it. Much like the All-Father, the stallion bore the same human semblance—even though all his features were equine, his form disdained walking the earth on all fours. He wore a silver shirt of mail, a loose pair of silk leggings, and a thick red cloak that was clasped around his neck by a fiery brooch. A fine sword hung in a scabbard on his left hip, balanced out by a large tome on the right. I watched him warily as his dark eyes rested on me, betraying not a single emotion. I found him strangely beautiful.

"So you are the wolf everyone is talking about." The horse spoke with a deep voice. He ran his eyes up and down me, and then nodded to himself. "You have strength to you," he acknowledged, his tone rising, "one I wouldn't expect from the Trickster's spawn." He fingers tapped the hilt of his sword.

"It's not just you who is grateful I don't take after him," I muttered, watching his hand closely.

The Aesir snorted, like a horse. "We'll see who you take after, though," he replied, chewing the words in his muzzle like a beast of burden does with its tack. I smelled the tang of magic again; I was certain I was somehow being judged.

"Really?" A snarl betrayed my distaste. "When Loki was done rutting as a wolf, he came loping back to your halls, where you have sheltered him since. Why should I care what you suspect, when you house the very being you hate?" I snapped my jaws, going further. "I swore your lord's oath, what more do you want?"

The horse rose in a start, his ebony hooves clattering against the stone floor. His nostrils flared, and then a great smile broke across his face. I blinked in surprise.

"You make a good point, Wolf," he laughed, slapping his thighs.

"And you are?" I spoke quietly, confused at his humorous response.

"The god Tyr. I wield Tiwaz, the rune of honour. Justice is my main keepsake, though."

"Really?" I tilted my head to the side. I was surprised such a concept existed here at all.

"Those are my aspects." He nodded.

"Hold true to them, then. Don't condemn me for my father's crimes," I growled, weary of how he kept narrowing his eyes at me.

"You speak with a sharpness." He paused. "I think that's your own wolfish tongue, not his." He frowned, tapping his hoof on the floor. "You understand why your parentage would warrant caution, though?" I didn't reply immediately to him, for I was too busy sniffing out the truth of his words, rolling them over my tongue, trying to find any hint of a lie in his breath. I didn't want to fall into another snare.

"Not one bit. I am no god, I am no shapeshifter. I am truly the flesh that I am." I laughed. It was true—I had none of the glamor the Aesir or Vanir possessed. I knew I was no threat to them, but from the way Tyr swallowed it seemed he had something to say, and I started to doubt that conclusion. I actually smelled a little bit of fear on him—not a lie - but it was gone before I could be sure of it.

"You speak well; not what I would expect from an animal," he murmured, scrutinising me with his unreadable brown eyes. "You did what was asked of you, and have done no wrong," he sighed, but he wouldn't admit that I was right.

I inclined my head respectfully; a gesture that internally, made me howl, but it wasn't like I had any other options—I needed to win some friends here, I wanted to know what he knew about the runes. "What am I to do now?" I asked, looking about the empty hall. Above, the stars showered their ethereal light through the arches, and all seemed quiet in the distant realms beyond the walls.

Tyr shrugged. "I don't know the full extent of Odin's plans." He paused, watching me again. "You should not worry. Most of the Aesir still remember our humble beginnings, when we didn't have runes. They still trust deeds over words—even runic ones. Prove yourself and in turn, they may give you their trust."

"May?" I snapped. I couldn't fathom the fickle nature of these beings.

"You're still the son of Loki," Tyr sighed. "I'm afraid that though you may hate him for what he did to you, he's done worse to the Aesir."

"Then you're all fools to keep him here," I growled. We fell into silence for a moment.

"Sometimes, Fenrir, it's better to keep your enemies within reach." I noticed how he looked away from me as he spoke, instead staring at the All-Father's throne. The runes upon it seemed to shiver in the faint light, as if trying to speak. "Odin is quite the pragmatist; as is the nature of a king. While others would've killed Loki outright for his slights, he keeps your father here because he has his uses." He shook his head slightly, as if he didn't wholly agree. The horse pointed at the gaps in the vaulted ceiling, from which beams of starlight fell down. "Take this hall. Thanks to Loki's tricks, it was built for free, our honor kept intact, and Odin got a new mount, too."

"What do you mean?"

"Probably won't surprise you," he said gruffly. "Loki changed into a mare, shagged the builder's horse, and so he lost the bet we made over how fast he could build our halls. Loki got pregnant...and that's how Odin got his horse Sleipnir." He grinned. "Like I said, Odin's a pragmatist. A good ruler needs to be."

"So I'm a pragmatic solution? To what then?"

"Yes," he said simply, refusing to say anything more. From the way he held his jaw shut, he seemed less like a horse and more like a stubborn mule, but again, I smelled no lies on his tongue. "Forget this business, though - the law says that between strangers, the hall-lord should offer his guest trust and hospitality," Tyr said sternly, his lips moving as if reciting some dusty old tome. "Come, I'll show you some of the delights Asgard holds."

I followed the warrior horse through the winding passageways, his mail glittering, his hooves thumping loudly against the floors. I hoped he would lead me past something that would give hope to my plans. There were all sorts of treasure here; piles of gold coins cascaded down from the walls. More importantly, the palace was full of swords, spears, coats of mail—weapons that glittered with the glamor they held, and bore points that were as sharp as stars. Though none of those things smelled like a rune, it gave me the impression that Asgard's real nature was a fortress, a place for war. The vague hope that I would taste blood again made me feel better. In spite of the cultured aspirations I held for my children, I still lived for the simple pleasures.

Tyr then opened a set of double doors, which led into a great feasting-hall, with a lofty ceiling carved out of eldritch wood—I recognised them as trees from the Ironwood itself. The dark lumber gave it a homely scent, one that had the faintest aroma of rain, of earth, of crushed pine needles.

"I know the scent of this wood," I said softly; it felt soothing with every breath.

"Remind you of home?" The black horse beamed with some genuine warmth, flicking his ears. "Please, sit," he said, pointing to the fire.

I settled down there, the heat pricking between my thick fur. I wasn't used to it, but I found it surprisingly comfortable as it washed over me, soothing my aching muscles. Yet still I found myself longing for the Ironwood, for its dark nights and ice to crunch beneath my paws…even if I might find someone to sire my children with.

"Now, you must have questions," the black horse breathed, brushing some stray bits of his mane from his face as he pulled over a bench and sat next to me. I was still suspicious of him, but I needed information, and at least for all the power he smelled of, I couldn't detect any hint of a lie. It wouldn't be wise to ask about runes outright though, so…

"Why do you dress yourselves as beasts—you were like men once, were you not?" I asked.

Tyr shrugged and ran a hand down his mane, his brown eyes staring up at the ceiling. He then reached over at the table and grabbed a shiny red apple, and began to crunch away into it, filling the air with its sweet scent. Noticing how my snout quivered, he took a silver bowl from the table and filled it up with a hearty draught of an amber liquid, setting it down before my forepaws and encouraging me to drink. I only did so when he drained a goblet of the stuff—all the while hating how he held his drink in his hands, and I had to lap away like a beast.

"Mead." Tyr grinned, pouring us both some more. "Like it?" I nodded. It tasted like honey but with a fiery aftertaste to it, but it ran down my throat so easily. I felt it work its magic on me immediately, making my limbs tingle and my muscles relax.

"So?" I pressed, reminding him of my question. The great horse nodded his head, but went on munching away at another apple - as if to remind me who was in charge. I swallowed my pride, though, remembering I needed his information, maybe even an ally. "I know my father was always a shapeshifter; sometimes a hawk, sometimes a *mare*," I said, emphasising the word, "a salmon, a seal, even a fly…a wolf." I went further. "What power let him do that?" I winced internally, thinking I'd been careless.

"Yes," Tyr swallowed, licking his fingers. "That's true, but Loki is of Vanir stock. Glamor, magic, call it what you will. It is in their blood, their very nature, to be formless." He paused. "The Aesir though? Not the case, but now we have their runes, and with such power, you see things differently, sharper. We were men once, but there are things in beasts that have we always desired. Their strength, their cunning, their stamina, their agility…" he trailed off, waving his hand in the air.

"Beauty," I offered, trying to keep him going. I now knew that the power of runes could be gained. I had hope.

"Yes." Tyr nodded. As a beast myself, his accord cheered my spirits.

"Humanity is something like a dull set of clothes—the power of runes lets you mix it with other suits until you find something comfortable to wear."

"And you happened to choose a horse?"

Tyr shrugged. "I've always seen horses as noble creatures."

"When they're wild," I replied flippantly, the sweet mead loosening my tongue, remembering the sleek forest horses' gallop between the trees. "Not once they're broken in by their rider," I yapped, only realising what I said too late. I had no stomach for that stuff.

"You have a problem with authority, don't you?" Tyr snapped, angry that I had insulted him, somewhat unintentionally, even if it was for telling him the truth. "Remember, wolf; Odin is a pragmatist. You may mistrust him, but as long as you obey him, there'll be no harm."

"I might not mistrust him if he had been truthful with me—I know what lies smell like now," I growled, my hackles rising. I'd muzzled myself for too long—I needed to snap at someone, say what I really felt. I hope he realised Odin's power was not the issue, it was how he abused it. However, just as quickly as my anger rose, it drained away, the tremors in my limbs reminding me how weak I was. "I'm sorry I bit you," I murmured, lowering my head as I sat back down by the fire, staring into its dancing flames. "I just...want someone to tell me why I'm here. My father is enough of a liar for all of us," I muttered, licking my tongue over my teeth consolingly. My head had begun to thud painfully. "I hope Odin wasn't lying with his offer," I whined. The mead had taken my tongue.

The black horse tapped his hooves against the stone, threading his fingers through his mane. After a moment, he gave a loud snort and spoke. "I don't think you realise it, having spent all your days in that body. I'd think you know its strengths better than anyone else," he sighed. "Remember what we've said about Loki? Vanir, liar, formless shapeshifter. Regardless of how he hides, all his fancy tricks, you can sniff him out. You knew he was there watching when Odin bound you, didn't you?" He dragged the bench closer to me. "Loki has a part to play in things...for the worse of us all. You can keep him in check. Do this and you need not mourn Ironwood."

"What 'things' exactly?"

"Even Odin refuses to tell me. I can tell it's not good—I've never seen the old man worry. Still...will you do it?"

Maybe it was his honesty, or maybe it was how the mead left my head throbbing, but before I knew it, I said yes. If I was sober, I would have snapped my jaws and snarled—it's not a wolf's nature to be so subservient. Instead, I felt joy creep into my heart as Tyr, my friend, gave a genuine smile. If I expected Tyr to stay though, I was wrong. No sooner had I said yes was he back on his feet, exchanging his mail shirt for a shapely tunic that I must say really showed off his chest.

"Where are you off to?" I asked, lifting my muzzle up off the floor.

"To tell Odin you've had a change of heart. Eat, drink, rest. It is late," he said, leaving without another word. I nodded my head as he walked out the door, giving me hope that my service would bring reward. I could swallow my pride for that.

I took Tyr up on his offer, but his food was too salted, too sickly, or too sweet, and none of it slid down with the warmth a chunk of steaming meat did—blood and all. The mead was good, though, so I continued drinking that. Soon I was stumbling about on all fours, my mind pleasantly numb to all my worries. I was even starting to feel like less of a prisoner, and deeper still in that part of me smothered by all my wolfish pride…I was secretly overjoyed that I would no longer be alone. It is a wolf's nature to be strong, but he also loves fiercely those dear to him. I was quite willing to accept Tyr into that empty space. I'd even love Odin for the stern father he seemed to be. As for my desire for children? I honestly forgot about that.

Maybe I was incredibly drunk. I had a thought—why not go to Odin and show my willingness, in person? With all my speed I leapt towards the hall's great doors, pulling at their iron knockers as best I could with my paws. The doors did not budge. I tried again, looking for a latch, but there was no keyhole or any sign of a lock. As I pounded my paws against the door, even in my inebriated state I scented a sliver of magic. Peering closer, I noticed a silver mist hovering over it. Carefully, I watched as it formed about my paws, almost invisible against my grey fur. Each time I reached out, it prevented me from ever touching the surface. With a sniff I slunk away, finding a cold spot in the corner. I turned my back on the fire, on the mead and meat. I closed my eyes and let sleep take me. That night, like every other one to follow, I dreamed of home.

* * *

Tyr was right. I was a second Sleipnir. The All-Father didn't care about anything other than my usefulness, and my nose was better than all the runes and animal guises Asgard could muster. To the Aesir I became both a valued addition to their house and a tool; one that to their annoyance would sometimes talk back. Yet with a stern hand Odin thought I could be trained, much like how the rider breaks a new horse.

With that runic oath Odin forced me to keep an eye on Loki. Day and night, sniffing him out—whether he was a fly, a seal, a hawk, a mare—he couldn't hide from me. There was no rest to it. Whatever Odin commanded, his fetter forced me to do. I didn't always hate it. I was always overjoyed to see my father fail. When I wasn't commanded to seek Loki out, Odin would have me guard wherever he wished my father not to be. I was the dog outside the doors while the other Aesir drank and feasted without any interruption. I watched over their secret meetings, where they talked about the prophecies the head of Mimir glimpsed. I even guarded that thing - a job I hated but still carried out, my mind full of the promise of my reward. The ugly thing kept mouthing the word 'Ragnarok' at me, over and over, with an evil smirk, like it knew something I did not. It made me realize carrion could actually smell bad, and that blind, severed head kept staring at me like a viper wanting to spit out something poisonous. I'd have crunched that smug head into bits if Odin hadn't forbidden it.

However, time winds on. Years passed in Asgard like days. With no sun or seasons to see there, time was hard to tell. I became respected, trusted, rewarded. I would have been accepted as one of their own, but my downfall was born in the aftermath of battle.

Blood, limbs, and feeble cries for mercy were all that remained of several Vanir-witches left over from their ancient wars with the Aesir. Huginn and Muninn, Odin's ravens, flapped their dark wings overhead, and wheeled down to earth, gleefully feasting on the steaming meats laid out for them—squawking and batting their wings at each other.

The Aesir weren't so animated. Thor stood in the form of a great stag, looking mighty in his mail even though he was breathing heavily. His ruby gauntlets were bloodied and stained, but he seemed oddly peaceful as he sat in a patch of unstained snow, carefully wiping them clean. The watcher Heimdallr was with him in his eagle aspect—strutting over the battlefield, ruffling his feathers, casting his great, beady eyes over the corpses, as if he could make the dead cough up their secrets. He looked ridiculous in that form, some weird halfway spat between human and bird. Behind Heimdallr was Vithar—wearing the form of a thin, blond-haired dog, brought along to carry swords and polish armour. Clearly, Vithar took too much after the handsome Baldr, god of beauty, as he was all that and no bite.

While the others stood idly, I held the last Vanir in my jaws, delighting in how her flesh quivered at my every breath. It had been too many moons since I last held prey in my jaws, and it was all I could to prevent myself from crushing her neck in a swift crunch and sucking up all her blood.

"It's a good thing Odin spared you, Fenrir," Tyr snorted, trotting over, his horse-coat riddled with sweaty foam. He stank, but it was a scent that made me happy—it was comforting, to see that the god's animal guises betrayed their fleshly nature. In a few places even Tyr's masterfully forged mail-shirt had a couple of holes rent through it.

I growled my approval to him, unable to speak as I kept my jaws wrapped over her throat. As the points of my fangs nicked her skin, my wolfish tongue lapped at her flesh—I was mad with delight for the taste of fresh blood, full of fear from the chase. In the long years spent in Odin's halls, I had grown in size easily matching Thor and Tyr in strength and stature—and that was when I prowled on all fours.

"He's right," Thor laughed in approval, slapping me on my back. "Why on earth did my father have you languish in his halls for all those years?" he asked, before snatching a wineskin from Vithar's fumbling paws and draining it in three hearty draughts. "You see that, Vithar? Fenrir doesn't even have a sword and he fights better than you!" he snapped, wrenching the weapon from his grasp. Though he grabbed it by the blade, the runic sword didn't dare cut Thor, unhappy as it was in the golden-boy's grasp.

"I'm sorry," Vithar mumbled, fumbling his hands about against his chest, but Thor was having none of it—he smacked him across the cheek with his hand.

"You're a warrior!" His eyes were wide. "You don't grovel, you don't apologise—and you don't let anyone disarm you!" he screamed, kicking the nearest corpse. "Go and clean my sword," he thundered, pointing. It lay inside a Vanir's caved in skull, the entire body stuck in an unsightly mangle of bear and horse—having never shifted from one form into the other before the moment of death.

Like a good dog, Vithar wordlessly obeyed, struggling to lift the mighty weapon, but no matter how he grit his flat little teeth, it would not budge. Thor shook his head, still fuming at the boy, whilst Tyr and Heimdallr chuckled gently to themselves. With a flick of a finger, Thor released his weapon—then it was lighter than the air, causing Vithar to fall flat on his backside, dirtying his silk robes.

A deep rumble of laughter clawed its way out of my throat, despite my jaws still holding fast around the witch's neck. Out of the corner of my eye, I noticed her gaze flick about, attempting to gauge the mood of the Aesir—but then she started to stare at me, as if she realized I was not one of them. In that moment, I clenched my jaw, and felt her blood trickle down my throat once more.

"Lay off, Fenrir," Tyr sighed, taking a seat on the chest of a corpse next to me. I'd torn the man's throat out as he begged for mercy. His blood was far sweeter to me than anything he could promise. "I don't want her dead—well, not just yet," he chuckled, prodding at the exposed spine with his sword. "Are you going to use your tongue to talk, then? If not, I see no need for you to keep it."

Before Tyr could begin his questioning, Thor strode over, interrupting. "To think I doubted you, Wolf-Fenrir! You are quite the monster in battle!" He laughed, slapping me heartily on the shoulder—a blow that should have knocked the wind out of me, but I barely even flinched. "Here, let go of her, Fenrir, I'll hold her fast with my gauntlets—you can snap your teeth at her if she refuses to talk."

Reluctantly, I let my fangs slip away from her skin, despite knowing that it would be hard for her to talk with them resting in her flesh. Without much of a thought, I licked my lips and placed myself between Tyr and Thor, licking away the blood that had marked my paws.

Heimdallr stepped silently next to me and whispered, "I'm surprised you didn't bite." He never was a talker, and when he did say something, it was usually monosyllabic.

"So," Thor began casually, showing off his impressive antlers, some of which were bloodied, "where are the others?" The witch smirked, pointing at the corpses. "No! No!" Thor laughed, "The living ones! We know this isn't the last of you."

"They're the only ones I know," she retorted. "Kill me if you want then, Aesir. You've already done enough to ruin me." She glared at me, wolfishly.

Thor was quick in his rebuke. "I'm not one to kill an unarmed woman," he snapped. The regal stag was indignant. "At least I have the honor your kind lacks!"

Heimdallr pressed his beak close to Tyr's ear and whispered, "Look at her lips, she wants to play a game of words. Kill her. Be done with it, we don't need her," he muttered, readying his sword. Meanwhile, Thor was becoming flustered as the witch's words ran circles about him.

"You'd let me win, then?" she laughed sweetly. Thor was fuming and would have hit her then—I smelled his battle-anger bubble up at her taunt, but she was a woman, and he would not sully his honor.

Heimdallr spoke again. "I say we give Fenrir new prey. Set her loose. Let her run. Let the wolf run her down. He's still lusting for flesh," he said, tapping his beak together.

The woman's eyes widened—the watcher had hit a nerve. There was a white flash as she tried to summon a rune, but Thor's mighty gauntlets sucked away any of her glamor; the rubies inside them gleaming brightly. He didn't let her free and fulfil Heimdallr's suggestion, but neither did he voice his outrage about the dishonor—he was quite happy to be rid of her, as long as it wasn't him bloodying his reputation.

"So you would have someone else kill your charge?" Tyr retorted, choosing his moment to revenge himself of Thor's insult by taking over his interrogation.

"You wanted to kill her anyway," the stag snapped, grinding his teeth as if he had fangs, but really it looked like he was chewing a mouthful of grass. "She is a Vanir, and must be slain."

"And yet you would go back on your honor and allow Fenrir to kill an unarmed opponent?" Tyr laughed. "The law is absolute, we cannot kill her." He swished his tail about.

"What about them?" Thor shouted, his hoof kicking a lump of snow onto the face of another dead Vanir woman.

"She attacked us. This one did not."

With Tyr refusing to compromise, Thor loudly proclaimed, "We must take her to Asgard then, and leave her to Odin's judgement. She can be made to swear an oath, or married into our house, like we did with Skadi and Njord," he muttered, disgusted, throwing the Vanir witch down on the ground. "That's the law!" He curled his tongue at Tyr, who pretended not to notice.

For a moment no one was holding her down. She could have cast any rune, but instead, she remained silent. I smelled her triumph. Her eyes met mine, and they flashed yellow.

"To Asgard, then." Heimdallr nodded, sealing the matter.

The proposal made my skin crawl on instinct. I didn't just not trust Odin to be as honorable as Thor, I feared what her plan might be. I don't know why, but though I should have voiced my concerns, I kept my silence about her. Odin's hold upon me was weakening.

* * *

I deliberately took my time as I scouted the way ahead underneath the snowy pines. These few days outside of Odin's halls were precious to me, and I sought to make sure I eked out every single moment I had. I loved breathing the crisp chill air once more, catching the fragrance of pine needles and the faint scent of the earth, released as my paws crunched down on the snow. In that aim, Thor's prisoner was my closest ally. If it were not for her, Asgard would have been reached before the end of the day, and I would be stuck, breathing in the stale air once more. But with a prisoner who could cast runes of her own, the gods didn't have the luxury of casting *Raidho*, rune of haste, and eating up the distance. Instead, it would be a slow, plodding pace towards the horizon and the golden hall.

For the most part, I was given the freedom to range ahead of the Aesir and find the best path home. Each time I contemplated giving them the slip, but I felt Odin's runic shackle pull at my soul whenever I took a step towards that aim, so I inevitably ended up coming back. When I returned to them though, I immediately wanted to leave. I was wary of her eyes upon me—calculating, weighing up the risk. She made my hackles quiver, rise, and worse—her scents barely gave anything away.

Unfortunately, I couldn't hide from her forever. When we set camp for the night, she made her move. Tyr, Thor, Heimdallr, and the coward Vithar were all asleep, and it was my turn to watch the charge. As they snored away, I lay on my belly against the fire, resting my head on my paws, watching the shadows dance between the gouts of flame. Just when I felt the gods fall into a deeper sleep, she began to speak.

"They call you Fenrir, don't they? Is that your true name?" She spoke softly, like the murmur of leaves. Perhaps it was a moment of weakness, or I knew what was to come on instinct. Instead of remaining silent, I answered her.

"My mother called me Fenrir," I said, still watching the flames. "She left me when she was young." I felt anger bubble up in my gut, seeking to pull away at my lips and form a snarl. I hid it from her, though. If anything, I resented my mother more than Loki. Fathers run away from their children all the time, especially if they sire a wolf, but mothers? They're meant to love you, no matter what.

"And the Aesir found you?"

"No. I lived free in the Ironwood for many years," I replied neutrally. I still missed its charms, the way the moonlight shone between the winter boughs, the way the water gurgled in the burns, the way the winter brought a perfect stillness to the earth.

"Then they found you?" I refused to answer her, but even my silence made it obvious to the witch. "He made you swear an oath, didn't he? The Old One?" I looked away. "Of course he would—you know, he fears you." I should have raked her with my claws for that tongue of hers, but that snake danced a beguiling dance, and like a silly bird, I was trapped by it.

"If you keep lying, I'll rip out your tongue," I growled, but really it was a hollow gesture. Her words stoked my wolfish pride. How I wished Odin feared me, that false wolf.

"Haven't you noticed it?" she winked coyly. "The Aesir fight with runes they stole from my people, but you match their strength without holding any of your own." As soon as she said that truth, I was hooked. I knew it to be true, and I couldn't resist the faint glimmer of hope that she might offer some escape from Asgard's service. After all, her words smelled of truth.

"You're lying," I replied, but she only smirked—she knew that I knew otherwise.

"When you caught me, I was using runes too. And yet you still overcame them."

I was silent for a moment, kneading the snow between my black claws.

"Do you know what the Vanir call you?" The fire cackled between us, as if it knew where this knowledge led. "The Father of Wolves."

I was no longer convinced that this woman was a stranger. But, as I searched my memories for a trace of her, all I found were distortions, like ripples on a lake. She sniggered again then, as if she was the one who held that knowledge back from me.

"What do you mean?" I finally replied. Odin's oath made it hard to speak to her.

She refused to respond, as if she'd pushed enough, and the rest would fall into place. Looking up at the stars, I noticed my watch had passed. With a growl, I woke Vithar, who, in his dog-aspect, whimpered pathetically as he was startled by my wolf form.

"Your watch," I grumbled, before moving away from the fire to sleep in the darkness—it was too warm and too light for me there, and I wished to savour these last few days of sleeping under the sky. In my natural state, sleep folded her blanket over my eyes without a moment's pause.

It came as no surprise that the Vanir escaped shortly into Vithar's watch. Thor gave the dog a deserving cuff around the head, but I was furious. I screamed at the stupid dog, catching his neck in my jaws with my fury. I felt his entire body flutter like a little bird; then his bladder gave way, ruining his silk attire. Tyr pulled me off before I did anything rash, believing I was merely expressing the frustration they all felt. I cared nothing for that whelp's shame. It was more than that—I knew she was my mother, and that meant I was pure-blooded Vanir stock. The ability to wield runes was in my very blood. I just needed her to tell me how.

We spent the entire day trying to find a trace of her glamor, but there was nothing to be found, not even a sliver of her scent. That was the only day my nose failed me. Without a prize, the gods cast *Raidho* once more, and still keeping pace, we sped back to Asgard, the she-witch's words echoing in my head.

* * *

I'll spare you the details. Vithar was punished, Thor was congratulated. I won the respect of the other Aesir, now that I'd shed their enemies' blood. Even Odin began to show me favor, bestowing fine gifts upon me—gold, mead, meat, but never what he promised. The years continued to pass, like the inexorable march of the stars overhead. The knowledge of my potential and my inability to wield runes clawed at the inside of my skull. I kept growing, exceeding even Tyr's height, and that was when I walked on all fours. Each day I felt more wolfish, and less like a dog. Something in me was burning out.

Still I resented their treatment of me—I served just as much as any other, and yet, I was granted none of the privileges they enjoyed. I still lived with Tyr. I had no runes or titles, or songs composed to my name. Every night I dreamed of the Ironwood, of my legacy, of being 'The Father of Wolves'. So, believe me, I leapt on my opportunity to take what I was owed when it showed. I had given up on waiting on a miserly ring-giver.

I was summoned in the middle of the night—the darkest of hours, when all the other gods slept. Odin sat alone, crouched over the stone-like head of Mimir, his brows furrowed. For the first time, he looked old, vulnerable, worried. I wondered if he ever slept.

"I have a task for you, one that's suited to your skills." I bowed wordlessly, showing my assent to his demands. Again, Odin appeared in his wolf form, now dressed in a mail shirt and gripping his spear in hand. "I've come to see your confinement to Asgard and its surrounding plains as a disservice—keeping track of Loki is the least you can do. After all, runes cannot mask the scents you track."

I bowed my head in thanks. Odin preferred it when you didn't talk at all, and I always wanted to be rid of Wolf-Odin as soon as I could, such was my jealousy.

"As you know, the Vanir are powerful rune wielders, and have access to ones still beyond the Aesir's knowledge. Thor and Tyr have made it clear to me that you can be trusted, so I'm giving you a task of your own."

Again, I nodded my wordless thanks. Odin appreciated that—he loved seeing me bow to him, as he sat, a poor excuse of a half-wolf, on his golden throne, as if one would be proud of such a thing.

"You know of Ragnarok, it is no secret to you. I want you to go to the realm of men, and using that nose of yours, sniff out any Vanir you find agitating the mortals. I need their loyalty and the souls of their dead warriors to fill up my halls for the upcoming battle."

"Won't the Vanir notice my presence? I have no glamor of my own, and even with magic to mask my presence - they would notice my size."

The All-Father nodded. At least he liked an intelligent question, even if he had already thought of a solution. It shows you're thinking, and it made him confident he wasn't sending some block-head to mindlessly follow his orders. Sometimes situations change, and that requires flexibility. Odin was a pragmatist, after all.

"I'm giving you the knowledge of the runes you need—ones to conceal your size, ones to change your form, and ones to conceal your glamor," he said, casually, as if it was no matter. I stood there trembling, excitement numbing me to any suspicion. Finally. Odin breathed the runes over me. "*Raidho*, to speed your journey, *Sowilo*, for luck, *Berkanan*, to change your size." His breath smelled of power. Then without another word, Wolf-Odin pointed to the door, where Heimdallr was waiting to usher me across the Bifrost. For a moment, I felt like something had been awoken in me, but at the same time, like nothing had changed.

* * *

I fell through the sky among a shower of ice and snow. The sun hung low over a vast pine forest, dancing between the trees with golden rays; I felt its warmth trickle between the tufts of my fur. Following my instinct, I cast around for scents but there was nothing out of the ordinary, just the wet scent of snow and the tangy aroma of pine sap. It was like a still pond waiting for a drop to disturb the waters; quiet, betraying nothing. Though I was confident in my nose, I felt the temptation to experiment with these newfound runes rise from deep inside my bones, but anyone could be watching. On a world far away from Asgard, the slightest hint of any glamor would stick out like a lightning bolt at night.

Whatever caution I felt for these woods faded quickly. This place felt much like the Ironwood, only lighter, with more space to grow. The trees held thick branches full of green needles, and their thick roots bulged, erupting swollen from the earth. I can't quite say how I felt after being locked up in Asgard for so long, but—ah, I felt like a ghost, like a shadow trying to claw its way back into the light.

Reluctantly then I set about Odin's commands, his oath feebly tugging at my mind. Was this some sort of test? Did he really trust his hold over me so much? I couldn't think of any other reason why he'd give me such knowledge if he didn't. My irritation only grew as I roamed about; the banks of snow held no Vanir, and the sleeping trees were just trees. I dived deep into the icy pools, searched the shores and scoured the fens, but there was nothing. This place was untouched, wild. The only sign of humans were their distant campfires at night, so far away they seemed like stars.

Deep inside my soul, I felt that little snare of Odin's snap, fizzing out into nothing. I remembered my wolfish nature—those hopes I had of waiting for a reward, I saw them now as thoughts of Odin's own. I was the Father of Wolves, a wolf who would show his teeth. I snapped them together, rolling my tongue over them as if they had been newly grown, and I laughed.

Just as the Vanir's runes had little effect on me, the same applied to Odin's runic oath. Like a chain, it had grown rusty over time, and without even a pull, it crumbled into dust. The 'All-Father' was a fool to ever think he could tame a real wolf. I howled for joy—this was perfect! Odin had hidden my glamor so I could stalk the Vanir, but in doing so he had blinded himself. Better still, he had given me the knowledge of runes, and so given me the perfect opportunity to realise my ambitions.

Odin could go to Hel.

In a burst of speed, I loped deeper into the forest. The trees coiled about behind my tracks, bent by the speed of my wind-rush lope. Behind me the dark-wings of Huginn and Muninn flapped in frustration, until distantly I heard them screech as I evaded their sight. The forest conspired with me, the branches thick enough to hide me, stretching out far to the horizon, with only the peaks of mountains briefly bursting from their depths.

I grinned, and ran about in a circle, giddy from my deception. Would Odin think I had betrayed him? I cared not—I was free again. Perhaps the old fool would believe I was on the chase of something? Whatever, I had slipped his leash, and put enough distance from his birds that they would only feel the ripples of my runes before it was too late.

Experimenting then, I rose up onto my hind legs, freeing my paws for the casting of runes. From the snow about me, I gathered up seven piles of snow, and shaping them into pillars roughly my size, I placed into them shards of ice, wood, and earth. Finally with my own fangs I snagged open a vein, and let my blood trickle into each, along with a tuft of fur. I knew Odin would never give me a wife, but with runes I didn't need one. Better, no Aesir blood would corrupt my children.

The pillars stood there lifeless, nothing but empty vessels waiting to be bound into living flesh. I practised with my runes. I thought of their meanings, and the ways they could be applied. I laughed, Odin truly had no grasp of them—of course, he had only stolen them from the Vanir. He literally believed their meanings, that the runes were rigid, unchangeable things. He was wrong.

I cast my rune.

"*Berkanan.*"

I stretched away at the word with my tongue. I pulled and twisted it, and found which ways it would go. It was not just control of growth - Odin missed the point - it was of sustenance, of fertility—a rune of life. Around me, the snow melted, grass and ferns began to bloom, birds emerged from their tree-holes and began to sing and find mates. All sorts of perfumed wildflowers burst up around me, in the very depths of winter.

I pulled, and as I strained, I channelled that life into the pillars I had made, willing the pure snow to become flesh and tissue. The ice melted away, flowing into earthly aspects of my wolfish nature, pure, wild, free. The blood frothed and boiled, the earth shivered with my fur and slipped over their icy forms as they wriggled and writhed, their senses firing as their souls flickered into being.

I shaped them to be beautiful, to be better. I molded their paws into slender arms and legs, shaping their muzzles into ones capable of speech. Each tongue I kissed with my own, so it knew the words I spoke. They would not just be wolves—animals, but people ready to make their own life here in this world that held beauty greater than the dark, dingy Ironwood I once knew.

I was not done with one rune, though. Emboldened by my success, I shaped their destinies. I cast *Sowilo* to wish success. I fused it with *Berkanan* so that their lives would burn for decades at a time. I blessed them with good fortune, and speaking *Raidho*, I blessed them with swiftness—they would run without tiring, as if they were born of the wind itself.

When I was done, I fell back to all fours, legs trembling. My children stood around me, a progeny of beautiful wolves—unlike me, they were free from Loki's taint, purified of all his deceit and trickery. But among them a pair seemed perfect, a white wolf and a black one, and instantly I knew their names—Skoll and Hati. They had wonderful blue eyes.

I never got to speak those names.

"Cark!"

The raven's call echoed from the trees above, and within that instant, I felt the runes I was gifted drain from me. Without them my children shrank, becoming small, mute animals that ran on all fours—except two, the first I had made, the first to be made complete. Their blue eyes watched me knowingly, as if they sensed what was about to happen. They certainly didn't flee as Thor swept through the skies. First the lighting ripped the branches from the trees, then I felt Thor's fist in my cheek.

"You stupid animal!" he screamed, his voice sounding like his father's. "You were given one task—one!" the stag ranted, pounding his fists against me, as if he was upset.

I snapped my teeth at him and snarled, like a wild thing does when it finally decides to free itself of its keeper. I swiped at Thor with my claws, gouging long red lines through his chestnut fur. But it was short-lived—in a moment he shifted from his stag form into that of a black bear. The change was so swift he had me by the throat in a second, and all I could do was bite down as hard as I could on his gauntlets—which began to crack under my jaws. Thor finally snapped out of his blindness and noticed my two remaining children. Those that had fled, now animals, meant nothing to me.

"What have you done?" he growled, but they didn't flinch. They just kept watching, waiting for something. I felt pride that they didn't turn tail and flee like the others.

Then Odin arrived in wolf form, striding out from the trees—his form matching that of my children. Immediately, they looked at him in awe, as if he had fathered them. He circled the two wolves, watching them from every angle and his ravens swooped and dived at them.

"Who are you?" Skoll and Hati finally spoke. They were still, swaying from side to side, mesmerised by everything they saw. It was all new to them.

"I am Odin, King of the Aesir, and the All-Father," he whispered, silently casting his runes, awing them with his power.

"All-Father?" Odin caught my eye. I whined, I sneered, I thrashed— but Thor held my mouth shut. The All-Father had timed his intervention perfectly; he had struck just when they were most vulnerable.

"I am. You are mine, and you will be forever loyal to your father."

"Who are we?" they asked again. Knowing nothing at all they drank his every word, their eyes flickering yellow with an impression of Odin's own.

"You are Freki," he said touching Hati on the muzzle as he bound him with the runes. "And you are Geri," he uttered, doing the same to Skoll. Wolf-Odin's face was emotionless, but I knew from his eyes that he was laughing at me.

"And who is he?" they asked, pointing at me. At this point, my monstrous strength got the better of even Thor, and I burst out from his arms, wrenching his hands free from my muzzle.

"I am your father!" I howled, hoping my call would trigger something in the blood we shared, but they just stared blankly at me, and looked up to Odin with adoring eyes.

"That animal is nothing; mothered by a witch, fathered by a liar. A beast he will always be. Think nothing of him, my sons."

I felt my hackles stiffen up like spikes of ice, realising what Odin's plan had been. He knew he couldn't hold me forever—I was by nature too unruly, too much a Vanir, too much like my father even. He knew I'd rebel. He knew I'd create my perfect children—he'd given me only the runes for creation, not destruction. And he knew exactly when to strike, so he could gain guard dogs that would be totally devoted to him.

I screamed. It was wordless, primal fury. Odin flicked an ear and watched me with his yellow eyes. Then his wolfish face twisted.

That was the only time I saw Odin smile.

* * *

It was dark. I could hear the drip of water on stone. I cast around for scents, and again, the familiar odors of Asgard—the stale air, the ale, the sweat—it was all there. I thought back to the woods on the mortal world, and I wished I could have stayed there. I felt a pang of fear, hoping my remaining children had not been found.

I scented Tyr before he entered.

"Why did you do it?" the horse snorted. "I wouldn't believe it until I saw them."

"Why do you think? Was Odin ever going to give me a wife, even if one was willing?"

"Odin screamed about killing you, like you kill a dog that bites its master."

"Then he's more of a fool if he ever thought he could tame a wolf. I was more than a guard-dog, you know that, Tyr."

"You betrayed your Oath." He stamped a hoof.

"Then Odin is equally guilty of betrayal for not honoring his terms. He gave me nothing, despite all he said. You tell me what's worse, Tyr, one who lies when making an oath, or one who refuses to honor his terms." He didn't reply to that. "I didn't turn against him. I didn't attack him, or conspire with his enemies. I've done none of that, unlike Loki, who's -"

"You betrayed his trust."

"You're a fool! He tricked me! Odin does not trust anyone—if you weren't so weak-nosed you could smell that!"

"Fenrir, stop - he wants to kill you!"

"Then why doesn't the old man come and do it himself? He's already taken my children from me, what more does he have left to do?"

"Odin may lead us, but he isn't in charge of the law." Tyr angled his head defiantly.

"And what do you want me to do? I've already told you why I did it."

"Apologise. Ask for him to forgive you."

"I'd rather let him kill me," I snarled, fangs flashing in the gloom. So, I knew Tyr was offering me a way out, but I wasn't willing to be bowed a second time. That time when he made me swear that oath was the first, and the last. Worse, for that humiliation, what had he done? I was given no gifts! No rewards were given for my irreplaceable service—only demands that abused any vows of fealty and companionship. I had learnt enough of what a Ring-Giver should be. I would give my life for Odin, and he would reward me and give me a place in his hall. Odin had turned them into chains.

"Do you really mean that? Don't think this is a game. I don't believe you want to die." Tyr's ears drooped.

"You're not listening to me, are you? I only did what I had the right to do—to have my own legacy—what he promised! What about you, Tyr? How many years have you served Odin, carried out the sentences he would never utter, and never been rewarded? Oh, he made sure Thor was married, and all the others, but what about you? Why are you still alone?"

"Don't make this about me—I'm only trying -"

"To help me? You know I'm beyond help now—Odin will find a way to do as he pleases, he always does! If it won't be you, then it'll be Loki, and my father will only be too happy to get rid of me after all I've done to him -"

"Fenrir. You can sit here in your anger, but Odin won't wait. When I leave, I need a decision. Please, as a friend, don't make this worse than it already is."

"Oh, come on. Odin's threat is an empty bluff. He wouldn't get rid of me—he needs his dog to keep Loki in check," I retorted, fluffing up my mane in pride. Inwardly, I wasn't confident at all—Odin had Skoll and Hati for that now, but a show of resistance mattered. I wouldn't let him break my spirit.

"Very well," Tyr said sadly. "If this is really what you want."

"It is. I won't let Odin keep me on a leash anymore."

I remember seeing Tyr look back as he stepped through the doorway, leaving me alone in the dark. There was a look of sadness over his face, and I would like to think he knew the injustice that had been done to me. I felt a faint flicker of hope rise within me, that he would rebel against Odin and pronounce me innocent, but it was short-lived. Tyr couldn't see what I had from Odin; he wasn't a wolf. He had his own hall, his own runes, his own sword…they were all things that had been gifted to him for his service. Odin had put gilded blinkers on him, harnesses and reins, and the only thing preventing him from becoming a second Sleipnir was that Odin did not ride him. Worse, he didn't have the nose to smell out the lies.

* * *

The great hall of Asgard looked more regal than I had ever remembered it. Maybe it was because I now entered waiting to be judged. The golden beams seemed to rise higher into the vaulted ceiling, the hearth-fires lining the isle roared with bright orange flames, crackling like gossiping tongues, and Odin's golden throne itself seemed higher, and shone brighter.

Thor and Heimdallr dragged me across the stone floor, the bones in my legs bumping painfully against the stones. Each one held a paw tightly, while a set of iron chains had been wrapped around my muzzle, and sealed with all the strength of the rune Tiawaz. I was thrown roughly at the feet of Odin's throne, just so I had to crane my neck up to see the old man.

Wolf-Odin sat there, proud as ever. His fangs were polished in a pearly sheen, his ebony claws were perfectly dark, and streaks of silver and grey wound through his pelt, like he'd spun fibres of moon-silk into a coat. His Star-spear rested across his lap like a sceptre, and at either side of his throne he was flanked by the only two sentient children left to me. I felt physically sick watching them stare at me with cold indifference, the same sort I would use when holding the doomed prey down, before closing in to kill with the final bite to the throat.

"You stung me, wolf," Odin began, his muzzle twisting as he minced the words. I could tell from the cruel glimmer in his eye that he was enjoying this; it was that kind of look you see in those who only find satisfaction when they have their rivals firmly under their boot. "I gave you everything."

I strained my jaw to speak, and though the chains screamed and groaned as I stretched them, I howled, but no one seemed to hear me.

Odin rose from his throne, grasping his spear beside him. "Look carefully, Freki and Geri. This is what ingratitude, deceit, and betrayal looks like. I gave a beast a home, and it bit my hand."

Then Odin cast the rune of pain, his lips flushing red as he spoke. I heard little else after that but a roaring in my ears, and I writhed like a snake cut in half as I tried to find somewhere to hide from it.

"This creature was born as a beast, the spawn of a liar and trickster. I took him from his miserable home among the rain and snow, gave him a home, a hearth." As my eyes rolled about in my sockets, I watched all the Aesir drink Odin's lies.

Stoked into life by the pain, anger began to flare through me. The chains binding me began to creak and groan, a sound that was only enhanced by the hall.

"And for these things, he betrayed my trust—which without it, we are nothing better than beasts."

It was a mockery; to hear him lecture my children, to hear him speak of trust when he knew nothing of it. I glared across the hall at Tyr, who stood there in his proud horse-form, daring him to be just. Throughout Odin's speech, Tyr stood there, flexing his fingers across the hilt of his sword. I was desperate. I even hoped Loki had come round, that he'd felt some sort of fatherly compassion for his own wolven spawn. I hoped he'd play some trick. But nothing happened, and I only scented Loki hovering about in his fly form, settling on my nose and biting it hard enough to draw blood. Bizarrely

I wanted to laugh—he wasn't the one doing the backstabbing for once, and I admitted, he was quite justified in hating me.

The horse-god walked up to Odin, his hooves clattering ominously upon the stone. Swishing his long black tail, he bowed at Odin's throne, and then turned to deliver his verdict. All the time, he refused to meet my eyes, though his ears twitched every time I howled in pain or my writhing made the chains squeal.

"The wolf Fenrir, son of Loki, you are guilty of betraying the trust of your lord, of abusing the authority given in his name, of conspiring with his enemies the Vanir, and of siring your own monstrous race."

I kept staring at Tyr, as he held his arm out, reading from script surely penned by Odin himself. I could almost see Odin pulling the on Tyr's reins. Indeed, he sat behind Tyr on his throne with a disgusting smirk stretched across his sagging lips, no doubt delighted by how my eyes cast themselves vainly upon Tyr, upon Loki, upon my children at his side.

"For these crimes, you are to be bound forever and buried deep in the earth."

That did it. I heaved, I pulled, and after a sickly screech, the chains began to shear off, ringing as they scattered across the stones. Thor was ever quick to leap against me, but I swiped him away with a claw, throwing him across the hall. I saw the little white tuft of his deer-tail as he flew backwards. Heimdallr tried to bind me quickly, but I was already leaping towards Odin who was sitting there, a look of fear stretching across his muzzle.

I would have taken my revenge then, but stupid, noble Tyr decided to try to stop me. I twisted my neck, and with a sickening crunch, ripped his hand, the one that held my sentence, cleanly from his arm. But in that second Odin had readied his spear, and I felt it sink deep into my shoulder.

It was over quickly. I felt Thor wrestle Gleipnir upon me, and I howled in misery as the silk band crushed down against me, forcing me to struggle for breath. My howls started to tremble, and gave way to some pathetic gasp. All the while, Hati and Skoll were standing there like idiots, listening to my howls like they were deaf to their native tongue. But I wasn't the only one who bled. Tyr clutched a bleeding stump. His severed hand, still gripping his sword, lay at Odin's feet—who glowered hatefully at him. I think I understood. Tyr glanced at me for a moment. If it were not for him, Odin's spear would have sunk down into my throat.

Odin was silent. He seemed to consider whether to kill me then, but something stayed his hand.

I wondered if he didn't really want to kill me. Maybe he still had a further use for me, now that I was tamed by chains, or maybe he realized his house wasn't so devoted to him, and it was better to keep me alive than risk rebellion? I don't know, but I certainly believe Odin was spiteful enough to keep me prisoner for eternity—the end that was death would be far too easy a way out for a god like me. I'm a little bit flattered at the thought, actually.

* * *

You know the truth now, skald, but how will you sing my story? You might wonder if I have regrets, but eternity is a long time to not just think over the past, but to tease out its possibilities, its imperfections and imaginations, like a smith forging a sword. If there's one thing I've learnt from Odin, it is that the truth is a pliable thing, bent so easily with well-placed words. I'm sometimes tempted to think that Odin and Loki are the same.

Still. I have no desire to torture myself over the past.

In time, all bonds break. You can never tame a wolf. Every year I keep growing stronger. I've felt Gleipnir creak and groan. Asgard has forgotten me. A chain is only as strong as its weakest link, and while Odin made sure those binding me were strong, he did not look for the weakness within his own house. Loki may be the herald of Ragnarok. I will be the end of Odin's world.

And I will certainly make sure that the pathetic whelp Vithar will not kill me.

The Egyptian Gods haven't been worshipped in centuries. Millennia! Are they cut off from today's world? How do humans look upon them today?

Anubis decides to find out.

The Three Days
of the Jackal

by Samuel C. Conway

"I am going, and you can't stop me."

"Anubis, be reasonable!" Thoth pleaded. "You can't go!"

An unfamiliar face poked through the doorway. "Hey, what are you guys talking about?"

"Nuby wants a Second Coming," Sobek grunted.

"Oh, I wouldn't," the newcomer said. "You know the rules. No Second Comings."

"That's what I keep telling him," Thoth sighed. "But he's not listening."

"The last guy who tried it got nailed to a tree, remember?" Sobek offered.

The newcomer shook his head. "If he's bound and determined to go, then let him find out for himself. I just wouldn't want to be in your sandals when Ra found out, Nuby."

Anubis watched in silence as the newcomer wandered off. "Uh, Guys, who exactly was that?"

"That?" Thoth said. "That was Set, of course."

"Set? *That* was Set? But he…I didn't recognize…"

"Nose job."

"Oh."

Sobek shuffled through his scrolls and pulled out *Nubile Nubians*, an old favorite. "Hey, if Nuby wants to go so bad, I say we let him. I'm kind of curious myself to see how the monkey-heads are coming along without us."

"No!" Thoth said. "There are rules!"

"And we are gods," Anubis said determinedly. "We should be allowed to make our own rules."

"Anubis, don't, please. You simply can't"

"No, Thoth. I'm off. I'll tell you guys all about it when I get back."

* * *

And the evening and the morning were the second day. "I'm worried, Sobek," Thoth said while wringing his hands. "He should have been back by now."

"Maybe he got nailed to a tree."

"Oh, don't say that!"

"Hey, it would serve him right."

"What? You were the one who was egging him on!"

Sobek grinned as only a crocodile can. "Why not? All he ever does is sit around whining about 'Oh, Mankind must not forget us!' 'Oh, why can't we be worshipped as we once were?' I'm sick of listening to it."

"It would help if you could be a bit more supportive," Thoth grumbled. "But I suppose you can't be bothered to look up from your smut long enough to offer him any positive reinforcement."

"It's not smut," Sobek snorted. "It's porn. There's a difference."

* * *

And the evening and the morning were the third day. "He's back!" Thoth shouted excitedly. "Here he comes!"

Sobek glanced up from his scroll. "Well, well, the Prodigal Puppy returns. How are the monkey-heads? And, dude, what the hell is that you're wearing?"

Anubis plodded in and dropped the parcels he had been carrying. "It's what Humanity wears these days."

"Wow. You've gone native. So, tell us how it went."

"Yes, tell us!" Thoth said eagerly.

Anubis sat down with a weary sigh. "It was not what I expected."

Thoth's feathers drooped. "So they don't remember us?"

"Oh, no, they still do. When I appeared I was shocked at how much we are still celebrated. I found a huge gathering, probably thousands. They were all wearing masks made to look like our faces and they were having a...a really, really good time, actually."

Thoth brightened. "Anubis, that's wonderful! Tell us, how did they receive you?"

Anubis rubbed at an ear. "Like I said, it really wasn't what I was expecting."

"How so?"

"Well, when I arrived, there were at least six of them disguised to look like me. I was flattered, of course, but then they all grabbed me and pulled me up onto a stage. When it was over they gave me this." He pulled a shiny blue ribbon out of one of his bags. "They proclaimed me First Place."

"Sounds like you really had them fooled," Sobek snickered.

"Sobek, be nice!" Thoth scolded. "Go on, Anubis, what happened next."

Reaching into another bag, Anubis withdrew a stack of parchments. "They celebrate us in artwork. See here?"

"Oh, my, those are lovely," Thoth said.

"Yes. I rather like this one. Oh, and Sobek, I picked these up for you. I thought that you would appreciate them."

"Yeah? Let me see. Oh...OH! Whoa, Niley! Dude, these are for me?"

"Of course. They seemed to be tailored to your particular tastes."

"Oh, Nuby, you're my new best friend!"

"I'm your only friend."

Thoth cocked his head and puffed his feathers a little. "This is all great news, Anubis, but I can see that something is troubling you. Did something bad happen while you were there?"

Anubis rubbed once more at his ear. "Well, there were these men in red tunics. They insisted that I come with them to a room. There was...well, there was beer. A lot of it. A whole lot."

"That doesn't sound so bad," Thoth said hesitantly.

"No, it wasn't. It was good, in fact. Good beer. And these men were grand company, for mortals. In fact, they drank so much that I suspect that they weren't as mortal as they looked. But there was a woman there. She was disguised as Bast. Beautiful, smooth fur, shining eyes." He shuffled his feet and wrung at his kilt. "Well...it's been sort of a secret fantasy of mine, for a long time, you see."

Thoth's eyes widened. "Oh, Anubis, you didn't!"

Anubis stared at the floor. "Yeah. I think there might be a little demi-god or two running around soon."

Sobek leaped out of his chair and scattered scrolls everywhere. "Oh, say it ain't so!" He rushed to the window and thrust his head out. "Hey, everybody!" he bellowed. "Nuby got laid!"

"Sobek! This is serious!"

"You bet it is! Our little puppy is all grown up! So, Nuby, what's it like to do it with a monkey-head? Did you do it jackal-style or what? Tell us!"

"Sobek, that's enough!"

"Oh, go sit on a pyramid, Bird-brain."

"What did you call me?"

Anubis held up both hands. "Guys, cut it out. Thoth is right. I...there was a lot of beer, like I said...and I had way too much."

Thoth sat down heavily and folded his arms around his legs. "Oh, this is bad. We're going to have to tell Ra, you know."

"What, with Mr. All-Seeing Eye always hanging around him?" Sobek said. "Why bother? He probably already knows."

Anubis nodded. "I know. I'll accept whatever punishment is due."

"Punishment!" Sobek spat. "What for? He should be proud of you. Besides, Zeus does it all the time."

"*Used to,*" Thoth corrected.

"That's what you think."

Thoth's jaw dropped, but before he could start sputtering Anubis stood up. "Thoth's right. I'll go right now."

"We'll go with you," Thoth said.

"What do you mean, *we?*"

Thoth glowered at Sobek. "*We!*"

* * *

They found Ra right where they had expected, seated along with his compatriots around a table scattered with dice. The game-master scowled when they entered and blew a puff of flame from his nostrils. "We're sorry, Lucifer," Thoth said sheepishly. "We'll have him back in just a minute. Ra, can we have a quick word?"

The sun-god pushed back from the chair and strolled casually from the room. After closing the door, Anubis hung his head. "Father Ra, I know that it is forbidden to procreate with a mortal."

Ra's subtle smile did not flicker. "Of course. The world is no place for demi-gods these days, after all."

Anubis winced. "I understand. That's what I have come to tell you."

"I know what you did," Ra said simply.

Thoth closed his eyes reverently. "No transgression can be hidden from The All-Seeing Eye of Horus."

"Actually," Ra said, "we could hear Sobek roaring all the way over here."

Anubis shot Sobek a sour look and then dropped his gaze to the floor again. "I am prepared to accept my punishment."

Ra shook his head. "Do not worry, Anubis. There is no need for punishment. May I get back to my game now?"

"But…but the child…"

Ra laid a comforting hand on Anubis's shoulder. "My gentle son, there might very well have been a child," he said with a warm smile, "had that actually been a woman."

So far, the Gods have remained largely separate from the humans' affairs. In "A Melody in Seduction's Arsenal", they get down 'n dirty into the humans' action.

The Western and Eastern Roman Empires have evolved in a different direction than they have in our history, and have acknowledged all the beings of mythology—including the Egyptian, Greek, and Roman Gods. How have those Gods fared amidst the affairs of mortals, including all of the politics and espionage?

A Melody in Seduction's Arsenal

by Slip-Wolf

Mere minutes from disaster, Thadeus was reading all the wrong signs. Whether overconfidence could be blamed, or the wine clouding his senses, didn't really matter. Hubris was about to find him again. "You've gotten much less talkative since we came up here, or is it just me?" he asked.

Breeze billowed in through the window's draperies carrying the distant calls of night fauna into the inn's room. This late at night, there were no pings of carriage engines, no rumbling trains, none of the calamities of modern life to disturb them. Captured theurgic wisps from the room's four lamps painted details into the shadows. Sleek ivory curves of skin languidly stirred on the bed's rippling silks, and chestnut hair spilled over the pillows. Thadeus' hot breath on Lillian's neck was warm and eager.

"I like secrets," Lillian teased as her fingers teased Thadeus' beard. "Can we stop talking?"

The satyr smiled toothily and shrugged in reply. He nuzzled the dryad's blushing cheek, bringing a delighted chuckle even as she pulled away. "That tickles." Green eyes narrowed teasingly as they briefly met Thadeus' needy brown ones. The hand that stroked his beard danced south through the fuzz of his chest.

"You wanted me to stop talking," Thadeus purred, no mean feat with his elongated goatish jaw and flat teeth. His hands slid up her arms and massaged her shoulders, bringing a smile.

"That's a step in the right direction," Lillian smiled. "I want to just forget about work and just enjoy myself. There will be plenty of time for nonsense later." The way she narrowed her eyes told Thadeus she was sure what he *really* wanted from her was something he'd get if he only stopped pretending to be interested in socializing. *Shut up and just let things happen.*

If only things weren't the other way around. He was enjoying her company, to be sure, and he was in no hurry to wrap things up. He was, to his regret, on assignment, however.

Reliable information from Section Intelligence had led to Thadeus' first approaching Lillian in the tavern below. His flirtations with the dryad hadn't been rebuffed. Humans around them had given the beautiful woman surreptitious appraisals, and Thadeus' open glares as the two of them shared wine and moved to a little song. Just the right tune on his syrinx pipes brought amusement to her cheeks. She opened up to his interest bit by bit.

They both had lodgings here. Thadeus gratefully accepted Lillian's invitation to hers, as the room the innkeeper had granted Thadeus was a second rate hovel commonly given to 'types like his'.

Her generosity helped. Intelligence gathering was greatly aided by seeing what was spread around someone else's room; right now, their clothes.

As the files told, Lillian worked in the employ of Seth Axbev, a man whom Thadeus had been trailing up and down the Mediterranean for months. Lillian expertly handled Axbev's client affairs, though what the dryad knew of the organization's inner workings was still in question.

"What are you thinking about?" she asked him. He realized he'd slowly stopped massaging her shoulders.

He put on a grin. "Putting a flower in your hair, perhaps a whole garland."

"That's sweet. Pity there aren't any here. You'll just have to bloom for me." She winked.

His brows rose. Why did the exciting people in his life always wind up as those he was sent to investigate? It was as though he couldn't be interested in anyone who didn't have a skeleton in their closet. He briefly thought back on a handsome male Sileni he'd dallied with last year who'd been suspected of selling secrets to the Eastern Empire. The literal skeleton in that traitorous soul's closet had been an arms dealer who crossed him. With any luck, Lillian wouldn't be tied to her shady bosses' goings on.

Her hands snaked around Thadeus' back. Her legs wrapped around his furry thighs and flipped him on his side, laughing. Thadeus landed on the feathered mattress with a huff. Hungry eyes drank him wordlessly and she kissed him.

Through the combined buzz of arousal and copious quantities of wine, the question came abruptly. Who was seducing who?

Thadeus' taught instincts tugged him as his pulse thundered. Lillian was letting him do the work, coaxing him to a state of relaxation that was all too accommodating too quickly. He could taste the sweat in the air, and something didn't seem right. Her aura was like a second skin hiding something else.

Lillian rose to straddle him but Thadeus' leaned the other way, gathering their wine cups by their wet brims from the bed table. "Have another with me."

Lillian grabbed playfully at one of his horns. "Can't I just have you? What is it with you goats and your drink?"

"Makes us more pliant, don't you think?"

"I really didn't think a satyr needed so much to loosen up." Lillian laughed and reached out to tickle at Thadeus' furred flank as he slid past. "Bring them quickly."

Thadeus, already tipsy, approached the porter's tripod that was tucked out of light's reach. He had a little surprise he'd picked out himself sent up with the libations, something he had intended to give to Lillian later. He finally realized what triggered his apprehension, something Lillian had dismissed. The absence of flora from the room was peculiar. Even his own meager accommodations had a few decorative thistles in a copper pot. Separation from Nature's physis made dryads melancholic, which Lillian seemed anything but. Yet the room was disturbingly bare of vegetation, save the orchids Thadeus had concealed under the cart's cloth covering.

That strangeness in her scent, it spoke from every pore on her, but only now was he listening. Thadeus couldn't see under the cart, but his fingers found the petals and recoiled. The orchids' shriveled remains were slimy with decay, days of neglect somehow elapsed in a mere hour.

But how? Nothing he had brought with him could cause that. Instinct clicked with reason. He knew the miasma had to come from Lillian, her enticing scent a mask. He hoped desperately for some other answer than the one that jumped out at him, but nothing else fit. Thadeus' arousal fled as he realized that Seth Axbev wasn't just onto him. He had firmly decided that Thadeus was a threat. Lilian wouldn't play with him for long.

Outwardly calm, he filled both cups with wine and set them on the cart before going into his cloak pocket for his syrinx pipes. He brought them to his lips. "Rhea," he whispered. The F pipe breathed back at him and the miniscule theurgic wisps in the instrument's compartment rummaged through thousands of formulas for just the right elements. A thin tendril of smoke crept from the "A" bar as alchemy churned along. There could only be one batch—Thadeus could only hope there were no mistakes this time. Drinking Lilian under the table was a poor plan to fall back on.

The bed rustled behind him. There was a fizzle as the brazier's spark was extinguished, casting the room into darkness. Soft things stretched, split and tore with wet rending sounds.

Thadeus felt his hairs stand up on his neck, back and legs. Sickly green light spilled over his compact muzzle, broad nose, flinted brown eyes, and the rolled horns cresting the brow. His stubby goat's ears were swept back to the sounds behind him. The wisp of his beard thinned out over his thickly downed chest. Lillian laughed in an icy rasp. "Unfortunate choice of gift, satyr. Seems you only get one secret from me."

Thadeus' charm dropped like a spent weapon. "You're cursed, aren't you? Descended from one of the Ash tree dryads who tried to kill the God Zeus when he was an infant in Rhea's cave. Legend has it that irritated him just a little bit. Any time you get near any flora, it withers away to nothing. That must be maddening." He turned around, and saw her in the emerald glow of her own gaze. Her skin had withered to bark, her limbs twisted into tree limbs scimitared with curved dagger-like digits. Vines slipped round her misshapen torso, glistening with the hooks of thorns.

"I don't traffic in myths of Gods or curses, goat. My *condition* makes my field of work so much easier."

"I really doubt you could sell me a relaxing day at Axbev's mineral baths." Thadeus kept the pipes close to his side. "Unless you could hold that wonderful disguise of yours indefinitely?"

Splintered teeth smiled in a rictus. "I didn't need to. I only needed an hour more while you drank yourself into complacency. Splinters in the right places collect more information than caresses, as I intend to show you."

Thadeus raised a brow. "Well then. Glad this room's under your bill."

Lillian surged forward. Thadeus turned, placed his palms on the tripod and kicked back, his cloven hooves striking something neither flesh nor tree bark. She staggered, groaning through a throat of branches as wooden talons sliced air. Clawed roots dug into the floorboards as she gained purchase to attack again.

Thadeus spun. Syrinx in hand, he formed an embouchure with his lips in a flute-player's smile and blew a bright C note. A mist erupted, spraying Lillian.

There was the barest moment of confusion in the cragged, knotted face. Then the transformed dryad sneezed, spitting rotten splinters. Her green eyes narrowed suspiciously.

Thadeus swallowed. "We can talk about this."

Lillian wiped the dribbled mist from her chest. A single finger raised and curled wickedly in the moonlight. "I'll soon be listening to all you have to say." By the crackling sigh in her voice, Lillian was even more aroused now than she was in his arms. Thadeus should have pegged her for that type.

The door to the room was locked and he'd need critical seconds to get it open. A naked satyr wouldn't be something they'd be too pleased to see down in the tavern. He marked the distance to the window.

Lillian flexed for another lunge, then buckled, hissing with surprise and pain. Thadeus had barely a moment to realize what was happening and duck before the afflicted patch of dryad burst into a gout of flame.

Lillian screamed obscenities in Latin, Greek and a curious bit of Gaelic as she spun around seeking relief and then threw herself on the bed to quench the fire. The disheveled sheets caught blaze almost immediately. As the dryad danced and flung herself around, so did the drapes.

Thadeus instinctively raised the wine flagon to douse her, realized what vintage he was holding, and took a swig instead as he backed away and processed the scene. The open window was a leap past the flaming bed away, the dryad thrashing and rolling on the floor before him. To one side of her was her stack of possessions, including her neatly folded clothes and a small satchel. To the other was a haphazard pile of Thadeus' own garments.

He sighed as the room burned. Was there really a choice? He leapt past the grasping talons of the cursed dryad, whose wound was now a smoking ruin, grabbed her satchel and then hurled himself past the flames to the open window, an inch from singeing his shin fur.

At the balustrade, he quickly gauged the distance to the gardens below, crouched on his sturdy goat's legs and leaped. The night air was cool on his naked frame as he landed, rolled and fled down the cobbled street passed the glow of theurgic lamps, to the dark at the edge of town.

* * *

Time being critical, a meeting was arranged by ether-line at least two jurisdictions from the mess Thadeus left on the coast.

The tavern was in a village tucked between the hills of Old Gaul Belgae, a rustic outlier in the Western Auguries Pact that had changed little in the centuries since the Western Roman Empire's final dissolution and the Pact's formation. It was a quiet little settlement where ethnic unrest, hazardous theurgic-industries and stern brinkmanship with the Eastern Empire were of little concern. Thadeus envied these people.

The tavern's hall was thick with stale kitchen scents and buzzing insects. The burly Roman known as Brand was hunched in a corner where a fetal sausage, greens and amber malt underwent his offensive. He typically met his agents in the field; not just because he could read his charges better right after a mission, but so he could visit more exotic restaurants that way.

Thadeus took a rickety seat and slid the syrinx over. "It needs topping up," he said without preamble.

Brand furrowed wiry eyebrows and spoke in halting baritone. "This is the third time you've arrived at a meeting wearing someone else's trousers."

"I traded an empty leather satchel for these breeches and a bottle of Tuscan at a border post. I couldn't do too much haggling with the midnight cold encroaching on, well, all of me."

"You traded for a pair of pants and some *wine*? Why not a shirt?"

Thaddeus looked down at his bare chest. "I needed to calm my nerves."

Brand grumbled as he took another bite. "Your missive was rather abrupt. So Lillian was a bent dryad sent to kill you?"

"She said as much. We didn't get to fully know each other, we were both a bit rushed."

"Thank the Gods you made it."

"Let's not."

Brand shuffled cutlery. "I trust you kept things tidy. We don't want a repeat of the Chiarianus affair last year."

Thadeus grimaced. "Will you ever let that go? I stopped the man from transporting that explosive-stuffed wine-press to the Parthenon. So what if I couldn't find the spark-box? The creditors were going to level his winery anyway. It's why the bitter bastard wanted everybody dead."

"There wasn't an unbroken cup or window from the Acropolis to the coast," Brand countered.

"Glassware merchants did so well as a result that the Greek recession likely ended." Thadeus shrugged. "They're welcome." He raised his arm to hail a server who ignored him. "Incidentally, back to this assignment, the room was on Lillian's tab, so if the place burnt down we won't have to pay for it."

Brand closed his eyes and shook his head. "Dammit, Thadeus. This Axbev character clearly knows you're onto him. That complicates things."

"For me."

"We know you can handle it."

Thadeus darkened. "No thanks to you. Your geniuses in the Palatine Bureau had Lillian pegged as an ambitious, eager-to-please dryad handling clients and making appointments, just another clerical worker. That's nine of every ten damn preternaturals who wander out of the mists looking for mortal employment."

"Effective assassins are the ones we don't know about. One of the dangers that you signed on for in protecting the safety and freedom in the Auguries Pact." Brand snorted. "And that's imperiled. The pressure from above has gotten worse. We have another body."

Brand was infuriating. No matter how many swords, bombs, and nooses Thadeus escaped out there, the *real* pressure always seemed to come to him from above. Thadeus set his anger aside. "Who now?"

"An Aegean league diplomat, Catoline Tulo out of the embassy at Crete, found in his home like the others, serene contentment glowing on his dead face. We know he was another client of Axbev's in a resort he had on the island."

"So, that's six dead now." Thadeus silently sorted the facts; six victims over the past two months spread throughout the West Auguries' states and territories. Venture merchants, populares, and politicos found in their homes with blissful, cherubic expressions on their cold dead faces. "Any results from examination?"

"No. Necromantics, Curses, Poisons: we've checked for everything. Autopsies and para-theurgic divinings have been fruitless. Their only mutual connections are as confidential clients of Axbev Recreational Facilitations. We've still failed to assemble any definitive history on Mister Seth Axbev, beyond his public prominence as an owner of several Mediterranean resorts."

"Well, now you know he employs dryad assassins. That seems rather important."

Brand nodded, knowing what Thadeus meant. Even after six hundred years of integration into the waning Roman Empire, many Mist folk showed no desire to integrate with Western society. Lillian's exceptionally rare curse made her kind extremely difficult to retain.

Outside the tavern's slatted windows, a carelessly driven stroke-carriage cut off a rickshaw, splashing its puller with gutter filth. The dripping centaur waved his arms, scuffed his hooves, and shouted in colorfully profane Germanic as his human fares cringed in one another's arms.

The sad show dragged Thadeus back to the present. "We also have more." He unrolled a small scroll onto the table. Julian calendar days were marked apart with slashes. A single notation marked the next. "This was in Lillian's things. It reads; 'her full entourage expected, guard exit six.'"

Brand sat back and set down his cutlery. "I think I know what that may refer to. Ledgers you recovered from last week's visit to Axbev's offices contained interesting expenditures. He's purchased box tickets for a performance of Apuleius' transformational memoirs at the restored Milano Theatre in two day's time."

"Her full entourage..." Thadeus muttered.

"The next step is to find out what that means." Brand put his elbows on the table, eyes hard with honesty. "Just remember, Thadeus, we'll support you with all the tools at our disposal," he deftly switched the syrinx for a stroke carriage primer key; "but unpleasant surprises are your job. We didn't select you for these assignments simply because you avoided drinking your way up through the service."

"That was an option?" Thadeus asked, realizing that after ten minutes none of the sleepy staff in this place had offered to serve him. Of course, there were no other preternaturals in here.

Brand hadn't noticed. "The carriage is fully fueled and waiting around back. You'll find everything you require stocked inside," he said by way of dismissal.

Thadeus didn't want to eat here anyway. "I'll send word when I have something." Thadeus retrieved the key and then lifted Brand's amber malt, downing it all in four swallows. He set the empty glass down and they regarded each other stoically.

"You have any pudding coming?" Thadeus asked.

"No."

Thadeus left.

* * *

The late afternoon sun painted Milano's edifices a coppery sheen, marred only by columns of rising steam and the climbing viscera of ether lines and junction boxes that bolted to the tulfa brick and spread cables from rooftop to rooftop. Thadeus sniffed at the heavy summer air that hung with the stink of warm trash. Despite the uniquely urban stench, he was hungry.

It was a short walk from where Thadeus stabled the carriage, having discreetly donned the low-buttoned rich blue tunic that revealed some of his broad furry chest and knee-length leather trousers inside. Another syrinx found in the boot storage weighed in a hip-side sling.

Late day crowds bustled in and out of tarp-shielded shops and taverns, haggling or joking in Latin, Greek, and other languages from the Pact's reaches. Thadeus lowered his ears against the bangs that came from a carriage shop where a thumping stroke engine was laid bare so a smithy could diagnose the integrity of the caged theurgic forces furiously turning its crank.

If one thing truly defined the fifty or so states that formed the Western Auguries Pact, it was the harnessing of theurgy. The scientifically applied opposing powers of creation and destruction had led to a vast Renaissance in the arts and sciences even before Western Rome's fall and the Pact's formation in its wake. Ether lines allowed cross-Western messages to be sent while powerful engines pulled trains and carriages and oceanic vessels across leagues.

Thadeus stopped at a shop to buy some bread and cheese. He paid the old Gaul baker two coppers, which the man accepted with a sour stare, after Thadeus declined a stale loaf and pointed at one that was steaming with freshness. The transaction settled, Thadeus went on his way. The cheese was hard, but by tearing the hot loaf open and stuffing the cheese inside to melt, Thadeus was able to make a decent meal.

Life for preternaturals, as the burgeoning sciences now demarked Peoples of the Mists, wasn't perfect. Even after hard fought concessions throughout the Western Auguries, centaurs still had difficulty accessing many human built spaces. Mariners still hunted leviathans rumored to be intelligent, and sileni were banned from many drinking halls for suspected behavior that made satyrs look comparatively sedate. Despite their precarious status in some circles, a wide majority of non-humans were allowed to go most places unmolested, providing they behaved in what the human majority considered a lawful manner.

And they were certainly useful. Banging hammers and creaking pulleys drew a scaffolded building up taller, guided by dust-coated humans below and frayed-winged harpies above who scratched at their beaks and swore at one another in comradely bickering that made Thadeus smile. His hunger pangs fell away and his mood brightened even if the dust in the air was settling on the meal he ate.

Despite his own status as a citizen being second rate to some, things were certainly better here in the West than in Constantinople and the conquered lands of the Eastern Roman Empire, which retained the Imperial title the West had discarded. Dictates from their Emperor held that preternaturals were infernal monsters consigned for enslavement or destruction. Fear of an Eastern invasion loomed largely. Peace was only just maintained through the same theurgy that kept the lights on at night, with massive weapons of incredible destruction pointed both ways across the Mediterranean border just off of Athens's shores, guarding the fragile sanctity of the two superpowers.

It somewhat helped interspecies relations in the West that the Pantheons of immortal Gods were seen as tangible forces by the few who still believed they really existed. The "Auguries" part of the West Auguries Pact was more wishful propaganda than celestial endorsement. Thadeus was pretty sure the last Western Emperor didn't actually declare his Empire defunct before throwing himself on the swords of his own honor guard, but who even cared anymore? The Pact managed to join city-state sovereignties with a mutual desire to prevent the East from overrunning them. Thadeus couldn't argue with that.

The working noise fell back as Thadeus approached the theater, another imposing architectural giant crowding the city's core. Corinthian columns cast its bulk in long shadows as Thadeus climbed its steps. A garland-crowned oracle working the door smiled wanly as she took a draw of Delphic incense from the tripod before her and offered a brief blessing on behalf of Dionysus in exchange for his entry fee, beckoning him to enter with a thin smile.

Thadeus entered the ornate lobby's bustling throng, upper crust Latins in rich tunics, togas and a smattering of excursionists from distant provinces wearing trim Gaulish and Frankish styles. Marble stairs led to the high boxes, the concession bar spread below. With the curtain an hour away and a dry throat, Thadeus chose the bar, lit by theurgic wisps in glass mountings, as his best vantage point.

He passed many groups, catching snippets of conversation that changed course to note the satyr with coinage for a show. While many preternatural folk had lost their exotic flavor over time, others still drew attention. The extravagant Frankish Countess holding court by the stairs didn't have a water nymph on each arm by accident. As a satyr, Thadeus had complicated impressions to deal with that went far beyond scowls from street vendors and innkeepers. The odd pair of eyes traced his stocky utility down to where hock and hooves escaped his leggings. One man instinctively put an arm around his companion to steer her from Thadeus' path. A dark haired, slender man at the bar held a kylix of wine under his nose and quietly wondered things that made him smile guiltily.

Thadeus accepted the glances. Whether satyrs really could pipe melodies that made people dance naked in the moonlight or suffer overwhelming panic in battles didn't matter much. Legend still surpassed empirical truth where many preternaturals were concerned. That could be an advantage in his work, but grudging respect from some circles gave way to scorn from others that led to various small complications. Many humans found satyrs physically unappealing. Others knew better. Thadeus' novelty would wear off and allow him to disappear into the background soon enough.

Thadeus perched on a stool and ordered a chianti, proffered by a bartender who studiously averted his gaze, took his coinage and escaped quickly. Thadeus sipped calmly, watching the throng head for stalls and boxes, waiting for something to draw his attention. Time passed languidly before his studiously indifferent gaze was drawn to the foyer.

The disturbance's effect was subtle at first. From the entrance, a small group crossed the threshold with patient deliberation. In the center of a smartly attired sea, a presence bloomed that tingled the hairs on his hide, even from a distance. Thadeus sat straighter on his stool and caught a glimpse that caught his breath, waves of ochre hair encircling radiant feminine features. Ocean-blue eyes consumed everything in their path. Thadeus' memory stirred, colliding hard with doubts.

It simply couldn't be her. Wonder, worry and other feelings he didn't know how to untangle rushed in as recognition dawned.

People in her wake seemed to react to something inexplicable. A young couple instinctively put their hands around each other's waist, ready to dance. A solitary soul became lost in a pleasing memory. People brushing past one another traded glances, wondering, appraising, coy. The hall warmed *en masse*, spreading tiny fires beneath the skin of everyone in sight.

Thadeus gripped his wine tightly. No one recognized her. Hell, Thadeus couldn't decide if he himself was merely mistaken or hallucinating. Her brood had become so elusive that their very existence was often doubted. Yet right here, a creature with all the power in the world appeared to pass Thadeus by on sandaled feet.

She ascended the stairs with her entourage of nubile cupids and nymphs, drifting forth in an elaborate stola whiter than a summer cloud. The air tingled long after she faded from sight.

Thadeus sat quietly, collecting thoughts and emotions like debris, his assignment nearly forgotten in the face of something that he couldn't explain. *Her full entourage...* No, they couldn't be connected. This had to be a ridiculous coincidence.

Ridiculous because it couldn't be true. Awe surrendered to weariness and annoyance. Of all the places to run into *her*—he really didn't need this.

And were they face to face, they'd want nothing more than to spit in each other's faces.

Thadeus knocked back his wine and swayed, feeling woozy. His heart had quickened with his old acquaintance's passage, but something else was also settling over him, something malevolent. The glass slipped and shattered on the foot rail. Colors began to bleed into one another.

Thadeus stumbled towards the lavatory, bumping into a coifed prig who watched him weave on his hairy legs and sniggered to his friends. *Yes,* Thadeus thought. *Drunken satyr on the move. Don't pass up a stereotype, you ignorant ass.*

Thadeus' world went milky as he slumped to his knees. The liveried arms of lobby attendants slipped under his, hauling him up. The opening of a server's curtain was the last thing Thadeus blearily saw before being thrust into a darkness that became everything.

* * *

Thadeus woke, tasting dust on a neglected floor.

In perfect unison, arms clamped his bare shoulders and pulled him to his knees. His tunic was gone, his leggings remained. As his head cleared, eyes throbbing under needling light, he saw the stifling confines of a wood-slatted storage room, empty save a dangling wisp lamp.

Thadeus craned to inspect his captors. The hands holding him were black lacquered like insect carapace. Red theatre attendant dress terminated under shiny dark orbs with white painted faces, serene and dispassionate.

"Ningyos?" Thadeus muttered through a cotton layer of numbness.

"Yes," the reply was deep and gravelly. "I used golems for awhile, but fired clay wears horribly in the wet months. I find the automata of the lands far East of Constantinople's reach much more reliable for my purposes, trade embargoes be damned."

Each of these theurgically-fired machines likely cost enough to pay Thadeus' own stipend for a year. Probably high-jacked with their loyalties re-cogged. Thadeus swallowed. "What happened?"

"Satyrs and their Tuscan reds," the voice chided. "You missed curtain call. No refund, I'm afraid."

Drugged wine. The barman hadn't looked him in the eye, but too few ever did. "Have we met?"

"Indirectly. You invaded my offices last week and went rather rigorously through my things."

Axbev.

Floor boards creaked as a slim human came around. Fine leathers, a tailored gilded jacket in Egyptian cut over a crimson cravat in Brittanican style collected upon a slender middle-aged mortal man. His black hair was clipped short and his eyes were darkly lined with kohl. "I've wanted to meet you in person ever since."

"Really? Wasn't your assistant supposed to kill me?"

Axbev coughed delicately. "I had other things in mind. Pity, you left her with quite the rash."

Thadeus frowned. "Don't go starting any rumors."

Axbev smiled.

"So don't keep me in suspense, Seth. What am I doing here?"

"Well, ordinarily it would be enough for me to extract the information from you regarding what you're doing here and kill you—"

"That's original."

"—but Lillian's detailed, rather caustic report of your few hours together has revealed you have talents that would greatly benefit me."

Thadeus raised an eyebrow. "Some rumors aren't so bad."

"You're a satyr. And I need a satyr, but for a different set of skills entirely. When you meet her, you'll understand."

Thadeus tread carefully, having no idea where Axbev was going with this. It still might be a coincidence. "Her?"

"Someone very special, right here amongst us in this very Opera house. A lover of the arts and an artist of loves, whom I've followed round this world. A precocious, rebellious flame who so rarely manages to slip free of her brood's overbearing clutches and bejewel this bleak world. You, lucky satyr, get to be in her presence today."

Oh damn, that sounds an awful lot like who I think it is. "So you fancy someone. You expecting me to offer you some pickup tips?" Thadeus baited, feigning ignorance with a shrug.

Axbev crouched and struck his blunt muzzle with a back-handed swipe. The sting lingered as the ningyos held him tightly.

"I expect you to make up for your transgressions, goat. Spying on *me* for your bureaucratic swineherders! It's thoroughly pathetic that such as you should serve the whims of slavemasters who debase you."

Thadeus blinked. "I don't work for anyone. And I'm feeling rather debased by *you*, if you want me to be honest."

Axbev's laugh rattled harshly. "Forgive me, of course! Spending your spare time seeking every bottle's bottom narrows your view of the world you live in. As for myself, well, I've been well versed in the Mist folk's usefulness while mixing with the self-aggrandizing masters of these Auguries. Copper mine dust won't choke a minotaur, mermaids have been trained to lay undersea ethercables for miles without tiring, and satyrs willingly lay down their lives for a loaded bed and few drinks! Like every creature that once graced the Gods, mortal man has you sorted and productively relegated; playthings for exploitation in their newly forged world."

Thadeus swallowed. "Is that so? I don't suppose Lillian received this wisdom before you relegated her?"

Axbev ignored him. "Such blessed wonders you used to be, shining bright among the base creatures littering this world. But you decided to throw that away to toil with mortals in their filthy industries; maligning theurgic powers to make carriages roll and voices fly. Such pointless waste." He sighed. "Hubris is not just a human foible, after all."

Thadeus could see where battle-lines were drawn in Axbev's head, but they didn't make any sense. "Barring insanity, you aren't who you pretend to be. So out with it. Who am I really dealing with?"

Axbev sneered as he stood to his full height and opened his collar. With a bubbling hiss his fair-seeming skin began to boil. A drop of wax sizzled the boards at his feet, then more and more drizzled down his attire as his human features stretched and fissured. Under squinting eyes, a slender black muzzle thrust forth. Tall black ears rose from under a wig that tumbled away. A kerchief in a black paw rubbed the thickest of the wax away as the dark jackal's head took a rasping breath.

Thadeus felt cold. The jackal's countenance before him was familiar, though by reputation rather than acquaintance. It certainly couldn't be who it appeared to.

"You know, someone seeing the real you might be tempted to think you're a God."

Axbev sneered. "Few believe in them anymore. What do you think, satyr?"

"I've found it best to keep an open mind. So I'll just go ahead and ask. How...familiar are you with Anubis of the Nile?"

The voice growled from that muzzle, the spell that animated his disguise now fully spent. Axbev tore away fake flesh from his fingers and put a dark paw on his chest. "I am his son."

Thadeus realized at that moment how utterly over his head he was and fought to think logically. That Gods were real and moving among mortals and preternaturals was in itself no real shock, not to him anyway. But that the offspring of one of Egypt's Pantheon of immortal Gods would be the man he was chasing, spanning the Auguries...and running pleasure resorts? The satyr needed a stiff drink just to make the whole thing seem less absurd. "I suppose the Axbev moniker is a Romanized derivation of the Egyptian phrase Ouaxbef, the bark of a dog." Thadeus shrugged as best he could. "Yes, that's right, I speak Egyptian. Did you pick that?"

"Irrelevant. All that matters is that I picked you." Axbev said. "So listen. I am not the only immortal in attendance here."

It took Thadeus effort not to swallow. "You're jesting."

"The Goddess Aphrodite walks among us. She will be brought here, and you will charm her to submission."

Much as he'd wanted to goad Axbev to keep him off guard, much as his heart wanted to sink at hearing that name, the snicker came first. "Thanks for preening my ego, but you're overrating me just a little bit."

Axbev raised a shiny brow, amused. His black furred paw withdrew a pale object from his jacket. "You will with this."

A syrinx glinted in his hand. It wasn't the one he'd brought with him.

Thadeus frowned. "Even if I believed that one of the Gods of Olympus was actually watching a play on the other side of these walls, I can hardly imagine what you want me to do with those."

"Why, play them of course. Play something very particular." Axbev grinned, canines glinting as he paced in a wide circle around his captive. The ningyos held themselves and Thadeus perfectly still so he couldn't follow the jackal's progress.

"One of my favorite, but little known tales of antiquity brings us together, my little friend. You will play a very old melody for our guest, one composed by your ancestor and benefactor, the God Pan over one lonely, fitful century. He intended to use it to seduce the Goddesses into loving him and decided to try it first on Aphrodite. In Pan's arrogance and urgency to gain favor he, well...overdid things."

Thadeus stared at the syrinx, then at Axbev as the jackal came around. He knew what Axbev was speaking of and felt the room grow smaller.

"Struck a nerve, did I? We both know Pan's musical compositions were highly cherished among the satyr tribes who dispersed during the first mass diaspora of preternaturals into the larger world. Those passed-down melodies were very rarely played and carefully guarded by satyr-folk for good reasons, weren't they?"

Thadeus wouldn't let Axbev see how fast his pulse was racing now. Axbev knew too much, but not everything. Thadeus phrased his question very carefully. "That's an extremely dangerous composition you're referring to, Axbev. It didn't succeed in seducing her or any of the other Gods. All it did was render her unconscious." Thadeus took a deep breath and grit his teeth. "And she was very furious when she woke. Do you know what happened to Pan for playing it?"

Axbev chuckled. "Aphrodite's lover Ares killed him, the only God ever snuffed out among Zeus' brood; proving that hubris even makes its way to Olympus if you're a cloven-hoofed moron seeking congress above your league."

Thadeus' expression hardened. He didn't want Axbev to see him fume.

The dog laughed. "Despite his dying, I discovered through painstaking research that Pan's melody found its way to other hands. The relics and refuse of Gods always manage to wash up somewhere. Satyrs kept the composition's power hidden to guard against the kind of persecution they now suffer under the Eastern Byzantines. Its effect is legendary, but I was excited to discover additional potential."

Axbev produced a scroll which he unfurled. The musical notes were rough, the parchment badly frayed. Thadeus' stomach churned as he recognized the arrangement.

Axbev rolled it up again. "While Pan's song can lull a God to swooning submission, slight tonal modifications, even on wax roll recordings, take the song much, much further with mortals. Too much bliss is fatal, did you know that?"

Axbev's deceased clients, dead with cherubic smiles. One veil of the mystery was lifted. "You…you weapon-ized a love song?"

Axbev shrugged. "What else is any tool of seduction? Pan intended no less. Nor do you when you coax an informant to bed. Love is the more comely face of war. You know this." His demeanor settled to wistfulness. "Sadly, it seems that a God's ears require a live performance with a soul breathing life into pipes for the composition to work. No song-grinder will suffice for this job." Axbev grinned. "You carry a flute like this as your only tool because you know how to wield it, and wield it well. I already had a satyr selected for this task, one playing flute in this very play's orchestra, but I would prefer one of proven skill. Lillian's debrief got *you* the position of first flutist."

"Oh, wonderful. Well, I play better with my own."

"Yours was damaged when we confiscated it. The theurgic forge inside made a fiery mess in the cloak room. Why don't you try and fool me some other way?"

Deal, Thadeus thought. "What do you want Aphrodite for?"

"Nothing that concerns you."

Thadeus met his gaze and held it. "Oh, but your victims concern me. An Aegean diplomat on the verge of settling the Lesbos conflict in Eastern Imperial Waters? The venture-merchant who acquired New Carthage's largest siege-weapon builder with intent to dismantle it? Am I getting somewhere?"

Axbev sniffed disdainfully. "Theorize all you like." He waved the scroll. "You will do as I say."

"If I refuse?"

Axbev crouched level with his captive and didn't blink. "I know every single part of you that doesn't play music. We won't need any of them, will we?"

Thadeus could smell the bloodlust on him and considered his options carefully. The ningyos had him. His weapon was gone. There was no means of escape, no assistance. The satyr down below whom Axbev had originally planned to abduct wouldn't have any reason not to comply with the Jackal's threats. Even if he did, Thadeus knew at least three others like himself between here and Rome who who would do it for a glass of cheap port and a laugh. There was only one thing he could do.

"I'll play it," Thadeus muttered.

Axbev's ears perked. "Pardon?"

"Yes."

Axbev blinked. "I was sure you would resist." His paws wrung fretfully. "I rather hoped you would, just a little."

Thadeus stared at the floor and sighed wearily. "I can't stop you, so I'll settle for keeping my hide. That means you have to do something for me."

"Do I?" Axbev rumbled dangerously.

Thadeus looked up. "Swear on Osiris' name that I go free after this. Neither you nor anyone with you can hurt me. That's a promise you can't break."

Axbev's muzzle hung open and he laughed. "Very astute! Your knowledge of the powers of our oaths impresses me. Certainly. By Osiris, your life will not be harmed if you do as you're told." Axbev licked his teeth, giving him a sideways glance. "There's just something about you that I can't put a claw on, you clever goat. Just don't disappoint me."

Thadeus said nothing, expression cold as he planned.

* * *

With Axbev's plan in motion, she came. Two mortals in subdued attire escorted Aphrodite between them. The Goddess ignored their proximity, her aura crackling. Even restrained and threatened, Thadeus was involuntarily drawn to her timeless beauty, a maddening effect under the circumstances.

"Please come in." Axbev beckoned. "I hope her entourage posed no difficulties."

One of the men responded tersely. "To the contrary, she only came willingly to keep them alive. She doesn't seem very threatened."

"You will regret this transgression." Aphrodite's voice rang the world like an assembly of bells, haughty and furious. "My husband will seek you out and you will perish with—."

"Hephaestus?" Axbev scoffed, fighting the urge to laugh. "Please save it. You're really going to pretend he's your champion? I suspect you still have Ares wrapped 'round your finger, but I doubt that clubfooted dullard you wed would miss you very much. Zeus probably let you stray to Earth to get a little peace from your mutual bickering."

Aphrodite looked as though she'd been slapped. Her eyes narrowed, glistening with deadly promise. The jackal merely shrugged.

Axbev produced wax ear plugs and flicked his tall ears as he blocked them. The ningyos' wooden skull's ear canals clicked shut. Axbev pointed to the open scroll on the floor and knocked Thadeus on the horns with the syrinx he handed down. "Play."

Thadeus gasped as the ningyos released him and took the syrinx, shaking numbness out of his shoulders.

Aphrodite's gaze finally found the kneeling satyr with pipes in hands and blinked, surprised.

"Hello, my name is Thadeus," Thadeus blurted with a pained smile. "We've never met, but—"

"I don't see you playing," Axbev snarled.

Thadeus had to act. If she recognized him…Putting syrinx to his embouchure-formed lips, eyes to the scroll, he obeyed.

At first Pan's final composition was slow and mournful, a lament stemming from longing and solitude, a fugue that quickly drew Aphrodite's attention like a moth to a flame, as powerless for her to ignore as her aura was for him. Gradually, coaxingly, the composition turned, swelling with a sliding melody that promised joys and pleasures far from the grip of a heartless diminishing universe. Reedy breaths whispered promises of eternal devotion, built on strong notes of hope for affection's return. Lustful lows and ecstatic peaks serenaded Aphrodite, who swayed on her feet, eyelids fluttering as the melody took full hold. As the tempo slowed, she sank to her knees, gazing wearily into Thadeus' eyes. All too soon, the song ended.

Moments passed. Axbev removed his plugs. "Did it work?"

Thadeus swallowed. The air was charged with the raw theurgic power that fueled immortal blessings—and curses.

He had to be quick. "It can't work yet. The song needs approval."

"What?"

Thadeus glared at him. "You have to know of the curse put on Pan's work by Apollo. No melody works unless someone judges it to be better music than Apollo's. If not, the composition fails. Please tell me you actually studied that."

"I've never *heard* Apollo's music. How should I know—"

"It's wearing off!" Thadeus hissed.

"Fine! I judge Pan's music to be better than that of Apollo," Axbev stammered, perplexed. There was a twinge in the air when he said it, a static crackle that made everyone who wasn't a machine wince.

Thadeus breathed one last note. Aphrodite sank to the floor with a yearning moan, eyes dreamily seeking something distant and wondrous.

"Done," Thadeus gasped.

Axbev's jackal nose tested the air. He crouched and sniffed carefully at Aphrodite's throat. His lips pulled back from dagger-like teeth. "Excellent!"

Axbev's attendants removed their ear plugs. One of the conspirators coughed. "Are we still needed?"

Axbev waved him off with a raised claw. "I shall join you for the last act shortly. You will both be rewarded for your assistance, now and in the work to come."

The mortals sauntered out, a distant murmur of a Greek chorus floating in behind them. Aphrodite was left crumpled in the dust as Thadeus stared uselessly. "I suppose you won't tell me what you want with her."

Axbev scratched an ear as he grinned. "I'll enjoy her company for awhile. After that…My father's family is of no help to me, so I've crossed the West Pantheon's boundaries to secure Ares' martial talents for a venture of mine, one that will require Aphrodite's presence as his inducement. He will do *anything* to get her back."

From what he knew, Thadeus realized that much was absolutely true. He weighed this against what he already knew, namely the significance of some of Axbev's victims. A peace envoy, a reformed weapons maker, politicians dedicated to the *status quo*. "You're going to start a war, the Auguries Pact against the Eastern Empire."

A shrug. "Really, I'm only nurturing the inevitable along. I wouldn't want to weigh on your conscience any further, so I must go." He stood, rubbing his ear lobe.

"Wait! All the thousands dead, with theurgic weapons of mass destruction, would seriously tax your father's ability to weigh the hearts of every soul, wouldn't it? The underworld Gods of the other Pantheons might suffer the same." Thadeus pressed. "A breakdown between the Pantheons would be some revenge for being neglected, wouldn't it?"

Axbev strode past, saying nothing.

"I understand your anger! You're just a forgotten bastard of his, aren't you? Axbev is the name you chose because he didn't care to give you one."

Axbev stopped at the door, lip curling from sharp teeth that ground together. "Did you know that promises to Osiris don't extend to automata? The ningyos had their final orders hours ago." He nodded to them. "Collect the Goddess afterwards. Don't get too much of him on that stola she's wearing."

The automata at Thadeus' sides clamped his shoulders again, drawing out a pained bleat. Axbev scratched his other ear distractedly and left.

Aphrodite's slumbering form was still as the free limbs of Thadeus' executioners dispensed short, wicked knives.

"Get up." Thadeus hissed. "Help me!"

A blade angled for the plunge into his furred throat.

Aphrodite stirred and opened her eyes.

The ningyos paused at their task, confused. One released Thadeus, stepping fluidly toward Aphrodite who narrowed her gaze. "You cannot harm me."

In a blink, she became a small gold-throated blue bird, fluttering to a low rafter. Thadeus twisted in the remaining assassin's unbreakable grip, the blade at his naked throat when the bird sang a trilling warble.

The ningyos froze.

There were sounds, slight at first, then loud like the snapping of lyre strings. Both ningyos shuddered as whale-baleen sinews and bone cogs within them began cracking and failing. A mask slipped off one of them, freeing pearlescent spinning brain-case cogs that danced across the floor. Within moments, the ningyos crumbled into broken detritus.

Aphrodite, back in her mortal guise, stood among the remains. "Oh, for a thing to face its own emptiness and yearn itself inside out! My voice has always carried far more power than those winsome pipes of yours."

Thadeus winced. "Luckily, I know which notes to flex so the spell is broken. Axbev would have smelled if you faked it, not that you two wouldn't have been a perfect match after what you put me through." Thadeus let words freeze the air that he'd been saving for centuries. "After all this time, you're still an overbearing, cruel bitch."

Curiosity subdued Aphrodite's fury, but only for a moment. "And to hell with you, Pan, you stupid goat. You're supposed to be *dead*."

The satyr who called himself Thadeus snorted. "I could slap you."

"I could kill you!"

"Obviously you can't, Kypris. Or have your sponge-headed sycophant do it for you."

That name hadn't been spoken to her in eons. "Ares told me he put an arrow through you," she sneered.

"Still have the scar. I'm dead as far as you're concerned, and that's enough for me."

Silence burned between them.

"You tried to violate me!" she hissed.

Thadeus grit his teeth. "No! I wanted your affections, yes, some manner of reciprocation from you, but when the melody put you asleep I didn't...I just went off and sulked for a while."

"Only because you knew what would happen to you," she rumbled.

"Damn you, Kypris, I wasn't just after sex. I wanted you to feel something for me, appreciate my artfulness. I thought you could see past this," he flicked a long ear, "that you could even love me."

She laughed bitterly "Sentimental, hirsute idiot. Do you have any idea what the rest of the Pantheon thought when you subdued me? What they concluded? Do you have any idea the whispers that chased me through Zeus' house?"

"Oh, and those snickers would be all my fault, would they? Playing around with Ares behind your husband's back wouldn't have contributed to that jibe? No, you blamed your whole lot on me and tried to have me killed. Enough pissed-off suitors of yours came after my tail to restock the Spartan army."

Aphrodite straightened her stola. "Ares told me he took care of business. How did you escape?"

Thadeus shook his head. "Worry about your botched murder attempt later. Your escorts are waiting."

"This discussion isn't over, Pan."

"Oh, you damn well bet it isn't. And don't call me by that name."

In a second store-room one floor down behind theatre boxes, they speedily dispatched the Ningyos holding the entourage at blade-point. Aphrodite strode forth, drawing their attention while the satyr took the first machine down with a hoof through the brain-box. The other raised its weapon, but could not kill Aphrodite as she approached. Her imitation of Axbev's voice was flawless after a few minutes hearing it, her command imperative. Two strokes of its own weapon retired it in the honorable tradition of its painstaking craftsman, theurgic discharge clouding from its belly.

At her strict command, the nymphs and cupids blew kisses and tearful prayers at their Goddess as they fled. Thadeus watched them depart, embarrassed by the sycophantic thank-you's that rained down on her. "Right, let's go. Axbev won't be preoccupied much longer."

"Preoccupied?"

Thadeus took the stairs, hooves clacking on the wooden planks and Aphrodite light on his heels as the third act swelled beyond the walls. "It's a case of curses overriding curses. Happens a lot after a while. Thank your vain brother, Apollo."

"I don't understa—"

"Thadeus!" A hiss roared up towards them and they froze. With the sounds of wood scraping on wood, a figure rose into view whom Thadeus recognized immediately. Lillian was back in her lithe nymph form, or most of the way. Along her chin and slender neck, a bark-like swath of scar tissue plunged down into the black-low cut stola she wore. Her slender white fingers grew wooden talons as she opened her palms menacingly. "I knew I would find you again!"

Thadeus frowned, realizing he'd forgotten something. "This is exit six, isn't it?"

Aphrodite shrugged. "Why would I know?"

Thadeus' shoulders fell. He realized that in addition to not having his armed syrinx, his fuzzy torso was still bare to the waist. He kept eyes on the wooden claws before him. "Hi, Lillian. You're healing well."

"And you'll *die well* for what you've done to me! It will take months for these scars to disappear!" She stamped one foot. Her bare toes were growing roots that scrabbled at the planks.

"Why should they matter? You look perfectly fine to me. And you kill people for a living, anyway."

"I *seduce* and kill people. And that was only part-time! How am I supposed to sell exfoliant and citrus skin treatments to the rich Romans who visit my master's baths when I look driven over by a wagon wheel! I won't hit my quotas!"

"Oh, that's no concern, trust me, Lillian. All Axbev's resorts will be razed or repossessed by the Auguries Pact authorities in a day or two. You won't have that job either."

Lillian's green eyes widened. Aphrodite coughed. "That will calm her down. I suppose you gave her that rash."

"Oh, shut up," Thadeus muttered. The next landing exit was two flights back up. They couldn't run back that way fast enough. Lillian crouched to leap and Thadeus prepared for a tackle, wondering how many of the cursed dryad's knives would pierce his flesh. He was startled by the snap of Aphrodite's fingers.

Lillian leaped.

Or tried to. With a roar, she glanced down to see her winding foot roots had buried themselves into the planks. She teetered, pin wheeling both arms and one grabbed the bannister. Her talons immediately wrapped round the polished wood, puncturing the lacquered surface and melding with the wood there. The dryad gasped in horror. "What have you done?"

"Facilitated my departure." Aphrodite responded calmly. "I am tired of playing games with you creatures. Do not cut us as we pass or you will live long enough to regret it."

As Lillian cursed and used one arm to try to pull the other away, Thadeus hurried past. Aphrodite followed slowly and deliberately, stopping to proffer an object for Lillian to take. "Cut below the knuckles. All will grow back. Do not cast your shadow upon me again." She left Lillian to stare at the hatchet in her free hand and walked calmly down the remaining stairs.

Thadeus forced his pulse to slow with effort. "Why did you have a hatchet?"

Aphrodite shrugged. "Gift from an admirer. You were saying something before about Apollo and curses."

Thadeus shrugged. "Oh, right. Where was I? Remember about seven hundred years back, that music contest we held with King Midas of Pessinus judging whether my pipe's music or Apollo's lyre played better?"

"No."

"Few do. That's because I won, and Apollo being Apollo, well, he was a vindictive whining bastard about it, and demanded nobody spread his shame. He placed a curse on Midas that still falls on any listener who dares to openly judge my music superior to his. You need only say the words."

"The jackal…"

"Said those words." Thadeus smirked as they neared the exit. "Axbev enjoys collecting musical cruelties. Let's see how he handles one he never studied…"

* * *

In the highest private box, Axbev watched as the mortal character of Lucius sonorously celebrated his regained humanity. With Isis' aid and roses consumed, he was no longer trapped in the form of a donkey. Stupid fool should have been sacrificed to her instead.

Axbev laughed at the tale's greater metaphor. This world was full of terrified animals, seeking gratification in love and lust and power. Fear of the East Empire, the border squabbles, the industrious weapon-smiths waiting to profit, all was in place. With countless hearts to weigh at the underworld's gates, Anubis would finally grant his son respect.

And his son would then usurp him.

Axbev frowned. The itching in his ears had finally subsided, but the acoustics in the hall seemed different. He asked if anyone else noticed. One of his human lackeys turned to ask what his master meant.

When his expression slackened with shock at the sight of him, Axbev knew something was wrong. He felt across his handsome jackal's features, fingers fumbling up the sides of his head to fleshy tatters of coarse hair over soft cartilage, his noble points gone.

The polished metal of the box's rail was dull, but as he lunged forward he could make out his bulbous reflection in its coppery surface, eyes wide with horror.

Seth Axbev, the self-proclaimed next judge of the underworld, had grown the ears of an ass.

* * *

Waves rolled off the Mediterranean as the sun dipped low, wind winding through the Goddess' gown as they stood on the winding beach. "I'll kill him," she declared.

"Don't bother. His plans are ruined and he's been humiliated. Where his father's from, that's worse than death."

"He'll be after you."

"I should be used to it by now." Thadeus shrugged, horns lowering instinctively. "We'll be dismantling his operation come morning, and I've got my mind on other things. You had me killed, and I'm not sensing much regret."

"You are not dead, even though you deserve to be," Aphrodite replied levelly. "And you are sensing no regret, whatsoever. I want to know how you escaped."

Thadeus grit his teeth. "I didn't. Ares' arrow caught me at Olympus' edge. I fell, long and hard; came to I don't know how much later with bruises, cuts, and the first of many broken bones. Those actually *hurt*, if you've ever wondered. Now I breathe and bleed, a satyr like any other. How that happened I don't know, but Ares succeeded. Pan died."

Aphrodite was silent for a moment as she studied him. "You seem more active than ever."

"That's only because it took centuries to find something to do with myself. I was in a period of reflection for about a century."

"Would that period of reflection by any chance have been a self-pitying drunken stupor?"

Thadeus shrugged and kicked at the sand. "I deal with grief my own way."

Aphrodite's lip turned with amusement. "So really nothing's changed, then or now. You still fight and drink and sleep around."

"As opposed to watching it happen on a stage? Living vicariously through others allows for easy judgment, doesn't it? Is that what all the Gods are doing these days? Do you even care that with the theurgic secrets unravelled people think you never even existed?"

"We handle that our own way. You're no longer in a position to understand. Answer my question. How did you come to do…this?"

Thadeus sighed. "A war found me—they seem to have lots of those. I got involved and distinguished myself. I kind of had to. It's a real mess here."

Aphrodite was confused. "How is any of that your problem? Why don't you just get far away from it all?"

Thadeus sighed. He'd asked himself that all too often "I've come to understand why powerful people create the havoc they do. Too many of these people think harnessing heavenly powers makes them Gods in their own right—uninhibited, unaccountable, using the theurgic sciences to play games that risk the lives of millions. It's all your past antics that inspire every megalomaniac's power bid I get sent to deal with. I'm uniquely experienced in handling with them."

"*Our* antics? You don't consider yourself one of us?"

"No." The word carried a leaden weight, and Thadeus wasn't at all surprised at the bitterness he still felt. His sulking was supposed to be behind him but his voice dripped malice that he couldn't hide. "If I had any inkling that you wanted the world back under your thumb the way it once was, I'd gladly oppose you. This world is much better off without you."

"So you put yourself above us now, do you?"

Thadeus snorted. "Not at all, even if you did murder me for a mistake."

"Mistake?" Aphrodite rounded on him and the waves beating the short began to chop with urgency as the sea responded to her fury. "Don't try to paint a pretty picture of what you did. You know exactly what you were after when you tried to seduce me."

"I was young and I was stupid, Kypris! We all were."

"And now you're old and stupider."

Aphrodite broke his gaze and turned to the sea, feeling none of the night's cold. She had ice of her own when she finally spoke. "Creatures like Axbev provide you with an outlet for revenge, but all you are is bitter for what you lost and still mourn for. You don't even know you could actually get full immortality back if you wanted it."

"No games, please."

Aphrodite curled her lip in a cruel smile. "The mists could give you what Ares' arrow took away."

"No. That can't happen and you know it." Thadeus growled through his flat goatish teeth. There was a slight hesitancy and he knew Aphrodite felt it, a tiny morsel of yearning that gave her a thrill when she tapped it.

She played her tune. "Yes, it can." She rounded on him. "You're far more jealous than angry." She walked behind him as he avoided her gaze, staring into the ocean as though he could boil it. Her fingers reached up, and caressed his rough cheek. The sudden contact burned like fire. "You want it back." Her voice had changed, become silkier. She stepped around and Thadeus saw that she had changed again. Goat's ears stood tall through her blond hair, her face long and beautifully tapered, downy fur catching the light. Under her stola, blond furred goat's legs sensuously arrayed, ending in shining ebony hooves in the sand.

Aphrodite grabbed his slender horns, pulling his head to her transformed lips. He thrashed and bucked, but his preternatural animal strength paled next to hers. "Stop it!" he barked.

Aphrodite laughed. "Play soldier all you want, but you aren't complicated to me. I bet you'd give anything to be immortal again. Anything." She trilled seductively, planting a poisoned seed in his mind with three carefully intoned words: "Remember Olympus' groves."

With his memories fired clear as glass blown in a furnace, Thadeus suddenly remembered being Pan. He could taste ambrosia on his tongue, smell endless wild fields surrender their perfume. The dryads, satyress', sylphs, the pipes, the drunken celebration. The honors burned to him on pyres by supplicating shepherds, hunters and their kings.

And everything he wanted, every hunger was sated without restraint through the hordes of supplicants that came to him. No guilt. No remorse. That was Godhood.

"I really hate you," Thadeus moaned, desire and bitterness battling in him with a force that shook his limbs.

Aphrodite purred. "I'll bet you could really go for a drink now, couldn't you?"

"Fuck you."

Her voice honeyed his ear. "Oh, satyr, don't you worry. I'm not going to tell the other Gods about you. I'd rather keep you my little secret, watch you realize just how close immortality is, and give up all this nonsense to crawl through the filth to get back to where you're really from. Or die trying."

With yearning burning through his veins, and an overpowering desire to just touch that splendid fur, just once, Thadeus' fists unballed themselves. Tears flooded his eyes as he reached out to her. "Kypris, just tell me if you feel—"

She released him suddenly, slipping free and letting him fall. Thadeus hairy knees beat the sand as he collapsed with exhaustion.

There was a thunderclap as a wave folded and the invisible door to Aphrodite's realm slammed shut. Her parting words threaded the air in her wake. "No, Pan, I don't! I will keep your secret and protect you from divine wrath. That's my only parting gift. Keep me entertained, will you?"

The tide was wetting him before he had the strength to rise again, senses twisted into knots. He simply couldn't think. He needed to minister to himself, get her out of his head. A few drinks would definitely do that much. He could wire Brand afterwards, let him know to move in when he got to an ether-box.

But how much about what really happened could he say to those he worked for?

Living behind a fake name, what legacy was he leaving?

Thadeus meandered along the shore as though already drunk, ancient regrets kicking at him like Furies. The waves crashed behind him, burying the syrinx in the wet sand with deliberate patience.

Sun Wukung and his pal Bajie (Pigsy) are two of the most popular folk gods in China. But what are they doing teaming up with the Singaporean Merlion? And fighting Baphomet?

Read on…

Adversary's Fall

by MikasiWolf

A splitting pain erupted through my skull and I screamed, falling hard onto my knees. Everything was completely washed out; the clatter of train wheels upon poorly-maintained tracks; the generic chatter of Mass Rapid Transit train commuters. I could feel the tendrils of my essence pulling itself apart as the lifeforce of one of my followers faded, a chilling echo that remained in my being.

"Run, my devotees, hide!" I hissed, willing my suggestion into their beings. I could see consecutively through several of my devotees' eyes as their vision lurched violently across furniture and altar accoutrements. They were escaping from something. Burning sections of my last shrine flitted across my vision, confirming my worst fears. One of my followers turned around, and I briefly caught sight of one of The Adversary's enforcers, a reptilian being slithering towards my field of view. Glints of steel were followed by a scream, and I saw through that follower no more. One after another, their point of views turned black, and I slumped listlessly forward as I lay on my knees. Nobody worshipped me now. Soon, I would be just another Forgotten God.

The silence of the train was deafening. Peering upwards, I saw both the surprised and enraged muzzles of the many different species of commuters looking down upon me. And through my sensitive irises, I saw their aura changing from calm to anger, be they oxen, civets and canids of every kind.

As one, they grabbed me. No monkey who screamed and talked to himself was just another mortal on his way to the city center. I tried willing my magic to get free, but my essence was too badly rended to commit more than a mere gust of wind, lifting the skirts and ties of my assailants. When an ox drew an arm across my neck from behind, and I couldn't break free, I realized that subtlety was no longer an option.

I drew my weapon, the Compliant-Golden-Staff. Magically scaled down to fit into my ear, I flicked it down onto the carriage floor. With a command, I forced what was nothing more than a gold toothpick among the thrashing feet of the crowd to grow.

The CGS swelled exponentially in size, punching an enormous hole through both sides of the train carriage. Its expanded girth knocked me and the crowd back in both directions, with the unlucky ones sent flying out of the train. I prized myself out of the grip of the stunned bull and stood by the gaping hole at the side of the train, shrinking my staff back into my ear. The wind gushing into the still-moving train buffeted me, but I held onto a handhold. With rails on an elevated track 10 meters high, I could tell from the presence of the Sports Hub building in the near distance that the train was now in the central township of Kallang. Once the train got into the tunnel leading to the next station, my chance of escape would be near-impossible. Every station had the serpentine Nāga agents of The Adversary waiting, and their weapons cut through gods like tofu.

Flipping the finger towards my stunned assailants, I leapt out of the train. Closing my eyes, I called on my somersault-cloud ability, willing myself to travel towards what was the last temple of my devotees.

I should have arrived at my destination in an instant. Instead, I found myself rushing to meet the ground. My eyes snapping wide open, a jumble of images flitted past me as I fell hard onto a row of parked Mag-bikes. I could actually feel the pain from each and every protrusion of the bikes as I rolled hard over them, each one adding a new dimension of hurt. My suit ripped as it caught against a handlebar in my tumble, and I fell face-first onto the concrete floor.

That was not supposed to happen. I groaned as I got up, taking stock of my surroundings. At 8am on a Monday in a residential township, I was fortunate no one was around to see my fall from grace. Where drops of my blood lay, I could see it solidifying back into the grains of rock I was from, traces of my essence going along with it. I didn't know what to make of it. Not once, in all of the battles had I fought with gods and demons had I ever bled before. And yet, a simple fall on the mortal realm had me as ravaged as any mortal would be. Granted, I could see my wounds and rips in my suit healing themselves quickly as I took a few steps forward. I needed somewhere to get my nerves back together, and being out in the open wasn't going to do it.

My stomach started acting up as I made the first few steps forward, and I stopped. Strange as it may sound, I had never gotten hungry before. Gods did eat, but it was as much an indulgence as acknowledgement of what our followers had spared for us. The first signs of the long-forgotten ache in my stomach reaffirmed itself, and so I went to the market.

On the way there, the seriousness of what had just happened turned into fear, and that was when I broke down. I knew why I was getting hungry. I knew why I could now be wounded. It was because the last of my followers were now gone, with no one left to worship me. I sat myself down on an old bench with a thump, ignoring its protesting creak.

There is a remarkable thing about Gods. When we first came into being, none of us had any followers to call our own. But our deeds and powers in both the astral and mundane realms soon gained the attention of mortals. As people respected and desired our abilities, we were paid tribute for what we could bestow upon them. Good health from the God of Healing? Check. Stronger-than-normal capabilities from the God of War? Check. And the list goes on. I knew a god who called himself Coyote who took up the challenge to bring fire to the mortals. On hindsight, that might not have been the best of decisions. Fire destroyed more than it served, in my opinion.

As the number of our followers grew, so did our powers, and with it came the ability to manifest ourselves fully in the mortal world. A chance to be among the very people we protect. It's hard to explain the spiritual and divine bond that we gods share with our worshippers. It may be easier to think of it as the bond a father has with his children.

When a god's follower dies or loses faith in him, his link to the mortal realm is weakened. His power then starts to wane. When none of their followers survive, the god soon ceases to be. There are some who say this veneration by our worshippers is the reason for the downfall of what were known as the Forgotten Gods. The world used to have a heckuva lot of gods, such that you could chuck a stone in any direction and have it pass through one or more of them. This was long before I, Sun Wukong, the Handsome Monkey God existed, mind you. I was born from a heavenly-infused rock much later. Many other gods that existed much earlier, along with the first mortals, had been brought into being by The Creation.

From what I understood, more and more people believed in a smaller selection of gods as the years passed. Then came the late 20th Century. You could then drift for miles in any country and not find any divinity to talk to. Not that all divinities make for good talking; I spoke to Cupid back in February of 2012; his power always seems stronger that month; and I had to clean my ears out after having heard all the filth he recounted. The 21st Century saw a marked disbelief in gods. With all the wars, disasters, crimes and whatnot mortals had a tendency of waging, I wasn't overly surprised. I mean, how could one believe in a divine being protecting them from danger when it happened anyway? I attributed it then to the results of their own folly. But what I and the other gods failed to see was that this was all the work of one who resented everything about The Creation. We called him The Adversary.

Some say The Adversary was one of the first gods brought into being by The Creation. Some say that he was stripped of much of his powers after his fall from grace trying to fight the very forces that made him. It is said he now manifested the form of a goat, while others testify they had seen him in serpentine form at least once. But the definite fact of the matter was that he was responsible for the corrupted state of the mortal world.

Much as how gods could influence our followers in their daily life, The Adversary could do just that. And the problem was that one worshiped The Adversary not by knowingly giving him prayers, but by being part of even a small act of evil. That was how he gained his hold on one's soul, and committed them to far more dastardly deeds. Where did all the wars and crimes come from? The Adversary. His hold on the people was a long time in coming, and some said he was the one who introduced weaponry to mortalkind. I lost many of my friends in the years that came. One week, they were listless from the loss of their followers' faith. The next, I couldn't find them. They had faded into Forgotten Gods.

The Adversary's hold reached throughout the world with his seat of power in the old island-state of Singapore. Because evil transmits by association itself, and with the countless links the cosmopolitan city had across the globe, The Adversary had the whole world under its grip by 2034. The mortals of the world used to take on the form of humans. But The Adversary's hold on the world had them revert into their true forms. Petty criminals morphed into foxes and weasels. Corrupt bureaucrats and police became the Serpentine Nāga favored by The Adversary. The rest took on other forms. This was known as The Changing. Not a single human existed after that.

Why didn't we fight him? The fact was that gods weren't as united as you think. With each having their own set of followers with different beliefs, it was little wonder that we did not trust one another. After all, one's followers may become another god's when their faith changes, and we only had each other to blame. It also didn't help that shortly after The Changing, The Adversary tasked his Nāga to eliminate the competition. All places of worship were soon destroyed, and even the surviving cults of followers didn't last for long. The few mortals that clung to their beliefs in the Old Gods were mercilessly executed.

Just like how my followers were. The Old Gods were now the Forgotten Gods.

* * *

I couldn't grieve forever, and so I found myself at the market. Having checked that my magical guise still worked, I changed my appearance differently from what I normally used. The law would have gotten wind of the ruckus in the train, and I didn't want the Nāga enforcers to pin it on me. They didn't have magic, but the Nāga had the technological capabilities of the police and military. You couldn't walk ten metres without at least two cameras scanning your mug with facial-recognition algorithms. After using my Golden-Gaze to check that none of the people around were Nāga in disguise, I bought a couple of peaches and ate, contemplating my next move.

If what had happened to the Forgotten Gods was any indication, I had until the end of the day before I phased out of existence. It was the time when the energies of the mortal and astral realm realigned itself, and not having any worshippers meant I would no longer have an anchor on earth.

So I considered my options. One, I could try winning over new followers. It shouldn't take too much effort on my part; it was a well-known fact that mortals could be lured into servitude by promises of power, with a couple of magical tricks thrown in for good measure. But this wasn't the early 1900s. Most mortals would have by now watched enough movies to know not to be fooled by such promises. Besides, the majority of the populace worshipped The Adversary in their own way. By hearing my offer through their eyes, he could always send his Nāga to wipe me out with their Godslayer scimitars. This was totally out.

Option two would have to be the direct approach. Killing The Adversary himself. It might not guarantee some of his followers turning over to my side, but I'll be damned if I didn't do something, at least. The only problem was that no one really knew if he had a physical form to speak of. He did speak on TV every now and then in that goat guise of his, but who's to say that wasn't one of his spokesdemons? I wasn't against killing his messenger, but it wouldn't do me any good. Besides which, I didn't have a location. The Adversary didn't have a place on any governmental seat, and instead rules through his Nāga bureaucrats. Otherwise, I would only have to go to his seat of power and thrash the essence out of him. I laughed to myself. Yeah, because I'm feeling in top form right now. No way was that gonna happen.

Option three would be…shit, I couldn't think of one. Except dying or phasing out of existence. A definite No-No.

I looked at the modern yet poorly-maintained buildings around me, the hallmark of places touched by The Adversary's influence. Cracks and mold had crept into the concrete, giving everything a dark demeanor. People shuffled past with scowls on their faces, swearing as another got in their way. Whatever The Adversary had a hold on eventually deteriorates, be it people or cities. To think that such a now powerful god ruled from such a small country really bordered on the realm of disbelief. But Singapore had come a long way in international connections ever since it came into being, and The Adversary knew how to take full advantage of that fact. If this country was defended by a National God, he wouldn't have let The Adversary take hold. National Gods existed not due to the existence of followers, but on the basis of the lands they were tasked to protect. It's a pity that this country didn't have one—

I jerked to the present. Now that I thought about it, this country used to be home to a National God. The local populace used to call him The Merlion. A being of half-lion, half-fish, he had never been thought of as anything more than a fairy tale. They couldn't have been further from the truth. When the Old Gods started making their way to Singapore since the 1800s to serve their migrating worshippers, they paid homage to him on account of his role as the island's protector. Needless to say, I didn't see the need for such formalities. Truth be told, I didn't know much about the guy, only that he tended towards the form of a lion, with a poker face to match. I supposed that fishy tail of his true form couldn't have helped him much on land. As the years passed, and we saw the island go through its changes, I never saw him again, not even during the God Wars of 1942-1945. The Oni and Kitsune had tried taking our places during the Japanese Occupation; all the gods had their paws full during then. It was a well-known fact that National Gods had the power to banish other gods from their domain, but yet the Merlion hadn't seemed to give a shit even now.

It was possible he wouldn't give a shit if I were to find him. But I didn't have a choice. If there was any chance that he could help me on my quest, I would have to take it. Or cease to exist by day's end.

I sighed, looking at the distance where the skyline of the city could just be seen. It looked like I was going to have to walk. I couldn't trust public transportation, not with my run-in from earlier. Besides, it wasn't like I couldn't walk long distances. After all, I did escort a priest all the way from China to India, and back again. I'll have to tell you all about it sometime.

* * *

Gods tended to stick to where statues of their likenesses were. I knew that the two most well-known statues of the Merlion sat at two places; one in Clarke Quay, which was at the river near the city central, the other on Sentosa Island. Given they had since been demolished, it was no good trying to find him there. But I did remember that he always hung around the mouth of the Singapore River when I and the Old Gods first arrived, so it was a good place to start.

If I still had my somersault-cloud ability, I would have been able to fly overhead and search for him with my Golden-Gaze. But now I had to do it by foot. The Golden-Gaze power in my eyes gave me the ability to pick out divines and otherworldly creatures from a crowd by their aura, and allowed me to see their true form. Helped me many a time during my demon-hunting days.

I had to have walked around the river for hours before I saw a bluish-green mist of an aura next to the dirty-looking Fullerton Hotel. Once a hotel for high-end clientele, it was now a hangout for the seedy. Next to it was a collection of bars which used to serve booze, but which now also dealt in other forms of vice. With not many people at this time of day, none of the working girls or junkies were around, and I could spot a lone figure seated just at the edge of the granite walkway overlooking the river. Walking purposefully towards him, with my eyes peeled for Nāga, I finally got a proper look at my quarry.

On the mortal plane, one could see a matted-furred lion slumped in a deckchair, his mane tousled and unkempt. With several halfhearted attempts to trim it, the lion's mane was uneven in places. His fur looked like it had been sandy-colored once, but was now a muddy brown. His tail slumped listlessly against the base of his chair, its tuft of fur caked with grime and dust. The lion put a bottle of beer to his lips. Some of it sloshed down his front, adding to the many stains on his clothes and pelt. Dressed in a greying singlet and shorts that would have been worn by a streetside vendor, or even a beach goer, the lion would have looked out of place if it weren't for the pile of Tiger Beer bottles littering his side. The astral plane did nothing to improve this picture of decline. Aside from his normal blue-green aura, I could also see the dark, smoky haze of astral decay. Overlaid over his form in the mortal plane was his true form, a ghostly image of a fish's tail over where his legs would have been.

I must have been staring at the lion for quite a while with my mouth open, when he finally spoke.

"If you want a drink, go get your own," rumbled the lion. "Otherwise, feel free to fuck off."

I opened and closed my mouth a couple of times. I must have looked like the proverbial goldfish as I did, so I said the first thing that came to my mind.

"Buy you a drink?"

The lion turned slightly, lowering his scratched sunglasses with a paw as he did. "That's a first. But how about you stop wasting my time and tell me what you want?" The annoyance in the voice stung, and I was ready to turn tail and leave. But my task at paw held me in place.

"Are you The Merlion?" I asked. "The Child of the Land and Sea? Guardian of The Island at the End?"

There was a long pause, during which I wondered if he had dozed off. "I used to be." The lion took another sip of his beer. "In case you haven't noticed, I'm retired."

"Sorry to break you out of retirement, O Guardian of..."

"I told you I'm bloody retired. Call me Sanga, if you so insist. And before you make your introductions, I know every god who came through this land. You're Sun Wukong, also known as The Handsome Monkey King, Great Sage Equal to Heaven. Though I have to disagree with the last two titles. Correct me if I'm wrong, but you're here because you're as screwed as the rest of the gods. Is that right?"

I looked at the sorry excuse of a god before me, fighting back the urge to draw my staff and thrash him. "You're pretty well-informed, Sanga." I said, trying to keep my fur flat.

"As the god of this domain, I know about everything that goes on around here," Sanga waved his paw before him. "I know about The Adversary reaching his claws into all aspects of society, giving rise to the demise of the Old Gods. I know about your attempts at rebellion you wage against The Adversary's Nāga, whatever little good it does. I also know about the last of your followers dying in one of their raids today." The lion dipped its head. "I am sorry to hear that."

"Then you know why I'm here." I stated, steeling my jaw. It was hard not to think about the screams of my followers as they perished, the resounding tearing in my essence a pain I wouldn't forget.

"You misunderstand, Wukong," said Sanga. He lifted his bottle, cursing as he discovered it empty. "I may know about the actions of those in my domain, but I have no claim over the thoughts of those involved. I don't even know what goes on in the mind of mortals. Do enlighten me."

"I need your help, Sanga," I said. Never in the history of my existence had I thought I would say that. I was pretty independent, as far as gods went. "By the end of the day, I am going to fade away, not having a single follower left," Sanga grunted. "But I am not going down without a fight, not as far as The Adversary is concerned. I know that when The Creation tasked you to protect this country, one of His edicts gave you the right to banish any god around here if you so wished. And yet, The Adversary reigns supreme. And in the last 200 years since the old gods and I first came, I had yet to see you do anything to protect this land. Not even when the Oni and Kitsune tried taking over."

"My duty is to these lands, not the petty squabbles between gods or mortals!" roared Sanga, and I kept my staff at the ready. "Oh, you're very high and mighty now, but do you know how painful it is when nobody acknowledges your existence?" The lion got up from his seat, flinging his bottle onto the ground. Now that he stood, I could see that I dwarfed him by at least a foot. Despite having a broad-chest that suggested great physical strength, a beer belly could be seen beneath it. "Ever since The Creation cast His edicts tasking me the guardian of these lands, I protected its natives on land and sea! I even risked my ass protecting them once from a great storm. Instead of thanking me for that, they attributed it to another higher power! And then came more mortal folk from afar, along with you and the other gods. Oh, sure, a couple of them greeted me when they came into my domain. But most of them, you included, wouldn't even acknowledge I existed. Don't think I don't know!

"One day, I realized something. The edicts never said I had to protect anyone, only the land itself. And then I figured I didn't have to interfere any longer. After all, all the mortals had their own gods like you and everyone else to protect them. And so I stopped giving a shit. Until The Adversary took hold."

I waited for Sanga to continue. When he did not, I said, "And you didn't stop him because…?"

Sanga's kicked hard at the pile of bottles. "I tried. But he got hold of the edicts The Creation tasked me to. Because he had it, I couldn't do squat to him."

I mused this for a moment. "I'm afraid I don't quite follow."

"Look, everyone knows that The Creation cast edicts for some of us in stone," said Sanga, falling back into his deckchair with a thump. It was a marvel it held. "I even heard of some guy in a land far from here receiving two tablets with ten edicts inscribed upon them. You know about what the mortals call the Singapore Stone?"

I nodded. When I first came, the Singapore Stone stood at the mouth of the river, right next to where I was now, actually. A large sandstone slab with lines upon lines of gibberish, it was destroyed by the mortal colonists to make way for some fort or other. All that remained was a single piece. "Nobody had been able to read them. I looked at the only surviving fragment years back when it was in the museum, and I didn't understand a word of it."

Sanga stayed silent, and my eyes widened. "The Singapore Stone carried the set of edicts The Creation tasked to you?"

"You got that right, Cloud-Soarer," droned Sanga. "Well, it used to contain all of them, but the fragment that wasn't destroyed holds the two most important parts of it. It may just be a stone fragment, but it gives me the authority to uphold the law in my domain. But it went missing some time before The Changing. If I wished to banish a god, I had to show the edict to him. This means that if The Adversary had it with him…"

"You could only banish him after getting it back." I finished.

I now knew what we must do. We would go to The Adversary's seat of power, kick the door down and…

… except I didn't know where it was. No one did.

"Where is he, exactly?" I asked. This didn't sound like the smartest of questions.

"I don't rightly know," shrugged Sanga.

"You just told me you know what goes on in your domain," I tapped my feet impatiently.

"The places The Adversary and his consorts call their own were shielded from my sight," clarified Sanga. "Think of it as 'private property', to use the mortal term. Surely you aren't thinking of taking on The Adversary on your own?" asked Sanga with the hint of a frown. It's hard to tell through all that mussed-up fur on his mug.

"I won't. You're coming with me," I said, increasing my size magically for good effect. "After all, isn't it your duty as guardian of this land?"

"Hey, I never said anything about helping you. I'm pretty comfortable where I am," snorted Sanga, throwing his head back. "I may have wanted The Adversary gone when he first came, but so far, he hasn't given me any trouble. And I aim to keep it that way." He slid down further in his deckchair to make his point. Though his paw scrabbled for an unopened bottle, I could see that all the bottles were either broken or empty.

"The people of your country need you," I said sharply. "Are you going to let The Adversary fuck them up even more than he already did?"

"What had the mortals ever done for me, huh? Tell me that!" Sanga jabbed a claw against my chest. Though it wasn't hard, it hurt my already unstable essence. "Because if I just open my ears wide enough, I could just make out the sound of them not caring! They never respected or valued me! Even before The Changing, they saw my statues as 'tourist attractions', nothing more! Mortals should never expect anything from gods they don't believe in. So don't say they needed me. They never did."

I looked at the poor excuse of a god before me. I took in his ragged features and appearance. Deep beneath the astral plane, I could see hopelessness and melancholy emanating from Sanga's aura. It is said that immortality is as much a curse as it was a boon. I couldn't quite say I understood Sanga's logic, but I could imagine how he felt. How a god would feel, if he wasn't wanted for centuries upon centuries? Sanga had nothing but an island of nothing but jungle to look after for years until 1819. And even his intervention against a storm wasn't enough to give the mortals faith in him. I knew how it was to feel useless for centuries. Due to my party-crashing antics before and after I attained godliness, I was pinned under a mountain as punishment for 500 years. It had given me plenty of time to think about things; such as what I had done wrong and how best not to get caught the next time round. I even got to beat the shit out of demons after I was set free to atone for my deeds. But for a god like Sanga, who hadn't been party to anything of significance to begin with, the centuries only gave cause for resentment.

"Have you ever done anything other than sit around or swim?" I asked Sanga. A shake of his head was his reply. I pulled up a chair and sat near him. "I think what you need is meaning in your existence. Something you can look back on and realize how fun it was when the going's good. If you want people to know what you've done, you have to do something noteworthy, something big enough that stories and sagas would be told about your deeds. You know why the mortals used to have so many stories and TV adaptations about me? Because I was an extremely skilled troublemaker. I fought other gods and demons, and there's nothing more invigorating than fighting against impossible odds. It doesn't seem like an interesting task, but when you defeat The Adversary, the people will know that you were part of it. They will rebuild your statues in your name, and make stories and movies about your deeds. If nothing else, it's going to be fun, Sanga. That much I can promise you."

There was a long silence as the two of us just sat. I could hear the sound of traffic somewhere in the civic district, the far-off voices of mortals having their arguments and disputes. The world had changed in the years gods had been in existence. A number of us had seen empires rise and fall, like countless risings and settings of the sun. Mortals could be counted on to do whatever it took to harm one another. But it was the duty of gods to try to guide them on the right path. We didn't always succeed, but we tried. That was what made us different from mortals. That was what made us different from The Adversary. I only hoped that Sanga could see that, despite the centuries of misgivings he may have on the world at large.

I got my answer soon enough. "Buy me one last drink and we'll be on our way," said Sanga, stretching himself out. Countless pops from underused muscles could be heard. "And I want the good stuff."

* * *

Sanga had puked most of his top-shelf vodka before we left. I figured that going without the good stuff for so long must have worked havoc with his beer-infused guts. Even gods had their limits with mortal swill.

Sanga had morphed his clothes to something marginally presentable; a faded Lionsdale Polo tee and pants. He kept his sunglasses on. I found out that he really didn't know where The Adversary was. I'd thought he was bluffing to shirk out of his duty. But he knew a servant of The Adversary who did, and that person was at the top floor of the Marina Bay Sands Hotel.

In its heyday, the MBS Hotel was of the highest end of the spectrum when it came to accommodation and performing arts in Singapore. Since The Adversary's influence, however, it has become home to entertainment of a different sort. Scantily-clad females and males alike beckoned passersby to their strip clubs and halls of vice. Just outside the main entrance, the smell of marijuana, cocaine and opium drifted out of strategically-placed vents, suggesting yet other choices of entertainment. It was known that much of the evil of the world congested in places like casinos and nightclubs. Much of The Adversary's followers worshipped him, if only through partaking in vices of their own.

I could already feel the tingle in my fur as we walked through the doors of the building. What was once the waiting area for hotel guests had its seats replaced with mattresses and recliners where the low-rolling junkies lay, syringes, bongs and opium pipes next to them. From the hysteric giggles and slurred mumbles they emitted from time to time, they were clearly enjoying their trips.

I made my way towards the main elevators, but Sanga dragged me through another door as they chimed. As I peeped through the pane of glass set in the door, I caught a glimpse of two reptilian figures exiting the lifts. With the lower half of snakes, the Nāga would have looked humanoid above the waist, were it not for the greyish-green scales of their torsos. They wore vests of green silk, and had their scimitars in sheaths across their backs. The aura they emitted betrayed their otherworldly nature, though a passing mortal didn't seem to notice. Forked tongues slid out and tasted the air as they slithered, and I ducked my head back as one of them tensed. I recalled the last thing my followers saw, and it was all I could do not to tremble.

Don't move, I heard Sanga's voice projected within my head. *They can't see through our guise, but these beings can sense our presence through vibrations in the ground and air.* I fought to keep my breathing level, as I imagined the Nāga jerking their bodies left and right, trying to find out where two gods were hiding.

I had to have been standing there for a while, because Sanga spoke. "They're gone. We'll have to take the stairs up to the top floor."

I pointed outside. "We could use the elevators."

"We can't risk the Nāga finding out we're here," hissed Sanga. "If they do, The Adversary's servant would be informed, and we don't want to risk a fight with him. Knowing him, he'll sooner escape. And anyway, you need a biometric chip with The Adversary's signature to get to the top floor with the elevators. That isn't something our magic can forge. Follow me, or you're on your own."

It was one thing to climb the stairs of an apartment or office building. It was an entirely different thing walking through 54 floors of the MBS hotel, without hoping my existentially-strained essence didn't spontaneously combust. Despite having chugged much more alcohol that was reasonably safe, even for gods, Sanga took the stairs without complaint, pausing only to wheeze every ten floors. The stink of clandestinely smoked cigarettes, piss and drugs lingered in the stairwell, adding to the already dizzying journey up the steps. Given that my legs ached with as much fire as I'm sure a mortal would feel, it was fair to say that the recent loss of my anchor to the mortal realm was fast taking a toll on my essence. It was fortunate that the Nāga didn't patrol the stairwells; if they had, I doubted that I could have caught my breath in time to handle them with my staff.

I didn't know it was possible to spend more than an hour of one's life climbing the stairs of any mortal building in the world, but by the time we reached, I couldn't help but look forward to the time I could do my cloud-soaring ability again.

"Is this the door?" I panted when the stairs ended. There was no roof access for this set of stairs.

"If the floor plan hasn't changed since The Adversary took over, then yes," wheezed Sanga, his body swaying as he stood. For a moment, I hoped that he didn't throw up all over me, but he would have done that on the 30th floor. Panting hard, with Sanga behind me, I turned the handle of the door. Judging by the door opening easily, it hadn't occurred to the Nāga that anyone would enter through the stairs.

Despite the squalor evident on the cracked walls and ceilings, the overall appearance of the dimly-lit carpeted hallway was a marked contrast to the lobby. Long-withered plants stood in their eternal watch at corners, with dirty lamps providing light for much of the hallway. A lopsided plaque in front of the elevators announced that the Chairman Suites of the hotel was just down the corridor. I let Sanga lead the way; after all, he knew where The Adversary's servant was. Despite the door up ahead being close to eighty feet away, the sounds of female laughter and unmistakably male grunts could be heard up ahead.

Sanga walked right up to it and knocked. The grunts paused for just a moment, before answering.

"We don't need no more pot, guys. Let us be."

Sanga rolled his eyes, and to my great surprise, turned the door's handle and went in. With the floor normally accessible only by Nāga guards with a biometric chip, the occupant of the suite didn't think he needed to lock it.

The first thing I was aware of as we stepped into the suite was how big it was. The Chairman Suite of the MBS had cost tens of thousands to rent per day during its heyday, and was complete with everything you needed for a lap of luxury; Jacuzzi, rain shower, and even a piano that nobody actually uses. The other thing I realized was that the enormous bed at the end of the suite was occupied by not one, or two people, but five. A nine-pointed rake leaned on the wall beside the bed, glowing weakly of godly magic in the faint light.

Back in the years when I was escorting a Tang Priest to collect a bunch of scrolls from India, I was part of his three-man escort team. Three-demon escort team would be a more accurate term; I wasn't a god then, and was only involved in the journey as a form of penance. My brothers-in-arms were Sha Wujing, a river demon, and Zhu Bajie, a boar demon. Now, there was many an occasion when Bajie caused the party much grief and delays with his enormous appetite for food, along with his penchant for women. Knowing his weaknesses, many demons wishing our party harm had posed as women in order to lure him away. That said, I had to risk life and limb to get him out of those predicaments. There was even an occasion in which Bajie egged our master, the Tang Priest, to punish me with a head-binding sutra on unfounded accusations. When we finally completed our journey, needless to say, I hoped never to see him again. Because of his traits, Bajie had since then been worshipped by prostitutes and the promiscuous. His worship at bars and nightclubs had led him to be associated as one of the primary gods of vice.

And yet right before me was Bajie, groping four different women at the same time, his prominent belly visible even among them. He must have had a thing for musky species, because I counted a fox, a weasel, a civet of some sort, as well as a small-clawed otter. All of them were giggling as they raked their own paws over Bajie.

"Lord Bajie?" said Sanga, his voice carrying well even in the large space. The giggling on the bed stopped. Bajie sat upright.

"Sanga?" Bajie's bristly snout twitched as he sniffed. His face creased in anger. "Hey, don't you know better than to barge into a man's home uninvited? I'm in the middle of something here!"

"That I can see," said Sanga, as he stepped forward, nose twitching. With five different scents of musk in the air, my nose was itching as I followed. "Unfortunately, there is a matter of great urgency we have to discuss. Privately." He cocked his eyebrows at the females.

"You barge into my home demanding an audience?" roared Bajie. The women flinched. "I ought to thrash you where you stand…" The boar leapt onto the floor next to the bed and reached for his weapon. It wasn't there.

"Looking for this?" I held up the rake.

"What the fuck. Alright!" Bajie shoved at the fox and weasel closest beside him. "Get lost, girls! Party's over! But you owe me for this, Maned One!" the boar snarled. The women scuttled out of the suite, and whether or not they had their clothes waiting outside remained a mystery.

"Spit it out, Sanga, I haven't got all day," snarled Bajie as he fumbled with his clothes. "Have you come to accept my offer? If so, you could have waited. And who in the name of The Creation are you?" Bajie snorted at me.

My jaw dropped. "What do you mean? Don't you recognize me? I'm Wukong!"

Bajie lifted his snout and sniffed. "You ain't the only monkey in the city, Wukong, and I don't have that Golden-Gaze of yours. Your guise was pretty convincing, and you'll pardon me if you're the last thing on my mind since that business with the Tang priest and the scrolls. My feet still hurt from that journey."

"Sanga, why are we even talking to this guy?" I demanded. "If we need anything done, I can guarantee doing it far better than this block of lard."

"Bajie here works for The Adversary," confirmed Sanga.

Bajie must have been waiting for his chance, because the moment I turned my head in shock, he went for his rake, ramming me with a shoulder as he did. My staff was out of my ear and extended to fighting size in an instant, parrying the hefty blows of Bajie's rake as he lashed. The clash of our godly weapons sent shockwaves that triggered cracks on the floor-to-ceiling windows, shattering in a satisfying smash by the third bout. I had no qualms with killing Bajie, despite any history we may have together. Whoever served The Adversary was my enemy, and I intended to avenge my followers where I could.

Sanga opened and closed his mouth, making an obvious effort in preparation to talking us over. Bajie and I ignored him. Gods should know better than interrupting their fellows in the midst of battle, and it was one of the many unwritten courtesies we showed each other.

Except Sanga wasn't a courteous god. One moment, I had the teeth of Bajie's rake locked against the tip of my staff; the next, what had to be the stinkiest spout of water in the history of godhood sent me and Bajie crashing into opposite walls. Fluid burned across my eyes as I choked and spluttered, wondering what had happened. The strong stench of stomach acid and alcohol permeated the room, and it was all I could do to not pass out from the smell alone. Sanga stood between the both of us, wiping his mouth with a paw.

"Did…did you just puke on us?" I queried, resisting the urge to lick my lips. Half the suite and its furnishings were ruined, and it would take a godly power to get it smelling clean again. Bajie groaned, massaging the side of his head.

"Drastic times call for drastic measures," stated Sanga as he paced. "It should wash off easily with a good fur shampoo. But we are running out of time, Wukong, you especially, so we had best get onto the topic at hand. Bajie can help us."

"Why are we talking to him?" I demanded, jabbing my staff towards Bajie. "It didn't take long for him to fall into darkness. Anyone who works for The Adversary is a blight against all gods. And how did you two know one another?"

Sanga took a breath. "The reason why I know Bajie makes his home here," at this, Sanga gave a sniff, "is merely because he offered me a position with The Adversary a number of years back. Needless to say, I declined. His offer still stands, however, showing how little he knew about me."

"I'm not so sure about you myself."

"Tough. You asked for my help, so you're going to get it," said Sanga with a clap of his paws. "As for why we're here, you must remember that taking The Adversary to task is impossible without knowing where he is. Not even the majority of the Nāga do. Only those directly involved with him, perhaps his royal guard, are privy to his throne. As the last god whose worshippers are tended towards vice, Bajie is the only other one who does. The Adversary sees the value of having a god among his fold, but I believe we can turn that to our advantage. I'm sure we can come to an understanding."

"What makes you think I'm going to help you?" spat Bajie. "I already have everything I can ever wish for. No end of women; loyal worshippers, as much food and wine as I can eat…"

"Table scraps, Bajie," reminded Sanga. If there was ever a lion who could smirk, it was him. "You and I know the only reason why The Adversary lets you exist is because you bring in more followers for him. Those who tend towards the vice you represent are after all drawn to The Adversary's allure. And the food you get? I'm sure the Nāga get far better than you do. Not to mention their Lord Takshaka."

"You're just jealous!" retorted Bajie, but I could tell from the flicker of his eyes that he wasn't so sure.

"Not at all. I hadn't exactly had the need for worshippers. You know that."

"Will you just get to the point already, lion-man?" growled Bajie. "You still haven't told me what you want."

"I'll need you to bring us to The Adversary. You needn't concern yourself with what happens after; Wukong and I will see to it personally."

"You're going to kill him, aren't you?" asked Bajie, trying and failing to keep the doubt out of his voice.

"I never said that." Sanga winked at me.

Bajie got up and I stiffened. The boar took several strides to the cleanest armchair he could find, settling himself into it. Grabbing a bottle of expensive rice wine, he took a gulp from it. When he next spoke, he sounded more confident, more in charge of the situation.

"Assuming that you do want to kill The Adversary, and just assuming I do take you to him, how exactly would it benefit me to do in the one who let me live?" asked Bajie. "The Serpent—that's what his servants and I call him— may have caused the fall of the Old Gods. But you have to understand that the time of the Old Gods is long past. With the state of the world as it is, people worship The Serpent because he relates to their wants and desires. He is already ingrained within them. If I let you guys kill him, who's to say that the world won't fall apart? The Adversary has been around since the dawn of time, Sanga. He's not going to be killed by two washed-up gods."

"Because all I'm going to do is banish him," said Sanga, whiskers twitching. "As National God, I have that right."

"Then why don't you just do it?" said Bajie smugly.

"Because he has the bloody edict that allows me to do so," said Sanga with an edge creeping into his voice. "It's the fragment of the Singapore Stone. And what's so damned funny?"

Bajie had started laughing, his rotund belly quivering as he shook. He laughed so hard that the nearby lampshades shook in their stands, and I was sorely tempted to give him a little tap between the ears to remind him who called the shots.

"The Great Merlion, steadfast defender of the Nation, unable to banish The Serpent all because he holds your little trinklet! My, that's rich!" Bajie downed another large gulp of wine, copious amounts dribbling down his front. "Looks like you can forget about your plan, Old Maned One."

"We don't have time for your comments, you overweight pillar of fat!" roared Sanga, and all of a sudden, Bajie started choking and gasping, his bottle dropping soundlessly on the carpet. I could see the shimmering wine snaking its way through Bajie's mouth and nostrils, effectively choking him as he tried vainly to claw the liquid away. "I can always choke you here and now, giving The Adversary one less servant. But instead, I am choosing to give you a chance for redemption! A chance to show the mortals of the world that you have a part to play in ridding the world of his vile influence! So I ask you just once more, Bajie. Will you help us in our struggle, and in doing so gain the respect and worship of many, or will you choke on a beverage that had been the downfall of many a mortal? The choice is yours, pig." Sanga let the wine do its job for a few seconds longer before releasing his hold on it.

The wine splattered before Bajie, who coughed violently. I had to admit that Sanga's control of alcoholic beverages was a pretty neat trick. As The Child of the Sea, I wouldn't have expected anything more than water manipulation, but all those bottles of booze the merlion consumed must have given him an affinity to it.

Bajie snorted out a last burst of fluid before speaking. "Point taken, Sanga. I can take you to where The Serpent makes his throne. I even know that he keeps what might be your edict close by. I had always wondered what that hunk of stone was. But are you two absolutely sure about this? It's one thing to phase out of existence, Wukong; there's always a chance some group of mortals would discover your name in the future. You might be able to return to this realm then. But if The Adversary or any of his agents kill you, you're gone. And I mean forever. Not even a billion followers to your name is able to bring you back. Many a civilization had fallen all because their National God fought some petty battle with another and got themself slain. Look at the Mayans! The Easter Islanders! Do you still want to go down that road? Or bide your time till The Adversary's hold wanes?"

"We all know that The Adversary is the strongest he has ever been. I don't think he's about to go anytime soon," I replied. I could hardly contemplate the prospect of living in non-existence, but it had to be a lot worse than my being stuck under a mountain. "And who's to say that anyone would even remember that I or any of the Old Gods existed? I'll take my chances."

Bajie and I looked towards Sanga, who had by now opened a bottle of rice wine for himself, sniffing its contents. His brow was furrowed, and I could tell it wasn't the quality of the wine that bothered him. When he looked back, I could see something in his blue-green eyes. Wisdom, tinged with regret.

"For years, I had been sitting on my tail, with nary a challenge to test my powers against," said Sanga softly. "The last two-and-a-half centuries brought with it challenges that I could have intervened in, but didn't. Did you know that I had more action in the last half-hour than for the past 700 years? So yeah, I'm in. You guys won't make it without me anyway." He downed the entire bottle of wine, paying no heed to its disgruntled owner.

"You're such the picture of modesty, aren't you?" I said with a smile. With two gods by my side, I already felt a lot more confident taking on the Adversary.

* * *

Bajie led us into his private elevator just as we heard the sounds of Nāga slithering into the suite. With the ruckus I and Bajie had made during our fight, not to mention the descent of the floor-to-ceiling window fragments to the street, I wasn't entirely surprised. I expected the lift to be stopped halfway in our descent, but it was clear that the Nāga hadn't yet factored on Bajie turning to our side. But we didn't have much time before they got the word out, so time was of the essence, no pun intended.

Bajie was typically chauffeured in a car parked just out the front, but given our circumstances, he took us to his other, nondescript car in the public garage. Despite the new-car smell that betrayed underuse, the Terimoto Roadster's on-board system greeted Bajie as he threw himself into the front. I rode beside Bajie while Sanga sat at the back.

"You don't normally use cloud-soaring to travel?" I asked as the car pulled out by itself. Bajie selected a command on a holographic interface.

"The Serpent doesn't want the mortals to think we're any different from them. It isn't good for PR. By travelling the same way they do, everything looks normal on the outside." The automated security barrier drew up and we exited into the road.

"So where's the big man at?" asked Sanga. I looked behind and I'll be damned if that wasn't yet another bottle of wine in his paws.

"At the Marina Bay Sands casino."

Well, that was as good a place as any. "That isn't far from here. Why are we even taking the car?" I asked suspiciously. "If you're setting us up, Bajie…"

"Because I'll be damned if I have to walk anywhere," said the boar with a smack on his belly. "You know how tiring going on foot is? Besides, the underground walkways are going to be crawling with Nāga. We can't risk getting boxed in all sides. It'd be a massacre. Not even Sanga can take on the might of an entire battalion."

"Won't they see us when we're there anyway?" I asked.

"As long as you stick close to me, my aura and scent will mask that of the both of you," said Bajie. "There's also a back door to the building we can use."

I wasn't sure if the reek of bedtime activities and alcohol counted as a scent, but I supposed I didn't have a choice. Night had already fallen, and the streets had already gotten crowded. I didn't have much time left, and already I could feel my essence fading along with my powers. I just hoped that it was enough to do what was necessary.

Bajie was as true as his word. His car passed a manned security booth without any trouble, and his car parked itself at the corner of a loading bay.

"Remember, you have to be right next to me, otherwise my aura won't be able to mask yours," reminded Bajie as we got out.

"If you want to get cosy you need only ask."

"Shut up."

A side door opened as Bajie neared, so he probably had a remote chip on his person. We walked along a winding corridor that was as ugly as service corridors went; half the lights were fused, and the reek of a thousand scents overlaid one another. Faint glimmers of aura still lingered, suggesting that Nāga had slithered through here some time before. At the end of a corridor, two cargo elevators stood, with Bajie and us entering the one on the left. Bajie pressed the button marked "B1" and turned to us.

"If any of you have any second thoughts, it's not too late to turn back now," he said as the doors closed.

"We're already in the building and you chose to remind us now?" I asked.

"Couldn't hurt to ask." Bajie licked his lips.

"Wukong, would you please show Bajie what your staff is capable of?" asked Sanga.

"Forget I said anything," said Bajie as the lift dinged. The elevator doors slid open to reveal a set of double-doors. "Here goes."

I was taken by how much activity was going in the hallway outside when the doors opened. Revelers, partygoers, and general high rollers either drunk or high staggered or otherwise danced towards their destinations. A large sign overhead listed the different casinos and amenities in both directions. Red and green banners with the insignia of The Adversary, a goat's head within a pentagram lined the walls. Televisions placed at 20 meter intervals showed The Adversary speaking on one of his talk shows that always seemed to air. But what kept me rooted to the ground was a patrol of six Nāga turning towards our direction.

"Lord Bajieeee!" exclaimed their captain in a hiss of fangs. Unlike his subordinates who wore green armor, the captain also wore a baldric of red and green, and was significantly larger. "We weren't expecting your arrival."

"Captain Vasuki," greeted Bajie. I tensed myself, but the Nāga didn't seem to pay me or Sanga any attention. "I was just on my way to meet His Greatness. There's a matter of great urgency I have to discuss with him."

"Yesss, we heard about the destruction of your suite. Several of our brothers are currently at the scene," hissed Vasuki. "Where were you when it happened?"

"If you must know, I was fighting for my life!" challenged Bajie. Vasuki's eyes narrowed into slits as he drew back. "While your brothers were whiling away their time elsewhere, leaving me undefended, two assailants came and accosted me during my rest. But they proved to be of no match to me and fled. I have thus come straight here to make a complaint to His Greatness regarding the tardiness of your men. As his most trusted servant, I deserve far better security than what your men had accorded me!"

"Lord Takshaka wouldn't like that. I urge you to reconsider your actions," hissed Vasuki. All his men were now tensed and at the ready, and I was starting to wonder if Bajie had intended to fight after all. It was clear that there was some bad blood between him and Vasuki, if not the entire Nāga Legion. Bajie never had the balls to pick a fight on his own, and I wouldn't put it past him to start one the moment he got the help of two other gods.

"That's his problem. I'll just be on my way," Bajie snorted derisively, elbowing the two of us. We followed quickly behind as he stalked off, taking care not to bump onto anyone else in the crowded hallway.

"Can't they see us?" I asked, chancing a look back. The Nāga were still glaring furiously at us as they hissed, but were making no effort to follow.

"Barely. I couldn't chance them asking who you two guys were, so I cast a concealment on you both," confirmed Bajie. "But Captains like Vasuki can still detect your aura, and that was why I needed you to stay close. Having your auras mixed up with mine would have them guessing."

Sanga scowled. "You mean you got us past only through an assumption?"

"Did you think there're that many gods left for me to have done this before? And anyway, I did ask if you still wanted to go ahead with it. So stop complaining."

Bajie walked towards the entrance of the biggest casino, and the Nāga guards parted without question. If the outside was chaotic, inside was even more so.

The casino itself had evolved in size and scale throughout the years, and the reign of The Adversary was no exception. Stretching out as far as the eye could see, it would have resembled an underground military bunker were it not for its contents. Heavy metal music blared from the speakers, in the midst of the clatter of dice and casino chips. Hundreds upon hundreds of gambling tables lay in the open floor space, each of them packed to the fullest. A number of the players were not just immersed in what was going on at the tables, but similarly engrossed in the women that had found their way onto their thighs. Most had joints of weed or other delicacies close at paw, and I supposed it wouldn't hurt to multi-task when it came to sinful pleasures. Pole dancers and strippers of all species plied their wares on platforms throughout, with catcalls and wolf-whistles surrounding them. I could see several fights breaking out at several corners of the establishment, some with weapons, but nobody, not even the scaly bouncers that called themselves Enforcers intervened. This was a temple of sin at its finest, and I was sure nowhere else in the world could rival this.

After what had to be over a kilometer of casino, we finally arrived at a reinforced metal vault door not unlike those you would find in banks. Two Nāga clad in golden armor and a more ornate baldric than that I saw on Captain Vasuki were stationed beside it. These had to be The Adversary's Royal Guard.

"I would like an audience with His Greatness." said Bajie. The Nāga nodded, and without any physical cue on their part, the locking handles of the vault squeaked and rotated by itself. The door swung open, and the three of us stepped in.

Lined wall-to-wall at all corners of the vast interior of the vault were piles upon piles of money in every denomination. From coins to bills ranging into the tens of thousands, this was supplanted by currency throughout the world, including gold and silver bullion. Seated on the bare ground in the center of all this was a goat-headed figure. Not in the dark robe he always wore while on TV, but in his natural fur. Where his torso had the smooth skin characteristic of humans, everything below the torso was covered in a dark fur that seemed to suck away whatever light shone upon it. I then noticed that the room was devoid of any furnishings, with not even a single light fixture in sight.

"I am disappointed in you, Lord Bajie," said the goatman. His voice was indulgent, yet hard. Calm, yet malevolent. It was a voice that consisted of all the malice and anger of the world behind it, ready to rise in crescendo when it saw fit. It was a voice from an owner who knew and saw all, who could not be surprised by any deception, no matter how elaborate it may have been. I could feel all that emanating from the figure before me, and from the fluff of Sanga's mane, so could he. Bajie was stock-still, his breath ragged.

"Leave us," commanded the goatman. The two Nāga left through the opening they had came through, and the door shut behind us. If it weren't for the remarkable eyesight all gods possessed, the room would have appeared pitch-black.

"Throughout the eons, there were many who thrived on lies and deception," said the goatman. "Many had served me, most of them not knowing who their true master was. But all sinners belong to me, as had been decreed by the false pretender calling himself The Creation. And for those I own, I know their thoughts, wants and desires. So believe me when I tell you that I know the reason for your being here."

"You see, Your Greatness," began Bajie.

"You are only here because I wish it!" roared the goatman. "For vengeance is mine alone!" Without any visible stimulus, Bajie was flung upwards, his head smashing hard against the high ceiling. He fell back down against the hard ground with a thud, lying motionless against it. A stream of red trailed from his cranium. The structure of the vault must have been reinforced with godly magic to have been able to cause an open wound on Bajie, and I bit back a gasp.

"And the two of you, mere flies in my game, were brought here only because I desired it," said the goatman. I fought against the urge to go to Bajie's aid. "I see you have a question, little monkey, so you may ask it." I could see those glowing red eyes burning into me, compelling me to speak.

"You are the one whom your servants call The Ad—The Serpent?" I asked.

There was no warmth or sincerity behind the figure's smile. "No, don't hold back. I have been known by many different names. The Serpent, The Dragon, The Fallen One, to name but a few. The contemptuous call me The Adversary, as I'm sure you and your lion friend do. In my current form, I am also known as Baphomet. But regardless of any form I may take, all you need to know is that I am all-powerful." Baphomet tilted his head knowingly at me.

I saw the Stone. Sanga's voice echoed within me. I looked, and right next to Baphomet was an uneven slab with inscriptions on it.

"Well, you see, your Greatness—" Here, I looked at Sanga. "The both of us are here because we would like to serve as your warriors."

"And yet I was under the impression that you needed the help of Lord Bajie to vanquish me," smiled Baphomet. Curse Bajie. His link to The Adversary would be our undoing, even if unintended. "So why don't you just tell me why you're really here, before I destroy you both?"

Sanga stepped up. "You have the edict The Creation tasked unto me, Your Greatness, and I wish to regain what is rightfully mine. I believe it is that slab next to you."

"And banish me from my rightful throne?" yelled Baphomet and before I knew what happened, he had transformed into an enormous serpent, the long coils of his being taking up almost half of the room. With scales the size of paving stones, The Serpent's head resembled more dragon than snake. A total of six horns manifested from his brow, their curved form forming a perfect crown across it. From within his otherwise featureless belly, a total of six clawed legs grew, the claws drawing gouges across the otherwise impenetrable floor. Each curved talon was a good thirty centimeters long, more than enough to rend the essence of a mortal-sized god. Across his back were six splines of razor-sharp bone, which folded and curved with The Serpent's movements. With a swift clambering motion, he swept Sanga and me into two separate paws. The Adversary's touch burned from malevolence as he held, and I struggled vainly to break free.

"Do you see all the gold and currency of the world around me?" roared The Serpent, such that I and Sanga had to flatten our ears to survive the din he made. "Can you smell the greed and want seeping from them? Do you see the depravity that mortals partake in just beyond the doors to this room, each new pleasure following another? I make my throne here because their wants nourishes me! Do you know why I transformed these mortals into so many different forms? Because with every difference comes enmity, and through it my power!"

"I take it that you won't accept me as your servant, then?" choked Sanga, gritting his teeth as he wriggled. "You and your servant made me an offer years ago."

"And you think you can crawl back after all those years?" hissed The Serpent. An orange glow could be seen at the back of his throat as he turned to me. Now that his eyes were so much larger, I could see the green slits of his irises in the midst of their red orbs. "No, you're here to help this pathetic little monkey. How does it feel to have no one left to acknowledge you? I had relished the death of your worshippers, and now I shall relish the taste of you. Gods taste so much better..."

This was it. As The Adversary brought me up to his jaws, I knew that my time had come. With my arms pinned to my sides, I couldn't reach for my staff. I would die not just as fodder for this overgrown snake, but without anyone to recount my name. I tried willing the last vestiges of my magic, but the sense of hopelessness emanating from The Adversary told me it would be far easier to just let it go...

A roar split the air, and The Adversary lurched violently to the side, slamming against the wall. Shakened by the impact, I fell out of his open claws, landing hard onto a pile of gold bullion.

Sanga had charged into The Adversary in his true form, a hulking merlion that had got to be at least 20 meters in length. With a mane of blue-green tendrils, and arms beside a silvery pelt, his resemblance to a humanoid ended at the waist level. Below it, a powerful tail lined with scales of silvery-green bunched as he kept The Adversary pinned against the far wall. Piles of money and the treasures in the room were scattered as the two titans fought. The Adversary roared as Sanga bit down hard on a paw.

"Get the stone, my friend!" mumbled Sanga between a mouthful of Adversary. The Adversary swung that paw hard against the wall, shutting Sanga up. The Merlion pushed back against the wall, sending the serpent rolling over himself.

With the enormous length of a demon serpent lashing about, along with an enormous fish tail thrown into the mix, it was no mean feat trying to find a slab of sandstone amidst the mess of strewn gold and bundles of money. For an entity without legs, Sanga was incredibly agile on land. As the two grabbled at each other, I saw a slab of stone springing up from the impact. Frozen in midair, I leapt towards it, propelling myself forward with the last reserves of my magic.

The Adversary arched around Sanga's bulk, and I felt the fires of his breath encasing me.

It wasn't the heat as much as all the thoughts erupting through my head. Everything bad that had ever happened to me played through my head over and over, each episode of grief and despair washing across me as the unholy fire did its work. My 49-day sentence in the fires of the Heavenly Crucible; the 500 years I was trapped under the mountain...being punished time and again by the torture band that the Tang Priest had installed around my head...the emptiness from the death of my last worshippers...

I had to be wriggling and squirming face-first on a patch of blackened floor for a while, because when my eyes opened, Sanga was lying against the far end, his form unmoving. The air in the room had gotten unbearably hot. Having also been hit by the flames, his essence sizzled from his person in the form of steam, the Merlion's mouth open and closing as he gasped, eyes wide and unseeing.

"Your time in the Heavenly Crucible may have kept you from immolation, but no one is spared the true horror of the fires of Purgatory," said The Adversary, wisps of flame trailing from his nose. He didn't seem to be hurt from the fight with Sanga. "Your very worst memories replaying itself over and over, with no means of respite. The emptiness you feel with each recounting. All those who trespass against me will face its true power. If you think that the last one minute was bad, you should try experiencing it for an eternity. After all, gods have all the time in the world." The Adversary grinned.

With my back facing him, I pushed myself upright, noticing for a moment the molten gold and burned piles of cash around me. "I'm afraid I'm going to have to pass," I answered, drawing my paws over the slab of stone I had clutched to my chest.

Fifty lines of previously unreadable script ingrained themselves into my consciousness, with fifty lines of words translating itself. I could hear a voice speaking within me. It was a voice that carried calm, yet authority, peace, yet justice. It was a voice that I recognized even though it had never spoken to me, a voice that was ingrained in the very core of what we gods and mortals are made of.

"… and let Edict 6 say that the appointed Defender of the Island, Sanga-Behaya-Laposka, The Child of the Land and Sea, does have the right to banish any divine intruder and their associates in his domain of protection. This edict must be presented as proof of My commission.

"Should The Child of the Land and Sea be incapacitated or otherwise unavailable, I give unto him the authority to appoint any divinity or mortal he deems a friend to take on his role. The appointed divinity shall be bound by the obligations to the before and aftermentioned edicts. This constitutes Edict 7.

"Edict 8 gives unto the Defender a place in my…"

The voice ended abruptly, and I knew it was where the stone remained incomplete at the break. Turning slowly to The Adversary, I smiled a little smile.

"Time to go, asshole." I said.

The Adversary balked for a moment, then stepped forward with a smile and a growl. "Don't you know? That edict can only be enforced by that sorry excuse of a god right there. That slab of stone is all but useless to you."

"He called me his friend," I said. And with an exaggerated flourish, I flashed the inscriptions towards him.

The Adversary let out a terrible screech. His essence quivered and shook, blurs of smoke pouring from him as he did. The door to the vault opened, with a squad of Nāga rushing in. Before they could make another move, they started fading away, hissed curses dying along with them. The many forms of The Adversary presented itself as his essence cycled through them all, and soon, his incarnation of Baphomet was left, kneeling on the ground as he panted. By now, I could see right through him, the ghostly shadow of his figure looking up at me.

"You won this time, monkey," whispered The Adversary in a snarl. "But the damned in the world belong to me, just as I had been promised." And with that, The Adversary faded away.

The building rumbled and shook, with cracks forming upon the walls. My first thought was that an earthquake was forming. I then realized that the entire building could have been held up by the will of the Adversary alone, being in such a state of disrepair and all. I had best hightail it out of here, but first…

"Sanga!" I yelled, prodding the Merlion's enormous form hard with my staff. His body was no longer sizzling from the fire he had been subjected to, and he blinked hard as he took me in.

"Is that narcissist gone?" he yawned, as if he had only been napping.

"Yes, but so would we be if we don't make a move!" I urged.

Sanga looked around at the room. Large segments of the ceiling had started to fall downwards, landing with a crash. A supporting column fell across the door to the vault, barring our exit.

"We won't be able to make it out by foot. Climb on my back!" urged Sanga. "And mind that you keep that stone with you!" I was about to do as he said, when I saw Bajie lying at the side. Despite his weight, I managed to drape him across the Merlion's neck, seating myself in the long fur behind him.

With a roar, the Merlion propelled himself forward with his tail, smashing the column barring our way. I dodged as shards of rebar and magically-tainted concrete rained down upon us, slapping aside larger pieces with my staff. Here, the former glory of the casino was gone. The gambling tables and dance platforms abandoned, I caught sight of what appeared to be piles of clothing lying all over the place. My mount dove his way through all this, splintering wood, plastic and steel as he made his grand exit, enormous paws clearing obstacles ahead of him. As we hit a particularly thick column, Bajie almost slid off, and it took a great deal of effort on my part to swing him back in place. We came out into the main hallway. Seeing an opening for an escalator to a higher floor, Sanga sprang upwards, landing right in the atrium. As he pushed his way through the glass and steel front of the building, Sanga turned to me.

"If we stop too close to the building, the shockwave of its collapse might do us a world of hurt," yelled the merlion, his mane now embedded with all manner of debris. "I'm going to leap across the river, onto the Marina Bay Floating Platform. We will be safe there."

"That's only a structure of steel! It'll break with your weight on it!" I exclaimed. The Floating Platform was a floating stage just across the river. Having been designed to be easily disassembled, I doubted its suitability for merlion-sized landings.

"They paraded military vehicles on it. It'll hold." Without waiting for confirmation, Sanga pounced. I held my breath as we soared high over the river, wind buffeting my fur.

As the flimsy platform loomed towards us, I got an idea of how a suicide victim must have felt. With a loud smash that must have echoed through both the astral and mortal plane, Sanga buckled as I tried and failed to hold onto his fur, tumbling off with Bajie in the process. Plates of metal making up the reinforced flooring flew in every direction, finding their way into the stands and river. Being fortunate enough to land on Bajie, I was only lightly winded, with minor bleeding across my knees and paws.

A thunderous rumble came from behind me, and I turned back. What was once the facade of the Marina Bay Sands hotel and the main casino building crumbled into itself. The smoke that trailed after it wasn't unlike The Adversary's during his demise. Once monuments that cost more than any other set of buildings in the world, it had served as a temple of evil until now. All that remained of The Adversary was a collection of rubble, and its untold number of followers. It didn't feel like much of a victory to me, but then, I hadn't really been expecting one. It was one thing to defeat an extremely powerful being whose only goal was to corrupt. It was another thing entirely to remain in the mortal world.

I looked up at the almost full moon high in the sky. Only less than an hour to midnight. Then I wouldn't have to worry any longer.

I walked over to the pile of steel plates marking the end of Sanga's journey. Buried under a pile of plates, the Merlion's eyes were closed.

"Open your eyes, Sanga." I said tiredly. I wasn't in the mood for his gags.

The Merlion cocked open an eye, fixing me with his blue-green gaze. "You don't sound overly glad of your success, Wukong." he commented, pushing the plates away from his sides. None of the debris had scarred him.

"What's there to be victorious about? It was your edict that banished The Adversary." I said bitterly. "And anyway, it won't be long before I'm gone from the world."

"But it was through your efforts and willpower that it happened," said Sanga calmly. With a shifting of metal, he propped himself on an elbow. "Did you know why you could pass Edict 6 on The Adversary, despite the fact that only I could do that?"

"Only because you threw the responsibility to me by means of Edict 7," I sulked.

"Edict 7 would never have worked if it was in pretense, Wukong," said Sanga calmly. "There is no lying when it came to The Creation's laws. I really did consider you my friend."

I could feel the tears welling up in my eyes at the thought. For years, I hadn't had any friends to call my own. All of them were now gone, all through the efforts of The Adversary, sowing disbelief in everything except the allure of the Seven Sins. And now, one out of two surviving gods had spoken his thoughts out loud. Pompous, disgruntled Sanga, once a bitter god who was all but forgotten, now a good friend of mine.

"I'm glad you're my friend too," I replied.

"So am I!" oinked someone behind me. I had forgotten all about Bajie. The boar hugged me. "You didn't have to rescue me from that death trap, Wukong, but you did. Despite the disagreements we had with each other, I'm glad you saved me. No god, not even you should ever be alone in this world."

"It's going to be midnight soon, guys, I'm afraid I may not have much time left before it's goodbye." I sighed.

"What makes you think you're going to be Forgotten?" asked Sanga. A knowing smile played across his muzzle. "Look around you."

I did that, and I saw all around us, on the bridges, at the windows of the nearby buildings, on the platform itself, crowds upon crowds of mortals stood looking at us. People young and old, species of every possible type. Emanating from them was warmth and gratitude. Gratitude at no longer having to live under the fear of the Nāga kicking their doors down, executing them for beliefs that they held dear. Grateful at being free of the control of a malevolent power that for years, had been all too dominant in their lives. There had to be hundreds, if not thousands of people here. These were the ones who didn't believe in the temptations of The Adversary. The ones who were truly free.

"Wonder how all these people know what had happened?" Sanga said. "Those who weren't entirely set in the ways of The Adversary had his hold broken on them. As the god of this island, all I had to do was whisper his demise to their minds, along with where to give their thanks to. For the ones that had been loyal to him, and given to temptation till the end…well, you heard what The Adversary said. The countless sets of empty clothes down in the casinos says it all. You'll find more on the streets if you care to look."

The damned in the world belong to me, just as I had been promised. I would never forget those words. For in every era, there will be those who are drawn to evil's might. And what better ruler than the evilest of them all? He may have offered them their wants and desires, but in the end, all they got was damnation.

"Citizens of my fine country!" spoke Sanga as he stood upright on his tail. His roar carried well across the kilometers, with a hush falling over the crowd. No one had ever seen The Merlion in his true form, let alone heard him speak. "You are assembled here today to witness the fall of the one you had been forced to call The Serpent. But the only right way is to call him The Adversary, because he goes against everything a virtuous person could stand for. He no longer exists in this realm, and we may all breathe easy now that he's gone.

"Some may think I was the one responsible for this great feat. A feat that no sane god or mortal would have undertaken. 'The Merlion did it?' I hear you ask. 'He exists?' Well, sure he does, he's standing right before you!" The crowd laughed politely. I and Bajie shook our heads with a smile at Sanga.

"But no, I was not the one who put The Adversary away. Wukong, please step up."

I looked at Sanga uncertainly before doing as he said. Everyone started chattering and pointing at me, a buzz of noise washing across the crowd.

"That honor falls to my dear friend Wukong," rumbled Sanga. "Also known as The Handsome Monkey King, or Great Sage Equal to Heaven. He fought against the odds in his favor, swathing through servants of The Adversary like rice to the scythe! As I lay wounded from the injuries our foul enemy had inflicted, Wukong called upon ancient magic to banish The Adversary to where he had come. It was only through his encouragement that I summoned the strength to pull myself from the crumbling ruins of The Adversary's temple, such that I may recount in detail the deeds of this brave god. I am honored to have fought by his side, and for saving this country I call home, I bow in deference to him." And with that, Sanga dipped his head in supplication.

As one, the crowd of mortals did likewise. I could feel the awe and respect emanating from the people, like a warmth of a fire to those around it. I could feel the fabric of my essence repairing itself, taking hold on the mortal plane as it did. Sanga may be pompous, but he was shrewd. By having the people know that I was their savior, I had gained more worshippers than anyone could have ever gotten by deeds alone. I would no longer fade away into nonexistence, but remain in this realm. And so I bowed both to Sanga and Bajie, knowing that even gods needed friends to help keep them sane in the eons to come.

And to help them out when the shit hits the storm, of course.

Civilization has wiped itself out in an apocalyptic war, and the gods wonder whether to start up Earth again, maybe with improvements? They ask the opinion of the last survivor, an astronaut alone on a space station.

What he asks is: if the gods are real, then who is really responsible for the death of Earth?

As Below, So Above

by Mut

He'd found the note clipped to Thomas's bunk with a magnet. It had been written in an urgent, passionate scrawl as uncharacteristic of the rat as the words. It spoke of sacrifice and redemption, temptation and past sins and a new world. Several times he wrote of Spirit talking to him, testing him, giving him instructions. At the end he apologized profusely to Jake, and hoped he might be forgiven.

Jake had put it out of the airlock along with the body, suiting up to send both drifting towards the graveyard Earth. He suspected he would regret that later, but that he would have regretted keeping those last, confused words more. Back before, there would have been no question: a death on the Station would have been an international scandal. Getting rid of evidence like that would have had the brass, the politicians, the press, and anyone with a keyboard and time on their hands after him. He would have been on trial as soon as they could figure out what law applied to this place. But now, none of that mattered. He did not feel liberated.

The recompression cycle took a long time, and the rat's body was almost invisible by the time he was out of his suit and staring out of the cupola window. His gaze slid away from the grey-blue planet, but he forced himself to stare even after he could no longer tell Thomas from the flecks of dust and debris. He let his mind drift, very carefully not thinking about the events of the past few days. He concentrated on making his tail wag slowly back and forth, on perking his ears up, on slowly breathing in and out.

It was the noise that finally broke apart his meditation. It had been bothering him for a couple of days now: an intermittent, irregular clicking. The Station made a great many noises, from the low hum and high-pitched whine of electronics to the regular whirr of fans to the gentle pinging of metal expanding after it passed out of the Earth's shadow, but this one was new. He'd asked Thomas about it but the rat hadn't been able to make it out. They'd gotten sidetracked by a discussion of the hearing sensitivities of rats and foxes that Thomas, predictably, had ended by claiming expertise in all things biological. Probably he'd been right, but now he was gone and Jake was still here, and so were the noises.

He kicked off from the window with practised ease and floated across the room, grabbing a handle as he passed through the doorway and bringing himself to rest with his paws against the wall. His ears twitched, flicking back and forth. That way, he decided, and pushed off again.

He let his instincts and his muscles do the work, leading him towards the source. He was having a dumb fox moment, a detached part of him decided. There were a dozen other things he should be prioritizing, starting with the communications systems. Depending on when Thomas had—on when he'd last been on duty, they might have gone unchecked for eight, ten hours. If, improbably, someone was still down there and had managed to get a signal up to him, they'd need a reply urgently. He leapt onward anyway, nose questing too now. He didn't want to deal with matters of life and death for a while; he wanted a nice, simple engineering problem to bang on.

Jake slowed down as he found himself heading into the experimental area. Even before, they hadn't come here often. It was a relic of another time, when the Station had had a larger, international crew. Some of the experiments were still live—still taking data, he supposed, counting cosmic rays as they flashed through—but anything that required the astronauts' participation was long gone. He wondered briefly whether he should shut the rest down, but shook his head. It would be disrespectful, somehow. Besides, there was no shortage of power; the boxes could go on counting long after the food ran out.

A scent he couldn't quite place caught his nose and he swung to a halt. It was almost like a person's—a dog or wolf, perhaps. It happened sometimes, up here, that the air recirculation system would play tricks, spreading smells through the Station faster than they had any right to travel, or trapping them in a loop so that you caught dull, mechanical hints of the past. He sniffed again, but it eluded him—but then the clicking started once more, and he knew what it was. Not one click but four together. Impossible footsteps. His tail wormed its way between his legs. The childhood stories came back to him: stupid, careless fox, caught in a dog's trap, jaws go snap-snap. He could smell it again.

He growled at himself. Stupid fox indeed. Couple of hundred miles of vacuum away from whatever life was left, and he was worried about not being alone enough. He kicked off hard in the direction of the sound, flipping through the doorway and coming to rest in a crouch on the floor. He glared around.

There was a she-wolf.

What his eyes, nose, and ears were telling him was not just impossible but ridiculous. She was naked and heavily pregnant, belly and teats both swollen, and yet somehow also on the verge of heat. She smiled at him. Jake put a paw over his nose automatically.

"You look tired, Jacob of Fox. Be at peace. You are safe with me." Her voice was low and soothing. Underneath it, Jake could hear not only her heartbeat but two or three more in her belly. He shook his head in disbelief.

"Look, lady, you can't be here. I mean, literally, you cannot be here. So either I'm going crazy—which is not unlikely—or you have pulled some major shenanigans to get here. Either way, I don't exactly feel 'at peace.'" He sighed through his nose. "Let's start with who you are and how the hell you got on board."

She lowered her ears. "My poor child, you have been ill-used. I am Merra She-Wolf. I bore the world. I bring comfort, warmth, love, cubs, food, life. I did not get here, but have always been here. I am everywhere that my children walk. Or float," she added with a smile.

Jake felt his ears splay again. "Crazy it is. So, okay, you're from the stories my mom used to tell me. Kind of makes sense, although her version had a lot less nudity. Not quite sure why I imagined you instead of Feyat. Must be just a teeny bit homesick."

"My brother?" Her ears raised. At the same time, the scents in the room changed somehow, but with his paw over his muzzle Jake couldn't make it out. "Do not worry about him. As for me, I am very real. Let me show you, child."

She began walking towards him, hips swaying. Something about the motion was off; he was already hauling himself up with one of the doorway handles by the time he understood. She was walking. As soon as he saw it, it was obvious; even the way her stomach hung down suggested a weight that was just not there in orbit. She was not real. Jake grinned with relief at the realization, even letting his tongue hang out, right up to the point when she took his forearm in her paw. Her grip was surprisingly strong.

"You see? No need to fear. I am flesh and bone and oh so much more. Do not hide your nose from me, fox; I want only what you want."

"Oh really?" Jake let her lower his paw. That other scent was stronger now. Mustelid, male. "Cuz what I want right now is for my husband and family and friends and colleagues and everyone I spoke to or met or saw or heard of to not be dead. Is that what you want, lady who— Spirit on a stick, I can't even say your name, it's that stupid. If that's what you want, I'm getting some seriously mixed messages here."

"Yes, that is what I want. That is exactly what I want," Merra replied, tail swaying slowly. "This world is dead, and you are all that remains. I would birth it anew. It will be filled with new life, and we will begin again, just as it was once before. But first," she continued, slipping Jake's arm down further so that his paw rested on her belly, "you must worship me."

"Lady—Merra—I'm really not the worshipping kind. Card-carrying atheist, that's me. Or I would be, if I believed in carrying cards around for that stuff. But, uh, bringing everyone back to life, that I like the sound of. So let's maybe talk about that once you have let go of my arm, which I would really appreciate, please."

She held on for a fraction longer, then released him, smiling brightly. "Nothing to worry about, dear fox. It comes naturally to all men to worship me."

"To most men, Sister. Not all." The source of the other scent, a tall and muscular weasel, sauntered through the room behind Merra, easing around her as he approached Jake. He wore more than her, though not by much, and carried a spear as long as he was.

"Feyat," she snarled, hackles raising. "I have this one. I bade you stay hidden."

"You did," he replied cheerfully, "but I find I am not so easily bidden. He is not one of yours, so the claim falls to me." He thumped the butt of his spear against the floor and bowed to Jake, who simply stared. "Feyat, at your service. As you are at mine."

Merra had shifted her stare to Jake, teeth still bared. He ignored it as best he could. "Uh, well. I'm pleased to meet you, Feyat. And honoured. Really. You were always one of my favourites, and— wait, is that Quill? You carved it from a yew that had been struck by lightning, and it was sharp as a needle and strong as rock? And you threw it at the sun and it was dark for a hundred days?"

"It is," Feyat answered, lifting it into the air for a moment before lowering it casually between Merra and Jake. "Not my most inspired decision, but I have learned a few things since then."

"Well, that's good. Listen, um, about what you and your sister were saying before, and us being at each others' service?" Jake spoke carefully, sensing the jaws of another trap. "I'm flattered of course, and honoured. Did I say that before? Well, I'm still honoured. You're a very handsome weasel, and I'm, well, I'm just a fox. But, you understand, I'm still in mourning for— still in mourning."

The god laughed and clapped him on his shoulder. "You two are as bad as each other," he said with a grin, pointing with his spear at the she-wolf, then at the fox. "Always it is about sex. No. You belong to me because you are a warrior," he continued. "Major, UCAF. You fought, did you not?"

"I did. But I'm a civilian now. That was a long time and a very long way away."

"Hah!" This from Merra. "Not one of yours either then, Brother? Perhaps he is mine after all. He was born from a womb."

"Be quiet, Sister. I am not done yet. No, once a warrior, always a warrior. Blood calls to blood, and he has spilled it. His heart is mine," the weasel said, tapping Quill against Jake's chest for emphasis. "Unless, I suppose, he has no heart," he added, letting the tip linger. "In which case he would be of no use to me. Do you have a heart, fox? Shall we investigate?"

Jake's tail froze. "No, that's fine. So you want me to… worship you too? Tell me, O Feyat, what would I have to do? Exactly?"

"You answer a god's question with a question? Very rude." The weasel made a tutting sound. "Fortunately for you, it is a question I like. There is a little ritual which has unaccountably fallen out of favour with warriors today. Some words, some deeds. Some blood, not too much. No sex, do not worry!"

"And then… you would remake the world? Like her?"

"I would remake it, but not like her. Bigger, better, stronger, fiercer. It was weak, this world. One short war and it falls. I fought the night itself, and pierced it a thousand times with my spear. The next will not be unworthy."

"And those who died?" Jake asked. "They were all unworthy, were they?"

"Oh-ho! Did I prick your pride, fool of a fox? Your lover was no warrior, and your warriors were no good. Worthy of you, maybe, but not of me."

"I understand now. Thank you. One last question, O Feyat, and then I think my worries will be at an end. Tell me, what would happen to your new world if I died, here and now?"

The weasel tilted his head for a moment, then narrowed his eyes and raised Quill. Merra snarled and leapt forward, jaws seizing his arm, but he flipped the weapon across to his other paw. Jake pushed himself away from the doorway but misjudged his balance, spinning backwards tail-over-head into a wall. Feyat lunged after him, stamping his foot down as he thrust the spear forward. Jake had just enough time to wonder at how little pain he felt before the shaft of the spear whipped up from the shallow cut and slapped him hard across the muzzle.

"This is not over, fox!" Feyat shouted. "You are mine, you will be mine, the next world will be mine! Do not forget it."

He must have stormed back off to wherever it was that the gods kept themselves, because when the pain in Jake's snout had quieted down enough for him to open his eyes again, the weasel was nowhere to be seen. Jake was vaguely aware of being patted and cooed at, and of something cold and damp pressed lightly against his muzzle. He gave a painful start upon realising that Merra was there, and tried to shuffle away but was pushed firmly back down by someone on his other side.

"Easy there." A new voice, older, female. His nose couldn't make out much beyond Merra and his own blood. "She's behaving herself, aren't you, poppet? And she's sorry for before."

"I am very sorry." The wolf didn't sound it to his ears, but he didn't feel in a position to argue.

"Who are—" he began, and regretted it at once.

"Tch, I said easy. That fool broke bones in there, and it's not so easy knitting them back together. My fingers aren't what they used to be. So don't you talk." He felt movement over to his right, and a moment later saw the face of a rat peeking out of a hooded cloak, fur greying but eyes still jet black. "Curiosity satisfied, hm? Good, then let me get back to work."

Work seemed to consist mostly of sitting back next to him and sucking on a pipe. "Funny time, though," she observed after a while, "when a weasel's the fool and a fox outwits him. O'course, every man's a fool when his dander's up, you know that as well as I do, I 'spect, but even so. Doesn't work like that in the stories, now does it? I knew you'd best him, though. Had my eye on you for a while, I have. You may have been a soldier for a bit, but you were a tinkerer first. Engineer." She stretched the word out as though savouring it. "Wise man. One o' mine. Oh, don't you worry, I ain't gonna hook my claws into you or anything. Wouldn't be respectful. Professional courtesy, call it. Like you an' our Feyat. I could've stepped in, told him no, I got a claim on this one too. He would've laughed, but I could've said it. But you were smart, got yourself out without help, proved it for me. And if you hadn't, mm, wouldn't've been mine after all. Same deal now: you'll come to me yourself, thinking I'm the right choice, or not at all. Oh, but where's my manners? I'm Skarra. Though you probably knew that, eh?"

Skarra Rat-Crone. Healer, elder, wise woman, scribe to the gods, gatherer of secrets. Yes, he knew her from the stories. She had been the midwife when Merra birthed the world. She found the dragons' lair by trapping one of their shadows, and drew the poison from Feyat's wounds after he slew them. She sewed Fox a new tail after he lost his to Rayfe in a bet, saved him from drowning after he tried to drink the ocean, and stitched him back together on probably half-a-dozen different occasions. She knew the uses of every plant, and where they might be found. Sometimes, though, she took on a more sinister aspect. She had a pet crow that flew overhead watching the other gods and whispered their secrets back to her. She poisoned Rayfe after he slept with her grand-daughter. Through her magic, she spread plague and famine among the tribes that displeased her.

"Aye, I think you know who I am," she continued. "Now, why don't I tell you what I see, hm? That weasel was right about one thing: we can't do the same with the next world. There was a rot in it, a sickness."

"Careful, old rat." Merra again, with a growl in her voice. "That is my world you speak of."

"Oh hush. No mother's love ever kept a cub from sickness, an' no father's pride shielded it from death. Mother's love and medicine, though, now that's a different thing." The rat drew on her pipe again. "If we make the world like before, they'll war and war and soon kill themselves off again. Oh, we could hide the stuff they used this time, but they'd just think of something worse. I bet you could come up with an idea or two here and now, couldn't you, ducks?" She patted Jake's arm and his ear flicked; he was grateful his injury gave him an excuse not to reply.

"So it's got to be different, an' it's the people that're the problem. Now, we could make 'em smarter, but then they'd just get themselves in a jam twice as fast, much as I hates to admit it. Or we could make 'em dumber, but then they'd never make it this far. Smart, dumb, rich, poor, it's the fighting that's the trouble. So, young fox, why'd they fight so much, eh?"

Jake shrugged mutely, splaying his paws. To his left, Merra sighed impatiently. "Because each wants what the other has, like cubs with toys," the she-wolf said.

"Aye, cubs with toys. So, how d'ye keep 'em from fighting?"

"Show them love, teach them to share."

"Hah! Easier said than done, even with two cubs. With a worldful? Forget it."

"Fine. Give them all the toys they want, then."

"Weren't you listening, girl? As long as fox has a toy, dog'll want it. Give 'em both more, you'll make things worse, not better. No, there's only one answer to the riddle. You'll never see it, though. What about you, fox kit? Dog got your tongue too?" She let the question hang in the air for a moment, then made a show of slapping herself between the eyes. "What am I thinking, the poultice is still on. Stay, stay, stay, stay, don't move, and… now."

With that, she tugged the cloth off. At the same time, something tingled and crackled in his nose, and suddenly smells were pouring in once more. "It'll be tender for a while," he heard the rat say. "Don't you go scratching at it or I'll smack it again myself. Now, have you got my answer?"

It took him a few seconds to gather his wits, during which he was all too aware of Skarra staring at him.

"Okay. Wow, huh. So, first, thank you for healing my muzzle."

"You're welcome, Jacob of Fox. Chest too, mind, though that was just a nick. Now, stop your stalling. I'm too old for that."

"All right. There're three solutions." He paused briefly, half-expecting an interruption, but none came. "First one, no toys. Works in the analogy, but not for real because that'd mean people have no lands, or crops, or whatever. Scratch it. Second one, no cubs. No fighting either, I guess, but not what we're looking for. Third one, one cub, all the toys. No fighting, no whining. That's what you want, isn't it?"

She gave a high-pitched laugh. It hurt his ears. "Exactly, exactly what I want! And you know what it means, yes?" she asked, poking at his chest with a claw.

"One species for the whole planet," he answered flatly.

"One species for the whole planet," she echoed. "Think on it! No more warrin' over who gets the gold, or the water, or the oil. No more gangs scrappin' it out in the big cities. Everyone workin' together, part of the same society. Part of the same family. It'd be peace."

"It'd be genocide."

"Pfft. Shoddy thinkin', cub; you know better'n that. Can't murder people who ain't even been born. But what happened down there?" She pointed in the direction of Earth. "There's your genocide. How many billions dead? How many species? That's a whole genus gone. You willing to do the same to the next world?"

Jake didn't look directly at her. "And the one species, just taking a wild guess here, that'd be the rats?"

"Makes sense, don't it? We're gregarious, smart, adaptable. Can eat anything, live anywhere. Nobody else could do it, 'cept maybe the dogs, and do you really want to hand the next world over to them? Oh, I'm open to reason, 'course, but I think you'll find I don't get persuaded so easy. Not even by you, my little engineer."

"There any room for otters in this new world of yours?"

She twitched her whiskers. "Otters? Not askin' about foxes?"

He swished his tail humourlessly. "Oh, I knew we'd never make the cut. Guess they're out too. Well, it's an interesting proposal, but I'll have to think about it." He tapped the side of his head. "I'm open to reason."

"Don't you get sharp with me, young fox. You're gonna need stitching up again soon, I reckon, an' next time won't be for free." She put a hand on his shoulder and pushed herself to her feet, joints clicking. "I'm right an' you know it. So you think on it." She started hobbling off down the corridor, then paused and looked back over her shoulder. "Just don't think too long."

Jake sat quietly until she was out of sight before breathing out and letting his head tilt back. The motion set him twisting very slowly through the air, to his mild surprise. In the rat's grip he'd almost forgotten that he was weightless. Merra extended an arm to him, and after a moment's hesitation he took it and lowered himself back down next to her.

"You should not have done that," she said. "Skarra does not forgive, and her vengeance can be terrible. Even the strongest must be humble before her."

"Eh, what's she going to do? I'm pretty sure I'm not long for this world—I'm no doctor but I think hallucinations are a bad sign, no offence—and I already lost everyone that matters to me. I'm basically a dead man walking."

Merra shook her head. "There is always something more that can be taken."

"You're probably right. Let's maybe talk about something else, though."

"Very well. Have you reconsidered my offer?" she asked.

He yipped a laugh. "Spirit's tears, you don't give up, do you? Still no on the bumping uglies, but maybe I'm coming round on the rest. I mean, so far you're the only one that doesn't want to erase my family, so you're ahead on points. So, are you guys taking turns or something? It feels like I'm being speed-dated."

"There are… formalities. I think I should not say more."

"Yeah, sure. You know who's up next, at least?"

"I do not know. Perhaps Fox." She had the courtesy to look away.

"Guess we'll see. I'm gonna go check the comms, maybe eat something. Had enough gods for a while," Jake said, drifting up gently and bracing himself against the wall.

"Be wary, Jacob of Fox." She paused. "And no, I do not give up."

A retort came to his lips, but suddenly he didn't have the energy for it. He nodded instead and kicked off, letting his paws do the work for a while. He whipped back up the corridor, breathing more deeply as the unsettling scents of weasel and wolf faded, replaced by oil and dust and the over-sweet powdered drinks. Rat was still strong here, a doubly unpleasant reminder. He looked away as he passed Thomas's berth.

The control room was much less grand than it sounded: a handful of terminals, a couple of workspaces mounted on the walls, some electronics, and an A/V rig. Most of it had been brought up years ago and was obsolete compared to his laptop, but it was here and still worked so it had stayed. He checked the network quickly but it was still down: all of the Earthside stations had dropped within minutes, and he doubted there was much left of them. But there was a ham radio, and if anyone was going to get through it'd be on that.

As he picked up the headset, he heard the door slide shut behind him. The scent of dog reached him. He did not move.

"Well, what do we have here?" The voice was dangerously light and friendly. "Smells like Fox. Looks like Fox. Standing still and hoping I'll go away, also straight out of the Fox playbook." The air moved behind him and the scent grew stronger. "Is this going to be a short conversation?"

"You're Rayfe."

"Sounds like Fox too. That's disappointing; I had hopes for you."

"You're not real," Jake said. His tail brushed against something warm and he drew it back quickly.

"An interesting gambit. Problem is, it opens you up to a response of 'If I weren't real could I do... this!'" Jake flinched, but the bite did not come. After a moment, the voice continued. "But that would be entirely too obvious, and I would never stoop to such depths, goodness me no. Why don't you turn around, hm? With such a delightful tail, I can't be responsible for my actions if you don't."

Jake let go of the headset, leaving it to drift, and gripped the wall, turning himself carefully. A couple of feet below him and to one side, the dog was waiting. His first thought was that Rayfe looked smaller than he'd expected: not a hulking brute of a mastiff, but leaner, sharper. Like Feyat he wore a loincloth, although his was a dirty black.

"What a revelation!" Rayfe exclaimed, following up with a big, toothy grin. His tail waved deliberately. "Isn't this nice? You do look comfortable, bobbing up there like an otter. I think I'll come join you." The dog kicked off and floated up next to him, rocking slowly back and forth as though in the ocean. For a moment it reminded him of Glen, and his ears flattened.

"Look, I'm not in the mood for this. What do you want?" he demanded.

"To get laid, duh," Rayfe replied promptly. "Oh, not with you, don't worry, you're 'not in the mood'. But Merra, now—you smelled her? Like honey and fresh hay. Makes you just want to roll in her, mm-mmm. And those titties!" He kissed his fingertips, smacking his lips. "Like little dumplings."

"Go tell her that," Jake said. "I hear women love being compared to food."

"Aw, does someone feel excluded from the conversation?" Rayfe slid an arm around Jake's shoulder; the fox shrugged it off. "Let's talk about men, then. Specifically, Feyat. How can you be so ripped and yet so straight? Do you know the story about how I fooled him into thinking I was a woman?"

Jake nodded, not meeting the dog's eyes.

"Hah, that was the best. I got him to sleep with me—and weasels may be macho idiots but they've got bags of stamina, let me tell you—and then he wandered the land for a year looking for the 'mysterious beauty' he'd lost." The dog sniggered. "Of course, then I found out he knocked me up, which was no picnic, let me tell you."

"What?" Jake stared, confused. He knew this story well; he'd asked for it often enough to worry his parents.

"What d'you mean, 'what'? I'm giving you the good stuff here," Rayfe said.

"No, I mean that's not the way the story goes," Jake replied. "You got him to sleep with you, sure, but you didn't get pregnant. That'd just be weird."

"Oh, it was weird all right. But where d'you think otters came from? They're not called 'river dogs' for nothing."

"That's just gross."

"Yep. Sex is gross, childbirth is gross, people are gross, life is gross. Sometimes people cut the gross stuff out of my stories, but they're not the same without it. Which brings me to my question: what was he like?"

Jake was lost. "Feyat?"

"No, fox-for-brains, my grandson, or great-grandson, or whatever. The one you were boinking within the bonds of matrimony, which personally I think is a great perversion."

"His name was Glen, you asshole, and he's dead."

"Lot of that going around. Death, I mean, but plenty of assholes up here too now. My question stands."

Jake threw his paws up. "He was smart and funny and kind, worth more than all of you lot put together. He loved wine, could drink me under the table. He taught math. He couldn't sing and didn't care. Are you happy now? Is that what you wanted to know?"

"For now," Rayfe said mildly. "You still think I'm not real?"

"Spirit's not real. You're just ridiculous. Gods are a lazy way to explain the unknown, and you don't even explain it."

"Sure I do. Look, you lived on a world where there were… how many different sentient species? Talking foxes, dogs, horses, rats, even pangolins, which I personally think I made up when I was drunk."

Jake's tail swished in anticipation. "Ye-es, and?"

"Doesn't it strike you as a bit of a coincidence? Like, how are there, simultaneously, all those intelligent species?"

"You're behind the times," the fox replied with a triumphant grin. "This is Evolutionary Biology 101. Anthropomorphic principle. One," he said, counting it off on his fingers, "we have to be intelligent to raise the question. Two, the conditions to produce intelligent life are very rare. Three, when you see intelligent life, those conditions must have been present in the environment. Four, they would've applied to multiple species, so when you find one intelligent species you'll generally find a whole cluster. QED."

"And just what were those conditions, would you say?"

"I don't know, ask a biologist. Oh wait, you can't, the last one killed himself."

"And now you're using his death to dodge the answer that's staring you in the face. Smooth, kid, very smooth. You sure you're not one of mine? Say, though," Rayfe continued, "isn't it a pity that he did? He could've cleared all this up in a heartbeat. Not the whole evolution thing, gosh, that seems way too hard. But whether we're really here or just… figments. But I guess the conditions for him to kill himself were just present in the environment."

Jake looked away. "Yeah, thanks, I'd almost forgotten that the world had ended."

"That probably didn't help either. Man, this is depressing. You got any wine up here?"

"What? No."

"Really? C'mon, anywhere people live there's always wine. Or beer, or rum, or something."

"This is a space station," Jake explained slowly. "It's not allowed. We're on duty all the time. And it costs a crazy amount to bring each pound of weight up here. They don't send us booze."

"Yeah, but there's food, right? Fruit, vegetables, even if it's just mush, you can ferment it. Any time you have a bunch of men with time on their hands, you've got booze." The invisible current brought Rayfe closer until they were almost touching. "You must have something tucked away. You can trust me. I mean, who am I gonna tell?"

"There's nothing," said Jake, though he wondered. Thomas would never keep a still, but maybe one of the previous crews had set one up. Perhaps he could sniff it out later.

"What a sad time we live in. The youth of today, no respect for tradition. Someone should do something about it. Shake the world up!" He locked eyes with Jake. "You got any thoughts on the matter?"

"On making moonshine?"

Rayfe tapped the fox's nose lightly. "Don't be coy, it doesn't suit you."

"I've had a few offers," the fox replied. "Are you going to make a pitch?"

"Nah, not my style. Making a new reality sounds like way too much work. And where would be the fun in breaking the rules if I made 'em in the first place?"

Jake looked back up at the dog. "Are you sure? Is this some kind of reverse psychology thing? Because the others seemed pretty intent. Like, assault and battery intent."

"They're gods. They can't stand the thought of someone else being more powerful. Forget assault, it moves them to murder. It's in their nature."

"But not in yours?"

Rayfe shrugged, brushing against Jake's shoulder. "Being contrary is in my nature. When they zig, I zag. When they suck, I blow. When they come—"

"Wait, wait, shut up," Jake interrupted. "You said something there, about their nature. What if there were only one god?"

"Well, that is an interesting thing to say, which you came up with entirely unprompted. Just one god, dear me. Such a strange arrangement. I wouldn't dwell on it. Here, let me distract you with my masculine wiles," the dog said, putting a paw on Jake's side. The fox's fur bristled. He put his paws on Rayfe's chest, pads flat against the god's dappled fur, and pushed. To his considerable surprise, Rayfe drifted away. Jake thumped backwards into a display panel.

He crouched instinctively, but there was no retaliation. If anything, Rayfe looked pleased, tail wagging as he came to a halt in defiance of mere physics. "Someone's a little agitated, I see. Did I make you uncomfortable? Give you a little god-boner? I can always kiss it better," he offered, licking his lips suggestively. It didn't ring true, though, and after a moment Jake understood why: the dog didn't smell aroused—at least, not more than before—and for that matter neither did he. He shook his head.

"There's something not right here. Someone missing. I've seen you and Skarra and so on, but not Spirit. How'd that happen? I mean, no offence but you guys are kind of obsolete. Stories for kids, and not that many kids either. But Spirit? They're a capital-G God. They're worshipped— were worshipped by billions."

Rayfe shrugged. "Maybe it's because you don't believe in them."

"Sure, but I don't believe in you guys either."

"Mm, I think perhaps you like our stories better? Mine, at least. Some of the Feyat ones get pretty repetitive."

"Your stories gave me nightmares," Jake replied, crossing his arms. "How many times did you kill Fox, or skin him alive, or leave him to starve in a trap? That's just sick."

Rayfe's tail stilled. "Yeah," he said after a moment. "That's in my nature too. We don't get to change it very often."

"You still didn't answer my question. Where's Spirit?"

"Well, I guess technically I can't stop you from talking to them," the dog replied. "What a pity, I tried, et cetera. Though honestly, I don't know what everyone sees in them. I mean, seriously, can you get any more cynical? Invisible, incorporeal, and genderless. Sure, it's genius marketing, no rough edges to offend any demographic, but they've got all the personality of oatmeal."

Jake chuffed in disbelief. "You_ think _Spirit_ is_cynical?"

"Take it from an expert," Rayfe said, with a grin. "That whole schtick about universal love and redemption? It's for the rubes. Never trust a god who promises eternal happiness after death. And have you seen what Spirit's followers get up to? They talk a good game, but they sure love blowing stuff up."

"All right, yes, but." Jake rubbed a paw across his face. "People are people. We'll always find an excuse. But if you're gonna have a god—and I can't believe I'm defending organised religion to a figment of my imagination—isn't it better to have one that makes us aspire to be better? Whose main lesson is about love and not chopping foxes into bits?"

"You want to be careful with that. Nothing as dangerous as righteousness, nothing as blinding as love. Skarra loves her people, and woe betide you if you get between her and them. Spirit, now, they love the whole world. What wouldn't they do?"

The door rattled. Fox and dog looked at one another.

"What was that?" asked Jake.

"Oh, probably Skarra. I don't know why she didn't butt in earlier; I was beginning to worry about her. Maybe something happened to her hearing aid," Rayfe said, waggling his eyebrows.

The door juddered again, and then something thumped against it.

"Why doesn't she open it? Or just, I dunno, walk through it?"

"We're gods, not ghosts," Rayfe answered. "And she can't open it because Feyat's spear has unaccountably got wedged in that cavity the door's supposed to slide into."

Jake's fur bristled. "You trapped me in here?"

"Oh relax, I'm not going to eat you. Besides, she's very clever, and very determined, and a little scared. She'll have it open in no time."

"Why would you do that?" Jake tugged on his ears. "She already basically threatened to have me gutted. Spirit's piss, why?"

"To spend another minute with the handsomest fox there is. And, more specifically, to spend it doing my third favourite thing: talking. So, last chance, Jacob of Fox: what do you want to know? Clock's ticking."

"What happened to Spirit? And give me a straight answer, for piss's sake."

Rayfe bowed his head and lifted his arms, turning around and floating down to the floor, claws clicking as his feet touched the ground. He gestured and the lights dimmed. A voice filled the room, soft and warm and reassuring.

"we are here, my child." The lights flickered in time with the words. "we were within you all along, as we are within every soul that longs for peace."

"So what happened? Why are these guys here too? What did Thomas mean in his note?" Jake hesitated, then pressed on. "How would you remake the world?"

"we have little time and there is so much to tell. above all, jacob of fox, you must know this: your butt stinks, and yet it is cute anyway, and lo we prophesy that rayfe shall hit that, and it will be divine."

By the end of the performance, Jake was growling. "You stupid bastard, we don't have time for this!"

"come now—I mean, come now. There's always time for innuendo." Rayfe turned back to him, tail wagging. The lights returned to normal. "No words of praise? I thought I made a very convincing Spirit."

"I don't care about—wait, wait, wait. You're Spirit? You, what, made them up and pretended to be them to trick all those people into worshipping you?"

"Oh please, no. As though I could keep a straight face that long. Nah, they've got Spirit down in the far lab."

"In the... here? On the Station?" The dog flicked an ear at him. "So why," Jake growled between clenched teeth, "could you not have told me that ten minutes ago?"

"Because you only get one shot at this, puppy dog, and you would've Foxed it up. Plus, it's in my nature. Get ready."

A crackling sound came from the door, lasting for a second or two, and then the whole thing—apart from a thin slice at the edge—floated slowly into the room. Clawed hands gripped it from behind and sent it moving sideways, and Skarra stepped into the room. She glowered at them, pulling a gnarled stick from somewhere in her robe.

"Skarra! What a relief." Rayfe beamed, tail wagging. "I was just saying to Jake here that you'd have us out of here in no time. Say, are we going to play the stick-toss game? Normally I wouldn't indulge, but after—"

Skarra's hand had swung to point it at the dog then twitched, silencing him. Jake thought at first that Rayfe had somehow been paralysed, but the blood soaking through the fur at the god's neck quickly put paid to that.

"You killed him?" he heard himself ask.

"Dead as a dewclaw. He'll be back sooner or later, more's the pity, but for now we get some peace and quiet. 'Course, you ain't a god," the rat said, pointing the stick at Jake, "so I'd tread careful if I was you, dear. Now, what did he tell you?"

Jake forced himself to look away from Rayfe's body, hanging lifelessly in the air. "I think you already know that," he replied. "Didn't you have a bird that spied for you, in the stories?"

She made a hissing sound. "I told you not to go gettin' clever with me, little one. If you know the stories, you know I always gets my way. Always."

"You did," he agreed. "But by stealth, or cleverness, or poison, never strength of arms. That was Feyat's business. Funny, I don't smell him. He not with you on this? Couldn't trust him not to grab me for himself, maybe?"

He saw the tip of her tail flick. "Still that tongue of yours or I'll cut it out, so I will."

"But you won't. We've been over this before: if you kill me, that's game over. No new world; no more rats, ever. I put the last one out the airlock myself. Not one of yours, though, even if he was a doctor and a scientist. He was a Spirit man, through and through. True believer. That must've been a terrible disappointment, am I right?"

"Maybe I won't kill you," Skarra muttered, "but I can take you down a peg or two." Her hand flicked, but Jake was already moving, shoving off the wall and tumbling through the air. Something stung his tail and he yelped but kept going, rebounding off a console. He needed cover, or a weapon, but the room was frustratingly open. He passed the radio headset and slung it towards the rat, cord and all. She cackled and a screen next to his head tore open, spilling wires and shards of plastic.

"Nowhere for you to go, fox! Maybe you should read how your own stories end, eh?"

But there was one piece of cover, wasn't there? He swung around, grabbing Rayfe's body and putting it between himself and the rat. Globules of blood shook free, hanging in the air like baubles. He braced himself and kicked off straight for Skarra. For an agonising second or two, he could do nothing but cling to the dog and hope. Spattering and tearing sounds came from the other side; he could see guts and bone trailing behind them. Then, with a whump, they hit the rat, knocking her over.

It was a tooth-and-claw fight now, brutal and desperate. He was stronger but had no weight, no leverage. He seized her wrist in his jaws and clamped down, tugging the stick loose and throwing it away. She raked his face with her other hand. He bit down harder and something snapped in her wrist. Blood filled his mouth. Her hind legs scrabbled, claws tearing gashes in his uniform. He twisted around, out of her reach. Her free hand slipped into her robe and he grabbed at it through the cloth. She screamed, painfully high, and kicked at him, sending him spinning upwards. He came to rest against the ceiling, panting, staring down at her. She lay wheezing on the floor. Between them there was a haze of blood.

"Come on, this is stupid," he gasped. "You don't want to kill me, and I don't want to kill you. What happened to winning me over with reason?"

She gave him a sickly smile. "Knife in the belly always was a winnin' argument. What you goin' to do now, little fox?"

"I don't know!" His tail flicked and pain jolted through him. He gripped it with a whine. "Talk to people, figure it out."

"Too late for that, I reckon. Once blood's been spilled, the talkin's done. Happened down there, now up here."

"But we're talking now!" His paw clenched and unclenched. "Rayfe was trying to tell me something about Spirit in this weird, roundabout way. Why?"

Skarra's back arched and she pointed up at him. "You stay away from that thing!" she said, voice sharp again, then sunk back to the floor. "Worship me, or Feyat, or even that twisted-up dog, but never that." She turned her head and spat blood. "Pure evil, it is."

"We'll talk it through, all right? Look, let's call a truce. Will you promise not to hurt me, if I promise the same?"

"Too late for that, my sweetness. You already won."

Jake looked at her again, seeing just how much blood was staining her robe. "Oh Spirit dammit, why didn't you say?" He launched himself towards her, stifling a grunt of pain. "Let me see. Shit, where's the first aid kit?"

"Stupid fox," she whispered, though not without affection. "I was doin' medicine—and butchery—afore you opened your eyes. Don't you think I know what my own knife does? You just promise me you won't go near that monster."

"Hang on. Just… hang on, okay?" The kit was in the crew quarters. He leapt towards the doorway, brushing through the mist of congealing blood, and swung into the corridor. There was someone else up ahead. "Get help! Move, quickly!" he yelled. All he could smell was blood. Why were they just hanging there? "Skarra's hurt. Go!"

It was Merra, he saw. He grabbed a handle on the wall, twisting to a halt. She wasn't moving. The wrongness of it was plain, but he had to know. He drifted over cautiously, arms extended, and caught her shoulder. The smell of stale blood intensified. He turned her, slowly, glanced at her belly, and looked away.

Skarra was unmoving when he returned to the control room. He felt for a pulse, just to be sure, then sighed and let go of the kit. He should probably see to his own wounds, he realised, but couldn't find the energy. First we killed ourselves off, he thought, and now these gods are doing the same. He wanted to curl up into a ball and have it all go away. Or a shower, a long, hot shower. But there was no shower, and there was unfinished business. Two gods left, and then he could rest. He pushed himself off and began making his way back down the corridor.

He listened carefully as he approached the end. Breathing, occasional gasps and movement of paws. The musk of a weasel. He had thought to creep up unnoticed, but as he approached the doorway Feyat sniffed and called out: "Skarra, is that you? Come and take my place. I tire of this." A pause. "Are you injured?"

Rayfe's ventriloquism trick would be useful around now, Jake thought, poking his head around the corner. "She is," he said. "By her own blade. It was an accident."

Feyat stood with his back to the doorway, next to one of the experiments. No, Jake realised, not one of the original experiments: this was something new, cobbled together from parts taken from the others. The weasel stood next to a humming rack of electronics, and his paws were clasped together between two coils of wire.

"The cowardly fox, then." Feyat sniffed again, back still turned. "You reek of blood. Have you taken to murdering old women now?"

"She killed Rayfe. And Merra. Look, I'm tired," Jake said. "I just want this to be over with."

"Then strike me down, coward, and be done with it. It will never go free while I draw breath."

"Oh, stop being so dramatic." Jake eased himself into the room and edged along the wall to get a better look. "What are you even doing?"

"We have bound Spirit! I did not think it could be done, and yet she did." He lowered his tail. "Did she truly kill Merra?"

"Someone did, and it looks like you've got an alibi. So, yeah. You don't seem too bothered about Rayfe."

"Him? I've passed wind that I'll miss more than that dog."

Jake looked down. The coils were connected to the rack, and the rack was connected to the Station's power grid. He had no idea what it did—besides imprison gods, apparently—but it looked pretty simple to switch off. "Skarra said he'd come back. The others too, I guess."

"For the next story, yes. So long as there is a next story. Where are you sneaking off to, little fox? I've killed better warriors than you in my sleep."

"Yeah, yeah. So what's this all for? What did Spirit ever do to you, anyway?"

"They conspired against us," Feyat snapped. "They schemed to remake the earth to their own vision."

"Sounds strangely familiar."

"It is not the same! There is a way these things are done. A god does not just wipe the Earth clean and begin again."

Jake's fur prickled. "What do you mean, wipe it clean?"

"Their followers built those weapons, and their followers fired them. It is plain to anyone with a nose."

"Was it their fault, though?" Jake asked slowly. "Seems like they're the only one with any followers left these days. Seems like you could pin all of the world's problems on them that way."

"What does it matter? I know they did it," Feyat said, scowling.

"Because you would have done the same in their place?" The weasel didn't rise to the bait, so Jake continued. "It matters to me, though. Got a decision coming up, remember? Look, if you let them out, can you recapture them later?"

Feyat looked at his paws. "Perhaps. Skarra could have. But I will not risk it, not to indulge your curiosity."

"Then I'll pull the plug and you'll never get them back in. Or I'll shut the grid down, or I'll log into the rack, or whatever. We both know how this ends."

The weasel's shoulders slumped. "On your head be it, then. Don't believe a word they say." He stepped back, and suddenly warm, amber light filled the room.

"we are free. we thank you, child; be at peace." The voice was soothing and familiar, eerily similar to Rayfe's impression—or, Jake supposed, the other way around. He half-suspected that the dog was in the room somewhere.

"You're really Spirit, then? The Spirit? And they had you locked up in here?"

"we are, and they did, for hours. we felt our last follower fall, and could not comfort him. we must away soon, to recover his soul."

"Thomas? Seems you could've saved everyone a lot of trouble by talking to him earlier. Could've told him to hang tight, saved him a crisis of faith. He'd still be here, you'd have your decision, and I wouldn't've had to deal with these maniacs," Jake said, gesturing towards Feyat.

"we did speak with him, and he was troubled. we sought to ease his mind, but those ones interfered."

"Interfered how, exactly?"

"we felt the touch of a false prophet," Spirit said. Feyat spoke at the same time: "That damned dog, doing Skarra's bidding."

Jake sighed. "I actually thought he was trying to help. Stupid, stupid fox."

"we love you, fox. we must finish together what he could not. we must set the world on a better path. we must remake it as a heaven, and bring all the lost souls from the last world safely home. we must have your worship."

"Yeah," Jake said. It was a relief to give in.

"No, you cannot!" Feyat shouted, but the fox ignored him.

"So, um. In this new world, would Glen be there? And would I get to see him?"

"we are moved by your love. we will see you reunited. we would not wish it any other way."

Jake broke into a smile. He could feel the tears coming, and did not try to stop them. "Oh, that's—I mean, I never thought I'd see him again. He was dead, and—" He took a deep breath. "Okay. Listen, I'm so sorry but I've got to ask this. This jack-off says you blew up the world, killed all those people. That true?"

"we did."

Jake stared, baffled, then suddenly found himself retching. His vision dimmed. He fought it, shoving his paw in his mouth and panting until he could taste nothing but grime and dust and himself, until the blood was overpowered. Eventually, he looked back up.

"Why?" he asked.

"we saw the world tilting towards doom. we looked in the hearts of its people and found them ill-made, grasping, hateful. we saw in our sorrow that it was not their fault, for they had been made in the image of their old gods. we prophesied that the world would end, and feared for the next one. we placed one of our faithful safely up here, where the end would not touch him."

"Thomas," Jake said faintly.

"we told him that he need only strike you down, and then he would be the last, free to choose us, and the world would be ours to rebuild."

"But he wouldn't. Because he was a true believer." Jake leant his head back against the wall and closed his eyes. "He actually believed in feeding the one that bites you and harming no one and all of that crap. Oh man, that must have burned. And then Rayfe comes along in disguise and says to him, what, you passed the test, my child, we call you to heaven. Or, maybe, we will accept your life in that poor fox's place. Gives him a way out." He opened his eyes, blinking. The light still suffused the room. Fayat appeared stunned. "But, okay. Help me with one last thing. You kill all the people and then bring them back. What's to stop them picking up right where they left off?"

"we would not allow it. we will remake them in our own image, and they will not know hatred, nor selfishness, nor deception, nor lust. we will remake them pure."

"Guess there was a fourth solution. Make the people not be people. Piss on you," Jake said, kicking off towards the doorway. "Piss on you all. Feyat, you can put it back in that trap. Or not, I don't care. Just don't come after me, either of you."

He made it back to his quarters without throwing up, and counted it a success. In his bunk there was another fox. He was too exhausted to be surprised.

"Hey," said the other fox. "Are you me? You smell kinda like me."

"I hope not, for your sake," Jake answered. He glanced around, then shrugged and slipped into the bunk. The other fox put an arm around him. It helped.

"You're not Rayfe, are you?" the fox asked. "I promise I didn't do anything."

"Nah, don't worry, I'm just some guy," Jake said. His fur was a sticky mess but the fox didn't seem to mind. "And Rayfe's not so bad. Well, I guess he is, but he doesn't want to be. And you'd be Fox, right?"

"Fox!" said Fox. "Rayfe is too bad. One time he found me in the woods, and he hunted me, and he caught me, and he ate me, and the next day he pooped me out and ate me all over again."

"Okay, that's way too gross. Maybe don't tell me any more about him, please?"

"Okay," said Fox. "Oh! Skarra had a message about you. I'm supposed to worship you, or you're supposed to worship her? I forget."

"Let's, um, let's not worry about worshipping right now, okay? I think I've got something better. Or, at least, not worse than the options on the table. How would you like to hear some stories?"

"Is Rayfe gonna be in them?" Fox asked, with trepidation.

"Yeah, but don't worry. I think you'll like these. Now," Jake said, dropping into the familiar patter his mother had used, "these are stories of when people—that's me—and gods—that's you—walked the Earth together. There were many people, and many gods, and sometimes they fought, and sometimes they loved, and sometimes they did both together. This is a story about Rayfe the Dog and Fox. Rayfe was a great friend of the people, and he loved them all, and they loved him. Now, one day Rayfe was guarding a great, fat chicken for them. He was worried, because he'd smelled the droppings of Fox the day before, and Fox was the quickest and slyest of the gods, far cleverer than he was."

"But I don't think I am."

"Hush," said Jake, "we're working on that. So Rayfe was pacing back and forth, sniffing the air, when he heard a voice come from the woods…"

Hundreds of miles below them, under its blanket of stars, the Earth shifted in its sleep.

Everyone knows the major Egyptian gods. Ra, the sun god, Cat-headed Bast, Jackal-headed Anubis, Falcon-headed Horus, Crocodile-headed Sobek, Ibis-headed Thoth, Lioness-headed Sekhmet, Cow-headed Hathor, Ma'at, the human weigher of souls, and her pet demon Ammut who eats the souls that weighed too heavily on Ma'at's scales. Even Osiris, the green-skinned human god of the afterlife and of resurrection.

But there were many other Egyptian gods. Khnum the ram-headed, Tawaret the hippopotamus-headed, Heket the frog-headed, Khepri the scarab-headed, and even Babi the baboon-headed. One who was not just an animal-headed human was Uadjet, usually spelled Wadjet in English, the cobra (although sometimes she was depicted as a human woman with one or two cobra heads). Uadjet was the patron and protector of Lower Egypt, the counterpart of Nekhbet the vulture of Upper Egypt. Together they were worshipped as the Two Ladies. Uadjet's temple was in the city of Per-Uadjet, the House of Uadjet, in Predynastic ancient Egypt.

Uadjet was pretty much forgotten by 2000 to 1000 B.C., the most prominent millennium in ancient Egypt. By today, in "The Going Forth of Uadjet", the cobra-goddess is roused from her millennia-long torpor by Ra the sun-god to serve vengeance upon the humans who have forsaken the old gods—and to personally seek her long-lost lover, Nekhbet.

The Going Forth of Uadjet

by Frances Pauli

Uadjet guarded an empty temple. She stood in the shadowed niche and watched the dust motes dance in the sunlight for enough years to eat the stones away, to pit the bricks and make softer edges of the once-sharp rectangular doorways. Golden light on golden stones, and a golden god long forgotten.

Uadjet hid in the niche and pretended to still be useful.

Her forked tongue slid between cracked lips at least once per decade. The twin tips gathered scents, tasted the world and found it lacking. No friends remained to leave their footprints in the swirling dusts. No glinting, animal eyes blinked back at her from the other nooks.

Alone, afraid to think of the future, Uadjet drifted into her memories between ancient breaths. In her mind, she played with Sekhmet's cubs on the terrace just to the right, her scaled head gleaming with Ra's blessing while the little lions batted and nipped at the lacings of her sandals.

The Nile still snaked below the stone shelf, glorious and full of Sobek's people. The mighty crocodile had bathed there once beside her. They'd lounged on the mud and talked of gossip, of how Set slipped into his brother's bedchamber when the great hawk was away, of how the hawk's lady had welcomed him.

Uadjet could still taste the dates, sun-filled and overflowing as much as Sobek's belly. The crocodile's laugh echoed across the desert while the rumbling of his great, green tummy stretched the limits of his kilt. She missed that laugh, the long snout studded with fat fangs. She missed the gossip and the Nile that, even now, rolled past her.

Past them all.

Snake eyes blinked in the darkness. Uadjet tasted the temple air and smoothed the cotton fabric of her dress with desiccated fingers. Still there. The Nile, sweet on her lips. Her thoughts turned on that note to Nekhbet, long lost to her. Sweet, sweet Nekhbet with eyes like pins and a neck so like the snake she loved. *Where are you my blessed? Should not the vulture still fly, when the whole world has gone to death and our glorious bodies to decay?*

The thought drew her like no other could, and Uadjet shrank to the cold floor. She slithered, the black cobra that might slip unnoticed, once more, into the sunlight. *One last kiss, one last taste of life.* Her body curved against the dust, marked the sigils of her passing there. Her tongue flicked and flicked, gaining speed as her impulse grew, the urge to be out and alive again... if only for a breath, if only to see the Nile shimmer.

She reached the terrace but hesitated at the exit to the temple. Uadjet tasted a single drop of sunlight as her tongue tips broke that invisible barrier. Instantly, the light of Ra entered her, a far off whisper. It filled her head and spread warmth down and out through every ebony scale. The cobra raised the front of its length from the stones, lifted toward heaven and slid forth into the light.

"Uadjet, you have kept me waiting." Ra's voice rained upon the terrace. It called her higher, and her body shifted and rippled until she knelt again, a woman with the cobra's head bowed in honor of the most high.

"You wait upon me?"

"You are the last of us, Uadjet. Does that not infuriate you?"

"Yes." She hissed it, spat venom to the stones and heard them sizzle.

"Then what would you do, goddess?"

Do? Uadjet shivered despite the sun's heat. Had she grown lax in her niche? Content to while away the centuries on pity and soft memories? She had. Of course she had.

"Whatever I might to serve you." She answered with a stronger voice, with determination pressing at her words. Oh, to be doing again!

"Not to serve me, child." Ra's voice turned on a note, spoke with tenderness now that she'd fully awoken. "Not for me. For you."

"For me?" Uadjet's mind filled with vengeance. She saw the black bull of Set's rage in that, but she also saw the lioness slain, the tawny pelts of her cubs crimson with their mother's blood. She would *do* something. She should have done something already.

"You have lingered alone, too long in shadow," Ra said. "I fear for you, last one."

"I will go forth."

"Yes."

"I must go." She would poison the world for their crimes next. She would slither. She would strike.

Ra's voice chanted in echo, carried on the sun and the sparkles bejeweling the Nile. "Go forth, go."

* * *

Uadjet, the cobra, took to the fields.

She'd wound between the reeds along the Nile banks, felt the cold mud, the silt of life, beneath her belly and grew stronger for it. Then she lay for three days in the full light of Ra on a flat rock beside a palm where the gathered force of her master's heat fueled her fury to be off and moving.

When the bloodlust grew too strong to restrain, Uadjet entered the realm of man. She followed the furrows between the crops and let the thumping of the shadufs beat her war march to the winds. Sweet water trickled here, kept the crops green and full and eased the passing of her scales, frictionless, silent, and so very deadly.

She moved ever away from the great Nile now, inland, to where the mud sprouted houses and the fields had been dotted by the tread of tender brown feet. Soft ankles, the tight skin of those who'd abandoned her kind long ago.

Uadjet's tongue danced, out and in. She tasted the world, and let the scents guide her.

Once, the acrid scent of smoke burned her tongue. She crossed the field then, veered over the ruts, skipping like a long black stone for a ways. Here she met the swollen ox, saw Hathor's brown eyes looking back at her, the slick, wet nose and kind expression hanging beneath a pair of curving, sickle horns.

Hathor, who had been mother to them all, who had steered Uadjet gently into Nekhbet's arms when she might have hesitated, grown shy and chosen to remain alone. Instead of broad maternal shoulders, this head hung from thin, sunken blades. Shoulders used to the yoke of man, meant to serve and haul and carry.

The great cow goddess stood always proud. Her arms had been wide enough to encircle them all, to hug the whole world to her nurturing breast.

Uadjet hissed and reared toward the sun's disk. She flattened her skull, spread twin spots and danced side to side for the burdened beast. A hoof stamped the mud. The animal snorted fear, tasted of a life of abuse and labor. Uadjet struck. Her needle teeth bit into thick skin and injected justice, relief, pity into the flesh below.

A mercy killing, really. Not quite vengeance. Not yet.

The blood lent her power. The great shaking of the ground, when the animal struck it, when the ox lay on its side with bony legs churning the earth… Through all of this, Uadjet grew stronger, more sure in her task.

She stayed until the beast died, until she felt its last breath whisper against her scales. *Potential.* Uadjet heard something there, something precious but slippery enough that she couldn't quite snatch it. *Go forth, Uadjet.*

She slithered on, angled away from the water again. Now, however, her thoughts rattled. There'd been a message there. Something she might have utilized to greater good. Her mind churned and her belly scutes riffled over soft silt. The rich soil that brought life to the region, that brought life...

The last breath had tasted of life.

Uadjet stifled a surging of hope. Not that. Ra hadn't possibly meant that, had he? She hissed and heard her own anger on the wind. The years were too long, the gap too wide to breach.

Not for me, Uadjet, for you.

Her double tongue flickered, filtered the air. Why had she gone forth? What did she want?

For you.

* * *

The house hugged a lumping of the earth, shaded by four trees and cracking at its mud corners. The woman emerged from a dark doorway. Her long neck twisted this way and that, and her long hair fluffed in the breeze like dark feathers.

Uadjet hid in the grass and watched her.

A screen of blades criss-crossed her vision. Her tongue flicked. Her eyes tracked the woman's feet. She heard the singing of a soft voice, words about life and joy and circles. Uadjet listened and waited. She felt the woman's song vibrate against her belly. She felt the gentle tread of brown feet as the quaking of the world.

The woman plucked a reed basket from beside her doorway. She carried it beneath one arm, came with her hips rocking from side to side into the field where the snake hid. Her long skirts played a harmony against the grasses, whisked in time to the words of the song. She smiled, and placed bare feet against the silt.

When she lay the basket down beside the cobra, Uadjet held still, became a twig among the blades. The woven vessel hid her. She lay in its shadow while the woman started her work, leaning over, plucking at the unwanted growing things. Soft hands, brown fingers, slim, strong shoulders.

Strong enough.

Uadjet flicked and slid nearer. She peeked around the basket at a dark foot, painted toenails, and an ankh tattooed just above the ankle bone. If she'd doubted once, that sign now proved her path was true. The cobra fixed upon it, targeted that golden loop, and struck home.

The woman shrieked. She kicked out, but the goddess on her heel would not be deterred. Uadjet tasted her sweet blood, rolled it over her tongue and let her teeth inject the woman's death. Quickly, quickly she must fall!

A second wailing rose from the basket. In the reed nest, an infant howled as its mother tumbled to her knees. Uadjet released the tender ankle and coiled in waiting. Her tongue danced, in and out, while the baby screamed and the mother's mouth opened and closed.

No sound now, only the sacred breath. The breath Uadjet must not lose again. She lifted herself high, spread her hood and danced from side to side. The woman's arms flailed. Her eyes grew wide as stars. When the cobra only stared back, she sighed and fell.

Uadjet rushed forward. She lay herself along the woman, a twist of snake up the body, a pair of hooded eyes and eager, searching tongue. She positioned herself to catch the last breath, and this time, she knew exactly what to do with it.

For me.

Pink lips parted. Uadjet closed the gap. The woman's last breath escaped her corpse, and Uadjet caught it, inhaled the life force, and spoke an ancient name. *Nekhbet. Nekhbet, my blessed.* The cobra held the moment still in time, held her breath and danced. She spoke the incantations, sang the words, and summoned all the hope she had left in the world.

* * *

Uadjet lay in the temple. Her nostrils filled with the scent of copal burning, and her body filled with the sensations of Nekhbet's arms around her. The soft skin of her lover brushed against her own, and Uadjet's snake tongue darted out and back, tasting honey flesh and smoke at once.

"Be still love. The boy sleeps." Nekhbet's voice was true and clear. Still, Uadjet struggled with the meaning of the words.

Her head tilted to one side. She tightened her hood to offer a clearer view of the vulture holding her in strong brown arms. A crook beak, hard as the black feathers were soft. Twin eyes like pins regarding her with traces of humor.

"The boy?" Uadjet's voice echoed against the temple walls, even at a whisper.

"Shh." Nekhbet stroked long fingers over Uadjet's arm. "It is okay, Uadjet. You are no longer alone."

"It was so long."

"I know."

The cobra sighed and leaned back against Nekhbet's chest. She inhaled the copal, cleared her thoughts, and remembered. *The boy.* The woman had carried a basket that cried to the sun. Nekhbet giggled, read her thoughts and pointed with one painted toe toward a brazier where the copal smoke rolled free. The ankh on her ankle gleamed now, touched with power.

Beside the burner, the basket waited. The child slept.

"We've been waiting for you," Nekhbet said. "He's been waiting for us."

Uadjet and Nekhbet, the red and the white. Together they were the crown that joined kingdoms, that made kings. Nekhbet's arms loosened. Her voice goaded the snake from Uadjet's heart. "Go to him, my love. Bring him forth."

The cobra uncoiled, a black goddess. It slithered across the temple floor seeking the last breath that might bring life again. In her heart, she readied the incantations, sang the name for him. For him this time. *Horus.* She sang for the baby as she came, as she lifted and as she struck.

According to Chinese history, the Celestial Zodiac of the 12 Animals dates back to the early Han Dynasty, beginning in 206 B.C. According to Chinese mythology, the Jade Emperor of Heaven asked all the animals of the Middle Kingdom (earth) to visit him, and decreed that the first twelve to arrive would be given one of the twelve years.

After Buddhism arrived in China around the first century A.D., an alternate myth had Buddha calling the animals to say farewell to them before ascending to Heaven, and assigning a year of the zodiac to each of the twelve animals who came. Most legends agreed that the cat was expected to be one of the twelve animals, but the rat tricked him and stole his place; so that is why the rat is in the zodiac and the cat isn't, and is why the cat and the rat have been enemies ever since. More realistic historians say that the housecat wasn't introduced into China until about the time that Buddhism was, and the Celestial Zodiac was already established by then.

Except that in Vietnamese mythology, the cat is in the Zodiac instead of the rabbit.

Anyhow, the Zodiac goes back over two thousand years, and has always been exclusive to Oriental animals. How do the New World animals feel about this?

That Exclusive Zodiac Club

by Fred Patten

The Animal Dimension is a large and busy place. It reflects, by and large, the developments of the material Earth. The titled aristocracy, dominated by the Lion dynasty for millennia, has been replaced by a democracy for the last couple of centuries. As new lands and new animals have been discovered, they have been integrated smoothly into the civilization and culture of the whole. Cacomistles, camels, capybaras, caribou, chameleons, cheetahs, chinchillas, chipmunks, coatis, cougars, coyotes, crocodiles—they are all full members of today's Animal Dimension.

Except in one respect.

One of the oldest and most imposing structures in the Animal Dimension is the Zodiac Club. Modeled after the British gentlemen's clubs of the past couple of centuries, it is actually far older, dating back into the origins of Oriental mythology. The building is large and dignified, signifying age-old seniority, precedence, and status. Like other societies of its nature, it is exclusive—to an extreme. Since its creation over two millennia ago, its members have consisted of the same twelve animals. No new species have been voted in, or are likely to be. Rat. Ox. Tiger. Rabbit. Dragon. Snake. Horse. Goat. Monkey. Rooster. Dog. Pig. They are the unofficial aristocracy of the Animal Dimension.

Some of the other animals think that it is time for this to change.

It began at one of the Zodiac Club's social events; exclusive, as always, but crowded. It was restricted to the twelve members, their guests of the same species—and there were always lots of other rats, rabbits, dogs, snakes, horses, pigs, and their husbands and wives who were invited—and the staff, who were traditionally as exclusive as they were. Butlers, cooks, and other staff were always selected from the same Asiatic animals—binturongs, great or red pandas, tanuki, Asiatic bears, and so on. Nobody recognized at first that there was an interloper among them: the North American Raccoon. When he was noticed moving sedately in their midst, there was shock, indignation, and anger.

"An outrage!"

"Surely he's not a guest!"

"What are YOU doing here?"

"Haven't we told you that you are NOT welcome here?"

Raccoon stood his ground. "And why not? I'm just as good as you are. I've tried to join, but you haven't let in ANY new species since you started the Zodiac Club so many years ago, much less any New World animals. Any time that there's an opening, you always elect another tiger, monkey, or whatever to fill it. It's time—"

That was as far as he got. The twelve members and their same-species guests didn't even allow him the dignity of leaving by his own volition. An Ox and a Dragon gave him the bums' rush. Marched him to the fancy entrance and kicked him out so vigorously that he sailed over the sidewalk and landed in the gutter of the street. Good riddance, everybody agreed, as the door slammed.

As Raccoon picked himself up from the street and dusted himself off, he was joined by a taller individual, looking somehow both confident and furtive. "Excuse me, but I couldn't help noticing your assisted exit from the Zodiac Club. Having one of their exclusive affairs, are they? I think that I can help you to get in. My card." He introduced himself as Wile E. Foxy, solicitor.

It was too late for Raccoon to reenter the same party. Fortunately, the Zodiac Club entertained frequently, and there was another, even larger affair a couple of weeks later; and the members were not loath to invite their cousins as guests, as well. Monkey invited Chimpanzee and Gorilla. Dog invited Dhole and Jackal. Rabbit invited Hare and Pika. Horse invited Donkey and Mule. Rat invited Mouse (but not Naked Mole Rat). And Goat invited Sheep.

Fox adjusted the thick Sheep's fleece around Raccoon. "If possible, avoid the members and footmen and get one of the other guests to let you in." This seemed to be no serious problem since the party was so crowded, with both members and staff far outnumbered by the guests. The pseudo-Sheep watched through a window by the Club's main entrance and waited for a guest to come near. He was in luck; another Sheep, slightly tipsy and wearing a fez, wandered up to the door. The disguised Raccoon rang the bell. "G'day, mate! I'm yer cousin from Oztralia!" The other Sheep stepped back and allowed him to enter without a word or calling Goat over. He was in!

Unfortunately, he didn't stay in for long. The party was very crowded and hot, even without the thick fleece. Someone brushed against him hard enough that the back of the fleece opened. His Raccoon tail sprang out for all to see, which they did as soon as another guest screamed, "The horror!" and pointed right at it. He was promptly thrown out again.

As Fox helped him up, Raccoon complained, "I don't want to sneak into their party, anyway. I want to enter the Zodiac Club openly." "And you shall, or just as well. I've investigated, and discovered that the Zodiac Club never copyrighted or trademarked its name! You can start your own Zodiac Club!"

That wasn't quite what Raccoon had in mind, but he didn't demur as Fox began inviting other animal passersby, "Hey, Raccoon is starting his own Zodiac Club! You're invited!!" It seemed to be a very popular idea. All of the invited animals enthusiastically accepted. Then a wolf asked, "Where is it?" Fox thought quickly. "At Raccoon's house, and the inaugural meeting is next week!" "Great!!"

Raccoon spent all week getting his house ready for the first meeting of his Zodiac Club. When the day arrived, he was gratified but daunted to see a large crowd descending upon him. "When do they serve refreshments?" was the first thing he was asked. Raccoon spent all day rushing about putting out more refreshments and paper plates, washing dishes (he hadn't set out any of his own chinaware, but the guests found it and used his plates anyway), emptying trash baskets and ashtrays, and racing to a nearby market for more food and drinks. He was kept so busy that he didn't have time to call the meeting to order and get anything done. As evening arrived and everyone departed, he was exhausted. Every room of his home was in a shambles. He cringed to hear a member of his new club—he had no idea of the animal's name—say, "This was fun. This new Zodiac Club is a great idea. Let's have another meeting really soon!"

Raccoon spent all night cleaning up. When Fox arrived the next day to congratulate him on his success, Raccoon set him straight. "I don't want to sneak into the Zodiac Club in disguise, and I don't want to start an imitation club. I want to become a full member of the famous club that everyone knows about!" "Okay, okay," Fox said. "Let me think about it."

Fox returned a couple of days later. "I've got it this time. The old laws of trial by combat and trial by ordeal haven't been practiced for centuries, but they were never actually repealed. All you have to do is challenge one of the twelve members for his membership, and win it. Make it one of the weaker animals like Rabbit, Rat, or Snake so you'll be sure to win."

The next day Raccoon clanked to the Zodiac Club, currently in a lull between events, in a full suit of armor. Fox's talking about how the old-fashioned trial by combat was still legal had caused him to think of appearing in old-fashioned knightly armor. He had thought as well of Fox's recommendation to challenge one of the weaker Zodiac animals. But Rat had a reputation for being sneaky and tricky. Raccoon thanked the Heavenly Emperor that Snake wasn't the giant Python, but was the current Snake poisonous? Raccoon wasn't sure. When he got to the Zodiac Club, the sight of an animal in a suit of armor nonplused the doorman for long enough that Raccoon pushed past him and entered. He looked around the large, now-quiet room. Aha! Rabbit was

345

present. Raccoon strode over to him, struck a pose, and loudly said, "Rabbit, I hereby challenge you here and now to a trial by combat for your membership in this club!"

"Er, very well," Rabbit replied. "But as the challenged, I get to choose the nature of the contest. And here and now? I see by your suit of armor that you're ready to have the trial by combat right away. Fine. I accept, and choose a foot race. One dash in our large garden, from the rear door to the farthest hedge and back." Raccoon had a sinking feeling that he'd lost control over the challenge.

As Rabbit changed from his suit & tie into his running shirt and shorts—they were on hand; he had obviously been using the club's grounds to keep in practice—Raccoon grumbled that this wasn't what a traditional trial by combat was supposed to be like. "Well, I am a rabbit. What did you expect?" The race was short but not sweet. Rabbit did not conveniently take a nap during it this time, and his natural speed was complemented by Raccoon's being encased in a heavy suit of armor. Rabbit completed the race to the far hedge and back, to the congratulations of the other Zodiac members present, before Raccoon was even halfway to the hedge.

As Raccoon dourly clanked out of the club's front entrance, the waiting Fox waved him over. "I know, I know, but I've got a sure-fire plan this time. An old-fashioned method won't work? We'll win with a modern one!"

Several days later, the members of the Zodiac Club were startled when their current chairman was served with legal papers. "Raccoon vs. the Zodiac Club." The Club was accused of violating Raccoon's civil rights by refusing to allow him to join despite his being fully eligible. The prestige of the Zodiac Club was sufficient to bring the case to the highest court in the Animal Dimension, Judge Owl presiding. The whole Dimension followed the trial avidly.

The Zodiac Club cited longstanding tradition, and that it was a private entity entitled to its own rules. Fox argued the rebuttal eloquently. So had slavery and the old monarchy been longstanding traditions. They had become passé and been discarded by the evolution of society. Organizations that had once been private male bastions had been made by both social pressure and law to admit female members today. The Zodiac Club might be loftier, but it was not immune from being brought into the present. All Animals Were Equal, were they not? Then why should the Zodiac Club be allowed to continue the hoary privileges of the old order?

Judge Owl banged his gavel. "The Zodiac Club is ordered to accept the plaintiff as a full member." Raccoon had won! The newspapers and the telenewscasts interviewed both Raccoon and Fox beaming broadly as they claimed that their victory was a victory for all animals.

The next day, Raccoon presented himself proudly but humbly at the Zodiac Club. He was admitted, and the twelve members watched silently as their chairman invested Raccoon as their thirteenth member; the first in over two thousand years.

The other twelve members were still cool to him, if not actually frigid, but Raccoon didn't mind. They would come around in time. Right now, the atmosphere didn't encourage a long stay in the Club. He left to return home, and stopped short, stunned, just outside the entrance.

"We want to become members, too!" A vast horde of animals was advancing upon the Club, from Alligator to Zebra. Raccoon recognized Armadillo, Bat, Camel, Dik-Dik, Elephant, Ferret, Gerbil and his cousin Hamster, Hedgehog, Ibex, Jaguar…Kangaroo and Koala seemed to be a team…Lemur, Meerkat, Numbat, Opossum, Otter…he noted that Badger, Porcupine, Ratel, Skunk, Tasmanian Devil, and Wolverine were each being given plenty of room…Rooster's being one of the traditional twelve animals was enough to encourage a vast flock of birds including Albatross, Blackbird, Crow, Duck, Eagle, Flamingo, Goose, Hawk, Ibis, Jay, Kookaburra, Loon, Mockingbird…the gaudy Bird of Paradise and Peacock, and the dowdy Sparrow…Raccoon stepped back, edged around them, and left unobserved as they began to ring the bell and pound upon the front door.

A few weeks later, Fox encountered Raccoon walking alone along the boulevard. "Hello there! I thought that you would be relaxing at the Zodiac Club at this hour. Why so glum? You're finally a member!"

"Oh, yes. But who isn't? I can't stand the madhouse! The old building is bursting at the seams today, deafening, and filthy. The chairman and the staff have written it off as hopeless and resigned—most of the former staff are full members now and too good to do any work—some of the original twelve have actually left the Zodiac…"

"Hmmm," mused Fox. "Then I guess that there's not much point in my applying for membership, too."

W. S. Gilbert of our Dimension said it best when he penned:
"When every one is somebodee,
Then no one's anybody!"

At first glance, you may wonder where the gods are in "Three Minutes to Midnight"?

Keep reading...

Three Minutes To Midnight

by *Killick*

Imagine a beach. Now let me assure you that whatever image you have in your head right now is not nearly good enough. This beach is like nowhere you have ever been or seen, or ever will for that matter. This beach is absolutely perfect. A stretch of bright white sand that is never too hot, only warm enough to completely relax the muscles in your feet. The gently lapping waves are the most exquisite turquoise gems that shimmer and sparkle as the sun's light bounces and dances off them in every direction. A few seagulls fly overhead, never squawking, only gently warbling a soothing song. A gentle breeze flows like cool silk, but never carries coarse sand with it. Behind the beach is a wall of palm trees that keeps the thick jungle from spilling out onto the sand. It rustles against the breeze with the most relaxing white noise that you will ever hear.

This beach is quite literally too good to be real.

There are no buildings, no ships, and no people. Except for five figures. It is with them that this particular moment in time begins.

Along the seemingly infinite stretch of sand stood a tiny wood and grass hut with shelves that somehow held every type of booze bottle you could possibly imagine, and behind the counter worked a slim, red fox. The fox was young, attractive, and strangely androgynous. Depending on how you looked at the fox, or possibly on what you preferred, it could either have been a very slim young woman or a rather feminine young man. A loose t-shirt and a tie-dyed sarong around the waist hid the more obvious indicators.

At that moment the fox was mixing a drink for someone.

"Try… Amarula cream, coconut rum, and orange liqueur. Over ice," said a deep voice. The fox silently followed the instructions and handed over the

349

tall glass. A black horse, short and stout, sipped the cool drink. A faded tank top was pulled tight over his fat gut, not quite meeting the waist of his board shorts.

"It's good. But it still needs something."

The fox frowned in thought, then took the glass again and squeezed in a single wedge of lime and popped in a tiny paper umbrella. He handed it back to the horse with a smile. The horse took a careful sip, then grinned widely, his tail swishing around a wooden bar stool that had been worn smooth by sand and salt.

"You," he said waggling a finger at the fox, "You are God's gift to cocktails."

The comfortably ambiguous fox gave the horse a friendly wink, then went back to cleaning glasses. The black horse took a more daring mouthful of the cool concoction and sighed with contentment, disturbed only by a loud huff to his right. Another horse, but scrawny, white and nearly a complete physical opposite sat at the very end of the short bar. He sat hunched and curled on top of another stool, wearing a polo shirt and pants that were not appropriate for the beach. A pile of transparent orange medication bottles covered the bartop around him as he nursed a glass of cold water.

"You know you shouldn't drink so much, Finn. It's not good for you."

Finn looked over to his brother, Peter, and smirked.

"How is alcohol not good for me?" He gave the glass a swirl and quickly slurped down a mouthful. "You're just jealous 'cause booze doesn't mix well with your meds." He gestured his glass at the orange bottles scattered around Peter like a protective barrier.

"I am not jealous!" the scrawny horse retorted, straightening up on the bar stool. "I just don't see the point in constantly getting drunk all the time. People shouldn't need alcohol to have fun." Peter smirked as if he had made a poignant, argument-winning remark, and sipped his spring water. But his grin tightened into a frown when Finn just laughed.

"I can't get drunk, not if I don't want to. Speaking of, what are all those pills for, anyway? You suffering from hypochondria?"

"Oh, har har har, very funny," Peter sneered. "I have a sensitive condition that you wouldn't understand."

"Man, the only condition you have is not knowing how to have fun." Finn turned back to the bar, handing off his now empty glass to the fox who immediately replaced it with a full one, although this time with a plastic fish on a stick instead of an umbrella.

"That's just not true!" Peter protested. "In fact, I'm having fun right now," he said, squinting in the bright sunlight.

"You look miserable," said Finn.

"That's because my idiot brother is making fun of me, again," Peter muttered as he turned back to his water and pills.

"Finn's right, bro." The shadow that cast against the bar led across hot sand and to the hooves of a third horse, the fur covering his body a dark wine. This horse, taller than both Peter and Finn, had a body that appeared to have been sculpted by the masters of old. Lean thighs bulged out of tight swim shorts, and bare abs that could crush granite led up to a muscular chest, thick neck, and a severely short crop of mane hair on the horse's head. His name was Warren. "You got no sense of adventure."

Finn raised his glass and pointed at his larger brother. "See?"

"I mean, seriously bro, when was the last time you went out and did something for fun?" Warren went on, grabbing a beer from behind the bar and flicking the cap off with just his thumb. The fox bartender shot him a disapproving look, but otherwise ignored him.

"I...I do things!" Peter spluttered. "Just because I don't go around hitting things..."

"It's called boxing, bro. Sport of champions." Warren tilted his head up and chugged the entire beer in one go. He wiped the moisture from his lips then threw the empty bottle over his shoulder and into a wicker rubbish bin without even looking. "C'mon, tell us bro, when was the last time you went out?"

"I'll have you know I quite enjoy films!"

Finn's ears perked up at this, and he leant towards his thinner brother, placing his drink on the counter. "Yeah? What kind of films? I don't see you as a Hollywood blockbuster kind of guy." Finn slowly ran his finger around the rim of his glass. "Lemme guess...Indie horror?"

At the question, Peter began to fiddle with one of his pill bottles, screwing the lid on and off repeatedly.

"I prefer older films," he said somewhat forcedly.

"Aha, an eighties man!" Finn clapped his hands together in excitement. "John Carpenter or Woody Allen?"

"Umm..." Peter barely choked out, his beady eyes darting back and forth.

"Finn, bro, he doesn't know who they are," said Warren. The red stallion conjured a hacky sack seemingly from thin air, and started to kick it expertly between his two hooves, kicking up little puffs of sand. His eyes followed the ball, not even looking up to speak to his brothers.

"Really?" Finn replied in genuine surprise. "What was the last movie you saw?"

"Well." Peter finally put down the bottle and crossed his hands in front of his lap. "I remember seeing a delightful film about a funny man with a mustache who kept falling down."

Finn could only blink and stare for a few seconds while his brain processed the information. "Chaplin. The last movie you saw was a Charlie Chaplin film?"

"Yes, that was his name!" Peter said happily.

"I'm not going to knock the master of physical comedy, but that was nearly a century ago, dude!"

"Oh, I didn't realize it had been that long." The scrawny horse turned back to his ice water, focusing on its surface.

"They even have movies in color now," Finn joked. "Do you even keep up with what humanity does? At least try to take an interest in them."

"I only have to keep up with all those awful diseases they keep propagating! The rest is just frivolities," Peter sneered and whipped his tail. He unscrewed a seemingly random bottle, not even reading the label, and threw some pills unceremoniously down his gullet.

"Well, my favorite movie," Finn said loudly, deliberately ignoring his brother to pursue a subject that interested him. He got up from his bar stool and planted his hooves in the sand, leaning against the bar with his drink in his hand, his gut wobbling as he moved. "My favorite would have to be John Carpenter's *The Thing*."

Peter wrinkled his muzzle in confusion. "The what?"

"*The Thing*."

"What thing?"

"That's the name of the movie," Finn smirked. "It's called *The Thing*."

"That's not a very good title. It's completely forgettable." Peter sniffed, and sipped again on his ice water. He grimaced when the ice made his teeth ache.

Finn snorted and shook his head. "You have no idea, do you?"

"I think I've seen that one," Warren piped up, catching the colorful ball one handed. "About a monster in Alaska or something."

"Antarctica," Finn corrected him.

"Whatever. Creepy shit."

"It is the crowning achievement of eighties horror and practical effects," he proclaimed, raising his drink to the perfect blue sky. "About a creature driven to survive and endlessly consume all in its path, adapting and changing to whatever suits it best at the expense of all other life forms, near unstoppable."

"An interesting synopsis," came a voice as cold and curt as a bitter wind. A fourth horse, tall, skinny and lean, with hair the color of pale soot, lay on a plastic deck chair a few feet from the bar. In a cup holder on one plastic arm was a glass of thick, red wine, and a book grasped in his long, spider like fingers. This horse's name was Ash. "Is that how you view all of humanity?"

Finn looked at him confused, scratching behind his black mane. "What? No. I was talking about the monster."

"Of course you were," Ash said simply, returning to his book. Finn shook his head, confused, not sure if his brother was making a joke or not. Sometimes he just couldn't read the guy.

"Well, what's your favorite movie, Ash?" Finn asked, searching for a way out of the awkward silence.

"*Bedknobs and Broomsticks*," he replied without hesitating or looking up from his book. Finn and Warren looked at Ash, confused and surprised. Peter was too busy concerning himself with the chemical ingredients of one of his bottles, not that he'd heard of the movie anyway.

"Isn't that a kids' cartoon?" Warren said.

"Only the sequence in Naboombu is animated," Ash replied, peering over the top of his book.

"Are you being serious?" Finn was flummoxed at his brother's nodding. "I figured it would have been *Citizen Kane*. Or maybe even *The Human Centipede*," he added, deciding to take guesses from both ends of the spectrum. Ash just smiled and chuckled.

"Okay, I give, bro. What's so good about *Bedknobs and Broomsticks?*" asked Warren. He had procured a couple of dumbbells from behind the bar and started working on his biceps. Ash placed the book down on his bare, flat stomach, spine up.

"It's a wonderful ode to demonic worship in disguise. Almost Lovecraftian at times."

"I don't even know what the hell you're talking about, bro," said Warren, quickly losing interest.

"I do, but still, what the hell are you talking about?" Finn leant forward on his barstool, clutching his drink, desperately needing to hear his brother's explanation. Part of him feared what he was about to hear, but he was also excited. Hearing Ash's opinion on something, anything, was a rare treat and not an event to be missed.

"For starters, Miss Price is looking for the Star of Astaroth. You know, Grand Duke of Hell and one of the evil trinity?"

Warren dropped a weight in the sand, snapped his fingers and pointed to his brother. "Douchebag with the first iPhone at that party last decade."

"Yeah, I remember him," Finn said nodding. The bridge of his muzzle furrowed as he worked to recall the events of the movie, not in an attempt to disprove his brother but to ensure he understood him.

"So the movie directly references a high level demon by name, and suggests, in its own Disney-fied way, that this sorcerer was performing magical experiments on animals to make them more human. He succeeded, but they eventually turned on him, murdered him, and stole his powers." Ash grinned and gazed into the perfect sky as he spoke, his thin fingers steepled in front of his long muzzle. He grinned, knowing his brother would have to work to keep up with his bizarre logic. "And so using the sorcerer's demonic artefact, the now anthropomorphized beasts cross into a different dimension. Did they create this dimension? Did they conquer it? Perhaps. But why does the land of Naboombu appear to the humans as an animated landscape?"

"Um, because it's a family friendly movie and cartoons are fun and colorful?" Finn guessed, trying not to shudder, already knowing his brother had a much more sinister answer.

"I think," Ash said and looked over at Finn, "It's because Paul, the child who has control over the magic bedknob, cannot process the true horror and madness of this realm of bloodthirsty talking animals. So his brain creates this colorful fantasy to prevent him from going completely insane. Much like Lovecraft's 'indescribable horrors' that he's so fond of." He stopped and smiled at his brother, obviously proud of his explanation, then went back to reading his book. Finn finished his drink and breathed deeply.

"Dude, that's messed up." He put the empty glass on the bartop, the fox appearing with another full drink. Finn shook his head and the drink quickly vanished behind the counter. Warren grunted loudly as he finished his set of however-many hundred bicep curls, before dropping the heavy weights into the sand.

"My favorite movie is *The Expendables*. It's got a bunch of fights and shit. Jacked guys killing other jacked guys. It's pretty cool," said Warren, flexing his aching arms and watching the muscles ripple in all the right ways. Finn snorted but was ignored.

"I'm not familiar with that one," Ash murmured. He put his book down again and closed his eyes. His eyelids trembled and flickered for a few seconds, as if he were in the middle of an intense dream. "Hmmm. I think I see the appeal," he said, opening his eyes. "But it's a little...obvious for my tastes."

"Whatever," Warren huffed.

"Why do we even care about these fake things that they make?" Peter suddenly blurted out. He had gone back to fiddling with his bottles, so much so that he had managed to put a neat crack in at least one white lid. "It's not like they'll be around much longer anyway."

Silence dropped over the beach. Even the birds grew quiet. The breeze, for barely a second, carried a cold chill with it instead of its usual comforting coolness. His brothers stared at him. Peter looked away and curled up on his stool.

"You really should just relax and have a drink, Peter," Ash said pointedly. His face was stony with a smile that held no humor or friendliness. It had not been a suggestion.

"Fine," Peter sighed quietly, resigning himself to the peer pressure, and certainly not wanting to start a fight with his eldest brother. He squinted at the hundreds of glass bottles in the tiny bar. Most seemed to occupy the same space as another. "Ummm..." he murmured. The red fox appeared in front of him, smiling as always. "Something light? And that won't mess with my meds." The fox produced a green bottle that sweated with condensation. The label on the bottle boasted it was 'low-carb' and '1.2%' in bright red colors. The fox popped the cap off with a handy tool and passed the beer to Peter with a wink.

Peter squeezed out a smile before he took the glass, and tried not to shudder. That fox was probably hiding a horrifying STD under that sarong, he thought.

"While we're getting more drinks," Finn hinted happily. The fox eagerly moved in front of the fat horse, cocktail shaker at the ready. Finn stroked the bottom of his lip in thought. "Try Midori, pineapple juice, coconut rum and…" He trailed off when he saw the fox's disapproving raised eyebrow. "Shit, you're right. That's just a Midori splice. Uhh," he paused as he rethought his strategy. "Screw it. Cake flavored vodka, white creme de cacao, simple syrup, maraschino cherry, and topped with marshmallow fluff. Neat."

The fox nodded in approval as they constructed the alcoholic monstrosity in a low glass. Peter made a not so subtle gagging noise as he watched his brother throw it all back in one gulp. Finn made several smacking noises with his tongue as the sugary liquid coated his mouth and teeth. He slammed the glass down, smiled and nodded, then slowly pursed his lips and turned towards Ash.

"So," he started slowly. "How much longer?" he asked quietly. Both Warren and Peter looked up, their eyes shifting from Warren to Ash. Ash sighed, and pulled a rusted pocket watch from the plastic cupholder. It opened with a loud click, and he studied the scratched face.

"Not much longer now."

Finn nodded sadly, but Peter just frowned at him.

"You've gotten way too attached to them," Peter said with a hint of disgust.

"Beg your pardon?" Finn frowned and narrowed his eyes. He sounded more than a little pissed off.

"You've grown soft on them," Peter accused, jabbing a finger at his brother. "I remember a time when you relished the idea of depriving them of their basic survival needs, food and water. And now you just want to watch their silly films?"

"They've changed, Peter. They've become more complicated, more imaginative. They used to be just about food and sex, but they crave so much more than that now. They need to create to survive. Not just eat."

"Oh, they've evolved, sure. But that doesn't change why we exist. They are still the same selfish, brutal creatures that crawled out of the mud all those years ago."

Finn fumed at his scrawny brother. He wanted to hit him, but it wasn't in his nature. Instead the beer that Peter held gently foamed inside the bottle, turning sour and wretched. Peter watched the bubbles burp from the neck of the glass.

"Oh, very mature," he spat, throwing the ruined beer over his shoulder where it landed with a soft thud in the sand. The fox, ignored by all, quickly retrieved the bottle and dumped it behind the bar.

"Warren!" Peter called. The red horse was now laying in the sand, soaking up the sun into his perfectly chiseled body. "What do you think of humanity?"

Warren sat up with next to no effort. "I like them, they're pretty cool."

"Hah!" Finn blurted in victory.

"They make all the best stuff," Warren continued. "Like the AR-15 assault rifle, the Heckler & Kock G36, the Trident D5 ballistic missile..." Now it was Peter's time to smile, as Finn's started to fade.

"Thank you, brother," Peter called, smiling. "I think I've made my point."

"Well, when you only look at all the bad shit, then yeah, of course they don't look great. But you're out of touch, man. I bet you don't even know what Netflix is. All you want to see are their guns and their sickness. You don't see what they've created, you don't even want to see."

"I still don't understand why you even care."

Finn shrugged. "When they became about more than just consuming food, I guess I got an insight into their soul."

Peter couldn't help but laugh, a sneering, cynical cackle. "Oh boy. I don't even know how to respond to that. Ash, tell us, do they deserve to go or not?"

Ash studied his book for several seconds in silence. His brothers eagerly waiting for his thoughts.

"It's not up to us," he said finally, not looking away from the pages.

"What? Yes, it is." Peter frowned, and started to hunch back against the bar.

"You have grown too sure of yourself, brother. We do not decide when humanity's end comes. That is up to them and them alone. We just come when we're called. There have been a few times when we almost *were* called. But almost isn't good enough."

Peter sullenly turned back to his pile of medication, hissing at the fox when they put a frosty glass of water in front of him. Finn sat and stared at the sand for a while, then looked up.

"So, can you tell us? How much longer we have to wait?" he eagerly looked to his older brother. He knew that, either way, he would not like the answer, but now he had to know.

Ash pulled out the pocket watch again and grinned at his brothers, a single finger brushing against the delicate gold knob on the top. He studied where the hands lay against the face. "I think this thing needs a little adjustment."

There are many forms of love. Can a god—or goddess—experience love as a mortal can?

Should she try to? "A Day With No Tide" presents one reason why not.

A Day With No Tide

by Watts Martin

In Asharia, thousands of years pass with the same leaves on the same trees, the same blossoms opening at sunrise and wilting by dusk. To mortal eyes no seasons pass. But the day the universe became aware of its own existence was the first day of Asharia's spring; the universe shall draw to a close on the last day of Asharia's winter, waiting to be reborn at the next great cycle.

It was a late spring day.

Maraiya often walked along the shore of Asharia's sea in the mornings, watching the sunlight from behind her reflected in the water, whether crashing vigorously against the sands or—as it was today—lapping gently at the shore. As often as not, her lover of the night before accompanied her. As often as not, he or she was mortal. Some day, she knew, she would be reprimanded—again—by Zanu for these dalliances, but she saw little harm in them.

This morning, Maraiya walked alone. Yet this morning, unlike nearly any other she could recall, another figure stood ahead of her on the shore just above the beach line, motionless, staring out at the horizon.

Maraiya adjusted her path, walking toward the other woman. She received no acknowledgement as she approached, but she expected none, even as she moved to stand beside her and face out to sea as well. They could hardly have made a more incongruous pair, she reflected in silent amusement. Herself, a tall feline woman with subtly mottled warm gray fur, golden eyes, and a form that had inspired countless statues, paintings and love songs across countless lands, under countless names and visages. The other, an even taller rabbit woman with bone white fur, ram horns and dragon claws, and solid moonlight eyes that even others of her kind, like Maraiya, rarely wished to meet for long. Extraordinarily—were they other than what they were—both possessed wings, but even in that they stood as opposites. The cat's shone with iridescent silver feathers, rainbows swirling about her as she moved. The rabbit's all but absorbed the light, blacker than a great raven's.

They remained in companionable silence until Maraiya decided the first words to be spoken would be hers. "You are an unexpected sight this morning, Lady Inanael."

The rabbit woman's wings rustled, but she remained silent.

"Although," she continued after a moment, "you are an unexpected sight in Asharia at all. Usually, if we see one another it's me making a visit to you." The cat tilted her head. "You rarely leave your land but for ill tidings, but since we haven't all been summoned to Zanu's palace, I trust you're not here to bring dire news."

Maraiya's voice, as always, was honey, satin, the hearth on a winter's night. When Inanael finally spoke, her voice, as always, was that of winter. "I am watching the ocean."

The cat clasped her hands in front of her, and waited for the horned rabbit to continue.

"What would it take for the sea to be still?" she murmured. "For the waves to pause, the tide to remain in balance, neither in nor out."

"That sounds like a riddle for Death rather than for Love." Maraiya gave a curious laugh. "And do you mean any sea, or *this* sea? You and I may cause kingdoms to rise and fall, in our own ways. And I think you could—and shall, when it is the right time—bring the stars themselves raining down around our ears. But bring the sea of Asharia to a stop?" She pointed, tracing her slender finger through the air. "We could build a levee, a seawall. We could dig, and fashion a tide pool. Any sea can be stopped in a small place for a small time." Maraiya considered several ways to frame her next question, then simply sighed, letting her arm drop. "Inanael, out of all of us you are quite possibly the least given to idle philosophy. Forgive my bluntness, but what is it that truly brings you here?"

At length, Inanael answered, again elliptically. "Of all of them, you are the *only* one who visits my land by choice."

"Your land is beautiful, in its own way."

"While I think so as well, I doubt any other would see that." The rabbit finally turned her gaze away from the ocean toward the cat. "You said that one day I should—I would—come to you with questions of the heart."

"A thousand thousand years ago." She folded her arms, giving the rabbit a half-smile.

At that, the rabbit smiled back, fractionally. Maraiya doubted someone who knew Inanael less well would notice it as a smile. "Love is not my domain."

"Death is not mine, yet come late winter even I shall die." She shrugged. "Or—whatever it is we do. Yet I can tell you aren't coming to me now because you're in love. I would see that even in *your* eyes."

"No. I..." Inanael trailed off, looking back at the sea, and flexed her wings. "We do not have the luxury of choosing our paths like mortals do, Maraiya. Yet despite that, you have always seemed so...carefree. One might say cavalier."

"One would be wrong," Maraiya said, tone dry. "We all must be what we are. The weight of my function is no less than yours."

Inanael made a soft *hmm* noise, and fell silent for a time. "And I am what I must be. But...we can make small choices. Once in a great while, I wish to choose...brief respite." She tilted her face up to the sky, eyes closed. "Of all of us, you are the only one who has ever offered to listen."

"You have always been the surest of us, and the most alone." Maraiya bit her lip, then held out her hand. "I have an idea. Walk with me."

Inanael turned to look at her, remaining otherwise motionless for several seconds, then wrapped her taloned hand around the cat's sculpted one.

She led the taller woman up the beach, away from the water, past the sand and the sea oats. Then she sat down and folded her hands in her lap, eyes growing unfocused as she started to look elsewhere, through other worlds, other minds, other lives—anywhere people fell in and out of love, Maraiya was there. "Her...no, *her*," she murmured. "A perfect moment." She returned her attention to where she was, looking up with a triumphant smile.

Inanael knelt beside the smaller woman, wings flexing. "You are about to interfere with a mortal on my behalf," she said, tone wary.

"No. I don't intend to interfere with them at all." She took both of Inanael's hands. "I intend to interfere with *you*."

The rabbit stiffened. "That is not wise."

"We shall only still the sea a brief while. And you might be surprised how many beautiful stories begin with those words," she replied, eyes sparkling.

After a long moment, the rabbit smiled her own fractional smile, and nodded her head once.

Lady Maraiya leaned forward and touched her lips to Lady Inanael's, and her silver wings spread to catch and then eclipse the sun. The world became brilliant darkness.

* * *

"—wake *up*, for Zanu's sake!"

She opened her eyes, looking up at a low wooden ceiling, then turned her head, looking across the pillow at the open window. Sunlight streamed in. She smelled salt air. The voice, along with irritated knocking, came from behind her.

"I'm awake," she mumbled, sitting up in bed. Not *her* bed, not the canopy bed deep in her suite, deep in her palace. A small bed, pink cotton sheets, a floral print cover. Wooden floor, oval throw rug. Pale orange stucco walls. Had she ever been here before?

"It's almost *nine*, Anna." The voice sounded just as irritated as the knocking.

Anna?

She looked out the window at the unfamiliar scene, over tiled rooftops following a steep winding hill road down toward the harbor. Unfamiliar? No. she knew most of the people in those homes, at least by sight. She knew that was Geoffrey's house, the baker with a crush on Anna's mother that would forever remain unrequited. She knew that was Amelie's house, the old woman who had been a friend of Anna's mother's mother, now lying on her deathbed. She knew where the markets were. She knew the person banging on the door was Anna's sister, Delphine.

Her sister, Delphine.

"I'm awake," she said again, more loudly, rising to her feet. White rabbit paws, as expected. She rolled her shoulders, then looked over each one in turn, feeling momentary puzzlement at seeing nothing, then looked around the— her room. She headed to the dresser, then the wardrobe, putting on a tiered blue and green sun dress, and studied herself in the mirror. The woman who stared back in shock looked…almost as expected. The blue in the dress was a shade lighter than her eyes.

"I swear, you'll be late for your own funeral," Delphine was saying, stomping her foot for emphasis even as Anna opened the door. Delphine had light brown fur rather than white and a round face, contrasting with her sister's delicate features, and she looked cute even when cross—a quirk, Anna remembered, which tended to make her *more* cross when mentioned. While Delphine stood an average height for a rabbit woman, Anna positively towered, something frequently lamented by her mother. *You'll never find a husband if the boys are intimidated by you! Don't stand up so straight. And smile.*

Anna smiled, brushing past her glowering sister. "I don't think that's any time soon." She knew her funeral would not be. Neither would Delphine's. Yet the knowledge was distant, remote, something she had to consciously call on. For the first time in a memory much, much longer than Anna's, it was possible to set aside. Not easy. But possible.

"Breakfast has been out for an hour," Delphine carped, hurrying to be in front of her sister as they headed down the narrow stairs. The steps ended alongside the kitchen, a small room made larger by huge windows, bright morning sun streaming onto the wooden counters and terra cotta tile floor. "It's probably gone sour."

Only one dish remained on the table, artlessly arranged rind cheese and hand-torn bread chunks drizzled with honey. "It's cheese. It's *already* gone sour."

Delphine was unwilling to be mollified. "Then it will be covered with flies."

Anna sat down, giving her sister an amused look.

"*Sticky* flies. Tracking honey everywhere," Delphine elaborated, looking exaggeratedly cross, then burst out laughing. She rested her hand on her sister's shoulder as she walked past. "I'm going to the well. Just *try* to wake up after the sun hits your face in the morning. You might have a good excuse tomorrow, but you didn't today. Or yesterday. Or the day before." She kept repeating *or the day before* as she grabbed two wooden pails by the door and walked out onto the cobblestone street.

Anna regarded the plate. She often skipped eating entirely unless she had guests at the palace, a very rare occurrence. She would never have something this—this simple when she did take meals.

What sat in front of her was what she'd had nearly every morning of her nineteen years. Alien, and so familiar.

After a few moments, Anna picked up one of the chunks of cheese and popped it into her mouth, honey dripping off onto her fingers. The flavor was creamy and briny and sweet all at once, unexpectedly intense, and her eyes widened. Honey dribbled down her chin. She wiped it off awkwardly with a piece of bread, then did something Anna did frequently—her sister might say too often—but that Queen Inanael had never been recorded doing in any of the many tales of her through many names and many centuries.

She giggled.

* * *

A glare from the returning Delphine reminded her there would be no servants to clear away the dishes and clean the kitchen. Anna's mother might do that, were she home, but her father was out of the village this week, off to broker deals for the spices and dry goods he sold. This left his wife tending the store rather than tending the house. As the eldest of the two children by a full three years Anna should be in charge of the household, but she remembered with some chagrin that Delphine did more of the work even on Anna's most helpful days—which today certainly hadn't started as.

She wasted too much water cleaning her own plate, and worse, nearly broke it twice, first from banging it against the side of the wash basin and the next from making it so soapy her grip slipped. On the next plate—Delphine and her mother had left both of theirs out, as well as the serving dish—she let Anna's knowledge flow to the forefront of her mind. Not only did she finish without any more close calls, she found she knew where everything was stored, and knew what the rest of her tasks for the morning were, including which of her parents' clothes needed mending and even how to do it. While she doubted menial labor was the experience Maraiya had intended to gift her with, having little weightier on her mind other than needle and thread left her strangely content.

When she finished the work, noon had just passed. She considered what she needed to do next. As her mother chided her on occasion, there was *always* something to be done. ("Stop admiring your eyes in the mirror, child, and *use* them.") But she didn't see anything truly pressing, and she was too distracted by her anticipation for...what? Something she had been looking forward to. Something tonight.

Tapping her foot in impatience, after a few seconds she shook her head at herself and headed outside, down the steep street. She had seen it nearly every day. She had *never* seen it until now. Brightly colored paint peeled off rough stone walls in the bright summer sun. The bay breeze carried the scents of ripe fruit, drying laundry, pungently cured fish, and the occasional unpleasant bucket emptied in an alleyway. Townspeople—mostly other women—bustled between the narrow, closely set houses and the market stalls and shops by the harbor. The grey cobblestones of the street warmed the fur on her paws as she picked her way along, waving to the people she knew, often receiving waves in return.

The street seemed busier than normal for a summer day. She could hear out of place, raucous noises off to the east from the more well-to-do part of town: hammering, occasional bursts of untuned musical instruments. And then she knew what she'd been trying to remember. Malgin Karanos, the village mayor for as long as Anna had been alive, sponsored two dances a year, claiming it was a religious duty—he was named after the god of music and dance, yet had no talent for either. The first was the winter ball at his estate, an exclusive and invitation-only event that she'd never been to (although her parents had, twice). The second was an outdoor summer dance on his estate grounds open to the whole of the town. Over the years it had evolved into a renowned festival, with performers and market vendors and musicians from across the land attending.

Anna *didn't* remember being that interested in it before, except as a sheer spectacle. She wasn't much of a dancer, and even if she were, she didn't know anyone she was interested in dancing with.

Wait. Was that still true *this* year? She didn't think so.

As she reached the level ground by the harbor, where the street met the wide central avenue running along the water's edge and through the commercial district, the breeze strengthened, a sharp tang of seawater and damp wood overwhelming all other scents for a moment. She stepped onto the weathered dock, passing a blood-covered table where two vulpine fishermen cleaned their morning's catch, and stopped to rest her hands on a piling. It provided an excellent view of the four-mast sailing ship moored there. This was not one of the town's fishing fleet, but a navy warship, by far the largest vessel in the harbor today. Unlike the low, small boats covered in weathered nets and barnacles, the galleon gleamed, some of its crew polishing the brass fittings and wiping down the cast iron cannons as she watched.

Her attention shifted to the sound of a wolf barking curt orders at the otter crewman who'd been polishing the closest railing. The otter looked younger than she was, the wolf at least a decade older. She couldn't quite make out the words, but the otter shot a guilty glance in her direction and turned his full attention to the brass, ears set back. The wolf shot her a dour look and stalked back below deck. She realized the otter must have been chastized for paying more attention to *her* than his work. She felt her ears color. While Inanael could certainly turn heads, her beauty was rarely written of without the qualification of *terrible* or *dreadful*. Anna had a similar build—nearly identical, truly—with no qualifications to it.

"Anna!" a voice called from behind her, back on the avenue. She spun around, searching for the speaker. *Rylan.*

The fox, there, waving, smile bright, standing taller than she did, handsome black hair drawn back in a ponytail. She knew him. She'd known him since they were both very young, starting out liking him in the way children did, then disliking him in the way older children did—then, as they began to like each other in the way of still older children, he was gone, his parents moving to a larger city in search of better work.

Six months ago, he'd returned. She'd barely recognized him then. But she'd barely been able to keep her eyes off him since. That had led Delphine to exasperatedly snap at her sister for keeping her *hands* off him so successfully. The conversation came back to her now: "He's not looking for a romance with anyone but a vixen, I'm sure. Mother wants me to look for other rabbits, after all."

Her sister had made a rude noise. "Mother wants grandchildren. But we're not talking about offering him a dowry, are we? Your heart doesn't always follow your race. Neither do your loins."

"Delphine!"

"Anna!" she'd mimicked, hands on her hips. "Stop pretending you don't know how attractive you are, even if your ears are scraping the clouds. I don't care if he thinks he's only looking for other foxes. Unless he's only looking for other men, he's looking at you."

Anna snapped back to the present as Rylan turned to the younger tod he was with—his cousin, Richard—and spoke a few words, then jogged toward her as his cousin continued on. "I hope you're still looking forward to the festival tonight. That you're still intending to come." The mix of hope and worry in his eyes turned it into a question.

"Of course. You're who I'm coming to dance with." She smiled, broadening it quickly as the fox's tail wagged. "I can't imagine anyone in the town *won't* be there."

"Ah, I know you've never been much for idle socializing. You've said as much to me more than once." He laughed. "But it's quite reassuring to hear you say that. I'll be there an hour before sundown."

He looked over her shoulder at the ship at something, and she turned as well. The otter sailor was looking in their direction. When he saw Anna had turned, too, he immediately began tending to a new section of railing.

"I trust this sailor isn't bothering you, is he?" Rylan kept his tone amused but projected loudly enough for the otter to hear.

"No, not at all," Anna said, laughing.

"I assure you I've been quite well-behaved, sir," the otter called, giving his tone a formal military cadence. He didn't look up from his work, but he did smile.

Rylan laughed, too. "Sorry." He addressed Anna rather than the otter. "I'm being less gallant than merely pushy, aren't I?"

"You're being some of both." She smiled, taking one of his hands in both of hers. "And it's sweet, but don't pick a fight on my account. I'll see you again in just a few hours."

His ears reddened at her touch. She hadn't been that bold before, she recalled—but even knowing that, she couldn't help but give his hand a slight squeeze before letting go.

He took a deep breath. "I'm quite looking forward to it." The fox took two steps back and bowed to her, then headed back down the street, stepping so bouncily his paws seemed barely in contact with the stones.

Anna giggled again, then headed back up toward her house, following a different street. She had more housework to do before the dance, and would likely have less time to get ready than she imagined.

* * *

"Are you sure it looks nice?" Anna spun around to face three-quarters away from the mirror, twisting her head about to see her backside.

"For the third time, it looks *amazing*," Delphine said tiredly. "With a tiara they'd be calling you queen."

She knew the kind of material and tailoring a queen would have, and as fine as this was, it was not at that level. Yet it was surely the best dress Anna had ever worn. It had been her mother's, refitted to her by a professional seamstress a few weeks ago. The white was so pure it made her fur seem cream-colored; the cloth had been layered in light blue at the sleeves, neckline, and hemline. The corset was dyed the same color, laced in the back with golden thread. Delphine had tied it so tightly Anna had complained, but she had to admit the look was splendid.

She took a breath as deep as the corset would allow and smiled uncertainly. "And you don't think this is too...too much?"

"Don't be dense. I'm *aiming* for too much." She crouched down and lifted up Anna's foot, slipping a leather sandal on, then did the same with the other foot.

Anna sighed. "Who's going to be wearing footwear at this? I don't think—"

Delphine gave her an exasperated look. "Beautiful women wearing gowns and corsets."

"I don't see you wearing *your* sandals." Her sister had dressed prettily but more simply, a light yellow blouse and forest green pleated skirt with a matching sash.

"If things go as I'm hoping with Joseph, by midnight I won't be wearing anything."

"Delphine!"

"And I knew you'd say that, so I don't think it matters that your outfit is harder to take off." She stood up, then grinned. "Although if he gets desperate, tell Rylan it's fine if he cuts the corset lacing. I have another spool."

Anna felt the color already in her ears reach her cheeks. She opened her mouth but couldn't think of quite what to say in response.

Delphine shook her head, clearly biting back a laugh. "I simply don't understand how I'm three years younger and still your elder. Now come on. Let's get you there before Rylan notices how many *other* girls are staring longingly at *him*."

While the sun hung low in the sky it had not reached the horizon yet, and while the music had begun—they could hear it from the street outside the house, even though the estate was a good ten minutes' walk—it wasn't dance music yet. From the occasional burst of laughter, Anna guessed they were accompanying a performance on the main stage. Or perhaps competing with it. Mayor Karanos spent lavishly, but rarely coordinated the entertainment nearly as well as he ran the city.

As the two rabbit sisters crested the last hill before the mayor's estate, the street seemed almost empty. At the top of the hill, though, they were just high enough to see the whole of the estate spread out like a living map. The crowd surged and ebbed like a living sea. It appeared that all the town and more filled the lawns and fields, spilling out into the surrounding streets. In the orange light of the sunset the mayor's mansion gleamed like a magical palace. Even though she'd seen it before—

and seen Inanael's palace, at which the mayor's whole grounds would fit in one of the smaller wings, or if the queen so chose on a servant's nightstand—

at that moment Anna thought it might have been the most beautiful thing she'd ever seen.

She made her way down into the crowd as quickly as she dared, feeling very mindful of her clothing now. It was too fine a choice for the summer dance, wasn't it? The winter, perhaps—but no, it might not be fine *enough* for that—

"Look." Delphine reached up to touch her sister's shoulder and pointed toward the gate.

Rylan stood by it, leaned against the high metal bars. He held both hands in front of him against his body, looking through the crowds inside searchingly, worriedly. Anna beamed and hurried toward him.

The fox's outfit might well have been tailored to his form, dark blue trousers and waistcoat over a ruffled white shirt. It maintained a perfect gentleman's look, while subtly displaying more of the shape—if not more of the fur—of the body underneath than the loose clothes he customarily wore. As she approached, she found herself amending her thought of the previous moment. The mayor's estate was the *second* most beautiful thing she'd ever seen.

"Rylan!" she called as she approached. His head snapped around and he started to say something, but stopped in mid-syllable, staring at her with his muzzle slightly open.

He found his voice again as she reached him. "You always look lovely, Anna, but you look—you look truly stunning this evening."

"And you're looking *very* handsome." She fought to keep the blush away from her ears this time even as her smile widened.

"Ah, that's sweet of you, but I feel quite outclassed." He managed a more rakish grin.

"Oh, Lord," Delphine muttered under her breath as she passed by, just loud enough for Anna to hear. "Will you two just get it—" She passed out of her sister's hearing range before she finished the thought.

Anna cleared her throat. "I think the dance will start shortly." She held out her hand. "Shall we?"

"Yes, but first." He held out his right hand with a flourish. Between his fingers he held the stem of a large red hibiscus.

She took it gently and lifted to her nose. It still had its scent, honeyed, exotic, more delicate than that of a rose. "It's beautiful."

He wrapped his fingers around hers and guided it up to her head, tucking it into her hair over her left ear. "They're said to only bloom for a day, but I have faith it shall last the night." Then he held out his arm for her, his luxurious tail wagging.

Anna beamed again and linked her arm with his. Together they headed through the gate.

The din of the crowd grew more intense past the walls, and the carnival atmosphere reached a cheerful delirium. Smoke from roasting vegetables and meats intermingled with scents of perfumes, shampoos, cut grass and dozens of species, with the occasional floral note from the hibiscus when a breeze caught it just so.

"The last time I was at one of these, I doubt I was much past knee-high." Rylan looked dumbfounded. "Was it always this much of a spectacle?"

"It's grown over the last few years. At least, I'm told so. I was at one two summers ago, but the time before that had to be…hmm. When you last lived here."

The fox lifted his brows in surprise. "That was eight, almost nine years ago. You've truly only been to a single one?"

She nodded. "Only one."

"I can't imagine how many eligible bachelors you've disappointed by not being here to dance with."

"You flatter me."

"Ah, but it's true. I should say I *can* imagine how many, as I've heard more than one pining for you."

"Men don't pine," she said with a grin.

"Of course we do, dear girl." He ducked a nearby juggler without unhooking his arm from hers, making her duck as well, and deftly led her through the crowd toward a larger lawn with an octagonal stage at its center. Musicians had begun to set up on the stage, and the mayor's servants were shooing people back to clear space for dancing. "We just express it differently. You knit things and sigh to one another, we get into drunken brawls. Truthfully your way is far more sensible."

She couldn't successfully repress her giggling, and just shook her head.

"Seriously, look around us." He indicated the crowd with a grand sweep of his free hand. "Do you see how many men look toward us longingly? I'm fairly sure most aren't directing that gaze toward me."

She let her own gaze follow his hand. "You're making me feel self-conscious. And I can see more than a few women looking toward us."

"They're clearly jealous of your beauty."

Anna laughed. "Are we going to spend the night deflecting one another's compliments?"

"No, I'm finished. For now." He grinned. "I'm hoping to spend at least some of the night dancing."

The musicians—a motley band of deer, mice and one skunk—had finished setting up; the servants were erecting wooden torches on tall poles within the circle they'd cleared out. The sun still outshone the firelight, but it nearly touched the rooftops now, and bathed the revelers with the bright orange glow of a bonfire.

When they had lit the last torch, the servants silently disappeared, and one of the musicians took up two huge mallets, approaching a kettle drum. He struck loudly enough for the crash to echo across the crowd, waited several seconds, did so again, then a third time. By now other couples—and a few solitary dancers—had begun to fill the open space around the stage, looking toward the performers expectantly. An audience of non-dancers had also paused, although twenty yards out from the stage the festival continued on without concern.

The drummer had picked up tambourines now, and joined the rest of the musicians—wind instruments and guitars—at center stage. She saw no signal pass between them, but they launched into a sprightly triple time piece.

"My," Rylan said with a laugh, tail swishing behind him. "So much for starting out with the traditional processional. Do you know how to dance a saltarello?"

"No, I don't. I've never even tried—"

But he'd already taken her hands and started to lead her toward the cleared area between the torches. Only a few other couples had started moving yet, most seemingly as taken aback by the energetic music choice as she was. "That's fine. Just twirl a lot and hop every ninth step and no one will notice."

She laughed. "Rylan!"

"It's true!" He started to move, counting his steps aloud as he circled about her. "One. Two. Three. One. Two. Three. One. Two. Hop! One. Two. Three." He spun on each *three* and the "hop" was more slide than leap. She did her best to follow, keeping her upper body straight and arms low toward her sides, mimicking Rylan and the other dancers. She felt her feet had become twice their normal size and three times as heavy, and she was sure her spins were merely awkward lurches, that each hop would bring a muffled cry of pain from the fox as she stomped on his paw.

But she never did. "You're a natural," Rylan said with a smile, looking into her eyes. She hadn't done anything like this—

in a hundred centuries—

since she was a child. By the end of the song, she'd stopped feeling self-conscious.

The next song, in quarter-time, moved at a slower pace, although still with more vigor than Anna remembered from dances in her childhood. Of course, at those dances she really *had* just been hopping about. Now she was moving precisely—as best she could—following Rylan's lead, arms held like *that* and feet moving like *so* and maintaining just the right distance from her partner.

It was easy until she put it to such analysis. Becoming that conscious of her motions just made her stumble; Rylan lifted an arm to steady her and grinned.

"I'm sorry," she said, breathless.

"You're doing fine. Don't think too much on it, just keep moving to the music."

She nodded, doing her best to follow the advice, now trying desperately not to think about not thinking. After a few more measures, the tension faded, replaced by a happier longing for a dance. Soon, she hoped, they would play a dance for which holding Rylan, feeling his arms around her, would be appropriate.

Such music was rare, though, and could be a little scandalous for a party held by a public official. The next number was less energetic than the first but no less than the second, and at its end they retreated to the side to wait out the next one.

Before it began, Anna found herself startled by someone approaching to her side. "Madam, I don't suppose you'd favor me with your next dance?"

She turned, then looked down at the hopeful face of the otter from the ship this afternoon, dressed in his finest naval uniform, smiling up bashfully.

She laughed and turned back to Rylan. "Do you mind?"

"You again." Rylan crossed his arms. "Well. If the lady will grant that, I won't stand in her way."

The otter lifted his hands. "Just for one number, and I promise I'll be nothing but a gentleman."

"You'd best," Rylan said, although he kept his voice light.

As the music began, the two stepped forward. This number was the slowest of the night, a more romantic melody. Fortunately none of the other couples touched one another for it, so she felt safe following suit. For his part, the sailor didn't seem to mind. "Your name is Anna, I overheard?"

"Yes, sir."

"I'm Edward. It's a pleasure to make your acquaintance, Anna."

"Thank you."

"I hope you won't think this too forward, but you're truly one of the prettiest women I've ever seen. Your gentleman is extremely lucky."

She felt her ears color. "That's very flattering, but come, sir. I thought sailors had a girl in every port."

"A slanderous lie, madam. It's at most a girl in every *other* port. Why, often barely every third." He grinned.

Anna laughed, unable not to smile back.

The otter was at least as good a dancer as Rylan was, adding the occasional flourish to his step and always remaining light on his feet. As much as she enjoyed the show of slight competition, Anna found her thoughts drifting toward the fox throughout most of the music.

As the song came to a close the otter stepped back and bowed deeply to her, arms out to the side. She followed suit. "Thank you. You're a lovely dancer."

"You are as well." He smiled wistfully. "I hope your gentleman fox understands how lucky he is."

"He does," Rylan said, stepping in from the side and taking Anna's hand. The fox's tone remained light, but she picked up the tension underneath.

The otter grinned rakishly. "You'd best." He bowed to Rylan as well, then moved off.

"Quite the dancer," Rylan murmured, watching him head off.

She tilted her head to the side. "You're not jealous, are you?"

"Perhaps a touch," he admitted. "He'd offer far more exotic a life to his wife than a fisherman would."

"A life of being left alone for weeks at a time, when she would be expected to do little more than tend to the house and count the days until his hoped-for return?" She smiled. "That's not the life I'd choose, if I had a say in it."

"That lifts a weight off my shoulders to hear." He offered his arm to her. "Shall we head to the vendors and find dinner before the next dance?"

"That sounds lovely."

They fashioned a meal of bread from one merchant, cheese from another, roasted meat and vegetables from a third, ale from a fourth, and took a seat at a wooden table shared with another couple.

While Rylan and Anna ate the sun finished setting, the last wisps of pink-orange light vanishing into the night. When they returned for the final dances of the evening, only the torches and the moon lit their footsteps. This time, Anna didn't worry about where to place her feet. She didn't need to. Following the music was enough.

After two more songs, one of the musicians stepped forward, and spoke in a voice that projected over the crowd. "I believe some of you have been waiting for this next song most of the evening." The stag waved his tambourine in the direction of Rylan and Anna. "Some more than others." The crowd laughed, with scattered clapping and a few hoots. Anna ducked her head.

"I told you, you attract attention," Rylan murmured as the music began—this time a slow, measured foxtrot. He clasped his hands with hers, fingers entwining, and they moved close together.

"I don't know if I know how to dance this," she stammered.

"You're doing beautifully."

Taking a deep breath, she nodded. And again—of course—just following the music led her feet to the right steps. She might not have been the most graceful dancer that evening, certainly far from the most practiced, but she could lose herself in the look that was in Rylan's eyes right now and that was good enough.

As the music drew to a close, as they stopped moving, Rylan touched his nose to hers, a bit of intimacy that few couples not already married would show in public. Without thinking about more than just following the music to its natural end, she tilted her head up a fraction, turned it just so, and the touch became a full kiss.

She heard a few gasps—and a few claps—from the crowd around them. Rylan's ears shot straight up. But he didn't pull away.

"I hope you two weren't expecting *us* to have brought the ring," the stag called from the stage, to ripples of laughter.

Anna pulled away, feeling that blush once again. An apology for her rashness came to her lips, but as she took in the expression on Rylan's face, his own blush, the wonder, the love, she let it slip away unspoken.

Hand in hand, they walked away from the stage, past the estate's gate, down streets that—thanks to the festival—were nearly deserted. The full moon, now above the rooftops, cast the cobblestones in a pale blue glow that muted the brightness of the painted walls. "You know, Anna," Rylan finally said, "I've had a crush on you since...well, since I was taller than you."

She laughed. "You're still taller than I am."

"Am I?" He made a show of moving one hand between the top of her head and his. "By a whisker, maybe. And when we were teens I'm quite sure you had a full foot on me for a while."

"Oh, not *that* much." She tilted her head. "I always had a crush on you, too." She was quite sure that was true.

He led her through a small wrought iron gate between two buildings, opening not onto an alley but a small courtyard garden. The moon's light reflected from a fountain pool, broken up by delicate ripples. They sat on the grass, and he gave her another kiss, still gentle, but lingering for long seconds, tongue touching her lips before withdrawing. She leaned against him, resting her against his shoulder as his arms wrapped about her.

"I think I'd best not keep going before I get that ring," he murmured, sounding regretful.

"I think it's all right if you kiss me again."

He looked into her eyes, his muzzle almost touching hers. "I think if I do that it might become very hard for me to stop at a kiss."

"I think that's all right, too," she whispered.

Rylan kissed her again, and he didn't stop at the kiss. And even with the hesitations, the uncertainty, the struggle with the corset's lacing, it became very much more than all right.

* * *

She stood on the shore of a vast sea, the colors—of the ocean, the sky, even the sand—supernaturally vivid. The water lay so still it might have been a mirror.

"Was it a beautiful day?" the woman standing beside her said, tilting her head and smiling obliquely, gold eyes shining.

"It was..." she trailed off, smiling.

"Oh, please tell me that's a blush." She clapped her hands in clear delight.

"It was a very beautiful day," she finished. "The day after tomorrow, Rylan and I—"

"Rylan and Anna."

"Rylan and Anna. Yes." She looked out over the still water, her smile faltering. "If they have long lives, they will have many beautiful days, I think."

"Their lives shall both be long. I know this." She sighed thinly. "I would like—I shall have a little more time with them."

The woman sounded startled. "I'm glad to have given you this moment, my friend. I'm very glad you enjoyed it. But it's time to return."

"Another few hours, another day, shall do no harm."

The woman spoke more sharply now. "That is not what you yourself would have told me. How long should the whole world wait for you? Until Anna's next date? The date after that? The wedding? With all that you must be responsible for—"

"Not yet." She spoke firmly, almost challengingly, but continued to look out across the sea. She would not be denied in this, and she felt certain that—despite the mounting exasperation of her companion—she could not be forced.

Anna blinked awake. Unlike yesterday, the sun had barely risen high enough to come in her window.

She sat up, unsettled, rubbing her forehead. What had the other woman been saying in her dream? She couldn't remember who she was now. Everything had begun to fade, so fast. Such was the way of dreams, though; she rarely remembered them on waking.

Throwing off the blankets, she slipped out of bed and to her feet, then opened the wardrobe, selecting a plainer outfit than either of yesterday's.

As she finished tying her blouse, she paused, looking at the bedside table. The red hibiscus lay there, as fresh as when Rylan had handed it to her last evening, despite his description of it as lasting only a day. Giving it a curious smile, she picked it up, then tucked it by her ear the same way he had.

This time when she came down to the kitchen, her mother stood at the counter, chopping vegetables. Delphine sat at the table, nibbling on grapes and flashing Anna a clear *batten down the hatches* expression out of the elder rabbit's line of sight.

"So," her mother began, without looking up. Even though she stood shorter than either of her daughters, she had a deeper voice than either as well. Her build was stout and she'd had grey fur for as long as Anna could remember, but she moved at only a fractionally slower clip than her youngest. "I'm given to understand you and that fox boy put on quite a show at the festival last night."

"I wouldn't say that, ma-ma," she replied with a smile.

"What *would* you say, then?" She pointed accusingly at the hibiscus with her chopping knife. "A close dance with a man you're not betrothed to? A kiss in front of the whole town? Disappearing afterward?"

Delphine perked her ears at the last. She'd also disappeared, of course, but she hadn't been at the dance, either.

"We didn't 'disappear,'" Anna protested. "We just—just went for a walk. Rylan was a perfect gentleman."

"'Just.' A perfect gentleman wouldn't have taken an unmarried young woman off on a walk." She harrumphed and resumed chopping. "And I'm not such a naif as to think those grass stains came from a dance."

Anna stammered, but Delphine came to her rescue, even as she flashed her sister an amazed—and approving—look. "Oh, come *on*, mother. Anna's almost an old maid by now, and she's finally been swept off her paws by someone. Be happy!"

Her mother scowled. "You watch yourself, young lady. 'Swept off her paws' is nonsense enough. I'm more concerned about her being swept onto her back."

Anna made a choking noise; Delphine covered a giggle.

"And marriage isn't about being swept off anything," her mother continued, voice growing even more firm.

"But isn't love?" Anna said.

Her mother stopped chopping, freezing for a few moments, eyes unfocused. Then she sighed melodramatically and resumed the knife work. "I suppose I can't keep waiting for your father to find another rabbit nobleman with an eligible son. We tried that. Twice. But a *fox*? What about my grandchildren? And a *fisherman*."

"Marcus was a merchant, not a nobleman, and Lord Shrimple? Please," Delphine cut in.

"Lord *Shimpel*," her mother corrected with another scowl.

Delphine waved a hand dismissively.

"You've always been impractical and starry-eyed, Annabelle. It's time to get your head out of the clouds and join the rest of us mortals. Always work to do." She sighed. "After breakfast, I'm going over to Amelie's with flowers."

"Dear. Did she finally pass?" Delphine asked.

Her mother nodded. "I haven't heard for certain, but I visited her yesterday afternoon and I doubt she made it to sunset. Anna, you go down to the fishmonger and find us a nice cut of salmon. There's a fine bunch of thyme and basil in the garden and it's put me in mind for doing a cure. We can have a special dinner in a few days."

They rarely had fish unless they were entertaining, and she remembered from dinners as a child that cured salmon was one of Rylan's favorites. Anna and Delphine exchanged a glance; the younger rabbit grinned manically.

"Yes, ma-ma," Anna said, not quite keeping the smile from her voice.

* * *

The harbor had less bustle this day than yesterday, as if the town hadn't fully recovered from the festival yet. But nearly all the merchants had opened for business and the docks buzzed with activity, several more fishing boats having joined the navy galleon at mooring. She had never asked which boat— if it were any of these—that Rylan worked on, and so she stepped out onto the pier, approaching the group at the fish table.

The stench of entrails had been strong yesterday but today it was all she could do not to gag. Several fish on the bloodied plank flopped and flailed vigorously despite being cut open and, in one case, having a filet already cut—raggedly—from its body. "Damn you," one of the vulpine fisherman was crying, "lie *still!*"

Another fisherman, who'd caught sight of Anna approaching, cleared his throat loudly at his companion's curse, gesturing toward the rabbit with a nod.

The cursing fisherman turned, scowl still on his face, then grimaced. "Excuse my language, miss. Hadn't seen you come up."

"It's all right," she said, holding a handkerchief over her nose. "Are they always that...energetic?"

He shook his head. "You always get a couple lively ones, but it's been every single one today." He added another curse muttered under his breath.

"Can we help you with something, miss?" the one who'd cleared his throat cut in.

"Oh, no. I mean..." She bit her lip. "I was curious. Do you know which of those ships Rylan works on?"

"Oh." The first fisherman's bushy brows lifted. "You're *her*."

She laughed.

The second one pointed at one of the boats. "He's a net handler on the *Rosetta* there, miss. Not on board now, though. They're stuck in port for a few days doing hull work."

She nodded and smiled. "Thank you." With a wave, she headed back along the pier, then made her way to the fishmonger's, the largest stall in the harbor market.

While Anna didn't know much about fish, she'd known the shopkeeper all her life, and trusted him to pick out and wrap the best piece for curing. She was startled, then, to hear a voice close by her ear as she left the market, fish in the basket she'd brought with her. "Oh, you don't want *that* one."

She turned, startled, to see a wolf, taller than she was, dressed in a naval uniform. He was accompanied by a shorter otter—not Edward, the one that she'd danced with last night. She didn't like the expression on either one.

The otter chimed in. "Rabbits don't know much about fish. She should ask an expert." He pointed, unnecessarily, at himself.

"The fishmonger said it was fine," she said curtly. "Excuse me."

As she stepped forward, the wolf moved backward, keeping pace with her. "You're the one Edward was dancing with last night, weren't you?"

"She is," the otter said. "But just one dance."

"Not very friendly." The wolf looked directly into Anna's face with a leer.

She felt her hackles rise, fighting down the impulse to—

take their souls where they stood for the affront—

run. She blinked, momentarily disoriented. Where had *that* thought come from? "I...I have to go. The fish will spoil if it's not on ice."

"You should give *us* a dance," the otter said.

The wolf reached out for her chin, still leering. "You're too much a beauty to waste on fisherman foxes." She jerked back a step, and he laughed.

"Leave me be." She tried, unsuccessfully, to keep her voice from quaking. "I'm taken."

"I don't see a ring," the otter said, grinning.

The wolf suddenly grabbed her shoulders. "And *I* don't think you treated Eddie with the respect he deserved. So we thought we'd give you another chance to—"

"She said to leave her be!" the fishmonger bellowed at them, stalking up toward their side. The old bear's ears were set back. He looked like an angry mountain.

The wolf relaxed his grip on Anna, but didn't completely let go of her. "This isn't your business, old man."

"Let me go." Anna managed to keep her voice steady this time. Having unexpected support helped.

The bear put his hands on his hips. "Your commander is Captain Williams, isn't he?"

The wolf straightened up and narrowed his eyes.

"Yes." The otter sounded less insouciant and more uncertain now.

"Grew up around here, you know. When he's in port he goes out drinking with his old friend the fishmonger." The bear looked between both sailors. "You might want to think long and hard about what we're going to talk about tonight."

The otter and wolf exchanged glances. "We're not meaning any harm," the wolf said, letting go and raising both his hands placatingly. "It's just a bit of friendly joshing."

The bear's scowl deepened fractionally.

The otter cleared his throat, then tipped his cap to Anna, walking off at a fast clip. The wolf made the same gesture, but with a slightly sarcastic sneer, ambling after his shipmate.

"Are you all right?" The bear turned toward Anna.

"Yes." She caught a flash of movement off to the left and turned, distractedly, seeing a fox tail vanish into the crowd. She didn't think it was Rylan, though—he'd have come up to challenge them himself, no doubt. "I'm fine."

"I do wonder what our taxes go to sometimes," he muttered.

* * *

The hallway felt cold, imperial: tiles of orange marble for the floor, solid white marble for walls and ceiling. A place a merchant's daughter didn't belong. She ran down it, past other halls, past forbidding metal doors. Was she being pursued, or was she late? She thought she heard voices behind the doors, but couldn't make out the words.

She couldn't find where she needed to be, and she heard other footsteps behind her, heavy footsteps, but saw nothing. She turned down a larger hallway, then a still larger one, then one bigger still. The doors towered over her now, the voices more insistent.

She paused to focus on the words. *Let us in. Please. We need to come in.* Shaken, she started to run.

Another turn. Another. Abruptly she faced two massive iron doors, a skeletal rabbit standing guard by each. The rabbits looked down at her. She barely came to their knees. They bowed, as if in recognition, and silently opened the doors.

The room behind had the same orange marble floor, the same white walls, but it lay in shadow, hazy light trickling down from high overhead, glinting off dust mote spirals, reaching only a few tiles. She picked her way from bright spot to bright spot, seeing—things—moving in the darkness. Glowing things. Fanged things. And sad, pleading faces.

Then, suddenly, she faced a column. Drawing back, she looked up. A vast throne, fashioned of bones and skulls, rose above her. The throne sat empty, but it seemed no less horrifying for it. *What kind of creature*—

"Take your seat," a voice said urgently in her ear. "Let them in. Now."

The scream woke her up, sending her bolt upright in bed. Even after she realized it was her own, she couldn't stop another from bursting out.

Her door flew open, Delphine plunging into the room. "What is it? What is it?" She looked around wildly.

"I—" Anna took in a ragged breath, rocking forward on the bed, tears suddenly streaming down her face. "I'm Anna! I'm Anna!"

Delphine looked puzzled, then swiftly sat down on the bed and drew her sister close. "Who else would you be?" she murmured, sighing. "I don't know what kind of nightmare you just had, but you're all right. You're home."

"Home." She swallowed, forcing her breathing into evenness. "I'm sorry."

Delphine shook her head. "No need to apologize. But no screaming again tonight, hmm? You're lucky mother's such a sound sleeper. I'd worried the White Lady herself had come for you."

Anna's brow furrowed and she blinked slowly, then let out a weak laugh.

* * *

She tried to go back to sleep. When the sun came, though, she doubted she'd managed to do more than close her eyes and shift restlessly under the sheets. But she had no more dreams. As soon as enough light had filled the room for her eyes to begin to pick up color, she dressed, then picked up the hibiscus. Still red, still perfect. She frowned at it curiously, unsettled by its persistence, and set it back on the dresser.

When she came down to the kitchen, her mother was already there. A basket of flowers sat on the table. "Didn't you bring those to Miss Amelie's family yesterday?"

"She isn't dead yet." Her mother shook her head. "I don't know how. Her breath's been a death rattle for over a day. The flowers look just as good today as yesterday, so I'm hanging onto them until she finally passes."

"I see." Anna's brow furrowed.

"She's a tough old tangle, but…" She shrugged, then took a kettle that had just reached a boil off the flame.

Delphine had come down as well, and gave her sister a disbelieving look. "You? Up *early?*"

"I didn't sleep that well."

Her sister's look changed to one of sympathy and shared secrets.

"Excitement for your date tonight, no doubt," her mother said dryly, starting to pour water over coffee grounds, thick liquid draining out through cheesecloth into the pitcher below.

Anna's ears colored. "How did you know about that?"

"Mothers hear everything. Your father should be back from his trip tonight. You remembered that, right?"

"I did, yes. But he'll be just as happy to see me seeing someone as *you* are, and more likely to admit it openly."

She grunted, but couldn't quite keep a smile from her face. In that moment she looked more like her daughters than usual. "Respect your elders."

Anna leaned over and kissed her mother's cheek. "I always do."

"Only compared to your sister."

Delphine snorted loudly.

* * *

The sun had traveled well past the meridian when Delphine ran up the road toward the house screaming.

Anna had been working in the garden; she'd been about to stop for the afternoon, to go in and cool off and prepare for the evening. She turned to her sister, eyes wide. "What is it? What's happened?"

"It's Rylan," she gasped, grabbing her sister's hand and tugging her along. "Lost his damned mind, is what's happened. Come on!"

Abruptly Anna found herself running alongside Delphine, careening dangerously down the hill. "What do you mean?"

"Starting a fight." Delphine spoke between sharp breath intakes. "With that otter. Over you."

"What? No!" Anna looked stricken. "Why would he *do* that?" She ran faster.

They'd almost reached the bottom of the hill when they heard the pistol shot ring out, followed by screams.

By the time the two rabbits had reached the crowd, whatever had happened was over; they had arrived only for the aftermath. Edward was being restrained by two burlier sailors, including Commander Williams. The otter looked anguished, his gaze turned to the ground, toward a vixen Anna recognized. A nun, one of the town's nurses. Her expression was grimly set, resigned, and her simple blue blouse was covered with blood—

Anna drew to an abrupt halt, staring numbly at the fox on the ground, under the nurse's hands. Then, without being aware of the steps she took, she was at his side, the shriek she wanted to let out caught in her throat like a fish hook.

"Oh gods." Delphine dropped to her knees by her sister. "He said—he said the otter had threatened you—"

"Rylan," Anna choked out, putting her hands on his chest. It didn't seem like all the blood pooling underneath, already starting to soak her dress, could have come out of such a small entrance wound—could have come out of such a small body. She shuddered. Had it gone through him? How big was the hole in his back?

He looked up at her, eyes locking onto hers, trying to speak. "He..." Bloody foam flecked his lips. "And the wolf...my cousin saw...you at market..."

"It wasn't him!" Her voice rose hysterically. "It wasn't him! It was someone else! And it was only just words!"

"I didn't want to shoot, I swear," Edward cried, sounding in almost as much pain as Rylan. "He attacked me. He wouldn't listen to anything I said!"

Anna's voice dropped to a hoarse whisper. "Rylan. This—this isn't like you. How—why?"

"Love...can drive you mad," Rylan got out, smiling almost apologetically. A spasm wracked his body.

She swallowed. "We—we have to get you to the hospital, take you—"

The nun took Anna's hand in both of hers, looking into the rabbit's eyes. "We can't do anything. Not after this kind of wound."

"What? No!" Anna's voice rose again. She yanked her hand free.

"There's nothing—nothing left inside him." The vixen looked haggard. "It's a miracle he's lasted long enough to say goodbye. Please. Say it now."

Anna's tears finally came at that, and she leaned over Rylan, giving his bloody mouth a kiss. His blood smeared on her lips.

"Wanted another dance," he whispered. "I love you, Anna."

"I love you. So much." She moved her hands to squeeze one of his. He clasped back weakly, then released his grip, eyes rolling back.

Anna let out a single sob. Over the next minute his breathing grew more ragged. But it never stilled.

"He's still alive," she whispered, then looked up at the vixen, speaking more loudly. "He's still alive! We've got to help."

"I told you—"

"He's still alive!" Anna's voice became a shriek.

"He shouldn't be!" the nun snapped, ears back. "I don't know what's keeping him here! Gods below, he's the fifth one in two days who *just won't die!*"

The nurse's outburst shocked Anna into momentary silence.

"He needs you," Delphine said softly.

Anna took a deep breath. "That's what I'm trying to—"

"No." Her sister put her hand on her shoulder. The cadence of Delphine's voice shifted, sounding like an imitation of someone else she knew, someone very different. "He needs to move on. He doesn't need Anna. He needs *you.*"

Anna turned, and stopped cold as she looked into eyes that were no longer her sister's—beautiful, immortal, golden.

"He needs *you,*" she repeated. "They all do."

Her lower lip trembled, and she took in a deep, ragged breath. Anna's will remained strong, but for Rylan's sake, for her function's sake, hers had to break.

Closing her eyes, she nodded, once, very slowly.

Then, before she opened her eyes again, she opened her wings.

Gasps and screams came from the crowd around her, but she paid them no mind. She moved to slowly kneel by Rylan, by the vixen. By Anna. The vixen had scrambled backward, making a religious sign with a hand and prostrating herself. Anna's tearstained face had become terrified.

Inanael glanced at Delphine, but she was back to being only Anna's sister, as frightened as the rest. She reached out and touched both of the sisters' shoulders very gently, looking into Anna's eyes as she spoke. "This should not have been, but I cannot unwind it," she whispered. "Forgive me."

The rabbit girl's expression shifted from fright to wonder, then back to sadness. She nodded, very slightly.

Inanael lifted her hands, then rested them gently on Rylan. His breathing stilled.

Rising again, she beat her wings once, and—to mortal eyes—vanished, a cold wind swirling out in all directions from where she had stood.

* * *

This time Maraiya sat watching the waves crashing against the beach. Unlike most days, the sky roiled this morning, fierce clouds visible against the horizon. They matched the expression on Lady Inanael's face as she stormed toward the winged cat.

"I am sorry." Maraiya spoke softly before the rabbit could say anything. "For your loss, and for theirs."

Her voice quivered with restrained anger. "That was not the way their story should have ended."

"Their story was not yours to play out," Maraiya said sharply.

"You put me in their story!"

"For an evening. You were to be there for an *evening*, Inanael." The cat sighed, closing her eyes. "All love stories, when followed long enough, are tragedies. They can only end in loss. I know that better than anyone."

"All stories must." The anger had seeped out of Inanael's tone, replaced by resignation. "You were right. I should have left that first night. But...that kind of experience..." She looked down at the sand. "It is something I can so rarely have. I acted...unbefittingly."

Maraiya smiled a little, without speaking, and turned to look over the sea.

Fire returned to the horned rabbit's voice again. "But I *saw* their lives. That is not when Rylan should have died. Something changed. Rylan—he said went mad—" Inanael stopped, then turned to look straight down at her companion.

The cat remained facing the ocean, unmoving.

Inanael spoke in a hoarse, dangerous growl. "Maraiya."

"You had to come back." Her voice was barely above a whisper.

For a long time no noise passed between them but the crashing of the sea. Then, heavily, Inanael's hand came down on Maraiya's shoulder. Death kneeled by Love, and looked down with her bone white eyes.

"Anna will find love again," Inanael said softly, "She will keep it while she is alive. You will promise this to me now."

She nodded, looking up at the rabbit, speaking more passionately. "She shall meet a merchant from another village, and he shall love her deeply. They will have two—"

Inanael disappeared in a flash of lightning that echoed across the dark clouds.

Maraiya took a deep breath and let it out in a slow sigh, then sank down, head on her knees, watching the storm come in.

"Repast (A Story of Aligare)" is set in Heidi Vlach's world of Aligare; detailed in Remedy: A Story of Aligare (February 2011), Ravel: A Story of Aligare (December 2011), and Render: A Story of Aligare (May 2013). It takes place among the three peoplekinds of Aligare who live in symbiotic neighborliness; the green-skinned insect/humanlike aemet (with prominent antennae), the tall dragonlike korvi (they are called dragons because of the similarity, though they have feathers instead of scales), and the small, weasel-like ferrin.

Vivia Ava, usually shortened to Vee, is a young ferrin who has settled in the town of Greenway. She has made a vocation for herself as a forager—she finds plants and animal bones in the nearby forest that the mostly aemet inhabitants of Greenway can use, and trades for what she needs. Vee doesn't really care what the aemet use her finds for, until she is introduced to the elderly Welsken, a calligrapher who needs her wildlife bones to make ink for his calligraphy.

To draw pictures of Aligare's gods.

Repast
(A Story of Aligare)

by Heidi C. Vlach

Mama said there was a legend about the gods giving out names. Long ago, when the land was new and the first trees were stretching toward the dome of the Great Barrier, the mortal peoples were nameless. That was unfitting for gods' children. The Great Ones discussed and disagreed, and in the end used their vast power to poke dimples into the peoplekind's inner essence. Not enough to hurt, only enough to make people want to prod that spot inside themselves. Smooth it over. Maybe fill it with something.

That something, Mama said, was a name. It was different for each peoplekind. The aemets—the betweenkind folk, both furkind and insect—got one given name, and held their family name close so they always had company. The korvi—dragons of the skies—got one given name, and kept their clan name, too, for something to be proud of. And then, Mama said, came their own ferrin race. Some ferrin were happy with one given name. One didn't always fill them up, though. So Mama's mother gave her two names so she could pick between them once she was grown, and Mama did the same for her own kits.

Choosing one's name was a summoning of strength and levity, a sure way to feel right in one's own fur. Mama smiled, her whiskers folding up fond, and said she was eager to see which names her kits would pick. Or maybe they would find a third name. Wasn't that right, Vivia Ava?

The twinkling in Mama's eyes was a thunderbolt through Vivia Ava's chest. A patch of longer fur—adult fur—was spreading wide across her shoulders and she still had no earthly idea whether she was Vivia or Ava. Neither sat right in her mouth. Neither pretty name, selected by her love-strong parents, felt like the one she should ask folk to call her by. But if even great Ambri thought she should pick for herself, then there couldn't be any shame in it. Gods, supposedly, knew best.

When Vivia Ava started exploring the oak forest by herself—though always within smelling distance of home—she took the solitude as a chance to mumble sounds. She listened to her own tongue smashing her names into new shapes. And soon enough, she began telling folk that she was Vivia Ava, call her Vee.

* * *

Vee left home soon after her adult fur filled in. She put on the scarf Papa gave her—the gold- patterned one that brought out the green in her eyes— and she left the oak forest behind, following the trade roads and their trace scents of travelers, until the oak trees gave way to plains grass and eventually, cornfields ushered a town into view.

This place was Greenway, a large village made up of mostly aemet people. Aemets were as green as their plantcasting magic and every two-legged step came smooth. They gathered together just like the corn they grew, slender and angular, and they smiled down at Vee like they could sense promise wafting off of her.

It was a fine enough town to live in. Vee chose a maple tree on the outskirts of town to make her nest in, after promising her aemet neighbors she would do no harm to this child of the plant goddess. No sap drawn, and no wood broken away unless it was diseased or dead. That was a reasonable allowance to make for folk of another kind; Vee would be uneasy, too, she supposed, if her goddess's storm clouds were able to burn or bleed. And more importantly, great Verdana didn't mind people or creatures eating her seeds. There would be meals of maple keys in Vee's future.

As much as Vee's neighbors guarded the trees, they still needed wood for their hearths, to cook food and ward the night's chill away. Vee gathered fallen branches, at first, and she traded them for juicy cobs of roasted corn. As months passed, her foraging took her farther and farther afield, out past the farmers' plots and into the forest so she couldn't smell the town's latrines or woodsmoke any more.

The maple forest had a greener tang to its scent than the oak forest back home. Fewer whiffs of basilisk and cavebird's scents. Fallen leaves becoming pungent earth. More thrushes' and jays' cries and a more robust voice to the wind. After an hour's quick journeying, the ground sloped upward into the rocky foothills of Hotrock Volcano.

And with each trip, Vee found things. Trinkets more interesting than firewood or seeds: she found treefruit, and pebbles glittering with minerals, and wood bent by the wind's persistent presence. She even found a rock-clinging lichen that looked like musty leather scraps but was actually worth an eightday of hot meals.

"What can you make of that lichen?" Vee asked the town seamstress, around a mouthful of scalding but delicious pigeon stew.

"Oh, wait until you see it," the seamstress enthused. "It makes a truly *striking* shade of pink dye. If you find me more of this, there'll be more stew for you—wager on that."

And that was when Vee realized that she had a line of work: she found herself a name and she could find other things, too.

She dug more intently under leaf litter, and climbed higher up the Volcano. Each day, her scarf filled with mushrooms and pebbles as she bore wind-carved sticks between her teeth, and there was never a day Vee didn't look forward to the search. After all, why would gods put so many things into the world if peoplekind weren't meant to find it?

"My, but you've got a talent for this," one merchant told her. He was Syril, a red-feathered chatterbox of a korvi, part of some far-spread family who had made their mark in the land—and more importantly Syril was always delighted to see what Vee had found. "Wager four apples on it, the gods have given you a gift, friend!"

Vee tilted her head up at him. "You think it?"

"I do!"

"Do you know anyone who's looking for forest goods right now?"

Syril chattered off a list of names—a long list, seemingly folk who had asked for herbs at any point within the last eightyear. But just as irritation was making Vee's tail flick, Syril's eyes bugged wide. "Oh, and I nearly lost this bit of news in my dustbin of a head! There's a fellow right here in Greenway looking for inkwork supplies."

"What sort of supplies?" Like any trade, inkworking had more nuances than Vee had strands of fur.

Shrugging, waving his arms so his bangles clattered, Syril said, "Oh, different things, by the sound of it. The fellow is Welsken—old aemet man, married into the Tennel family? Not quite a hermit but certainly a rarer sight than a rainstorm. I came upon his daughter, Clematis—"

Whom Vee already knew: Clematis kept an eclectic vegetable garden and she was happy to buy all the herb and shrub seeds Vee could find.

"—and do you know what my dear friend Clematis told me? That Welsken is looking for some particular bones." Syril squinted, his voice lowering slight. "Grazing creatures' bones—and only wild ones, no farmed horses or any such thing! I keep a goodly stock of trinkets and rabble in my pouches, gods see that I speak the truth about *that*, but I had nothing within a shade of what Welsken wanted. He wouldn't even take a bargain on pigeon bones!"

People that discerning usually had the barter goods to back up their tastes. With her ears folding thoughtful, Vee nodded. "I cover a lot of forest when I'm foraging. I'm sure I can find what he needs. Where can I find this fellow?"

* * *

The next day, with a scarf full of new treasures, Vee began following Syril's suggestions. She went first to find Clematis, lolloping on four quick feet down the town's main road. Daybright winked through the tall maples; neighbors walked between houses, made with the aemet technique of boards tied gently around tree trunks. As the leaf canopy thickened, the path led to the Middling circle, that sacred aemet place full of pungent stacks of rotting plant trimmings. Clematis wasn't there—just three farmhand ferrin dumping a bucket of vegetable peels—and so Vee headed for the next most likely place. Clematis kept Greenway's Middling circle and oftentimes, she guided folk to the Garden.

Vee had visited the Garden once. It was a gathering of large, etched stones propped up tall, each one kept company by flower-speckled patches of daisies and yellow gelsemiums. The stone etchings were pictures of the gods—flat depictions of the stories Vee knew, cool and motionless rock that was nothing like a storyteller's voice.

But that was why Clematis spent time here, telling the stones' tales. Today, she was explaining a stone to two other aemets Vee had never seen nor smelled before.

"And after the rain stopped, great Ambri came down from the thunderclouds to see the result of her work." Clematis was fiddling with her braids as she usually did, smoothing them around her antennae's bases in a way that never satisfied her. "Her mighty lightning had filled the quartz stone with electric magic, so she had electricstones to bury for later. But there had been a tree too close to the strike point. One of Verdana's children, now blackened and smoldering."

Blunt-barbed aemet fingers gestured to the stone, to its chiseled sketch of a bird-like Ambri with her head bowed before a stick of a tree.

"So," Clematis went on, "Ambri sought out her mighty sister. She fluttered through every treetop until she was in the calmest heart of the forest, and there she found Verdana, our mother of green."

Vee stifled a sigh: this part of the legend always dragged on when aemets told it. But after long moments talking about the lush-leafed haven Verdana lived in and the clean air filtering through the leaves, Clematis got to the point.

"Ambri and Verdana talked for four weeks, though more like the wink of an eye to the gods. Verdana said that her flora were fragile; that was the beauty of them. Sometimes the other elements would harm plants, but that only made ash and charcoal and, eventually, new soil to nourish new life. Lightning was no enemy of plant life. Why, not even Fyrian's ever-hungry fire was truly an enemy.

It was then that Ambri called out to her same-element children, the larks and swallows in the sky and the lizards creeping under rocks. Birds came and alighted in the trees, and lizards lined the clearing—and ferrin people came, too, peering out from leafy branches.

Let the land know that lightning might do harm, Ambri said. Folk needed to mind thunder's rumbling warning, and seek shelter. But though it could wreak destruction, Ambri's element tried always to do good, as well.

The birds took off, chattering the message to all who would hear it. The ferrin nodded to their High One, and took the message into their hearts. So it has been, ever since."

The visitor aemets touched their palms together in quiet applause, like they might break the atmosphere of the Garden. Clematis looked bright-eyed with her own storytelling, but thankfully she turned a glance to Vee; the visitors drifted away toward the next story stone.

"Good day, neighbor," Clematis told Vee. "You need something?"

"Your father is Welsken Tennel—is that right?"

"He is."

Her tone carried a heavy *but*; Vee's fur prickled with possible unwelcome.

"I don't want to bother him for no reason," Vee added, "but I'm told that he's a calligrapher? I found some plantkind bones he might like to trade for."

"Oh," Vee relented, "that's a different matter. I'll take you to him!"

Every town had its hermits. Folk who decided that their best friends were quiet and solitude. Folk who hid themselves like moles. Welsken wasn't quite one of those—but Vee wouldn't have known his face or his scent if she had to find him on her own. All she knew was the kind-tongued gossip about him, and the seamstress's set of ink-painted clay dishes that she said were Welsken's handiwork.

Clematis led her along a narrow path at the back of the Garden, through rustling boxwood and sumac. They came to a house surrounded tight by hazel bushes, its wooden walls hardly visible through the meshed leaves.

Clematis rapped her blunt-spined knuckles on the door pole. "Father? There's a forager to see you, with some bones for trade."

Silence answered. Nervousness sparked electricity under Vee's skin and she reined it in: her ears fanned forward at the faint scuffling of movement within the home. Welsken's footfalls approached and stopped before the door curtain. Hesitating, maybe. Or considering. Vee had always wondered what aemet people's airsense could actually show them, other than a mound of fur and whiskers.

Finally, the door curtain was whisked aside—by the shortest adult aemet Vee had ever seen, his posture so stooped that his tunic hung like an empty sack. Faded brown eyes mirrored his tacked-on smile. He seemed rusty at meeting guests.

"Suppose we can talk for a moment," Welsken said.

Clematis hummed a satisfied note. "I can't stay, is that well with you? Travellers are viewing the Garden right now."

"Go," Welsken grumbled mild.

Then Clematis was gone and he was lifting the door curtain, waving Vee inside.

The close-walled home smelled like its waxy-skinned resident, and burned cornstalks and dust. Beside the central hearth pit, there was plenty of room for Welsken and Vee to sit—but any other visitors would have had to sit on his bed and he didn't seem like the sort to offer it.

"Ah, humph. Something to eat?"

"No, thanks."

For half a heartbeat, Welsken smirked. "Good. I'd rather see to business, if you don't mind."

"Fine by me." Vee was unknotting her scarf, and she snatched a glance at him. "Um, I heard you wanted bones, so I searched the northeastern forest and brought back what I could. If I might be blunt, too, do you mind seeing the cartilage bits still attached?"

Welsken was silent again. Vee looked up to find those puddle-brown eyes fixed on her again, like he was drawing a net through his memory for something she reminded him of. She held the stare, mild but with her ears canting a question.

And Welsken laughed suddenly, a dry little bark that Vee wouldn't have known for a laugh if she hadn't seen the crinkle of his crows' feet. "It's nothing. You remind me of someone, that's all. What was your name again?"

"Vivia Ava. Call me Vee."

"Hm. Knew another ferrin named Vivia, once."

"Oh. Was that her choice name?"

"It was."

They avoided gazes for a moment. Then Welsken tossed one wizened hand, shooing away the thought. "Ah, let's head back toward the point. Bones with gristle still on, you said? That's no trouble. Have you got any from a deer?"

With her spirit lifting, Vee drew open her scarf full of treasures. "You tell me, please."

Once his gaze locked onto the trade goods, Welsken seemed to forget he had company. His splintered nails ran over the planes and crevices of the bones. His brow worked, tugging his antennae bases this way and that. And his scent changed gradual—to a warmer smell, a happier smell.

"Mmm, this is from a nurl," he mumbled. "Foreleg, looks like. Makes a fine shade of red-black, though I've got plenty of red-black still. Ribs, breastbone…

What's this, a squirrel? Little rotten, but still good. Maybe I'll take those from you some other time. Ratkind don't graze."

"Are you working on something particular?" Vee asked.

She hoped powerfully for an answer. Welsken flicked a glance at her, put the squirrel's bones aside, and picked up a large, promising joint. "I mostly record the Great Ones. What they look like."

"Oh, you're *that* sort of artist!"

"It's something to do," Welsken said. "This, now, this has got to be a deer. Whole leg of it, too! Great green, a small one like you carried these all over creation?"

Vee couldn't help herself: she sat taller on her haunches.

"I'll take these bones, Miss Vee. What's your price?"

She had planned to ask for food—for corn, barley, potatoes, or whatever else this aemet fellow kept around. But the words stopped in Vee's throat. There was knowledge here, hidden in this neighbor's hands and heart, and Vee felt like she did when she was Vivia Ava, full of an encompassing need to know and to *find*.

"Can I see your art?"

Silence thundered. Welsken's lips pressed thin.

"It's mostly just patterns. Decorations on bowls and such. Ask Clematis if you'd like to see them."

"No, I want to see them. You draw them, don't you? If you use ink, that means you draw with a split reed, right?"

His face stayed stony but his warming scent gave him away. Without a word, Welsken pushed stiffly to his feet and produced from a storage box one long strip of softened parchment. A grey strip.

No, Vee realized—it was beige parchment, just patterned lavish with ink. Grand whorls of outlines, filled with flowing currents of scritch-scratch textures. As Vee's eyes adjusted to the flattened-out image, she saw a deer-like creature with endless antennae wafting on wind. And another creature, a beetle-shelled woman with hooves. More and more divine beings as Welsken unrolled the parchment, but all of them looked like the goddess of green, Verdana.

"Ohh!" she breathed, hopping closer. The sheet was an object that smelled like stale leather and solvents, but this was still the excitement of meeting someone real. "So many Verdanas! Wow, this must have taken you months."

"Years," Welsken murmured. "They're all from different... Different people's thoughts on what Verdana looks like. Legends from here and there."

The inkstrokes led Vee's attention up and around the sheet. She floated on the sight of it, on the dawning thought that the gods must have textures to their bodies like mortals did. Wouldn't they? Maybe they didn't. Vee had always dimly supposed that the gods had touchable fur and hair and feathers, when listening to her elders' stories.

Then she noticed the quiet, and the weight of Welsken's stare on her. He was thinking about the past again, said Vee's gut.

"What is it?" she asked him.

"Nothing. Anypace, there's a bug-shaped Verdana I'm trying to finish. Just needed more ink to finish her, and it wouldn't be right to use ink from anything but a plantcaster's remains."

"Can you draw Ambri for me?"

A hesitation like a hook in Welsken's mouth, before he grumbled, "Not for just those bones."

"I'll bring you firewood. Because you have to burn the bones, don't you?"

She could feel her own whiskers vibrating with burning hope. And when Welsken sighed and shook his head resigned, Vee let her grin spill out over her snout.

"The bones," Welsken said, "the firewood, and some more parchment. I'll take that deal."

* * *

Of course, she had to ask Clematis to escort her again. To bring Welsken the firewood and soft hide for their deal. And she asked again five days later, when she found the remains of something else with hooves. And once more the following eightday, to show Welsken a wind-warped maple branch that reminded her of the way he drew plantcasting energy, roiling like vines.

And after that, Clematis told Vee to go ahead to Welsken's home by herself. "I'm sure you know your way by now," she said, low but fond. "And I think he likes you."

That was enough of an honor, glowing ember-warm in Vee's chest. But when she knocked on Welsken's doorway that day and he called her inside, there was more: he was hunched over his worktable already, reed scratching out long strokes. Like feathers, Vee dared to hope.

"What are you drawing?"

"Come here and see," he said with a smile touching his voice.

She was across the room and at Welsken's side in one bound, then standing tall on two legs and gasping at the sight. Electric goddess Ambri spilled glorious across the small square of parchment, her weaselkind body curled graceful. She had the long, pointed ears of a ferrin, pale-tipped like Vee's own ears, and a mane of feathers filled with zig-zag textures like woven lightning.

"I'm nearly finished," Welsken added. "This'll be yours before darkfall today."

Vee had a powerful need to butt against his arm, to express the joy built up inside her. That would jostle his drawing arm, though, so she stifled herself. "Can I watch?"

He huffed a chuckle. "If you'd like. It's no thrill to watch."

That wasn't true at all, in Vee's mind. She pulled over a storage box full of blankets, hopped into it, and watched for the next hour as Welsken's hand finessed lines and dots into place. Ambri filled up real.

"There," Welsken sighed. He straightened with a grunt and rubbed his clenched drawing hand.

"She's beautiful!" Vee tipped her head against her fur-pillowed arms. The only part of the drawing she was unsure about was the mystery in Ambri's clawed hands—a round object shaded in like it was shiny, like its surface glint hid secrets. "Which legend were you thinking of?"

"Mm, no legend in particular. I was thinking of Ambri as she appears on the Garden stones. Always thought myself that she should look strongly like a ferrin."

Like a family resemblance. Vee climbed careful out of the storage box, to walk four-footed around the edge of Welsken's tabletop and consider his art from new angles. "Oh, that's fine, I was just wondering what she's holding."

Welsken paused. Confusion tugged at his features. "I don't rightly know. She needed to be holding a found treasure, since this artwork is for you. Can't say what that's supposed to be, though."

"It looks like a gemstone, maybe?" Vee tipped her head farther, ears fanned low. "You just felt like the thing Ambri is holding... needed to look like that?"

With a shrug—a limited movement, given his stiff shell plates—Welsken hummed. "Cicada alighted on me, I suppose."

"Maybe..."

The Legend Creature of creativity probably liked Welsken well enough. That thought didn't sit flush in Vee's mind, though; there was something more here. The gods put potential out into the world. If they could make people want to name themselves, why couldn't they put a vision into an artist's head?

"What's wrong with that," Welsken grumbled, "hmm?"

"I don't know. You seem close to the gods."

He laughed, sharp as vinegar.

"No, you do! Could it— Could you have imagined that gem for a reason?" Maybe Welsken's antennae were sensing the far-off shape of a treasure, meant for one of Ambri's ferrin children to find.

Welsken was frowning at her now. "You're making too high a wager on my whims."

"It's not a wager. Just a guess."

He frowned for another moment. Then he rose on his sticky joints, and went to the water pail to clean his reed. "All I do is put legends down into pictures, Vee. There's ink in it, and an old man's efforts, and some stories he's heard bandied around from mouth to mouth. That's all."

Her ears fell against her neck. Welsken saw clouds even in clear skies; that was his way. But Vee had never heard him gloomy enough to doubt even the Great Ones.

Working a wet rag against the reed's stained tip, Welsken glanced sidelong at Vee. "Ah, forgive me, friend. If you want to go search for a trove, don't let me talk you away from it."

Her heart lifted a fraction and so did her ears. "Searching is what I *do*."

"And it seems like your calling. Well, anypace. Keep alert for electric creatures' bones, if you would. I've nearly used up my Ambri inkwell."

Vee agreed—and as she watched Welsken's back bend into a tighter arch, she assured herself that the land had plenty of riches for the finding.

The winds blew fiercer, as Vee collected enough sticky tree sap to glue her Ambri drawing up on the thatch wall of her nest. And as aemet farmers dried corn for the coming cool weather, Vee combed the Volcanoside forest, more diligent than ever before.

There was glittering mica on the hidden sides of pebbles. Boleta mushrooms and hazelnuts abounded. Maple keys showered down from brown-touched canopies, and Vee found all the dry sticks she could carry—but though she collected those things, they weren't what she was looking for.

Welsken kept drawing. He produced delicate renditions of water god Okeos, and the high gods Bright and Dark, images that swirled in Vee's mind like festival dancers. Maybe Welsken was so productive lately because he was pouring out his own essence onto the pages. Maybe that was why he looked older, Vee noticed with a start one rainy afternoon: he had more brown spots peppering his skin, and straightening from his worktable was more labor every day. He was going to be forty-six years old once sowing season returned. That was far longer than any ferrin had ever lived, and nearing the end of aemetkind's measure.

Through it all, Vee wanted more legends. She knew the basic stories of gods and creation—Mama and Papa told her all of those before she and her littermates saw their first year pass by—but maybe more legends would give Vee clues on where to look.

She asked her trade customers for legends, whenever she brought them supplies. Farmers talked about lightning bugs befriending aemet ancestors and aiding them against a plague of gasterslugs. The town seamstress told her a legend about tinctoria lichen gaining its hidden colors. Fine legends, but not what Vee craved.

After much hesitation, she asked Syril.

"Begging your pardon, dear friend, but I'm no more a bard than I am a pikefish!" He puffed out his chest, flicking his wing quills like a second greeting. "We Reyardines are merchants first and foremost, say that four times because it's the utmost truth!"

"Oh," Vee said. "That's fine. I only thought I'd ask…"

"Why don't you ask that artist fellow, ah, what was his name? Welman? No, no, Welsken! I've heard tell that you two get along like sparks and tinder. And if any Greenway villager has a headful of legends, bet a turnip that Welsken does!"

Canting her head, Vee asked, "Why is that?"

"You don't know? He gathered up all of those legend-etched stones that make up the Greenway Garden! I remember it clear as air! He put out a call for miners and diggersfolk and led them here and there, all over the land. Said he knew whoever it was that chiseled the stories out, too. Goodness, but old Welsken must have a thousand stories to tell, if only his mouth weren't clamped shut like a dog on a bone."

An inkling of success grew in Vee's gut—like she had picked up a promising scent. "I'll keep that in mind! Thank you, Syril. Now, if you can't trade me legends, might I see what else you have today?"

With a beaming grin, Syril began unknotting one of his cargo pouches.

With a newly acquired sack of thornwood roots clamped between her teeth, Vee ran to Welsken's house. He had a fondness for ground vegetables and, hopefully, enough fondness for Vee to tell her some tales.

"Well?" he asked. Welsken knelt by the hearth, raking its coals into an even cooking bed. "How goes your search for Ambri's jewel?"

Vee smirked up at him. "That sounds like a legend I've never heard before. Would you tell it to me?"

"Heh. There once was a ferrin, call her Vee, who searched every knucklewidth of the land." He paused. "That has a half-decent rhythm to it."

Vee couldn't help but agree. "I don't think I'll get to *all* of the land, though. I'm already nine."

Grumbling agreement, Welsken inspected a thornwood root. "You might need to search beyond Hotrock Volcano. That's Fyrian's domain. Ambri visits, but I wouldn't wager that she'd hide anything of hers up there."

"Mm, you'd likely know best."

He gave her a look: *what is that supposed to mean* formed clear on his features.

"I've got a question of you, Welsken," Vee murmured, "if it wouldn't bruise your patience."

He set down the ash rake and rubbed his drawing hand, out of habit more than any clear need. "What is it?"

"I've heard tell that you started the Garden, and arranged to bring the legend carvings here?"

"I did."

"Why?"

Welsken sighed, shrinking with the loss of air. "You want a legend? Vee, I already talk to you so much, you're going to wear out my throat."

"I could find you some honey? To soothe it."

His laugh was gentle this time. "I've already got you running all over creation, looking for things. No, I'll tell you. Put the roots into the fire, would you?"

Vee bounded to get the hearth tongs: ferrin had much shorter arms than aemets and she didn't want her fur singed. While she arranged the bristly-skinned roots onto crackling coals, she kept a sidelong watch over Welsken, his back toward Vee while he ladled himself a drink from the water pail. He swallowed once, and twice. He knelt on the swept dirt floor. Then he began.

"My grandmother and great-uncle were wandering sorts. Azalea Tennel and Falwith Tennel. They were close as could be, ever since they were born. They followed the winds across the land, partly to forage but mainly because they wanted to meet the gods."

He drank from the ladle again. Vee held her tongue against her mouthful of questions.

"It's a fool thing to go looking for the gods. They visit peoplekind when they wish to, and no sooner. But my family says that Azalea and Falwith did meet our great Verdana in a quiet glade. They searched farther and found Fyrian by a flow of hotrock. Then Ambri at the site of a lightning strike. And Okeos by a lake at duskfall. All of the Legend Creatures, and even great Bright and Dark."

Vee was staring bowl-eyed at Welsken, before recalling the tongs in her hands. "They must have been very lucky."

"I don't believe it's true," Welsken snapped. "My family swears by the legend, but if you want my measure of it, the story warped with the telling."

Another of Welsken's dour moments. Vee held her ears neutral; there was no sense in disputing his belief.

"But whatever Azalea and Falwith found," he went on, "it... it was something that gave them inspiration. They left carvings all over the land, to mark down what they couldn't put into words. Those carvings show the Great Ones of this land."

"And you gathered them into one place?"

"I did. Recruited korvi to chip the carvings free and load them into horse carts. Brought them here so folk could see them, without having to spend their own lives wandering."

"And Clematis tells the carvings' stories?"

"She tells whichever legends she feels like. No one knows what Azalea and Falwith were trying to depict!" He ran a hand into his umber-streaked hair. "I could guess but that's all it would be—a *guess*. I don't even know if I found all of the damned things."

Vee had no words. Just trembling, as she lolloped to Welsken's side and nudged her head against his arm.

"And I have no more time to find them," he sighed.

"You have time. You're still here."

"I've been in no state to *travel*, these last years. Sitting in a cart hurts my shell something wretched."

"Oh," Vee said low. "And if you wanted to check everywhere, you'd have to run…"

A smile hid at the wrinkled corner of his mouth. "Really, Vee, I wasn't that fast twenty years ago. It's all right—I'm just keeping up the tradition of taking down legends. There'll be plenty of pictures of the gods, in all their appearances, piled here in this house. All here in this house, in one place—except for a few outliers, of course. Like your Ambri drawing."

"I'll try to bring it back before I pass?"

"Nonsense, it's yours."

They sat together in the quiet. Then Welsken rocked to his feet and took up the rake.

"I thought I asked you to cover those roots. They won't cook even."

"Ah, sorry!" She snatched the tongs back up, poor rake though they made. "Thanks for telling me all that. You didn't have to."

He hummed. And while he worked the hearth, washed in warm light, Welsken came to some decision.

"I do hope you find it," he said. "Ambri's gemstone."

"I'll show it you," Vee said firm. "I'm going to find it, and show it to you. And *tell* you about it."

* * *

Vee set out early the next morning, when the purple light of evening still muddied the dawn. She would search Hotrock's slopes today. Higher than usual. Thinking of Welsken's ancestors—happening upon a lightning strike, meeting Ambri in all her galvanizing splendor—had given her an idea.

It had stormed through the night. Damp loam filled her nose, streaked with green each time she brushed past a shrub. Wet, felled branches blocked Vee's usual paths. She stopped often to shake herself dry, and knew that she wouldn't smell much variety today.

And yet, Vee was climbing an ironwood for better vantage when a scent grabbed her nose—something burnt. Only a whiff of it, smothered in the wet air, but she lifted her ears to gauge the wind and she chased that scent up the volcanoside.

Under bushes, over stones. Wet leaves slapping all around. Vee kept travelling upward and another hint of the scent gusted through the cliffside forest. Definitely a burnt smell. Vee hoped for a stricken tree, as the forest thinned and boulders broke through, as the distant clouds drew closer.

She reached a plateau, and stopped short as her paws sank into sand. Clean, flat-spread sand with not a single sprouting plant in it. Undisturbed stones and cliff maples stood around the perimeter. Vee's ears folded back as she stared at her own pawprints. This was too neatly placed to be natural. She wracked her mind for sources of sand. A miner might throw such a quantity of sand out of their mine tunnel—but no such openings showed in the nearby rock. The sand was speckled with pinholes from the rain: any footprints had been long since washed away.

Vee was crossing the sand field, intent on the trees and checking them for lightning strikes, when a powerful scent seized her. The burnt smell was coming from under her feet—like a lightning bolt had been stripped of its ozone aura, and that aura was then buried. Vee found a few sticks and turned the earth away—and under clumps of fused sand was something shiny, something pungent with the electric element. It was a lump of natural glass.

This was what Vee had been searching for. This, she knew as she flipped the glass onto cool sand and waited for its heat to disperse, was Ambri's jewel.

Maybe Welsken was thinking vaguely of the Garden stone with lightning carved painstakingly into it. Maybe he wasn't thinking, but merely channeling an idea that wanted to be drawn. Either way, Welsken was right, he was *right* and it made the electricity in Vee's chest sing with joy.

Once the glass cooled, Vee sat on her haunches and held it, staring at the iridescent yellow depths that warped the shape of her own pink hands. Then she wrapped it deep into her scarf, and ran down-mountain.

* * *

When Vee arrived at his door, Welsken was just beginning to draw by the light of a beeswax candle. Sketch lines spread across his parchment; charcoal dusted his fingers as grey as lichen.

"I think I ought to draw Verdana meeting Fyrian," he said. "This arch is Verdana, and the swooping shape is Fyrian, like he's greeting her with open wings. She's bringing tree wood for his flames to consume—from the legend of the first hearth fire, you recall?"

Vee remembered that. It was a story about fire being a friend, if a ravenous one. Mama told her the legend beside a temporary hearth scratched into the forest floor, her voice a harmony with the snapping of roasting acorns.

"That's a good legend. Um, maybe you should draw Ambri today, though."

Welsken stared at her, shrewd eyes taking in her posture. "What do you mean?"

Vee didn't answer. She only untied her scarf, held up the lightning glass and murmured grinning, "I found it."

"Great green," Welsken breathed. "This is… glass?"

"Made by Ambri, up at the top of Fyrian's volcano."

In reverent fingers, Welsken accepted the glass and turned it, his brows drawing up toward his peaked hairline. The lightning glass grabbed candlelight, the inner surfaces shining like it was really a quartz stone charged with someone's magic.

"Ambri is an artist," Welsken decided. A pause hung pregnant while he stared at the glinting contours. "Well, friend, you were right. Let me never question your faith again."

Vee retied her scarf around her neck, slowly, with fingers that felt thick as clay. "I didn't mean to prove you wrong. I just… knew there was something out there."

"Do you feel like this glass was meant for you?"

She stopped, her ears working. She never had liked trying to decide the greater meaning of things. Vivia Ava, call her Vee, was just one grain of sand in the whole wide land.

That thought yanked the sand plateau back into Vee's mind. In her eight years of foraging, Vee had never seen a neat field of soil that hadn't been laid for a reason—by another person.

"I," she ventured, "don't know if the glass was for me. I can't know what others intended. Especially not Ambri, if she had a particular wish for that one lightning strike."

Welsken waved a dismissive hand. "Put aside intent for a moment. Do you feel like this," and he held up the glass to glow in the firelight, "is in any way *yours?*"

"Oh, no, not at all. I don't feel like that except when I've foraged my own lunch."

Welsken hummed gruff, and set the lightning glass down. He scratched out a few more inkstrokes—sweeping strokes, maybe Fyrian's wings—before he spoke again. "So you could sell it to someone. Get a few copper pieces from Syril next time he comes trading. Or you could go seeking for yourself. Find who it belongs to."

"Yeah," Vee decided, hearing her own words and knowing them to be right. "I'll find them. This jewel's owner."

"That's the spirit." Wearing a wry smile, Welsken returned to his worktable. He had gods to honor.

* * *

Sowing season came. The scent of plantcasting rolled in from the fields, vividly green, and neighbors' pigeon coops grew louder with the added peeping of chicks. It was a good time for barter, and whenever Vee wasn't foraging she went to the market street and spread her scarf on the ground as a sales blanket. Her forest findings sold quickly; she kept the lightning glass hidden under the scarf's corner, so that no one would ask for it.

And she visited the sand plateau nearly every day, sniffing, searching. Rain came and went, and tufts of grass pushed up through the brown plainness.

Finally, after another thunderstorm, a clue showed itself: new scrapes in the rain-dappled sand, too broad to be made by a bird or a mouse. Burnt ozone lingered in the sand but the scent of the digger was there, too: feathers, lizard skin, and a hint of leather. It was a korvi person.

Vee had guessed that already, since the sand plateau was so high up and removed from any roadways. The other visitor probably had wings. But now Vee knew for sure and she inhaled deep, trying to learn more.

They smelled female. They couldn't have left more than a few hours ago. The sand didn't hold more secrets than that.

Well, Vee supposed, now she had a few truths to run with. She just needed to keep searching.

* * *

Korvi visitors were a common sight in Greenway. Messengers landed and hurried straight to the mage's home; merchants grinned with all their fangs while describing their wares; bards stood within gathered crowds, spinning tales and flaring their wings dramatic.

Vee considered all the scents around her, each day in the market street. The sandbringer korvi wasn't someone familiar-smelling—or maybe she was, Vee's doubts murmured. The scent on the sand plateau was always faded, stripped down to nothing by the high winds. What if the person Vee was looking for was actually a neighbor, someone who walked Greenway's street every day, and Vee simply couldn't tell?

Doubt wouldn't help. Hope might. Vee checked daily with the handful of neighbors who hosted travelers overnight; she met new faces but didn't find who she was looking for. She even tried checking with the mage, since the casting-gifted leader of Greenway was someone strangers came to see. The mage let Vee sniff a circle around her hearth fire, wearing a pleasant smile plastered over her bafflement. She said she would keep alert for that certain korvi—but the mage was an aemet, sense-gifted and smell-blind. She couldn't possibly detect what Vee was searching for.

Days became eightdays. Vee ate succulent, fresh-roasted corn again. And at his worktable, Welsken brought a lavish-finned Okeos to life, drawing the water god with a jewel between his wolfish jaws. That gem also wasn't meant to be anything, Welsken said, but there was a prankster's spark in his eye.

Welsken seemed happy and that was a blessing, but Vee wasn't finished: she had to know who the lightning glass belonged to because it *meant* something, it had to. She might actually need to travel the land, despite the lightning glass arriving so close to home.

On a warm morning, mid-growing season, Vee followed her circuit path along the main street. Scents billowed and faded; neighbor folk of all kinds bade her hello.

In the distant street, where Vee's vision showed her only misty blurs, she saw the spread wings of a korvi descending to land—someone scarlet, flashing with heaped jewelry. Syril of Reyardine. Maybe he knew a cultivator of lightning glass, Vee hoped as she ran toward him.

She was so focused on navigating the crowd, she belatedly caught a familiar scent. Something burnt. Clean like ozone. Someone was carrying more lightning glass.

Vee skidded and stood two-legged, sniffing in all the air her body could hold. Behind her. She bolted around aemets' feet, turned a corner, sniffed again and found the scent closer. A family of barrel-maker aemets walked past around—and beyond their antennae was one set of curved korvi horns, vanishing again.

Vee chased her. The korvi came into view, her whip tail and bead-trimmed pant legs; she was walking leisurely but on such towering legs.

"Excuse me!" Vee cried, "Korvi friend!"

The korvi stopped short. She was average size for her kind, well-muscled in her arms and shoulders, with feathers richly orange like daylily petals. Her eyes were mismatched, one pale grey and the other honey brown. Both of those eyes took Vee in, the korvi's brows lifting.

"Yes?" she asked mild.

"Oh, pardon my yelling. It's just that you have a scent I'm looking for. Um." Vee hopped closer. "My name's Vivia Ava, call me Vee."

After a baffled few heartbeats, the korvi obliged. She knelt down as near to Vee's height as she could manage, folding her two bird-like legs underneath her, and she held out one long-fingered hand, palm up. "I'm Ghilaine of Oriel. What scent would that be...?"

"Sand. And lightning." Vee took the chance to sniff Ghilaine's palm—not because this new kinship stirred any uneasiness in her, but because the telltale scent was clinging to Ghilaine's dragon skin, that clean earth smell with a sharpness like the sky. "Ah, I thought so. Have you been digging in storm-struck sand?"

"I— Yes?"

"At the middle-top of the Volcano's south slope?"

"Somewhere near there, yes."

"Did you put sand up there?"

Ghilaine's odd eyes were wide, like she was suddenly lost. "Yes. Friend, how do you know that?"

Vee released Ghilaine's hand and searched for words. She couldn't find any good ones—just long-knotted stories of gods and fates, practically nonsense in this moment—and she untied her scarf instead. "Ah, well. I think this may belong to you."

And she held up the lightning glass to dazzle in the sunlight. In an instant, understanding washed over Ghilaine, a smile drawing along her snout as she took the delicate omen between her fingers.

"Gods," Ghilaine said, "I hope so."

The two of them went to the town square. Vee bought them drinks from the apple cider vendor and, sitting by the silver chromepiece, they began to talk.

"Glassmaking isn't in my blood or any such thing," Ghilaine said. "I'm a stone block carver, from a long line of jack-of-all-trades. But lightning does what it wishes anypace, so I just thought I'd help some natural glass along on its way. It always seems that lightning storms strike that south-side plateau. A few buckets of clean sand was all it needed."

"A few buckets? There's a lakeshore up there! Only without the lake!"

Ghilaine laughed, sudden as a breeze. "Well, I didn't count how many trips I flew. I only wanted there to be enough sand for a good chance at glass."

Here was the answer Vee had been hunting. Here it was before her, a morsel for the savoring. "Why do you want glass, though?"

"Ah, hmm." Ghilaine's feathers shushed against each other as she resettled her wings; her sharp canines worried the side of her lip. "I've been having dreams… Where I'm flying and storm clouds gather around me so I can hardly move. Or where I'm digging and finding chunks of electricstone, only they don't hurt when I touch them. Strange things like that. Electricasting dreams."

Vee didn't know how to feel—but her ears did, lifting high. "Are you an electricaster?"

"No, not at all! I only have the fire I was born with." She shrugged, feathers ruffling. "I was planning on asking the mage back home for casting lessons. But I thought, on the off chance that a good storm strikes us tomorrow…"

Another person with a bizarre pull inside them, a wordless wish for something they didn't understand. Maybe there was a reason so many legend-folk went on grand quests.

"Huh," was all Vee said. "You should come see the Garden. There are some etching of great Ambri, an old one made generations ago. And if you'd like to hear the legend of the first lightning-stricken tree, the garden-keeper would be happy to tell you."

"I'd like that! I've never seen one of those old scratchworks that had a body there to explain it."

"Mm, they're not the same when they're silent."

"That's what I figured."

Realization stirred in Vee, that wriggling sureness that a discovery approached. She stared up at Ghilaine. "What you figured…?"

"When I was putting the sand down. There was some sort of chisel marking in the rock. It didn't look like a miner's claim or anysuch like that, so I thought I'd bury it for the time being and figure out later what it meant."

Later, to a korvi, might mean decades. But here Ghilaine was, giving Vee more possibilities.

Welsken had set out searching for chisel markings, once upon years past.

"Um, could you draw it?" Vee asked with excitement ballooning inside her. "The part of the carving you could see, anypace."

Ghilaine blinked her mismatched eyes. "Ah, I'm not sure I remember it," she said, but she touched an ivory claw to the street dirt and she tried. Lines scraped into being. Ghilaine mumbled doubts to herself and kept drawing, and soon Vee understood the lines as a head. A head with feathers and long, pointed ferrin ears.

"Ambri! I...that's Ambri!"

"Maybe," Ghilaine agreed brightly. "And there was another part, a stone's throw away." She added more scratches, this time rounded nubs like the tips of tail feathers.

Vee's excitement was too big to hold; she clasped her hands to her mouth and resisted the urge to bite them. "Ghilaine? Could we go look at the carving? I'm sorry, I'm asking heavy favors of you right after we met, it's just that I know someone who would be so, *so* happy if the carving is what I think it is—please, can we go?"

With a puff of a laugh, Ghilaine offered her arms to climb into. "You bought me a drink. Let's call it a trade."

The sand was piled deep, but it gave readily enough for Vee to dig with her paws. Ghilaine helped, and soon a hole opened up to reveal the carved Volcano face. It was definitely Ambri, swooping over a laughing Fyrian, each of them holding an opposite end of the same looping string.

"See, I don't remember any legend like that," Ghilaine commented. "Do you?"

"No. But my friend and his daughter might know. Can— Can you remove this carving? Dig it out...?"

Mouth writhing around her snout, Ghilaine folded her arms pensive. "I'd bet that I can. This is basalt, it'll cut into good blocks. It'd be hard to move the piece without help, but I know a fellow who might take a bit of grunt work. You're a forager, Vee?"

"I am! Tell me what forest goods you'd like, and I'll find them."

Ghilaine's mouth settled into a long smile. "Then I'm sure we can arrange something."

* * *

Ghilaine and her hired fellow—Peregrine, an old, mine-scarred korvi who looked wise enough to manage anything—began work three days later. And it took the two of them an entire fourday to cut the carving free of the volcanoside and wrestle it down the Volcano's slope. Vee rode back to

Greenway with them, bouncing along in a borrowed horse cart; the entire way, she stared at the dusty relic that had been hiding right below her feet.

Welsken's brow bunched like cloth when Vee told him he had a delivery, and he needed to come outside and see it. He hoped it wasn't going to be a fuss, he said. But when he saw korvi driving the creaking cart and its precious burden, Welsken ran from his home and laid shaking fingers on the stone.

"That's Azalea's hand, I'd know it anywhere! She always gave Ambri these rounded tail feathers like a magpie! This is— Bless you, Vee. And Ghilaine, Peregrine—all of you, I just," and his voice cracked as he confessed, "I never thought I'd live to see a new addition to my Garden. Gods *bless* you."

This was a good find, Vee thought. She had found a coincidence that wouldn't have happened if Vee hadn't been searching, if she hadn't held questions in her heart and gone out rummaging through everything of gods' design.

There had to be more forgotten carvings, secreted away in the wide, green land. There had to be more jewels and more names worth knowing. With a joylight kindling in her heart, Vee knew that she would never run out of treasures to search for.

"Origins" is another story set in an entirely new world with entirely new animal gods. Meet Raarbaash, the Great Chimera, who taught humans to create Pegasi and Capricorn; Gryphons and Simurghs; Cockatrice and Bat-Drakes; and a hundred more. Meet Tira-Khessst, the Many-Headed, the Dragon of the Abyss. Meet the Beast-Folk of Amalcia, a fusion of man and wolf. Meet Wolluh-Gurath, the mighty Wolf-God, the Lord of the Wild. Meet Xolhut, the Earth-Shaker, the Emperor of the North, Lord of Mammoths. Meet Rutara, the Horned God, Master of Animals, who has the body of a man and the head of a great stag.

Meet these and others; the deities and progenitors who might have been.

Origins

by Michael D. Winkle

AANUU, the World

First came AANUU, the Material World, the Universe, and from time immemorial the Ancient Ones of Aanuu believed that to be all of existence.

The Ancient Ones dwelt in all lands of Aanuu and ruled the land and the sea and the sky. Their towers of crystal and silver and orichalc rose like mountains above the plains. Their proud ships visited all countries, and even the Moon and the Stars. The Ancient Ones called lightning from the Heavens and fire from the Sun, but even their powers came to naught in the time of the First Catastrophe.

* * *

DURUWOM-AZ, the Cosmic Tree

One spring morn, as the Ancient Ones sculpted islands and valleys and clouds, Aanuu shook to its very foundations, although the Ancients' sages and instruments predicted no earthquake or burning volcano. Thunder deafened the people, though rain fell not. Forestfuls of animals fled danger that no human could see.

The Ancient Folk watched in horror as roots, as of a vast and speedily-growing Tree, burst from the northernmost point of Aanuu. The roots cracked continents, dammed rivers, and wrinkled up sea-reefs. The First Folk abandoned their cities and palaces as mighty branches split the firmament and replaced gray clouds with green leaves. They prostrated themselves as a gnarled Trunk swelled between the Roots and the Leaves, shifting mountain ranges and draining ocean beds, for they beheld DURUWOM-AZ, the Cosmic Tree, which had sprouted into Aanuu from OUTSIDE. And in this harsh manner the Ancients learned that there existed realms Outside, beyond the World.

So great was the power of Duruwom-Az, the towers and temples of the Old Race fell. The mighty ones of Aanuu stood humbled, bereft of their magicks and riches and knowledge, and they could only begin again, as savages. Yet, though the bursting of the Cosmic Tree into the Universe bought devastation to Aanuu, it betokened also a new beginning; and so the First Catastrophe was named the GERMINATION.

* * *

THE HYPERBOREANS

The roots of Duruwom-Az dug down to the nethermost vaults of Aanuu and passed beyond the Veil into that which lies Outside. And no man could say what lands or beasts or peoples lay Outside, or say how Duruwom-Az pierced the Veil. But after the Germination, when countries vanished and mountains bled, a new nation appeared in the northernmost lands. It was rumored that the New Race passed from land to land and from world to world along the roots and limbs of Duruwom-Az, as moisture in the soil is conveyed to the topmost leaves of a mortal tree. The new people knew Duruwom-Az as the Opener of the Way, the Keeper of the Gates, the Bridge Between Worlds, and theirs was the secret of coiling the Tree's roots into Gates, through which they could traffic with the realms Outside.

And as the new race entered Aanuu through a Gate at the northern axis, arriving as it were from beyond even the Pole, they were named HYPERBOREANS, "from beyond the north wind."

* * *

RAARBAASH, the Great Chimera

Before the First Catastrophe, each living creature bore a single form, that with which it was birthed or hatched. There were Aurochs and Goats, Horses and Deer; there were Lions and Wolves, Bears and Pards; there were Serpents and Lizards and Dragons; there were Ravens and Eagles and Storks.

The Beasts and Birds and Reptiles sprang from sires and dams like unto themselves, and the progeny thereof were also like unto themselves.

Then came the Germination, and forests burned, and cities fell, and the great ice melted. Floods washed across the land, and the hoofed and pawed and scaled creatures, and even the feathered avians, were smitten like midges and washed into the Great Sea Ocean, which is the place of Chaos.

And down into the Abyss drifted the bodies of the beasts of Aanuu, like meat and lentils in a stew.

But Chaos cannot lie still, and the dead beasts were stirred about, and broken up, and their pieces mingled, as flour and salt and eggs mingle in the baker's bowls.

And the pieces fused together in the Abyss and grew large, as dough rises in the oven, and they formed Order in the womb of Chaos. And from the depths of the ocean there sprang a new Being, born of no single sire or dam, a beast pawed and hoofed and scaled and winged in one: and this was RAARBAASH, the Great Chimera.

Raarbaash passed over the lands, and over the seas, and over the mountains, but never did She find another like unto Herself. And saddened was the Great Chimera.

She spotted beasts that had survived the Cataclysm, and in one She saw an aspect of Herself, and in another, a different aspect; but there existed no single creature like unto Raarbaash.

She spied humans who had survived the Germination, and She set Herself down amongst them; and they fled from Her, or threw themselves flat as if dead, or knelt to worship.

To these last Raarbaash spoke: Go hence, when the Moon is right, and create Beings like unto Ourself, partly of one creature, and partly of another, fused into a Whole, so that We may not be unique amongst living Beings.

And Raarbaash gave the humans the Ritual of Fusion, the Rite of the Chimera, and they became the priests of Raarbaash, and they ordered temples and altars built in Her name.

They studied in their temples, and they brought beasts and birds of various natures to their altars when the Moon was right, and with keen blades the beasts and birds were slain.

And to watchers outside the priesthood it seemed that the altar was a place of sacrifice, and that blood must be spilled to satisfy the Gods; but in the beginning this was not so.

The priests of the Great Chimera took the limbs and vitals and brains of one creature and combined them with another, fusing the disparate pieces with the Ritual. And from the slain beasts there rose one living being, combining the features of both. Thus were new beings brought into the world: Pegasi and Capricorn; Gryphons and Simurghs; Cockatrice and Bat-Drakes; and a hundred more.

* * *

TIRA-K'HESSST, the Dragon of the Abyss

Before the Germination, before the First Folk, the Scaled Ones ruled the earth and sea and sky. And of all Scaled Ones, the mightiest and most magical was TIRA-K'HESSST, the Many-Headed, the Dragon of the Abyss.

The Scaled Ones stomped across the world and slew one another and paid homage to Tira-K'hessst, and they thought in ponderous arrogance that it would always be so. But the sea turned to fire and scoured Aanuu, then the sky turned to fog and froze it, and the Scaled Ones dropped like very flies.

Tira-K'hessst heard the death-cries of Her children, and She knew they would rule Aanuu no more. Thus She sank into slumber in the vasty Deep, and for Aeons She slept.

Then came the First Catastrophe, the Germination, which awakened Tira-K'hessst as the ancient cataclysm marked Her entry into sleep. She watched the dead beasts of the surface world drift down into the Abyss like soft snow into a valley, and She watched the Chaos of the Abyss give rise to Raarbaash, the Great Chimera.

But the newborn Chimera was a weak and floundering thing, which could survive neither the crushing pile of beast corpses nor the cold waters of the Abyss.

And Tira-K'hessst, bereft of Her scaled folk, took pity on the struggling Chimera, and imbued Her with the Power of the Abyss.

And Raarbaash grew strong and resistant to hurt; and Her skin became as bronze, and Her claws as iron.

And Her wings spread as the butterfly's upon emergence from the chrysalis, and solidified like brass; and She flew up from the Abyss into the heavens.

And Tira-K'hessst remained alert, and Her many eyes and ears strained, so that She could see and hear the activities of the new world above, though She stirred not from the Great Abyss.

* * *

ATARAN

Those of Aanuu who still held the knowledge and machines of the Ancient Ones thought to flee the world to some new realm Outside, as the Hyperboreans had invaded it. They brought to bear their magicks and devices and alchemies, and anon they created Gates of their own.

Across the wide continent of Sakria did the Ancients open their Gates, and within the Kronian Sea; deep within caves and high on mountaintops did they open them. The First Men looked over the world of their birth, once a kingdom of peace and forests and magnificent cities, but now a pit of fire and mud and God-Things of frightful power. And they passed through their Gates to the realms Outside.

Many of the Ancient Race perished amidst forces never before known to mortals; others passed beyond these perils to fates unknown. A contingent of thousands, however, appeared on a wide island amid salt waters; a precious gem, as it were, in the empty sea. Here they built their cities anew, and they called their new kingdom ATARAN, "The Unyielding Jewel."

* * *

THE RENDING OF THE VEILS

Upon Aanuu, however, the Gates of the Ancient Ones twisted and tore reality, as holes and fissures weaken a wall of stone and mortar; and anon the Veils separating Aanuu from the Outside collapsed. Once more ice sheets melted and mountains fell; once more deserts became oceans and rivers shifted from their beds. And into Aanuu entered new invaders from Outside: humans, and creatures like humans, and creatures utterly different: the Hurrgo, the Arimaspi, and the Enochai; the Hulldre, the Oni, and the Argippae; and others besides. And this second catastrophe was called THE RENDING OF THE VEILS.

* * *

THE HURRGO AND THE WAR-BEASTS

In the first years after the Hyperboreans passed through Duruwom-Az into Aanuu, there were many wars, with other bands of humans, with the One-Eyes, with the Hurrgo, and with other hostile races. But the Hyperboreans knew little of warfare.

In the months-long Darkness of the eighty-ninth year since the Germination, a band of Hurrgo emerged from their tunnels and harried the folk of Amalcia by the Northern Ocean. They bore wicked spears and swords and arrows, and before them ran their War-Beasts: wolves and bears and huge felines.

The folk of Amalcia fought as best they could, wizards and priests, warriors and peasants; but the Hurrgo slaughtered them and burned their villages.

On the plain of Laddith did the Hyperboreans meet the Hurrgo and their War-Beasts; but so superior in the art of battle were the Hurrgo, that they lost only a few wolfen, while the rocky earth grew crimson beneath the humans' corpses.

Abaris, the most learned wizard of Amalcia and also a leader of warriors, looked over the field of slaughter, and he cursed the Hurrgo and the Catastrophes and the lands of Aanuu, where all creatures reviled the presence of the Hyperboreans.

Abaris heard a whine, and also a moan, and he found a warrior of his acquaintance, Garrm, and also one of the wolves of the Hurrgo. Both lay near death, Garrm's body and limbs broken, and the wolf's intestines opened and its throat gashed by a sword.

Abaris stood grimly, and thought he, If only our fighters had the claws and teeth of the War-Beasts, and the animals' knowledge of fighting, and also their memories of the Hurrgo's tunnel-kingdom, but were in mind and temperament still men, yet could Amalcia survive.

And Abaris thought, Such a thing *is* possible, but not even the priests of the Thrice-Great One have ever combined man and animal in their mortal chimerae; it is a thing forbidden. And whether this dying soldier would be grateful for a life extended in so strange a fashion, I cannot say.

But the fate of the Northern Folk lay in the balance, so it was that Abaris retrieved the Scroll of Joining from the Temple of the Chimera and returned to the battlefield where lay Garrm and the wolf.

The Wizard Abaris looked over the fallen warrior, and marked that his legs hung by mere strips, and that his flesh was punctured as a wineskin by a blade, and that his blood flowed as wine from a skin. So Abaris fastened the wolf's pelt about the torn and bloodied corpse, and over the shattered head he affixed the brute's gaping jaws; then fitted he the fore-feet to the crushed hands and set the hind feet where once were legs.

And Abaris the Hyperborean spoke the Words of Fusing, and called he upon Tira-K'hessst, the Dragon of the Abyss, and upon Raarbaash, the Great Chimera, and Behold! From the remnants of two dead Beings there rose One, alive and whole; one both beast and man, yet neither.

And the wolf that was also Garrm rose, and knew what the War-Beast had known; and Abaris bespoke him, and the Man-Wolf nodded, that the Ritual was for the best.

Again and again during the Dark Time Abaris performed the Ritual, and soon there existed creatures with the seeming of beasts and possessed of their feral knowledge, yet controlled by the reason of humans.

And the Beast-Folk entered the tunnels of the Hurrgo, as stoats enter the rabbits' den, and the Hurrgo now fought an enemy that knew war, and knew the ways of the Hurrgo, and knew the maze of the underworld. And thus the Hyperboreans invaded the lands of the Hurrgo, and finally the Enemy Beneath fled Amalcia.

* * *

THE WERE-FIRE AND THE SKIN-BELTS

In the days and seasons following the great victory, the Beast-Folk found the forests and mountains more attractive than the lands of men, and one by one they forgot their human lives and drifted into the wilds.

Abaris thought to reward Garrm and the warriors who bore now the aspects of wolves and bears and pards and lions; thus took he the skins of dead men, and of War-Beasts, and sliced them into strips; and he attached buckles of brass and bone to make of the strips belts; and he sewed them so that one surface was smooth human skin, and the other, furred animal's pelt.

The wizard performed the Invocation of the Moon, infusing the belts with his magicks, and one he wrapped around the waist of the wolf-Garrm, who had remained faithfully in his service, and Lo! The wolf's fur and tail and muzzle receded, and the warrior Garrm stood before Abaris, naked save for his belt.

In man's form again, Garrm spoke of the magicks of certain herbs, and of the scents that human animals enjoyed above all others, and of the voices of the Moon and the Sun and the Spirits of the Wood, which did tug upon them like ropes.

Thus Abaris gathered together wolf's hair and human hair, and rye bread, parsley, and monk's hood. And he traveled far into the wilderness, and built himself a great fire, and cast he the herbs and hair therein. Then appeared in his mind a chant to speak:

"Hunter of the Night, hear me! Walker in the Light, hear me!
I summon thee, Beast-in-Man and Man-in-Beast.
By the Sun in the West and the Moon in the East,
By the Lord of the Wood, the Lady of the Moon,
Come to me, Dual One, soon, soon, soon!"

And before the night ended, the human-animals who inhabited the forest came before him. Abaris told the Beast-Folk of his skin-belts, the which they accepted, and when they wore the human skin outwards, they walked as men, and when they wore the fur outwards, they walked as animals. And the warriors returned to their wives and children, but they did not renounce their beast-sides, and they vowed to become wolves and bears and pards and lions to defend Amalcia from her enemies.

* * *

WOLLUH-GURATH, the Great Wolf

Beyond Noori, a kingdom of the Northern Folk, Ullugwer, the Howling Wilderness, stretched endlessly to the north and west.

Around Koralek, where ruled Angyarl, the king of Noori, the folk set to pasture many sheep and kine, and also goats and horses, which provided the great city with wool and milk, meat and draught-beasts.

In the pastures dwelt shepherds, and often from the Howling Wilderness there echoed the cries of wolves. And when the winters were harsh in Noori, which was more often the case than not, the wolfen packs emerged to take sheep or kine or even horses, for there was not enough game in the forest to feed them.

The shepherds feared for their flocks and for their very lives, and the people feared for their meat and wool, and the king feared for his prosperity.

The king looked to the west and north, where stretched Ullugwer. At the edge of the woodland, where the pastures ended, he marked a crater, like the mouth of a sleeping volcano.

So Angyarl, King of Noori, proclaimed: Let all the hunters and soldiers and trackers of my land slay wolves; and let them hurl the carcasses into the Pit at the edge of Ullugwer; and for each dead beast a man brings, he shall be paid ten dekam.

Thus the hunters and soldiers and trackers entered the Howling Wilderness. They spread poisons and set traps and dug pits for the gray hunters, and they dug into lairs and stole cubs, and they took up their bows and spears against the packs.

And they slew a thousand wolves, and were paid, and another thousand, and the bodies they tossed into the crater north of Koralek, which was called the Wolf-Pit. And they slew ten thousand wolves and were paid, and another ten thousand, and those corpses, too, they cast into the Pit, and the rotting flesh of the gray beasts befouled the air, and their lean skulls and greasy bones piled high in charnel pyramids.

There were men who made a living at no more than slaying wolves. Tame wolves were stolen from menageries, and from the Forest Folk who loved all beasts, and from the Groves of the Earth Mother, where no animal may be harmed; and these were slain, and paraded before the king. And dogs that looked like wolves were slain, and paraded before the king. And for each death Angyarl paid ten dekam, and it was a price he happily parted with, for Angyarl wanted no gray hunters near the herds of Noori.

And the piles of bloodied fur and bared fangs in the Pit became rotting hills, and the rotting hills became pestilent mountains, until it seemed as though all the wolves in all the world lay dead in the Wolf-Pit of Koralek.

* * *

There entered into Noori Garrm, warrior and wolf, who had wandered south across the Rhipaean Mountains from Hyperborea.

Garrm heard of the slaughter of the wolves, and looked upon the Pit of putrid death, and he marched to the market square in the center of the city.

And there Garrm spoke: The Wolves have not attacked thy lambs and calves, save in times most dire; their prey is the deer and rabbit and coney. Nor do the wolves hold danger for the Noori themselves, even those who dwell outside the high walls of Koralek; for the Gray Hunters know better than to approach humans.

Garrm explained that the herds of the antlered beasts needed wolves to harry them, lest they grow slow and lazy. He spoke of the kinship between hunters two-legged and four-legged, and of how the packs of the wolves were like the communities of men, and of sigils and herbs that would make hoofed beasts unpalatable to wolves, so that they would avoid the herds of humans.

But the people of Noori laughed, for they grew rich on the wolf-bounty, and they carried Garrm beyond the outer walls of the city and there dumped him like so much offal.

The Moon rose with a full and angry face as Garrm returned to the Wolf-Pit. He found in the crater new-slain packs, and also a dozen mewling survivors, torn and bleeding from the spears and arrows of the Noori.

Garrm felt pity for the gray beasts. Against better judgment, he drew together the injured wolves, and he cut from their dead fellows whole legs, where the living had lost legs, and eyes, where the survivors had lost eyes, and tongues, where the crippled beasts had lost tongues. And he set legs, and tails, and eyes, and tongues, near the torn and bloodied wolves. And he drew forth his yellowing scrolls, and he called upon Raarbaash, the Great Chimera, and performed the Ritual of Fusion.

An ominous breeze stirred the trees of Ullugwer, and the floor of the Wolf-Pit shuddered as though flinching from the stinking carcasses. The walls of the Pit cracked like children's castles of sand. Darkness drew over the Moon, and a howl so deep and vast as to shake the stars in their courses echoed over the land of Noori.

The dead cubs and grizzled oldsters, the fallen leaders and crippled pacers, the torn limbs and rotting hides, spun skyward in a mighty whirlwind. Trees threw up their roots, and boulders shattered into pebbles, and Garrm himself flew skyward.

And the thousands upon thousands of wolves became One, a Whole greater than the sum of its parts: they became WOLLUH-GURATH, the Wolf-God, the Lord of the Wild.

The people of Koralek entered the dark streets, wondering at the noises from the Wolf-Pit. Then the sentries at the walls cried out in amazement; for there approached from the north a humped mass like a cloudbank, from which lightning flashed and thunder boomed.

But the lightning was the glare of eyes, and the flames of hot breath; and the thunder was a deep growl, and the thud of cottage-sized paws upon the earth; and the cloud was no storm, but a hunched Wolf vaster than a hundred Mammoths.

The sentries blew their horns and rang their bells, then stumbled down the steps or leapt from the battlements. The Great Wolf loped nearer, shaking the ground with each step. The archers in the towers loosed their shafts at the Wolf, but they would have more easily halted an storm-wave, or a volcano's fiery flow.

Wolluh-Gurath paused before the walls of Koralek, muzzle low and nostrils flared in the manner of a wolf. Then the God-Beast raised His head and howled. And the walls of the city crumbled like strawless brick, and the Great Wolf stepped unchallenged into the streets.

The folk of Koralek fled helter-skelter. Wolluh-Gurath sprang like a fox upon mice, and smashed some flat on the earth. He snapped up others as a dog will catch tossed scraps, and yet others wilted and died beneath His burning gaze.

The people hid within their inns and hovels and shoppes, thinking the God-Wolf would leave if He spotted no prey; but Wolluh-Gurath knew them in their concealment. The Lord of the Wild dug into towers of stone and houses of wood like a badger into loam, and He gulped down the tiny folk within. He howled like the North Wind, and the roofs were ripped from temples, and the walls of lowly taverns were stove in. He glared with eyes of flame, and trees shivered into splinters, and the cobbles of the streets smoked and shattered. And the Beast devoured the hunters and woodsrunners who had slain the myriad wolves—the wolves that *were* Wolluh-Gurath, in truth.

Angyarl emerged from his palace and watched the Great Wolf lay waste to his city. He commanded his guards and soldiers to attack the Lord of the Wild. Spears and arrows rained upon the shaggy hide of the Great Wolf, but they did no more harm than the wisps of a thistledown. Wolluh-Gurath raised His muzzle to the heavens, and commanded the skies to open, and rain and hail and thunderbolts fell upon the archers and spearsmen.

And siege weapons were brought forth, and filled with stones and burning pith. And these missiles hailed upon Wolluh-Gurath like so many cockleburrs.

The Wolf howled in anger, and now poisonous vipers and vast spiders and giant wasps descended upon the siege-men.

And Angyarl grew sore afraid; he commanded the sages to draw forth their scrolls, and the priests to pray for miracles, and the magicians to conjure demons.

But Wolluh-Gurath's gaze fell upon the College of Sages, and a thousand fleas and ticks and crawling mites, like unto those that infest the Gray Hunters, struck every scholar, and they fell to screaming and scratching, their runes and tomes forgotten.

And Wolluh-Gurath looked upon the Temple of Twelve, and the priests felt their throats constrict and their faces grow into muzzles; and they could only howl and yip as they tried to call upon their gods.

And Wolluh-Gurath padded past the Guild Tower of the Wizards; and the mages' arms and hands became the legs and paws of wolves, and they could not hold their magic chalks, nor wield their wands, nor make the divers signals needed for their sorceries.

And Angyarl fled to the deepest recess of his castle, but Wolluh-Gurath tore through granite and marble and basalt as into a vole's nest, and the God-Wolf found the King of Noori cowering at the end of a dark tunnel, as many a cub had been found by human hunters.

And Angyarl threw himself flat before the Lord of Wolves, and there he groveled and begged for mercy. And Wolluh-Gurath bespoke him:

Always have humans mistrusted the Gray Hunters, and always have humans trapped and slain My packs, for their skins and teeth and cubs, or because they imagined them rivals for the game-beasts of the forest.

But *thou*, Angyarl of Noori, hast encouraged a slaughter unlike any My packs have ever faced; thou wouldst happily see the end of every dam and cub and tracker and scout in every land of Aanuu. This I know, for I *am* the multitude thou hadst slain, each whelp and hunter and grizzled elder.

Know this, mortal: The one called Garrm (who has joined the legion within Us) became a wolf to aid Mankind; now Man will aid Our kind in turn. From this night hence, there will be humans chosen to become Gray Hunters, and they will have fur and tails and fangs and claws, and they will hunt and track and eat raw flesh, and they will know the wilderness and the ways of the Wolf. In all climes that know wolfen, let there be human-wolves, and where wolves are little known, let there be human bears, and pards, and lions, and others of the furred and feathered tribes. In this way will a few redress the ill done to millions.

Wolluh-Gurath withdrew His monstrous head, as long as the steam-breath'd Snow-Drake, from the narrow corridor. The God-Wolf padded back as He had come, each footfall like the thud of a hundred drums, and He entered the Howling Wilderness as a normal beast might enter a field of grain. And the winds stilled, and the clouds parted, and the Moon shone down silver bright.

Angyarl dared breathe again, and he marveled that he had not been swallowed whole, or transformed into a beast. But he saw his city and his palace in ruins, and his shops and houses burned, and his army routed.

A thousand of his subjects had been crushed, or burned, or poisoned, or devoured. A thousand more suffered from the wolf-madness, crawling on hands and knees and growling. And yet a thousand more bore the Mark of the Wolf: sporting now a tail, or pointed ears, or a paw for a foot or hand.

The King of Noori could not prevent his people from abandoning Koralek; and soon the lands roundabout looked upon Noori as a country accursed; and trade and barter ground to a halt.

And Angyarl knew, though he lived, and had not been altered in mind or body—his reign would not be a happy one.

And from that night unto this day, there have existed, chosen by chance or design, humans who become beasts: the *Therianthropi*.

* * *

XOLHUT, the Earth-Shaker, the Emperor of the North

Atop Mount Meru, the Diamond Mountain, the Navel of the World, Raarbaash brooded. It seemed to Her that Chaos grew strong in Aanuu. The Great Chimera owed Her very existence to the roiling turbulence of the Abyss, and in the forests of Ullugwer She saw Wolluh-Gurath, the Lord of the Wild, born of the quirks of men and chance.

From her perch on high, the Thrice-Great One espied a troupe of shaggy Mammoths marching in a gray and brown carpet through the snow, their trunks upraised and their voices extolling: "Xolhut! Xolhut!" Whereupon Raarbaash spread Her dragon wings and sprang from Meru and soared down before the Shaggy Ones.

The Mammoths bellowed and dispersed, for even their heavy forms seemed small and ineffectual before the Great Chimera. Thus Raarbaash called out: Flee not, Shaggy Ones! We mean thy herd no ill; We are Raarbaash, the Great Chimera, the All-in-One and One-in-All, and We would have words with thee!

And long-nosed faces peered from behind pine trees, and wide ears opened and shut like doors; and soon a Matriarch of the herd, her tusks yellow and cross-tipped with age, stepped from the forest.

What wouldst Thou of the Children of Xolhut? queried the elder.

And Raarbaash spoke: Thy people the Mammoths are ancient in the land, as is thy Lord, Xolhut, the Earth-Shaker, dwelling in Sakria before the Germination, before Our own existence. We would hear of Xolhut, a Power not born of the Rite of Fusion, a God of the elder times.

And the Matriarch drew near, and she bespoke the Thrice-Great One concerning Xolhut:

Catastrophes beset Sakria before even the Germination. In the ancient times the ice covered the seas and filled the valleys and crushed the forests. The Deer and the Horse and the Aurochs fled south, leaving the lands to the Mammoth.

The Mammoths ruled the country between Pterophoros and the Southern Sea, tall and massive as hillocks, but their domain was vast, and snow blurred the features of the land, so the Shaggy Ones wandered from their herds and lost their ways, and they died far from their mates and foals, without the prayers of passing.

Xolhut, Lord of Mammoths, Emperor of the North, heard the cries of His lost children and emerged from the tundra like a very mole. He discovered a valley ringed by mountains, and therein he pawed the earth with his hoof, and the glaciers split to allow His children entrance. He let his great curved tusks fall away, and these He planted to form an Arch, so that His children would recognize the valley as sacred to Xolhut. Then He raised his serpentine trunk and trumpeted until the moon and the stars wavered like reflections on the water. All the Shaggy Ones who were lost or dying heard the call of Xolhut and made their way across the ice fields to the Ivory Arch.

And Xolhut spoke: Let those who are nigh to leaving this life pass within, and they shall dwell with Me under the earth forever.

Let those who were separated from their herds leave again, with the knowledge they require to return to their mates and foals.

And let it be known to My children everywhere that they may come to this Valley when their final days are upon them, and that here they may rest, free from hunger and fear and the eternal chill, until the time comes for them to join Me under the earth.

And since that time the Mammoths have had foreknowledge of death, and they make their way to the Valley of Xolhut in their final days.

And though their flesh and their fur and their bones crumble away, and their ground-shaking mass fades to naught, they live again in Xolhut's country under the earth.

* * *

So the Matriarch ended her tale, surrounded by her fellows, the which had crept from the pine forests as she spoke. And Raarbaash nodded Her vast leonine head.

Thy Lord, Who appeared into the world without benefit of Our rite, is a great and benevolent spirit, said She. We now will seek Powers who have arisen since Our birth, who arose from the Ritual of Fusion, to judge whether any be so righteous.

And Raarbaash lifted Her pinions, like two wide pavilion tents, but stayed Her departure a moment more. She raised a monstrous paw, so large as a plainsman's yurt, and passed it over the Matriarch.

Great is thy Lord Xolhut, and He will greet thee and keep thee well in His valley, said Raarbaash. But not soon.

And the elder Mammoth's tusks uncrossed, and shone brighter than the snows, and her ragged hair became as well-carded fleece; and her withered legs grew sturdy, and to the eye she appeared of fewer years than her own sons.

* * *

RUTARA, the Horned God, the Master of the Hunt

Raarbaash betook Herself west over the lands of Sakria, overflying wood, lake, river, and prairie. And from the leafy forests of Hylaea rose lamentations as of people in the grip of terror and despair. The Great Chimera swept low, and from the trees onto a clearing burst humans fleeing and stumbling and fleeing again, as from some barbaric horde. Puzzled was the Thrice-Great One, and even nearer She soared. But simultaneously thunder rolled in from the north and east. But was it thunder, or the pounding of hooves? Or the baying of a pack? Or the trumpeting of a forester's horn?

Dark clouds, like a jet of ink in water, drew across the crescent moon. They angled toward the needle-strewn earth in their advance, as though the air could not support their vapors. Within the storm burned orange embers, revealed as sparks appear behind the scaled surface of hearth-logs.

Raarbaash circled, and now the storm cloaked the forest like the dust of charging horsemen. The clouds faded, and in their stead raced two score hunting hounds, some black, some white, their eyes the orange embers of the storm.

Behind the hounds galloped a coal-black stallion, from whose nostrils blew sulfur and from whose hooves flew sparks, though it did not touch foot to earth. Astride the dark steed sat a man in leather, a coiled hunter's horn in his hand and an ebony longbow across his saddle. He glared with eyes of cold white marble, and above, sprouting from jet-black curls, he boasted many-tined antlers, for his was the head of a stag.

Raarbaash set Herself before the demon-horse, and the stag-man drew up short before Her.

The Thrice-Great One spoke: Who art thou, Huntsman, and why dost thou persecute yonder mortals?

And the Huntsman replied Her: I am RUTARA, the Horned God, Master of Animals. Yonder men are trappers and archers of great renown, of such skill that no beast of the earth or bird of the air may elude them. Tedious became their professions, and unchallenging the wilderness, until they said amongst themselves, Let us bring into existence a new order of being, a creature like unto a man, with a man's reasoning and cleverness and dexterity, yet still a prey animal, and it we shall hunt with great clamoring and cheer. And so they stole the Ritual of Fusion from the Temple of the Chimera, and brought down the most powerful and swift of the forest animals, and slew they a captive taken during a tribal raid, and beneath the Moon they performed the Rite.

But the woodsmen wrought too well, and I, the hunted, became Master of the Hunt.

420

And Raarbaash queried no more, but rose again into the star-sprinkled night. And She glanced not behind, for in sooth She was of a mind that the men below had brought this fate upon themselves.

* * *

YAN-TIKUH, the Rat-King, Ruler of the Hidden Places

Far to the east sailed Raarbaash, and in the kingdom of Chaitan She entered vast black grottos beneath the steaming jungles. And bats swirled around her like so many swatches of cloth, and rats spilled into the shadows like a foul liquid draining. And within a dripping cavity She discovered a gray beast so large as the hairy Rhinoceros, with two pairs of gray arms before but one set of legs and one scaly tail behind. Upon its shoulders the head of a whiskered rodent, the size, perhaps, of a wine cask, grew; yet also a rattish head sprouted to the left and to the right.

And Raarbaash spoke: Who art thou, Gray One, and how camest thou to be?

And the Three-Headed One replied Her: Beneath the temple raised in Thy name dwelt the gnawing rats, so despised by Man. The priests above thought to drive them out with smoke and poison and cantrips, but they knew not of Rat-Kings, rodents with tails joined at the tips, who pull this way and that in their movements and finally move not at all. And the priests performed Thy Rite of Fusion, whilst the Rat-Kings squirmed and squeaked below; and the Many became One; We became YAN-TIKUH, Rat-King in sooth, Ruler of the Hidden Places below, above, and between.

And as the priests sanctified the temple above unto the Thrice-Great One, so shall that be, in sooth; We lay claim to Thy title and Thy edifice, and We shall evict Thee from Our kingdom.

And anon the rodents spilled from the shadows and holes in a river of beaded eyes and squared teeth. But Raarbaash deigned not to acknowledge their legions, and stepped from the grottos unconcerned, shaking their bodies as She would droplets from her paws.

* * *

ZHEBUB, Lord of the Flies, Father of Ghouls

So Raarbaash betook Herself south, to the empty desert of Cisthene, and here She overflew a great city, as it were, of sepulchers and tombs, wherein the Ancient Folk once interred their dead. And in this necropolis the Great Chimera espied movement. Down She soared from the dust-filled sky, and

421

beheld She a huge pale form seated upon a granite throne, and She set paws and hooves to the sere earth before it.

The figure on the throne possessed the body of a man, bloated and white and with coarse bristles covered. Upon its shoulders sat the tusked head of a boar, leprous, scabbed and bald in patches. Of eyes there were none; there remained but sockets oozing green corruption. Flies lit and speckled the figure with black, to buzz away and light again elsewhere.

Emaciated beings clambered over the boar-headed one, some like men, some like yeenas, some like swine, all emaciated and pale and unstill as maggots moiling within a corpse. Some knelt at the hooved feet of the pig-demon; others clambered into its monstrous lap or clung to its burly arms. The carrion-crawlers did not so much adore their Lord as bite off gobbets of flesh and lick away ichor; the enthroned one took no notice of their battening. Its scabrous head turned slowly, dislodging one mewling feaster, and the pus-oozing hollows, which could not see, yet focused someways upon Raarbaash.

And Raarbaash bespoke the figure: Who art thou, Charnel One, and how camest thou to be?

And the enthroned one answered Her: I am ZHEBUB, Lord of the Flies, Father of Ghouls, Feaster from the Grave. There came to Mesalam, City of the Dead, a caravan of Hyperboreans, the folk of the north, who thought to create a new race, partly human and partly beast, to serve them as slaves and warriors in this harsh and rainless land. And to this purpose they disinterred the dry corpses of the honored dead. And they performed Thy chimerical Ritual, reckoning not on the curse their desecrations had drawn upon them. And upon their sacrificial slabs bone joined unto bone, until there rose from blood and dust I, Zhebub, the Dead-Yet-Living.

And through Zhebub the forgotten dead enter again into the world and feast upon corrupt flesh and living flesh. For the dead hunger in the tomb and fain wouldst feed upon Me, their Father, and upon Thee, their Mother.

And forthwith the ravening parasites dropped from Zhebub and sprang like locusts upon Raarbaash. And from the black openings of sepulchers tumbled figures like unto skeletons, but little covered with skin and musculature; and from the dry earth reached hands and arms like brittle dead branches.

And the Great Chimera reared high upon her goat's legs and twitched as a horse beset with stinging flies, and to the very Heavens She bellowed, Enough!

And the Thrice-Great One spat fire upon the Dead-Yet-Alive, and upon the sarcophagi of Mesalam, and upon the withered brush of Cisthene, and She rose and winged away over a sea of flame.

* * *

KARUTA, the Lawgiver, Lord of Gryphons

Raarbaash betook Herself to Meru, the Navel of the World, and lit upon the summit, troubled in mind and heart.

When came Duruwom-Az, the lands and the seas exchanged their holdings, and the furred and feathered and scaled were swept into the Abyss, thought the Thrice-Great One. And from this maelstrom We arose, Order from the womb of Chaos, and We marked this a good thing. And mortals knelt to worship Us, and We bestowed upon them Our Power and Our Ritual, that creatures like unto Ourselves might walk the earth, and We marked *this* a good thing.

But some mortals have invoked Our powers and performed Our rites for gain, or mastery, or mere entertainment, and the Chimerae arising therefrom reflect these low desires; do We now regret Our own organization? Do We now regret the new beings wrought in Our honor?

A year and a day sat Raarbaash in contemplation atop the Diamond Mountain; and from Her lofty perch She observed Her priests and their creations, of the which some now were part human.

Handsome are these Chimerae that have been created in Our name, thought the Thrice-Great One, these Gryphons and Minotaurs, these Satyrs and Pegasi, these Lycocephali and Bat-Drakes.

Raarbaash noted that many Chimerae could speak and reason like humans, and they cast their gazes to Heaven, and worshiped the Gods, and thought the Powers to be beings like unto themselves.

And Raarbaash thought: Though born of Chaos, We, the Great Chimera, will work to bring Order. We shall create children of Our own with Our own Rite; and these lesser gods may seek out Chimerae like unto themselves, and the mortal Chimerae will pay homage to them, and it will be like praising Us for Our accomplishments.

Thus Raarbaash reached down from Meru and caught up in Her paws a hundred mighty lions. And She spread Her wings like thickening clouds and netted a thousand soaring eagles. And together did Raarbaash mix the spirits and bodies of the King of Beasts and the Lord of Birds, and to them She added the sharp ears of the Desert Ass, which could catch a whisper half a world away; and from the Many rose One: KARUTA, the Lawgiver, Lord of Gryphons.

And Raarbaash stepped back, and stretched out as does the panther, and did but observe that which transpired, as the craftsman watches his apprentice.

Karuta spread His wings of brass and copper, and stretched His legs, tawny like the savannas of Duat, and flexed His talons, black and solid as ship's anchors. Karuta twitched His sword-sharp ears and blinked bronze eyes like city gongs and clacked His beak, long and pointed like the prow of a warship. And Raarbaash saw that this was good.

Karuta soared westward, to the range of peaks called the Rhipaeans, and landed upon Lattipor, the highest mount beyond Meru. And Karuta spoke: Here will My Folk, the Gryphons, dwell in a vast Eyrie like unto a human city. And on other mountaintops will My Folk found more Eyries, as their numbers and clans grow and prosper.

And from valleys and hilltops, and small caves and single nests, the Gryphons sallied forth unto Lattipor Mountain, and here they found a vast warren of tunnels and grottos, and into these they carried their hoards of gold and jewels, and the scrolls and trappings of humans they found of use, and the materials to make many nests. And Lattipor became the first of the mighty Eyries, and the Gryphons bred and prospered and sent new clans out to found other Eyries.

And upon Meru Raarbaash smiled toothsomely, for Karuta's Folk lived not as beasts or savages, but as wise and civilized beings.

Wethinks the world and all in it require both Order and Chaos to prosper, the Great Chimera spake as to the empty sky. Law without Freedom becomes Tyranny; Freedom without Law becomes Anarchy. Without Order, the mind develops no plan, the body grows weak and clumsy, the heart reaches not beyond itself. Without Chaos, the mind thinks no new thought, the body seeks no new horizon, the heart learns no new truth.

Let Our Power remain in the world, and let Us welcome the Chimerae created in Our name. Yet also let Us create spirits of Order to guide them, that the new will not destroy the old.

Thus will Chaos and Order join, and the two disparate concepts will become as One; which is Our way after all, the way of the Chimera.

—The End and the Beginning—

About the Authors

M. R. Anglin

M.R. Anglin is a YA author who was born in Jamaica in 1980 and moved to the U.S. while still young. Despite her initials, she is in fact, female. She started writing in middle or high school and has not stopped since. All of her books, including those starring humans, have some sort of mythological, alien, or anthro creature featured in them.

She has self-published four books in her ongoing *Silver Foxes* anthro series—*Silver Foxes* (April 2008), *Winds of Change* (June 2009), *Prelude to War* (October 2013), and *Into Expermia* (July 2015); all published by CreateSpace and Kindle; has a traditionally published Middle Grade novel called *Lucas, Guardian of Truth* (Lamp Post, May 2012) available; and has written several other stories that are available to read online.

Samuel Conway

Samuel Conway (1965-current) holds a Ph.D. in chemistry from Dartmouth and spends his days in a laboratory in the Research Triangle area of North Carolina. He is also the chairman of Anthrocon, the world's largest furry convention, held annually in Pittsburgh, Pennsylvania. Some of his duties in that role include serving as an unofficial spokesperson for the "furry" fandom, and he has devoted a good deal of time and energy to dispelling the myths and misconceptions surrounding the world of anthropomorphics.

In what spare time he can find he likes to write short stories, including his 1999 "Tweaked in the Head" which was included in *Flights of Fantasy* (DAW Books, December 1999), an anthology of bird-related science fiction tales assembled by Mercedes Lackey, and two other tales that appeared in Ms. Lackey's *Elemental Magic* (DAW Books, December 2012) and *Elementary* (DAW Books, December 2013).

Alice Dryden

Alice "Huskyteer" Dryden's stories have been published in anthologies including *Inhuman Acts; A Collection of Noir,* edited by Ocean Tigrox (FurPlanet Productions, September 2015), *The Furry Future; 19 Possible Prognostications,* edited by Fred Patten (FurPlanet Productions, January 2015), and several volumes of *Heat* and *ROAR*. Born in Dorset in 1977, she now lives in southeast London near a pizza place called 400 Rabbits, where she first learned of the drunken Aztec rabbit gods. This is the first and only time a pizzeria has provided her with a story idea, but she continues to eat a lot of pizza in the hope that it will happen again.

She can be found at huskyteer.co.uk, or as @Huskyteer on Twitter.

Kyell Gold

Kyell Gold has won twelve Ursa Major awards for his stories and novels. His acclaimed novel *Out of Position* (Sofawolf Press, January 2009) co-won the Rainbow Award for Best Gay Novel of 2009. His novel *Green Fairy* (Sofawolf Press, March 2012) was nominated for inclusion in the ALA's "Over the Rainbow" list for 2012. He helped create RAWR (Regional Anthropomorphic Writers Retreat), the first residential furry writing workshop, and was one of the instructors at its first five-day session in 2016

He was not born in California, but now considers it his home. He loves to travel and dine out with his husband Kit Silver, and can be seen at furry conventions around the world. More information about him and his books is available at http://www.kyellgold.com.

Alan Loewen

Born in late 1954 in Easthampton, New York, Alan Loewen is the product of a long line of German Mennonite farmers on his father's side and a long line of Episcopalian whalers and fishermen on his mother's side. His stories come from a plethora of experience he has gathered over the years in working as a factory worker, inner-city security guard, park ranger, youth worker, radio personality, stage actor, stage and parlor magician, an ordained member of the clergy, computer salesman, counselor for mood disorders, life coach, and a host of other vocations.

A lover of anthropomorphic art, cinema, cats, Neolithic survivals, oriental cuisine, gardening, used bookstores, old houses, and sacred architecture, Loewen presently lives in Gettysburg, Pennsylvania. Married and with three sons, he shares his home with a Sheltie, a sun conure lovingly dubbed "The Death Chicken," and way too many cats. You can read more about Alan on his Amazon author's page.

Mary E. Lowd

Mary E. Lowd writes stories and collects creatures. She's had more than seventy short stories published, and her novels are available from FurPlanet Productions. So far, her novels include *Otters In Space* (CreateSpace, August 2010; 2nd edition FurPlanet Productions, January 2012), *Otters In Space 2: Jupiter, Deadly* (FurPlanet Productions, July 2013), and *In a Dog's World* (FurPlanet Productions, July 2015). Her fiction has won an Ursa Major Award and two Cóyotl Awards. Meanwhile, she's collected a husband, daughter, son, bevy of cats and dogs, and the occasional fish. The stories, creatures, and Mary all live together in a crashed spaceship disguised as a house and hidden in a rose garden in Oregon.

Learn more at www.marylowd.com, or read a great deal of Mary's short fiction online for free at www.deepskyanchor.com.

Watts Martin

A native Texan who really never lived in Texas, Watts Martin grew up around Tampa Bay, Florida, and lived there for the better part of three decades. Despite a stated career goal at 20 of becoming a famous novelist by 30, Watts instead drifted into computer work, and now lives in Silicon Valley working as a technical writer.

Watts's stories have appeared in small presses, mostly furry, from the early '90s onward. Books include the short story collection *Why Coyotes Howl* (Sofawolf Press, January 2005) and the Cóyotl-winning novella *Indigo Rain* (FurPlanet Productions, January 2013), as well as contributions to the FurPlanet anthologies *Five Fortunes*, *Inhuman Acts*, and *The Furry Future*. A full-length science fiction novel, *Kismet*, will be published by Argyll/FurPlanet in early 2017.

MikasiWolf

MikasiWolf (1990-present) started his journey through the labyrinth of prose and wordcraft since 2007, months before discovering furry fandom. He has never been without inspiration since. Though he occasionally dabbles in the wetwork and complexity of art, he considers himself more of an artist of words. His stories have appeared in *The Furry Future; 19 Possible Prognostications*, edited by Fred Patten (FurPlanet Productions, January 2015), VancouFur 2015 conbook, What The Fur 2015 conbook, Anthrocon 2015 conbook, and *Claw the Way to Victory*, edited by AnthroAquatic (Jaffa Books, January 2016), as well as in this here anthology. ;)

Despite the sweltering heat, he currently resides in the midst of an urban jungle. He spends his time picking up the pieces after his dog codenamed Taro, writing, and enjoying video games with a good premise. He can be found on: https://twitter.com/MikasiWolf, and http://www.furaffinity.net/user/mikasiwolf. Feel free to DM him with any comments you may have! Or if you just wanna talk. He doesn't bite…yet.

Field T. Mouse

Born in 1984, Field T. Mouse is a harvest mouse and lifelong resident of rural Indiana. He has been part of the furry community for nearly fifteen years. Though he went to college for fine arts photography and is particularly inspired by television and film, he's been keenly interested in writing from a fairly young age.

Having an affinity for prey species (particularly rodents) and their point of view, they tend to feature in most of his stories. For this reason, he was immediately drawn to the squirrel character Ratatoskr for the focus of "Contract Negotiations". The Norse messenger seemed as if he would make a particularly good catalyst for the inspiration of silly shenanigans, and he didn't disappoint.

Tom Mullins

Killick/Tom Mullins was born in England in 1988 and brought up in Australia, and has the inconsistent accent to prove it. He is a librarian at a Queensland university where he assists medical students and doctors with referencing software and improving research skills, yet he still struggles with PowerPoint. Tom lives with his amazing partner in Brisbane, Australia, a city with summers so humid you could swim through them. At home he enjoys playing board and video games, if only for a few hours each weekend, and he has begun to fall in love with classic and cult movies that he's never seen before.

This is his first published piece of work and he is very excited to show what he can do and be a part of this anthology. His arch-nemesis is cheesecake.

Mut

Mut is a dog, but it's not his fault. He was born in 1977 and grew up in the U.K., then absconded to California, Switzerland, and now France. He's not really a real writer, but he likes hanging around with people who are and pretending he knows what's going on. In his day job, he studies very, very, very tiny explosions. He has over six hundred publications to his name somehow, but most of them have weird symbols in the title and you should probably not read them unless you have SAN to burn. This is the first time anyone has paid him to write fiction, though, so please buy lots of copies. Makes a great birthday present. Surprise your parents!

If found, please return to the Bay Area, preferably near a sushi place.

NightEyes DaySpring

NightEyes DaySpring is a known troublemaker who is rumored to have a penchant for coffee and an interest in dead, ancient civilizations. His stories have appeared in *The Furry Future*, edited by Fred Patten (FurPlanet Productions, January 2015), *FANG 5* and *6*, edited by Ashe Valisca (Bad Dog Books, January 2014 and July 2015), *Trick or Treat 1* and *2*, edited by Ianus J. Wolf (Rabbit Valley, September 2013 and October 2014), and other anthologies. Currently he resides in Florida with his boyfriend. In his spare time, he masquerades as an IT professional.

More information about NightEyes can be found at: http://www.furaffinity.net/user/nighteyes/ and https://www.weasyl.com/~nighteyes. For day-to-day nonsense, follow @wolfwithcoffee on twitter.

BanWynn Oakshadow

BanWynn Oakshadow, aka Uncle Oakie, has been writing since about two years before he was born (1962=Greymuzzle). He was published as state and national finalists while in high school. The coyote was the first in gym class to get fur all over. The tail, ears and muzzle also made him feel out of place. He found Furry in 1974, and, comfortable in a world full of lunatics where they fit in, Uncle Oakie and BanWynn began writing. When someone started erasing his name and replacing it with their own, BanWynn switched to private peer-to-peer writers mailing lists such as TSA, critiquing and growing with other writers like Phil Guesz, who tossed "Shepherd's Song" back to BanWynn five times before saying it was ready. The 2007 anthropomorphic recommendation it received agreed. He jumped at FANG, and FANG nomnom'ed several of his stories and a novella. After almost a decade of not writing and two strokes, he is back and productive once again.

He is Mated to Snout, a husky sled dog trapped in a human body. They live in a forest in southern Sweden in a cottage built in 1754 with their flatulent dog, Biscuit.

Frances Pauli

Frances Pauli (1971-present) writes multiple books and series across the speculative genres. Though she has difficulty sticking to a particular box, her fiction usually touches on themes of magic and spirit, often includes romance, and occasionally wanders into dark or humorous corners at random. Frances posts furry serial and short fiction on various social sites as Vandisar, and maintains a blog and listing of her works in print at francespauli.com.

When not writing, she crochets, shows hairless dogs, and keeps far too many tarantulas for her family's comfort.

Michael H. Payne

The stories about Cluny the sorceress squirrel by Michael H. Payne (1965-current) have been published in every issue of the annual *Sword and Sorceress* anthology since 2008, and his novels *The Blood Jaguar* (Tor Books, December 1998; reprinted by Sofawolf Press, June 2012) and *Rat's Reputation* (Sofawolf Press, July 2015) are currently available. His webcomics *Daily Grind* and *Terebinth* appear six times a week at pandora.xepher.net, and he hosts *The Darkling Eclectica*, a weekly radio program full of music and stories every Sunday afternoon from 4 till 6 over KUCI in Irvine, California.

He would like to give extra special thanks to the writing community at writeoff.me, without whom his story in this volume simply wouldn't exist.

Slip-Wolf

Slip-Wolf (1975—the moment he least expects immortal wrath) has been wandering the furry realms of the western world for a scant three years, spooling tales for the publishing houses who control all writers' destinies. When not reconciling legends from lies for coin and drink, Slip convenes with other writers in the digital ether and the panel shrines in conventions where the writerly arts are worshipped, flaunted and sinned against. He has burned offerings in the halls of Sofawolf with *Heat* issues 11-13, FurPlanet with tales in *ROAR 6*, *FANG 6* and *7*, *Will of the Alpha 2* and *3*, the *Inhuman Acts* and *Dungeon Grind* anthologies, and with Rabbit Valley in its *Trick or Treat 2: Historical Halloween* anthology. He most recently placed an offering in *GoAL*, issue 2.

Slip occasionally leaves word of his doings on: http://www.furaffinity.net/user/slip-wolf/ He also can be marked on twitter: @Slip_Wolf

James L. Steele

James L. Steele, born in 1983, currently resides in Ohio. He builds worlds across multiple genres including sci-fi, bizarro, non-traditional fantasy, dark fantasy, anthropomorphics, and a little bit of horror. His short stories have been published in the *Planet* and *Solarcide* online magazines, the print magazines *Bourbon Penn* #9, *Fictionvale* #2, and *The Magazine of Bizarro Fiction* #3, and the anthologies *Allasso* vol. 2 & 3, edited by Brian Lee Cook (Pink Fox Publications, April 2012 & May 2014), *Different Worlds, Different Skins, vol. 2*, edited by Will A. Sanborn (Anthropomorphic Dreams Publishing, November 2010), and the 2011 Bram Stoker Award-winning *Demons: Encounters with the Devil and His Minions, Fallen Angels, and the Possessed*, edited by John Skipp (Black Dog & Leventhal Publishers, September 2011). He is the author of the novel *Huvek* (FurPlanet Productions, July 2014).

He likes his fiction with as few humans as possible, and prefers characters who are as far from normal as they want to be. For him, these are the two most interesting elements in reading and writing because they push us to see things from a perspective that is unlike anything we are used to.

Jefferson P. Swycaffer

Jefferson P. Swycaffer (1956-current) has been a furry fan since just about the beginning. He came within a fine camel's hair of naming the genre, referring to it as "fuzzy fandom" in an article around 1984. He has published nine science fiction novels, and several more on Amazon as Kindle E-Books; several of these books have been "furry" to one degree or another. In science fiction, his "Marterly Trilogy"—*The Empire's Legacy* (New Infinities, August 1988), *Voyage of the Planetslayer* (New Infinities, October 1988), and *Revolt and Rebirth* (New Infinities, December 1988)—examined the question of genetically engineered "slave races" and the morality of altering nature to serve mankind.

In somewhat less serious work, he wrote an X-rated crossover with Steve Crompton's "Demi the Demoness" comic book. Jefferson is emphatic in considering himself a fan first, including service as the Secretary for ConDor, San Diego's longest-running annual science fiction convention, and a professional merely as a matter of fortuitous contingency.

Televassi

Televassi is a writer currently living in south-east England, but secretly wishes to move back to the south-west where he studied for a degree in English Literature so he can resume exploring the beaches and woods there. He is fascinated with imagining the world as other animals see it and combining it with our own human perspective—naturally leading to his participation in the Furry Fandom. Televassi writes both poetry and prose, and has a slight obsession with *Beowulf, The Elder Edda,* and Celtic La Tène and Germanic cultures. Considering these interests, it is ironic that his nickname is TV. Yes, as in a television.

You can find Televassi's work in *Civilized Beasts, 2015 edition,* edited by Laura Govednik (Weasel Press, December 2015), Sofawolf Press' *Heat #13* (June 2016), and the present *Gods with Fur.* He has submitted to *Fragments of Life's Heart* (Weasel Press, June 2016). You can find him on Twitter regularly talking about writing, history, and rock climbing; or bring him to you by collecting lots of books on the Celts.

Heidi C. Vlach

Heidi was born in 1985, in northern Ontario, Canada. She graduated chef training at age 19, and now works as a professional cook or an overqualified waitress (depending on her mood). Video games were her gateway to the fantasy genre: Heidi still enjoys a story-rich video game as much as a good book.

Currently, she lives with her best friend and two very loud cats.

Michael D. Winkle

Michael D. Winkle was born in Oklahoma in 1959 and has lived in the same general area ever since. He has worked as library assistant, bookkeeper, and in the usual array of "writer experience" jobs, from car washer to postal worker. He graduated with a B.A. in English from Oklahoma State University. He is the author of thirty or so professionally published stories and articles, including "Wolfhead" (*Tales of the Witch World 3,* edited by Andre Norton; Tor Books, July 1990); "The Autumn Beast" (*Here & Now Magazine #5/6,* Spring 2005); and "Curious Adventure of the Jersey Devil" (*Panverse 2,* edited by Dario Ciriello; Panverse Publishing, September 2010). He also had "something", whether article, story, or serial chapter, in all twenty-five issues of the lycanthropic fanzine *Fang, Claw, and Steel.*

He hopes that his trickle of published short stories will eventually gather into a torrent of published novels.

About the Artist

Teagan Gavet

Teagan Gavet is a professional illustrator, graphic novelist, and freelance rambler. Find more at: http://www.teagangavet.com
http://www.furaffinity.net/user/blackteagan

About the Editor

Fred Patten

Fred Patten (1940-current) joined the Los Angeles Science Fantasy Society in 1960 while in college, and has been an active s-f & fantasy fan ever since. He began writing for and publishing fanzines in 1961 (see http://www.zinewiki.com/Salamander), and has written over a thousand reviews of anthropomorphic literature since 1962, irregularly for s-f fanzines in the 1960s, 1970s, and 1980s; for *Yarf!* from 1990 to 2003, for *Claw & Quill* in 2004-2005, for *Anthro* from 2005 to 2008, for *Renard's Menagerie* in 2008, for *Flayrah* from 2011 to 2014, and for *Dogpatch Press* since 2014. He has written two non-fiction books and edited eight anthologies of furry fiction. He founded the Ursa Major Awards and has been on its administrative Anthropomorphic Literature and Arts Association since 2001. He is a member of the Furry Writers' Guild and the Furry Hall of Fame. He co-founded Japanese anime fandom in 1977, and was awarded the Comic-Con's Inkpot Award in 1980 for helping to introduce anime to America. He writes a weekly column on animation, *Funny Animals and More*, for Jerry Beck's Cartoon Research.

A stroke in 2005 has left him hospitalized, from which he carries on his fan activities via a MacBook Pro laptop.

www.ingramcontent.com/pod-product-compliance
Lightning Source LLC
Chambersburg PA
CBHW071142020726
47502CB00002B/238